GOLDEN HILL

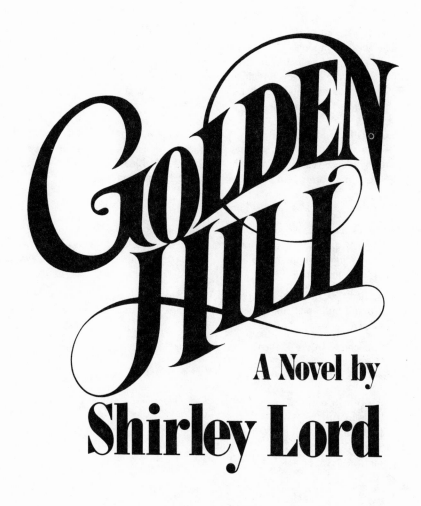

GOLDEN HILL

A Novel by
Shirley Lord

CROWN PUBLISHERS, INC., NEW YORK

Excerpts from "Parades, Parades" from *Seagrapes* by Derek Walcott. Copyright ©
1971, 1973, 1975, 1976 by Derek Walcott. Excerpt from "The Train" from *The
Gulf* by Derek Walcott. Copyright © 1963, 1964, 1965, 1969, 1970 by Derek
Walcott. Both are reprinted by permission of Farrar, Straus & Giroux, Inc.

Published by Crown Publishers, Inc., One Park Avenue, New York, New York
10016 and published simultaneously in Canada by General Publishing Company
Limited

Manufactured in the United States of America

Library of Congress Cataloging in Publication Data

Lord, Shirley.
   Golden hill.
   I. Title.
PR6062.0724G6 1982   823'.914   82-17240
ISBN: 0-517-54741-4

10 9 8 7 6 5 4 3 2 1

First Edition

To my Husband David

ACKNOWLEDGMENTS

Thanks to my husband, David Anderson, who first taught me to love life in the Caribbean and to understand some of its complexities, anomalies and undercurrents; to my sister-in-law Eve, whose hilltop house built on the Anderson family estate in Trinidad is surrounded by the scenery I describe in this book, scenery that inspired me to write it; to Anthony Camps-Campins, a Caribbean artist of note, for his paintings and the historical commentary that often accompanies them; to P.E.T. O'Connor, who wrote *Some Trinidad Yesterdays* (Imprint Caribbean Ltd.), for his glimpses of life in the tropics long ago; to the authors Jan Knippers Black, Howard I. Blutstein, Kathryn Therese Johnston and David S. McMorris of the *Area Handbook for Trinidad and Tobago* (U.S. Government Printing Office) and to James Trager, for his *The People's Chronology* (Holt, Rinehart & Winston, Inc.), for facts and figures past and present; to John K. McKinley, chairman, president and chief executive officer of Texaco, and Robert M. Bischoff, president of Texaco Latin America/West Africa, for helping to ensure certain portions of this book are technically correct; and to Alvin Lindsey, president of Roure Bertrand Dupont, for his enthusiasm and generosity.

My thanks also to David Brown, Morton Janklow, Anne Sibbald, Audrey Del Rosario, Jan Chipman, Joanne and Robert Herring and Carole Baron for their early support and encouragement; to my editor Betty Prashker for her superb judgment and advice, and to my son Mark Hussey for his valuable suggestions.

Last but in no way least, to Eva Clementi and Rob Murphy for their diligent transcribing and help in typing some of the *Golden Hill* manuscript.

1

Margaret
1974

IT had been an unsatisfactory day. "Unsatisfactory" was a word Clare
Pollard was known for. She used it a great deal, believing its crisp
British understatement best conveyed her displeasure over a variety
of displeasing occurrences, ranging from the trivial (the late arrival
of a new couture dress) to the major (the dismissal of a maid for stealing). She believed a certain enunciation, a studied attempt never to
raise her voice, helped establish the reserved, even austere image she
wished to foster, separating her with every trained syllable from her
Texas roots, and the "black muck" that was the source of her fortune,
linking her instead to all the expensive, exclusive things her father's oil
money had been able to buy. Small things in life, she had learned long
ago, emphasized the difference between *nouveau riche* and—a small
joke she allowed herself—*"riche d'habitude."* The small things propagated what one wanted propagated: words, tones, gestures—as well as
the more obvious "give-aways": menus, clothes, places and people—all
helping one to "belong," to become accepted by the "old money"
group, where the merest hint of *striving* to do or achieve anything received a cold, distant stare. As the custom-built Rolls turned off Park
Avenue, a traffic light away from the Pollard townhouse, Clare took out
her small gold compact with the magnifying mirror to inspect her face

thoroughly. It was an involuntary ritual before arriving anywhere, even her own home, where more often than not there would be only servants to greet her, often the same servants who were allowed to see her early morning unmade-up face.

Today she had a special reason for wanting to look as cool and as perfect as possible. She checked her watch for the third time since leaving Bill Blass's fitting room. It was four-fifteen. Margaret would have arrived an hour ago. Roger, damn fool that he was, would probably have decided to meet her himself at Kennedy—which meant she would have the unusual experience of seeing her husband three times in the same week and in the afternoon of his working day.

As she walked into the house, ramrod straight with a well-rehearsed slight smile, she pulled up so sharply the new maid almost collided with her. What stopped her was the usual sign of Margaret's intrusion and yet the one she always forgot. Invisible, yet just as pernicious to Clare as her actual presence, Margaret's perfume was already in the house: a haunting mixture of patchouli and rose, a scent Margaret had made just for herself.

There were voices coming from the library where the nervous maid informed her that Mr. Pollard, his niece and the lawyer were having tea. Lawyer! Clare's pulse quickened as rage flared inside her.

How dare Roger use their home as a meeting place to discuss Margaret's latest catastrophe! She had totally disassociated herself from Margaret's problems just as long ago she had disassociated herself from so much in Roger's life.

As quickly as the emotion came, she contained it, tightening her lips in contempt as she imagined the earnest conversation in progress. Let the "poor little rich girl" enjoy her moment of attention. She decided to go to her room, telling the maid to call her on the house phone as soon as the lawyer left.

On her desk was a list of instructions she had given to the housekeeper before leaving the house that morning. Each instruction was neatly checked. The clothes she wanted sent to the Southampton house for the summer season ahead had been sent. The swimming pool had been summerized and was open. The new wing of the pool pavilion was finished. Bloomingdale's had delivered the new wicker furniture, the extra monogramed towels, robes and slippers. A third gardener had been hired, following the usual reference check. Clare went down the list in a cursory way. She knew if she saw a check beside an item she needn't really read what the item was. Her houses, unlike those of many of her friends, were run by professionals. She could afford the best. She had the best.

Clare jumped when the house phone rang at five-fifteen with the news the lawyer had left. A familiar throbbing had started in her right temple, the beginning of a migraine headache, the price she often paid for her enforced phlegmatism. But now she ignored it, carefully looking at herself in one of the many full-length mirrors in her bedroom before going downstairs to greet her husband's niece.

Whenever she thought of Margaret, which was as little as possible, Clare employed a form of "myopia" she'd learned from her father, visualizing a person so devoid of any special characteristics, there was scarcely any need to consider her at all. If anyone brought up Margaret's name, Clare usually referred to her as "the daughter of my husband's half brother, you know . . ." followed by a pause and then a faintly deprecating laugh. "Only half a niece, don't you think?" She then made it clear the subject was to be dropped. Because of Clare's successful attempts to submerge the reality of Margaret, the first sight of her, on the rare occasions they met, invariably induced a stab of raw envy . . . of her large gray eyes, dark gold hair, her long slender legs and feet and even the graceful way she moved, as she sprang up from the sofa to kiss her aunt's coolly proffered cheek.

"You've had tea?"

"Yes, thank you, Aunt Clare."

"And how was Grasse?"

"Oh, very interesting. I loved it. I hope to . . ." Clare cut across Margaret's reply, clearly uninterested in any of her hopes.

"Roger, I rather imagined that in view of Margaret's appearance I might have the pleasure of your company. Does this mean you can join me at the party tonight after all?"

There was no trace of anticipation in Clare's voice. As Roger understood only too well, Clare was merely envisaging a possible change of escorts, because on the frequent occasions he was away or "unavailable," his place was readily taken by "stand-bys" or "walkers"—as they were described in *Women's Wear Daily*, one of her favorite papers.

God forbid, he didn't want to provoke her today of all days—to ignite any sign of feeling in this plaster-cast model of perfection that passed for his wife. He sighed. There was no alternative. Whether Clare liked it or not, as a Pollard she had to be prepared for what might happen now; a new barrage of questions from the press, followed by newspaper stories which would link her to a world he knew she despised, although she had never set foot in it.

For all his knowledge of his wife's attitude, Roger still exhibited a courtly, old-fashioned charm toward her. He couldn't help himself. Now, with an almost wistful movement, he leaned over to touch her arm. "Clare, we've heard that Rose is sinking fast. I'm taking Margaret down to Golden Hill on the morning plane."

It was as if he had said he was taking the dog for a walk. "You haven't answered my question." Clare gave him a short, tight smile. "Can you take me to Mary's tonight?"

Another sigh in this house of so many sighs. "I think it's best you don't change your plans, dear. Margaret and I will have a quiet dinner and an early night."

"Oh, yes, dinner." Another item. "Something light I imagine?"

The question was addressed to Margaret, who looked at Clare with a mixture of disbelief and resignation, a look that emphasized a new assurance Clare didn't like at all. There was a new cool reserve that was in direct contrast to the overanxious Margaret of the past.

"Yes, something light, Aunt Clare. I'm not really hungry."

Her aunt's disregard for other people's feelings never failed to amaze Margaret, even after years of trying to cope with Clare's hostility. How was it possible her aunt could pose a question about a light dinner on receiving the news someone was dying? All right, so it was her grandmother whom Margaret knew Clare had never met, although Rose was also Uncle Roger's stepmother.

Margaret caught her uncle's eye. "Relax," he seemed to be saying. "She'll leave us in a minute. It really doesn't matter."

Poor Uncle Roger. What a life he must lead, Margaret thought as she so often did, watching her aunt call through to the kitchen. The emptiness of it all, despite the fancy trappings. Margaret looked around the familiar room, remembering her first visit when, overpowered by events, every piece of signed furniture, every valuable painting and collector's item had deepened her sense of loss, her feeling of isolation.

How long ago it seemed and then, just when she'd begun to get on her feet to feel like a real person again, came one blow after another. First the challenge to her own inheritance and now the news of her grandmother's stroke. . . .

The strike of the library clock brought Margaret back to the present and to Clare again, who was leaving the room with the sort of careful "you must excuse me" sentence that Margaret suddenly thought, with the trace of a smile, her aunt must have learned at her European finishing school . . . and practiced a thousand times since.

The warmth in the atmosphere, which had disappeared with Clare's arrival, returned immediately once the door closed behind her. Roger took his niece's hand in his own. "Don't be upset, Margaret. She . . . she . . . doesn't understand."

And has no intention of understanding, Margaret thought, but she returned her uncle's squeeze affectionately. "Uncle, believe me, I'm not a bit upset. I would have been once, but I feel so different since I began working. I just *love* my work. It's even helped me through all these horrible months of lawyers and reporters."

She jumped up, and this time there was something wonderfully innocent and tender in the kiss she gave her uncle.

"What on earth would I have done without you, Uncle Roger." Sudden tears came to her eyes. "I've tried to feel upset about Grandmother's stroke, but you know I can't feel anything. I've never really had a chance to know her."

Roger put his arm around her shoulders as he said softly, "Of course you haven't. We're in the same boat. I never allowed myself to know her either . . . yet she's affected all our lives so much, so very much."

Margaret was silent, her eyes luminous with unshed tears. She was about to speak when the butler came in to ask them what time they would like dinner served.

"It's only from the air now that Golden Hill looks like a great mansion," Margaret said suddenly as she peered out of the plane window. "You can't see the potholes, the broken flagstones from up here. . . ."

Below her, thousands of cocoa trees marched row upon row in sharp precision, it seemed, almost up to the house itself, while the driveway looked as it had originally been planned to look, like a straight white arrow, pointing with no diversion directly to the house on the hill, Golden Hill, the shining symbol of one man's superiority.

As the jet carrying Roger and Margaret Pollard landed in Port of Spain, Trinidad, a distant roll of thunder echoed through the Northern Range, warning the cane planters to finish harvesting their crop before the June rains began in earnest.

The heat, like an invisible blanket, swaddled them the moment they left the plane. But even as tiny beads of perspiration broke out on Margaret's forehead, she shivered, feeling the sense of dread and fear she always felt, even when, thousands of miles away, only her thoughts returned to Golden Hill and Trinidad.

At the bottom of the plane steps was an unsmiling immigration officer who peremptorily pointed to a small dusty car that took them across the tarmac to a side door leading directly to the customs chief's office.

The immigration officer's obvious resentment of the VIP treatment he'd been ordered to deliver was a reminder to Roger that this was "lip service"—proffered with just enough arrogance to ensure they realized they were receiving it, not because they were the white Pollards of Golden Hill estate, but because they were kin of Ambassador Bracken, the closest confidant of Trinidad's prime minister, Eric Williams.

They were received with more civility in the customs chief's office, where all VIP passports and customs forms were checked to spare important visitors to the island the indignity of waiting in a line, which moved at a snail's pace in the unair-conditioned immigration hall.

Airport personnel came and went, not bothering to hide their curiosity as word spread that Margaret Pollard herself was in the chief's office.

Every minute seemed like hours and although this office was air conditioned, Margaret felt her palms and armpits growing slowly damp as her nervousness increased.

Her grandmother was dying. Didn't they know there was very little time left, that she had to hurry? She heard raised voices outside.

"Man, yo' canna go in dere. . . ." And then the chief customs officer himself booming, "Yo' boy, be mor' respec'ful t' Mistah Finch! Right here, Mistah Finch. . . ."

Margaret jumped to her feet. "It's Theo, Uncle Roger."

The door opened and the customs chief ushered in with his own idea of ceremony a dark, strikingly handsome man, who rushed over to hold Margaret to him for a brief moment, kissing her on the cheek before turning to shake Roger's hand.

"A few minutes of privacy, please." It was a command, not a question, and the customs officer withdrew with an obsequious leer.

Theo leaned toward them, hunching his shoulders, clenching his hands together as Margaret had seen him do so many times when he was about to say something important. This time she had a premonition about what he was going to say.

"Your grandmother died at daybreak."

Daybreak. It was typical of Theo to use a planter's term and later,

looking back on the moment, Margaret remembered her feeling of gratitude, not because Theo had taken the time and trouble to come to the
airport himself to tell them the news, but illogically because he'd used a
word that for her had conveyed hope instead of despair, a word which
hadn't invoked the true picture of Rose's solitary death.

"What's happening outside?" Roger asked. He was surprised at how
shaken he felt. He went on quickly, "Are there any press?"

"Plenty." Theo looked grim. "I think I can shake them off now, but
they're like vultures. I don't see much chance of avoiding them later."
He took Margaret's hand. "Are you up to it? Have you got your 'no
comment' ready?"

She tried to smile, but the initial sense of security Theo's arrival had
brought was waning. "I'll try." She gave both men a sad look. "At least
it can't get any worse. . . ."

Roger and Theo exchanged glances and she felt a lurch of apprehension. They knew something she didn't know, but there was no way she
could ask what it might be. She was too frightened of the answers she
might receive.

As her feeling of panic increased, logistics intervened. The customs
chief returned to say their papers were ready and their luggage had been
cleared. They were free to go. They went out as they'd entered—
through the side door back onto the tarmac, where now, instead of the
immigration officer's car, stood Theo's station wagon.

He drove fast, confidently, around a disused hangar to an abandoned
weed-choked landing strip, which eventually led to a road away from
the terminal buildings. Only then did the atmosphere in the car relax,
and Theo briefly explained that Rose had apparently died around six
that morning. Her brother, the ambassador, had immediately taken over
the arrangements for the funeral that would take place the next day.

"He has arranged a lying-in at St. Joseph's Church, but unless you
feel you must, I don't advise you to go there. Reporters have been hanging around all day to see who'll turn up to pay their last respects. I
assume you want to go straight to Golden Hill?" Roger grunted his
assent as Theo maneuvered the car to miss a procession of strutting
chickens.

The sights and sounds of Trinidad slowly penetrated Margaret's consciousness as they drove, often bumper to bumper, in and out of native
settlements. There were the *marchandes* perched at the roadside, their
heads tied in brilliantly colored bandanas, calling out their wares in a
variety of high, singsong voices. "De bes' cow'eel soup in town, mistah"

. . . "shark'n' hops" . . . "peanut cakes, me darlin'" . . . "sweet 'tater pr'serve" . . . "Mamie's cush-cush, sapodillas, black puddin', dumplin's an' pigtails."

Bursts of music—steel bands beating out "Yellow Bird" and "Give Me Love, Give Me Peace"—mixed together with quick gusts of high-pitched laughter, raised voices, screeching hens and barking dogs to produce a nonstop cacophony, which Margaret didn't think could exist anywhere else in the world. She loved it. She loathed the mixture of blood, races and peoples it stood for, yet, to Theo's amusement, despite her tension, her fingers involuntarily started to tap to the beat of the teeming streets.

Roger, half asleep in the back seat, made a perfunctory attempt at conversation. "How's your family, Theo? Are Paulette and Tommy with you?"

"Yes, they're out at Arima." Theo hesitated before adding, ". . . with my mother." He touched Margaret's hand. "They're looking forward to seeing you, Margaret—to hear about your trip to Grasse."

Grasse! Margaret closed her eyes, trying to recapture the feeling of freedom she'd had there, studying the intricate, and, to her, endlessly fascinating business of essential oils and perfume making. It had been hard for her to believe anything could have taken her mind away from the case endlessly thrashed over in the papers and discussed by teams of lawyers, a case that not only threatened her inheritance, but everything she had been brought up to believe.

But Theo, who had persuaded her to make the trip, had been right. She *had* been able to escape from the burden of it all there, even beginning to believe that, whatever happened, life could start over with fresh possibilities.

As Theo maneuvered his way in and out of the traffic up toward St. Joseph, Margaret heard with foreboding the unearthly yell of the wild red monkeys in the wooded foothills, a sure sign of approaching rains and the all too abrupt end to daylight, something she hated about the tropics. She sighed painfully. How well she remembered her beloved father telling her with his special smile, "Twilight here passes in the twinkling of an eye, my darling, so grab every second of the day."

On the few occasions she'd gone back to Golden Hill since her parents' deaths, Margaret had always been initially shocked by the signs of so much neglect, the peeling paint, broken shutters and cracked flagstones trying to break out of the wide terraces, because in the more frequent—if reluctant—visits she made in her mind, she saw only the

Golden Hill of her childhood and adolescence, pristine white under a burning sun, surrounded by immortelle trees, their showy orange flowers giving the plantation its name. But if the house had been allowed to age and crumble without dignity like its last owner, Rose Pollard, the land around it was a different story.

Roger occasionally boasted that his niece Margaret, who'd inherited over a thousand Golden Hill prime acres from her father, certainly had the "Pollard business flair." For although an absentee landlord, like those of old, through the efforts of an experienced overseer, each year she made a tidy profit from the land, as well manicured and looked after as her own fingernails.

It was dark by the time they reached the imposing gates at the bottom of the Golden Hill drive. Although they were open and the gate lights were on to show they were expected, a parked car blocked the entrance.

Theo sounded the horn insistently but the car didn't move. Instead, a severely dressed black woman got out and came over to where Margaret was sitting to tap on her window. Sure she was a reporter, Margaret ignored her, staring straight ahead, praying somehow she would go away and not cause any problems.

Theo got out and said courteously, "Would you please move your car. You're blocking this entrance."

The black woman flashed a wide grin of recognition. "Mr. Finch, I'm sorry, but I have my instructions from Am-bass-a-dor Brack-en." She rolled out each syllable with exaggerated deference. "I have to give this per-son-al-ly either to Mr. Pollard or Miss Pollard. I reckoned this was the only way I could be sure of carryin' out my instructions." Only the dropped g linked her accent to the islands, as she held out a manila envelope stamped with the Trinidad government seal.

Roger slowly unwound himself from the back seat of the car and got out. "I am Roger Pollard, Miss . . . ?"

She simpered. "Aimee Atkins, Mr. Pollard. Personal assistant to Am-bass-a-dor Brack-en. Thank you. Would you please sign this for me to show you received it per-son-al-ly?"

"What is it, a summons?" Roger asked sarcastically.

A sly look of amusement crossed her face. "Certainly not, Mr. Pollard. Ambassador Bracken told me to tell you—or your niece"—she threw a casual disinterested glance in Margaret's direction—"he assumed you would prefer not to see each other more than was necessary . . . in view of the, hmm, other matter . . ." She paused deliberately, as if to show her respect, ". . . still not bein' resolved." Obviously

warming up to her task, she fluttered her lashes before carefully artic-
ulating as if in an elocution class. "Am-bass-a-dor Bracken has made all
the arrangements for his de-part-ed sister Rose's burial. The de-tails are
herein enclosed. The lyin'-in has been observed and . . ." Departing
from the words she had typed only an hour or so before, she hurriedly
went on, "Yo' all still have time to get to see her at rest in St. Joseph's
Church. The service is at eight sharp tomorrow mornin' and after. . . ."

Aware how much Aimee Atkins was now enjoying herself, Roger put
up a staying hand. "Thank you, Miss Atkins. We don't wish to detain
you any longer. I'm sure Ambassador Bracken has taken care of everything. Let me sign your note."

By the gate light, Roger signed the proof that he had personally received the details "pertaining to Rose Pollard's funeral." Then, click-
clicking her teeth in approval, Aimee Atkins returned to her car with a
"mission accomplished" flourish and drove off into the night with a
noisy meshing of gears.

They were silent as they drove up the long drive to the colonnaded
entrance where Margaret could see a small cluster of servants waiting,
among them Obee and Maize, who had been with the family for as
long as she could remember.

"How old is Obee?" she had once asked her father.

"Nobody knows." He'd laughed. "Least of all Obee himself. Old
Negroes in the islands hardly ever know their age, but I remember him
telling me, 'Me mudder made me de year of de cholera. Dat be long
time now and I feel very weary, so I must be well old.'"

As the car drove around the familiar saman tree in the courtyard she
closed her eyes again, trying to blot out painful memories, concentrat-
ing on inhaling from her abdomen, then exhaling in a long, low whistle, helpful in lessening both mental and physical pain her doctor had
told her, and to her amazement she'd found he was right. It did help—
sometimes.

Later, in the dark-paneled library with its thousands of vellum-covered
books, shipped in decades ago by Piper Pollard, Roger's father, Roger
opened the Aimee Atkins special-delivery envelope.

"Would you read it out?" Margaret asked. "I just want to know the
worst, then try to get some sleep."

She looked strained, Theo thought, even older since she'd stepped
inside the house than when he'd first seen her at the airport. It was too
much for her, coming back while the wretched case was still going on.

As the old grandfather clock in the hall chimed the stanza announcing the first quarter of the hour, Roger started to read in a dry matter-of-fact voice: "'According to my information, my sister Rose wished to be cremated on the Golden Hill Estate. Therefore, although to my knowledge my sister had not set foot in a place of worship for almost half a century . . . '" Roger grimaced, adding, "he couldn't resist getting a jibe in . . . 'after a short service conducted at eight A.M. by my friend Archbishop Smallwood at the St. Joseph Church in the Parish of St. Joseph, the coffin will return to Golden Hill and from there be carried by estate workers to the highest part of the estate where a pyre has been made ready for the cremation.'"

Margaret recoiled. "Oh, no . . . that's . . . that's barbaric," she gasped.

Theo turned to her quickly. "It isn't unusual, Margaret. You must understand that. On the great old estates it's a tradition for the owners . . . even the workers to want to be buried on their land, or for their ashes . . ." He didn't finish his sentence as Margaret burst into tears, burying her face in his shoulder.

"There, there." He rocked her back and forth until her tears subsided and she made an effort to compose herself.

"I'm sorry," she whispered. "It's just so primitive, so strange . . . but if that's what Grandmother really wanted. . . ." Her voice petered out.

Theo got to his feet, looking concerned. "I must be going, and, Margaret, you should go to bed early, don't you think?"

"Yes, boss." Margaret made a valiant effort to smile . . . to feel again like the person she'd been in Grasse, determined not to let the ghosts of Golden Hill overwhelm her. "Does the letter say anything more, Uncle Roger?"

"It's just a pompous timetable," he answered. "Nothing for you to worry about. The Am-bass-a-dor is a-name-a-dropping. What else d'you expect? It says here, 'Except for un-fore-seen cir-cum-stances, the Prime Minister Eric Williams himself may attend with other dig-nit-aries!'"

Roger's imitation of Aimee Atkins made Margaret laugh despite herself.

"That's my girl," Roger said, relieved. "Let's meet for breakfast on the east veranda at seven o'clock, okay?"

"Okay," she replied, trying to sound cheerful for her uncle's sake.

"The best time of day . . . when Trinidad is the best place in the world," Theo said lightly as he walked with Margaret out to his car. "Try to smell the plumbago hedge just after dawn; then remember its scent when you're next in the lab."

Normality was resumed. The primitive, the barbaric, the raw edge of Trinidad never far below the surface was, for the moment, forgotten. "I wish you could come back here for breakfast," Margaret said wistfully.

"I wish so, too, kitten." Theo kissed the tip of her nose. "All the same, smell the plumbago for me and remember it for Tropica!"

As he drove down the drive Margaret's sense of loss returned. There was a stirring inside for something . . . someone. . . . She shuddered and resolutely inhaled and exhaled as she went to face a night of trying to sleep in her old room.

The Catholic Church of St. Joseph in the Parish of St. Joseph—Trinidad's capital in the eighteenth century—was packed to its old rafters by 7:45 A.M. the next morning.

As Griselda Monk, on her first overseas assignment for the *New York Times*, wrote in her notebook, "The haves, the used-to-haves and the have-nots are gathered together to pay their last respects to an unusual woman, Rose Bracken Pollard, a descendant of the black slave Louisa Calderon, whose arrest and controversial torture at the command of Trinidad's first British governor, Lieutenant Colonel Thomas Picton, caused the scandal that led to his censure and eventual removal from office at the beginning of the nineteenth century.

"Rose Bracken Pollard—who three generations later revenged her ancestor when she married Piper Pollard, to become mistress of Golden Hill, the great house of the Picton estate, taken over by Pollard in 1911 from Picton's descendant, 'Finchy' Finch. The Finch family is represented at the funeral today by Thomas Finch, named after his controversial ancestor, and his parents, Theo and Paulette Finch—who founded the successful Tropica beauty company in the United States twenty-three years ago."

As the funeral procession moved from the church through Maracas Valley back to Golden Hill, Griselda thanked her lucky stars she'd been able, with the help of her *New York Times* credentials and her own brand of "promise now/pay later" flirtatiousness, to ingratiate herself with Ambassador Bracken's press secretary.

Instead of riding with all the other "scribes," it meant she was up in front—in fact in the third car behind the principal mourners and well ahead of the "gorillas," as Griselda had named the muscular aides in army uniform who so far had been able to block all interviews with members of the Bracken family about the juicy case going on.

As a feature writer, Griselda considered herself a cut above reporters.

She didn't intend to grovel for any salacious details. Leave that to the *Star*, the *National Enquirer*, or come to that, the *Daily News*. The hard facts were fascinating enough.

A colored, illegitimate child was challenging the white legitimate heiress for a substantial share of her huge inheritance, in particular a share of valuable Golden Hill land. According to Griselda's scrupulous homework, Golden Hill had long been responsible for a family feud, which had produced tragedy, arson and death.

A trickle of perspiration further defined Griselda's generous cleavage. In this ferocious heat, feuds must be a daily occurrence, but not many attracted the attention of a government. For Trinidad's prime minister, it must be a public-relations dream, she thought cynically, and would continue to be—providing he could still support the black offspring's "right-to-sue," without losing the clever veneer of "impartiality" he'd displayed to date. The case seemed to have been going on forever, with enough new facts emerging every few months to keep the press returning to it like bees to a honeycomb. Now with Rose Pollard's death and apparently a new will to be read, there was a flurry of renewed interest from all over . . . even Murdoch's papers in London had sent over a hack or two, Griselda noted disparagingly.

She was first out of the car, hoping to get a word from Margaret Pollard herself—that would be a real coup. This was Griselda's first sight of the "tormented heiress," as the gossip columns had christened her over the months. She was standing on the Golden Hill veranda with her uncle, Griselda supposed, and the Finches, who, according to the most recent coverage, had given Margaret a trainee job at Tropica where it had been discovered she had a natural gift for creating "unusual perfumes."

Griselda was beginning to move toward the tightly knit group when a black hand firmly clasped her plump upper arm. It was the press secretary, who from the look in his eyes had no intention of letting her "pay much later" for his favors.

"Come with me, madame! We'll follow the procession together." She tried to extricate herself, but the black fingers held pincer firm, maneuvering her into the shade of the huge saman tree dominating the courtyard in front of the house. The fingers withdrew quickly, however, when a distinguished-looking, balding black man started to walk toward them. It was Ambassador Bracken, the deceased's brother and a key figure in the *Bracken* v. *Pollard* case.

To Griselda's distress, before she could fire the fusillade of questions she had ready after hours of studying the family histories in the pock-marked Port of Spain public library, the ambassador was distracted by an agitated female, answering to the name of Aimee, who dashed up to inform him she had just heard from the Red House that the prime minister was on his way.

Furious, Griselda watched her quarry hasten inside the house, while Aimee was sent to give the news to the Pollard group, isolated on one side of the colonnaded veranda, away from the sea of mainly black faces.

A motorcycle escort, followed by the prime minister's car, soon arrived, and, like a well-choreographed production, six young Negroes in spotless white shirts and well-washed dungarees effortlessly swung the small cedar coffin onto their shoulders to follow the archbishop and two young black priests up a newly pruned trail.

After some stilted introductions, the prime minister, flanked on each side by a bodyguard with a rifle, walked with Margaret Pollard and her uncle behind the coffin, followed by another group of bodyguards. Then came Ambassador Bracken and his wife Emerald, his one-armed brother James (Griselda had been told he was one of the originators of the steel band), with his wife Carmelita and son Frederick, then Theo, Paulette and Tommy Finch with the mayor and row upon row of dignitaries.

Despite the drama of the funeral procession, the "importance" of those attending and the exotic surroundings, Griselda decided it could almost be described as an emotionless occasion. She jotted down a few notes, waiting for the press secretary to escort her to the trail where, with some apprehension, she realized they were at the end of the long line of mourners. But they were not going to be the last to join the procession.

Griselda missed the chance of a scoop for the second time that day as, within minutes of leaving her privileged position under the saman tree, a gray Mercedes screeched to a halt in the courtyard and an elegant black couple jumped out to race inside the house before most of the press assembled on the veranda realized who they were. Those who did, scrambled to follow them inside and were rewarded with an impromptu interview—before one of the army guards quickly came to stand in front of the main door, blocking the way for the others.

It was all over in minutes, for on learning the funeral party had already left for the cremation site, the couple rushed out to the trail, leaving the press under guard once again.

If I try, I can pretend I'm somewhere else, back in Grasse, anywhere but here, Margaret thought as she stood before the pyre of immortelle and tonka-bean wood, stretching well over eight feet into the air. She averted her eyes as young estate workers climbed and scrambled to place the coffin on the uppermost branches, where it balanced precariously, looking small and defenseless.

Unexpectedly, Margaret caught the eye of her grandmother's younger brother James, who, lighter skinned than the ambassador, bore more of a resemblance to his dead sister.

Margaret blushed and looked away, suddenly remembering her grandmother's fragility, her tiny hands and feet, hands her father had told her that could sew like an angel, feet that had once loved to dance all night. They had belonged to a person Margaret had never known and could hardly believe had ever existed, seeing only a shuffling, pathetic old lady who'd hardly ever joined her parents at the dining table, who'd lived in seclusion in her room most of the time.

The archbishop started to chant the prayer for the dead and swung the censer. The smell of incense was intoxicating as it mixed with scent from the oleanders and morning glory in the hedgerows.

A soft breeze sent a shower of tiny pink and yellow blossoms from the poui trees over the coffin and there was a tense moment of stillness as the estate boys started to saturate the rubber tires at the base of the pyre with gasoline, its pungent smell assailing everyone's nostrils.

It was as if suddenly everyone there held their breaths at the same time to stay the moment they knew had to come next.

The boys threw burning torches onto the pyre and with a sharp explosion it ignited, flames tearing through the rubber-and-wood construction.

Margaret swayed as if she were going to faint, feeling violently sick, groping for Roger's arm for support.

As leaping fingers of fire crackled upward, moving fast toward the coffin, Margaret prayed, hoping there was a God to listen, trying to keep her thoughts away from the body beginning to shrivel inside the coffin, the hands crossed over the heart, the small feet that had loved to dance being burned to pulp and ashes.

She squeezed her eyes shut, her face red from the heat, praying now that those who were trying to besmirch her father's memory would fail and that the world would know they had failed.

The crowd gasped as the wood immediately beneath the coffin began to burn so fiercely, the coffin slipped on its side with no more support to hold it in place. Margaret opened her eyes, panic-stricken to see it hanging perilously between two fragile struts, looking as if it might easily fall to the ground to open and spill out its contents.

It was then she saw the two latecomers to the plateau, the young black couple, standing across from her with their heads bowed in the shimmering heat haze that enveloped everyone, their bodies looking curiously as if they were vibrating.

How dare they show up! Margaret's rage rose in her throat like bile. Did they have no shame? No respect for the dead? She had a mad impulse to rush over and push them back down the trail, to scream, "Go away! You don't belong here! This has nothing to do with you!"

As she seethed with fury, above the roar of the flames came the voices of other estate workers, standing so still behind the bushes that she hadn't even seen them. They brought her back to the grim reality of the moment.

"Madame, sh' be goin' straigh' t' heav'n, Lord save us," they began to chant, their bodies heaving backward and forward. "Madame, sh' be goin' straigh' t' heav'n . . . Lord save us. . . ."

As their chants grew louder, the fire reached the coffin itself and eerily, as if with renewed strength, brilliant red and gold flames shot over twenty feet into the clear sky, accompanied by clouds of black smoke. "Lord save us," the natives cried hysterically, cringing back from the fearsome sight.

The archbishop signaled everyone to kneel on the rough paragrass as he prayed sonorously, "The ashes of the deceased will bring a blessing to this beloved land. . . ."

At last, tears for the grandmother she had never really known started down Margaret's cheeks and the coffin slid into the center of the pyre to disappear in the holocaust. Slowly the fire, with nothing left to burn, sizzled into a glowing mass of red embers.

Rose was gone.

Her brothers knelt, inscrutable, each consumed with his own thoughts of the sister who'd made them suffer as nobody else had done, who had changed their lives and channeled their energies to outwit her, although she had never permitted them to know her except from a distance.

The natives continued to chant, their voices reduced to a steady hum like the drone from thousands of bees. The procession returned down the trail to Golden Hill.

It was over. The last car had disappeared down the drive and Obee and Maize hobbled about collecting dirty glasses and plates as Margaret and Roger sat together on the old veranda swing seat.

"How long do we have to stay, Uncle Roger? There's no movement on the legal front, is there?"

He sighed. "I didn't want to mention this last night, Margaret—you were too upset, but Roland's letter did mention your grandmother's will, apparently a comparatively new one drawn up only a few years ago following—hmm—Drum's—your father's death."

Margaret paled but was silent as Roger continued. "There's going to be a reading of the will tomorrow at noon—at Gellen's, the family lawyer. I think we must be there in view of the case going on over your inheritance." He turned to her almost eagerly. "It could play a decisive part in settling everything. If there's any truth in the girl's claim, your grandmother would surely have left her something, whereas if there's no truth to it, she won't be . . ."

Margaret interrupted him angrily. "Uncle Roger, how can you even mention the word 'truth.' You know it's a stinking lie, dreamed up by Jack Bracken and probably his father the ambassador too." She almost spat out the word "ambassador." "You've only got to read the papers. Even the worst ones say the case couldn't have come at a better time for Eric Williams to be able to demonstrate he's 'no tool of the whites,' that he 'thinks of people of his own color first and last.'" She pushed back fiercely against the swing, causing it to crack with the unaccustomed strain.

Roger put a placating hand on her knee. "Margaret, you've faced up to everything marvelously—but you've got to go on being strong. Don't get your mind fixed on what is or isn't the truth. You have your memories of your father. Nothing can ever change them. But you *must* be prepared for anything. Otherwise you'll just go under again—and it isn't necessary."

Margaret fidgeted, her lips set in a grim line. "I won't go under, Uncle Roger. Nothing will ever convince me my father could have done this to me . . . to me. . . ." She repeated the words in anguish.

Roger didn't know what to say.

He ached for this girl he loved like a daughter—the daughter who should have been his—not knowing how to help her face the shocks he feared might still be in store.

He sighed again, then, taking the easy way out, said in a deliberately cheerful voice, "Well, it will all be over soon . . . perhaps tomorrow . . . with the reading of Rose's will. . . ."

Margaret's thoughts were far away as she looked into the distance over thousands of her cocoa trees to where heavy rain clouds were beginning to settle around Mount El Tucuche's three peaks.

For a split second Roger saw—as he had so often seen—her startling resemblance to her father Drum, his younger half brother, who should have been "second" but had always been "first" in his father's eyes.

How he'd hated him and how he'd hated Rose.

Roger dug the nails of one hand into the other. Tomorrow—for once—Rose had to come through for him . . . then perhaps he might be able to forgive her. Perhaps.

2

Rose
1922

Iᴛ was her first tram ride, Rose told the conductor with a shy smile.
That was the reason she hadn't got off at her chosen stop but had
ridden all the way to the terminal in St. Ann's, to watch him reverse
the boom on the top of the tram for the return trip. She told him
how clever he was to connect the overhead boom at first go. It wasn't
the reason she'd stayed on the tram at all, but, like many men before
him, the young conductor swallowed Rose's compliment, and with a
proud little bow announced that as it was her first trip, for such a beautiful lady he would forget about payment for the fare back to her original
destination. Rose accepted the gesture graciously, outwardly the same
composed Rose most people saw, inwardly churning with a mixture of
emotions she'd never experienced before.

By the time she stepped off the tram at the northeast corner of the
Savannah, turning left and then right as her aunt had directed her to
reach Maraval Road, her nervousness had turned to real terror. Her
heart pounded so heavily she was sure anyone passing by could hear it.
Her hands trembled so much that the precious jar and the sewing basket
she carried trembled, too. Her legs were turning to jelly. She literally
couldn't go a step farther and she stopped to look around, half expecting
to be struck to the ground by someone demanding her right to be there.

She couldn't believe herself. She wanted to scream and scream at the nameless fears that transfixed her, at her body letting her down on this day of days. Even as she stood shaking in the shade of a palm tree, her mother's face flashed across her mind. How she would love to see me like this, Rose thought bitterly. How she would wag her calloused finger to say, "I tol' yo' so, me girl. Yo' wid yo' big ideas."

Thinking of her mother momentarily stiffened her resolve. Even if the houses were bigger and more magnificent than anything she'd ever dreamed could exist, even if the ladies and gentlemen driving around the Savannah in their carriages and open touring cars were all like kings and queens, she, Rose Bracken, *wouldn't* be overpowered. She'd walk straight up to the front veranda, *not* the back, and she'd walk straight into the marble entrance hall, and she'd . . . although she'd rehearsed her arrival a thousand times in her head, she invariably drew a blank at this point, for what would she, in fact, say to the servants who let her in? Once she gave her name, would they send her around to the back porch to announce herself in the servants' quarters where she belonged or, knowing nothing about her background, would they accept her at face value as a visitor? (Although she was a visitor come to work in a special way for their mistress?)

It wasn't surprising that Rose Bracken, just turned seventeen and in a city for the first time in her life, felt so out of place.

Charles Kingsley, the author, had been accurate when he'd described Queen's Park Savannah, the beautiful meadow of over two hundred acres in the center of Trinidad's capital Port of Spain as "a public park and racecourse as neither London nor Paris can boast." It *was* magnificent, surrounded by palatial residences, including the most palatial of all, the governor's mansion set in botanical gardens full of rare and exotic flowers and trees from all over the world.

From where Rose now stood, Maraval Road stretched to the west, lined for as far as she could see with grand residences, each one appearing to want to outdo its neighbor in opulence and splendor: the turrets of a Scottish baronial castle reared above the royal palms lining its driveway, while next door a Moorish palace of white coralstone glistened in the sunlight, each minaret decorated with a tiny crown. Châteaux, castles, palaces . . . Rose became more and more awestruck as she walked—increasingly slowly—along the most famous road in the Caribbean, realizing that here, it was not a question of choosing to arrive at a front or back veranda, but of choosing between the grandest, most stately looking entrance and a gate clearly defined for "trade."

In the distance on a slight incline was the pink house her aunt had described. Shimmering in a heat haze, Rosefleur, her destination, could not be missed. The gloves she'd been so proud of, the first she'd ever owned, were wet with perspiration. Her hair, cut so meticulously into the latest bob, each black strand emphasizing the beautiful shape of her head and the whiteness of her skin, now hung in lank wisps.

She'd been counting the hours to this day, ever since she'd agreed to help her aunt with her dressmaking business, and now she was going to make a fool of herself. Perhaps her mother was right. Perhaps, despite her light skin, she didn't belong in the white people's world of power and privilege after all.

As she hesitated outside Rosefleur's towering gates, seeing through the wrought iron a curved drive lined with hibiscus of every rose-toned hue, she was on the point of returning to the tram stop, defeated, out of courage, when a Model T stopped at the curb and a swarthy man in a loud striped suit called out, "Are you lost, little lady? How would you like to climb in my dicky and be shown the way?" As he started to get out of the car, Rose bolted through the gates, one fear driven out by a more familiar one. She ran panting up the drive, thinking bitterly, Men, black or white, they're all out for the same thing—whether they're on Maraval Road or "dancin' the cocoa" in Santa Cruz. The man was still there as she approached the impressive double doors. There was nothing else she could do. She lifted the gargoyle-shaped knocker and let it fall.

She was so nervous that she hardly knew what she said to the East Indian servant who opened the door, then silently showed her into a huge drawing room. First she sat, then she stood, then sat again, gingerly on the edge of a plump pink satin armchair. It was one of a suite of six, she noted with amazement, each of which had a contrasting pink-lace stuffed pillow. After a few minutes when nobody came, she dared to raise her eyes from the marble floor to look around, marveling at everything. There were flowers everywhere, in Dresden china wall vases, in crystal, in silver cups and jardinieres, even growing in a miniature garden where china figurines appeared to be tending each bud.

A crystal chandelier hung from the paneled ceiling along with crystal pendants that slowly turned, reflecting in miniature every object in the room and the vista of pink blossoms outside. Everything was pink or gold or silver. It was dazzling.

Across the room, Rose realized with a start, she could see her reflection in a long gilded glass, and her crushed demeanor shocked her anew. It was incredible how quickly her dreams of a new life, of independence away from the shackles of her family, could be wiped out with one brief glimpse of the reality of white power.

She was biting her nails, something she'd vowed never to do again if she could only leave Santa Cruz, when the door opened and Madame Vincent, her aunt's most important customer, swept in, chattering excitedly, clanking with bracelets and necklaces and followed by two yapping white poodles.

"But you are *vraiment belle, ma chérie!*" Madame Vincent cried. "Let me regard. . . . Can you really sew like the angel you look?"

When Rose knew Madame Vincent better, she learned that no questions were ever meant to be answered except when, following a few glasses of rum and milk, Madame Vincent needed to be reassured as to the durability of her own voluptuous looks. On this first day Rose stuttered, stammered and tried to break through the torrent of words, all to no avail.

Rose could, indeed, sew like an angel. She didn't know why. She had never had a lesson. Who was there to teach her in the wild country place she came from? Who there had even understood her passion for fabric, for needle and thread, which in her hands gave a certain look, a line to the old clothes handed out to the workers by the wives and daughters of the Santa Cruz gentry.

How she hated their smug, charitable faces. It gave her a certain satisfaction to rip away at "their" seams, their "safe" necklines . . . to create all manner of extraordinary garments. Oh, the battles she'd had with her mother over her clothes. Battles that she always won, for her mother wasn't only colored, she was stupid—stupid enough to get pregnant practically every time her husband condescended to pay her a visit, which, as Rose grew up to discover, was luckily only every few years.

It wasn't until her aunt made the arduous cross-country journey from the city to visit them on Rose's fifteenth birthday that Rose discovered her aunt was actually a kindred spirit, not only because she was almost as light-skinned as herself, but because her aunt had the same kind of quick, deft fingers that could tie a bow like an artist, could drape a piece of sacking around her and still make it look like something. And it was her aunt (unbelievable, Rose often thought, that she could actually be her mother's sister, they were so unalike) who detected Rose's ability not only to sew but to design. Her aunt hadn't laughed at the wild and fanciful things Rose designed, made and wore out of the scraps that came her way. Instead she had urged Rose's mother to let her seek a future in Port of Spain because, she'd told them all, now that the war was over, there were many parties being given to celebrate the return of the heroes from the trenches.

"I'm workin' me fingers t' de bones, Aggie. Rose be a big help t' me. Yo' know I'll look aft'r her lik' mah own."

But her aunt's request had fallen on deaf ears. Her mother was scared, as she said at least twice a day, that Rose would come to no good in the city. Her skin was too light, her head too full of grand ideas. No, it was better Rose stayed on the farm where her mother could keep an eye on her until she found a local boy to bed with and settle down.

It had taken two years of cajoling, begging, scheming and finally scaring the daylights out of her mother for Rose's prayers to be answered. She didn't pray to God. She was sure He didn't exist. How could He exist, bringing her into a world where she so obviously didn't belong, for Rose had known since she was a small child that she had been born to the wrong mother. She prayed instead to her aunt, by then back in Port of Spain far away across the valley. Every night she knelt on the hard clay floor of the mud-and-wattle hut in which she lived with her mother and an ever increasing tribe of multicolored sisters and brothers, beseeching, "Auntie, please don' forget me. Please rescue me. Please com' bac' an' tak' me wid yo' t' de big city. I'll work mah fingers off for yo'. Please. . . ." The mud-and-wattle walls heard the same pleas again and again, but if her mother—and father, on his infrequent visits—heard her, they never mentioned it.

If it hadn't been for the events of the Harvest Festival, Rose was certain she would still have been working "as a skivvy" on her mother's cocoa patch—ten acres of nothingness, as she scornfully described the place of her birth. The more her mother took pride in her acres, the more Rose derided her. "What good is it t' grow an' sell 'nough cocoa t' feed us, clothe us year in, year out, wid ne'er a penny ev'r for anythin' else?" she'd yell. Being brought up in the depths of the Santa Cruz valley was full of endless trials and tribulations as far as Rose was concerned, for then it was a long way from the civilization of Port of Spain.

Only one unpaved road lay over the mountains, with the alternative in the dry months of trying to get down the hills to the road that led to the railway station at San Juan. In the rainy months, from June to December, the latter route was too dangerous, for there were no bridges over the river, which crossed the road at several points.

How Rose hated the rainy season, when everywhere she went she was ankle deep, if not knee deep, in mud. How she loathed her regular tasks, in particular looking after the beehive mud oven outside the hut where she did the cooking for the family while her mother looked after the cocoa. She'd have to wait for the fire to burn itself to embers and rake them through before putting in a slab of meat—when there was enough money for meat—sealing up the oven till the meat was cooked, then clean it all out again. The monotonous drudgery of it all slouched her shoulders, and turned her mouth down until sometimes she thought she'd forgotten how to smile.

The Bracken cocoa patch wasn't the only small one in the area. There were many, because it was the richest cocoa-growing area on the island, and under Spanish laws (which the British had continued to observe after their capture of the island in 1797), a slave was allowed to plant cocoa on land allotted to him for growing his food. If and when he raised a thousand cocoa trees to bearing stage, the law stated the slave had to be given his freedom. The sugar industry didn't have a similar law attached, so naturally the slaves loved cocoa and formed hundreds of small cocoa groves in order to be free.

By the year of Rose's birth in 1905, 41 million pounds of cocoa had been produced in Trinidad, and by 1911 cocoa had superseded sugar as the island's main crop.

For as long as Rose could remember, she'd formed the habit of grinding her teeth whenever her mother boasted—as she often did—in her high singsong voice about her illustrious ancestors, in particular the fine French gentleman who'd bedded down his slave, her mother's great-great-grandmother, who'd given birth to a "beaut'f'l light-color'd son an' name' him Maurice, a fine, fancy French name. . . ."

It was Maurice who'd been left the land they lived on, and Rose's mother constantly tried to make Rose, her eldest child, appreciate their good fortune, that despite attempts of Sir Ralph Woodford, the British governor of the time, to stop bequests by foreign settlers to their illegitimate colored children, their noble ancestor had honored his promise so that "no-on' an' nuttin' can ev'r tak' our land away."

Sir Ralph Woodford *had* tried—to no avail—to do away with many of the laws originally drawn up by the Spanish to attract their people to the island in the late eighteenth century, and he'd especially frowned on the habit of landowners sleeping with their slave women. As he'd frequently pointed out, whenever the women became pregnant and paternity was acknowledged, it hoisted the offspring on to an "intermediate" level between white (their father's race) and black (their mother's). This, Sir Ralph correctly predicted, would lead eventually to racial friction, for it was commonly accepted that the West African slaves brought in to cultivate the land were a rank below those of mixed blood!

Rose cringed when her mother preened herself to speak about her distant French ancestor—exhibiting a pride that had been handed down by one generation to the next, for Maurice's pride in his French father now far transcended any thought of his black slave mother, a prevalent attitude among "free coloreds," leading a wit of the day to say, "It's as if they were born in the land of the rooster egg!"

If her great-great-grandfather Maurice had had any sense, Rose often reflected, he'd have continued to strengthen his white strain, not his black . . . for her mother omitted to mention all that came after: that Maurice, secure on his ten acres, had married another "free colored," who'd given birth to a light-skinned daughter, who'd gone with an African black to give birth to a black daughter who, in 1886, aged fourteen, had given birth to Rose's mother, Aggie, in a sugar field alone under the stars.

Aggie's father had also been a white man, but "no gentl'man" Aggie would hiss at Rose, taunted beyond endurance by her high and mighty ways. "He may hav' help'd yo' git yo' Trinidad white skin . . . but he nev'r gave me mudder or me nuttin'."

"Why didn' yo' watch out for yo'self den," Rose would cry. "Why tak' in a man lik' me father?" But Rose already knew why. It was said her father Bert Bracken could "charm the birds off the trees," and she believed he probably could.

Light skinned, Bert's African roots nevertheless made themselves visible in flaring nostrils, tight curly hair and whiter than white fingernails, but—something not unusual to see in Trinidad—Bert also had vivid blue eyes as a result of his ancestor's follies, eyes that always seemed to be laughing, as he promised Aggie and the children the moon . . . until the sun came up to reveal he'd already moved on.

It had hurt Rose agonizingly once, but as she grew up and her father's visits became fewer and the length between them longer, Rose had built a wall of indifference against him, despising her mother's weakness for always taking him back, haughty and cold whenever he tried to win her over.

Rose's French great-great-great-grandfather wasn't the only ancestor talked about in the Bracken home.

There was another, a celebrity in a way, whom her mother would refer to—another reason, apart from Rose's growing beauty and amazing white skin, to single out the Brackens on their paltry cocoa patch. For the female slave who'd caught the attention in no uncertain way of the French landowner was (and here Rose's mother would puff out her cheeks and straighten her shoulders before making her announcement) a niece of Louisa Calderon.

It was a name that produced low whistles and incredulous stares. Louisa Calderon was part of Trinidad's colorful history, a black slave girl who'd caused a major uproar in Port of Spain, when after three hundred years of Spanish rule, Trinidad had passed into British hands at the end of the British-Spanish war and Trinidad's first British governor, Lieutenant Colonel Thomas Picton, had ordered Louisa Calderon to be tortured when she wouldn't admit to a charge of petty theft.

Aggie loved to deliver the gory details: "Her right han' was tied t' her right leg, her lef' han' t' a rope an' dat rope i' be tied t' a big beam, de rope passin' through a pulley . . . her lef' foot dat be lef' t' hang ov'r a sharp wood'n spike . . . an' sh' be lift'd up an' down on dis big spike . . . ." Aggie's voice grew high with excitement as she came to the finale. "Sh' couldn' bear de pain an' in de en' sh' 'fess'd sh'd help'd her man steal de money. . . ."

When news of Louisa's torture arrived in England, Governor Picton was severely censured, and in order to show the world the British know how to shoulder their responsibilities—however many thousands of miles away they might be—the British government reduced Picton's authority, setting up a three-man commision to ensure British "fair play," a two-to-one vote deciding any future controversial matter. Joining Picton in Trinidad came the aristocratic Colonel William Fullarton and a naval officer Samuel Hood.

At their first official meeting Picton and Fullarton clashed violently, Picton already judged in Fullarton's mind as a man unworthy of his stewardship. This early conflict was fanned by members of the local elite, mainly Spanish but also many full-blooded French aristocrats who, during the Jacobin terror, had emigrated to Trinidad from their homeland as well as from Haiti and other French possessions.

At the turn of the century, encouraged by local society in his outspoken criticism of Picton, Fullarton brought criminal charges against his co-commissioner on the Louisa Calderon issue. Picton's defense: that Castilian laws, which allowed torture to be used during the questioning of an accused, were still in force at the time of his administration.

At first Picton was condemned, but on his appeal he was granted a second trial when Fullarton, to arouse public feelings still more, took

Louisa Calderon to England to parade her as a "blessed innocent." Despite these efforts, however, the jury finally returned a verdict in favor of Picton, although it did him little good. Soon after, in 1815, he died in action leading his men in a bayonet charge at Waterloo.

Deep down, Rose was proud of her distant relationship to Louisa Calderon. In her fantasies she often saw herself as a heroine, dangling above the pointed spike, turning Louisa into a kind of Joan of Arc, conveniently overlooking the reason for Louisa's travail.

After her aunt left, as one dreary day followed another, Rose withdrew more and more into her fantasy world, imagining herself one minute as a great dress designer, the next as a martyr suffering on the spike.

She thought of running away, but something always stopped her: her very real fear of men, who, to her innate disgust, seemed to be increasingly aware of her body, always wanting to touch her.

To her mother's relief, Rose was not only uninterested in men, she made it clear they were to stay out of her way. Rose knew she could look after herself in the small community where she lived, where everyone knew each other and the men knew they were likely to get a stick poked in their eye if they so much as tried to lay a finger on her. But, Rose thought, who knew what she might encounter on the long journey alone over the mountains to reach her aunt's place? She'd heard stories about what bands of roaming young men could do to a woman, stories that were enough to curl the straight black hair she was so proud of.

A mile away from the hut where Rose lived was the Fedder plantation, one of the biggest estates in the valley. Aggie often went there to make extra money as a washerwoman, taking Rose with her—protesting all the way—as well as Rose's younger sister, to work in the kitchens whenever the Fedders needed extra pairs of hands.

Although it was the biggest estate around, there weren't many amenities or certainly any luxuries at Fedder, where the emphasis for over a hundred years had been on work from dawn to dusk. The large single-story estate house had been built of native hardwood and cedar to survive the extremes of the tropical climate and there was nothing fancy about it; everything was functional, plain.

There was no laid-on water supply, and the Fedders had to rely on four tanks, one positioned at each corner of the house to catch the rain from the roof. As the dry season approached, the tanks were locked and bath water was rationed.

The Brackens had no tanks, but they did have a waterhole, which worked well enough, except during the dry season when it became black with the falling of leaves and flowers and the Brackens resigned themselves to going dirty.

If water was a treat to Rose, ice was a luxury and one she surrounded herself with in her fantasies . . . ever since the time at Fedder she'd actually seen someone put a piece of ice in a drink! The sight had filled her mind for days. Until then she had only been familiar with the big dirty slabs of ice hauled to Fedder from the train at San Juan and used solely for the purpose of keeping huge raw chunks of meat fresh.

Only the Fedders' dripstone compensated Rose for the indignity of having to work in the kitchen there. At least from the dripstone she knew she could get the occasional sip of cool drinking water which after working in the kitchen's steamy heat tasted like nectar and was so much better than the water from their own waterhole. After dripping through a porous coral vessel to another set immediately below, the water poured in became filtered and cooled by evaporation.

Life in the valley was tranquil ("deadly dull and dreary" to Rose), its rarely changing routine interrupted only by two social events each year: the Catholic church's Harvest Festival celebration and the Discovery Day race meeting on the beach.

Even the Fedders opened up their house for Harvest Festival, for it was traditionally expected the "gentry" should offer hospitality and invite house guests over the weekend in order to swell the coffers of the church.

After high mass, people came from far and near to Fedder for an annual fair and auction of bags of cocoa and other provisions, all donated by well-to-do planters, the proceeds of which also went to the church.

For once Rose didn't argue with her mother when she suggested Rose might like to make something for a needlework stall, an idea brought back from England by one of the Fedder granddaughters. Rose was determined to show those stuck-up plain janes what she could do and, to her mother's surprise, Rose volunteered to run the stall as well, providing she didn't have to wash any dishes following the big buffet which, along with a well-stocked bar, remained open until long after nightfall.

Rose was proud of her efforts—toy animals made out of fabric scraps, stuffed and padded, with funny expressions sewn on their faces. And just as she'd expected, they sold out long before the other donated needlework items.

Crowds strolled by, laughing, carefree, happy that something different was actually happening to relieve the day-to-day monotony of life spent on the land.

Rose felt restive, hot; her tongue was parched, and worse, her body was grubby and sticky with heat. The waterhole had been dry for five days now, and she yearned for the feeling of water on her skin.

To her annoyance, trickles of perspiration started to run down her nose. She was sure she looked a sight with her usually pale cheeks flushed and sweaty. Well, at least the day was coming to an end, and with nightfall, she thought, she could slip away and drink to her heart's content from the Fedders' back veranda dripstone.

At that moment, as if he had read her mind, an elegant young man dressed in the *de rigueur* linen suit, soft shirt, bow tie and panama hat stopped at the stall and said, "Would you like a drink?"

Rose smiled gratefully. "I'd lov' one. D'yo' kno' where de dripstone is? At de bac' porch . . . ?"

"Oh, I can do better than that," he said with a languid smile, and before she could say another word, he strolled toward the bar, returning in a few minutes with a tall glass of what looked like icy water.

"What's dat?" Rose asked suspiciously.

"Better than water, believe me. Very refreshing." He had an accent she'd never heard before, a soft drawl that was very soothing.

She took a sip. It was delicious. "Coco'nut wat'r?"

He laughed and nodded as he watched her greedily drink it down. When he suggested another, she couldn't resist.

Suddenly, everything stood out in greater relief . . . looked sunnier, more colorful. The world—even at boring old Fedder—wasn't such a bad place after all, and she felt a surge of optimism that soon she'd be able to join her aunt and conquer the world.

The young man was back, and, looking at the sophisticated cut of his clothes, his air of self-confidence, Rose was flattered, even excited by his attention. "You still look very hot," he said. "Can't you come into the shade?"

"It'll soon be dark. It'll be cool an' I ca' leave. . . ." She felt like singing and leaned forward, resting her full breasts on the counter, cupping her face in her hands. She didn't understand why, but she heard herself saying, "Ca' I tell yo' a secr't?"

The young man laughed again and obligingly bent his head to listen as she whispered in his ear, "I'd love t' tak' a bath in dis icy drink."

He whispered back, "That would be too cold. What about a cool shower?"

She giggled conspiratorially at his crazy suggestion. "Dat's a lov'ly idea." Like magic, another glass of the delicious mixture appeared at her elbow and this time she savored it slowly through a straw, her black silky lashes every so often closing over her eyes. She felt strangely sleepy, relaxed, although it was hours from her bedtime.

Music started up on the long gallery. She could hear the Charleston, and she started to move her body sinuously from side to side in time to its rhythm.

The young man was now stroking her arm, something she usually hated, but the nearer he came the more she liked the smell of lavender about him, the smooth pink of his boyish cheek.

"Oh, there you are, Charles. You *are* a naughty boy wandering off like that."

It was Clarissa, one of the Fedder granddaughters, recently engaged, so Rose had heard from local gossip, to an American. Was this the American? If so, she liked Americans; they were much more attractive than Trinidadians. She hiccuped and laughed at her thoughts, but Clarissa didn't seem amused.

"How are you, Rose?" she asked loftily. "I hear you've made some pretty little toys out of the old cushion covers Grandmama sent you." She turned to the young man who still leaned against the stall. "Rose is a talented seamstress, darling. Perhaps one day we may even ask her to join our household. It's always useful to have a few sewing women around." Without another look in Rose's direction, Clarissa tucked her arm through her fiancé's with a proprietary air and they walked away in the direction of the music. Rose's cheeks flushed with anger. Damn dem, she thought, as she took a greedy suck of the last drop of coconut water. Damn dem all t' hell!

Colored lights went on around the gallery as dusk fell with tropical suddenness, and Rose heard a familiar buzz of mosquitoes arriving. She started to lock up the proceeds from her sales in the metal box provided by the church when to her surprise she found the young man back at her side. "Charles, yo' naughty boy," she mimicked, not believing her own cheek. "What ar' yo' doin' bac' wid de lil' ol' sewin' girl?"

He gave her a playful whack on her bottom and whispered, "Do you still want to take that icy bath?" An unusual feeling of excitement flooded through her as she nodded vigorously. "Yes, oh, yes."

"Guess what"—his drawl was as soothing to her as a snake charmer's—"I know how you can get your wish."

"Yo' do?" The thought of giving her body the same kind of drink she'd been sipping all afternoon was glorious.

"Come with me," he said, and like a child Rose placed her hand innocently in his and followed him behind a grove of breadfruit trees, avoiding the front gallery now packed with rocking, pitching couples dancing the Charleston as if their lives depended on it. Through a gate marked PRIVATE, she went with her guide to a side of the plantation house she'd never seen, where with an exaggerated bow the young man brushed aside a cluster of coconut palm fronds that fell naturally to the ground to show her they enclosed a slab of concrete set in the earth to make a "natural" bathhouse.

"Where's de ice?" She giggled nervously.

"I am at your service, Mistress Rose. Just get ready for your bath and the ice will suddenly enfold you." She shivered in anticipation as he continued, "I will now leave you to your pleasures, madam." He bowed ceremoniously again and ducked out under the fronds.

"Ar' yo' sure no one will com'?" she called out.

"You have my word on it, pretty Miss Rose."

Her heart beating fast, Rose slipped off her frayed ankle-strapped sandals, loving the feel of the cold concrete underfoot. She peeped her head out of the fronds but there was no one in sight. She decided she didn't care even if there was anyone around and, humming under her breath the current favorite, "The Sheik of Araby," she let her short dress (too short by far, her mother had snorted) fall to the floor, then wriggled out of her first camisole bra. Her mother would faint, Rose thought, if she ever saw she'd made one of the newfangled underpinnings for herself.

High above her from the coconuts came the by-now-familiar drawl: "A little to the right, please." As she squealed in alarm, a bucketful of ice came showering down all over her, followed by a bucketful of water. "Oh, oh, oh!" she cried as the cold water flowed over her hot skin. She tried to hide, to curl up in a corner, as the horrifying realization came that the American was actually looking at her undressed.

The euphoria of the afternoon washed away as fast as the water washed over her and she realized with a sick jolt she must be drunk. Frantically trying to find her clothes in the now almost totally dark bathhouse, her hands flew over the ground and among the coconut fronds, but she couldn't locate them. Now she was crying. What had she done? In her naked state how could she ever get home past all the people outside?

Ankle deep in lumps of ice that floated in the water slowly seeping its way into the earth, Rose had visions of herself spending the night there, half naked, waiting until just before dawn to creep home. Yet, at the same time Rose knew her mother would have long before sent out a search party.

"Oh, oh, oh," she cried over and over, wrapping herself round with her arms, moaning as if in pain.

The American boy was suddenly in the bathhouse with her, his hands forcing her arms away from her breasts, his knee pressing her legs open, his mouth brutally bruising hers, his tongue pushing itself down her throat. She wanted to die as she realized he was naked. She could feel him, huge, bulging, pressing into her body through her saturated pants as his hands squeezed her breasts.

He released her mouth and she screamed.

He slapped her sharply across the face. "For God's sake, be quiet. I thought you wanted a little fuck, you stupid fool. Open your legs like the fast little native girl you really are. Shut up and let's have some fun." But her scream had been heard. Outside were voices, and to her desperate shame Rose recognized the voice of old Mr. Fedder and the nightwatchman, one of her mother's closest friends.

She had nothing to lose now. If they passed by, who knew what this American fiend might do to her.

She screamed again, coughing and hiccuping, as the boy suddenly pushed her violently out of the coconut fronds to sprawl on the ground in front of the two astonished men. The American didn't lose his cool manner for one second. Poking his head out from between the fronds, he drawled, "This little miss surprised me in the shower, sir. I don't think she realized you only have enough water for one . . . hmm . . . I believe she's been partaking a little too freely of the coconut gin fizz." With that he withdrew his head inside and splashed the remaining water about noisily.

It had been the worst moment of her life, but afterward, as she constantly said to herself, at least it had meant her mother couldn't wait to get rid of her.

The next morning, after hearing the sordid details from the night-watchman, who came to deliver a stern message from Mr. and Mrs. Fedder that none of the family were ever to come near the Fedder plantation again, her mother, with lips clamped together, marched her down the valley to put her on the train to Port of Spain. She left Rose with the ultimatum never to return unless she got herself "resp'ctbl' married t' one o' our own kind."

Rose felt soiled, dirtied by the American boy's touch. She wasn't sure if the bulge pressing into her stomach would give her a baby. If it did, she was determined to drown it at birth.

Late at night she finally found her way to her aunt's house in Laventille, a poor suburb of Port of Spain. Her aunt's house came as a terrible shock. In Rose's fantasies she'd imagined it with bougainvillea growing around the door, with even two or three steps leading up to a front veranda and with real curtains at real glass windows. Instead, Rose found a single-room wooden house, the lumber blackened with age, the plank floor raised a few feet off the ground to fight the ever-encroaching damp and mildew, while in a corrugated shed outside was the same kind of mud oven she'd toiled over in Santa Cruz . . . and just beside it a pit latrine.

The one room was about fifteen feet square and cut almost in half by a battered screen that separated her aunt's large bed from the rest of the room, a bed that Rose found she was expected to share, as she'd always shared her sister's or mother's bed. Another disappointment, for she'd been sure her aunt would have a bed (or at least a cot) just for her.

Everywhere was evidence of her aunt's dressmaking business. On both sides of the screen the room was covered in bits and pieces of fabric, cotton, buttons, paper patterns, old newspapers, pins, needles, cotton spools.

Her aunt tried to keep everything clean, using the few tattered sheets she possessed to wrap around the dresses she was working on, but when the tradewinds blew, clay dust from the potholed track below covered everything in sight.

Rose was determined to make the best of it. She had nothing to lose, nothing to go back to. It was now or never . . . she had to move forward and whatever happened, she was going to treat white people as she'd been treated by them—with condescension or contempt, one or the other, taking, never giving and never, ever being led astray by a white man's charm again . . . or any man's for that matter!

The important thing was that she had arrived at an opportune time, for, as her aunt had predicted, parties were going on "roun' de clock," roaring away to the sounds of the newfangled jazz.

The "brigh' young t'ings," as her aunt called them, weren't content with evening parties any more. "Dey're dancin' in de aft'rnoon," she told her wide-eyed niece. For the Queens Park Hotel had just introduced a new idea called *thé dansante*. "From France, yo' know," which not only meant afternoon dancing, but afternoon dance frocks, too!

Her aunt spread out her fingers to show Rose how red and sore they were with sewing day and night . . . and yet there was still one lady, she told her sighing, she hadn't been able to please. She was the most important lady of all, Madame Vincent, a very rich widow, who went to and gave more parties than anyone else in the whole world.

Her aunt, cackling away with hoarse laughter, told Rose Madame Vincent was out to catch a man, not just any man but *the* man, *the* catch of Trinidad, Mr. Piper Pollard of Golden Hill, no less.

"She's bin drivin' me silly," Rose's aunt confided a few days after Rose's arrival, as they sat sewing together by the light of a kerosene lamp. "Yo' see, she's givin' dis costume party in his honor, dis Mr. Piper Pollar' o' Gold'n Hill, an' sh' wan's a dress lik' nobody has ev'r seen de lik's o' befor' an' dat no one will ev'r see again . . . dat will keep de world talkin', talkin'. Ever' time I tak' a pattern or pickt'ure out o' de pap'r, she runs roun' de room lik' a wil' wom'n. Now, I'v' got t' go bac' up dere by Sat'day wid somethin' sh' says ev'n de queen o' Sheba, whoe'r sh' may be, don' hav' de lik's of. . . . I don' know what I'm goin' t' do, chil'. . . ."

Her aunt rattled on nonstop as she sewed . . . about the miracles of Madame Vincent's house . . . about the brilliant and handsome American oil millionaire Piper Pollard, who with his colleague, Captain Arthur Cipriani, had returned from the war to change things for "de poor color'd folk, t' see dey get a fair share o' everyt'in'" . . . about Golden Hill, the finest old plantation in all of Trinidad, practically rebuilt by Piper Pollard since he bought it from Lieutenant Colonel Picton's heirs. . . . But Rose hardly listened and hardly spoke.

That world had nothing to do with her. Anyone who believed a white man—especially an *American* white man—would care tuppence for poor colored folk deserved what they got, including her aunt. Even the word *American* made Rose sick to her stomach. If Madame Vincent was stupid enough to want to dally with an American, all her money wouldn't save her from misery.

But Rose had no time to worry about that. In her mind she was busy designing the most incredible dress anyone had ever worn. She had the beginnings of an idea that might be able to surprise and satisfy even Madame Vincent. The idea consumed her, and long after her aunt started snoring the night away, she silently sketched and cut up any bits of fabric she came across, easy to find under every cushion, under the bed, on shelves, even in cooking pots.

When her aunt returned from visiting Madame Vincent on Saturday, she was close to tears. "Sh' didn' lik' me ideas. Sh' frew dem on de floor an' her lil' dog, he did tear dem up. . . ." Her aunt, biting her lip, sniveled. "I tol' her 'bout yo', Rose. I said mah lil' niece ca' sew lik' an angel . . . dat sh'll know what t' do. Dat Madame Vincent just 'bout has ev'r' pair o' fing'rs workin' for her now for dat ball sh'll be givin' in de most beaut'ful house in all de world. . . ."

It *is* the most beautiful house in all the world, Rose thought as, two days after meeting the volatile Madame Vincent, she sat sewing as fast as her fingers could move, looking out over the pink blossoming gardens of Rosefleur. She couldn't believe her luck in one way, yet in another she felt she deserved every bit of it.

Events had moved swiftly, her nervousness subsiding when she realized with a flash of joy that Madame Vincent was so enchanted with her design . . . *"ravissant, incroyable . . ."* she was actually stamping her tiny feet in impatience wanting the dress to appear like magic at once.

"If you could only stay here, *chérie*, and make the dress now," she'd wheedled. "But I suppose your aunt would not like zis? No?"

The lie had slipped out effortlessly, as smoothly as Rose's needle moved through the silk. "Bu' Auntie tol' me t' stay wid yo' if yo' lik' dat—'til de dress . . . dresses —she'd hastily corrected herself (the more she could do, the longer she could stay)—"are t' yo' likin'. Sh' doesn' expec' t' see me bac' 'less yo' didn' lik' de dresses, Madame Vincent."

Like an excited little girl, Tilly Vincent had clapped her plump hands together, making her bracelets jangle all the more while the poodles barked and raced around and around jumping on and off the plumped-up pillows. *"Merveilleux!* It is settled then, *ma chérie.* We start now." And, running out of the room, she had beckoned Rose to follow her to her dressing room where, lined up like giant dolls were six dummies, all replicas of Madame Vincent's shape. Rose had learned, to her astonishment, that Madame's shape varied wildly, going in and out and up and down with the help of vigorous massage, salt baths and a native concoction called "rurue," all dictated by whatever the latest fashion happened to be. When hips were "in" Madame Vincent was at her happiest, because, as she cried to Rose, "Ze rurue doesn't work so fast any more. My waist is tiny but"—she patted her plump behind—"zis does not go down so fast . . . does not look so good in the flapper dresses."

Rose had been given a toothbrush (the first she had ever seen), a can of salt with which to scrub her teeth, a piece of soap, a bowl for washing, some faded but clean cotton smocks and a tiny room off the sewing room with a small cot, on which she learned to her joy she would be sleeping alone.

Now, just as she was beginning to feel more at ease, Sam the East Indian butler came to tell her the dressmaker was in the servants' quarters asking to see her.

Rose was torn with indecision. Even though two days had passed, she hadn't yet set foot in the servants' quarters and it appeared she didn't need to, providing she could continue to hold Madame Vincent's interest with her sewing and designs. She'd been told to take her meals with M'selle Marie, an ancient French lady, who had been with Madame Vincent since Madame's birth, first as a nanny, then as a tutor and finally as a responsibility, when arthritis crippled her arms and legs.

To Rose's astonishment she had even been waited on in M'selle's little dining area. Now, she decided, if she acknowledged the dressmaker as her aunt, it would bring her down to the servants' level. It was far better, she thought, to see her aunt later—much later—when she could send her something nice as a farewell present. And Rose was determined that it *was* farewell, forever. She would never go back to that shack. She'd rather die.

Rose sent a message downstairs via Sam that Miss Bracken was too busy to see the dressmaker, but would certainly think of her, if there was any sewing work needed in the future.

On the day he was to be the guest of honor at Madame Vincent's ball, Piper Pollard met with his wartime colleague and friend, Captain Arthur Cipriani.

A Creole of Corsican extraction, Cipriani was the man often described as the "knight errant" of Trinidad politics, ever since his unanimous election to lead the Workingman's Association, the first masses-based force in politics on the island, uniting many colors and creeds.

The formation of the Association had staved off an explosive situation in the early twenties, when black soldiers returning from the Great War had found themselves poorer than when it began. They had gone on a rampage—striking, rioting, leading to what was called a "crusade against the aristocracy," in which the entire city of Port of Spain had been held to ransom by demonstrators, forcing shops, offices, even the waterfront to close down—when domestic workers had been called out from the fine residences to rebel against the white man's domination.

"The mob has tasted blood," one editorial of the day had stated. "Its leaders have envisaged the delight of power and are threatening 'more to come.' The rioters are anarchists, myrmidons of a gang of skallywags from other islands, who have hoodwinked the Trinidad masses. . . ." To defend property, people and honor, Piper Pollard had formed a "vigilante platoon" of two hundred and seventy planters and merchants, but the situation had worsened, until Cipriani stepped into the breach.

It was typical of the many anomalies of the times that no serious objection had been raised over having a white planter lead a predominantly black, lower-class, social-protest movement, for in the early 1920s, Trinidad seethed with the greatest mix of races and religions in the world.

The old French and Spanish Creole families, who could trace their land ownership back over hundreds of years, still felt a sense of superiority over the British "interlopers," although over a hundred years had passed since the British had begun to rule the island from London.

The Negro was no longer a slave, but he felt like one. His position hadn't been improved by the island's liberal immigration policies either—ironically put into force as a result of his refusal to work in the cane fields following emancipation. In order to save the sugar estates, the British government had given permission as far back as 1844 for the West Indian colonies to import a massive labor force from China and India.

Cipriani, decorated for gallantry during the war, as Piper had been, had gained the confidence and respect of black servicemen, who believed him when he said, as he often said publicly, "I represent the unwashed, unsoaped, barefoot men. I believe in agitation . . . for education and confederation."

"I'm optimistic," Cipriani told Piper now, as they sat together in his inner sanctum. Only recently returned from London, Cipriani was bringing Piper up to date on the recommendation contained in a government report regarding the number of "serious disturbances" taking place on the island. "In short, for the first time since 1831, we are to have a say in our own affairs," Cipriani said dryly. "This report recommends a very thorough parliamentary reform, my friend"—he shut the government document on his desk with an air of satisfaction—"a chance

at last for the West Indies to speak with its own voice." His face lit up
with his usual charming smile. "You see, dear fellow, you were quite
wrong about the British Empire and the English gentleman. We *are*
listened to and our request for more participation in our own affairs is
not doomed to be ignored."

Piper laughed, but Cipriani went on undiscouraged. "When the Labour Party comes into power in Westminster, you'll see, they'll show
the world they mean what they say about anti-imperialism. One day we
can hope for universal suffrage here."

Piper snorted. "That's a fantasy, Arthur, and you know it. One man,
one vote will never happen, and probably never should."

Despite his comments, Piper was really thrilled by Cipriani's news.
His two passions in life, gambling and politics, were intimately related—and the biggest gamble of his life had been to stay in Trinidad,
an island he freely admitted he found intoxicating. Piper had come to
Trinidad in the early 1900s, and had struck oil at Point Fortin in 1911.
With his early oil strike he had had money from the beginning to take
advantage of all the good things in life that were so easily to hand, as
well as to enjoy the exotic beauty of the surroundings. And now, he
reflected, the time was coming when he might be able to influence, if
only in a small way, events happening on the world's stage.

Piper reveled in being the confidant of Cipriani, who he knew was a
natural-born leader. As power and influence on the island changed—as
one day Piper believed they would have to change—he reckoned he'd
still be on top . . . providing he continued to use some of the revenue
from his oil wells to cultivate and manipulate the right people.

"The Corsican" (as Cipriani was known in the press) stretched his
arms up over his head lazily and said, "Well, I mustn't keep you from
your afternoon poker. Or are you taking a nap to build your strength for
the French onslaught tonight?"

Piper laughed easily again. "*Chacun a son goût*, my friend. Just
thank your lucky stars you're not a widower like me. Thank goodness,
my social conscience keeps me so busy, I have little time for frivolity."
Piper reached up for his panama hat, tilting it at a rakish angle over his
tanned forehead. He winked and then swung out of the room, raising
his hat and throwing a kiss to Cipriani's secretaries in the outer office,
who agreed yet again that "Mr. Pollard has to be the best lookin' man
we've ever seen—next to Rudolph Valentino."

The ball dress that was to make Trinidad history was in place on

Madame Vincent's number-three dummy—a little rounder than the number-two version, because Madame Vincent had been right—the rurue wasn't working so fast for her any more. Only the all-important additions from Rose's precious jar had to be added and sewn into place.

By seven o'clock, an hour before the dinner that preceded the ball, Madame Vincent had changed from one dinner gown to another, finally deciding, much to Rose's chagrin, on a deceptively simple sheath by a French designer called Coco Chanel. When M'selle told her with an air of triumph that Madame Vincent had chosen a French dress to wear to the dinner over the one Rose had designed, Rose sniffed. "Hmph," she said, "whoev'r heard o' a great design'r nam'd aft'r de cocoa bean?"

When Rose saw that the straight lines of the sheath gave Madame Vincent a svelteness she didn't naturally possess, she was impressed. She vowed to herself that once Madame Vincent changed into the ball gown, she would try to take a close look at the seams and, with luck, if there was the right opportunity, she would unpick them, too, to see just how the "cocoa bean" worked such magic.

Rosefleur was illuminated inside and out. It glowed like a great rose-colored bonfire at the end of the drive, which itself was a river of light from flaming torches, brands and flares casting a golden radiance over the guests, as they arrived at the marble entrance in their cars and carriages.

Inside, the hall had been transformed into a garden at twilight, the twilight that promises but never comes in the tropics. A soft pink light filtered through a ceiling made of interlocking tropical foliage—wild poinsettias, oleanders, lady-of-the-night, orchids of every color and combination—while in the background could be heard the sweet bird-song of the kiskedee (named after the song it sang) and yellowtail birds. It was breathtaking, even Piper had to admit that, more impressive than anything he had ever seen in any capital of the world he told a spar-kling-eyed Madame Vincent.

The dining room, forty feet long, was surrounded by a wide covered gallery on three sides onto which eight pairs of double doors opened. Rose had not only been allowed to watch from a dark corner of the gallery, she had been commanded to, for at a certain signal she was to rush upstairs to fit Madame Vincent into the ball gown, which only she could do.

Although the fear she'd felt so acutely on her arrival at the house only ten days before had been evaporating during long days of unceasing

sewing, cutting, fitting, sketching, Rose again felt the same sense of
nervous awe, as she saw through the open doors reflections in several
long mirrors of the huge silver candelabras blazing with light on the
long Chippendale table.

Although Madame Vincent had shrewdly decided on an understated
dress for dinner—in order to make the impact all the greater when she
appeared later dressed anew for her ball—her guests, without the opportunity to change, were already in ball gowns, so different from the short
flapper frocks they usually wore.

Not only were they enjoying the "return to the past," as the ball was
themed, in billowing skirts and tightly boned bodices that cinched their
waists and showed off their bosoms ("out of sight for far too long," as
one happy elderly man guffawed), they were also enjoying the novelty of
the hairpieces dressed high on their heads with osprey feathers, flowers
and jewels, while their arms were encased in long white gloves. "They
must be four fingers above the elbow," Madame Vincent told Rose,
who eagerly lapped up every piece of information.

How she longed to be part of the parade, while at the same time the
practical side of her nature told her how infernally hot the ladies must
be, despite the servants behind every chair, fanning them hour after
hour. Although Rose knew she had at least a couple of hours before the
signal, she didn't dare take her eyes away from her employer for more
than a few minutes at a time, so it was easy for her to observe the guest
of honor sitting with such confidence and charm on Madame Vincent's
right.

As one sumptuous course followed another, Rose's mouth curled in
contempt as she saw how easily he made her mistress twitter and flutter
and blush. Another American fiend, she thought furiously, may he boil
in eternal damnation.

Every so often she felt herself go hot all over as Piper Pollard's eyes
seemed to look directly into hers. It was an illusion, she knew. He
couldn't possibly see her crouched in the corner, yet again and again it
seemed to happen.

From the ballroom came faint strains of the orchestra tuning up, and,
as Sam came in, followed by ten other waiters all bearing jeroboams of
champagne, Madame Vincent stood up and then sat down again. It was
the arranged signal and Rose hastily got to her feet, not noticing a heavy
jardiniere to her left. Her foot caught in the iron leg and she fell with
what sounded to her like an earth-shaking crash, but with all the conversation and clinking of glasses and plates in the dining room, only

Madame Vincent, her concentration now only partly on the dining table, heard it. She got up in a flutter of consternation to go outside to the gallery. Nothing must happen to the sewing girl *before*. *After* it didn't matter what happened to her. Piper Pollard, seeing his hostess's agitation, followed her, gesturing with his hand to the guests nearest to them to remain seated.

"Rose!" Tilly Vincent's voice shrilled hysterically. She came outside to see Rose holding onto the gallery balustrade. "Rose"—again the voice came out like a screech—"what is it?"

Piper Pollard strode over to Rose. "Is your ankle twisted? Let me see." He started to inspect her foot but was stopped in his tracks, shocked by the look of virulent hatred on her face.

"I'm al' right, I'm al' right!" Rose cried, limping past him as fast as her injured foot would allow. Piper followed her to the back stairway, still attempting to help her, but Rose hissed at him violently, "Don' yo' com' near me. Keep away, yo'—yo'—" She didn't finish her sentence, but rudely shut the staircase door in his face.

By the time she reached the dressing room, Madame Vincent was already there. In her anxiety over her dress, Madame Vincent hadn't even noticed Rose's rudeness to her guest of honor, but he had certainly noticed it and it disturbed him considerably.

What on earth could he have done to receive such a look of passionate hate from such a beautiful young girl? He wondered if perhaps she could be the sister of somone he'd squired around since his wife's death, but then Tilly Vincent had told him she was the sewing girl. But what on earth was a girl who looked like that doing as a sewing girl?

Rose momentarily forgot the pain of her ankle as she helped Madame Vincent into the delicate lace and gauze dress and added the finishing touch from her jar, "the *pièce de résistance*" as Madame Vincent referred to it: for the bodice, already a miracle of puckering, was now glittering, alive with flashing light, as between each pucker small and great fireflies were imprisoned for the night of the ball to flash their special tropical light on and off, on and off until dawn.

It was a sensation. As Madame Vincent stood at the top of the ballroom stairs, even the diamonds in her hair couldn't compete with the fireflies in her bodice, so brilliantly trapped by Rose that they didn't realize they were trapped at all and sparkled with their unique radiance in the specially dimmed lights. As cymbals clashed and the drums beat a tattoo to announce the hostess's arrival, slowly, like a queen, Tilly Vincent descended while the orchestra played "Mademoiselle from Armentiers." And like a dutiful swain, Piper waited at the bottom of the staircase to bow low over Tilly's plump hand. He could hardly hide his amusement as the fireflies flashed in his face. What an act! What a dress! Well, Tilly had certainly made her mark in Trinidad history tonight—dubious mark though it might be. It was as well, Piper thought, as he waltzed Tilly into the ballroom, that there was no Royal Society for the Prevention of Cruelty to Insects. With everyone stopping them to exclaim over the dress, it was easy for Piper to bring up the subject still nagging at his mind. "Tilly, you're a genius," he said. "Only you, with your French sense of chic, could have found a country girl who knows how to sew and how to tame fireflies at the same time." It was just the right bait.

"Chéri, of course, I have always wanted to show you my love of nature, and this was the right way, was it not?" As his flattery continued and he pressed her into dancing one dance after another, he learned all he could about the young girl with the face of a Botticelli angel, who so obviously loathed him. He found out very little because Tilly Vincent obviously didn't know much, except the girl—Rose—had colored blood, despite her camellia-white skin.

After three dances, Piper, with seeming reluctance, relinquished his hostess to dance with the man of the hour, Captain Cipriani. And certain she was well on the way to winning Piper as a husband, Tilly Vincent celebrated by lifting up her voluminous skirts to cross kick back and forth to the beat of the Charleston, the fireflies flashing back and forth with her.

Piper wasn't known as a man of action for nothing, and Rose intrigued him. It was unusual enough for a woman to look at him with indifference, let alone loathing. For some unaccountable reason he realized he wanted to find out why, and in any case, he said to himself, he should at least inquire after a damsel in distress.

Her creation a success, Rose's moment of glory was quickly tempered by the pain from an ugly bruise spreading across her instep. She lay down on her cot trying to sleep, but the pain throbbed with every beat from the music downstairs . . . which seemed to be invading her room, urging her to come down to listen. As the orchestra struck up her favorite, "The Sheik of Araby," despite the black memory it stirred, she limped down the back stairway to slip into M'selle's little dining area beside the conservatory. There she could feel a soft breeze and the music was softer, more muted. As she held her bruised foot, rocking back and forth, a stern voice said, "Let me see the damage."

It was Piper Pollard, bending over her, touching her instep with sure, cool fingers. Indignantly, she tried to pull her foot away, but it was too painful and his fingers too strong.

"What d'yo' wan' wid me?" She longed to slap his self-confident face, but her hand was stayed by his commanding manner, subduing her into silence.

"It isn't broken, I don't think," Piper said, ignoring her words, her glowering attitude. "I don't think it's twisted either, but you probably need tincture of iodine, young lady." He strode out, returning in only a few minutes with a slim young man whom he introduced as "my friend, Dr. Packer." Rose sat pale and silent as the doctor examined her foot and agreed with Piper that it was only bruised and that tincture of iodine would help it feel infinitely better. When the iodine was produced and applied, Rose tried to leave with the doctor, but Piper in a matter-of-fact way said, "No, stay here. I want to talk some business with you. You're a talented young lady. I gather you designed and made Madame Vincent's spectacular dress?"

He made no further attempt to touch her but sat, arms folded, watching her with the air of a stern schoolmaster. She felt uncomfortable, yet flattered that he'd recognized the effort behind the dress. Twisting uncomfortably in the chair, Rose nodded abruptly, not trusting him but not hating him with as much passion as she first had either. He asked a number of questions, which she answered either with a nod or monosyllabically, and when he finally got to his feet, he told her he was going to ask Madame Vincent if she could make some special shirts, for him, the new cool kind of dress shirt called "liki-liki"—half shirt, half coat—that men in South America were beginning to wear in the evening. "Do you think you could manage it? If I gave you a sketch?"

"I'll try. If Madame says I ca'," she replied offhandedly . . . and what is more, Piper thought much later as he drove back to Golden Hill, she really doesn't care whether she makes them or not, or ever sees me again, either. As Piper expected, Tilly Vincent was titillated by the thought of Piper wanting her seamstress to design and make his shirts, for Tilly construed that it brought their relationship onto an entirely more personal level. And in one way she was right, but it was to be in a way that she would forever curse.

To Piper's amazement—and alarm—as the weeks passed and he made no impression on this strangely impassive girl, he realized he was becoming infatuated with her. It was the first time he'd allowed his thoughts to dwell on any woman since the death of his wife. By now he'd taken it upon himself to learn a little more about Rose and the family she'd left behind in Santa Cruz—a result, he'd gathered, of her entanglement with the fiancé of one of the Fedder crowd. Every so often he would remember the look of absolute hatred she'd displayed toward him the first night they met. He had never seen such a look on anyone's face, as if she were willing him to drop dead beside her bruised foot!

If Rose didn't look on him with the same venom now, there was no sign of any other feeling either as she carefully measured the length of his arms, his neck, his shoulders, while fittings for the liki-liki shirts took place under Madame Vincent's approving and now openly proprietary eyes.

Piper had plenty of other things on his mind, yet the thought of Rose penetrated his usual carefree, happy-go-lucky nature in an increasingly irritating way. As a much-sought-after widower, he was used to dealing with all kinds of women, of light-heartedly accepting their favors and just as light-heartedly bowing out whenever he sensed a more serious relationship developing.

Madame Vincent didn't know that she had Rose, not her own special charms, to thank for the fact Piper was visiting Rosefleur more often since the night of the ball. However, Piper was shrewd enough to make sure Tilly Vincent thought he couldn't stay away from her, so it wasn't surprising that when she asked him whether she should make her annual visit to Europe—to look up friends and relations and visit salons to choose more clothes for the season ahead—she was sure he would want to accompany her.

So diplomatic was Piper that Tilly, instead of being upset, was highly flattered when he told her in "strict confidence" (as she then told her "closest intimates") that because he was working on an entirely new structure of government with Captain Cipriani, he couldn't possibly get away, not even to take his son Roger to his first boarding school in England. Tilly Vincent simpered and even blushed as she explained to her closest *amies* that Piper had told only her that he'd chosen to send Roger to an English school in deference to his first wife's memory. "She was English, you know, and well, it's so *charmant*, he is such a gentleman. . . . But Roger will learn business later, of course, in America."

Confident that her absence would make Piper's heart grow even fonder, Tilly sailed to Europe with her usual battalion of servants. Initially, to Piper's alarm, she had announced she would take Rose with her, but when Piper insinuated that the French designers wouldn't hesitate to snap up a talent like Rose's and that she might never get her back to sew and design for her exclusively, Madame Vincent knew only too well what he meant and the idea was promptly dropped.

Piper vowed to himself he'd stay away from Rosefleur for a couple of months. And he threw himself into his work on the Golden Hill estate, the most successful on the island, his oil business and, for him, always an enjoyable—and profitable—sideline, gambling with his cronies.

At the same time, although Rose never knew it, through his own intelligence network he kept tabs on how she was spending her days— diligently designing and sewing for her employer's return . . . hoping that as each day passed without a word from him she would at least feel lonely and neglected.

On the day Tilly Vincent's servants received the order to get ready to sail back to the tropics and start packing the mountain of luggage full of new purchases (she'd bought up half the stock of the Paris salons), Piper drove over to Rosefleur for the first time in nearly three months and ordered Rose to come with him to Golden Hill in his new Bugatti. He noticed with satisfaction that her lip was trembling as they drove toward Maracas Valley. She should be nervous, he thought, glancing at her from time to time, and when I tell her what I have in mind she will be even more so.

As he helped her out of the car, he couldn't help admiring the straightness of her back, the beautiful shape of her head held so haughtily, as if it was the most natural thing in the world for a sewing girl to be visiting a gentleman at his residence in the late afternoon.

She refused a sherry, refused water, sat with her hands held tightly together, her large golden eyes staring into space, as usual silent and seemingly . . . serene.

But Rose did not feel serene at all. She was quaking inside as she saw Piper's beautiful house for the first time—beautiful not only because of the undoubted high cost of its contents.

At Rosefleur everything said "money." At Golden Hill Piper's love of beautiful things and inherent good taste showed up in a mellow, restful way. Golden Hill was a home, whereas Rosefleur was a showplace, and Rose sensed it almost mournfully, realizing anew how little she really knew about the real world, Piper's world.

"Why did yo' brin' me here?" she asked in a meek little voice that didn't sound like the usual Rose at all.

His absence *had* hurt her, and just when she'd thought she was resigned to not seeing him until Madame Vincent's return, there he had been, his bright blue eyes sparkling with mischief. It had been a surprise, even an unnerving shock, because she'd realized immediately how much she'd missed him and she hated herself for her weakness. He stood over her now, the slightly mocking smile on his face she'd come to know so well.

"Well, Rose, why don't you guess why you're here?" He laughed when, as he placed a hand on her shoulder, she cringed back in the chair.

She looked up at him defiantly, determined not to be bowled over by the charm she'd seen exhibited so expertly and easily on other women. "I sup'ose yo' wan' some mor' shirts, liki-likis." She wrenched the words out and for the second time Piper saw the flash of hatred he'd seen over a year before. He moved away abruptly, stung as he had been then. But now, worse, bewildered, feeling emotions he'd forgotten.

As he stood with his back to her by the long window, Rose felt a surge of excitement. She suddenly knew, as if she'd read his mind, that she'd hurt him, that she must mean something to him. She knew it as if he'd sworn the words on the Bible and she savored the fact, going over in her mind that she, Rose Bracken, from the cocoa patch, could actually mean something to the high and mighty Piper Pollard of Golden Hill. But even as the realization exhilarated her, she felt cornered, in danger, because at the same time she had to acknowledge that she also very definitely felt something for him. As one fevered thought followed another, she saw Piper, his face set and determined as if he'd finally made up his mind about something, go to the library door and slam it shut, then cross the room swiftly to kneel before her, his hands tightly gripping hers.

"Rose!" he cried. "Why do you hate me? Did the American boy hurt you so much? Did you love him so much that you now hate all men?"

Rose opened her mouth in astonishment, while a slow blush reddened her face, her neck. "Love him?" she repeated. She wasn't only astonished that Piper Pollard knew about the episode with the American boy, but that he could think she ever could have loved him. She spat out the answer. "Love dat—dat verm'n, dat rot—" He didn't let her finish the sentence, but gave in to his overwhelming desire to crush her to him, smothering her face with kisses, burying his face in her neck, almost moaning her name, "Rose, Rose. . . ." He scooped her out of the chair as if she were a child, cradling her in his arms while she wildly tried to escape. The more she struggled, the more excited she became, knowing she didn't want to escape. She wanted this man as much as she knew now that he wanted her, yet even as she became wet with longing as his hands touched her breasts, she forced herself to resist. He could have any woman he wanted; she knew that. If she were just like the rest, welcoming him with open arms, what would become of her?

Piper carried her through the double doors at the end of the library into his darkly paneled study and laid her down on the large old-fashioned sofa. He watched her large nipples stiffen through the thin cotton of her dress. "You don't hate me?" he tried to joke, fighting his desire to rip off her clothes, to ravage her, to lick every inch of her petallike skin.

She answered almost gravely, as she still tried to move out of his arms, "I don' hate yo'. I—I lik' yo', but what d'yo' wan' wid me?"

What did he want? It was a fair question. He knew he was totally infatuated with her; she was rarely out of his thoughts and his self-enforced absence hadn't helped. If anything, it had made his longing for her worse. He'd seen a multitude of women since, but his thoughts had always strayed to this mysterious, cool-mannered girl. It was like a disease, Piper thought. He needed to sleep with her, to penetrate and violate her calm in order to be cleansed, rid of his obsession.

From his investigations of the Bracken family in Santa Cruz he hadn't found out anything more damning about her than the tangle with the Fedder girl's fiancé. Goddamn it, he didn't even know if she were a virgin. It was highly improbable, yet something about Rose's demeanor made him think she could be. The guarded way she moved her body, the fact that, unlike every other woman he knew, only Rose constantly went out of her way to avoid coming into contact with him, even trying deliberately not to run the risk of brushing by his body.

That morning, on receiving an overly amorous letter from Tilly Vincent announcing the date of her ship's arrival from Europe ("I cannot wait for our reunion," she had written), Piper had made a decision. He couldn't, wouldn't see Rose under Tilly Vincent's roof and patronage any longer. Rose would have to come to Golden Hill to work for him, and the more he'd thought about the idea the more it had appealed to him. Magnanimously he'd decided he wouldn't only pay Rose well, he would see to it that she received a proper education and learned to speak the king's English like the lady she looked and could be.

It had all seemed so simple in theory, and, once he'd decided on the plan, he'd seen no reason to delay carrying it out, giving in to the impulse he'd had so often to drive over to Rosefleur and take Rose back with him to Golden Hill.

Now, with this beautiful girl-child in his arms, looking up at him so questioningly with her soft golden eyes fringed with the most delicate black silk lashes, he wondered how on earth he'd ever be able to do a day's work knowing she was in the house. He'd forgotten how exquisite every inch of her was, how perfect her skin, how intriguing her proud air of indifference to him and everyone. If he brought her to Golden Hill, his obsession with her would grow worse . . . and yet he couldn't let her work in that overstuffed French catastrophe of a house and put up with Tilly Vincent's whims until Tilly grew tired of her or, more likely, threw her out, realizing his interest in the girl was not confined to her shirtmaking. What on earth was he going to do?

Rose broke through the tumult of his thoughts. "I'v nev'r loved anyon'," she whispered, "an' no one's ev'r loved me." As his arms tightened around her, she added vehemently, "an' no man has ev'r had me, no matter what anyone has tol' yo'." He knew she was telling the truth as her eyes blazed and she searched his face, longing for him to believe her.

So she *was* a virgin, a sweet, untouched virgin. As if sensing the impact of her words, Rose almost demanded, "D' yo' love me, Piper? D' yo' really wan' me?"

He nodded slowly, his face taut, almost with a kind of anger. Rose stood up with her back to him and slowly untied the bows of her dress, letting it fall to the floor along with its petticoat. Then, just as deliberately, as he watched, she stepped out of her panties.

"I'v bin savin' meself for de right man," she said proudly.

Piper, using all his willpower not to drag her on top of him, drew in his breath sharply as she turned toward him, revealing her nakedness, showing him, to his wonderment, the one sign of her black heritage: her large nipples were as black as the most luscious blackberries, standing out in startling contrast to the rest of her creamy white skin. It was the most erotic sight he had ever seen, and a half cry escaped him as he could hold back no longer and pulled her to him, fastening his mouth first on one, then on the other nipple, while his hand moved down her belly to explore her silky tangle of wet hair.

Time stopped for both of them, and, experienced lover though he was, Piper was lost in a paroxysm of joy he'd never encountered before. The smell of her intoxicated him as he buried his face in her wetness, hearing her groan with ecstasy as with practiced control he brought her to orgasm after orgasm, holding his penis back until, aching for more of his body, she tried to push his mouth away, begging him to enter between her wide-open legs and take her. As he pushed his swollen shaft deeply in and out, hearing her wild cry as he broke through the virginal skin, in a moment of sanity he withdrew at his climax to flood her belly with semen.

"Why . . . why . . ." she almost sobbed.

His answer thrilled her to a new surge of passion. "I don't want to give you my child . . . yet."

It was true. As he'd entered her, he'd known this was not going to be the casual affair he'd envisaged. He was not infatuated. He was in love. . . . At the same time he felt an ominous foreboding that it could bring him nothing but disaster.

Later, in the candlelit study she lay curled in his arms, still naked, while he studied and stroked her magnificent body, every so often unable to resist fastening his mouth on her jet-colored nipples. . . . "Your wonderful present from Louisa Calderon," he teased her. He couldn't bear to let her go and yet, like a splash of cold water his common sense told him she couldn't stay . . . not if he wanted to maintain his position as a man of integrity, a leader in the community.

As the grandfather clock chimed eight times for the half hour, Piper gently told Rose he had to take her back to Rosefleur. She didn't speak as she dressed, and he couldn't look at her or his resolve, he knew, would have broken. He longed to have her in his bed, to be able to turn to her throughout the night, to make love to her again and again, but he said nothing.

It wasn't until they were nearing the turn to Maraval Road that, drawing the Bugatti to the curb, Piper turned her face to his, seeing her eyes bright with tears. "I wanted you to come to work at Golden Hill," he began, and as anger blazed in her face he hastily went on, "but after tonight I know it's impossible." Still angry, she tried to get out of the car, but Piper's arm shot around her shoulders, forcing her into the seat. "Stop that," he said fiercely. "Don't be a little fool. I'm going to look after you, don't you realize that. Before Tilly Vincent returns you'll be gone from there."

"Where will I go?" Rose asked bleakly, shocked that after all that had happened he could have ever thought she might work for him . . . making shirts all day and being fucked all night, she thought bitterly.

"I have an idea, but first I must make some inquiries, Rose, sweet lovely Rose." His hand crept under her dress, feeling for the soft flesh beneath, but she clamped her legs together tightly.

"Tak' me t' Rosefleur an' don' com' t' see me 'less yo've anoth'r home t' offer. I won' be yo' slave. . . ."

For hours that night in their separate beds a few miles apart Piper and Rose tossed and turned, Piper working out one plan after another, only to discard them, Rose certain now she had given herself to Piper he would no longer want to see her. The memory of their lovemaking filled her with longing and she squirmed on her cot, forcing her fingers into her bloody vagina trying to recapture the delirium of the hours just gone.

It was Arthur Cipriani who gave Piper the solution days later, days Piper had spent agonizing over what to do about Rose, fighting his obsession for her, returning again and again to think of her astonishing rich, dark nipples, the way she moved, the smoothness of every inch of her. He had to have her. His body ached for her as it had never ached for any woman, yet he couldn't see how he could have her by his side without ruining the position he'd achieved in society. He'd stayed resolutely away from having a mistress during all the years he'd been a widower. That kind of messy entanglement wasn't for him, and he knew he couldn't degrade Rose by expecting her to work as a sewing girl by day and look after his sexual needs by night. How the gossip would spread through the valley, the island, all the way to Westminster. He could hear it. Piper Pollard taking advantage of a poor "Trinidad white," as the white-skinned offspring of mixed races were often called . . . and a descendant of Louisa Calderon, too!

After a week of considering many possibilities, a week that brought the ship bearing Tilly Vincent nearer and nearer to Port of Spain and a week in which Rose grew thin and even paler with remorse as no word came from Piper, it was a chance remark of Cipriani's that suddenly gave him the solution.

They were talking as they frequently did now about the British government's proposal for parliamentary reform, about the continuing rising prices with more and more disgruntled ex-servicemen unable to afford the basic necessities of life. This was true particularly since world cocoa prices had collapsed, bringing ruin to the small cocoa producer as well as to many merchants and outside speculators.

"The problem is too much talk and not enough action," Cipriani barked in a sudden flare of exasperation. "It's time there was a strong outward sign from the British to show they mean it when they pledge allegiance to the underdog cause. If they don't make it soon, there's going to be an explosion. I can feel it coming."

Piper looked at his old friend as if he were in a dream. Then, like a young schoolboy, he shouted at the top of his voice, "Yippee, yippee . . . that's it! That's my sign of allegiance. Arthur, my friend, that's it!" He started to dance around the office while Cipriani regarded him as if he'd gone out of his mind. He stopped to perch on the corner of Cipriani's desk. "Arthur, I have to tell you. I'm in love! Yes, I'm afraid so. I've got the disease well and truly. And know this, not only with a beautiful girl young enough to be my daughter, but with a descendant of none other than Louisa Calderon. . . . Yes, a colored girl who happens to look as white as driven snow, but her family certainly doesn't. You've solved my problem, dear fellow. I've just decided to make an honest woman of her. I'm going to marry her"—Piper roared with happy laughter—"to show my allegiance to the underdog cause."

Cipriani looked aghast. "Piper, do you hear what you're saying? Is this one of your poor jokes?" But it was no joke. In a flash of inspiration Piper saw how he could have his Rose legitimately in a marriage 'that would add tremendous validity to his outspoken support for the masses and so be a very useful tool for his political ambitions.

By the time Madame Vincent stepped onto the seething wharf at Port of Spain, anxiously scanning the crowds to see if Piper had come to meet her, Rose was already ensconced with a tutor and a chaperone in a cottage on the Golden Hill estate, engaged to be married and preparing for her wedding to Piper while learning how to speak and act like a lady.

It wasn't only Tilly Vincent who received the news with a sickening shock. (It sent her to bed for four weeks.) On the same Harrison Line ship was Roger, Piper's motherless son, eagerly returning to Golden Hill for the holidays after his first homesick term away at an English preparatory school.

Unlike Tilly Vincent, Roger didn't expect his father to be at the dockside to welcome him home. Much as he longed for his father's love and attention, he knew for a terrible reason he couldn't expect it, that the most he could hope for was his father's indifference—far preferable to his anger, which although rarely expressed, made Roger's already lonely life intolerably miserable.

For five years his mother, Faith Summerton, Piper's childhood sweetheart, had waited for Piper's summons to his side to honor their engagement to be married, but it wasn't until 1911 when Piper became a rich man on striking oil and took possession of the then deteriorating

Golden Hill estate from Finchy Finch that she received word she wouldn't have to wait much longer.

Even then Piper had spent almost another year putting the great old estate in shape, lavishing money and attention on every aspect of the house and grounds, importing large quantities of furniture, crystal and porcelain from Europe and modern paintings from American artists. When he was satisfied that it was the most beautiful home in the West Indies, he'd sent for Faith and married her in the chapel he'd built in the grounds. Piper was then thirty; she was twenty-eight and ten months later she'd died giving birth to their son Roger, who became a walking reminder to Piper that he was responsible for Faith's premature death. As Roger's resemblance to his mother grew, the blame had grown into antipathy, which Piper had never tried to understand or control.

Roger was never told directly about his father's impending remarriage, but he overheard the servants chattering away about "phony Rosie," whose skin was like white rose petals, giving no trace of her black grandmother and mulatto mother and father. "Phony Rosie," whom, he learned, at first to his disbelief, his father was actually going to marry, who would then become mistress of his beloved Golden Hill. He was sick, literally sick, vomiting into his basin when Em, the fat black cook, finally got it into his head that he was going to have, as she put it, "a new ma."

"She'll never be my mother!" he had screamed as if in pain. "I haven't got a mother. I'll never have a mother. . . ." And he'd run to his room, sobbing, to throw up again and again—until Em had sneaked up and crooned him to sleep on her ample lap.

When the dreaded confrontation with "phony Rosie" took place, it hadn't helped. Roger could see she was very beautiful, like a china doll, almost too perfect, but he'd hated her all the more, watching the way his father's eyes followed her wherever she went, how his father, usually so undemonstrative, continually went over to touch her arm, her hair, or to peck her cheek. It was disgusting because even to Roger's young eyes she looked so young herself. He would never have believed he could actually long to return to his dreary school in the English Pennines, where the constant rain made the memory of Golden Hill so precious, but now he wanted to be as far away as possible from the house he loved so much. To Roger's ears even Rose's voice sounded phony. Little did he know the long hours of practice Rose was putting in with her patient English tutor, trying to remember to sound her g's, to finish her words and, above all, to obliterate the singsong Trinidad accent.

Rose was quite aware of all the eyes on her, of all the talk she was causing in the house, throughout the estate and probably through the island, too—and she enjoyed thinking about the fuss and commotion she was causing. Even when the workers and servants weren't talking about her she was sure they were, and she held her head more haughtily than ever.

As her wedding day came nearer, she often thought of her ancestor Louisa Calderon, hoping that somehow, somewhere, Louisa knew that she, Rose Bracken, was at last going to vindicate her. Because next to her growing love and lust for Piper (just as great as his for her), she was overjoyed by the fact she would become mistress of Golden Hill, not only the finest estate in Trinidad, but once the property of Picton's heir . . . Picton, the man responsible for Louisa's torture. She hugged the thought to herself. Now it had come full circle—for now she could make sure her heirs (and so Louisa's) would possess it forever.

How brilliant and handsome her future husband was, she reflected with fierce pride. They lay together in the long grass on the highest point of the estate, surrounded by a circle of giant immortelle and poui trees, exotic with scarlet and salmon-pink flowers, while far below, sheltered by hundreds of other immortelles, stretched the precise line of Piper's cocoa trees for as far as the eye could see. She still could hardly believe her effect on him. She had only to loosen or touch the bodice of her dress for him to be almost feverish in his attempt to undress her and make love to her hour after hour. Piper couldn't believe the change in himself, either. He was a man bewitched, willingly subjecting himself to her spell, wondering how on earth he'd ever thought he was "living" before he met Rose. He still forced himself to withdraw his penis at the crucial moment, but he longed for Rose to become his wife so he could freely flood her body with his seed . . . and she would have one baby after another.

It amused him to see the dramatic effect the history of Golden Hill had upon her, for he'd forgotten momentarily that Picton, her ancestor's torturer, had originally bought the land on which the house was built. What fools the Finches had been to let it slip through their fingers, Piper mused. Finchy Finch, Golden Hill's last owner, had been the biggest fool of all, mortgaging off parcels of Golden Hill land to pay his gambling debts, until the day came when Piper revealed he'd bought up the mortgages and now wanted to buy him out for good.

How lucky he'd been, for now Golden Hill meant even more to him, knowing how important it was to his child bride to reign over what had been Picton property. As a hummingbird buzzed around them, he tickled Rose, rolling her over onto her belly, lifting her skirt to pull down her panties and greedily feel the firmness of her plump white buttocks. He pushed a lean finger lightly along her crease. She begged him to enter her. This time he lay back, enjoying the passionate look on her face as she tried to pull him to her. With one swift movement she sat astride him, straining back to insert his full length into her, pulling her bodice open to let her unique breasts hang over his face. This time he couldn't, wouldn't withdraw. If she became pregnant—the wedding day was only days away. He caught hold of her large black nipples, pulling them like reins as she rode him, urging his penis deeper and deeper into her until with wild cries of ecstasy they came together in a long, fulfilling orgasm.

Only one thing marred Rose's approaching wedding day, and it was the only thing that Piper was adamant about. Her mother, and if possible, her father and brothers and sister had to be present. Piper insisted upon it, however much Rose railed and cried and said it would ruin all the work she'd carried out learning to speak and act like a lady. Why, she wailed, did all his friends have to see her multicolored kin? They would never accept her. But Piper wouldn't listen, even arranging for a car to go to Santa Cruz to bring them to Golden Hill where, on the day, to Rose's mortification Piper told her they would sit in the same pew as Captain Cipriani.

When the wedding day finally dawned, for the first time in her life Rose decided she had to be blessed after all, because she received word that her sister and one of her brothers were stricken with cholera. None of the family would be able to attend, but they would pay her a visit just as soon as they recovered. Over my dead body, Rose thought grimly. Once she was mistress of Golden Hill, there was no way her family would ever see her again.

As the bride walked slowly down the aisle on the gallant captain's arm, there was nothing virginal or even demure about her appearance. On the contrary. Through the fine lace veil, it was easy to see the bride's eyes were not cast downward but rather looked from side to side boldly, taking in with great satisfaction the many curious looks directed her way from the "gawking gentry," as she described them to Piper later. Her dress, which she had made herself, was copied from a Chanel design with a few modifications. No frilly lace or decorous neckline for Rose. Instead, she'd taken a leaf out of Madame Vincent's book (who hadn't answered the invitation but had sent it back torn to shreds in the RSVP envelope), choosing a deceptively simple dress, cut to show off her perfectly shaped breasts and to remind Piper of what lay beneath the white swell she exposed, the back a miracle of tiny pleats, rounding her already round behind. It was a sinuous, subtly sexy dress meant to convey to Piper that just as she was pledging her mind to him, her body came, too.

After the ceremony, Piper roared with laughter at her pitiless descriptions of the guests and their reactions. "How they longed to see me stumble or faint, anything to stop me from reaching that altar," Rose laughed. They drove back from the chapel to Golden Hill, decorated throughout with thousands of yellow roses, chaconia and bright golden poui flowers, turning the house into a golden palace. Side by side they greeted their guests, among them the most important decision makers in the West Indies, as well as the richest and most influential landowners.

Rose had pouted on seeing the Fedders' names on the long invitation list, reminding Piper of their refusal to believe her innocence that terrible night. Easily he'd acquiesced to her plea to have their names removed. How happy she was to think of their chagrin, knowing they were the only important landowners in the whole of the Caribbean left off the guest list of what the press was calling "the wedding of the decade."

As the long line of guests filed past, Piper longed for the formality to be over, so he could be alone with Rose. Oh, the joy ahead!

He gave her behind a quick little squeeze as the toastmaster announced the next in line, "Mr. Thomas Finch and Miss Magdalen Finch." Piper hastily whispered to Rose, "Here comes two of Picton's descendants. Remember, I told you about Finchy Finch, the last owner of Golden Hill. . . ."

Rose prepared herself to be gracious but condescending, as she'd seen other ladies behave, delivering a touch of disarming sweetness while thinking nothing but sour thoughts. She was therefore all the more disconcerted when Finchy Finch and his red-headed daughter Magdalen hardly seemed aware of her, barely touching her outstretched hand as they imperiously passed by without a word of congratulations, to shake

Piper's hand thoroughly, wishing, as far as she could hear, only *him* all good things.

As the toastmaster cleared his throat to announce the name of another guest advancing, Rose was infuriated to see Finchy's daughter—not that much older than herself—still holding Piper's hand. Why, she was actually ogling him! Rose tugged at Piper's sleeve irritably to attract his attention, and dutifully he excused himself to turn to welcome the next arrival.

The malevolence of the look Magdalen shot at Rose did not go unnoticed. I wonder if Piper and Magdalen Finch ever had more in common than an interest in Golden Hill, Rose thought pensively as she stood with a fixed smile, being introduced to one new face after another. I must remember to ask Piper what he thinks about that young lady. . . .

Years later Rose had plenty of reason to remember that look—and to realize too late she had never asked Piper the question.

3

Magdalen
1924

THE guttural belches of the Trinidad bullfrogs were incessant as Magdalen stood on the wide portico of Golden Hill waiting impatiently for her father to join her. Their rude cries, heralding approaching summer rains, made her shiver as they always did. They reminded her of another summer long ago and of a day that had started as every day had started then, bright with promise, but a day that had marked the beginning of a totally different kind of life.

She looked around restlessly, hoping to see someone she knew leaving the wedding reception, someone who might give her a lift back to town so she could leave the gig for her father and not have to travel back with him, his alcoholic breath fouling the atmosphere. As she stood hesitating as to whether she should go back inside to seek someone out, her father emerged, a familiar hangdog expression on his face. She didn't know which was worse. His "eat-humble-pie-forever" look or the one which indicated he was in his belligerent "I-am-the-master-of-the-house" role. Whichever way he looked, Magdalen now saw him clearly for what he was—an inferior man, who'd done a good job of wrecking the lives of those closest to him.

"Mags," he bleated, "did you see what he's done to our place? Did you see the wanton waste of money? Oh, the pity of it, the pity of it."

She looked with disgust as a dribble of saliva rolled from his mouth down his chin.

"Our place?" she retorted coldly. "You mean the home you gave away, don't you, Pa?" Finchy Finch blinked watery eyes, then lurched forward to catch her elbow. "He's a wicked man, Magdalen. Never forget that . . . wicked, wicked. He tricked . . ."

It was a familiar diatribe and she cut him short. "I don't want to hear about it; let's go. I can't stand to be here for one more minute. I told you we shouldn't have accepted this invitation. It's . . . it's degrading."

She was dying inside, a slow death withering her away cell by cell at twenty-two years of age, with no hope now of retrieving her home, her lost life. How could Piper Pollard have married this—this *Creole* creature, all got up to look like a lady? She reflected with bitter satisfaction on the way they'd sailed past Rose's outstretched hand and pathetic attempt to act like Mrs. Piper Pollard. But that was the terrible thing. She *was* Mrs. Piper Pollard and, worse, she was mistress of Golden Hill, the house in which she, Magdalen Finch, had been born, the house that had been built by a Finch almost a hundred years before.

Magdalen looked with even greater loathing than usual at her father, who'd given up her birthright so feebly. For if Piper Pollard was wicked—and deep inside her she was beginning to accept that assessment—her father was weak, spineless, stupid, which she believed could be viewed as just as bad.

Magdalen drove their old two-wheeled gig back to Port of Spain, cracking the whip viciously in the air, both to force the mare into a brisker trot and to relieve her feelings of frustration.

As she drove with tightly clamped lips, Finchy Finch started on his usual drunken monologue . . . how badly the world had treated him, how the world should be rid of vermin like Piper Pollard. She paid little attention, until, giggling foolishly, he started to drool about Piper's beautiful new bride and the price he'd have to pay one day for picking such a luscious young fruit.

"Shut up!" she screamed, cracking the whip wildly, "shut up!" The look on his daughter's face cowed Finchy as nothing else could and he sulkily shrank back into a corner of the gig, which rattled over the cobblestoned roads, swerving dangerously on one wheel around corners. There was no knowing what his wild daughter might do when she was in this kind of mood.

The more Magdalen thought about Rose, the more recklessly she drove. She even tasted bile in her throat as she imagined Rose and Piper embarking that night on the big liner to sail past the five islands into the Grand Boca and out into the Caribbean on their way to America—for she'd been told at the reception that Piper was taking his Rose on an extended honeymoon to the country of his birth.

She remembered the diamond flashing on Rose's finger as she'd raised her glass to Piper, but most of all she remembered with a stab of pain the possessive, almost hungry look on Piper's face as he'd returned his bride's toast.

By the time Magdalen drew in the reins outside the old rectory where she'd lived with her father for the past thirteen years, her jealousy of Rose was like a living thing inside her, as painful and as real as an abscess ready to burst. She flew upstairs to her bedroom, locking the door before throwing herself down to weep hysterically, pounding her hands and feet against the counterpane. There was no one to comfort her. No one even to hear her suffering, for Finchy Finch had gone like a homing bird in search of his own refuge from memories, to the first bottle of rum he could find.

As she often did when depression descended, Magdalen took out her diary and began to record the events of the agonizing day and her feelings on entering Golden Hill again after so many years. But even as she wrote the first sentence, tears of self-pity splashed down on the ink and she threw the diary back into a drawer to pace the room like a young lioness in a cage, pushing her dark red hair away from her swollen eyes.

How lovely, how truly golden and glittering Golden Hill had looked. To Magdalen's adoring eyes, not so very different, despite her father's words, from the last day she'd lived there, when as a terrified nine-year-old she'd been wrenched away so suddenly from all she loved and held dear to live with her grandfather, the vicar, at the rectory. The rectory was a place she'd always dreaded to enter, as somber and as dark as Golden Hill was sparkling and full of light, for, as a child, Magdalen had seen only the beauty of her home—so remembered none of the ugly signs of its neglect.

Golden Hill had been a magnificent home, years before Piper Pollard first set eyes on its fine coralstone structure, each precious piece brought by sloop from Barbados in the early nineteenth century. For months enormous crates, full of the best that money could buy, had arrived from all over the world—for Golden Hill hadn't been built just to be a house or a home. It was built as a tribute—by his heir—to Lieutenant Colonel Thomas Picton, a tribute that was meant to last forever, "thumbing its nose" at the house across the valley built by Picton's co-

commissioner and archenemy, Colonel William Fullarton. Fullarton had gloated publicly that, although he was no longer in command of the island, Belmont, his own home had been chosen, with his blessing, to be the official residence of Trinidad's governors forever.

Unfortunately, Picton's zealous heir, who built Golden Hill on the thousand-acre sugarcane estate first purchased by Picton, soon tired of life in the tropics and returned to England to become an absentee landlord. He was like so many of Trinidad's new landowners at that time, who, after investing in Britain's new colony, returned to the mother country—considered to be the seat of education and culture—or went on to America where business opportunities were so much greater.

It wasn't until 1850 that Golden Hill again had an owner in residence, when, after an arduous and lengthy sea journey from London, twenty-seven-year-old Thomas Finch arrived to inspect the property recently inherited by his widowed mother on the death of first her uncle and then her aunt by marriage, one of the few remaining Picton relatives.

Thomas had heard enticing stories for years about the easy life "down the islands," where the glorious rays of the sun woke you in January instead of icy drafts announcing another freezing winter day . . . where all around was an abundance of delectable fruit just waiting to be picked from the trees—where it wasn't necessary to try to find something edible from a barrel of bleak apples stored from a summer that was invariably too cool and too short. Best of all was the news that the islands teemed with blacks, only too eager to satisfy every whim of their masters. A perfect idea as far as Thomas was concerned, since he'd always been noticeably indifferent to lifting a finger for himself.

With letters of introduction and his link to the governor of the past, Thomas had quickly swung into the top echelon of Trinidad society and his position was all the easier to maintain since he had his own fine perch from which to swing.

As he wrote early in 1851 to the mother he was never to see again, "Golden Hill is both a pleasant surprise and an unwelcome responsibility. . . ." For although both mother and son knew a sugar plantation went along with the inheritance of the Golden Hill mansion, as city folk born and bred, it was the mansion that had captured their attention. They'd taken for granted the sugar-producing land, counting it as an extra windfall that would automatically go on producing the same profits every year to take care of their present and future.

In practice, as Thomas quickly discovered, the house had to be relegated to a back seat in importance to the sugar. There were acres and acres of it, requiring an immense labor force to produce and a quick business brain to unload for a profit in an increasingly competitive marketplace. Unfortunately, he had neither and he was unlucky in his timing.

Up until the Emancipation Act, which abolished slavery, the Golden Hill sugar estate had produced an enormous annual income, due to a series of efficient foremen and the efforts of loyal native workers, who'd been born as slaves on the estate like their fathers before them. Once slavery was abolished, however, many natives refused to work in the cane fields. There was a good reason. Along with their freedom, the British offered a considerable inducement to former slaves who cleaned and cultivated a piece of land for themselves, giving them ownership providing the land wasn't claimed by another after one year.

By the time Thomas arrived, the number of loyal workers left at Golden Hill who wanted to die where they'd been born was so diminished, that in order to save the crop the main foreman, who'd kept everything in top running order for years, had been compelled in common with many others to import a new labor force from India.

With no knowledge and little interest in sugar, Thomas didn't care whether "niggers or half castes ran the show," as he pompously crowed in the Port of Spain clubs, "providing the sanctimonious souls in the British government don't make us pay for it." But that was just what the British government was forced to do a year later, levying a heavy tax on planters to help pay for the indentured workers' passages from India and China, plus increasing duties on rum and many other "necessities" of Thomas's life.

The year his beloved mother was to have joined him in what he still described in letters as "the most idyllic place you have ever seen," she died of pneumonia and Thomas turned to the rum bottle for solace. Like so many who crossed the oceans, leaving behind the cold of Europe to live in the heat of the tropics, he didn't realize how easy it was to slip into a life of mental and physical indolence, each year drinking more, eating less, moving about as little as possible. And as he continually complained, he was hot twenty-four hours a day. It wasn't surprising. Then, anyone not wearing a broadcloth coat and silk tie to go about his business—although the temperature was usually in the high eighties—was simply not considered a gentleman.

At forty, although he still had a superior swagger, Thomas knew Golden Hill didn't have anything like the same shine it had had thirteen years before. How could it have? The estate was now only producing a quarter of the profit of the past. His affairs in shambles, he finally decided he'd better marry for money (as it seemed he couldn't get it any other way) before his own money ran out altogether and before he was too old and his looks were gone.

A flashy and fleshy Spanish widow, loaded with what looked like gems from the Spanish Armada, encouraged him to believe she had her own fortune, while she had covetous eyes on Golden Hill's rolling if now unkempt acres and its crowning glory of a house, run-down, she believed, because it lacked a "woman's touch." In fact, it lacked the necessary money for refurbishment, but neither found out the other didn't have it until after the wedding day.

Thomas's troubles worsened the next year when his bride died, aged thirty-two, giving birth to a son whom he named after himself, but who was to be called Finchy all his life. Thomas tried desperately to recoup his losses on sugar by gambling. Sometimes he won. Sometimes he lost, but the biggest loser of all was Finchy. He was brought up by an ever shifting staff of servants, who even as a little boy he despised, because he quickly learned his father despised all blacks, so it seemed perfectly natural for him to do the same.

As the nineteenth century drew to a close Finchy, like his father, already drank too much and—when he was allowed to—gambled away on illegal cockfights his small allowance.

Neither father nor son comprehended that the writing was on the wall as far as the West Indian sugar industry was concerned. Ironically, although sugar consumption in the British Isles was increasing, the government, indifferent to the needs of its subjects so many thousands of miles away, earning their living raising sugar, wanted only to buy it as cheaply as possible. That meant sugar from European beets, not from the cane raised and obtained so expensively in their own colonies.

More and more planters, aware of the shriveling market, were replacing their sugar crops with cocoa, but Thomas plodded on, oblivious to the approaching near collapse of the industry, blaming the "gross negligence" of his fewer and fewer workers and the world in general for his disappearing fortune.

By the time Finchy decided it was time to find a wife, as there were now too few servants left in the big house to look after himself and his almost senile father, he was twenty-nine and not much of a catch— except to Mary Walters, the highly strung, "left on the shelf" daughter of a rigid cane-wielding Anglican parson.

The Reverend Walters had come to Trinidad to teach the Holy Romans the "errors of their ways and spread the faith among the heathen," as he stentoriously told anyone who would listen. Mary, his red-headed daughter, was twenty-seven when she went to the altar, relieved to be able to leave her father's morbid rectory at last and to have a married woman's status, no matter what it cost her. It was to cost her plenty.

From the beginning, Mary was bewildered by the lack of difference in her life. Brought up on the fairy tale of "happy ever after," she had lived for the moment she would be married, but in just twenty-four hours she learned she'd merely exchanged one morbid home for another, much bigger, and more run-down, with two men, not one, to feed and look after. Worse, her husband demanded her body, not just at night in the bedroom, which she'd known she had to endure, but at all times of day and night anywhere—in the kitchen, in the library—wherever she was, whenever she saw his hand stray to his britches and she couldn't escape on a pretext fast enough.

Nevertheless, two years passed before Mary could tell Finchy joyfully she was pregnant—joyful more because of the respite from his attentions she now expected, than because of any thought of bearing his child.

But if anything, the news seemed to whet Finchy's already overwhelming sexual appetite, until she would scream for mercy. But it was all to no avail, as up until the last months of her pregnancy, he would unbuckle his belt and lay her back clumsily, lifting up her skirt, pulling down her bloomers, even if Thomas, his father, by now totally senile, sat laughing to himself watching them from a corner.

It was into this family atmosphere in 1902 that Magdalen Mary Finch was born at Golden Hill, to a mother who hated not only the touch of her husband, but the very sight of him.

Through Magdalen's eyes, though, Golden Hill was an enormous playground, with ever moving toys—lizards, iguanas, agoutis, frogs, spiders, centipedes and butterflies by day, giant night butterflies at night—which she dimly remembered had terrified her mother, as they rushed on soft wings into the room to beat against the oil lamps, always seeming to want to touch the one person, her mother, who loathed them. Her mother would run out of the room sobbing, while Magdalen tried to catch her skirts to hold her fast, so that she would enjoy the pretty flutter of the winged insects. "They won't hurt you, Mama," she would cry, but it was too late. Mary was gone, barricading herself in her room, where the sound of her sobs would make Magdalen's heart ache until something else took her attention.

Magdalen innocently sugar-coated the memories of her childhood at Golden Hill because they were the only memories without flaws. She cherished them: riding with the stockman as he drove his cart into the paragrass field to bring in bundles of grass for the stables . . . returning perched precariously on top of the high stacks . . . raiding the sugarcane fields near harvest time to return laden with juicy stalks that she would suck for hours in the shade of the saman tree.

The memory of her mother was confused, but all through her life Magdalen clung fiercely to the fact she'd loved her more than anyone else, although she'd known her for so short a time. By the time Magdalen was nine, her mother was dead by her own hand and so were her brother Thomas Finch III and her young sister Sarah, born between two miscarriages in 1904 and 1907.

She hadn't known what the word *suicide* meant that day in August, when she'd rushed into the house soaked to the skin after being caught in a sudden thunderstorm. As she'd hurried home a worker had told her her mother had been looking for her hours before to take her for a walk, but instead she'd been roaming through the estate in search of a place to set up her "lagglee," the little trap cage in which she constantly hoped to catch a bird or a butterfly just as the natives did.

Suicide. She'd known the word meant something bad, something frightening when she'd heard her father cry it out, as drenched, she'd crept by the library. From that moment nothing had ever been the same.

It was years before she learned the whole truth: that her mother, only recently out of bed after giving birth to a stillborn child, had been seen walking over the hills with her two younger children . . . that a native had seen her at the edge of the riverbank watching the Maracas River, flooded to a depth of forty or fifty feet with heavy summer rain, rush toward the sea . . . that just as he'd gone to warn her of the danger, he'd seen her leap into the swirling torrents, taking her two small ones with her. Magdalen often wondered what would have happened if her mother had found her that day. . . . But instead she'd been roaming the estate, so she was alive—and alone.

It was all Piper Pollard's fault, her father had told her then, and when the next month she'd learned they had to leave Golden Hill, because it now belonged to Mr. Pollard, she'd believed her father had spoken the truth. She was nine years old and Piper Pollard was only a name, but it was one she learned to hate early.

What Magdalen didn't know, but grew up to guess with increasing contempt for her father, was that from the moment Piper Pollard saw Golden Hill he'd set about trying to buy it. He'd found after a few inquiries that it was going to be easy, for in 1909, on his father's death, Finchy, after already losing a substantial sum himself, had started to mortgage parcels of Golden Hill land in order to settle some of his father's debts. Without Finchy's knowledge, Piper bought up every parcel, until in 1911, just before Finchy's fortieth birthday, Piper put his cards on the table, proposing to buy for a generous price whatever was left free and clear.

Finchy, his back to the wall, had blustered, fought, put off accepting what was a foregone conclusion to the "people watchers." The day he told his wife Mary they'd have to leave Golden Hill and go to live for a time with her old father back at the rectory was the day she'd decided she preferred to drown herself and her children.

Before Magdalen ever set eyes on Piper, her adolescent hatred of his name was largely fed by her own imagination, not by her father's constant condemnation of him, because by the time she reached her teens, she'd already made up her mind how much her father's many weaknesses and drinking habits had contributed to her mother's death and to their poverty.

Now as she sat brooding in the gathering darkness with no more tears to shed, Magdalen reflected it had to be almost a year since she'd met Piper Pollard for the first time, a meeting that still burned in her memory. What a little fool she'd been, knowing now that all the time she was mooning over him he must have been seeing Rose Bracken.

As she did most things, Magdalen rushed to light her lamp, impatient to find her last year's diary, where sure enough, there on Discovery Day, the first Monday in August, she had marked in large letters: "Met the Monster at Last!!!"

It wasn't surprising that twelve years had elapsed before their first meeting, because although Finchy rambled on endlessly about retrieving his family property, each year he deteriorated further with drink and indolence. As Piper's wealth and standing in the community grew, the distance between the two families' social levels became as wide as a crevasse, until one by one, those who'd known the Finches at Golden Hill—who at first had been anxious to show kindness to the "poor Finch girl"—forgot they even existed.

In any case there was no way Finchy could have reciprocated, even if he'd wanted to, which he didn't, so as Magdalen's childhood ran out, she'd found herself living in a strange no man's land, with few friends or social ties with members of the influential white families or with any of the blacks, Indians or Creoles who, in the main, worked for them.

Only one family, the Middletons, had occasionally been smitten by conscience, inviting Magdalen to join them for a house party or vacation "down the island," where they had a cottage on Monos, one of the many tiny islets dotting the straits between Trinidad and Venezuela.

In the years immediately following her mother's death, Magdalen had longed for the Middletons' invitation to arrive, knowing for two precious weeks she was going to be part of a happy, carefree throng of brothers, sisters, cousins and friends, all about her age. They'd board the *Ant*, a paddle steamer that laboriously churned across the waters of the Gulf of Paria three times a week eventually to reach Monos. Magdalen had thought of the tiny island as paradise—and each spring until she was about sixteen she'd managed to recapture there some of the idyllic moments she remembered she'd spent at Golden Hill. Always inclined to be a tomboy, she'd shrimp, fish and wade among rock pools with the Middleton boys and swim from dawn to dusk in the frisky ocean.

Then one year the Middletons had simply forgotten to include her, and when they'd apologetically proffered another invitation the year after, the whole atmosphere had changed. The girls had simpered and whispered about people Magdalen had never heard of, they'd cared about getting their hair wet, shrieked when a bat flew in the window— and as for the boys, they hadn't seemed to want her along on their climbing, fishing and rock pool expeditions any more either.

As each day passed she'd felt more and more self-conscious, aware that her old swimming costume didn't perfectly cover her large breasts that the girls even laughed at pointedly, and probably the boys too. Her obvious lack of knowledge about fashion, dancing and all the things the rest of them seemed to be doing back in the city had made her feel totally left out. She'd vowed never to see any of them again, refusing the invitation the next year, although, sitting in the drab rectory, the thought of the silver sea and the hummingbirds darting in and out of the brightly colored cottage had been so painfully tempting.

If her father hadn't started to nag her, saying it was time she thought about getting married, she would never have accepted the Middletons' invitation to join their house party for the Discovery Day race meeting, which took place on Manzanilla beach every year. But she had just begun to think she'd go mad if she didn't get away from her father when the invitation arrived, and on the spur of the moment she'd accepted it, although she'd regretted it almost the next minute.

The fact was she was suspicious, sure her father was up to something as, day after day, he'd warned her she was going the right way about ending up as an old maid. She'd discovered she was right the day before she'd left for the Middletons' house, for her father had sulked ever since she'd told him she was going away for the weekend.

Finchy had known there was nothing he could say or do to stop her, so he'd slammed his door and locked himself in his room for a twelve-hour rendezvous with the rum bottle, only opening it to repeat his "old maid" warning in a drunken burble. But this time he'd let the truth slip out without realizing it: he was "negotiating" to marry her off to a very rich planter . . . so rich that neither of them would ever have to worry about money again.

As she sat reading her old diary, Magdalen could still remember the rage that had welled up the year before as she'd driven off to catch the train to the Middletons'. Now her rage was coupled with a sense of helplessness, but even the year before she'd known only too well the identity of the rich planter her father had been "negotiating with." Joseph Acerra was certainly rich, but also ugly, and a widower at least thirty years her senior, who had been pestering her to come to lunch or dinner for months.

Perhaps it had been the thought of her father's disloyalty, perhaps it had been the years of frustration, and anticipation, but, whatever it had been, twenty-four hours later when Magdalen had come face to face for the first time with the man she'd always thought of as her worst enemy, instead of hate she'd found herself overwhelmed with a different kind of passion.

Now as she stared out at the darkened Port of Spain street, she could see in her mind the scene of almost a year ago, everyone gathered under the coconut trees that fringed the long Manzanilla beach, on horses, in buggies and in estate carts, ostensibly there to watch the races—for horses, mules and donkeys—but in reality to see each other, to flirt and socialize and drink planter's punches and munch on East Indian *rotis* (curried pancakes), Accra cakes and "kisses angostura," a concoction of egg whites, vanilla, chopped nuts and angostura bitters.

Magdalen had sat stony faced, preoccupied with her thoughts, while all around her the young Middletons had blown kisses to their friends and alternately cheered or booed as their bets either succeeded or were lost, although the animals had seldom completed the course, but bolted either into the coconuts or into the cool of the sea.

Henry Middleton had tried to make the unhappy-looking girl join in the fun his children, nieces and nephews were so obviously having, but he'd had little success until his old friend Piper Pollard had appeared in a buggy from out of nowhere.

"Well, Piper, so here you are." Henry had laughed. "We'd quite given you up—yet I had a feeling the poker game we're going to have tonight might be a draw you wouldn't be able to resist." Remembering his manners, Middleton had turned hastily to Magdalen sitting woodenly beside him in the estate cart. "Piper, I'm not sure if you've had the good fortune to meet Finchy Finch's young daughter Magdalen?"

Magdalen had felt herself blushing—it seemed from the root of every red hair on her head. It had been the moment she'd dreamed of so often, the opportunity she'd waited for to revile the monster, the man responsible for the death of her mother, her brother, her sister, and every moment of her own happiness since, but instead, as if in a trance, she'd looked into the bluest eyes she'd ever seen on a man and, not saying a word, had given him her small hand to be shaken by his.

Until Henry Middleton had mentioned her name, Piper had hardly been aware of any girl, or indeed of anyone sitting next to his host. He was hardly aware of any woman these days, he'd irritably noted. Rose Bracken had taken over his mind, which was one of the reasons he'd almost decided not to make the tiresome journey to Manzanilla from Maracas, until at the last moment he'd forced himself to come, and to continue his self-imposed ban on seeing Rose during Tilly Vincent's absence overseas.

So this was Finchy Finch's daughter. Piper had looked at her with his usual charming smile, little realizing the havoc he was causing. A red-headed, voluptuous little thing, he'd thought, and then he hadn't thought about her again until later that day when he'd found himself sitting beside her in the Middleton estate cart. They'd both laughed until they'd almost cried over the antics of the clerk of the course who, having quenched his thirst too often at the rum booth, had lain slumped across his saddle, his formidable hunting crop hanging limply from his hand, hiccuping and singing loudly "Auld Lang Syne."

Magdalen had felt like a bird, a swooping, light-hearted bird, as she'd looked into Piper's devastating eyes. What a lot of time she'd wasted, she'd thought. If only she'd known how handsome, how distinguished, how really outstanding he was—for suddenly it had all seemed so simple. The monster wasn't a monster. He was a wonderful man, who would fall in love with her and she with him and they'd live together happily ever after at Golden Hill.

On the way back to the Middletons' coconut plantation she remembered now with a twist inside her she'd sung her heart out, her arm slipped through Piper's as if it were the most natural thing in the world.

The Middletons had marveled over the change in her, at her witticisms at dinner, at her spirited dancing. "Why," Henry Middleton had remarked to his wife, "I never realized before that Magdalen is growing into quite a handsome woman."

The evening had grown more and more boisterous, until the men in the party had disappeared for an all-night poker game. By the time Magdalen had joined the family at breakfast next morning, she'd learned to her annoyance a group of them had already decided to blow the cobwebs away by having a race of their own over the hills to the neighboring valley. She'd spent the day getting ready for Piper's return, certain he must be as eager to see her as she was to see him, but when the men had returned, the party spirit had enveloped them again and they'd drunk and drunk to Piper's victory in the race, which he'd kept insisting modestly had really been no race at all.

Magdalen had realized with alarm that time was running out, that she had no time to make Piper realize she didn't hate him, that—in fact—she was almost sure she loved him. Love at first sight? She'd heard it could happen, and she'd been sure it was happening to her.

Now, thinking back to that night made her sick. How she'd degraded herself . . . waiting hour after hour, listening for Piper to come upstairs to go to his room after another poker game that had gone on into the small hours, rushing nervously along the corridor in her nightgown with her red hair brushed out so it coiled around her shoulders like a flame. She shuddered at the memory.

Oh, he'd been civil enough as she'd knocked, then entered his room.

"Well, Miss Magdalen, and what do you think you're doing?" He'd laughed, standing by the long mirror in only his shirttails.

She'd gone over to him, longing for him to take her in his arms, half expecting it, then realizing with revulsion he was tight. His breath had reminded her instantly of her father, whose breath was never free of the smell of rum. And yet she'd tried not to notice or care, putting her arms around his neck, nuzzling him, whispering shyly, "I forgive you."

He'd laughed even more, tipsily rocking back on his heels as he'd gently pushed her away. "My little one, *you* forgive *me?* For what, pray? No, don't answer that. . . ." He'd stretched and suddenly cried out, "Oh, but I'm saddle sore! I'm too old to be so long on a horse." Then he'd slurred, "If you really forgive me, Miss Magdalen, you have to prove it. Here, help me put these sticking plasters on my confounded behind."

To her mortification, he'd lifted up his shirttail and tried to examine himself in the long mirror by the light of a candle. "Well, my new friend, come on, help me."

With angry tears, Magdalen had snatched the plasters from his outstretched hand, and, as he'd pointed at the mirror at the sore marks on his bare buttocks, she'd angrily slapped the plasters onto their reflection, before running out of the room to hurl herself, sobbing, onto her bed.

She'd never seen him again until today, the day of his wedding to the sewing girl, Rose Bracken. She'd tried to see him, if only to thank him, as she'd told herself, for the flowers that had arrived a week later with his card and a scrawled message. "Thank you for the first aid to the mirror. I deserved it, Piper Pollard."

In the weeks following Piper and Rose's wedding Magdalen's sense of helplessness and lovesickness didn't go away. As she'd imagined herself into a situation at the Middletons' plantation, she began to dream of another likelihood, realizing she wasn't yet willing to relinquish her grand plan for a return to Golden Hill as Piper's wife, even though he was newly married to somebody else. In common with many others, who hadn't stopped gossiping about the unlikely match, Magdalen started to think that once Piper got over what could only be an intense infatuation, he would come to his senses and see Rose for the inferior being she was, leaving her the perfect opportunity to pick up the pieces. Perhaps, she thought, things will even be different when they return from their honeymoon.

Piper and Rose were away for almost four months in America. At the beginning of the trip Piper had even been thinking of reestablishing himself in Cleveland, where his father had been born and had died a disappointed man, having repudiated with scorn in the 1880s the notion that the newfangled petroleum business could have any long-term benefit. Piper had grown up determined never to make the same kind of massive mistake. That was the reason he was usually ready to try anything, to gamble and explore. That was the reason he had decided to go to the West Indies in the first place, and his innovative entrepreneurial flair had always paid off.

But not only was the U.S. business climate hopeless in the early 1920s, Rose didn't like America, and that was much more important as far as Piper was concerned. As their honeymoon continued, Piper became more besotted with his bride, not less. He showered her with jewels and clothes, taking her to the opening of Saks, a ritzy new store on Fifth Avenue, even buying her a one-thousand-dollar raccoon coat there, one she would have little use for in Trinidad, watching with pride as people stopped to look at her in the coat, as she stepped gracefully out of a limousine on the opening night of the *Ziegfeld Follies*.

When, after days and nights of parties, theaters, shopping trips and a long and tiring visit to the citrus groves of Florida, Rose announced fretfully she wanted to go home to Golden Hill, Piper realized he was relieved. He knew Rose couldn't wait to adopt her role as mistress of Golden Hill, and now he was also willing to admit America was not for him.

Instead, with Rose at his side he would prove his commitment to the people of Trinidad and was hopeful the dual British and American nationality he had now adopted would mean he could win a seat in the new Council at the first election coming up in 1925. It was now entirely possible, he reflected, that he could become a major influence in Caribbean politics.

Unfortunately, Rose didn't seem to understand how important a part her family played in this plan. In fact, her family was the one subject that had managed to mar their honeymoon. On the ship back to Trinidad, Piper decided to bring up the matter more decisively. "I think we should move your family to one of the cottages on the estate," he said gently, stroking her arm as they stretched out in deck chairs on the upper deck.

Rose recoiled as if she'd been stung, even forgetting in her anger to sound her *g* as she was usually so careful to do. "Livin' with us? Oh no, Piper, I couldn't bear it," she cried. "Please don't suggest that."

He couldn't stand to see her tears, even ones like these that he knew were shed in anger. "Well, you must welcome your family to our home, Rose," he said quietly but firmly. "It's important for me—for our plans—that we should seem to want to share our good fortune. In any case"—he tickled her, trying to get her into a sunnier mood—"surely, you don't want your mother, your sister and brothers to have the same wretched life you tell me you had? Or perhaps you made it all up?

Perhaps you were a little princess, sitting on a silk pillow, being fed strawberries and cream."

She refused to be placated, crying stormily, "Piper, I've escaped! Don't bring the prison to me. I have nothing to say, nothing in common with my family. I've told you that many times. But—well, yes, all right—if you really want me to. Of course I'll welcome them when we get home. . . ."

But Rose had no intention of welcoming them. As far as she was concerned, she wanted complete severance from a family that linked her through their color to an existence several rungs below that of the white man. And the more she lived as a white man's wife the more she realized it was only an *existence*, not a life, and one she was sure would never change for colored people no matter what her husband or his friend Captain Cipriani said or did.

A few weeks after their return to Golden Hill, Rose received word from Maize, one of the upstairs maids, that a Mrs. Bracken was downstairs in the servants' quarters with her brothers, the masters Roland and James. She'd been expecting it and she'd made up her mind what to do.

She went into the cold room at the back of the house and surreptitiously took from the pocket of the raccoon coat what she'd been hiding there—two hundred American dollars, carefully saved during the months of her honeymoon, either from money Piper had given her or money she'd taken in small amounts from his pocket when he was out of the room.

While Maize waited, Rose wrote speedily what she couldn't say to her mother's face. "You said you didn't want to see me until I was properly settled. Well, now, I am settled and I don't want to see any of you. Take this money and don't bother me again. It just wouldn't be right."

When the maid left the room with the sealed envelope, Rose sat staring out of her bedroom window at Mount El Tucuche, its three majestic peaks just showing through a haze of heat. Her heart was beating wildly as she sat stiff and rigid, for she half expected her mother to rush into the room to curse her for turning her back on her own flesh and blood. But as the minutes went by and the old stone house remained as silent as ever, except for the steady tick-tick of the grandfather clock below, she slowly relaxed, and she went to her bathtub to soak in a lily-of-the-valley milk bath in readiness for Piper's return home.

Another week passed before Piper learned by accident from Obee, his new young black valet, that Rose's mother had paid them a visit in the servants' quarters, and how she'd told them Miss Rebecca, Rose's younger sister, had died from cholera.

For the first time Rose could see Piper was angry with her as he strode into her dressing room where she was trying on a dress just arrived from Saks. "Why didn't you tell me your mother was here?" he demanded. "Or that your sister died from cholera? What happened? What did you say to her about your sister's death? Did you arrange another visit?"

Rose flushed. Rebecca dead? She looked down at her hands, her head spinning with the news. "Well, I—she. . . ." She decided to risk a lie. "My mother was very happy to see me look so well," she said lamely. "Yes, she'll return, but she really prefers to live in Santa Cruz, you know. I gave her a few dollars for Rebecca's—" She couldn't bring herself to say the word *grave*.

"Are you telling me the truth, Rose?" Piper asked coldly. "You know the eyes of the island are on us. If I'm to have a political appointment I *must* live up to my words." He walked up and down agitatedly. "Rose, we'll visit your family without fail this weekend and we'll invite them to come to live in one of the cottages."

Rose paled, but she knew Piper was much too angry to be placated or to change his mind. "If you wish," she whispered. "If that's what must happen, Piper. . . ." He strode out of the room, sure Rose was not telling him the truth, determined to waste no more time on words.

His resolve was further strengthened that day in town when Cipriani asked him casually if he'd seen Rose's family since his return. Piper's abrupt no told the wily politician all he needed to know and he also knew that just by asking the question, Piper was alerted to its importance in the scheme of things. Others were getting into the political race, Cipriani told him over a quick lunch, men for whom money was no object and who were beginning to spend it freely, hoping to "buy" their way into a decision-making post.

By the time Piper reached Golden Hill that evening he was determined to make Rose realize once and for all that he meant what he said, that he wanted no more nonsense from her over her sensitivity to her colored relations.

He knew exactly what he was going to say, with even a reference or two to her ancestor Louisa Calderon, when, as he went toward the library where they usually met for a predinner cocktail, he was told, "Mistress Pollar' she not feel so well, today." All thoughts of his fight to acknowledge the Bracken family went out of his head as he raced up the marble staircase to their bedroom, where Rose lay, her black hair flowing over the lace pillows, her eyes red with weeping. "Rose, Rose, what is it, my darling, my darling?"

She flung her arms passionately around his neck. "I thought I'd die all day," she sobbed. "You were so cross with me."

"Is that all?" He sat back dejectedly. "You mean I made you sick." To his bewilderment she started to giggle even as tears continued to trickle down her face.

"No, Piper, you didn't make me sick. I think it was your—your baby."

For a long moment the word didn't sink in. She lay languorously back, the movement exposing one full breast, its dark nipple looking riper and richer than ever.

She did nothing to cover herself, but looked at him with a proud little smile as he repeated the words, "Baby—my baby? Oh, Rose." He groaned with happiness. "You mean you're pregnant? But why didn't you tell me? Are you sure?"

Rose nodded slowly, arching back against the bed, running her hand beneath her breasts as if they were too heavy, cupping them out of her nightdress. Piper covered her white skin with kisses, running his tongue again and again around her swollen nipples.

"When, when?" he asked feverishly, as she started to stroke his groin, pushing a finger between the buttons of his trousers.

"In late July or August—perhaps on our first anniversary."

With his penis wanting to burst out of his trousers, Piper sat back with a hungry yet resigned look. "I've never been happier, but I suppose I can't touch you, can I? Nothing must happen to you or our child. I don't know how I'm going to get through the next few months without your body. . . ."

Rose kissed him, her tongue darting in and out of his mouth quickly, lightly. "It's all right, Piper," she whispered. "I asked the doctor today."

"You what?" He was scandalized.

"Oh, I asked in a very ladylike way—for the sake of the child—and the doctor said he believed lovemaking from the second until the sixth month was perfectly acceptable . . . even beneficial." As she spoke, Rose was unfastening his belt, his trousers with deft fingers, taking out his thick penis. Piper pulled the bedclothes away from her, spreading her long slender legs, pushing her nightdress up to her waist to expose the bush of her curly black hair. They fell upon each other as hungrily as ever.

If Piper thought he loved Rose before, as each month passed and her belly grew larger and her breasts more swollen, his feelings surpassed anything he ever thought a man could feel. He spent every possible minute with her, an ominous terror descending whenever he had to leave for a few hours, making him rush back to Golden Hill to see she was still all right. His common sense told him the reason he acted so illogically was that his first wife had died in childbirth, but he couldn't control himself.

When on one occasion he attempted to bring up the subject of her family again, she became so distraught and hysterical that he promised her on his knees he would never mention them again. He resigned himself to the fact he couldn't join Cipriani's crusade on behalf of the black majority for the first election. Instead, he would give his old friend every help possible behind the scenes. Cipriani would know he could count on him for funds and speeches, but he would wait until the next election to gain his own position, because, by then, he reassured himself, Rose would have calmed down and become more accustomed to her position in society, so that the thought of any familiarity with her family wouldn't threaten her self-confidence.

The thought did cross Piper's mind once or twice that he might possibly see signs of Rose's mixed heritage in their own child, but he dismissed it as unworthy, not even realizing the ambivalence of his attitude.

As for Rose, it was a thought she lived with day and night as the child moved inside her. What if he was to be born black? She would wake up in the middle of the night with Piper sleeping like a blond angel beside her, worry gnawing, sick with guilt over her treatment of her family. During the last month of her pregnancy she was racked with nightmares. A black baby pointed an accusing finger at her from the cradle, screaming in her mother's singsong voice how much he hated her. The strange thing was neither Piper nor Rose ever considered the likelihood of having a daughter. Although Rose was nervous about the color of her baby's skin, she was always convinced she had Piper's son growing inside her.

And it was the news of Arthur Donald Pollard's birth the first week of August that finally put an end to Magdalen Finch's dreams and desires about Piper and Golden Hill. She had just returned to the rectory from a shorthand and typing lesson, when Finchy burst in yelling belligerently, "Another damned Pollard up there on my hill. . . . Another blue-eyed bastard to grow up on my land!" When he'd calmed down,

Magdalen learned with a heavy heart that there had been much celebration at the Port of Spain Club that day, as Piper announced the birth of an eight-pound-three-ounce, blue-eyed baby boy. Not only was he blue-eyed, as Rose had wept tears of joy to discover; he was white from the top of his tender head to his minuscule penis right down to his ten tiny toes.

Finchy Finch never understood why his unmanageable daughter abruptly agreed to meet Joseph Accera.

In his increasingly addled mind he didn't spend a second wondering why. Putting it down to the perversity of women in general and Magdalen's in particular, he hastened to capitalize on his good fortune and drove Magdalen over to Accera's plantation. For once he was almost sober, anxious to wheedle and whine his way into becoming part of the deal—if his wildest dreams came true and Magdalen actually consented to marry the old planter.

If he'd been able to see inside Magdalen's mind and obtain even a glance at her wounded pride, her feelings of despair at having to accept she'd lost Piper forever, Finchy would have been astounded. If he was sure of anything, it was that his daughter loathed and detested Piper Pollard and everything to do with him as much as he did.

After a month of meeting Joseph Accera with her father acting as chaperon, one day Magdalen agreed to go alone with Joseph to see a new plantation he told her, with a meaningful leer, he was considering buying, because it had a house on it a woman might like.

God, he's ugly, she thought, as stiffly upright she sat beside him in his buggy. Even his hands were hideous she noticed, covered in brown spots from the sun, so they looked almost diseased. She shivered at the thought of hands like that touching her, but as they drove through imposing gates and she saw a porticoed house up on the hill, she began to resign herself to what she would have to give in order to get what she wanted.

The house was much smaller than Golden Hill, but it had possibilities, and according to Accera the property was going for a song, so he liked the idea as a business proposition.

As he went over the land with the estate agent, Magdalen wandered through the well-proportioned rooms, mentally visualizing the kind of furniture they needed, hanging pretty curtains, amusing herself as she placed in her mind the kind of plates she'd want for a Welsh dresser in the large tiled kitchen.

As she started to go upstairs, she could hear somebody whistling off key a rendering of her favorite song, "Jealousy." Nervously, she went down again, when a door opened on the landing and a tall, darkly tanned young man came out, smoothing down his silky mustache. "Oh, *pardonne*," he said. "I do apologize."

As he came toward her, Magdalen received a flash of white teeth. "Allow me to present myself. I am Theodore Bartrième. I own the land next to this. I was going to buy this house, but I kept changing my mind, and now I believe I am too late, am I not?"

She was about to answer when Joseph Accera and the estate agent came into the house.

"You're too late, too late," the agent said excitedly. "You shouldn't be here, Monsieur Bartrième. This is not correct."

Magdalen tried to hide her amusement as the Frenchman bowed from the waist and mimicked the little man. "I know, I am too late. Please forgive me, good sir, but I couldn't resist one more look. I found the door open. I came inside."

Boldly he held out his hand to Accera. "Allow me to congratulate you and your daughter, monsieur. . . ."

Accera withdrew his hand abruptly. "Miss Finch is *not* my daughter, sir." And with that he stumped out angrily, calling to Magdalen over his shoulder, "Come along, Magdalen, let us not waste any more time."

As she left she couldn't resist looking back once more at Theo Bartrième who, grinning widely, gave her an audacious wink. "Well, really!" She rushed to join Joseph, who set off in the buggy at a fast pace back to Port of Spain.

Two weeks later, with Finchy Finch and Joseph Accera's lawyer as witnesses, a document was drawn up, stating that Magdalen Finch would inherit all of Joseph Accera's worldly goods and land should she be married to him at the time of his death; and that for the duration of the marriage Mr. Thomas Finch, Jr. (otherwise known as Finchy), would receive a monthly stipend during Joseph Accera's life and on his death a certain sum, not less than ten thousand British West Indian dollars and not more than twenty-five thousand dollars, again, providing Magdalen Finch was married to Joseph Accera at the time.

Magdalen read and reread the document that her father had brought home as fast as the gig could carry him. "What about it, Mags, what about it?" He giggled nervously, watching his daughter's face like a man in pain. "Look at it this way, you're twenty-three and he's—he's—" Finchy hesitated, wishing he hadn't started the sentence. He floundered, obviously trying to think of another way of saying the same thing. "Look at that Piper Pollard, that fleshpot up on our hill . . . fathering a child with a child. It's not decent. Why, he's fully twenty years older than his bride, yet he expected her to have a child. You won't have to worry about that sort of thing with Joe Accera. No, my golly, he just wants a pretty young thing to dress up his house, to show off in his last remaining years."

"How old is he, Pa?" Magdalen shot out. "How old?"

"Well, I think—"

Magdalen screamed at him, "You don't think. You *know*. Tell me, how old is the old bugger?"

Finchy blinked. "Well, he's just turned sixty." Then he muttered defensively, "And he's got a heart murmur just like me."

Magdalen rushed upstairs to her room and locked the door, impervious to her father rattling the handle and bleating on about not turning down the chance of a lifetime.

He didn't need to worry. Magdalen had already made up her mind to stifle her aversion and marry old Accera. For, as she told herself grimly, it wouldn't be for long. He was as good as on his deathbed, and she was determined to aggravate his heart murmur in every possible way to make sure he didn't take long getting there.

Even on her wedding day, however, Magdalen learned her husband wasn't going to be a pushover. Halfway through the reception he received word that some of the workers in his citrus fields had gone on a go-slow strike for better working conditions and were actually sitting down on the job.

"Stop serving!" he bellowed at the waiters. Then, turning to the startled guests, he said gruffly, "I'm sorry, but the reception's over. You can all go home now—I've got to get back to work to protect my livelihood."

Magdalen, who'd decided to drink herself into a stupor to prepare for the night ahead, looked at him, aghast. "You can't mean it," she wailed, but he certainly did mean it, and it was only a small indication of the cantankerous and ruthless nature she soon discovered her new husband possessed.

Hours later, as she undressed and lay on the old oak four-poster bed, waiting for Joseph to return from dealing with his workers, she found herself shaking with fear. She'd hunted through the house for a drop of drink to subdue her nerves, but she had found only locked doors and padlocked cupboards.

When she finally dropped into an uneasy sleep, she dreamed she was in Piper's arms, yet as she tried to draw closer, he retreated farther and farther out of her reach. When she woke with a start, dawn was just breaking. With a heave of relief she realized she was still alone.

As the sun came up in all its glory, its golden rays flooding the bedroom with light, Magdalen heard the front door open and the stump of boots up the stairs. She cowered over to one side of the bed as Joseph burst into the room.

Dear God, don't let him touch me, she prayed. Dear God, don't let him kiss me, but even as she prayed, he stood over her, the smell of drink filling her nostrils. To her horror she saw his hands were black with dirt and his knuckles crusted with dried blood.

"What happened?" she cried, not caring, but desperate to put off the dreaded moment of his touch. Joseph gave her a sinister leer.

"Nothing for you to worry about, my pretty puss. Just some well-deserved punishment delivered. Now let me see, my pussy. Let me see what I've paid for here. . . ." He yanked the bedclothes away from her and went to lift up her nightdress with one blackened hand, but Magdalen quickly dived to the other side of the bed.

"So, that's what you want, is it? A little game. All right, my girl, that's all right with me." He ran around the bed, huffing and puffing, as she again threw herself away from him, but this time he caught her ankle and pulled her toward him like a sack of potatoes.

"You're hurting me, Joe. You're hurting me. Let go . . . let go. . . ." But her words were useless as with his other hand he ripped open the bodice of her nightdress and pulled at her nipples viciously.

"I'll get the strap to you, my girl, if you defy me!" he shouted. "I had to do it before with my last wife and I'll do it again unless you obey me." Beads of perspiration broke out on his head as the sun beat through the unshuttered windows.

Magdalen felt all the fight go out of her as he pinioned her half on, half off the bed and grunting and straining tried to insert his limp penis between her clamped legs. He brutally drove his knee between her thighs to force them open, cursing as he found he still couldn't maneuver his way in.

Just when she thought she would die, asphyxiated by his foul breath and the smell of manure and blood about him, he slumped across her, one filthy hand clawing at her breast. For a moment she thought God had miraculously answered her prayers and that Joseph Accera had died as he deserved to die, but he started to snore, the sound reverberating through the room, and she realized with a mixture of disgust and relief that he'd simply fallen into a drunken sleep.

It was the first of many similar encounters, until Magdalen learned how to deal with them. She learned the hard way, enduring a number of beatings with a thin strap across her buttocks and breasts before she realized she didn't need to fight off Accera's advances. He was impotent, but as long as she could make him think she was encouraging him in his efforts to get inside her it was enough. It was only her attempts to foil him that sent him into an ugly, uncontrollable rage.

The only escape she had from what was turning into a life of drudgery and fear was on horseback, for Accera kept horses on the property, sure that the "newfangled" motorcar would never permanently replace the horse and buggy as a form of transport.

As soon as he left to make the rounds of his various plantations in the early morning, Magdalen would saddle up and ride off across the land to get rid of her feeling of suffocation, her red hair free and loose in the breeze, enjoying the feeling of the saddle between her legs.

The first time she crossed onto Theo Bartriève's land she saw him waving to her in the distance, beckoning her to come nearer. But with the memory of a beating she'd received only that morning fresh in her mind, she didn't dare respond.

By the time she'd been married to Accera for three miserable months, however, she'd begun to learn how to handle him with more skill, so she didn't shy away when Theo Bartrième rode up beside her one day and invited her back to his veranda to take a glass of wine with him.

He was the strangest looking man she'd ever seen, she decided, as she sat sipping from a huge goblet, strange and yet fascinating with dark blue eyes that were almost black: hypnotic all-seeing eyes.

She was apprehensive as he casually showed her his cramped bachelor's living room, where guns, boots and saddles were strewn about with what appeared to be half-finished canvases, paints, brushes and large art books. After her second glass of wine, Magdalen relaxed a little yet knew she shouldn't stay. She felt in danger—from what she didn't know—yet at the same time she wanted to experience that danger.

"I thought you were a planter, Monsieur Bartrième, yet it seems you are also an artist. May I ask what you are doing here so far from home?"

He stroked his mustache with one lean, sensitive finger before he replied lightly, "I am admiring you, Madame Accera, and I am also wondering why you *are* Madame Accera."

His words were impertinent, insulting, Magdalen knew, yet she couldn't take offense; his tone was so light, skillful, teasing. "That is not what I meant and you know it." She got up to leave, but he remained seated, looking at her now in almost a mocking way.

"I am here because my father came here from France, and now I don't have to stay, but it suits me at this moment to stay. Would you like to see my work?" He seemed to ask the question impulsively and Magdalen nodded excitedly. This was the most fun she could remember having since the Middleton weekend, but even as the thought flashed across her mind the pain associated with the memory came too.

Theo Bartrième led her up a rickety stairway to a large loft where at one end on an easel was a half-sketched, half-painted canvas.

As she went to examine it more closely, she gave a startled cry and backed away, confused and embarrassed. Although there was a great deal of work needed to finish the painting, the canvas clearly depicted a group of naked black women all touching each other in various intimate ways. She turned haughtily, but Theo Bartrième blocked her way. "Let me pass," she said, feeling excitement rising inside her.

"Don't you like to see the truth?" the Frenchman asked insolently. "Didn't you know, Madame Accera, that women like to touch each other?" Suddenly he firmly fastened his hands over her breasts, but seeing her wince with pain—from cuts still not healed—he immediately withdrew them, his languid insolence gone, replaced by a look of concern.

"What is wrong? Did I hurt you? I am sincerely sorry. Please believe me." His sympathetic tone was too much for Magdalen's overwrought emotions and she collapsed in a flood of tears, burying her face in her hands. "Oh, leave me alone," she moaned, "just leave me alone."

As he started to descend the narrow staircase, she called out, "No, don't go, Theo. I'm sorry. I'm sorry."

"I will return at once," he said in his stilted English, and soon he was back with an open phial in his hands. "Smell this," he said. "It will calm you."

She timidly sniffed at the pale green liquid inside, and sure enough it did help, almost immediately. She sniffed again and again until she realized she was beginning to feel light-headed.

"What is it?" she asked.

"Oh, something one of the servants made for me. I like to dabble in perfume you know. I am a Frenchman. . . . I like wine, women, perfume and song—" He started to whistle "Jealousy" again in the same off key way she'd heard when they'd first met. She had to laugh.

From that day, except on Sundays when Joseph Accera was at home all day, Magdalen visited Theo Bartrièye for a glass of wine in his home.

Occasionally he would ride back with her to the stables, but he never came inside the house and he didn't attempt to touch her again. As each day passed, Magdalen realized she wished more and more that he would touch her. At night, listening in the darkness to Joseph's snores rise and fall, she lay wide awake, wondering how many reasonably attractive women of twenty-four were married virgins. For she was sure that, for all his fumbling, Accera had never been able to penetrate her. One late afternoon Joseph sent word he would be very late home for dinner and Magdalen, restless, unhappy, decided she would ride back to see Theo for the second time, having left him only hours before as she always did just before lunchtime.

With her heart racing at her bravado, she urged her horse to jump over the low fence separating their land and rode up to his funny little tumble-down house.

Although she could hear voices and laughter, nobody came in answer to her knock, so she pushed the door open, calling "Theo, Theo, it's me. I've come back for a few minutes." There was sudden silence; then she heard him call down, "Come up, my dear. I'm working up here."

Magdalen climbed the stairs nervously, not certain of what she was going to see, yet not expecting to be too surprised either.

In the loft studio, standing out in stark relief against a white sheet pinned from floor to ceiling, were three black women, naked except for a few colored beads around their necks, their nipples and belly buttons painted with brilliant splashes of vermilion.

"Come in," Theo said courteously, as if he were inviting her to a vicarage garden party. "I am happy you're here."

Magdalen didn't know what to do. She stood hesitating on the stairs as Theo lifted his paintbrush like a conductor in an orchestra and commanded, "Back to your positions; my friend is also an artist."

Giggling, the youngest of the group—she looked about twelve to Magdalen—went down on all fours, poking an amazingly long, red tongue out so that its tip touched the bush of hair of the fattest woman, who in turn pushed a fat finger in the vagina of an older woman standing beside her, who held a whip as if to slap the buttocks of the little girl on the floor.

Mesmerized, Magdalen watched as the black women writhed and cavorted about, every so often switching positions, obviously enjoying every touch they received. As they moved, Theo alternately beat a tattoo on a drum beside him, drank from a slim phial and splashed paint on the canvas. And, as Magdalen saw clearly, the bulge in his trousers began to swell.

There was a sweet insistent smell in the air coming from a tall cluster of candles, and, as Theo kept up the pulsating beat, Magdalen started to squirm and moan just as the black women were beginning to do.

"Theo," she murmured, without even realizing she'd mentioned his name. "Theo—"

He turned abruptly—his dark eyes on her. "Would you like to join us, my friend?"

She longed to shout no, to run away and never return but, her head reeling with the scent, she heard herself say yes.

"Would you like to be undressed?"

Again she meant to say no, but heard herself say yes as Theo's eyes seemed to stare into her innermost being.

She was just like child's putty, she thought, as the black women, ordered curtly by Theo to "undress madame," slowly removed every piece of her clothing until she stood before them, trembling not with cold or fever but with a long-buried aching desire, her pallor strikingly evident as she stood beside their gleaming blackness.

"Matilda, you may begin, and then Ruby and Angel. . . ."

The fattest of the group took her by the hand, to place her like a precious object on a chaise longue in the corner, where her arms were placed one after the other languorously above her head, her legs opened wide, so that one lay along the chaise longue, while the other touched the floor. Each of the women started to massage a different part of her body, slowly exciting her nerve endings, stopping just on the edge of her vagina, every one of their fingers touching her in the most tantalizing way. An unaccustomed wetness filled the pink mouth between her legs and she yearned for the women to play with her there, arching her body to attract their fingers inside her, but always they withdrew.

Theo suddenly clapped his hands and said, "Enough. Leave us. Go about your work." And immediately, chattering and giggling, the black women picked up their cotton shifts and scampered down the stairs.

"What's happening to me, Theo?" Magdalen asked drowsily.

"Do you want it? Do you want the only truth, Magdalen?"

"Oh, yes, oh, yes . . ." she pleaded. He never took his hypnotic eyes away from her as he now undressed himself, showing her an enormous, ramrod-stiff penis. He stroked himself as he stood observing her, quietly saying again, "Do you want it?"

"Oh, quickly, quickly. . . ." She had never wanted anything so much in her life.

"Then you must ride me as you ride your horse. I am your horse. Ride me, ride me. . . ."

She followed Theo to a large chair that looked almost like a throne, placed beside a mirror in which she could clearly see their reflections.

"Come, Magdalen," he commanded, and like a sleepwalker she mounted him, climbing onto his lap to open her legs wide, feeling an agonizing, piercing pain as he broke into her, forcing her down, down, onto him, pulling her bare buttocks closer toward him. She thought she would faint with the pain and screamed as he suddenly lifted her off of him only to pull her down again. At no time did he kiss or caress her, but as if they were engaged in an act of warfare, more and more forcibly lifted and lowered her onto him, until blood splashed onto his legs. But still he went on, his eyes fixed on hers, hers on his, it seemed for hours, twenty, thirty times. She tried to kiss him to get close to his face, to feel his mouth on her mouth, but always he held her away, now shouting, screaming, "I am your horse, ride, ride, ride!" Finally exhausted, painfully sore with the friction, she slumped against him and with a shuddering sigh he ejaculated, his sperm shooting down their legs to mix with her blood.

He didn't take his eyes away from her as almost immediately he said, "Magdalen, dismount. It is time for you to go home."

As she rode back across the field, darkness fell abruptly but she felt no fear of the angry husband probably waiting at home for his dinner.

She felt alive, every part of her body tingling where the black women had massaged her, enjoying the pain, even the searing soreness she felt between her legs. "I'm no longer a virgin," she said. She was delirious with joy. "Oh, Theo, Theo . . . "

She didn't know how she could wait for the next day, but it was not to be the next day—for she'd forgotten it was Sunday. As much as she racked her brains, Magdalen couldn't think of an excuse to sneak away from Joseph's brooding eyes.

As Monday's light dawned—after the longest hours she ever remembered spending, she was sick with impatience as Joseph seemed to take much longer than usual over his breakfast, mumbling and bumbling away about the cost of everything. As he went out the door, he sneered, "You be ready for me when I get home. I felt you squirming in the bed last night, you red-headed witch. You're getting used to it, aren't you, me girl?"

She shivered as she saw him drive off toward Arima, but even the thought of what was probably in store on his return couldn't quiet her excitement as she approached Theo's house for their usual morning rendezvous, only this time it wasn't going to be the "usual"—a little walk, a glass of wine. She ached for Theo's hands on her. She said his name silently to herself. Theo, Theo, Theo. . . . But when she arrived it was as if nothing had ever happened . . . except he was a little more distant, more polite than usual, despite her obvious eagerness to touch him.

"Don't rush things, Magdalen," was the only intimation he gave of understanding her need. "It will happen, but give it time. We must be careful. We must be patient."

"But why? I don't want to be patient!" she cried, even attempting to undo the bodice of her dress. "Where are the girls, Matilda, Angel?"

Theo sighed. "Magdalen, not every day. I haven't the strength. I must wait until my mood demands it."

But she couldn't wait. At home after a frustrating morning when Theo refused to satisfy or even acknowledge her passionate desires, Magdalen paced her bedroom up and down. Perhaps Accera would be late again. Perhaps he wouldn't even notice she wasn't home.

At four o'clock she could bear it no longer. She saddled up, telling the stableboy she was going to deliver a note.

As she entered Theo's house, she immediately smelled the familiar, enticing, heady smell, but this time it was coming from the main room, where Theo sat cross-legged on the floor smoking a long, thin reed, his face a phlegmatic mask.

"I knew you would come," he said. "I realized it was inevitable, so I willed myself to accept it."

"You willed it?" she cried excitedly.

"Yes, as I am willing myself now to respond to your new needs. You were a virgin, were you not, Magdalen? I didn't know that before. Now I am going to begin to teach you how to bear the greatest torture of the senses—torture and ecstasy—to explore your body, to give and receive exquisite pleasure."

The note in his voice frightened even as it exhilarated her, and as her eyes became accustomed to the dim light, she saw Theo was only half dressed. From the waist down he was naked, his penis as swordlike as it had been the evening before. "Take off your undergarments." It was a command she instantly obeyed.

"Sit here." She sat in front of him, inhaling the smoke he blew into the air, until the room began to whirl around her, but nothing could obliterate the excitement she felt, the shameful feeling of nakedness beneath her skirt. Theo inhaled deeply, and, lifting her skirt, blew the smoke deeply into her vagina before inserting his lean fingers inside, moving them slowly, expertly, in and out.

She was writhing now in frenzy as he made her open her legs wider, wider, each time coming near, then moving away again, tantalizing her, while she saw his penis grow even bigger.

Suddenly he clapped his hands, and from a side room came Matilda, the fattest Negress, this time a bright cotton skirt tied around her middle, her huge bare breasts glistening with oil, the nipples still painted with the bright paint. "Suck her breasts," Theo commanded Magdalen, and, as Matilda hung her fat teats toward her, Theo drew aside the Negress's skirt to show she was naked beneath, poking his fingers in her as she stood there, until she squirmed and whimpered, her huge body heaving, Magdalen realized, as an orgasm shuddered through her.

Theo dismissed her peremptorily, and again moving a chair to a long mirror, beckoned Magdalen to mount him as before. This time, hardly had she felt him thick inside her before she began to respond, quivering with pent-up desire. Before she could give herself up to the overwhelming sensation, again he lifted her bodily away from him, lifting and lowering her, oblivious to her cries to let her stay as she reeled in a haze of sexual ecstasy and frustration.

They were so lost in a world of their own making they never heard the heavy banging on the door, never saw it spring open in the cloud of heavy, musklike smoke that surrounded them. It wasn't until Magdalen heard the crack of a whip across her back that she felt the pain and realized she'd been knocked halfway across the room by a towering Joseph Accera, ranting and raving, "I'll get the police. You thieving whore! Don't you ever come back to my house! You're finished. You're dirt; you're lower than sewer muck. You're—" His bellows of rage could still be heard as he rode off, after Theo managed to manhandle him out of the door.

Magdalen cowered in a corner, the ecstasy of the minutes before threadbare, barren. "What shall I do?" she whispered again and again, but Theo, rocking backward and forward with his eyes closed, never answered or even looked at her.

When he finally turned to her, his gaze was as hypnotic as ever but his words were cold. "Mr. Accera means what he says. You can stay here tonight but tomorrow you must leave or he will be back with the police."

Magdalen lay awake all night on the chaise longue upstairs where only two days before she had been introduced to a totally new world of idyllic lovemaking, petting, fondling. Now, everything she saw around her looked tawdry, ugly, and in the love-reflecting mirror she saw herself for what she was: a scared waif, a stupid fool.

In the morning, with the smell of coffee and the sight of fruit and fresh bread on the table, there was some degree of normalcy, Theo acting overpolite as if she were an unexpected but not unwanted guest. As if to answer her unspoken questions, he told her gently that she could return in a week or so, when things had calmed down. He laughed as he said, "You have only just begun your studies in the sexual arts. There is much to learn." And then with an intense look, he said, "I want you to come back."

Suddenly the world wasn't such a screaming black hole, ready to pull her down inside to hell itself. Theo wanted her back, perhaps forever. Perhaps it was all for the best.

Her horse was gone, but Theo told her she could borrow his horse and buggy to collect her things from the Accera house. He didn't suggest coming with her and her heart thumped nervously as she drew near and saw a pathetic-looking heap on the servants' back doorstep. It was everything she'd brought with her following their marriage and not one item more. As she looked in the servants'-hall window, the ambling foreman approached, half embarrassed, half smiling. "Missus, I can' let yo' go inside. De master, he say he'll skin me aliv' if I let yo' in dere. Dere's yo' tings. He says t' tell yo' he's gone t' de town t' get one o' dem divorces."

Divorce. The full significance of what had happened was beginning to overwhelm her as, eyes cast down, she picked up the bundle and climbed into the gig.

There was only one place she could go—the old rectory. It was the only place she had left where she could gather her wits and her strength, waiting until she could win Theo's love and convince him they should be together forever.

A week later, unable to bear the separation a moment longer, Magdalen risked returning to Theo's house. And so began a life of furtive visits, of nights and days of feverish lovemaking, of masturbation at

Theo's command, of being loved by and loving back a never-ending parade of different black women under Theo's hypnotic stare, of having her body painted, her pubic hair shaved, acting in a series of erotic charades—until the day came when she could no longer ignore a nagging suspicion.

Now, after the ignominy of returning to live at the rectory with her father, who cursed her from morning to night, she knew she was pregnant. As she dressed to visit Theo to tell him the news, she had a new sense of self-confidence, of power. For only two nights before, during their last intense hours of sex, Theo had told her she was helping him find himself, that until she came into his life he had had years of darkness, of near madness, unable to reach a climax, rarely able to find relief—until the day she first rode him to ecstasy.

She was helping his painting, he told her, and soon he would take her to Paris where he intended to hold his first exhibition of black nudes. And there he would introduce her to the women who had first taught him about the art of sex, the most beautiful women she would ever see, who lived in a house devoted to exploring its passion, pain and pleasure.

"Where are you going, you slut?" her father roared as Magdalen came downstairs. Her inscrutable look was still one of contentment and it infuriated him. But before he could stop her she was out the door and in the gig, her red hair waving like a triumphant flag as she urged the mare away at a fast trot.

By the time Magdalen neared Theo's house, however, her mood had changed. Now she was nervous, not sure how to tell him about the baby, wondering how she would feel on the long sea journey to France.

The house was different and it took her a while to realize why. It was tidy. The tumble of objects that always littered the large sitting room was gone. Instead, arranged in neat piles were boxes, trunks. Theo had obviously already decided to leave.

Tremulously she called upstairs, "Theo, Theo, darling, it's me, Magdalen."

He came to the top of the stairs, shirtless, the dark curly hair of his chest matted with paint.

"Come here." His voice was strangely high pitched. "I've been painting all day and all night since you left."

A surge of love flooded her. She *was* good for him. It was all going to be all right. He did love her and he would love their baby. She ran up the stairs and he crushed her to him. The delirious feeling of abandonment he always ignited in her now, even with a look, made her groan, while between her legs she felt the familiar longing for his penis.

But after only a minute he pushed her away to pick up his long, thin reed, striding to his canvas, where among a medley of black bodies Magdalen could make out a figure that bore a strong resemblance to herself, held aloft as an offering, black fingers touching, probing, pinching. She shuddered and turned away. "Will you use that in the Paris exhibition, Theo?" she asked plaintively.

He laughed, and again she heard the high pitch in his voice. "It is pivotal, pivotal, my darling, but we will see."

She didn't understand him but knew better than to interrupt as he painted. Minutes passed like hours as she sat waiting for him to throw down his brush as he always did eventually, to come to her, the bulge in his trousers growing as he stood there.

She was determined to give him the news before she acquiesced in whatever he wanted her to do this time, but as he stood over her, his hands poised on his hips like a ballet dancer's, all the clever ways of telling him deserted her. She blurted out, "Theo, I'm going to have your child."

He stared at her in disbelief, his eyes like an animal's eyes, soulless, away in another world. As she began to repeat the sentence in an imploring tone, he brutally slapped his hand over her mouth and then ran downstairs.

She followed him, hearing his sobs, hysterical, high-pitched sobs mingled with terrible shrieks of laughter. She would never forget the sound as long as she lived. "Theo, Theo." She went over to him as he sat hunched, his shoulders shaking. "It won't make any difference. It will be wonderful. We will—we must have a beautiful child. You will see, it will—"

"Careless whore!" he shrieked, slashing his hand out at her, his eyes blazing with fury. "Clumsy, careless whore. . . ." He hit her again as she stumbled back, grief gripping her throat, unable to speak, unable to cry.

For two hours she sat like a piece of stone as Theo alternately raved, ranted, sobbed, paced, went up and down the stairs, laughed and screamed like a madman.

Then just as suddenly as it began, it ended. He came down, a fresh shirt covering the paint stains on his body, the smell of lavender on his skin.

He came to her, buried his face in her skirt. "Forgive me, forgive me.

It was a shock. It is such a change to our plans. I am bereft. You must let me think."

She still felt as if ice and not blood were running through her veins, but she sat motionless as he pulled open the bodice of her dress to run his tongue over her blue-veined breasts. There was no joy in her as she followed his commands later, straddling him in front of the large mirror while he pulled her breasts painfully toward him, heaving himself inside her as if to break through to the embryo. He used her to no avail as no climax came for either of them, and finally, tired, he pushed her away to turn silently to face the wall.

As the room became dark he told her to go home to prepare to sail with him the following week, but to tell no one she was leaving. It was a joyless parting, as unemotional as that between two acquaintances, as Theo led her to the gig and briefly brushed her cheek, asking her for the sake of secrecy not to return until the day before the ship sailed.

How she lived through the week, Magdalen didn't know. Her emotions, always volatile, changed even more radically as she went over and over in her mind the wide gamut of Theo's reactions to her pregnancy. One minute she felt as if her body were charged with electricity, with visions of the new life she would lead in France . . . next, a wash of depression brought into focus only Theo's blackest moods, his silences, his unexpected vicious flashes of temper as he smoked one long reed after another.

The day of departure arrived and Magdalen left the rectory at dawn without a backward glance, a brief letter in her pocket that she intended to mail from the docks, telling her father she would probably never see him again, which would be the best thing that could happen for both of them.

As the mare broke into a faster trot as the turn to Theo's property came near, only the thought of seeing him again and being held in his arms mattered to Magdalen. She'd let the future take care of itself. It was enough for the present that she could be by his side. But when she hurried to the front door it was secured with a large padlock, and when she went to the back it was to find that locked, too. She pounded on the shuttered windows, crying as if her heart would break, "Theo, Theo, Theo . . ." but nobody answered; only a yellow bird swooped out of the sky, crying its sweet cry.

As she stumbled back to the gig, sobbing silently, not sure where she was going, or what she was going to do, she heard the sound of somebody moaning, groaning, crying. It was coming from the stable, and when she rushed inside she found the black woman Matilda crouched in a corner, her foot roped tightly to the stable post.

"Where is he?" Magdalen shrieked, trying to untie the rope. "What's happened?" Her questions made Matilda sob all the louder until Magdalen slapped her, screaming, "Tell me!"

"He be gon', Mistr's Magdal'n. He promis' t' tak' me but he be gon' wid dat Angel an' dat Ruby but no' wid me, an' he promis' me an' now de police be lookin' for him an' he be gon' an' he tie me up t' stop me comin' aft'r him."

"Gone where?" Magdalen asked the question, although she already guessed the bitter truth.

"On de big ship, he be gon' for two days an' de police—"

Magdalen ran to the gig, half demented, gagging, a pain stabbing her side as she raced the mare down to the docks, where she burst into the main office of the Royal Mail Steam Packet Line.

"Has the ship gone?" she asked the startled clerk.

"Which ship, miss?" he asked pompously.

"The one to Paris—to Europe . . . I don't know . . . the big ship."

"If you mean the *Victoria*," the clerk replied as ponderously as he could, "the *Victoria* left for Southampton Docks two days ago, miss, and yes, there is a connection from there to Cherbourg and, of course, to gay Paree." He allowed himself a knowledgeable little cough.

Blushing even as she mentioned his name, Magdalen persisted desperately. "Would you possibly know if there was a Monsieur Bartrieve on board—with—with his maidservants?"

The clerk shook his head as if she were a lunatic. "Miss, there are hundreds and hundreds of passengers. I couldn't poss—" Then a thought seemed to strike him and he looked at her craftily. "Wait a minute. Monsieur Bartriève? Yes, we had an inquiry about him earlier from a police sergeant, concerning a strange case of goings-on—witchcraft. . . . What will the country come to next? Yes, as we told the sergeant, I'm afraid their man got away. A Monsieur Bartriève *was* on board with his staff. . . ."

Their man got away? It was her man who had got away. The father of her baby. The man who was going to give her a splendid new life in Paris.

Blinded by tears, Magdalen stumbled out of the office to the dockside to look down into the filthy water as it slapped against the concrete wall. She felt a strong urge to throw herself down in the mire, to be sucked under along with all the worthless trash. . . . She took a step nearer,

nearer, leaning forward. Her mother had done it. Now she knew how her mother had felt. It would put an end to everything. It would be so easy—no more pain or poverty or humiliation.

As she swayed, a hand clamped down on her arm. It was the clerk, an idiotic look of disbelief on his face. "Are you all right, miss? Can I get you a glass of water? You look a bit faint."

She shook him off. "I'm all right . . . I'm all right."

For months afterward her mind returned to that moment at the docks and she wondered whether she would have had the guts to throw herself in the water just as her mother had done if the clerk hadn't intervened. As her belly started to swell and she felt her child move inside her she began to be glad she was still alive, spending most of the time in her room to avoid her father's constant taunts and threats to throw her out into the gutter.

She vowed she'd make sure her child received a better break in life than she had received. Now she realized she loved Theo's seed as she loved all growing things and she started to guard her body and look after it, following her doctor's orders, not seeing with her preoccupation with herself and her growing fetus how her father was shrinking into a decline, moaning more now about his pain, which rum was no longer able to dull.

The day Magdalen's son was born—three weeks earlier than the doctor had predicted—was stifling. On waking that morning Magdalen found herself soaking wet with perspiration and soon the most terrible cramps started, which worsened as the hours went by. If it hadn't been for the old *marchande* outside the rectory crying out her wares as she'd cried them out for decades, Magdalen wouldn't have even known her "cramps" were, in fact, labor pains, first coming every four to five hours, then every hour.

She tried to get to the gig to ride over to the doctor, but she couldn't make it and the old *marchande* summed up the situation with one withered glance.

As Magdalen endured the worst pains she'd ever experienced, shuddering through her in ever-increasing crescendos, she could faintly hear her father crying too, almost as if he were echoing her screams, until the sounds merged together in a cacophony of agony.

It took twenty-two hours for Magdalen's son to be born, a long day and most of a grueling night, during which time Finchy Finch's own life started to slip away. After the *marchande* washed the baby and then her own gnarled hands, she went at last to see what all the screams had been about from the downstairs room. There on the floor beside his bed was the master of the house, Thomas "Finchy" Finch, dead of a mammoth stroke, an empty rum bottle beside him.

Magdalen didn't waste any tears over a father she'd long ago given up for dead. To her he'd died the day they left Golden Hill.

As she rocked her baby son to sleep, Magdalen went over her few assets: an unexpected insurance policy on her father's death that netted a thousand or so dollars, a shorthand typing diploma, still reasonable looks, a voluptuous figure and—if it could be considered an asset—a heart as cold and as calculating as it was possible for a heart to be, except as far as her son was concerned.

She looked down at his tiny perfect features, cherishing his tight, curled fists, the few dark curls on his head, his deep set eyes so like those of her faithless lover. Drug addict, pornographer—now Magdalen knew the worst about Monsieur Bartrière. It hadn't taken the pain away, but it had strengthened her resolve to get back at the world, to fight for the sake of her son, who, in a perverse mood, she christened Theo so, she told herself, she would never allow herself to forget her foolishness and make the same mistake again. She was through with men and she'd legally taken back her maiden name, so that Theo could grow up as the Finch he was meant to be. As she told him fiercely over and over again, even as he lay in his cradle, "Theo Thomas Finch, you are the *rightful* master of Golden Hill; it is your heritage . . ." and one day, she vowed, she would see he retrieved it.

By the time he was six, Theo, a slender, delicate-looking boy with a mass of dark chestnut hair and deep blue eyes, could repeat word for word the stories his mother told him about her "carefree, idyllic, flower-filled childhood at Golden Hill," the big house that had been stolen from her father by the wicked Piper Pollard. Theo also knew from his mother's stories that he was a descendant of a very important man, Trinidad's first British governor—so important there was even a statue of him in the main street of Port of Spain. Yet, Theo thought, perplexed, his loving mother had work-scarred hands and was often so tired at the end of the day that she fell asleep over her dinner. He couldn't really understand it all. . . . Theo knew the wicked Mr. Pollard had an eight-year-old son, and a daughter, too, but he didn't care about her.

It was the little boy, nicknamed Drum, who concerned him . . . Drum, who was in his place up on the Hill. But one day, as Theo told himself, his mother had promised him it was all going to change.

4

Jack
1933

HIS mother had been ill for days. None of the cures she'd used on the family had been able to stop her sickness, her diarrhea. Jack had beaten a bunch of ripe bananas and heated them into a mush, just as he'd seen her do so many times to cure a stomach upset. He'd tried to make her drink coconut water for her fever, but he hadn't been able to get a drop between her lips. Now, even after a visit from the Fedders' own servants' doctor, his mother still lay moaning and throwing up. Every so often in anguish and frustration he had to rush outside to bang his head again and again against the wall.

With his elder brothers away—Roland trying to find work in the oil fields and James on a sugar plantation down south—Jack knew he was the man of the house. He was expected to look after what was left of the cocoa and to keep everything running smoothly just as Roland had told him . . . but no one had told him this was going to happen.

It wasn't fair. Although he didn't know exactly how old he was, he knew he had to be about twelve because his mother had told him long ago he'd been born at the worst time in her life, when the cocoa market collapsed and nobody wanted the few pods she was able to grow.

He stuffed his fingers in his mouth, trying to stop the noisy sobs that kept bursting out. He was frightened. He wanted his mother, his brothers. He didn't know what to do any more. The thought of his older sister flashed across his confused mind. Should he try to get over the hills to where she ruled the roost at Golden Hill, while the rest of them scrambled for a few measly cents in the valley?

The bold idea faded as fast as it came. What good would it do? She thought of them as lower than animals, not fit to set foot in her fancy place. So what could he do to change her mind, particularly now that he knew why she hated them so much. He, of all the family—except Roland who was as black as he was—probably wouldn't get past the main gate or certainly past the servants' quarters once they saw his color.

Jack heard his mother moan in pain. He couldn't bear it a minute longer. He ran like a wildcat out of the yard along the dirt track to find the wise old man of the village. He knew his mother would be furious, for she'd forbidden them all ever to seek out the old man, but there was nothing else he could do. The doctor's magic hadn't worked; his mother's remedies hadn't worked. Even if the old man was the evil spirit his mother said he was, he had to be able to do *something*, for Jack had heard he could turn day into night, a child into a man, fire into water. . . .

By the time Jack begged, implored and finally persuaded the wise old man to come back with him to help his sick mother, the sun was blazing down and every step the old man took seemed to take forever, each one marked by a screech from the blue-and-red macaw, almost as big as a hen, that perched on his skinny shoulder.

Along the way the villagers they passed bowed their heads low to show their respect. The old man was known to be able to work "Obeah," as his supernatural power was called, so wherever he went he was regarded with a mixture of superstitious dread and reverence. Jack trembled at his own temerity in doing something he knew his mother would condemn, and also because every second he expected something bad to happen to him. He eyed the ground nervously as he walked behind the old man, expecting it to open up and swallow him like a giant beast. But nothing changed, until they reached the little house where Aggie Bracken now lay so still it was as if she were already dead. Her light brown skin was a curious ashen color and her tight black curls glistened with perspiration as if she'd just taken a dip in the waterhole.

The old man, his face as wrinkled as a walnut, took out a blackened box from which he produced a number of ugly little wisps. Jack watched, open mouthed, as slowly and methodically the old man started to grind the wisps into a fine powder, which he then moistened with a few drops of liquid from a phial. Every so often he would close his eyes as if in a trance, place his gnarled fingers on Aggie's pulse, then open his eyes wide again like a yawning trapdoor to place a pinch of the powder mixture on her tongue. He sat, stiff, silent, eyes mostly closed, delivering pinches of the powder for hours, until he gestured for Jack to come and take his place and watch the shadows made by the sun in order to time when the powder should be given.

With a sense of majesty, the old man got to his feet and left the room. It was only when Jack saw him outside that he realized the macaw hadn't made a sound until it reached daylight, when its soulless *caw-caw-caw* could be heard once again measuring the old man's steps.

When the old man returned next day, Aggie's diarrhea had abated and she was sufficiently conscious to realize who her savior had been. Jack never knew why his mother didn't like the old man, for he obviously respected her well enough to explain his magic and tell her why her sickness was now, "on de way out o' yo' body" . . . because of the wisps, which came from a gizzard's lining, he told her, rich in a natural healer, pepsin, moistened with his own special brew of witch hazel.

When she grew well again Aggie no longer forbade Jack to go near the old man. Even if she had, he wouldn't have taken any notice, for now he knew for himself the old man's powers. He would saunter down to the village, feeling like a hero, hoping to summon up enough courage to ask the old man to change him into a man, not just any man, but a white one, so that he could be as high and mighty as his white-skinned sister. How he longed to show her what he could do if only he were as white as she was. But something about the old man's actual presence always stopped him from asking for that special piece of magic, even when the words were on the tip of his tongue.

Jack had been born after Rose left home and so he had never set eyes on her, and yet he was intensely curious about her, the only member of the family who ever asked why she never came to see them or why they never went to see her.

When he saw Golden Hill for the first time, he started to grasp the meaning behind some of his mother's words. It wasn't that she often talked about Rose . . . if anything she was inclined to be silent on the subject, preferring to act as if Rose had died, until something happened to make her suffer Rose's abandonment all over again.

Roland and James never seemed to worry about Rose. Like all native children, they'd worked in the fields since the day they were old enough to lift a spade, and they were usually too exhausted after laboring all day to bother their heads about the life Rose was leading.

Although Piper Pollard had long supported Cipriani in his petitions to the British Colonial Office to stop child labor and institute compulsory education, the majority of Trinidad's leading citizens, many of them his friends, were opposed to change. As one wealthy landowner testified, "This is an agricultural country and unless you put children to work in the fields when they're young, you will never get them to do so later. If you want to turn these people into clerks, all you have to do is to prevent them from working in the fields until they are fourteen years old. Then I guarantee you will have very few laborers left in the colony."

So the Bracken children had always risen at dawn and worked until dusk—except for Rose Bracken, now Pollard, the sister Jack thought about compulsively as he swung his machete into the weeds forever clogging the sandy clay around the cocoa trees, the sister living a life that was so very different from their own.

After Rose had humiliated her mother so dreadfully—"an' in fron' o' all thos' servin' people," as she would cry long after the event—Aggie vowed never to speak of her eldest child again, let alone attempt to see her.

Although Aggie often broke her vow of silence on the subject, she never dreamed she would ever change her mind about her second vow, but then she never dreamed she would become pregnant again after giving birth to Jack. After twenty-three years of childbearing, she'd made up her mind that if her lying, deceiving, whoring husband ever came back she wouldn't allow him near her.

But like every other time Bert Bracken had whirled into the house flashing his white teeth, and before Aggie had time to think about it, she was in his arms, loving every thrust of his body against her.

She was never to see him again. A fast car crushed him to death as he made a dash across a Port of Spain highway, but nine months after his visit the last Bracken child was born, a light-skinned daughter, whom Aggie named April after the month of her conception.

Why did Aggie, after recovering from her mysterious illness, decide to try to see Rose one more time, risking the possibility of another snub?

There was a reason so overwhelming that it overruled her previous experience . . . and in any case the memory of that terrible visit had diminished. Eight, nearly nine years had passed since she'd made that first trip to Golden Hill, confidently expecting to be comforted following the death of her second daughter from cholera.

Now, Aggie reasoned, as Rose had two children of her own, a handsome boy and girl, she would surely understand a mother's longing to achieve the very best for her own. For Aggie desperately wanted the best for little April and her illness had frightened her, making her realize she was as perishable as a cocoa bean or a piece of fruit. She wasn't worried about the boys making some sort of life for themselves, mean and unrewarding though she expected life to be for anyone with black skin, but April, little April—who would look after the little girl if she were suddenly to die?

In the middle of a restless night, the solution had come to her, an idea that in the morning had seemed as crazy as something her youngest son Jack might dream up, but an idea that kept returning.

As she dressed April in her best cotton dress and tried to fix a ribbon in her tight black curls, she told the little girl she was at last going to meet her big sister and her little nephew and niece. She didn't tell April the real reason they were making the journey to Golden Hill, for she knew April would scream the place down if she knew the truth. Aggie's grand plan was that when Rose saw the light color of her little sister's skin, she might allow April to stay there to grow up at Golden Hill alongside her own children, giving her all the opportunities she would otherwise never have.

At the last minute she agreed to take Jack along, not so much because of his plea to be included, but because deep down Aggie was scared, although she wouldn't allow herself to admit it. How could a mother be afraid of her own daughter? It didn't make sense, but with Roland and James both away, she needed some support even if it had to come from the youngest and most unstable of her sons.

It was the first time Jack had ever been away from the village and Aggie continually had to urge him to hurry. He stood dumbstruck in San Juan at the end of the first half of the journey, watching the cars and endless parade of different-colored people, Chinese market gardeners carrying their wares in baskets slung from both ends of bamboo poles balanced on their shoulders, Negroes trundling barrows full of turtle eggs from the Manzanilla sandbanks, East Indians with donkey carts full of green coconuts and charcoal for kitchen braziers.

By the time they drew near to Golden Hill it was Aggie who was dawdling, no longer sure the visit was such a good idea. As they stood at the bottom of the drive and saw the great house in the distance, Jack looked at his mother in disbelief. "Dat's wher' Rose lives, Ma?" The words almost choked in his throat as he looked up at what appeared to be a castle, as unreal as anything the wise old man of the village might dream up. His palms started to sweat as he thought of having to walk up the imposing driveway to where a huge saman tree divided its path into two neat curves.

April started to cry, tears splashing onto her dress, which already showed signs of the journey. "I wanna go home, Ma. I don' lik' dis place, I'm hot. I'm tired." To Aggie's dismay, a trickle of urine ran down April's leg as she stood there in misery, hopping from one leg to the other.

Aggie had turned away dejectedly, as if to leave, when a horn from a low-slung white Bugatti roadster tooted musically at them from the road. It was Piper's latest acquisition, with Obee behind the wheel. He recognized Rose's mother at once and beaming said, "Madam Bracken, ar' yo' payin' us a visit? Ca' I giv' yo' all a ride up de hill?"

Jack, beside himself with excitement, needed no encouragement to clamber inside, leaving Aggie no alternative but to follow with April, who continued to wail she wanted to go home.

Obee was naturally shrewd. He knew enough not to risk any trouble by arriving at the front entrance. Without saying a word, he drove around to the servants' quarters, which to Jack's eyes were more magnificent than anything he had ever seen.

Instructing Maize to give Aggie and the children some "refres'men'," Obee went happily through the bougainvillea-covered walk to the main part of the house, knowing this time his master, Piper, was at home, so sure Rose's mother would receive a different reception from the one he'd been forced to deliver eight years before.

Rose's continued adamant refusal even to acknowledge her family, let alone improve their lives, had hurt Piper's chances politically and he was well aware of it. As he tried to point out to her every so often, he was living by a double standard that could be dangerous. He was making endless speeches throughout the Caribbean, in London and the U.S. to support Cipriani's plans to alleviate years of economic injustice to Negroes and coloreds, through the introduction of old-age pensions, an eight-hour working day and compulsory education. At the same time he was privately shutting his eyes to the fact his wife's younger brothers, all under fourteen at the time of the last legislative council election in 1930, were hard at work in the fields, as they had been since they were six or seven years old, not only deprived of an education, but working much longer than eight hours a day.

Cipriani himself made Piper uncomfortably aware that, until he lived by the policies he advocated, it was impossible for him to gain a place on the all-important legislative council. For Cipriani knew—and Piper knew that he knew—what the truth was, that although he meant what he said as far as blacks and coloreds in general were concerned, when it came to the Bracken family, he was totally under Rose's influence.

When Obee knocked on the study door to announce Aggie's arrival with two of her children, the news agitated Piper considerably. He immediately wondered how on earth to tell Rose, who was upstairs suffering from a bad headache. In one way he told himself it was a godsend he was home and could deal with the situation correctly. In another way, now that he was faced directly with the problem, he found he didn't really know what to do. The fact was he didn't care to be too close to his colored relations, either. He raced upstairs and gently tapped on Rose's door. Her voice was drowsy with sleep. "Who is it?"

Piper was struck as he still could be by her erotic beauty, the white flesh of her now plump body emphasized by the black lace nightdress Rose knew Piper liked her to wear. "Rose, darling, wake up. I hate to disturb you, but I must."

Alarmed at the note in his voice, Rose sat up quickly, breaking the thin strap of her nightgown as she did so.

"You're not going to like this," Piper said abruptly, certain of her reaction to his words. "Your mother's in the servants' hall with your young brother and, I'm told, a still younger sister."

Rose gasped, a red flush building up from her neck to her forehead. "How dare she come here!" she cried.

"Now, Rose, wait a minute. This may be the best thing that could happen, don't you see?"

She cut across him, snapping, "How can it be the best thing? They've come to beg. Piper, I implore you, give them some money but send them away. I *can't*, I *won't* see them." Her voice rose hysterically. "Tell them I'm ill. Tell them I'm in Europe . . . tell them anything . . . say I've become a nun. I can't see them. . . ." She clutched Piper's arm feverishly. "Where are the children? Where are Drum and Rosetta? They mustn't meet them. I couldn't stand it." She gasped as if fighting for breath.

Piper pulled her to him, feeling her large nipples against his chest. "All right, all right, Rose. I'll see them. I'll deal with them, but you know you're wrong. I love you so much, but I shouldn't give in to you like this. This is your own flesh and blood you're turning away—I know you'll regret it one day."

He propped her back against the pillows. "This will probably be the last time they'll ever come. Are you absolutely sure you don't want to see them . . . and meet your little sister? It has to be a younger sister? One you've never even known. There has to be a reason for their visit."

Calmer but still trembling, Rose cried, "Piper, they mean nothing to me. It will ruin my life if I start seeing them now. Please don't forget that when you speak to them. . . ."

How often she was to remember her words years later, but that day she smiled with satisfaction as Piper left her to go downstairs, repeating he would "deal with them." She knew he would. She knew she wouldn't have to see them, and this time she prayed her mother would finally get the message they had nothing more to say to each other.

Piper found Obee waiting silently at the bottom of the marble staircase. He knows, Piper thought, he knows what went on upstairs, just as if he had actually been in the room. Well, it can't be helped. I can't change Rose and I'll be damned if I'll ruin my wonderful marriage for the sake of a lot of half-caste relations.

"Bring Mrs. Bracken and the children to the study, Obee," he said casually. "I'm afraid Mrs. Pollard isn't feeling well enough to join us, but I will explain."

They stood before him, pathetic in their attempts to hide their fear, looking as if they expected him to slap them in irons. Piper felt an unaccustomed flash of irritation that he should even be put into such a position. "Do sit down," he said, as if he were entertaining a group of business colleagues.

Aggie looked around hesitantly, not daring to sit on any of the plump upholstered furniture she could see. In the corner of the room was a straight-backed wooden chair and she went toward it, but Piper intercepted her and gently propelled her to the sofa, beckoning Jack and April to sit with her.

They looked as if they were waiting for the dentist, Piper told Rose later, surprised that she kept asking him to tell her exactly what transpired, to describe how her mother, Jack and little April looked, what they said and in particular how little April behaved.

Aggie didn't know how to begin, particularly when Piper broke the news that Rose "is under the weather and can't join us this afternoon."

With skillful prodding, however, Piper soon had Aggie bursting with pride over the achievements of little April. "As bright, Mistah Pollar' sir, as young Rose ev'r was. . . ." She stopped, wondering if she'd ruined her case, but Piper, who immediately guessed Aggie's objective, tactfully "dealt" with what could have been "a very delicate and embarrassing situation," as he later described it to Rose.

Using all his charm, Piper suggested that in view of little April's obvious brilliance the family should move nearer to Port of Spain, in order for April to receive a proper education at one of the better church schools.

"You can do me a favor, Aggie," he told the still frightened woman with a disarming smile. "I have an unexpected responsibility on my hands—a small house in Port of Spain given to me as payment of a debt. It would make Rose and myself very happy if you would avail yourself of this house. Consider it a present from us for April's future if you wish. . . ."

Aggie went back to the cocoa patch in a daze, not fully comprehending what had happened until a week or two later a messenger arrived with the deeds of the house in April's name and the news that a bank account had been set up for her with a monthly stipend to be paid in to cover all bills.

If Aggie felt a sense of pride and appreciation for Piper's generosity, Jack certainly did not. He smoldered, particularly when they went to inspect April's windfall. As he snapped to his mother, "It coul' fit in de space o' Gold'n Hill's sam'n tree." But Aggie was happy—not for herself, but for April. Aggie knew, as soon as she set foot in the smelly, fishy street and dodged the splashes as cars sped by in the summer rain, that city life was not for her. It was decided her sister, the dressmaker, who had originally set Rose on the road to fortune, should leave Laventille and move into the new house to look after April when she started school. Aggie would return to the Santa Cruz property she was still so proud to have inherited from her French ancestor.

From the moment Jack was able to make the comparisons between Golden Hill, April's little house in Port of Spain and his own mud-hut home, his hatred for Rose and Piper began to grow, fed with a mental manure as fecund as any fed to the Trinidad soil, which could transform minuscule seeds into trees and trees into forests in months, not years. Everywhere Jack went, he began to meet people who smoldered like himself at the injustice of everything; although Jack knew he suffered from the greatest injustice of all, cold shouldered as he was by his own flesh and blood.

Although Rose seemed satisfied with the arrangement Piper had made—as much to assuage his own conscience as hers—inside she was uneasy.

Giving April the tiny house in Port of Spain was one thing, but the fact that her mother had even *had* such a crazy idea—that April might be brought up with her precious children, Drum and Rosetta, troubled her. What would her mother think up next? And if not her mother what might her crazy brothers dream up? What might Jack do, who Piper told her looked around the study nonstop as if to tabulate everything in sight. Piper had laughed, but Rose didn't think it was funny. It was unnerving, particularly in these troubled times they were living in, for she was becoming more and more aware of the tensions in the world, reflected so clearly in the island.

While President Roosevelt grappled with massive economic depression in the U.S. and Hitler promised a new order in Germany based on racial purity (depriving Jews of German citizenship and making intercourse between Aryans and Jews punishable by death), there was just as much unrest in Trinidad, aggravated by another race factor.

As Piper lightly chided Cipriani, when the British Labour Party at last had been voted into power under Ramsay MacDonald, they didn't seem to be about to honor their promises to promote more self-government for the island, giving the black majority a greater voice in their own destiny. "Where are those promises now, old friend?" Piper had asked, as he read in the *Trinidad Guardian* that Prime Minister MacDonald had been asked at the annual Labour Conference to explain his party's refusal to promote a trade-union movement in the colonies.

Piper knew a trade-union movement in Trinidad was long overdue. Many workers didn't even receive a living wage, for low wages had long been the main reason the island's sugar producers could afford to pay such high dividends to shareholders year after year, despite the stabilization of sugar prices.

Piper was no fool. He could smell trouble coming, and he did his best to fight what he considered was a damn fool move on the part of some of his competitors in the oil business, who not only passed over educated local blacks to offer plum jobs to white foreigners, but worse, employed whites used to dealing with Negroes in South Africa. And those whites were now trying to introduce segregated facilities in the oil fields and refineries.

"I tell you, Arthur, this island is going to crack at the seams!" Piper warned Cipriani. "It's no wonder we're having so many strikes. There's got to be more of a change. Can't you talk some sense into Westminster? I'll do my bit with my myopic friends in the oil business whose brains I'm beginning to think have become soft from too many gushers. . . ."

Cipriani was silent, rueful. He felt old, ineffectual, unable to stop or control the sweeping surge of anger behind every strike, every outbreak of violence. He had been let down and mystified by the Labour government's failure to fulfill in any way the anti-imperialist pledges they'd made while they were in opposition. He was a disappointed man, but he didn't intend to let his hypocritical friend Piper know it.

If Cipriani felt uneasy, Rose felt a thousand times more so. Since her mother's unwelcome visit, the news in the papers played havoc with her nerves. It concerned her more and more that Piper's name, always linked with Golden Hill, was mentioned so often as he attempted to pacify agitators and mediate in the disputes occurring almost daily now in the island's main industries of sugar, cocoa and oil.

One night they lay in each other's arms, relaxed, their desire sated as Rose had lulled Piper into forgetting his daily worries, holding her nipples out for him to suck, almost nursing him into her body until they came together in a fulfilling climax.

For a while she was silent, listening to the night music from the frogs outside. Then, Rose began to tell Piper what had been on her mind for some time. "You know how much I love Golden Hill," she whispered. "I'm so proud of it, but I'm beginning to be nervous. It's too big, too well-known and it's so near town— When you leave me you don't come back for hours. . . ."

She started to whimper, knowing Piper couldn't bear to hear her cry, trying to break down his defenses before she came to her objective. As she expected, he cradled her closer to him.

"There, there, Rose. You know I hate to be away from you any longer than I have to be. I am your slave, my Rose. . . ."

She placed a finger across his lips. "Piper, wouldn't it be wonderful if we could spend more time together? You know you want to send Drum away to school and soon it will be time for him to go. Before we know it, he'll be a young man. . . ." She drew a deep breath, then in a rush went to her real point. "When he goes to school, couldn't we find a place farther away . . . perhaps in the next valley, a smaller place where we wouldn't be so on view? Where you'd have a chance of some peace and quiet, where we could be more . . . more private?"

Once she started she couldn't stop and Piper, although half asleep, thought Rose must have been thinking this way for quite some time. To stop her talking so he could go to sleep, he promised her he would consider the idea, although he had no intention of doing so. When he remembered their conversation in the morning, he dismissed it as foolishness.

He should have known that when Rose had her mind set on anything she never gave up until she got what she wanted.

Drop by drop, like water from the dripstone, she relentlessly returned to the idea of moving away from Golden Hill. "It's mentioned in the papers at least once a week. We have no privacy," she would wail, pointing out that Roger—the stepson she privately acknowledged hated her—would shortly receive his degree from the Imperial College of Tropical Agriculture and that to make him manager of Golden Hill on his twenty-first birthday might be a meaningful way to congratulate him.

Piper was at first amazed, then disturbed as he realized how serious Rose was about moving. To think of leaving Golden Hill was like uprooting him as a sturdy tree might be uprooted from the soil. It was traumatic. He wasn't sure his roots could take hold in other soil; yet as time went by he began to view Rose's persistence in another way.

It was true he *was* caught up in a whirlpool of activity, with endless appointments, so he reached home later and later. He also had to admit that Golden Hill was mentioned in the press far too much. It had become a political center, its spacious rooms providing the perfect accommodation for the meetings that went on late into the night, as ways were sought to quell the increasing number of riots taking place.

Armies of black men marched through the streets with banners that proclaimed the misery of their lives. They were led more often than not by Uriah Butler, once one of Cipriani's most loyal lieutenants, now no longer willing to wait patiently for change.

The masses were spellbound by Butler's speeches, which repeated in many ways the message: "White employers think and say 'Ignore niggers. Blacks only bark. They can't bite.' It's time, my friends, we showed them blacks have teeth. . . ."

Roger's twenty-first and twenty-second birthdays came and went before something happened that finally galvanized Piper into action. He'd managed to put up with Rose's increasing pouts, complaints and almost continual nagging about finding a safe sanctuary. He'd tried to tease her out of it, reminding her—and himself at the same time—how once she'd longed to be "mistress of Golden Hill" and how quickly she seemed to have tired of the role, now wanting to conquer fresh fields. "Does this mean you're tired of your husband too? Do you want a new husband to go with a new house?" But she wouldn't acknowledge his teasing, not even bothering to answer him, knowing he was as sure of her love as she was of his.

Just when she thought that for once she would never be able to change his mind, events on the island, one following another, helped her in her mission.

It started with a report in the Port of Spain *Gazette* about a party they'd given for an old classmate of Piper's. Although Piper disliked the press writing about the parties they held for VIP's, he'd found it impossible to avoid this one. Golden Hill *was* a landmark and so in a way was he.

As he read the report aloud to Rose over breakfast, it irritated him considerably that the journalist had captured his endeavor to show his old friend that living in the tropics didn't mean living like primitives, that any of the splendor and culinary skills found in Washington could be matched at Golden Hill.

"Goddamn it, Rose, it sounds as if we're the reigning monarchy here," he snapped. Then, as another thought came to him, he smiled and said, "Well, at least that means you're Queen Rose. . . ."

"That's exactly what I've been trying to tell you!" Rose answered sulkily. "These days it's not *safe* to be a queen. Oh, Piper, why won't you listen to me!"

The next week, with a grim expression, Piper told Rose he had decided to listen. They would close up the big house and move out of the neighborhood for the time being, leaving Roger in charge of the agriculture just as Rose had been suggesting for so long. He didn't need to tell her what had changed his mind, for she had been in the room when the news had come from Cipriani's office that Uriah Butler was at the head of a long "hunger strike" march, intended to draw attention to "unlivable conditions in the oil fields."

"Men are joining in droves from Point Fortin, Palo Seco and Fyzabad." Cipriani's assistant had cleared his throat nervously and looked at Rose for a moment before adding, "It's believed, sir, that Roland and James Bracken are now among Butler's leading supporters and are marching up front with him. They're headed for Port of Spain. . . ."

Rose was pale as she worked her fingers together, but still sounded imperious as she'd interrupted, "But the oil fields must be fifty miles away. How can they march so far?"

She'd slumped limply in the chair as Piper had snapped at her,

"They're used to marching, walking, running. Their feet are their only form of transport."

Cipriani's man had gone on. "Sir, I should warn you, there's been talk about the newspaper article about the party. Butler and the Bracken brothers have stuck on banners the headlines about your magnificent home. . . ."

Despite Rose's protest, Piper had motioned the man to go outside with him to the veranda, where he'd heard of Butler's plan—to ram home on the doorsteps of the oil magnates responsible the magnitude of the oil-field workers' plight. According to reliable sources, Piper was a key target. The men had been further incited, the official had pointed out, by an underground oil-field newspaper that stated the truth: although profits from the oil companies had jumped sky high in the past year—increasing dividends to shareholders by thirty percent—oil-field workers had only been offered a two-cents-an-hour raise and no benefits.

Piper padlocked the gates at the bottom of the drive, barricaded the doors and windows of the house and prepared for a siege as Butler, followed by over a thousand ragged men, neared Port of Spain. On the outskirts of the city, however, Butler was arrested for causing a "disturbance to the peace" and the Bracken brothers, along with the rest of the men, dispersed, disappearing like gaunt black shadows in the night.

The papers lost no time in reporting that Butler had been headed for Golden Hill, "the magnificent residence of Mr. and Mrs. 'Piper' Pollard who so recently gave the party of the year for a leading American citizen. . . ."

Now Rose's fears had real meaning, and Piper lost no time in making arrangements to leave. As he gruffly explained to Roger, he intended to close up the main house until the trouble calmed down. "I'll get one of the best cottages ready for your use and I'll leave Obee's brother and sister here to look after you, but Roger, you're a man now. Realize I'm depending upon you. . . ."

Even as he spoke Piper couldn't bring himself to look his oldest son in the eye, but fussed with the papers on his desk. "I want regular reports at least once a week when I'm on the island and I don't want you making any newfangled changes without getting my approval first. I know you have some fancy ideas, but this estate is very profitable as it is. Your job is to keep it that way—then in a year's time we'll see about adding improvements or making any amendments."

Roger looked steadily at the father he hardly knew. He saw a man little changed from the day of his wedding—eleven years before—to "phony Rosie," as Roger still referred to his stepmother privately. His father was a little more robust, with a sprinkling of gray in his fair hair, but otherwise he still looked full of vitality, strong, tanned and handsome. Roger was annoyed to feel his heart begin to beat faster as his father continued his lecture on what he expected from him and how he should conduct himself when running the estate.

There was a tap on the door, and Roger knew without looking around who had come into the study, for his father's face instantly lit up as if somewhere inside him a light switch had been turned on. Jealousy gnawed at Roger's stomach as his young half-brother, Drum, raced over to Piper, who swung him high in the air. "Papa, Papa," Drum cried out excitedly. He's like a yelping pup, Roger thought contemptuously, as Piper tousled his young son's hair.

At ten years old, Drum was still small for his age, but he'd inherited his father's striking looks and coloring; even his hair, which although curlier than Piper's was the same color of dark straw.

Although he'd been christened Arthur Donald after Cipriani, Rose had once or twice playfully called him "Piper's little Drum," and the name had stuck, however many times she'd tried to insist on the use of his proper Christian name.

Now, Drum looked shyly at his older half brother, who never seemed to want to play with him, who always made an excuse whenever he asked if he could come to his room to talk.

"Papa, is all the commotion over? Can I ride Bessie as usual? Mother says I can't."

The fond look Piper focused on Drum was more than Roger could stand. It was a look his father had never given him, and although he was grown up now and supposed to understand the reason why, Roger increasingly felt it was a penalty he should never have had to pay, a penalty he would suffer from all his life.

"I'll be going now, Father," he said coldly, as Piper continued to tousle his young son's hair, but Piper wasn't listening. "I'll talk to your mother, young man. I'm sure you and Bessie can go off on your travels again now. . . ."

As Roger went toward the door, Piper looked up absent-mindedly, as if he wondered what Roger was even doing there. ". . . Oh, yes Roger, all right. We'll discuss the planting in detail tomorrow. I'll get Watkins over, so we can draw up some plans, and meanwhile I'll take a look at some of the cottages to see which one will be most suitable for you."

Like a general planning a campaign, Piper swiftly organized the move away from the house he loved so much. He knew he had to "cut the cord" quickly. Otherwise he might have been tempted to risk staying, putting off what he was now beginning to view as inevitable.

Six months after Uriah Butler's abortive march on Port of Spain and Golden Hill, the Pollards were established in a smaller but still elegant house on Mount St. Benedict. It was not really that far from Port of Spain, but through a curious quirk of topography it was so secluded that Rose felt she was in another country entirely, and miles away from rabble-rousers like Uriah Butler, who having been released from jail, was once again storming around the island. He was often accompanied by Rose's brothers ("the Bracken boys" as they were beginning to be called) spouting his favorite speech which began, "Our miserable lives are not as a result of world depression, but because of the machinations of the 'blue-eyed devils!'"

Rose felt safe for another reason. She no longer feared any "unexpected" visits from her family, for Piper had gone to considerable lengths to keep their new location a secret. The new house had been bought in the name of a trust, and the only "leak" in the press had been a small paragraph to the effect that Piper Pollard was going into semi-retirement to allow his eldest son, Roger Pollard, the chance to manage Golden Hill and other Pollard agricultural interests, while he concentrated more on his oil business and, in particular, attempted to rectify some of the oil-field workers' grievances.

When Jack Bracken learned the news he scoffed. From the moment he'd heard Uriah Butler mention the "blue-eyed devils" he'd known exactly who Butler meant. He had to be referring to Piper Pollard, the blue-eyed devil to end all devils—Jack didn't need Uriah Butler or the wise old man of the village to tell him that!

Aggie was beginning to despair over Jack. He was the misfit of the family, lackadaisical about the house, careless and uninterested in their cocoa crop, so she was greatly relieved when Roland, her favorite son, came home from the oil fields for a visit and agreed with her it was more than time for Jack to do some real man's work.

Despite Jack's protests, Roland hauled him off to return to the oil fields with him. There Jack found himself living in squalor in a ramshackle collection of cast-iron shacks with no sanitation, while to his unsophisticated eyes the white workers lived in neat bungalows that were palaces by comparison. Enviously he watched the "whiteys," young geologists and civil engineers, hop into their two-seaters to roar over Pointe à Pierre hill on their way to a night out in San Fernando or Port of Spain.

Violent emotions churned inside him, which he longed to make as visible and ugly as the black oil bursting out from the earth. After a backbreaking day of wielding an ax, cutting through forests to get to a new well site, he'd scream out his anger during the three-mile walk he had to make to get back to the hut he shared with his brothers.

It didn't take him long to decide he had to escape at the first opportunity, and that wasn't long in coming.

As he neared the end of the weary trudge to start work for the day, he heard a thundering explosion as the area surrounding a well site ignited like a firecracker. There was a foul smell of burning oil, burning flesh, screams and commotion as people shouted and ran hysterically in all directions.

"My God!" Jack heard someone scream. "He tried to cap the well. He couldn't see . . . he tried to use his headlights. The sparks from his engine must have started it. Oh, my God, there's nothing left of him. . . ."

Jack ran, too, not knowing what was happening or where he was going. As men jumped into cars to get away from the holocaust, he leaped without thinking onto the first running board he could find.

"Hold on, nigger," said the driver, a freckled Scottish driller, who drove without stopping, bumping and pitching along a dirt track until he reached the main highway where Jack was allowed to climb inside. It was, he considered, the first and only act of kindness he ever received from a "whitey." The driller took him all the way to Port of Spain, ruminating out loud about the dangers of any sparks getting near a "drop of gas! My, but we're lucky, laddie, we only got our eyebrows singed. Don't want to spoil our looks for Carnival, do we now?"

Carnival! Jack hadn't even realized it was Carnival time. Whatever happened he *had* to persuade his aunt to let him live with her and April in the little house at the south end of the city, and when he pointed out he'd certainly be killed if he had to go back to the oil fields, his kind-hearted aunt agreed he had to stay.

As dawn broke the next day, Jack heard singing and the insistent beat of calypso bands. It was time to go out into the streets.

Jack, his aunt and April stayed out all day, dancing, singing, swigging rum punches, eating sweetmeats, listening to the calypsos—which from time to time as Jack strained his ears to hear—would even mention Piper's, Cipriani's or Uriah Butler's name.

He felt ten feet tall as he strutted about, loving the swirling, sweating activity, lapping up the sights, smells and sounds.

"Oh, dis is where I sur' do belong, Auntie!" he cried. At that moment April dashed after a dark, intense-looking boy in frilly shirt and blue cotton breeches.

"Theo, Theo," April screeched in delight. "Come here. Yo' mus' meet mah big brudder!" Jack turned up his nose rudely as he came face to face with the "whitey" his sister seemed to know.

The next day he decided to give April a lecture. "Who be dat wut'less pusson? Yo' don' wanna mak' frien's wid dat white trash."

April bristled, already benefiting from her introduction to education, for, true to his word, Piper had helped her gain a place at one of the better schools in Port of Spain where, despite the British government at last making education compulsory, schooling was still mostly in the hands of the churches.

"He's no' a wut'less pusson. He's mah own bes' frien'. He's teachin' me mah A-B-C." April shook her fist at Jack, who stepped back bewildered by his little sister's championing of a white boy.

It was true. Theo Finch was helping April. Through a coincidence, the school started by Magdalen's grandfather, the forbidding reverend, was the school chosen by Piper for April's advancement. As far as Theo was concerned he didn't have any choice. He had to go to the church school founded by his grandfather. There was no money for him to be sent overseas to be educated as his birthright entitled him. There was only enough money available for Magdalen and he to live—to provide food to eat, to keep a roof over their heads and occasionally—when Magdalen could scrape it together—enough money to buy him a new pair of boots and a new shirt for Carnival.

Theo was Magdalen's life. She scrimped and scraped, saving as much as she could from her secretarial job with a Chinese merchant, to give her son as many good things as possible, but it was never very much. They were "poor whites," she would think bitterly, neither fish nor fowl in the social order of things. . . .

When Jack fell into the habit of taking April to and from school in the weeks that followed Carnival—eager to please his aunt, in case she decided to send him back to the oil fields or to the Santa Cruz cocoa patch—he realized with a certain amount of pride that Theo obviously wanted to hang around him, walking part of the way with them, soaking up Jack's words as he told bizarre stories of his heroism in the forests, prospecting for "black gold."

It didn't take long for Jack to move on to his favorite subject, crowing about "fightin' de blue-eyed dev'l" . . . and in Theo he had the perfect audience. Since he was a baby, Theo had been filled with stories from his mother about his grandmother "dying of a broken heart because of the evil Piper Pollard" . . . about his "rightful heritage, as master of Golden Hill" . . . about "the little boy who was up there in his place. . . ."

Although Theo was blue-eyed himself, as Magdalen teased him when she first heard him use the phrase, he didn't comprehend the ambiguity of his childish threats to avenge his family's honor and at the same time help his new friend Jack Bracken fight the "blue-eyed devil."

It took a long time for Magdalen to realize the "blue-eyed devil" Theo so often referred to was actually Piper Pollard. It took an even longer time for her to understand, to her revulsion, the extent of Jack's influence on her sensitive, lonely son—and when she did, it was too late.

She had other things on her mind. Her lack of money for one, and the advances now being made by her Chinese boss for another. She tried to ignore the "accidental" touches, the innuendoes, the brushing by her body as he dictated a long letter.

With increasing dread she guessed from Mr. Tong-Li's sighs, looks and the excuses he gave for asking her to stay later and later at the office that soon she was going to be faced with a "situation," and it was one she didn't know how to cope with.

She couldn't afford to lose her secretarial job, but if she didn't accept his advances soon, she was sure she would be fired.

The solution was presented to her in a way she never expected, "almost a matter of killing two birds—two problems—with one stone—one body." She grimaced as she wrote in her diary what happened.

She had been typing a lengthy report in the office she shared with a colored clerk when Tong-Li entered with another well-dressed Oriental. The clerk had been shooed away, and Tong-Li had asked her to accompany them to his private office upstairs.

Because of his companion Magdalen hadn't felt her usual trepidation, only curiosity as she'd been asked to sit down and offered a glass of Chinese wine. As she'd taken the first sip, she'd nearly choked when Tong-Li said calmly, "My friend and I admire you. We would be willing to come to an arrangement with you—for money. My friend and I. Shall we say we have agreed to provide an alibi for each other." His words had seemed to amuse him, for his shoulders had shaken up and down, while his face creased in mirth, although no sound left his lips.

Magdalen had attempted to get up to leave, but the other man easily and silently had pushed her down again. "What do you want me to do?" she'd asked as meekly as she could.

"We would like to inspect your body," Tong-Li had said, using the matter-of-fact tone he used to say, "Take a letter, Miss Finch," and suddenly she'd found herself holding a crisp one-hundred-dollar bill.

"Do you want to keep it?" Tong-Li had asked.

She'd stared at the plaited floor mat noticing the pattern was irregular in one or two places. She had seen no way out. She needed the money. She needed the job and, who knew, she might even like whatever it involved. The two men had sat watching her impassively, smoking cheroots as she'd slipped out of her simple gray-and-white dress, iron-ically embarrassed that they would see that her old brassiere barely con-tained her large breasts.

She'd leaned back on the couch and spread her legs wide as directed while Tong-Li watched, fondling himself as his friend slipped a condom over his penis. With impatient jerks he pierced her and, with a sharp cry, withdrew, letting his semen drip onto the floor.

She'd shut her eyes as within seconds she'd felt another penis, larger, and stiffer, probe into her slowly, deep, deeper, until against her will she'd felt the stirring of her own orgasm. She'd fought to subdue the feeling, but Tong-Li, unlike his friend, had not been in any hurry. A master of control, he'd tooled her almost languorously, until she could no longer hide her own frenzy.

That had been the first of many late nights at the office, where Mag-dalen found—at first to her self-disgust—that, providing she couldn't see the Oriental color of the skin looming over her, she enjoyed the way her body was being handled.

There was a certain highly strung delicacy about most of the encoun-ters. Before any sexual activity took place there was the ceremony of the glass of wine, money changing hands and sometimes another "friend" of Mr. Tong-Li's to meet.

After the first evening there was another ritual Tong-Li insisted upon. The ritual of the bath, which followed sexual intercourse . . . some-thing he told her in almost a shamefaced way he'd learned from the Japanese. It was a bath not only to cleanse, but to prolong excitement, as Magdalen discovered when the Chinaman soaped her most intimate parts in a nerve-tingling way, rinsed her with a soft natural sponge, then stood back observing, knowing her body was again heaving with desire, just when the evening was almost over.

She quickly came to realize it increased Tong-Li's gratification to leave her sexually unfulfilled, the wine having relaxed her inhibitions. He obviously wanted to see her wind her legs one against the other, knowing she was sexually on fire, longing for more . . . which sometimes he would gratify, sometimes he would not, telling her instead to be ready for another "interesting occasion" in two or three evenings' time.

Her neglect of Theo because of this regular "overtime" was brutally revealed when, with some of the extra money she now earned, she gave a special party for his eleventh birthday.

When Theo begged her to invite Jack Bracken, she acquiesced, stifling her innate dislike of him, but Jack ruined everything. His bombastic, tribal whoops and cries as he stuffed himself with the creamy cakes and puddings frightened the other children into silence, and when the birthday cake was brought in with eleven candles burning brightly on top, even Theo squealed in alarm as Jack plucked one out and darted it quickly in and out of his wide-open mouth, grinning inanely, shouting, "I learn'd dis trick from de wise ol' man o' de village. I ca' do mor' . . . I ca' turn de night int' day, I ca' turn yo' all int' frogs. . . ." He belched hideously like a Trinidad bullfrog, sliding along the floor on his belly until Magdalen, her patience exhausted, yanked him up by the collar and told him to leave.

"I don't want you ever to see Jack Bracken again," she told a sullen Theo later, who sulkily pushed her present of a wireless to one side to clutch the Obeah doll given to him by Jack.

"Why not, Mama? He's my friend!" Theo cried. "We're going to beat up that old Piper Pollard and Jack's sister. . . . We're going to get even. . . ."

Magdalen looked at her overexcited son in horror. "What are you saying? Are you crazy? You must never say anything like that again!"

Theo blushed, but stormed angrily, "You've always told me Pollard's wicked. You told me I should be up at Golden Hill and not that Drum. You've said so over and over. . . . He's wicked, you said so, that Piper Pollard. We're going to get him."

Magdalen, her heart heavy, the scene spoiling all she'd set out to do, tried to calm Theo down, speaking as light-heartedly as she could. "Well, in any case the Pollards don't even live at Golden Hill any more. They've moved to a new house on Mount St. Benedict. The big house is all shut up, so don't even think about it again." Even as she spoke, remembering Golden Hill as it used to be, the familiar old ache came back to touch her in a way she'd thought she couldn't be touched any more.

She was hardening, she knew it. At nearly thirty-five, the kind of life she was leading was beginning to show. Only Theo touched the tenderness she had buried inside her, and now Theo seemed to be under the influence of this terrible older boy.

Magdalen shuddered and made him promise he wouldn't see Jack again, but a week later as she came home unexpectedly early with a roaring headache, she could hear Jack's hysterical voice as she walked into the rectory.

She stood outside Theo's room, her head throbbing, a premonition of danger stopping her from bursting in to throw the boy out.

"Fire!" she heard Jack cry. "I've seen wha' it ca' do, fast, easy . . . fire, fire, fire, fire."

He sounds mad, she thought, clutching her throat in alarm. He *is* mad, and he's affecting my little boy.

She pushed open Theo's door to see Theo, chin in hand, sprawled on the floor looking up in awe at Jack.

"Theo, what did I tell you?" Magdalen was so frightened, her voice came out in a high squeak.

Theo flushed as red as she always did and jumped to his feet. "Mama, Jack wasn't doing anything wrong. He's my friend."

Magdalen ignored him. "Jack," she said coldly, "I would rather you didn't see Theo any more. He's far too young to be your friend. I suggest you find a friend your own age. I don't want to see you in my house again."

With a sneer, Jack edged past her, creeping out like some wild coyote, she thought, while Theo tried to rush after him, kicking and screaming as Magdalen blocked his way, trying not to show her fear as Theo squealed, "We're going to get vengeance against the blue-eyed devils . . . we're going to do it. . . ."

Magdalen talked to Tong-Li about the scene the next day, for slowly their relationship was beginning to grow more into one of friendship, although their evening sexual encounters continued as before. She'd begun to feel she could confide in him and seek his advice. In a curious way she realized he was her only real friend. She'd always respected his shrewd business sense and the way he frequently outwitted his competitors. Now, when she praised him, she knew he genuinely valued her opinion.

As he finished dictating a letter, Tong-Li looked at her penetratingly. "What is troubling you?"

Magdalen didn't hesitate to tell him about the conversation she'd overheard. "I'm frightened," she confessed. "I don't know how to stop Theo seeing this boy and I'm beginning to think he's unhinged, unbalanced. Every time I see him he seems wilder. . . ."

Tong-Li told her to come and sit beside him on the sofa. He spoke to her calmly, soothingly, making her think she was overreacting because of the troubled situation all around them, for the many elements of strain in Trinidad were beginning to reach the breaking point so often predicted by Cipriani and Piper. It *was* easy to overreact when everywhere were signs of a simmering populace.

But Tong-Li didn't know all the facts and neither did Magdalen. Jack didn't care about Magdalen's ban. He was sure enough of Theo's devotion, treating him as a lacky, frequently tormenting the lonely child with his own mother's words . . . that he was indeed "too young" to join him in the "big league." Jack was now a member of Trinidad's newly formed Youth League, often out in the streets trying to cause as much trouble for "whitey" as he could.

When Uriah Butler was imprisoned again, following the first general oil strike, there was immediately a noticeable intensification of class consciousness on the part of the workers; black against white, Indian against black, both against mixed color.

Jack's violent feelings found expression as he roamed through the city with a band of hooligans, breaking windows, stealing, setting fire to property, and generally causing havoc.

He no longer feared his aunt might send him away. On the contrary. Now, it was she who lived in fear, for Jack was beginning to terrify her. Once he woke her up in the middle of the night to show her a snake he'd trapped in a cage, a snake that he told her, rolling his eyes up into his head, only hours before had been a man . . . a snake that would suck out every drop of her blood if he only gave the word. His aunt cowered against the wall as Jack advanced, swinging the cage casually in his hand, the snake's tongue flickering through the netting.

"Gimme, gimme, gimme," he snickered, as she rushed whimpering to give him every penny she had in her purse. From then on she never knew what to expect. There would be a hideous centipede on her pillow, a spider in her teacup. She began to despair as Jack became more uncontrollable.

Only one person had any influence over him and that was Roland, his oldest brother, whom Jack both feared and revered. When Roland learned on a visit to his mother in Santa Cruz that Jack still wasn't working in Port of Spain, but was stealing his way through life, even taking money from the aunt who'd befriended him, he arrived at the house one morning, intending to teach Jack a lesson.

He found his aunt screaming for help, her wrists and ankles tied to a chair, while on the floor in front of her was the ugliest tarantula Roland had ever seen.

"Where's Jack?" he cried, as he crushed the dangerous spider to pulp with a shovel. His aunt was so hysterical that he couldn't get any sense out of her for a good half hour, but finally, as she sobbed on his shoulder, the story of the horrendous treatment she'd been receiving from Jack during the past few weeks came out.

About midday, Jack sauntered tipsily into the kitchen, yelling, "I wan' my dinn'r. Com' on Auntie. I com' t' let yo' loose for dat ol' spid'r . . . yo' bett'r be good or . . . " He stopped in midsentence, as he saw Roland, thunderous with rage, by the door.

Jack tried to dash out but Roland was too quick. He grabbed his brother by the neck, smelled the strong drink on his breath and threw him violently to the floor. Using all his strength, he smacked his fists and feet into Jack, screaming, "Dis is jes' de firs' lesson . . . an' 'til I'se tol' yo' chang'd yo' ways, I'm comin' bac' agin an' agin t' giv' yo' de same lesson 'til yo' does learn. . . ." For two days Roland continued to "give Jack a lesson," and when he left, he took his aunt and April with him, telling Jack they would stay on the cocoa patch in Santa Cruz until Jack scrubbed and painted every inch of the house, and until Jack was able to tell him on his next visit that he had a paying job and would never let "de dev'l an' drink tak' ov'r yo' spirit agin. Yo' sho'd be 'shamed. . . ."

Of course, Theo didn't hear the truth behind Jack's horrible swollen black eyes, missing teeth and bruised and battered body. He listened with a mixture of awe and fear as Jack recounted how he'd beaten up a couple of blue-eyed devils and sent them packing off the island forever.

As Jack spluttered on, Theo remembered to tell his hero what his mother had told him . . . that the Pollards were no longer living at Golden Hill, that it was shuttered up and empty. "They've gone away,

Ma told me, to Mount St. Benedict, so I suppose you've scared them too?"

"Yeah, yeah," said Jack, a crafty look coming over his face, "but dose folk, dey don' stay scared for long. . . ."

If Magdalen could have heard the conversation that followed, she would have sent Theo away from the island, as she'd been thinking of doing ever since Tong-Li told her he would help her with funds for Theo's education overseas.

If only she'd heard Jack and Theo that day, but she was nowhere near, confident that Theo was at last listening to her, never guessing that he was now seeing Jack at his aunt's house instead of having Jack over to visit.

Magdalen continued to be torn, not wanting Theo to be so far away from her—in a school across the ocean in a strange country, even though it was the country of her ancestors . . . and not wanting to put herself so totally in Tong-Li's debt either.

While she racked her brains trying to decide what was best for Theo, he was hanging on Jack's words as much as ever, while Jack—hysterical and immature—made less and less effort to find a job, fueling his bravado with the drink he'd discovered, brewed in a village to be almost ninety proof.

As Jack drank, he rubbed his large hands together gleefully. "We'll show dem fancy Pollar's wha' it's lik' t' b' poor an' black, man! We'll show dem folks!" He danced demonically around the room, swigging from the bottle. "I've seen what dat ol' man fire, he ca' do . . . he ca' turn de nigh' into day . . . he ca' kill, kill, kill. . . ."

Theo shrank back in terror as Jack, eyes blazing, advanced toward him, swinging the bottle as if he were going to crash it over his head.

Jack laughed like a hyena, as he threw more of the native brew down his throat. He pushed the bottle at Theo and demanded that he take a swig, too. Soon Theo was dancing around the room, singing with Jack, "Death to the blue-eyed devil. We're going to burn him into the ground . . . into the ground . . . fire, fire, fire. . . ."

Roger
1939

As Roger drove past a large plantation on the way to visit his father, the sugarcane was in full flower, its tall white plumes waving and ducking in the warm breeze, reminding him of the great wheat fields of the northern prairies.

North America! What a wonderful continent it was, so full of enthusiastic people, so abundant with opportunities for anyone with guts and drive! After his most recent visit to Canada and the United States, Roger was impressed all over again by the potential for success he felt was there, ready and waiting.

Did he have the guts, the necessary drive? That was a question he often asked himself, especially on days like today, when he was already nervous and keyed up for what he knew could easily turn into a confrontation with his father, as it so often had before when he attempted to have a straightforward, man-to-man discussion about introducing some far-reaching changes at Golden Hill.

This time, Roger reasoned, his father *had* to listen. The facts and figures he was about to show him were irrefutable and, a big plus, the idea was American in origin. As his father had been born in that land of initiative, surely he would immediately see the possibilities, which could swiftly add to the family fortune. More important, as far as he was concerned, his ideas would prove to his father he'd inherited at least a fraction of the Pollard business ability.

As Roger neared the turn to the Mount St. Benedict house he slowed down. It was a treacherous corner with a driveway so well concealed it was easy to miss. As Roger drove under a low archway, thickly clustered with bougainvillea, he quickly had to steer his car to the side to allow a Bentley to pass. He saw Rose, erect, immaculately groomed, in the back with Obee at the wheel. There was a quick, cool flicker of recognition, but to Roger's relief the car didn't stop. Thank goodness he wouldn't now run the risk of being interrupted by *her!*

Roger's determination to get his point across to his father intensified as he parked in the shade of a palm grove. In the four years since he had stepped into Piper's shoes at Golden Hill, the estate had prospered. Little by little, Roger had weeded out old-fashioned, time-consuming habits, and he had concentrated on improving productivity by introducing some of the techniques and labor-saving equipment he'd learned about at the College of Tropical Agriculture.

Piper never praised him, but his silence and noninterference, providing he stuck to a strict agricultural program, were rewards enough for Roger. He'd grown up without praise, without love, except for his old black nurse. He was a solitary soul, who didn't expect to receive anything and who had never learned how to give of himself either.

Despite his resolve to speak out and impatience to move quickly into a venture he felt certain could be immensely profitable, Roger suddenly felt tongue-tied as he often did before a meeting with his father. But when he walked into the study, Piper was on the telephone, irritably shouting into the receiver, repeating himself over and over again, so that Roger guessed it had to be an overseas radio call.

He sat quietly, sure his father was speaking to someone in England as every so often he would yell, "Do you believe Chamberlain or not? 'Peace in our time,' he said. 'Peace in our time . . . Peace in our time.' Goddamn it, should I bring Drum back or not?" With a sigh of exasperation Piper slammed the receiver down. "What's the good of this bloody thing? I'd be better off without the aggravation of trying to use it." He shook his head; then, with an unusual betrayal of his feelings, he slumped back, saying, "I don't know what to do, Roger. Do you think I should bring Drum back? He's only just gone to this highfalutin' school. . . . I believed in Chamberlain when he came back from Munich, yet now I'm beginning to think I've made a dreadful mistake. Perhaps when Drum comes home for Easter I should keep him here with a tutor? What do you think?"

Before Roger could reply, the phone rang shrilly, but this time it was a call from Port of Spain and Cipriani, telling Piper he wanted to see him urgently, as a copy of Lord Moyne's report had just reached his desk.

Roger sat downcast as Piper talked excitedly with his old friend. He'd obviously chosen the worst possible day to capture his father's full attention, for Roger knew, as every thinking person in Trinidad knew, that Moyne's report was of the utmost importance, destined to bring about big changes in Trinidad.

Lord Moyne had been chosen by the British government the year before to head a Royal Commission sent out to investigate the rights and wrongs of the black man's status in the West Indies, and it had already been hinted his report was devastating, outlining clearly for the first time the main cause of unrest in the Caribbean: that government officials responded more to the financial needs of "absentee landlords" in Britain than to the needs of the inhabitants. Among Moyne's many findings (some of which had already found their way into print, although they were supposed to be top secret) was the fact that wages on sugar plantations had risen only ten cents an hour in one hundred years!

When Piper put down the phone, Roger looked at his father expectantly, hoping he might give him a hint as to what the report contained, but Piper said nothing, just sat frowning at the papers on his desk. He looked outwardly calm, but inwardly he was shaken and uneasy. Cipriani had just told him somberly that Moyne's overall opinion of what could happen in the Caribbean was so serious that the British government had decided to hold up publication of the report in view of the possibility of a war in Europe and "in case it gives gratuitous propaganda to the enemy."

"Well, Roger . . ." Piper finally looked at his son. "You said it was important we meet today. What is it this time?"

The moment of intimacy, the chance to become closer to his father even if it had to be over something connected with Drum, his brat of a half brother, was lost. They were back, balancing uneasily on the usual tightrope of their relationship.

Roger cleared his throat and hesitantly began to explain. "Dad, you know I've just been in Canada and the U.S.A. for that agricultural conference. I ordered the Allis-Chalmers Harvester we discussed and you were right, it's a little gem, light and . . ."

"Yes, yes," Piper interrupted, pointedly looking at his watch. "I know all that. What else? I want to get over to Captain Cipriani's office as soon as possible."

Roger was never at his best when he had to explain something in a hurry and particularly not to his father, but this time, rather than suggesting coming back when it was more convenient, a surge of anger made him forge on. This time, goddamn it, his father was going to listen or . . . well, he didn't know what he would do, but he'd damned well do something.

"Dad, you've got to listen to this. . . ." Roger pulled out a sheaf of papers from his briefcase, and in his anxiety a paperclip came loose, spewing them all over the floor. As he picked them up, he continued to speak more and more quickly. "I've mentioned it before, the icebox business . . . here, look at these figures." Roger pushed some of the papers under Piper's nose. "The icemen have to make almost daily deliveries to U.S. households now— See how the figures are up year after year. Even home freezers are becoming commercially important."

Piper hardly glanced at the papers, not trying to hide his irritation as Roger went on, words pouring out of him. "I saw this new invention in Boston—the Cryovac deep-freezing method of food preservation. It's incredible, Dad, it has a big future, I know it, and especially in America where people love to try new tastes, new things, where experiment is the order of the day. . . ."

"And so is failure," Piper growled. "What are you trying to say, Roger? Get to the point, man. We're not in the icebox business, thank goodness. Messy, stupid, uncontrollable kind of business, if you ask me. What are you aiming at?" As if to finish the conversation, Piper stood up and started putting things in his briefcase, pushing Roger's papers to one side.

Roger flushed. "Sir . . . I want to build a deep-freezing plant at Golden Hill. I want to export tropical fruits, vegetables, perhaps even plants and flowers in ships' holds, and one day when aviation is more developed, in airplanes, too. I have the figures worked out. It can bring us a valuable return. Frozen food is going to be the convenience food of the future just as Clarence Birdseye predicted it would be. . . ."

"Rubbish!" Piper growled this time loudly. He shut his briefcase with an emphatic snap. "Rubbish. Nobody's going to want to eat old food, and that's what frozen food is, *old* food. For goodness sake, Roger, I thought you had more in your head than that. Where have Birdseye's predictions got him, I'd like to know? He started with the frozen fish he found in Alaska, and ended up bankrupt a few years later."

"That's not so," Roger answered heatedly. "He was bought out for twenty million dollars by General Foods and . . ."

"I don't want to hear another word of this harebrained scheme, Roger. I think I'll put a stop to your attending these conferences, if this is what you come back with. My God, the world is falling apart around our ears, and all you're thinking about is iceboxes and frozen mangoes. I think your own brain must have been deep frozen over there. . . ." Piper walked past him, throwing over his shoulder, "Think about increased productivity. That's what you *should* be thinking about. We may have a war-torn Europe to feed shortly. You'd better take a look at that sugar plantation that's just come on the market. We may as well increase our sugar production."

When he heard Piper drive away, Roger, his hands trembling with anger, went over to his father's bar to pour himself a stiff scotch. That's done it, he thought, as he threw the drink down his throat, then poured himself another. That's the last straw. His father's words still rang in his ears. *"I'll put a stop to your attending these conferences. . . ."*

How dare he! How old did his father think he was? Drum's age? Here, he was a man of nearly twenty-seven and his father still talked as if he could forbid him to attend important agricultural conferences.

Rage engulfed him. He paced up and down his father's study, increasingly incensed as he relived the scene that had just transpired. He *had* to get out from under his father's thumb before it was too late, and his self-confidence was totally sapped like coconut milk from its shell. The only way his father would ever listen to him would be if he made it on his own.

As the weeks went by, the news from Europe worsened, but it wasn't reading about the greatest pogrom in German history that made up Roger's mind to see Europe before it was too late. It was the paragraph beneath the shocking story that made Roger start to organize his affairs in readiness to get away. "Newfangled Freeze Idea for 'Old' Food" was the headline, and the story announced that "soon precooked frozen food in the form of 'chicken fricassee' will be introduced in the U.S.A., under the Birdseye label, now owned by the General Foods Corporation. . . ."

Although the piece was written in a tongue-in-cheek "what-can-we-expect-next-from-the-good-ol'-U.S.A." kind of way, for Roger it came at a resolve-making time. He'd never been able to get his father to discuss the subject again, and if the world really was falling apart (as was now being predicted daily in newspapers and on the wireless), Roger decided he had to see more of it before the collapse actually happened.

He worked out a plan. He would spend about three or four months looking around Europe—the maximum time he estimated his savings would last—then he would cross the Atlantic and approach General Foods in the States to try to get a job in the frozen-food end of their business, learning as much as possible, before setting up on his own, when he'd prove to his father he didn't have a "deep-frozen brain" after all! He longed to fly as far and as fast away from Trinidad as possible, for flight, he felt, would emphasize his longing for freedom, but planes were few and far between. Although a flying boat could take him to Miami, he would still be thousands of miles away from Europe.

When Roger learned that Drum was not going to return to Harrow, his British public school, after the Easter holidays because Rose and Piper had decided it was now too dangerous for him to be in England, Roger immediately went to the shipping office to discover when the next liner would leave for Europe. So the journey would take weeks instead of hours. Anything was preferable to staying in Trinidad to witness all the fussing and cosseting over Drum that would go on on his return. Roger booked to sail out of Trinidad on a ship going to Rotterdam only three days before Drum—Rose and Piper's "precious little darling"— sailed in.

Piper, who'd always vowed never to repeat his father's short-sighted repudiation of the "petroleum business having any future," failed to see the irony in his peremptory dismissal of Roger's belief in the new frozen-food industry. By the time he received Roger's letter, Roger was already twenty-four hours out to sea on board the *Simon Bolivar*, the pride of the Royal Netherlands Steamship Company.

Exultant as he watched the proud bow of the liner rhythmically break through giant Atlantic rollers taking him farther and farther away from Trinidad, Roger wondered why it had taken him so long to leave. He cherished his new-found sense of freedom as he strolled around the deck, making endless plans for the frozen-food empire he intended to build.

At first Piper couldn't believe Roger's act of defiance, and his incredulity was swiftly followed by a blaze of anger. "Ungrateful devil!" he cried, as he handed Roger's letter to Rose to read.

Rose gave him a warm, understanding smile. "There, there," she cooed. "It's his loss, darling, not yours. He'll soon discover what a cruel world it is out there and how endlessly good and kind you've been to him."

On Sunday as the family relaxed on the veranda after a big welcome-home lunch for Drum, Piper squeezed Rose's hand and announced emotionally what a lucky man he considered himself to be ". . . surrounded by my loved ones in this paradise so far away from the terrible happenings in Europe."

Rosetta's cat, Posie, chose that inopportune moment to jump on Rose's lap, causing Rose to squeal. She hated cats and it had taken all of Piper's charm to persuade her to let Rosetta keep Posie, who'd wandered in from the nearby native village as a scrawny kitten.

"Get that animal away from here," Rose screeched as Rosetta started to cradle Posie in her arms. The little girl reluctantly shooed the cat away into the palm grove and to change the subject, Drum began to ask where Roger was, but his father cut him short. "He's a fool, Drum. He's gone to Europe just when it's about to explode, leaving me in the lurch at Golden Hill, but he'll pay for it. Remember that, Drum. I don't look after those who don't look after me!"

If Rose expected Roger to come crawling home "to ask forgiveness" nothing could have been further from the truth.

As time passed he reveled more, not less, in his independence, carefully working out how much he had to spend each day, avoiding what he decided were likely to be overpriced "tourist traps."

From Holland he went by train to Paris, then on to Rome, then Berlin, spending only forty-eight hours there, quickly sickened by the sight of so many bleak-eyed people with the six-pointed yellow Star of David prominently displayed on their clothes, people who were being pushed and shoved around by police and pedestrians alike.

He was on board the *Queen Mary* en route to New York to put the second phase of his plan into action—to obtain a job with General Foods—when he read in the ship's newspaper that German troops with aircraft support had invaded Poland.

By the time he stepped onto American soil, Britain and France had declared war on Germany and already a German U-boat had sunk the British ship *Athenia* off the Irish coast.

Roger was totally unprepared for the American "let's stay out of it" attitude, boosted by speeches he heard on the radio, especially those given by one of his heroes, Charles A. Lindbergh, who stressed why anti-intervention had to be America's stand. Roger listened, inwardly protesting, but said nothing. Other than the radio and newspaper reports, it was hard to realize there was a war going on in the countries he'd so recently visited. It was all a gigantic pity. He tried to push his thoughts to the back of his mind. He didn't have any time to waste. If he was ever going to be able to prove himself, he had to get into the frozen-food business without delay.

In Trinidad, there was no sign of any war going on either. Those with relations, lovers and friends overseas in Europe, sat glued to the BBC Overseas News and waited with mounting trepidation for mail to arrive.

Magdalen thanked her lucky stars she'd decided not to send Theo away to school in England. She knew he still saw the repulsive Jack Bracken, but she decided it really wasn't doing much harm. . . . So they chanted their ridiculous chants against the blue-eyed devil and she knew now Piper was Jack Bracken's real target, but what of it? Piper Pollard *was* a blue-eyed devil, she could vouch for that, and probably so could many women in Port of Spain. However, Magdalen solaced herself, living with that vixen Rose Bracken couldn't be a bed of roses, so perhaps Piper had paid for his devilry by now.

Every cent she earned, Magdalen saved for Theo's future, planning to send him to an American college when he was eighteen. To her delight, he easily passed the stiff entry examination to secondary school and displayed such a quick, natural intelligence she was beginning to plan for the day when he would be able to make a success in the business world, and live like the gentleman he was born to be.

Magdalen was no fool, but like so many mothers, her vision was clouded by a haze of love whenever she looked in her son's direction. She never noticed the uneasiness in his eyes whenever she came unexpectedly into his room; the small deceits he practiced when he was planning to meet Jack late at night. She didn't know that as soon as she switched out his light, Theo would frequently skip out through the back window for a nightly prowl with Jack . . . or, if he wasn't meeting the "revolutionaries," as Jack proudly called the gang of hooligans around him, how often he would switch the light on again because he was frightened of the dark.

In one way Theo longed to break away from Jack, yet in another he was too intricately caught up with him, trapped by years of listening to his mother's stories about Piper Pollard's acts of injustice to them, and, more binding, trapped by an increasing fear of what Jack might do to him and his mother if he tried to break away.

Then one night Jack was arrested, caught painting "death to the blue-eyed devil" on the wall of the Prince's Building, as he caroused up and down, screaming out profanities, interspersed with Piper Pollard's name, taking hefty swigs of a potent native beer. He was jailed for a month, but as far as he was concerned, it was a profitable stay, because who should be one of his cellmates, but the brother-in-law of his own high-and-mighty sister's upstairs maid at her secret home at Mount St. Benedict.

"A verree us'ful pusson t' know," Jack told a subdued Theo on his release, when he immediately rounded up his gang.

Later, the brother-in-law took Jack on a two-day hike through the back woods, showing him a way to look down on Rose and Piper's house almost from the top of the mount.

Well, what of it? Theo wasn't interested and only half listened as Jack made his usual wild boasts of what he had in store for his lily-white sister and her devil of a husband.

The blitzkrieg rained bombs down on Rotterdam and other Dutch cities while German armies swept across the lowlands without warning, moved on to overrun Belgium, then raced toward Northern France.

In Jack Bracken's confused mind, a plot began to formulate, relentlessly taking shape as he sat, open-mouthed, watching the pitiless war scenes on Movietone News.

Thousands of miles away in Hoboken, New Jersey, Roger wrestled with his conscience as he watched a similar Movietone News showing pictures of bombs falling, of grieving faces, of miles and miles of refugees moving slowly along desolate, seemingly never-ending roads away from the advancing army.

Through a contact from his last visit, Roger had landed on his feet. He was working on a secret U.S. project to produce an instant coffee to compete against Nescafé, the instant brew brilliantly developed by the Swiss and introduced in 1938 after eight years of research.

In one way Roger was in his element, happy to work a twelve-hour day, knowing he was in at the birth of one of the most important developments in freeze-drying processes. On the other hand, when he went across the George Washington Bridge at night to the simple apartment he'd rented on the west side of Manhattan, he was torn by the feeling he wasn't doing his part, that he was behaving dishonorably, selfishly. Here he was working on ways to preserve coffee and its flavor, when he should have been working to help preserve his fellow man.

His father's words often came back to him in the middle of the night—and sometimes during the day too. ". . . the world is falling apart . . . and all you're thinking about is iceboxes. . . . I think your own brain must have been deep frozen . . . "

The full reality of war was brought home to him with sickening clarity one evening when he received a long letter from Watkins, the Golden Hill foreman, enclosing a newspaper clipping that reported the sinking of the *Simon Bolivar* after it struck one of Hitler's magnetic mines in the North Sea. It had gone down carrying mostly West Indian passengers, who were returning to the Caribbean at the outbreak of war. Although the foreman wrote, "Fortunately there were many survivors," some of those lost had been well known to Roger.

He stared gloomily at the sliver of the Hudson River he could just see between two tall buildings. Unexpected tears pricked his eyes as he remembered the uplifting surge of relief, of freedom he'd experienced as he sailed out of Trinidad on the *Simon Bolivar* only the year before . . . and now she was at the bottom of the ocean.

Roger suddenly felt he couldn't live with himself anymore, listening, saying nothing, never attempting to contradict his colleagues in the lab as they bemoaned the uselessness of the British attempts to defend their little island. He couldn't swallow his pride day after day. He had to do *something* for the war effort, to show respect for his mother's country, even if it meant delaying the creation of his own frozen-food empire for a few years.

Within days Roger had resigned from General Foods and was on his way to Toronto to enlist at the first Royal Canadian Air Force station he could find.

As he scribbled wryly on a postcard to his father, "I'm on my way to help pick up some of the pieces of a world that's rapidly falling apart— just as you predicted."

In the early hours of New Year's Day, on the steep slope leading down to Rose and Piper's Mount St. Benedict sanctuary, Jack Bracken, Theo and the brother-in-law of Rose's upstairs maid crouched in the paragrass that stood as high as a man. Far below, a thin gray mist trailed like a gauze scarf across cliffs and valleys, encircling the green slate roof of the mansion, which on one side was partly covered by a cat's claw vine, that fell like a shaggy cloak from the uppermost branches of a huge saman tree, soaring beside the house to a height of over fifty feet.

As they inched down the slope toward the tree, a breeze caught the branches which started to sway and rustle, almost as if to alert the house it was in danger, but as quickly as the breeze came, it went, passing on down into the valley, leaving the branches to stand out from the mighty trunk like the upraised arms of a conductor about to begin a symphony.

"It b' time t' b' goin'," the brother-in-law croaked with an alcoholic giggle. He plunged away from the other two and slid down a sandy track as if he were on a chute, landing in a muddy brook. Jack followed, dragging a reluctant Theo down with him. Now they were almost on a level with the top of the tree, and it looked easy for the brother-in-law to jump up and catch hold of a giant branch, along which he swung, hand over hand, whistling softly until he maneuvered himself onto a safe perch.

Jack followed his movements exactly, and sure enough the man was right! It *was* easy. Theo cowered back against the hill, waiting for them to return the way they'd gone, which they soon did, jumping easily back onto a large stone by the brook and retracing their steps, climbing up the steep hill to reach the gravel bar, which stretched for almost a mile to reach the main road.

In exchange for ganja, Jack had persuaded his jailbird friend to take him again to look down on his sister's house. Now he knew the route by heart and he was going to make use of it, he told Theo. "T' giv' ol' whitey, dat blue-eyed dev'l, de fright o' hi' life. . . ." Theo protested he wanted nothing to do with it, but, when Jack threatened to put the curse of Obeah on him and to turn his mother into a red-bellied snake unless he came along, Theo gave in.

Two weeks after their first foray with the brother-in-law, Theo, shivering with fear, accompanied Jack back to Mount St. Benedict, this time in a stolen car with a drum of stolen kerosene in the back.

Jack had waited for the light of the full moon to carry out his act of vengeance against his sister, her husband, their two children and the whole white world in general. But it was dark and menacing under the foliage from huge spreading trees and clumps of bamboo as they climbed from the main road to reach the gravel bar.

Theo sniveled as he edged along the narrow path, clinging to the hillside, scraping his hands and knees on the rocky soil, getting soaked by rivulets which fell from the hills above. He was terrified by the sudden silence, by the omnipresent blackness made by the roof of slender trees high above them, their limbs totally entwined with luxuriant festoons of thick creepers.

"Don' worry," Jack hissed as Theo and he neared the end of the bar that led to the steep hillside. "Nobody's goin' t' get demselves hurt. Jes' scar'd. Dem folks down dat hill, dey d'serv' t' be scar'd an' we're goin' t' giv' it t' dem." As before, they crouched in the tall grass to recover their breath. Theo watched Jack unstrap the kerosene drum from his back and roll it down the hill to land in the muddy brook as effortlessly as he himself had done at daybreak two weeks before.

Now, the valley below and everything around them—flowering trees, shrubs, vines, poinsettias, flamboyants, hibiscus, forest orchids and lady-of-the-night—were all bathed in the unearthly pale light from the moon and millions, billions, trillions of stars in a velvet sky, turning everything into a hauntingly beautiful and awesome paradise.

"Jack, let's go back. I'm scared. It's wrong. It's bad. I don't want to," Theo whispered, tears pouring down his face.

Jack bared his teeth in a look of hatred. "Wha' di' I tel' yo'? D'yo' wan' ol' Obeah in yo' mudder's bed dis night?" Theo shook his head, biting his lip until he could taste blood, trying not to howl out loud. Now he realized how much he hated Jack, but there was nothing he could do, except obey his dreaded orders if he and his mother were going to live another second. . . .

Jack motioned violently with his hand for Theo to catch hold of the outstretched branch of the saman tree that on their earlier visit the brother-in-law had bent nearer to the boulder on which they now stood. Theo jumped up and easily caught the branch, which momentarily sank as if it were going to break, then bounced up again, taking him with it. Once he was balanced on the stalwart arm, he leaned forward, as he'd been instructed to do, to take the drum of kerosene from Jack. He placed it carefully on the flat place made by two branches crossing each other.

Now Jack swung himself up and along the branch, arm over arm, until he reached Theo, when slowly, together, they edged their way toward the roof of the house and the room in which the brother-in-law had told Jack that Piper and Rose slept.

Jack was humming a calypso under his breath, every so often rolling his eyes back in a horrifyingly eerie way as he neared his destination. Nodding his head backward and forward in a kind of ritual, he slowly unscrewed the cap from the kerosene and, lifting the can high in the air like an offering, he began to pour the dirty yellow liquid over the branch that brushed the roof's gutter, the cat's claw vine spewing from it to drape decoratively around the top of open shutters through which, in the ghostly light of the moon, Theo could see a pale curtain sway.

When the branch and the cat's claw vine were saturated, the raw smell of the kerosene smacked Theo's nose so hard he only just managed to stop a sneeze, almost falling onto the roof in the attempt.

Jack edged back, ordering Theo to hold on to his ankles tightly, as he stretched himself out to lie full length on his stomach along the branch. Before Theo could guess what he was about to do, with a wild whoop Jack struck one match after another, throwing each one onto the oil-soaked wood.

With frightening speed, the branch ignited, its fire sweeping along to the vine, devouring the dry twigs, moving on to the shutters and curtain. In no time, the whole east corner of the house was crackling and spluttering, fingers of fire creeping down the window frame onto the floor of the bedroom, catching the muslin around the huge canopied bed and the delicate mosquito netting, roaring through like an inferno, throwing red-gold sparks far out into the garden.

Jack was laughing so hard he was crying. His whole body shook with mirth, maniacal, guttural sounds coming from his mouth, as his large red tongue flickered in and out in a hysterical outburst of joy.

Theo, with his back pressed into the trunk of the tree, hidden by the branches, was transfixed, as below he saw people start to run out of the house screaming—a little boy, a little girl, a beautiful woman, with a long black plait that looked as if it spliced her bare white back in two.

Directing people in a calm but authoritative voice, Theo realized, had to be the blue-eyed devil himself, Piper Pollard, who sent servants running in all directions with buckets of water, while others tried to fix up an antiquated-looking hose.

As Theo stared, his stomach churning, longing to be sick, Jack touched his arm and motioned him to follow him back up the hill. But Theo couldn't move, couldn't take his eyes away from the moonlit scene.

He could hear the little girl crying, "Posie, Posie . . . where are you? Come back here, come back. . . ." She ran inside the house and next Theo saw Piper Pollard pull himself away from the arms of the beautiful woman to run inside after the little girl. Theo waited and waited for them both to come out again . . . but they didn't come out.

It took six months for Roger to learn the facts surrounding the deaths of his father and half sister, six months for a letter to follow him from the General Foods laboratory in New Jersey to a pilots' training unit in Montreal to a gunnery station in Winnipeg, Manitoba, to another operational training unit in Halifax, Nova Scotia, where, along with ten thousand other men, he was waiting to embark on the S.S. *Normandy* en route for Greenock, Scotland.

He'd received a telegram with the news shortly after it happened but he'd refused to take compassionate leave, because even as he sat stunned in his commanding officer's study, crushing the telegram into a tiny ball in his hand, he'd decided he had no one to go back for. Who needed him? Rose? Drum? Neither of them wanted *his* compassion, *his* comfort, and neither of them could give *him* the slightest comfort either.

He'd tried to get through on the telephone a few times to speak to the Golden Hill foreman to find out exactly what had happened. But, as the operator had told him every so often after he'd waited six hours with no success, "There's a war on, sir. There *are* priority calls, you know. . . ." So he'd given up. It wasn't until he was about to get on the ship for Scotland, headed toward active duty at last, that the envelope, stamped with all his different forwarding addresses, had finally been put into his hands.

Even after he'd read it there were many things he didn't understand. All right, so it was a clear case of arson and his stepmother's younger brother Jack Bracken and Theo Finch, the even younger grandson of the original owner of Golden Hill, had been apprehended and accused of the crime, but did anyone know why the crime had been committed?

On the perilous journey across the Atlantic, Roger had plenty of time to think about things. Somewhere deep inside him he'd buried his grief for his father for the duration of the war. When the war was over he hoped to see Golden Hill again and then he would release his grief, let it all flood out so that it didn't consume him, as his lifetime grievance over "what might have been" consumed him now.

The new relationship he'd sought with his father, based on respect, if not love, was now never going to be. . . . Now he'd never see the look of approval on his father's face that he'd always yearned for. It was all such a terrible waste.

The ship would heave and pitch, bringing Roger back to the reality of the cabin he shared with three other men, all of whom were suffering because they'd just left their loved ones, whereas he was suffering because he didn't have a loved one to leave.

By the time Roger completed his training, received his wings and became attached to a bomber command squadron in the south of England, his father's death and Golden Hill seemed a very long way away and so, for that matter, did the frozen-food business.

Returning from one dangerous mission after another, when all too often someone he'd come to know and like was lost, his dreams for the future were centered on learning how to live, *really* live, with a lovely, peaceful girl at his side, most probably at Golden Hill, which he would run as his father had run it, like a gentleman farmer, not as a frozen-food tycoon.

Peace was uppermost in his mind as it was in everyone's . . . peace and settling down with the lovely, peaceful girl he hadn't yet found.

There was to be no peace for the criminals. Jack Bracken was arrested only hours after the fire and accused of arson and murder. He immediately blamed Theo, who was also arrested and imprisoned awaiting trial, despite Magdalen's desperate plea that he was only a baby and in any case had to be innocent.

But he wasn't a baby and he wasn't innocent. He was in his fifteenth year, five years younger than "mad" Jack, who in a crazy fit in the courtroom jabbered on about how much he'd enjoyed lighting the matches that had started the fire to cause "dat ol' blue-eyed dev'l's death, dat dev'l, h' b' rottin' in de hellfire. . . ." There wasn't much chance for Jack after that outburst, and a year after the fire he was sentenced to death by hanging. Theo, as a minor but still an accomplice, was sentenced to ten years in prison, the first three to be served in a boys' reformatory.

Magdalen aged ten years herself waiting for the sentences to be passed, while it seemed her long-time antagonist Rose turned into an old woman in one night, the night that took her husband's life.

The only time she seemed to come to life and show signs of the vibrant, volatile woman who had so totally captivated Piper Pollard, was when she went to the preliminary hearing against Jack.

She looked like a wild gypsy on the witness stand, her eyes glassy, her long black hair unplaited, uncombed, falling over her shoulders, a curious yellow tinge to her skin. At first she sat looking down at the floor, speaking so quietly when answering the questions that twice the judge gently had to ask her to speak up.

Then looking around the courtroom she saw her other brothers, Roland and James, sitting toward the back. It was as if a wand had been waved over her. She stood up, her eyes blazing with hatred, hissing like a hyena, pointing a finger directly at them, screaming at the top of her voice, "Don't let those two escape! See those two black men there. They are just as guilty. They planned my husband's and my daughter's . . ."—she began to choke on the word—"m-murder. Don't just take the insane one. They're just as guilty, look at them! Take them now before they—they escape!"

An officer of the court rushed over to her, while the judge, insisting she stop her verbal attack, rapped his gavel. Rose broke down, sobbing until she collapsed on the floor. After a nurse administered a sedative in the rest room at the back of the court, she was driven to Golden Hill, where she didn't leave her room for months.

She was back at Golden Hill by her own wish, because after the fire there was no way she could bear to live in the Mount St. Benedict house again, the house she'd persuaded Piper to buy.

Again and again she tortured herself with the thought it had all happened because they *were* so well hidden, whereas if they'd still been at Golden Hill, up on the hill where all the world could see them, it could never have occurred. . . .

She never allowed herself to think of *why* it had happened. All thoughts of having anything to do with the reason behind the tragedy were so deep down in her subconscious, they never surfaced except in her blackest nightmares. She'd pray for hours on end for the end of the world to come soon for her . . . and certainly for all the members of her loathsome family . . . for Roland, James, Jack and April, and her mother.

As Arthur Cipriani said sorrowfully, "Rose Pollard has had a complete nervous breakdown, and is it any wonder? What a tragedy. What a totally avoidable tragedy. . . ."

Tragedy was a word that kept coming into Roger's mind these days . . . for quite a different reason. Tragedy or farce? Which way should he look at it? For while his friends were dropping like ninepins all around him, he seemed to lead a charmed life, no matter how many risks he took or how careless he was with his own life. He had even acquired the nickname "Lucky Roger." And there were even plenty of girls around, girls who seemed to find him attractive. They teased him, touched him for luck, but none of them ventured beneath the surface value of their words . . . because what were they really saying? That he was lucky still to be alive? Lucky to be still breathing, eating, sleeping? Because that's all my life seems to be about, Roger thought bitterly. What am I being saved for?

As he went up to London on a rare forty-eight-hour leave, Roger read for what had to be the sixth or seventh time the cold phrases of his father's will where, to his hurt and shame, all too obviously their relationship was exposed to the world for what it had always been: a non-relationship, an "accident" of birth. The fact that his father had bothered to leave him anything, Roger reflected grimly, didn't in any way make up for his act of injustice. Looking out at the neat English hedgerows as the train rattled across southern England, Roger felt the same burning tears behind his eyes he'd felt as a small boy, being shunted off to boarding school thousands of miles from home. He groaned inside. . . . His father hadn't left him *any* part of Golden Hill. That was the worst hurt of all. He could put up with Rose and Drum receiving the lion's share. He sneered at himself. The "lion's share"? What was he thinking about? It was a royal flush, the king and queen's share, the royal right of inheritance.

For the length of the train journey from Bournemouth to Waterloo Station, Roger burned, plotted and vowed to himself he would fight the iniquitous will once the war was over, for Piper hadn't changed the will he'd drawn up following Drum's birth in 1925. Then he'd left most of his worldly goods to Rose, including the "star" in his crown, Golden Hill and half its enormous acreage. The other half was left in trust for Drum to inherit on his twenty-first birthday, along with the major holding in his Point Fortin oil company.

To Roger, Piper had left—it appeared almost as an afterthought—a generous annual income from the oil royalties and a coconut plantation at Cedros that Roger had even forgotten his father had bought as a speculation—only to lose interest in developing it when he married Rose.

The air raid warning started to wail its crucial message as Roger grabbed a taxi and on the spur of the moment decided to "splurge" and see if he could get into the Savoy. Within minutes of crossing Waterloo Bridge, the heavy throb of German bombers sounded overhead and the ack-ack guns started up.

"Going to be another noisy night, guv'ner, but then you'd know all about them there buggers up there, wouldn't you?" To Roger's alarm the taxi driver was more interested in turning around to look at him and chat than in keeping his eyes on the road, but he gamely answered the driver in the way he'd found Cockney drivers liked to be chatted to, sighing with relief when the cab soon turned into the darkened Savoy forecourt.

The receptionist at the front desk said they'd probably have a room if he didn't mind waiting for an hour, so, leaving his overnight bag with the hall porter, Roger walked slowly into the blacked-out Strand. He recalled once wandering into a little bar nearby, where he'd met the prettiest girl he'd ever seen in his life. She'd been very obviously "attached" to an RAF pilot who never let her out of his grip, but they'd all chatted together about wonderful times they'd had in the Caribbean—and Roger remembered it as one of his happiest times.

As he groped his way toward Charing Cross, trying to locate the steep steps that led down to that same little bar, the wall he was holding on to came to such an abrupt end that he would have fallen down the steps he was looking for if there hadn't been someone blocking his way. As it was, he knocked the person over, but before he could apologize, a bomb exploded across the river and for a few stark seconds a searing yellow torch of flame illuminated the sky, the Thames and the steps that Roger saw he was on the brink of.

"I'm terribly sorry. Have I hurt you?" He thought he'd stumbled over a child, as, totally enveloped in blackness again, he couldn't make out any features and had to bend down to hear the muttered response. Another bomb came whistling down to the west of where they stood and Roger involuntarily moved nearer to the little figure, trying to protect it, while irritably thinking it was just his luck to run into a child, whom he'd either have to take home or to the nearest police station.

"Are you lost?" he asked, realizing the arms he'd involuntarily clutched as the bomb came down were shaking.

The small figure seemed to stretch up as if to get up to his level. "Certainly not," came a clear, well-educated, girlish voice. "Would you kindly move away from me, so I can get some air. First you try to stampede me to death and now you're trying to suffocate me. . . ."

Roger was totally confused. He couldn't work out whether the person was serious or joking. He decided to get the boring business over with. "Miss, I said I'm sorry and I am, but I don't know why you're allowed to be out on your own like this. Whoever allowed it should be ashamed. Now, if you'll tell me where you live, I'll try to get you back there. . . . We should probably phone your parents first to tell them you're okay."

She was laughing: the little wretch was *actually* laughing at him! Roger was infuriated.

As he heard another bomb explode in the distance, he snapped,

"This isn't a funny situation, miss. You shouldn't be out in the blackout like this. Where do you live?"

"At the Savoy."

"Where?" He couldn't believe his ears. What on earth was this little creature doing living at the Savoy? Why hadn't she been evacuated away from the blitz with all the other London children? He was getting out of his depth and she appeared to know it, for she started laughing again. He felt himself flush and, losing his temper which he'd been on the verge of doing ever since he'd received the copy of his father's will, he yelled, "Goddamn it, I can't see your face! You're either a midget or a child . . . perhaps both. As far as I'm concerned you should be at home in bed playing with your teddy bear."

He heard the slap before he even realized she'd struck out at him, missing his cheek, but knocking his cap sideways.

"How dare you speak to me like that? Let me pass this minute." She tried to push past him, but, embarrassed as well as intrigued by now, and realizing the girl's small stature must belie her age, Roger held on to her arm.

"Look, I'm sorry. I'm a bit overwrought, but this *is* a crazy situation. Neither of us can see the other. Won't you risk a real blind date?"

She was quick to laugh again and the throaty chuckle made him suspect she really was very young, a suspicion that wasn't totally put to rest when in a few minutes they reached the confines of the old tavern he liked so much and the girl looked up at him with cool, amused gray eyes. As if she guessed his thoughts, she said, "Are you worried they won't serve me? Do you still think I'm a child?"

He knew she was teasing him now, but as he thought over several rejoinders he might make, the subject was changed for him. "Alicia, darling, is it really you?" A languid young man in a well-cut gray flannel suit slipped off the barstool and came toward them.

"Toby, how divine! I didn't know you were in town. . . ." She turned her back on Roger and talked animatedly for a few minutes, before turning back in an offhand way to say, "Toby this is my blind date for tonight. He just knocked me over in the Strand and he's trying to make amends. . . ."

"Roger Pollard." Roger gave his name curtly, irrationally longing to throw this pixie of a girl over his shoulder and carry her back to his room at the Savoy . . . if he ever got a room. Just then he saw a couple leaving a cozy spot in the corner and, tapping Alicia on the shoulder, he beckoned her to follow him there. Self-consciously he put his cap on the other chair in order to hold it, and, as he sat watching her, for a few irritating minutes, he thought she was going to stay chatting away with Toby at the bar. He was just about to give up and grope his way back to the Savoy, when she joined him, a broad smile on her face. "Toby Plugge's an old, old friend, so I was lucky you bumped into me tonight after all. . . ."

"Hmph, why isn't he in uniform?" he heard himself say grumpily. Why he'd asked her, he couldn't imagine. What did he care if Toby was in or out.

Alicia pouted like a spoiled child. "For the same reason I'm not. We've both got asthma. That's how we got to know each other so well, heaving our guts up in the foggy, foggy dew, trying to breathe during a particularly fog-infested weekend in Dorset."

She spoke so quickly and with such clipped enunciation that Roger had trouble following all she said, and as she chatted on he gave up trying, sitting back and letting the tension seep out of him.

Like a contortionist, she sat cross-legged on the chair, her arms around her knees, every so often pulling down the skirt of her tweed suit to cover what little showed of her legs.

Although there was nothing particularly elaborate or chic about her suit, its cut and the way she wore it, her well-worn crocodile bag, the shine on her sensible tan shoes and above all the way she spoke, all indicated to Roger that, adult or child, this little sprite must come from a good family.

When the atmosphere between them relaxed over a glass or two of warm beer, her rate of speech slowed down and with a warm feeling Roger realized she probably talked fast because she was nervous, and perhaps she was even as shy as he.

Now he felt he could risk a question without getting slapped down, but he still took the precaution of asking it in a roundabout way. "I just left the Savoy when I ran into you. . . ." She laughed with him over his choice of words. "I was trying to find this place again to kill time because my room wasn't quite ready. I was here about eight months ago, but tell me, do you *really* live at the Savoy? Isn't it very expensive?"

She chuckled mischievously as before. "*I* don't pay for it. My uncle does. He thinks I'll get into less trouble if I'm staying at a hotel where he's so well known. I'm in the press office at the Admiralty just down the road, so it's very convenient. When Uncle Robin heard I was going to offer my brilliant services for the war effort, he made me promise I'd stay at the Savoy so he could keep tabs on me. The staff there has known us all for years. . . ."

Roger couldn't believe it when he heard the familiar call, "Time, gentlemen, please." He'd never known time to pass so quickly.

They walked slowly back to the Savoy, Alicia's hand clasped in his, the wonderful, warm feeling he'd experienced earlier welling up inside him. "Can we meet tomorrow?" He was on tenterhooks as they arrived in the Savoy forecourt. "I've got a forty-eight-hour pass."

"Let me think. Yes, of course we can. It's a Saturday, isn't it? D'you want to get some sea air? Toby was saying he thought he could wangle a rail pass to Southend on Sea."

"No," he said. He hadn't meant to sound so forcible, but the word shot out. By now they were in the lobby, Roger looking down at her, miserable that in a few minutes she'd be gone.

She pouted again. "Toby is loads of fun—you'll love him." She wandered over to the reception desk with him, where to his relief he heard a room was ready and waiting. "What have you given my new friend, Arthur?" the girl asked the receptionist cheekily. "Not the room with all the mice, I trust. We *do* have to be good to the boys in blue, you know."

The elevator was out of order. "As usual," she chirped as Roger followed her through a confusing labyrinth of corridors, up and down stairs that she seemed to know well. Finally they arrived at the back of the hotel, where most of the rooms overlooked the Thames. She stood on tiptoe to kiss his cheek, but he wasn't putting up with that. He swiftly caught her chin, propelling her mouth to his.

He'd expected some resistance, but instead she opened her lips, darting her tongue in and out. He pulled her closer. God, there was so little of her that even as he enveloped her with his arms, he felt nervous he might break one of her tiny bones. She pulled her mouth away. "I must go. I really must. . . ."

He released her immediately. What a clumsy, enormous bear he must seem, but she was smiling, so perhaps she didn't think he was so bad after all. "Can't we spend tomorrow together, just the two of us? Can't you give up the sea air this time?"

She leaned lazily against the door, enjoying the sensation of having this intense, worried-looking young man plead to see her. She loved the brief moment of having some mastery over a man's emotions, a mastery no one had ever expected *she* could exert. In only a few months, ever since she'd come to London, she'd learned her little-girl look could be enormously appealing to men, particularly when they learned she knew how to act like a woman.

Roger waited for her answer, not daring to say any more. As she turned her key she said lightly, "I'll call you. I know your room number."

"When? When?"

But she closed the door—little did he know—only to lean against it on the other side savoring to herself the dejected look on his face. Oh, what a great time she was having, blitz or no blitz!

Early the next morning a tug mournfully blew its horn going down-river toward the London docks and the English Channel beyond, and a watery sun tried without success to dry the rain puddles on the Embankment. Roger pushed open the musty brocade drapes and sent the black-out blind hurtling into its slot at the top of the window frame. The cheerless gray outside reminded him of the times he'd stared out of his boarding-school window in the Pennines, trying to block out the dreariness by visualizing instead the brilliant colors of the tropics, where even the shadows were golden, glorious reflections of the sun's might.

He tried to read the morning paper, but there was nothing there to cheer him up. He stared glumly at the phone, realizing that he didn't even know Alicia's last name, only her room number, and, as the operator had made embarrassingly clear the night before, no calls were connected without the knowledge of a surname. "Not at the Savoy, sir." Every syllable had been a reprimand.

As he started to shave, a rat-a-tat-tat on the door made him jump and cut his chin badly. Cursing, he attempted to stop the bleeding as a second tattoo was rapped out. He draped the bath towel around him. "Wait a minute, can't you. What the hell is it?" he cried. There was no answer.

Roger wrenched the door open, intending to give a piece of his mind to whoever was thoughtless enough to disturb him almost at the crack of dawn.

Alicia stood there, smiling broadly, immaculate in a riding habit that had obviously been made for her with loving care, the dark jacket stroking her body, whittling her waist, the pale jodhpurs adding just the right amount of fullness to her shape and disappearing into soft, weather-beaten leather boots. She knew she looked her best in riding clothes, and she leaned coquettishly against the doorjamb. "I said I'd call. Am I too early? I thought heroes always rose with the dawn."

Roger grabbed her, slamming the door behind her. "You little devil," he said, admiration shining out of his eyes. "What d' you think you're up to?"

"I came to take you riding in the park," she replied calmly. "You're from the colonies, aren't you? Colonists always ride. I thought you'd enjoy that before I go off for the day with Toby."

"No, you're not." It was as if she'd kicked him in the stomach with the pointed toe of her faultlessly polished Lobb boot.

"Oh, who's going to stop me?" She loved teasing, flirting with this serious man. He was like Rochester in *Jane Eyre*, she'd decided the night before, strong and silent, already suffering from her jibes.

"I am." He didn't know what came over him. He was acting totally out of character, but something made him lock the door and take the key with him as he went back into the bathroom to work on his chin. He couldn't bear the thought of a drop of blood falling on her.

She was staring at the river with her back to him when he returned in his dressing gown. He hesitantly wrapped his arms around her, burying his face in her hair, momentarily, like the night before, expecting to be repulsed. Instead, she immediately pressed back against him, wriggling her behind up and down against his thighs until his penis began to swell. She slipped out of his arms and went toward the door, asking him with her most charming smile to unlock it.

He would have done, too, if she hadn't started to laugh at him again—this time at the wrong moment, because suddenly his rage and frustration welled over.

Why should he put up with her tricks? Endure her obvious attempts to play games with him?

He lifted her high into the air above his head, shaking her hard as if she were a rag doll, until tearfully she begged him to put her down.

So the bear was not so tractable after all. Alicia's heart beat faster, as back on the ground she looked at Roger surreptitiously.

For the first time since they'd met she began to feel unsure of herself. She was no longer certain this cozy Canadian was a man to play games with, to tease until the moment came (as it always did) when she had to run away as fast as she could from any danger of encountering what in her mind she always called the "real thing."

"Who are you, little Alicia?" Roger asked in a quiet, sad voice. He didn't attempt to touch her, just stood, hands in his dressing-gown pockets, looking at her steadily. "Why bother to come here at all if you want to spend the day with Toby?" She didn't answer. Now she was the one afraid to say anything that might jeopardize their relationship.

Roger unlocked and opened the door. "I mustn't keep you from your riding. . . ."

"Won't you join me?" Her voice was a little girl's voice, timid, scared.

"Not if you're going to spend the rest of the day with Toby, no. I'm not interested." He meant it, for he'd decided if she really intended to go off with that Toby individual, it was far better to end it there and then.

If she could hurt him when he hardly knew her, God knew what she could do if it went any further. He'd already been hurt too much in his life to start seeking out a woman who seemed to know where the cuts were still bleeding.

Alicia looked different now from the girl who'd arrived only a short while before, challenging him with every word and gesture. Her shoulders were slumped and she moodily twisted the riding crop in her hands as she hesitated in the doorway. Roger was about to shut the door firmly behind her, when she said plaintively, "You win."

"Win?"

She stretched up and quickly threw her arms around his neck, pulling his head toward her and crying, "I never had any intention of going off with Toby Plugge. He's a big bore. I was teasing you. Sorry."

The next thirty-six hours were the most ecstatic Roger had ever spent. He rode beside Alicia in Hyde Park's Rotten Row, strolled with her along Park Lane to Marble Arch where over tea in a Lyon's Corner House he learned his "little elf," as he'd begun to call her, was, in fact, the Honorable Alicia Forrester, niece of the Earl of Chingford, who had taken the place of her father, his brother, who'd suddenly died from a heart attack when she was still a baby.

For the first time Roger had someone to talk to about his fears, his hopes, his aspirations for the future. He only lightly touched upon his life in the tropics, although Alicia was obviously fascinated by the subject. It was his *future* he wanted to dwell on.

By the time they reached the Mall to walk through a light drizzle back along the Embankment to the Savoy, it had begun to be *"their future"* they were discussing.

It was only when Roger impulsively lifted Alicia up to carry her into her room that he realized she was soaked to the skin and so was he. He hastily ran a hot bath for her, letting the tap run for longer than was expected of a patriotic citizen, then poured into it, at her called-out request, some of her favorite jasmine bubble bath. The sensuous scent was all over his hands as he waited impatiently in her tiny sitting room, noticing with a sense of dread the clock on the mantelpiece inexorably moving on to the time of his departure.

She called out, "Roger, oh, Roger . . ." and he rushed into the bathroom to see her in a sea of pale green bubbles, her silky hair stuck close to her scalp, making her look like a well-scrubbed cherub, soapy suds only partly concealing her small pink-and-white breasts.

"Wash my back," she commanded languorously, moving her torso forward to hide herself in the suds. It was the same flirtatious, half-teasing, half-terrified Alicia emerging, living out a fantasy of her erotic imagination, but Roger didn't know that. He saw only the girl of his dreams, as he tremulously began to massage soapy bubbles all over her pale back, then tried to rinse them away.

He picked up a huge pink bathsheet, noticing the small coronet embroidered in the middle. "Come, my little elf," he said gently. "I'll dry you." She continued to sit in the tub, bubbles dispersing around her, suddenly certain she'd gone too far, that this time there was no easy way to draw back.

The quandary was so obvious in her face that Roger longed for her all the more. "I won't hurt you, darling," he said gently. He scooped her out of the tub, wrapping her up in the bath sheet, carrying her into her lacy white bedroom, patting her dry, feeling every curve of her body through the fleecy towel. He ached for her and she could see the aching, the longing on his face.

She both longed for it and dreaded it at the same time. In a little voice she asked if he'd go outside while she slipped into a robe. Then when he obediently went out, she hunted until—perverse as ever—she found the most seductive negligee she owned, one Roger would think of every day and every night for the next few months.

Roger gasped as, in the doorway, she posed in the low-cut, flesh-colored gown. Tiny holes were set in the top for her pink nipples to pop through, while the lacy skirt split at the back stopped short of her boyish behind, and at the front to show just a trace of the fair fluff covering her vagina.

She curled on his lap, allowing him to caress her breasts, to lick her stiff nipples. She fondled his penis through his uniform till it grew so large and rigid she quickly moved her fingers away. But when he didn't demur, she couldn't resist opening her legs wide to show him her fair bush of hair, allowing him to push his fingers into her, to work her into a frenzy. When he could control himself no longer he rolled on top of her, racking himself up and down until his semen flooded out to soil the negligee and darken his uniform as he cried, "Alicia, Alicia, you're mine. I'm yours."

6

Roland
1944

WHEN Roland Bracken looked out of the barracks window at the Chaguaramas Naval Base, he didn't often see what other people saw—the alluring deep blue of the Caribbean stroking a slice of pale beach and, in the distance, a crop of verdant islands growing out of the sea.

For him it could never be an idyllic view. For him any view from Chaguaramas could only be a gut-twisting reminder of all that had happened during the past three years. Out on the horizon he could easily see Carrera, an island that from the shore looked just as entrancing as all the other islands, but was, in fact, the home of Trinidad's maximum-security prison, where his "baby" brother Jack had been incarcerated for so many months before his final transfer to death row in the Royal Gaol.

Even now Roland went to great lengths to avoid going anywhere near the jail's main entrance on Frederick Street. It wasn't easy. Frederick Street is one of Port of Spain's main arteries, but, luckily, the commander's wife was a kind woman and, unless she was in a hurry, never said a word when he'd veer off to take a circuitous route to drive her to her destination. When it was unavoidable and he found himself in the vicinity of the jail, his arms would sweat as if he'd dipped them in water, while at the same time an eerie cold enveloped the rest of him as a picture of Jack's tortured face came into his mind and he remembered how Jack had clutched him so fiercely that last day before the noose went around his neck, he'd torn a piece off his shirt before the guards came in to separate them.

Within days of Jack's arrest, just as Rose had screamed out at the preliminary hearing, Roland had realized his younger brother was terribly sick in the head. "The insane one," Rose had screamed, and it hadn't taken Roland long to learn that if a plea was made that Jack was "guilty but insane," it could save his life.

He'd gone to Uriah Butler, who was his god, hero, father, mother, savior of the people and—he believed and blindly trusted—the only man who could rescue Jack. Butler had painstakingly explained what had to be done to save Jack from the gallows. The defense lawyer provided by the government had to prove to the jury Jack didn't know the difference between right and wrong. From then on Roland had gathered together every scrap of evidence he could find to substantiate that claim, trying to get the cold fish of a lawyer to recognize Jack's wild behavior in jail for what it was—an inability to judge between right and wrong. He'd pored over law books with Butler's help, looking for a word, a sentence that would make the lawyer listen and act and send Jack safely off to St. Anne's lunatic asylum.

But during the weeks and months that Roland agonized, the lawyer hadn't listened, acted or even defended Jack in any proper sense of the word, and no one, least of all Roland, was surprised when Jack received the death sentence—not just once, but three more times over the next two years, as, following the usual agonizingly slow judicial process, his case moved to the High Court, to the Court of Appeal and finally to the Judicial Committee of the Privy Council, where a final appeal was made and refused.

For Roland it had been two years of striving, of knocking on doors that never opened, of crying out to people who never listened, of listening to people who openly showed their distaste for him and anyone like him. Two years of getting nowhere, except, as Roland now knew, *he* was getting somewhere all the time—not helping his brother, but inadvertently helping himself.

As he often thought with a curious pride, it certainly wasn't his looks that had brought him to the notice of the commander's wife and then to the attention of the commander himself.

Looks only counted when you were either extraordinarily beautiful

like his sister Rose or extraordinarily ugly like the hunchback of Notre
Dame. No, thank God, his looks were ordinary to say the least. It was
his brain that was extraordinary—and he'd choose a brain over looks in
God's gift department every time. A good brain was a wonderful gift to
have, offering, as he was beginning to appreciate, more and more opportunities every time you sharpened it, whereas looks faded fast, even
overnight, as he'd seen happen with his own eyes in the case of Rose.
He would never forget the way she'd looked in the witness box, like a
scarecrow put out in the fields to frighten the buzzards away. He would
never forgive her—or hers—for what she had perpetrated—for in Roland's mind *she* was the criminal, not Jack. She was the one who'd
caused it all, inciting his brother to bring about the deaths of her husband and child through her willful neglect of the family, her years of
insulting them, making them feel ashamed ever to have been born.

And then he would never forgive her for her attempt to bring James
and himself tumbling down along with Jack, accusing them at that first
hearing of being just as involved in the fire as Jack had been.

It had been lucky they'd both had cast-iron alibis, proving they were
nowhere near Mount St. Benedict the night of the fire, for if there had
been the slightest doubt, Roland was sure they'd both be in jail, probably to rot there for years, if not forever.

As he put on his uniform—the open-necked short-sleeved shirt and
shorts the tropics demanded—the intercom linking his quarters with the
commander's house buzzed. "Yessir," he answered. That it could also
be the commander's wife, Mrs. Brett, at the end of the line didn't affect
the way he answered. "Sir" was the most respectful form of address he
knew, and Mrs. Brett deserved the best of everything as far as Roland
was concerned. If it hadn't been for her . . .

By the time Roland put the phone down he had his orders for the
day. He would deliver and collect some important packages; he would
chauffeur Mrs. Brett to and from lunch at Government House; he
would then drive the commander to a meeting in the oil fields (during
which time Roland knew he'd be expected to continue telling the commander all he knew about the fields they were visiting, plus anything
else he felt was relevant about Trinidad's oil situation).

It was the usual full day, when Roland knew he'd be likely to see
some of the leaders of the community, if not a familiar face from overseas, the kind of face that once before he'd almost greeted, thinking he
knew the person, although he couldn't place his name. Then he'd
blushed under his black skin realizing in time the face was "familiar"

because it belonged to a famous member of the armed forces who regularly appeared on Movietone News.

As usual his mind was ablaze with ideas as the day went on, and he observed from the background the workings of power, the ostensibly smooth, yet intricate relationships between people at the top, who pulled and maneuvered, each one wanting his own way, just as Uriah Butler wanted his own way, but with a big difference. No voices were raised; hardly a brow was furrowed. Nobody ran the risk of being called a "rabble-rouser," let alone being shoved in jail, where, as he knew and Uriah Butler knew, you could yell and scream and gain nothing except laryngitis.

It was a revelation to Roland that so much *was* gained with apparently so little effort. Initially he had been amazed to realize how much white men differed in their opinions, too.

Roland watched, listened, learned, knowing all the time he himself was being watched and assessed by the commander, who, by now, knew everything there was to know about him—his rough country background; his mother's cocoa patch that would one day be his as the oldest son; his life of toil on the land as a child, his rampages on and around the oil fields as a teenager, and—most important of all—his allegiance to Uriah Butler. As he'd attempted to explain to his boss, it was Uriah Butler who'd forced Westminster to wake up from its long sleep to find out what the trouble was really all about in the island. Butler was the man responsible for Lord Moyne's report which, Roland had been told (although he didn't believe it), actually recommended elections in which *every man* over twenty-one, no matter what the color of his skin, would be allowed to vote . . . "to lead to more representative government."

And what could that "more representative government" mean?

To Roland it meant the chance to make that leap out of obscurity, to show the world the kind of brain he had—providing he could become educated, keep out of trouble and, above all, be *patient*, for now he knew it was possible to get what you wanted in life with guile, with smiles, even with silence. . . .

If it hadn't been for the war, Britain's prime minister, Winston Churchill, would never have agreed to the Americans establishing naval and army bases in the Caribbean, exchanging the granting of that privilege under the Anglo-American Lend Lease Agreement for fifty old American destroyers, "mothballed" since World War I, but desperately needed by the British in 1941.

The agreement between Churchill and Roosevelt had been signed in March, and it seemed to Roland that almost overnight Trinidad became a hive of industry and money as construction crews moved in, followed by a flood of American and Canadian military and naval personnel, the army going to Waller Field, the navy to Chaguaramas.

Roland and James didn't waste a second longer working in the oil fields for starvation wages. On the construction sites springing up everywhere, anyone who could lay his hands on a hammer or saw was considered a craftsman and got paid accordingly—often in American dollars. It was "get-rich-quick time" and soon Roland was swept up to work on the Chaguaramas Base itself. Even though the U.S. Navy had only moved in a few months before, it was already functioning like a corner of the "good ol' U.S.A."

If things hadn't been different, Roland would have been working all day and carousing all night as many locals were, living it up as they'd never had a chance to do before at parties where, as one young ensign described it, "everyone's color-blind." But things *were* different for Roland. Only a few miles away from the base, Roland's youngest brother lay in a dank cell waiting to be hanged by the neck to die at twenty-one years of age, and so Roland didn't party or carouse at all, but worked all day and many nights, too, in order to earn as much as he could to pay the so-called legal experts, each of whom gave him a different piece of advice as to how to make the thick-headed defense lawyer change his brother's plea.

As a determined "do-gooder," one of the first things Emily Brett had set her mind to on arrival at Chaguaramas was to install a lending library on the base. She then put her considerable energies to work organizing night classes in elementary subjects for the "native workers."

It was at night class—night after night—where she first became aware of Roland Bracken, who sat with a kind of dignity, apparently totally absorbed in the three R's, often when Emily knew there was a "jump-up" going on, attended by most, if not all, of Roland's black fellow workers.

Slowly—"like visiting an unknown land" was how Emily described it to her husband—Roland had begun to talk to her.

At first, he'd been suspicious, not understanding *why* Mrs. Brett could possibly want to talk to him, but then he'd been so sunk in despondency that it had been a relief to unburden himself, and he'd begun to believe she actually cared about the tragic events surrounding him.

Things had improved speedily when she'd made him a part-time aide in the kitchen, then a part-time chauffeur of the commander's car. He often worked under the car, too, when it was discovered he was also an excellent mechanic. Soon it seemed he had always worked in some way or another for the Bretts.

Roland knew, with a survivor's instinct, he *had* to appear to be will-ing to do anything and do it well until he became "indispensable," a key word in the white world.

It became common knowledge at the base that Roland Bracken, for some reason, had become the commander's "old lady's pet." In fact he had become something far more important. He had become Emily Brett's star pupil, and here Roland didn't have to "appear" to be willing. He gobbled up every scrap of knowledge like a starving man gobbled up crumbs.

Mrs. Brett gave him a subscription to *Negro Digest*, which came from the States every couple of months with all the other magazines for the household. There he read with excitement a piece called "If I Were a Negro . . ." written by Eleanor Roosevelt, actually the wife of the *presi-dent* of the mighty U.S.A. He began to grasp the fact that even without his sister Rose's white skin and beauty, he might be able to achieve something, and he threw himself passionately into his studies, moving up through the grades, passing exam after exam with ease, until Mrs. Brett told him with pride he was now at college entrance level and, she thought, might be able to obtain a scholarship that would enable him to enter a university after the war.

University. It was a hallowed word. The idea consumed him, while the thought of a future as Trinidad's leader became less of a vision, more a practical possibility. For now he knew Uriah Butler wasn't the man for the job of kicking the British back to their little raincloud of an island. Butler could mesmerize with screams and shouts, but, when his words were examined, Roland now realized they merely repeated the same empty promises the British had been making for over a hundred years . . . the stuffing in a turkey and none of its meat.

The Anglo-American Lend Lease Agreement that had modernized Trinidad at such a rapid rate—a new network of roads opening up the island from east to west, and north to south—was now helping to change the direction of the war. The Allies were gaining ground against the Axis every day.

And just as the Agreement—and the advent of the Chaguaramas

Base—had indirectly led to Roland Bracken's advancement, so did it now begin to influence the life of Magdalen Finch.

When Theo had been sentenced and sent away to an "industrial school," the euphemistic term used to describe the reformatory for criminals under the age of sixteen, Magdalen hadn't wanted to go on living. It had become too much of an effort to get out of bed in the morning and eating hadn't seemed worth the bother either. So the weeks had passed while she stayed in bed for most of the day, eating less and less.

If it hadn't been for her employer, Tong-Li, as later she would tell him over and over again, Magdalen probably would have slipped out of life as easily as she'd slipped into it from her mother's womb. But Tong-Li missed her, not only for her voluptuous body and stupendous breasts, but for her quick wit, keen business sense and perhaps most of all (although he never admitted it) her obvious respect for *his* business acumen and the praise she'd given him, praise he'd never received from any members of his family.

One day Magdalen became aware that the pounding she could hear in her head wasn't the pounding she'd grown used to from a throbbing headache. It was a pounding on a door. Her bedroom door? No, the front door. It took her quite a while to assemble her muddled thoughts and even longer to get down the stairs, her muscles aching with disuse, legs wobbly and hands trembling on the banister rail. She opened the door a crack to see Tong-Li outside, bowing while he wedged his foot in the doorway.

"Go away," she wailed. "I'm sick. I sent a message to the office. I can't come back. Go away." He didn't answer, but simply pushed the door to open it wider, while she cowered back into the shadows.

"You are not sick," he said in his usual clipped way. "But you will be sick if you don't return to your duties. In any case we have business to attend to."

"No, no, no," she wailed. "I can't type . . . I can't think." He slapped her across the face, his hand as sharp as a thin whip, leaving a red mark on her cheek.

"Can you think now?" he said without changing his calm tone. She started to sob hysterically, hiccuping and panting between sobs, until her body was convulsed, her chest heaving. She started to crawl toward the stairs, when he grabbed hold of her robe at the back, pulling her around to face him.

"You smell," he said coolly. He wrinkled his nose in distaste to emphasize the words. "You are dirty. We are going to the bathroom."

Protesting, sobbing, dribble running out of her mouth, Magdalen nevertheless found herself leading the way to the dingy room that housed her grandfather's old tub. To her amazement Tong-Li carefully took off his jacket and proceeded to wipe the grimy surface before filling the tub with water. "It's cold water," she sobbed louder.

"Get in." It was an order. She looked at him in disbelief.

"I'll die . . . *d-i-e* if I get into that c-cool . . . cold water. . . ." Even as she spoke her teeth chattered and she started to tremble. He came toward her menacingly and ripped her smeared disheveled robe apart, tearing the old material to expose her breasts. She tried to escape from the room, but he was immovable, his hands tearing the cloth from her body as if it were wrapping paper from a parcel. He lifted her as if she were a child, dunking her into the cold water, impervious to her screams and sobs. With a scrub brush he attacked her soiled skin, scrubbing her back, her arms, her legs until the blood came, when he threw more cold water over her, letting the water out only to refill it again and again. Only half conscious, Magdalen felt him lift her out of the bath and wrap her in the only towel he could find.

She must have fainted, because when she opened her eyes she was in a room she had never seen before, lying in a four-poster bed, every detail of which was reflected in mirrors on every wall.

As she turned, she yelped with pain. Her skin felt as if it were on fire and she quickly remembered the scrub brush taking away her flesh. She gingerly turned down what she realized was a thin silk sheet. Silk! She couldn't be in a hospital if there were silk sheets on the bed. Now she realized she was naked, nothing between her and the sheets that here and there bore faint traces of dried blood from her scratches and wounds. Where was she? She hadn't even the strength to get out of bed, but lay trembling, pulling the sheet right to her chin like a shield, sure Tong-Li had brought her somewhere to punish her further for staying away so long.

She felt someone was looking at her, yet as her eyes explored the room, she could see no one and no door either through which to escape. Only when she looked up did she realize why she had the feeling, for there above her was a mirror fitted into the top frame of the old bed, so she could see herself from every angle. She started to cry as she realized how drab and dull her hair looked, no longer red gold, but brown like mud—and it had been her most prized possession. Her face

looked thin, too, drawn, gray. I'm getting old, she thought, misery en-
gulfing her. I *am* old, and now Theo's gone—there's no one left to love
me.

The only light in the strange room came from windows set high up
near the ceiling. She fell into an uneasy sleep, moaning and groaning
with menacing dreams in which she was Tong-Li's prisoner, about to
endure another scrub-brush session.

Her pillows were being propped up. A soothing cool cream was being
applied to her sore body. She was terrified, afraid to open her eyes, but
when she did, all she saw was a small wizened Chinese woman in a
black smock and white trousers bending over her. Expressionless, she
motioned Magdalen to lean forward so she could slip her arms through
a delicate lace bed jacket.

"Where am I?"

The Chinese woman shook her head vigorously, placing a finger
across her lips as if to say she couldn't speak or at least speak English,
but Magdalen continued to plead, "Please tell me. I want to go home
. . . where is Mr. Tong-Li?"

The woman pointed to a covered tray but Magdalen turned her face
into the pillow, moaning she wouldn't eat until she knew where she was
and why she was there. When there was still no response, she turned
around to discover the woman had disappeared. Now, the room was
well lit and she saw pink lamps set cleverly into the mirrored walls cast a
rosy hue all around.

She sulkily took the cover from the tray and to her surprise felt hungry when she saw a perfect breast of chicken and a salad arranged artis-
tically on a porcelain plate. First, though, she sipped the tea that she
recognized as one Tong-Li occasionally served in the office. It was like
nectar, soothing, calming, and she remembered with a familiar pang
another potion had once soothed her long ago in the strange cottage in
the country.

When she had eaten, she felt sleepy again, and this time Magdalen
slept soundly. She woke at the sound of the cock crowing, refreshed and
ready to face the world, even Tong-Li himself. She didn't have to wait
long. As she stretched herself languorously in the bed, Tong-Li entered
silently from behind one of the mirrors. So that was where the door was
concealed! She looked up at her reflection and fleetingly felt pleased she
looked more like her usual self, with more life and color in her face.

As he came near her she pulled the sheet up to her chin once more.
What was this mysterious man going to do to her now?

"Why are you so frightened, Magdalen? Am I not your friend?"

She nodded quickly. "But you hurt me. I'm still in agony. Where am I?"

"It is your room, your floor, your private quarters." His body started to shake with laughter in the soundless way she had grown accustomed to.

"What do you mean?" Now she was getting impatient.

"Ah, that note sounds more like the Miss Finch I know and respect. You see, I had to be cruel to be kind, did I not?"

She flushed angrily, wincing as her shoulder came into contact with the pillow. "If you wanted to skin me alive like a chicken, you did a good job of it."

He stood over her and flipped down the sheet, quickly opening the bed jacket to expose her breasts. "You will see I scrubbed only what needed to be scrubbed." She looked down against her will to see the folds of her bosom were as smooth and as creamy as ever, but she petulantly covered herself up. "I am still not well," she began to say, but he interrupted her.

"Get up now. You and I have things to discuss, something I have been working on for some time, which I believe is going to interest you."

"Discuss?" she asked in a quavering voice. "What is there to discuss?" He ignored her question and went to the mirrored door. "You will find clean clothes in the mirrored cupboard to your left. Dress and then join me in your sitting room." His shoulders shaking with mirth once more, he left her as silently as he had arrived.

It was like a dream . . . one which went on and on until in the weeks that followed, she knew she had begun to live . . . and there was no going back to any other life.

In the cupboard, just as Tong-Li had said, were certainly clean clothes, but they were not only clean, they were *magnificent!* Magdalen had never seen such dresses, all in different shades of yellow, which later when she washed her hair several times to retrieve the red gold glints, emphasized its special color, just as the fit and style, all similar and deceptively demure, emphasized the swell of her breasts, her neat waist and generous hips.

It was just as well, because although she looked through all the drawers and cupboards, there wasn't a piece of underwear to be found, not one brassiere or one pair of knickers.

Timidly, she'd opened the mirrored door to find herself in a small dark room with floors so impeccably waxed and polished that she thought at first they might be mirrored, too.

Tong-Li was seated behind a French writing desk, studying a document as she stood hovering in the entrance. "Ah, yes, there you are. . . ." He looked at her so penetratingly, it was as if she were standing there naked. "Turn around." By the tone of his voice she knew better than to disobey him, but the mystery surrounding everything was now beginning to infuriate her.

To her surprise, he started to talk to her in the way she had frequently heard him talk to business associates, cut and dry, no-nonsense. "Because of the tragic circumstances of the past years, my dear friend, you have not been aware of the many changes taking place in this island. If you were to walk down this street now . . ."

She interrupted. "Which street, where am I?"

He shut her up with a look and continued. "You would realize Port of Spain has become a port of the world. There is now an important American naval base not more than ten miles from here. . . ." At her startled look, he nodded gravely as if to impress on her the importance of his words. "There is an army base at Waller Field, where thousands of acres are being cleared at this very hour. Americans, Canadians, people of every nationality—except perhaps Germans and Japanese." Again he permitted himself a soundless moment of mirth. "They are all here, but the war is not here. The air is balmy, seductive. The tropical nights are full of sweet, sensuous sounds and scents. . . . At the end of their working day, which is never too arduous, never reminiscent of the ugly things happening across the seas, the men are restless, lonely, bored." He looked at her in almost a whimsical, old-fashioned way as he saw she still had no idea of what he was about to propose. "During the last few months of your ordeal I have been busy—planning your future."

"My future?" Magdalen leaned forward anxiously, resting her square capable hands on the fine wood of the desk. "What possible future can I have? Oh, Tong-Li"—tears filled her eyes—"I haven't wanted to live for that very reason. I don't have a future and neither does my s-s-son. . . ." Her shoulders started to heave as tears coursed down her face.

The Chinaman ceremoniously gave her a silk handkerchief from his pocket. "This is not the moment for tears. It is a moment for celebration."

She stared at him as he pushed the document he had been reading into her hands. "I am offering you a partnership in a new business. You can take this and read it thoroughly later. I have spent a great deal of time thinking about it . . . ever since the first evening you confirmed to my friend and myself what I had suspected from the first moment that I saw you. You possess a special talent that even now you are unaware of . . . but you are not unaware of your hunger, your sexual hunger, are you, Miss Finch? Your insatiable sexual hunger that has punished you so severely already?" His voice slashed into her, and she felt defenseless as memories of her abandoned lovemaking with Theo's father and his "harem" poured into her mind. How much did Tong-Li know? What did it all mean?

In her agitation, she started to rip at his handkerchief, crying out, "What are you trying to do? Stop torturing me like this."

If anything the unusual wide smile that lit up the Chinaman's features unnerved her even more. "My dear, I am not going to torture you. You are torturing yourself, and it is no longer necessary. Now, you are going to be rewarded for your talent. It is going to be put to work . . . and . . ."— he leaned over the desk to squeeze her hand so tightly she winced—"you are going to make a great deal of money for yourself and for me."

As she looked into his face, she suddenly knew what he meant. A brothel. He was offering her a partnership in a brothel which she would run. He was offering her a job as a madam.

She started to laugh hysterically as she got up from the chair, turning to leave the room. A madam! "How dare you!" she screamed.

As she turned, he caught hold of her arm and cruelly forced her to the floor, ripping open the bodice of the yellow dress, fastening his lips onto her nipple as his hand easily opened the one hook which held the skirt together.

In seconds he had her writhing at his touch, longing for him. But as she felt her orgasm mounting, he quickly withdrew and jumped to his feet looking down at her with a sneer as she ground her legs together on the floor. "I can control myself, Miss Finch, but I do not think you can. With my guidance, however, you will receive all the satisfaction you require and will train others to give the exquisite pleasure you know how to give so effortlessly . . . but please . . ." He put a hand over his mouth to hide an exaggerated yawn. "Don't bore me with legends of your virtue. You lost that long ago. . . ." His shoulders started to shake as she looked at him with unconcealed hatred, knowing he was right. She had lost her virtue . . . there was no turning back. . . .

Her adoption of the madam role had been effortless, Magdalen reflected six months later, as she sat in the same drawing room, writing up figures, noting with satisfaction that since August—on the day the island received news of the liberation of Paris—business had become so overwhelming, they had doubled, then tripled their prices and still couldn't fulfill all the demand.

She was tired, but it was a healthy tiredness, both mental and physical . . . although she rarely allowed herself to be booked to a client. She was "reserved" (unfortunately, she occasionally thought, when through the two-way mirror she caught sight of a magnificent specimen of manhood) for her secret partner in the operation, Tong-Li, who as part of the arrangement insisted on total anonymity. No, now her physical tiredness came from being on her feet all day—not on her back—supervising fifteen little prima donnas.

As Tong-Li had predicted, the job suited Magdalen perfectly. She was efficient. She selected only the choicest girls of every color and ethnic group. She knew instinctively, with one glance through the peephole mirror looking on to the elegant ground-floor sitting room, if any customers sitting there might cause trouble. There was a burly black doorman to take care of that! Then she enjoyed the "creativity" of inventing delightful, unusual "experiences" for those she could also tell were much-traveled, experienced and so often jaded men of the world. Theo Bartrieve would be proud of me, Magdalen thought wryly from time to time, and now she found she could even think of him without pain.

She had nearly collapsed the first month when—nervous and unsure, surrounded by chattering, excitable girls (all of whom she was sure knew more about the business than she did)—she had seen through the peephole one of the island's most prominent citizens, a man known to be a close associate of the governor, and more important, as far as she was concerned, the chief of police. Certain she was going to be closed down before she'd even started, Magdalen had put a smile on her face and welcomed him with one or two rum cocktails. As she had been instructed to do, while they drank, she arranged for some of the girls to parade around the room. It was then she learned her important "guest" was not visiting to condemn or even scold. He indicated with an experienced nod, as if he were at an auction, that he wished to spend some time with Reza, a reed-slim, coffee-colored East Indian girl, who moved with the sinuous slide of a snake.

That was the first and last day Magdalen worried, or even gave any thought to a girl making love to a man old enough to be her grandfather.

Reza's crone of an aunt, who had brought her to Magdalen in the hopes of finding her "good employment," had already boasted of what her niece's tongue could do to a man, just as if she were praising her housekeeping ability. Now, still sick with worry that the law was about to pounce, Magdalen saw for herself through the two-way mirror Reza's tongue go to work, reducing the prominent citizen to a pathetic, panting fool, begging for more and more and still more. . . .

It was a propitious beginning and the day when Magdalen realized if she was careful not to tread on any toes, she could perhaps, little by little, influence someone in authority to recognize that an injustice had been done to her son. With Tong-Li's permission, she began to petition for his release and even pardon, never pushing too hard, just a word here and a word there, as her "house of pleasure" began to please more and more men in powerful positions.

Ironically, despite the nature of her "business," as time went by and without even realizing it, Magdalen became more and more "ladylike" in both manner and dress—for now she was able to afford her own clothes, which, she told Tong-Li coolly, she had no time to take off, even quickly. She ruled the establishment with an iron hand, offering many of the girls their first real home. She knew behind her back she was often called "the missionary," but it was with affection, and with a curious quirk of her mind, it was a nickname that helped her reconcile what she had become with the lady she knew her mother would have wanted her to be . . . a lady with a conscience.

Roland drove the jeep along the road leading to San Fernando and the oil fields in the south. Although the Americans had brought signs of twentieth-century progress to the island with their roads, radio communication and technological expertise, it was still possible to see the Trinidad that had sleepily remained the same for hundreds of years. Under a dazzling sun coolies stripped to the waist were working in the cane fields, cutting and chopping down six-foot-tall stems of cane with their machetes and casting them onto cumbersome two-wheeled carts drawn by water buffaloes. The air was filled with a sickly smell—a sign that the cane was at that moment being crushed under rollers in the cane factory into a sticky translucent juice on the way to being processed into sugar. Soon the swaying cane gave way to signs of Trinidad's more important natural asset—oil—as in the distance a number of derricks could be seen pointing their girders at the sky. "Have you thought of what you'd like to do after the war?" the commander asked abruptly, as they approached the Pointe à Pierre Oil Refinery.

"Yessir."

"May I ask you where you're headed?"

"I wan' t'be a lawy'r, sir."

The commander was silent for a moment. Then he snapped, "How old are you, Bracken?"

"I'm not sure, sir, 'bout mah late twenties, early thirties, sir."

It was incredible, the commander thought, that this bright young man didn't know how old he was, although while holding down a number of menial jobs during the day, Roland had reached the point in his education, according to Emily, when he could sit for a college entrance exam and possibly even win a scholarship. "You're a bright young man," Commander Brett said slowly, "but I would suggest perhaps it's a little late for you to embark on legal training. It all depends where you see your future—here or overseas?"

"Here, sir."

"Well, have you thought about politics? That's a fast way out of obscurity, and great changes are coming to this island—as we've discussed before. The war is well on the way to being won and the British know they'll have to let the people have more say in their own affairs after this one. . . ."

"Yessir." Roland pulled up at the checkpoint guardhouse by the gate of the refinery, but on being waved through he said nothing more.

. . . And he won't say anything, Commander Brett thought to himself. He knows where he's going all right, but he's not about to tell me or Emily, for that matter, and perhaps he's right not to.

The meeting took less time than the commander had expected. Everything was easier now that the oil magnates on the island were vetting their own affairs, ensuring that the yield from every well drilled justified the tonnage of steel used to obtain it.

As he approached the jeep, he could see Roland immersed in a book. It was an unusual sight to see a black driver awake when he had five minutes to himself, let alone to see one reading, and, looking around,

Commander Brett saw without surprise a couple of other drivers dozing in the shade of a breadfruit tree.

"What are you reading, Bracken?" He knew it was likely to be the kind of book that would bore most of his officers, let alone a struggling young black. Even more extraordinary, as the commander had discovered months before, Roland had an amazing retentive memory and could often repeat verbatim what he had read days before.

"Sir. Cald'r Marshall, sir."

"Tell me about it."

Without hesitation Roland launched into a monologue which, if the commander hadn't known him so well, he might have thought Roland didn't understand, but was merely repeating like a parrot. However, from the many conversations they'd had he knew that Roland absorbed what he read, drew conclusions from it and, for all he knew, acted upon it in some way or another.

"If Trinidad be a true example of a crown colony government, sir, den dis is a myth, sir. It covers a history of savage exploit'tion. Trinidad has never been a poor place, sir. It's a rich island wid ninety percent of its people impoverished. De benevolent tyranny is close to de demand of de big businesses but distant from de workin' people an' blunders on deaf to de cries of distress because it hasn' tried t' listen. . . ."

"All right, all right, that's enough, Bracken." The commander sat back, amused in one way that, whenever Roland was emotionally moved by what he read, his speech invariably deteriorated with the force of his feelings.

As they reached the turn to the base, a familiar figure came toward them, followed by a group of ragged men rolling empty oil drums. The commander was in a benevolent mood, so he instructed Roland to slow down. "It's your brother, isn't it, Bracken?"

It was another incredible facet of Caribbean life, the commander thought, as he looked at Roland's brother James, that members of the same family could be so many different shades of color . . . although God knew, white, black, yellow or brown, aptitude and intelligence so often differed from brother to brother, as well as from father to son.

Roland mumbled a reply as he stopped the jeep. He looked straight ahead as James came up to them. "E-e I'se glad t' see yo'," James said cheerfully. "Command'r, God res' yo' soul . . . dese 'ere drums, dey're jus' what we need fo' we all . . . it be gran' day fo' we all. . . . You'll be first t' hear de Sunbeams. . . . Right, Rollo ol' boy?"

Mortified, Roland stared ahead as if none of the remarks were meant for him, and soon, to put him out of his misery, Commander Brett told him to proceed, waving a cheery hand at the motley crew. "It's a new kind of music, Roland, isn't it? Your brother isn't the only one to ask for these empty drums. Apparently they are perfect for this new kind of . . . what is it called . . . tin band?"

"Steel band, sir." As if he hadn't had to suffer enough, Roland thought, first a brother like Jack and now a brother like James, who'd given up all pretense of trying to study. However much help and encouragement Roland gave him to work, James was hellbent on starting this crazy new steel band. Well, good luck to him. As long as he didn't give their mother any more worry, Roland wasn't going to stand in his brother's way, but he wasn't going to listen to him make a fool of himself either.

Around seven o'clock the next morning, when Commander Brett asked Roland to come to his office, there was nothing in his voice to suggest it was going to be a different day from any other. As usual, the commander was playing it cool and, with a great deal of effort and swallowing, Roland found he was able to receive the news just as coolly. But when he was dismissed and allowed to go back to his room, he threw his head back and with a mighty bellow yelled "Whoa!" at the ceiling. Then he found he was wet through, although the sun wasn't even half up in the sky over the tropical sea. He gave himself a cold shower, which was just what he needed to let the news really seep into his overexcited brain.

He was going to the U.S.A.! Commander Brett had requisitioned him to accompany him as his aide on an important mission.

They were leaving tonight for the land of the free. . . .

Drum
1945

NOBODY stirred in the old house as the boy came to the crest of the hill with his conch shell to sound the 6:00 A.M. angelus, blowing the shell like a horn, its mournful, hollow ring echoing down through the valley to bring the workers to the fields.

As the sky lightened, and cocks crowed and dogs barked, the ground floor of Golden Hill came slowly, laboriously to life. Shutters were opened, verandas were swept and the downstairs reception rooms, already spotless from little activity, were tirelessly polished. The same ritual was followed every day under Obee's sharp eyes. Obee was in total charge of the household since the master's death and as fussy and as particular as Piper had ever been about every square inch of Italian marble floor and wood-paneled wall.

It was just as well *he* cared, as Obee occasionally rebuked his woman Maize, when she moaned that he worked too hard and wasn't appreciated. Young Master Drum, like all young people nowadays, never noticed anything in the house—and as for the mistress, well, as all the servants knew, Mistress Pollard had really only come back to life in the past few months.

It was true. Until Drum told her sheepishly he'd decided to join up and do his bit for the war effort, Rose hadn't really been living at all.

Rose's shock at her son's words had been as penetrating and as effective as a surgeon's knife, able to get to the blockage in her brain, which in the days following the fire had stopped all feeling, all caring, as the realization came she would never feel Piper's arms around her again or see the look of baffled adoration in his eyes.

Until the day Drum unexpectedly knocked at her door and told her what he intended to do, Rose hadn't really seen him clearly in four years.

She hadn't been aware of anything or anybody. Keeping her bedroom door locked day after day, shut in with her memories, barely sleeping or eating, she had taken only scraps from the trays left outside her door to tempt her appetite. She'd left everything to others, including even daily contact with Drum, and sometimes a week or even two would pass before she'd come downstairs, a ghostlike figure, her hair prematurely graying, her perfect porcelain skin yellowing like some forgotten piece of paper shut up for too long in a drawer.

Many of Piper's friends and business associates had tried to break through Rose's desperate grief, to force her to pick up the pieces and start out on life again. But as they advanced, doctors among them, she retreated, until regretfully one by one they'd given up the effort and a pattern had become established . . . with Obee running the house and Piper's trustees, Cipriani among them, looking after the assorted Pollard business interests, as well as slowly introducing Drum to his father's world. It had already been noted he was a true Pollard, as quick-witted and charming as Piper had ever been and "a born politician," as Cipriani would chuckle to his wife. "How proud Piper would have been."

The same thought had flashed across Rose's troubled mind that day Drum's words jolted her out of her sick lethargy, opening her eyes to the realization Drum was no longer a little boy. He was a young man, obviously embarrassed to be in her bedroom, averting his eyes, stumbling over his words, blushing as he tried to explain just why he felt he *had* to leave Golden Hill to go to war before it was all over. With a sickening lurch she had also realized he was a young man she didn't even know.

She'd put out her arms to him, crazily expecting him to clutch her to him, as his father would have done, but instead Drum had backed away in alarm, apologizing for troubling her, trying to escape. She'd responded with panic, trying to make up for all the lost time, and had fallen on her knees, clutching his trouser leg, screaming she'd kill her-self if he left her, that he was all she had left to live for.

It was something she found herself saying again and again in the weeks that followed, because Drum *was* a reason for her to want to live. At the same time, the thought of her neglect of him was a new torture to endure. It meant that although Drum finally gave in to her frantic pleading, telling her in a sullen voice he would stay at Golden Hill at least until Roger returned to the island, she never really believed him and just as there was a housekeeping ritual instituted by Obee down-stairs—one she knew little about and cared less—she had her own ritual to follow upstairs.

Long before the conch shell sounded the angelus and night lifted, Rose was up, stealthily creeping along the corridor to Drum's room, where she would slowly turn the handle of his door. For the past few weeks since he'd wakened unexpectedly to find her staring down at him, the door had been bolted, but that didn't upset her. If anything it was even more comforting, for it meant Drum had to be behind the door in order to bolt it. It meant he was still in the house and Rose was deter-mined to keep him there for as long as she lived . . . which in one way she hoped would not be long, yet in another way, seeing every day how Drum was beginning to resemble his father, she hoped would be long enough for her to see him achieve the position of power Piper had always wanted for himself.

In her anxiety to make up for the lost years, Rose clung to Drum increasingly possessively, forever checking on his whereabouts, ventur-ing onto the main veranda to look through the telescope, hoping to catch a glimpse of him as he moved about the estate.

Now she tried to look like Mrs. Piper Pollard again—or as she mut-tered to herself before her long mirror, "Mr. Drum Pollard's mother," not seeing the swathe of gray in her hair or the way her clothes hung on her, accentuating the way her body had grown bent and gaunt.

His mother's renewed interest in him came at the wrong time as far as Drum was concerned. It was too late. He didn't need it or her now. He'd had to learn to live without her at a time when he'd needed her the most; when, lost and afraid, no one had been able to give him an explanation he could accept as to what really lay behind the tragedy which in a matter of hours had so totally transformed his life.

Drum wasn't his father's son for nothing. In the same way that Piper would have ferreted out the hidden truth, so, from his sixteenth birth-day on, did Drum piece together in his mind the reason behind his mother's reluctance to face the world, the reason she had changed so dramatically.

She was doing her penance, he thought, suffering for inadvertently fostering the insane hatred that had caused the deaths of three people— and he suffered with her, trying to come to grips with his own feelings about his relationship to the Bracken family.

At twenty, every Golden Hill acre seemed like a stone weighing him to the ground; every balance sheet, reflecting the vast Pollard oil holdings that he was being taught so painstakingly to understand and evaluate, tied him to his father's old desk. Now, he was more stifled than ever by his mother. Since waking from her long sleepwalk, she looked at him so intently, it was as if she was willing him to be a reincarnation of his father, clutching at his arm as if it belonged to her.

It made Drum's flesh creep when he saw her hands. It was macabre, but they reminded him of the perishability of them all—of his wonderful father, his little sister, and—because he remembered so well the laughing beautiful woman who had been his mother—of Rose herself, now a walking skeleton with clawlike hands ever stretched out to trap him.

He longed to escape, but whenever he mentioned his longing to travel—and perhaps even to live abroad for a time after the war—to men like Bill McMurtrey, one of Piper's closest friends and a man to whom Drum took many of his problems, even he made Drum feel like a traitor.

Sometimes he felt his life was already over. With few friends of his own age—they were all away at the war—he was hemmed in, suffocated by his father's contemporaries, members of Cipriani's inner circle, who, from his eighteenth birthday, made sure he realized the big plans they had for his future, plans they were determined he should follow.

First it had been hinted at; then, as his "education" under their strict supervision had gathered momentum, it had been said more openly that he had in him the makings of a future leader. He had the most perfect qualifications for the job, they'd explained, able to unite the disparate groups, colors, religions, without, as one of Cipriani's closest aides put it, "rocking the boat or disrupting the life our kind have led for the past three hundred years." He had the money, the land, but most important was his "bonus" of mixed blood, which stretched all the way back to the island's first heroine, Louisa Calderon. It was a heritage he was not to abandon or abuse as his mother and father had done.

Drum wasn't averse to the idea, and he knew very well from his own investigations how his father's policy of "do-as-I-say-and-not-as-I-do" had precluded him from obtaining any real power in the colony, and in many ways had led to the final tragedy. He also realized his training by many of the island's decision makers and his careful inclusion in certain political meetings were tremendous advantages. But as World War II ended in Europe and the action moved to the Pacific, his sense of frustration, of being cheated out of many of the things his money and background entitled him to, wiped out everything else. He knew he was "privileged"—he was told so often enough by his father's friends—but the gnawing feeling continued to grow that he was missing the main show by staying at the sideshow for too long.

On the surface he followed the rules and directions of his peers, sitting in on boring meetings on the island's economy, on long heated debates held by franchise committees—planning ahead for the election that would be held once the war was over, trying to decide which qualifications, if any, should be required of the populace in order to vote. Should eligibility be determined by a certain level of income? Or knowledge of English? Or other literacy qualifications?

Drum, who had a witty way of writing as well as of speaking, found it easy to get his pithy reports on these debates and other events into print, writing for the *Trinidad Guardian* that "Nobody points out that English has not, so far, been a required qualification when it comes to the Indian members of our population going to war. . . ."

At last the day Drum had been waiting for so anxiously arrived: VJ Day—Victory in Japan—as President Truman announced over the radio.

The war was over. At last life could begin again. Drum was lightheaded with excitement as, with Rose proudly at his side, he gathered the Golden Hill household together on the veranda and announced the joyous news, ordering an astonished Obee to crack open some bottles of French champagne from his father's cellar for all to enjoy.

Later he drove into town on the way to a big party at the Chaguaramas Naval Base, stopping his car every so often to jump out and dance in the streets, adding his voice to the frenzied cacophony from rattles, bells, whistles, hooters, trumpets, clanging cymbals.

At the base he danced like a dervish and sang at the top of his voice "It's Been a Long Long Time" and "Shoe Shoe Baby," realizing at one moment in a tipsy haze that one of the steel bands belting out the music was the Sunbeams, a band he'd heard had been started by his own Uncle James.

He scanned the row of grinning, shining black faces. Which one belonged to his uncle? He hadn't a clue, but he knew he loved them all. So what if they were black? Why had his mother worried about a silly thing like that? He started to stumble over to them, intending to kiss them all, when a pair of predatory female hands grabbed him and pulled him close, urging him to dance with her out into the tropical night.

The next morning, nursing a sick head, the first time he'd ever had such a hangover, Drum could hardly remember a thing about what happened after. Whatever it was, he was sure he hadn't broken any bones. It was only soft flesh he remembered touching, nothing angular, nothing to remind him of skeletons and death, only soft living flesh, which had tasted sweet, too.

In the next few months, life in Trinidad became even more turbulent as blacks, Indians, and coloreds started to return home with a very different outlook than they'd had before the war. For the first time in their lives they'd been in contact with white people who treated them as equals in equal situations. They'd seen with their own eyes, something they hadn't believed could be possible—white men and women performing the kind of menial jobs they'd thought always had to be carried out by blacks.

Self-government was the urgent cry from one end of the Caribbean to the other, but as stated in Lord Moyne's 1939 report (now published for the first time in its entirety), "Although the idea of self government, indeed one day of a West Indian Federation, is attractive and desirable, it is not practical in the near future." Drum knew why. Although the first election to be held under universal adult suffrage was months away, there were already more individuals than united parties fighting for the nine seats available.

To Drum's sorrow, his mentor and guide Cipriani suddenly died, before he could see his dream of universal suffrage come true. Even before his burial, a herd of candidates started to promote themselves as logical "successors" to the "man of the people."

All thoughts of leaving the island vanished, as Drum threw himself into the job of supporting the United Front, a party led by Jack Kelshall, the man Drum felt sure Cipriani would have chosen himself as his ideal replacement—until he was ready! Now, he knew he was too young, although he was equally sure he was as wily as many would-be politicians twice his age.

Uriah Butler was back on the scene, as wild and noisy as ever—

mobilizing his British Empire Workers and Citizens Home Rule
Party—"but every bit as influential," Bill McMurtrey told Drum as they
sat together after dinner at Golden Hill. "And I hear Roland Bracken is
back on the island. Apparently he decided with the election date fixed,
he wouldn't waste any more time on a university education overseas!"

Drum didn't miss the ironic note in the older man's voice. He said
quickly, "You mean my Uncle Roland?"

McMurtrey laughed heartily. "I'm glad you said that, my boy. It
shows you're made of the stuff we all think you're made of. Yes, your
Uncle Roland and, believe me, he's a much smarter operator than
Uriah Butler will ever be. His year in the States hasn't hurt either. I'm
told he's become a very smooth operator. We'd better watch out. He'll
be after a seat and I guarantee he won't hitch up with Butler this time.
I've heard he's been seen quite a bit with Gomes."

"Gomes?" Drum was shocked, for Albert Gomes presented a real
threat to Jack Kelshall and the United Front. An active trade unionist
for years, he was now trying to capitalize on Cipriani's name, boasting
that only he could bring about the changes for the masses that were so
urgently needed. Gomes was real competition, that Drum knew, for, a
Creole like Cipriani before him, Gomes had been able to make what
was called the "racial leap," belonging to the "middle minority group"
between Negro and Indian, therefore "acceptable" to all. Not only that,
he had an electric personality and an irrepressible sense of humor that
cloaked a calculating, nonstop ambition to boss the island, the Caribbean and then whatever else was available. Was Roland Bracken now
teaming up with him? It was unthinkable. It would have to be stopped.

Drum was deep in thought when Rose joined him as she now did
nearly every morning on the east veranda for breakfast. "A penny for
them?"

"Oh, nothing, Mother, nothing . . ." Drum answered absent-mindedly, then stared at her intently. "Well, as a matter of fact, that isn't
entirely accurate. My thoughts *are* really worth something for once.
Mother, I've made up my mind. I'm going to write a letter today, a very
difficult letter, which I want you to sign as well. . . ."

Rose smiled—a real smile of happiness, which for a fleeting second
showed a glimpse of the Rose of the past. At last her son was beginning
to share some of his life with her. "Anything, anything," she said, clasp-
ing and unclasping her hands in her anxiety to please.

"Well, we'll see." Drum got up abruptly to go to the study, where for
three or four hours he wrestled over a letter he found more difficult to

write than anything he'd ever attempted for the *Trinidad Guardian*. After many attempts he was finally satisfied and carefully wrote out a copy.

Knowing his mother tended to become more vague as the day went on, Drum decided to wait until the next morning, when at breakfast he produced the letter, holding it so tightly that Rose could see the whites of his knuckles. Even before he spoke she had a premonition of fear.

"I've written to our relations," Drum said in a careful, controlled voice. "Yours and mine, Mother. Your brothers and sister, my uncles and aunt. . . ."

Rose gripped the arm of the chair, choking back tears. "Why, Drum, why?"

"I want a reconciliation," he said. "A public reconciliation and a public forgiveness."

Rose looked at him piteously, feeling as if the ground were falling away beneath her feet. She saw the familiar dark gold curly hair, the piercing eyes that were Piper's eyes . . . in a face that no longer resembled Piper's, a cold young face that held no pity, no sign of caring as tears poured down her face.

"No, no, no . . ." she whimpered. "Do I have to go through this again after all—all—they—they—did?"

"Yes, Mother." Drum didn't raise his voice, but his tone sharpened. "*They* did nothing. What did *they* do? What did *you* do to them? After all that's happened, don't you think it's time? Your brother Roland may end up running this island. What do you think is going to happen to you, to us, to Golden Hill then? Read it."

He thrust two closely written pages into her quivering hand. "Read it and sign it, Mother. I'm not asking you. I'm *telling* you to do it."

The pages slipped from her fingers onto the floor, but Rose made no attempt to pick them up; instead, clutching the balustrade, she tried to creep back to her room.

Drum could feel rage rising from deep inside him. He tried to control it, but it was coming too fast and too powerfully. "Sit down!" he shouted. He pushed Rose back into her chair with such force it would have toppled over, taking her with it, if he hadn't caught the back in time. He picked up the letter and forced it into her hands. "It's the only copy I have. Read it," he hissed into her face. "And then sign it. I am not leaving here until it's done."

In the afternoon Drum made the rounds of the cocoa fields, trying to forget the scene of the early morning. The letter, signed by his mother and himself, was already on the way to Roland, inviting him, together with the rest of the Bracken family, to dinner at Golden Hill in order to start a new chapter in their relationship.

It *was* a good letter, Drum thought, trying to justify his actions to himself . . . in no way cloying, simply stating that now the war was over, it was time to seek the proper communication between people in order to preclude more wars, more bloodshed, more estrangement. He had lost his father and sister; they had lost a brother. Drum Pollard was prepared to forgive and forget the tragedy of the past and shake their hands . . . and so was his mother.

Drum shut his eyes for a second, blinking away the memory of his mother's hysteria, which had ended in Obee having to get the doctor to come and administer a sedative.

Although his mother had accused Drum of cruelty, he didn't consider he had acted cruelly at all. In the long run, she would realize he had acted wisely. If it went well and the Brackens did come to dinner, his mother didn't have to appear . . . probably wouldn't be *able* to appear. Drum gritted his teeth. He'd make damned sure there was some sign of welcome from her.

Cocoa pods in many stages of ripeness and color—from deep dark green to magenta and gold—hung from the trunks and branches as Drum deftly rode down the long alleyways. As usual some harvesting was going on, because, on such a large estate as Golden Hill, besides the two annual crops there were always smaller pickings to cull.

God knows, they look happy enough, Drum thought as one by one the workers acknowledged him with a shy nod of the head and an occasional "Good day, Mastah." They weren't abused or overworked. They had a regular roof over their heads and food to eat . . . but that was it. No more, no less. Drum gripped his reins tightly as he thought of his uncle and others like him—the Roland Brackens of this world, who wanted the workers to take over, to own and run places like Golden Hill. It was inconceivable, impossible.

The next day Drum received a letter that for the moment put all thoughts of his own "olive branch" to the Brackens out of his head.

As Obee told Maize, "I'v' n'v'r see' de Mastah so excit'd. Yo'd t'ink it be his own reel brudder instea' jes' half a one."

Roger was coming home. It was the best news Drum had had since the morning he'd heard President Truman's voice on the radio announce the end of the war. What was even more exciting, Roger was bringing a fiancée with him.

"Well, well," said Watkins the foreman dryly, when Drum burst into the estate office waving the airmail envelope. "So Mr. Roger's going to settle down after all. D'you think he's coming back to develop his Cedros place?" The dour foreman looked at Drum curiously, wondering if he even realized what a bitter blow it must have been to his elder half brother to learn he hadn't inherited any of Golden Hill, not one golden acre.

Drum scratched his head ruefully. "I don't know. I'd like to think so . . . but I really don't know."

In fact, Drum had often wondered how Roger had taken the news that Golden Hill had been left to his mother and himself. During the war, in his plans for the future, he'd even visualized giving Roger some of his Golden Hill acreage, which would soon really be his on his twenty-first birthday—a noble gesture, he'd daydreamed, which might gain him Roger's respect, if not his love.

Now, with so much going on in the island, and with himself at the center of it, Drum didn't feel so inclined to such an act of generosity. After all, he reflected, Roger had been left a sizable piece of land at Cedros and a generous income for life, so why should he carve up his own estate?

One thing he was sure of. There was no way Roger could criticize his management of Golden Hill, young though he was. It was making more money than ever and looked impeccable. By the time Roger arrived perhaps the reconciliation with the Brackens might have taken place and there'd be an altogether different atmosphere about the place . . . providing his mother behaved herself.

It took two months for Drum to accept as final that Roland Bracken wanted nothing to do with "any reconciliation" with the Pollards. Roland hadn't even bothered to acknowledge, let alone answer, Drum's letter. He hadn't needed to.

From the hustings he cried out against the many injustices perpetrated against men just because of the color of their skin. He used Golden Hill as an example of white elitist power, pouring scorn on those who "cover up their black heritage, cowering beneath the camouflage of white skin."

Drum heard about his uncle's soapbox oratory from everyone . . . of Roland's pledges and promises for a better tomorrow . . . about his warnings that "even now those in power are training their chosen one for the tomorrow that will soon be here . . . the white heir apparent who will try to trick you and lie to you that he has respect for black skin.

Don't listen, black friends. You are merely a number, a vote to him, which he will want to cull, as his overworked, underpaid workers cull the cocoa pods from his golden trees. Pods which once culled are thrown into the sweat box. Just more pods to add to his wealth, more votes to protect his wealth and the wealth of his children to come . . . with no more thought of adding a cent to your measly earnings. No, my friends, don't listen to the forked tongue of the Golden Hill heir apparent. Listen to me, your black brother, who really cares for your opinion, who will use your vote as a form of your self-expression to bring you and your children what you deserve. . . ." And so it went on, day in, day out, all around the island.

As Drum received another letter from Roger, with the news he was bringing his bride-to-be to Trinidad by ship, he was feverishly planning a retaliation to Roland's campaign.

The date of Roger's arrival propelled him into action. Drum had already begun a long article detailing his attempt to "bury the hatchet." Now, on the advice of Bill McMurtrey, he carefully traced for the first time his link to Louisa Calderon. "A link I share through my mother with my uncle—Roland Bracken—a man I would be proud to work with in the future for the good of all the people on this beautiful island."

A week before Roger and Alicia's arrival, the article was published, leading to a barrage of admiring letters and comments, praising Drum's magnanimity and breadth of character, despite his youth.

The day the S.S. *Antilles* from Southampton sailed past the Five Islands, by Pointe Baleine, Todd's Bay and Monos with its green peaks and silver bays, a major editorial in the *Trinidad Guardian* stated, "This shows an outstanding young man, one eminently suited to represent the people in the true sense of the word. We will wait to see if Roland Bracken has the same strength of character . . . to stop flaunting the fact he has what he considers to be the predominant—and apparently—the predestined color and skin to lead the people. We will wait to see if he agrees to meet and be reunited with the nephew he considers has the misfortune to be 'camouflaged' white. . . ."

It was a table-turning exercise against Roland, cleverly masterminded by those around Drum. It was further announced that Drum still felt a reconciliation should be possible. "To this end . . ." droned on the *Guardian*, "swallowing his pride, despite Roland Bracken's cold shouldering of his first invitation, Drum Pollard has now invited every member of the Bracken family to Golden Hill to celebrate his twenty-first birthday and also the return of his war-hero half brother, Roger Pollard, who is bringing to the island for the first time his fiancée, the Honorable Alicia Forrester."

There wasn't a trace of condescension in the story . . . of the hand outstretched from a position of power and wealth to an estranged, much poorer, black member of the family, a reconciliation for the sake of Trinidad. It sounded good, and the addition of the Honorable Alicia Forrester's name made it sound even better. Except Drum knew and his advisers knew that Roland Bracken wouldn't go near any of them. At least they were 90 percent sure he wouldn't. If he did accept this time, then their plot to discredit him as a fanatic, not fit or able to unite anyone or anything, was sabotaged.

The sun, a golden ball of fire, was sinking into the horizon and the sky was a miracle of purity, azure without a fleck of cloud, as Roger stood on the deserted boat deck, an hour away from docking in Port of Spain harbor. A lump rose in his throat as he saw in the distance the violet-colored mountains of the Northern Range. Trinidad. He loved the island after all. How could he have thought he hated the place so much that he never wanted to see it again?

Despite the nostalgia that engulfed him as the ship started to slow down, Roger felt as he'd felt many times during the last few years, like a man about to go into battle—except this time he wasn't about to climb into a cockpit. He was readying himself for the legal battle that probably lay ahead, once he put his cards on the table and explained to Drum and "phony Rosie" that part of Golden Hill had to be his, that there was no way they could expect to get away with it all.

He hadn't wanted to bring Alicia with him. Even now, he wondered how she somehow always managed to get her way. It would have been so much more sensible for him to have flown over to deal with the ugly side of the business first, hoping that Drum and Rose might even see the justice of his case and agree to a reasonable settlement without the help of the law. But Alicia had pouted and sulked in that childlike way of hers. . . . Then, when that hadn't produced results, she'd disappeared for two days, turning up just when, demented, he'd been about to call the police, sobbing that she'd drunk herself into a stupor because he'd made her so unhappy, that he obviously didn't love her as she loved him. It was so palpably absurd, because everyone could see he was crazily in love with her—yet he had this inflexible side, which he knew could be his undoing . . . and perhaps hers, too.

Even Alicia's uncle, the Earl of Chingford, had warned him. "Alicia's a baby. You're going to have your hands full if you take her on, old chap. For goodness sake, don't let her start on one of her crying jags. She can switch on the old waterworks for two days and then fill up again with gin. . . ." Roger hadn't known how to take the earl's warning.

In the gloomy ancestral house in Essex where Alicia had grown up, she had indeed seemed to grow younger before his eyes, dressing in old gym slips, wearing socks instead of stockings, talking in a baby voice to her uncle and mother. He hadn't liked it. It had depressed him, but as soon as it had stopped raining and they'd gone riding in the park surrounding the mansion, the spirited girl he loved had returned and he'd thought he understood why she hated to spend any more time than she had to in the family home.

"That makes two of us, darling," he'd told her and in bits and pieces had explained, without revealing the extent of his bitterness, how his father had passed him over to give his family home to his second wife and son.

When Roger received the cable from Drum, saying how thrilled he was that Roger would arrive in Trinidad in time for his twenty-first birthday, Roger found it hard to grasp the fact that Drum was nearly twenty-one.

As the ship slowed still more, Roger felt a pair of arms encircle his waist and, as he expected, a small hand crept down the front of his trousers and started fondling his penis, stirring it into life. How Alicia loved to play with him, tease him. Roger sighed. He had to be the most patient of men that he let her get away with so much playing and no real lovemaking, yet at the same time, illogically, he knew he wanted her to be a virgin until their wedding night.

Looking around to see the deck was still deserted, he pressed his hardening penis against her, lifting her blouse to stroke her bare little breasts. "I'm so glad you don't wear those complicated contraptions," he'd told her on their first date after the Savoy weekend, when with his arm around her in the back row of a cinema, she'd guided his hand on to a naked nipple beneath her shirt.

She's really aroused tonight, Roger thought happily, as the soft warm wind of the tropics ruffled their hair and, as he rubbed against her, her nipples hardened and she began to moan and open her legs.

A deafening roar from the ship's horn blasted them apart and, as they moved their bodies together again, the ship shuddered to a halt and they heard the rattle of the huge anchor as it was released into the water.

"Welcome to my island in the sun, little elf."

Alicia kissed him passionately. "I love it already. I want to stay. Why can't we get married here?"

"You know very well why, Honorable Alicia. What would all those loyal Chingford tenants say? They'd never forgive you."

Alicia giggled as they started back to their cabins, but Roger, suddenly serious, without even knowing why, caught her by the arm. "Alicia, don't get carried away. You know why I came back. I want to settle everything or at least get it under way in about a month. That will give me time to take a good look at Cedros and perhaps get a good price for it. This isn't the place for us to live now. Perhaps later—to retire to, if all goes well with the world, but not now. I only want the Golden Hill land because it's rightfully mine and it's valuable . . . but we've agreed haven't we, we're going to live in England."

Nothing's changed, Roger thought the next morning, as he looked out of the window of his old room to see the northern view of the plantation, where verdant low hills, their slopes planted with cocoa, were shaded by row after row of immortelle trees, brilliant with golden red blossoms.

Down below he could hear an excited murmur of voices, a cackle of high laughter, singing, the special sounds of the tropics. He smiled, wondering how Alicia was and whether she'd recovered from her first encounter with a lizard, which had been perched above the cotton canopy of her bed the night before. As he shaved, he continued to smile happily, remembering her look of shocked disbelief as he'd told her, "Lizards only visit people with titles, and it's a special honor when they decide to spend the night."

Whistling away, Roger couldn't remember when he'd felt so well . . . and, as for Drum, well, he seemed to have turned into a decent young man, after all.

He had yet to meet Rose who, to his relief, had been "indisposed" the night before and unable to welcome them. The thought of seeing Rose again was the one jarring note, for in his heart he blamed her for what had happened to his father. If Piper hadn't become entangled with phony Rosie. . . . Oh well, there was no point going over it now. The past was past and the future was . . . Alicia!

As he went toward the veranda where he remembered breakfast had always been served, he could hear Alicia's baby voice prattling on. Why on earth was she talking that way? He frowned. He had to get her out of that habit.

He pushed open the screen door to see Drum stroking a pure white rabbit on his lap, while Alicia knelt before him in apparent rapture. "Oh, Roger, Roger, it's beautiful. It's paradise." She leaped up to kiss his cheek. "Drum has just given me this bootiful little baby wabbit. Aren't you mine, you bootiful booty. . . ."

"Cut it out!" Roger didn't even know why he'd spoken so sharply, but the sight of Alicia's light brown head so close to Drum's unnerved him. In a second, though, he'd forgotten his feelings as he heard a hesitant cough and turned to see a graying, emaciated-looking woman come through the door.

Drum hastily put the rabbit down and stood up. "Mother, Roger has arrived with Alicia. Isn't it wonderful?"

Mother? Roger was so shocked, it took him a few seconds before he could speak. This was Rose? Beautiful, haughty Rose?

Alicia also looked confused, bewildered, as she stood up to shake Rose's hand, looking from her weary, thin face to Roger's and back again. She couldn't believe this was the evil but outstandingly beautiful woman Roger had described, the *femme fatale* who had ruined his father's life and very nearly his own.

As Roger looked at the woman he'd hated for so long, the resolve to fight her for his share of Golden Hill went right out of him. He was shattered as the thought struck him for the first time! Rose must really have loved his father after all. Or was her woebegone appearance yet another trick to make him feel sorry for her, so that he'd abandon his plan. Could she possibly have guessed the real reason for his return?

Later that morning, happy to find his old high boots still fitted him, Roger accompanied Drum around the estate with cutlass in hand, waiting for an opportunity to see the reaction he'd get if he mentioned their father's will. Their feet fell soundlessly on a thick carpet of leaves, and the air was heady, sweet with scent from the cocoa lilies whose petals fell like long satin streamers along the trail. It *was* paradise, and Roger could see that Drum obviously loved it every bit as much as he did.

Just when he'd decided to wait a few days before saying anything, to see whether Rose really was as pathetic as she looked, Drum burst out with, "I love this place and I know you do, Roger. Are you intending to stay?"

"I don't . . . don't know. It depends."

"On me?"

"What d'you mean?"

"Well, you know, I'm not sure I was cut out to be a planter . . . many of the people around here seem to see me more as a politician."

"So how do you see yourself?"

Drum laughed without humor. "As a trapped man. My God, how I've envied you during these past few years. You know I wanted to join up, but Mother . . . well, you can see for yourself how she is. I couldn't leave her. I didn't know what she might do if I did."

Only the sound of the ramier pigeons repeating endlessly *chookety-coo, chookety-coo*, broke the silence as they strolled under the golden arches of the immortelles.

Drum suddenly said excitedly, "Remember your ideas about the frozen-food business? I've often thought you were right."

Roger felt himself flushing. "How on earth did you know about that? You were just a little whippersnapper when I left."

"Oh, I heard Dad . . . Dad talk about it sometimes when you'd gone overseas. He never believed in the idea, but I did. Roger, there's land available at Golden Hill where you could start a business if you were still interested. I'd go in with you. . . ."

Roger looked at Drum in amazement. "You mean it?"

"Of course, I mean it." Drum sounded almost shy as he continued, "I just hope you might stay around now, Roger, so we . . . we can really get to know one another. Families have to stick together, you know."

By the time they returned to Golden Hill, Roger was very impressed by all that Drum had accomplished on the estate during his absence. As well as starting an apiary, already producing a sizable amount of Golden Hill honey, bottled and sold in Port of Spain, Drum had laid out citrus orchards to the east and west, grafted mangoes and other fruit trees in the south. His obvious knowledge of world agricultural markets and of the progress that had been made in the frozen-food and freeze-dried business impressed Roger, too. For the first time in his life he felt relaxed with Drum, able to talk to him, man to man, without the specter of his own jealousy coming between them.

Preparations for Drum's twenty-first birthday party went into full gear about ten days after their arrival. Em, the cook, bustled about with new importance as she supervised a group of giggling girls brought in from the village to help her with the marinating of the wild pigs, the mixing of the *temi-pain mals* made from bread and corn and wrapped in plantain leaves, the bowls of huge salads with four kinds of lettuce, avocados, artichokes and eggplant, the picking of only the choicest fruit—bananas, guavas, mangoes, Oriental figs, watermelon sea grapes and the making of every kind of pastry and pudding from coconut, banana and cinnamon, to chocolate and peppermint. Two gaily striped marquees were being erected, one for the bar, the other for the dance floor, much to the relief of Obee, who'd wailed, "Mastah Drum, Lawd ha' mercy, yo' don' wanna dem folk dancin' on yo' marble floor. It'll be ruin'd, dat it will, I t'ink so, don' yo' Mastah Drum?" It had already been decided to risk having the dancing outside in a marquee, where it was hoped the evening breeze would keep everyone cool and that there would be no heavy rain to dampen spirits.

Roger had intended to go over to Cedros to see his property before the party, but, as usual, in the tropics, one day melted into the next and, only twenty-four hours after his arrival, there suddenly was no longer any urgency about anything. He took Alicia down to Maracas Bay to bathe, rode with her over the mountains and strolled along the shady immortelle walks, but the heat affected her badly, so that most days, by early afternoon, she usually pleaded she wanted to nap.

The day of the party, Drum heard the Sunbeams were not interested in coming to play. He hadn't expected any different answer and it all helped to bolster the image of obstinate ignorance he wanted bolstered. "There are enough musicians coming to keep everyone dancing for a week," he said at breakfast with a laugh.

There was so much more laughter at the house these days since Roger and Alicia's arrival. Drum found himself looking forward to their early breakfasts together, sometimes the only meal they shared, as he was often gone until late in the evening, so by the time he returned, they'd already eaten and gone to bed.

"I'm not used to getting up so early, but I can't bear to stay in bed here either," Alicia told him. "I don't want to miss one second of the beautiful day . . . but I don't like the nights. I hate the sound of the insects. I keep thinking they're going to swallow little me up."

Drum was more and more fascinated by her . . . by the funny baby talk she sometimes used, by her girlish mannerisms, even by the quick way she'd run a comb through her short curly hair.

"You're going to stay up tonight, aren't you?" he teased. "After all, this party is for you, too." He suddenly thought of something. "There's going to be some 'dancin' the cocoa' today. Would you like to see it?"

"Oh, yes, whatever that means!" Alicia clapped her hands together excitedly, her cheeks getting pink as she turned to Roger. "Shall we, Roger? Shall we 'dance the cocoa' together?"

"You don't 'dance the cocoa,' elf," he replied lazily. "The natives do . . . but I'll snap you watching them in action. . . ."

By the time Drum was ready to go, Roger remembered he had to go into town to pick up something from the customs. He winked at Alicia to remind her that the American tape recorder he'd ordered specially for Drum's birthday, and which had been in customs awaiting their arrival, was at last going to be released. "You go with Drum," Roger said. "It's too hot for you in town, and anyway it's time you saw how the Pollards earn their money. . . ."

They looked like two children, Roger thought, as he watched Drum help Alicia onto the mare brought round from the stables. As they rode off toward the cocoa houses, their hair shining like halos in the sun, he felt a wild urge to stop them, to bring them back and let the day start over again. He shrugged his shoulders, not understanding his sudden uneasiness. Rose, with unusual warmth, wished him good morning as she joined him on the veranda. "I had my coffee with Drum ages ago," she told him. The smile disappeared from her lips when she discovered Drum had taken Alicia to watch the 'cocoa dancing.' "Why didn't you go with them?" she asked pointedly.

Roger explained about the present he was going into Port of Spain to collect, but Rose was not mollified. "You should be with your fiancée," she said firmly, not once, but twice, her tone reminding Roger of the old days when for him there had always been a "put-down note" in her voice, a bright, sharp voice that had then belonged to the most beautiful woman he had ever seen. Now, in the short space of five, almost six years, the beauty had withered away with grief. Roger felt uncomfortable even looking at her, and soon he excused himself to get ready to go into town.

Alicia rode beautifully. She knew she did and she also knew that Drum was giving her admiring glances.

There was something unusual about him, and about his mother, too, who, in answer to her torrent of questions, Roger had explained in his typical matter-of-fact way, had "just lost her looks, that's all. There's no great mystery. . . ." He'd sounded irritable when she'd pressed him about the great beauty he'd always described. "She lost her husband and daughter the same night in a fire deliberately set by her younger brother. Is it any wonder she lost her looks, too?"

Furtively, Alicia glanced at the slim man riding beside her, the golden boy of Golden Hill. She was glad to have a chance to be alone with him. She loved the way his eyes seemed to blaze with life whenever he was amused or interested in something . . . and now, in her riding clothes she knew suited her best, she was thrilled to see his eyes were blazing for her.

Squirrels, flicking their tails from their perches high in the trees, peeked at them. There was a continuous melodious hum from the insects, and birds chirped as they flew higher and higher seeking the warmth of the sun on the highest branches of the trees. As they neared the turn to the cocoa houses, Alicia heard the rhythmic notes of a calypso, happy laughing voices and the babble of a fast-running stream as it wound beside them over beds of white pebbles.

By the time they dismounted, her cotton shirt was wet through with perspiration, her small breasts clearly outlined through the clinging thin material.

As Drum saw them and thought of the soft pale flesh they represented, he felt his groin grow hot.

Pink with heat and excitement, Alicia tapped her feet in time to the fast calypso being strummed on a quatro, watching a number of natives on a raised platform treading on the cocoa beans all over the floor, their feet rubbing away the beans' slimy film as they danced and gyrated. The men, stripped to the waist, gleamed with sweat as they moved faster and faster in time to the music, the breasts of the women bounced up and down beneath their cotton smocks.

One of the laborers spotted Drum and quickly they improvised a calypso, singing, "Happy birthday t' yo', Mastah Drum; happy birthday, t' yo'. . . ."

With an easy smile, Drum acknowledged the workers he'd known since he was a child. Then he turned to Alicia, noticing the brightness of her eyes, the faint trace of sweat across her freckled nose, her mouth open in wonder.

"Do you want to 'dance the cocoa'?" He laughed.

"Oh, yes, oh, yes." She kicked off her boots and socks and before the natives could help, Drum lifted Alicia up on to the drying floor, his hands on her bare waist, as her shirt slipped out of her jodhpurs.

The beans were raked to turn them over to dry evenly on both sides, as the old man playing the quatro glanced up to keep a careful eye on the storm cloud gathering up on the hill. As he strummed more and more energetically, Alicia danced with as much abandon as the natives around her. She looks like a gazelle, Drum decided, as she swayed her body from side to side.

Suddenly, the music maker gave a warning cry: "Rain!" and Drum quickly moved to help the workers pull together the two halves of a sliding roof to cover the beans. If the slightest drop of rain fell on them, it could ruin the lot.

One by one the natives shuffled out through a door at the back. Drum dropped his boots into the yard below and drew the outer doors together as rain started to fall violently on the corrugated iron roof.

Alicia leaned back against the wall panting for breath, her shoulders still moving to the rhythm. In the peculiar half light, the atmosphere in the shed was as electric as the storm outside. Drum came to stand so close to her, she could feel his breath on her cheek. "You liked dancing the cocoa, didn't you? You looked very pretty . . . like a gazelle . . . or perhaps a spirit of the forest."

She looked at him with wide eyes, loving the sudden feeling of danger . . . of being away from everyone. A spirit of the forest? It was her kind of language. As if to intensify the magic of the moment, the rain started to pound even more loudly on the roof. Rat-a-tat-tat. Rat-a-tat-tat. "There are more spirits trying to come in," she whispered.

"We won't let them, will we, Alicia?" He came closer, but not close enough to touch her unless she moved a fraction forward. He could smell her fresh sweat, mingling with the flowery scent she wore. Just then a jagged flash of lightning lit up the shed, illuminating her upturned face, her mouth still open as she gulped in more air, her pink tongue just visible.

The thought of her baby breasts outlined by her damp shirt came into his mind, and, without any more hesitation, as thunder cracked above them, he slowly started to undo the buttons, opening her shirt to kiss each of her naked breasts lingeringly, running his tongue around each nipple. Her protests changed into whimpers as she first arched back, then crumpled toward him. But he made no other attempt to touch her with his hands, instead again and again ran his probing tongue around each areola, then kissed and sucked each nipple harder and harder until they stiffened in his mouth.

When she began to put her arms around him, Drum moved back and just as deliberately buttoned up her shirt. As if on cue the rain stopped, and in a few minutes the drying shed was flooded with sunlight as Drum started to slide open the roof.

Neither spoke on the way back to the big house, until, as they neared the end of the long avenue of immortelles, Drum caught the reins of Alicia's horse and tersely told her to dismount. She slipped off the horse, trying to look at him with bravado, to scold him in her usual coquettish way for his naughty behavior, but a look in his eyes stopped her. "Do you love Roger?" he asked hoarsely.

She scuffed the paragrass underfoot. "Of course I do," she said sulkily.

"Are you sure?" He tied the horses to a bar and came close to her again, forcing her back against a tree. His nearness made her giddy. Without realizing what she was doing she arched back again, aware of the soreness of her nipples, longing for him to take them again. "Are you sure?"

Now he sounded thunderous, looking down at her as if he might whip her into a different answer. "If you're sure, why do you behave like a whore?" She gasped but he went on, "You know as well as I do that you may as well go about naked the way you cover your breasts with that stupid little cotton top, don't you? Who are you trying to tease? Do you want a black lover? Have you thought about that? Don't you know a black man's cock is easily excited by the sight of a white woman's breast?" He hardly knew what he was saying as Alicia started to sob, her shoulders heaving. He felt violently angry, longing to tear her clothes off and beat her pink bottom until it was raw. But instead he rammed his mouth over hers, tight and hard, kissing her hungrily, his tongue searching for her tongue, his hands on her breasts, squeezing, molding, one hand slipping down inside her jodhpurs, his fingers on her belly, moving down. Her vagina flooded with juice. "Do you love Roger?" His voice was in her ear, insistent, beating into her brain, while his fingers stayed agonizingly an inch away from her wet hole.

She groaned. "I'm not sure, I'm not sure, I don't know anything any more." His fingers shot into her, cool, long, touching her in a way she'd never been touched before. She writhed as he played with her exquisitely, oh, so slowly, slowly, bringing her to the first full orgasm of her life. "Oh, Drum, Drum, don't leave me," she cried. She couldn't bear for it to be over as once again the heavy rain started to fall and his fingers moved away. "Let's stay here."

"No." He pulled his hand from her, holding it out in the rain as if it was unclean. Now he felt sick, ashamed, horrified at how easily he'd given in to the feelings Alicia had so unexpectedly aroused. Roger's fiancée. He wanted to hate her but he couldn't. The smell of her and the memory of her small, tight vagina stayed with him all day.

At eight o'clock, with the driveway packed with arriving cars and people pouring into the house, Roger was still outside Alicia's door, waiting to take her downstairs and introduce her to all his old friends. He'd been up and down for the past hour as she gave first one excuse, then another for not being ready.

Finally, he kept knocking angrily on the door until she opened it a crack. He was shocked by her paleness, her red-rimmed eyes. "What is it, are you sick, darling?" he asked anxiously, his anger dissipating.

"No, I've had a bad headache. I'll be all right. You go down."

"No, I'm not leaving you. Are you sure you can make it? I want you to be there when Drum opens his present." He tried to coerce her. "I'm sure it's the first ever seen in Trinidad. It's a beauty."

Alicia left the door ajar for him to come in while she tried to fluff up her hair, which obstinately clung to her head in damp tendrils. Roger felt terribly disappointed. She certainly didn't look her best, poor girl. The tropics obviously didn't suit her. She looked wilted, downtrodden, instead of like the mischievous, sparkling-eyed girl she really was.

"Do you think this dress looks all right?" Alicia held up a simple strapless cotton evening dress. "I'm so hot. I was going to wear this"— she pointed to a white-and-silver lace dress on the bed—"but I feel drowned in it."

"You'll look lovely in anything. Just hurry up, be a love." Roger tried to sound convincing. Alicia went into the bathroom to dress and when she came out Roger saw she'd put on some rouge, but he sensed there was still something worrying her.

As they walked down the long curved stairway there was a burst of applause from a group of guests standing in the main entrance hall. The faces were familiar, although Roger couldn't remember all their names, but in minutes they were surrounded by well-wishers who shook their hands, and slapped them on the back. He couldn't remember ever feeling so popular.

Up on the grass knoll Alicia could see the huge suckling pigs turning on spits, basted every so often by Em and a retinue of servants. The sight made her feel even more sick, but her adrenaline started to flow as, in the distance, she saw Drum receiving guests with his mother at his side.

Also rouged up, thought Roger as, with Alicia looking more cheerful, they went over to greet them and he saw an unusual slash of pink on Rose's cheeks.

Later, after dinner there were a series of toasts calling attention to the fact that this was a very special coming of age ". . . of a young man," said Bill McMurtrey, "who one day will help this country of ours come of age . . . a young man already noticed by the people for his compassion, his judgment, his amazing grasp of the complicated problems we face. . . ." So the compliments went on, to be answered by Drum in a brief witty speech, which ended with his request for all his honored guests to rise and drink a toast to his wonderful brother Roger and charming fiancée, the Honorable Alicia Forrester.

Roger stood up proudly, expecting Alicia to do the same. When she sat stone-faced, he whispered pleadingly, "Alicia, *please* don't embarrass me." She slowly stood up with a bleak smile, interpreted by everyone as "natural shyness" . . . except by Drum—and Rose, who looked at her searchingly, noticing the beseeching way Alicia looked at Drum, while Drum languidly raised his glass to her once more, a half smile, which seemed to mock her, on his face.

What did Alicia's look mean? Rose reflected. Was she starting to imagine things? Improbable, impossible things on this all-important night of her son's life?

As Drum cried, "On with the dance!" and encircled the waist of the lovely blond daughter of one of the Pollards' oil managers, Rose sat back reassured. She *was* imagining things. Alicia is Roger's fiancée, she told herself, and soon, thank God, they would both be returning to England, leaving her in peace again with her beloved son.

To Alicia, the evening was interminable, as she watched Drum dance with one girl after another, studiously avoiding coming anywhere near her. Pleading that her headache was worse, Alicia finally managed to persuade Roger to stay while she crept upstairs to bed, longing to let the tears burst out. She went over in her mind every minute she'd spent with Drum that day, in the drying shed and in the forest.

Was she in love with him? The thought both exhilarated and terrified her as she lay tossing from one side of the old canopied bed to the other. There was an undercurrent of . . . of excitement about him . . . of sexual pleasures she couldn't even guess at . . . of danger.

But why had he ignored her? Why had he made such a point of toasting her engagement, when he knew what she had allowed him to do to her only that afternoon and what he must know she longed for again?

Outside heavy summer rain swept down once more from the mountains, and at last she heard the sound of car doors slamming, hooters hooting. The party was over. Had he persuaded the blond girl to stay? Was he at this moment making love to her? Alicia pressed her face into her pillow, biting her lip. She wanted him, more than she'd ever wanted any man. He was different. She was different with him. She couldn't tease him like she teased Roger. There was nothing of Roger that she could see in Drum. . . .

When Alicia woke in the morning, it was to hear a tap on the door. For an ecstatic moment she thought it was Drum and flew to answer it, only to see Roger's worried face outside.

"I should never have stayed on last night. I should have made sure you were all right. Forgive me?"

Suddenly everything she'd always thought she loved about Roger irritated her intensely. He was a bore, a clumsy, predictable bore who always took no for an answer. She stomped back to bed. "I'm all right. I was just fed up hearing your precious little brother being swamped with praise. How big is his head this morning? It must be a monstrous size. . . ."

Roger laughed, relieved to hear Alicia sound like herself again. "No, I think his head was swollen before we arrived. He's quite a little hero, isn't he? Preferable I must say to the little horror I expected."

When Alicia later arrived on the veranda looking, Roger thought with relief, like his own "special girl" again in a neat tailored summer dress, Drum had already had his breakfast and, Roger told her, wouldn't be back until evening. She felt like weeping as the empty day stretched endlessly before her.

She snatched up the morning paper and tried to get rid of her frustration, making a series of sarcastic, biting remarks as she came to an article about Drum, which pointed out that despite all Drum's efforts, his uncle Roland Bracken hadn't been man enough to show up at the twenty-first birthday to "bury the hatchet" for the sake of the general good.

"I don't suppose for one minute Drum *wanted* him to show up. It's all a plot to make himself look like a man with a halo," Alicia snapped. "If any of the Brackens had come near, I'm sure he would have been very disappointed."

Roger could do nothing to please her that day. Whatever he suggested, she showed it couldn't interest her less. When he tried to hold her in his arms, he teased her that she felt like an arrow in a bow, quivering to be let go. Finally exasperated, he left her in her room, saying he hoped she'd be in a better frame of mind by dinner, as he still hadn't given their present to Drum and intended to present it then.

Drum would be joining them for dinner! Alicia cheered up immediately and, contrite, pecked Roger's cheek saying, "Sorry darling. It's the heat. I'll have a cool bath to get rid of my jitters!"

She lay down on the cool white bed to try to calm her rising excitement and sense of anticipation, all the while thinking, Drum, Drum, Drum . . . surely you must be thinking of me?

He was. As he drove back from Port of Spain, Alicia's cheeky little face, with the runaway freckles over her nose, came into his mind and his penis hardened as he thought of her perfect small breasts. She looked so amazingly young, like a bamboo shoot, with her slight measurements, her neat, small head. It was strange, Drum reflected, that although he might go through the motions of being initially aroused by a normal rounded figure, he found himself increasingly attracted to the slight, the immature, the budding body, where there was nothing to remind him of aging flesh, where everything was hopeful, growing, fresh.

As he pulled up with a screech in front of the saman tree in the courtyard, he wondered why he'd agreed to join Roger and Alicia for dinner. It was asking for trouble, playing with fire, yet he knew he had to face Alicia again at some point and fight his sudden "itch" for her.

He showered in cold water, knowing it was stupid—that cold water in the tropics was guaranteed to make one feel hotter than ever in an hour, but he needed the sharp sting of the spring water to slap him to his senses.

By the time he walked into the library, wearing one of his father's best liki-liki shirts, the fine white linen emphasizing his dark tan, he looked like the master of the house should look: cool, calm, totally in control. Alicia and Roger were already there—and, an unusual sight, so was Rose, smiling, sipping sherry, while Roger mixed martinis for Alicia and himself.

"How is the man of the hour?" Even to herself Alicia's voice sounded unnaturally high pitched.

Drum gave a self-deprecating little bow in her direction. "In perfect health. And how is the Honorable Miss Alicia? Did you help the natives clean some more of our cocoa crop this morning?"

He was glad to see her blush. He wanted to unnerve her, even hurt her with words, almost as much as he knew immediately once he set eyes on her again, that he wanted to make passionate love to her. His eyes had the curious blazing look. Alicia found her hands trembling as she yearned, Oh, is it because of me. *Please* let it be because of me! The tension between them was like a tangible, living thing in the room.

Drum looked hurriedly at Roger, but he seemed to sense nothing as, like an overgrown schoolboy, he rushed over to the library cupboard and lifted out a large box. "Here's your present Drum, something from Alicia and myself that we hope you like. . . ."

Now it was Drum's turn to blush. "Oh, Roger, that's awfully good of you . . . really unnecessary."

"Well, wait till you see what it is before you say anything." Roger guffawed, enjoying himself hugely. "You won't have seen anything like it before, I guarantee! You may not even know what it is."

Drum was overwhelmed with the tape recorder. "I've heard about them, of course, but I've never seen one. This is magnificent. Roger, really, it's too good of you."

The present saved the evening as after dinner they all recorded their voices, sang, recited nursery rhymes and generally played the fool, enjoying the unusual sensation of hearing their own voices played back. When Alicia's baby talk came into the room, Roger frowned. "Now you know how silly you sound, A," he said. "I wish you wouldn't do it."

"Oh, don't be such a stuffed owl," she said sharply.

Drum laughed quickly. "'Stuffed owl,' that's a new one. I never heard that expression before. What does it mean?"

"Twit, twoo, twit, twoo . . ." Alicia giggled. "Twit, twoo. . . ."

Roger was furious. "Alicia, you're making a fool of yourself. Stop it."

"Oh, Roger, she's rather sweet." Drum started to say something more, but thought better of it as he saw Roger catch the look on Alicia's face as she turned to look at Drum, a strained, wistful look of longing.

Roger didn't like the look one bit. What did it mean? Were the tropics really going to her head?

Later, when he kissed her goodnight, Roger pressed her to him, hoping to feel her fingers begin to fondle and excite him as she so often liked to do, but she felt like a dead weight in his arms. "What's wrong, elf? What's biting you?"

"Nothing. I'm tired, that's all," she moaned.

"You're always tired here." Roger made up his mind. He had been wavering for days as to whether to proceed with an attempt to wrest part of the Golden Hill property away, but he felt defeated before he even spoke to a lawyer. Drum had accomplished too much for him to be able to say his contribution before the war entitled him to some acreage. If he wanted to proceed with his prewar ideas of expansion into the frozen-food area, Drum would probably go along with him anyway, but now Roger knew it couldn't be in Trinidad. He didn't belong there any more after all. He both loved and hated the place, but in particular he hated its effect on Alicia. "We're going to Cedros tomorrow, and, once I've worked out what kind of price I can expect, I'll put the property on the market and then we'll leave," he told her grimly. "We've already been here nearly a month and it's a month too long. I'll book our return flights for next week—at the latest on Wednesday."

"Oh, no." Alicia put her hand to her mouth. "Roger, don't let's leave. I love it here, really I do . . . and anyway, what about Golden Hill? You haven't even mentioned it to Drum or his mother. What are you going to do about that? That's going to take time. You can't leave yet. . . ."

"I'm not going to do anything. It's finished. Over. A closed book. I'm going to make a fresh start in fresh clean air in England with you." He turned to go out of the room, but she rushed over to throw her arms around his neck.

"Please, don't take me back so soon . . . please. . . ." Her fingers were at work, touching him as she hadn't touched him in days, until, his penis throbbing, he pushed her down on the bed and locked himself against her, feeling her respond in the usual way, pulling down the straps of her nightgown to give him her breasts. She shut her eyes, trying to imagine it was Drum who was with her, Drum whose groans she could hear as the thick rod pushed against the space between her legs. "I'm coming, I'm coming," she could hear him say, but it wasn't Drum. It was Roger, a heavy weight across her nightdress. She hated him for it. His mouth on her nipples repulsed her. She bit her lips to keep herself from screaming at him to leave her alone.

The drive to Cedros was not a success. At first, remembering his adamance about returning to England, Alicia tried to act as if she was interested in everything he told her—about the sugar plantations they passed, about the meeting with his father so long ago when he'd tried to interest him in the frozen-food business. But as the rolling green hills gave way to the long flat stretch of road leading to the oil fields, Alicia's replies became more and more monosyllabic and her sighs more frequent.

Roger felt helpless, uneasy, as if he were trying to grasp a butterfly, within easy reach but always eluding him.

In Bonasse, the village on the outskirts of the property, Khano, the East Indian caretaker, was waiting to show his new master Roger around. First they drove, then walked through groves of spiraling coconut trees to the boundary, which Roger found stretched all the way to Icacos Point. There they sat on a small hillock to eat the delicious rotis the caretaker had provided, stuffed with chicken, coconut meal and raisins.

Below on one side of the hill the sea constantly churned while on the other side it looked smooth, peaceful. "What causes that?" Alicia asked, trying again to show some interest in the surroundings. "I' be de remous," the Indian said, forcing the word out like a curse. "De remous dat caus's death."

Alicia shuddered. "What does that mean? Is it a shark, a whirlpool?"

Between them Roger and Khano told her that since the days of Christopher Columbus seamen had been unexpectedly sucked under to their deaths by the treacherous crosscurrents called remous, which were formed by the tide of the Caribbean meeting waters coming down from Venezuela's Orinoco River.

"Crosscurrents," Alicia repeated dolefully, looking at the battling waters. "Trinidad is full of crosscurrents. . . ."

Before they started on the return trip, Khano asked permission to show Roger something of interest. Alicia, pleading tiredness, settled herself back in the car, where Roger found her sound asleep on his return thirty minutes later.

By the time she opened her eyes, for some perverse reason he decided not to tell her what he'd seen. He really didn't know what to think of it himself, for as Khano had led him silently through some uncultivated bush a sickening smell of gas had assaulted his nostrils, and he'd had to jump to one side to avoid a thick smear of black oil in his path. It was coming from the ruin of what had once been an engine house, where a rusty, foul-smelling pump cylinder still gurgled and creaked as black oil trickled out to merge with the earth.

His father had obviously had hopes of gaining something other than coconuts from Cedros. Had he abandoned the shaft after discovering it was not worth proceeding with the drilling venture? Had he forgotten about it? Or had he just started the exploration when he'd come to such an untimely end?

Whatever the answers, as Roger turned in to the Golden Hill drive, he still felt he couldn't wait to get away from the island. He had the facts and figures about Cedros, and now he decided he wouldn't rush to get rid of it. He'd wait until Alicia and he were safely married and then make up his mind what to do.

When Alicia came down for breakfast the next morning, it was to receive the warmest "good morning" she had so far received from Rose. It didn't take long for Alicia to understand the reason.

"Roger has gone to Port of Spain," Rose told her with a wide smile. "He tells me you're leaving next week— He has gone to inquire about the air tickets. What a wonderful world it is. To think you can be back in England in only one day—it hardly seems possible."

She knows, Alicia thought. Like a witch, she *knows* there has been something between Drum and myself, and now she can't wait to see me gone. Alicia threw her head back in her most haughty manner. "Well, Roger may be going back, but I'm not sure that I am. . . ."

"Oh!" The effect was instantaneous. Gone were the charming smile and the polite words. For the first time, Alicia had a glimpse of the old Rose, who had taken Maraval Road and Piper Pollard by storm, as, eyes flashing, Rose hissed ". . . And *who* has asked you to stay?"

Rather than giving Rose the satisfaction of knowing she could not supply a truthful answer, Alicia abruptly went inside, slamming the screen door behind her.

Where was Drum? Oh, where was he? Feeling the lump in her throat about to turn into tears, Alicia ran up to her room to stare moodily out of the window. Leaning her head against the shutters and listening to the sound of moving wings and unseen voices, she smelled the humus from the soil, the powerful scent of tropical flowers. She bathed again to feel cool; then the next minute she decided she would go mad if she didn't do something, go somewhere. She ran down the back stairs, terrified of running into Rose, for who knew what that mad-looking woman might do. Summoning up her courage, she asked if there was a horse she could ride and soon she was off, not bothering to change out of her cotton skirt, riding sidesaddle along the trail, not caring where she was going, feeling the tears coursing down her hot cheeks. As she walked the horse down a steep hill, she could hear voices at the bottom and realized that without knowing it she had arrived at the main estate office. With a flash of recognition, she saw Drum's car parked outside.

She didn't care what his reaction might be. She had to see him and tell him how she felt. She jumped off the horse and would have careened inside to throw her arms around his neck if Drum hadn't wandered out at the moment with an older distinguished-looking man.

"Alicia . . ." He was startled by the look on her face. He quickly turned to say, "Bill, have you met my about-to-be sister-in-law, Alicia?" The coolness of his tone was like a slap across the face, and she hardly knew what she said as she shook Bill McMurtrey's hand. Drum took no further notice of her, as she stood there like a little girl, waiting for the "grownups" to finish their conversation. "Well, I think this overture from Gomes is a good sign, Bill. Obviously, he's going to bring his trade-union people in along with him. . . . I wonder what my Uncle Roland thinks about that? A change of heart on Mr. Gomes's part that can't please him. Does this put Roland back in Butler's camp?"

McMurtrey went toward his own car. "I'm not sure Roland knows yet that Gomes is coming with us. . . . As you know, once upon a time he was trying to form an association between Butler and Gomes—a perfect triangle, but it didn't work out. Now, Butler is coming out of the oil belt to fight Gomes for Cipriani's old seat, and Gomes is joining our United Front. I think this leaves your dear uncle very much out on a limb . . . but we can never be too sure of that one. Glad to meet you, eh—eh—Lady Alicia. Congratulations . . . I hope you'll be very happy. 'Bye, Drum. Speak to you tomorrow. Let's hope that there's no rain. We need every man to turn out for this one."

As Bill McMurtrey drove down the lane leading to the main Maracas road, Drum looked at Alicia sternly. "What are you doing here?"

She tried to sound as light-hearted and as carefree as possible, but her voice cracked. ". . . I didn't know where I was going. I didn't care. Roger's . . . Roger's . . . gone to get . . ."

"Yes, I know. It's for the best, isn't it?" He sounded colder than he'd intended to, but, seeing tears start to pour down her face, he looked around hurriedly. "For goodness sake, Alicia. . . . Oh, wait here." He went inside and gave instructions for someone to take her horse back to the house. Then with scant courtesy, he pushed her into his two-seater, to roar back up the trail, until he reached a cul-de-sac formed by a cluster of bamboo trees. "Come on, we'll have a swim," he said. "That should cool you down and make you see sense. . . ." He drove under the bamboo fronds until the car was practically hidden from the trail. Into her mind came the agonizing question: How many times has he driven here with other girls to disappear from the world for a few minutes or hours?

Whatever the answer, just as minutes before she'd thought her misery would break her wide open, she now felt ecstatic as she followed Drum, scrambling over boulders and tree roots, scratched and dirty, her cotton skirt and top sticking to her with perspiration. On and on they went through thick undergrowth toward the sound of a waterfall.

When they reached a flat slab of rock patterned with mosses and ferns, Drum sat down to stare moodily into a deep blue-green pool fed by a crystal clear rush of water from the hills above. It was like being in a dark green cavern, she thought, as high overhead the trees entwined with exotic creepers blocked out the sky.

Drum peeled off his bush jacket and pants and dove into the clear water. Even the shadow of his body underwater stirred her. He reappeared to beckon her mockingly to join him and she slipped behind a rock about to take off her skirt, when his cool strong hands came around her, and his mouth was on hers. Her cotton panties were soaking with a thick wetness from deep inside her as with sure hands he helped her out of them, burying his face in the wet crotch before carefully placing them with his clothes.

"Drum, Drum, now, now. . . ." She couldn't believe the begging note in her voice, she who had always been terrified of "the real thing," who had always cock-teased and then retreated at the moment of decision.

"Let's swim." He turned to dive back into the pool, before she could see the swelling she was causing. She dived after him, the water like a blessing on her skin. From the depths he came up under her, forcing her legs apart to hang over his back while he buried his face in her. She was delirious with longing . . . but now she pushed away, swimming to the farthest, deepest green corner of the pool. If he wanted to torture her, she wouldn't let him see how much it hurt.

They swam like children, splashing, darting, chasing, catching an ankle, touching, kissing, cool clean lips coming together innocently until a tongue tip probed a mouth open.

Later they lay side by side, breathless as much from the powerful sexual attraction between them as from their activities in the water. "What do you want, Alicia," Drum whispered as he tried without success to control his feelings. He turned to lie on his stomach, determined not to give in to his longing to ram into her, all the same not able to resist running his hand over her cool pink nipples.

"You, you, you . . . I love you, Drum." She snuggled up to him and would have climbed on his back if she'd been sure he wouldn't tip her back into the water. She had never felt so unsure of a man or wanted one more.

"But you can't have me. You belong to Roger."

"I don't belong to anyone. Oh, Drum, I thought I loved him, but I don't. . . . Don't send me away."

The whining note in her voice did more to control his feelings than anything else could have done. He jumped up to fetch his clothes, but she was too quick for him, flinging her arms around his strong frame, pressing herself against him to feel her nipples against his chest. "Don't you love me?" The sobs were in her voice again, her shoulders shaking. There was something irresistible about her when she was so defenseless. He didn't know what to think. Did he love her? Certainly she was driving him crazy with her availability, her obvious longing to give herself to him.

He knelt on the mossy slab, prying open her pink mouth with his fingers, looking at the plump folds of skin that came together like the most perfect virgin shell. Without words they lay down again, but this time in perfect harmony, in a position that allowed his tongue to probe open and find her hot spot, while her mouth could envelop his growing penis. Around them the green cavern began to grow darker and the crescendo from the insects grew louder as the afternoon went on. Over and over they explored each other, groaning, crying out in the dark, oblivious of time, Drum trying to exorcise his demon once and for all. Orgasm after orgasm flooded through her as his mouth returned to excite her until at last in a rush of semen he gave himself up to her, hearing her half-choke as she swallowed, her tight little mouth holding on.

She didn't care if the world saw them. As they stumbled back to the car all she could think of was "the next time" and the next and the next until finally she had his penis deep inside her, breaking through her virgin skin. Drum's emotions were in havoc. He could still feel the screaming delight of her tight little mouth. He loved it, but did he love her? He was fascinated, but was it enough to wreck his brother's plans? As they sat together in the car he tried to work things out. "Alicia . . ."

"Yes, yes, oh, yes, Drum." Her eyes were so bright, he could almost see his reflection in them as the sun began its descent into the other hemisphere.

"Alicia, you must go back to London with Roger. Think things over.

Get away from here, then if you still feel the same . . . write to me. I'll
come to see you. I promise. . . ."

"I can't," she wailed distractedly. "How can you say that after this
afternoon? I'll never be able to let another man touch me as long as I
live. . . ."

The same wailing note reminded him of his mother and he shivered.
"Of course you can. You must if we're ever to have any kind of life
together. And now, what are we going to say? We can't arrive back at
the house together. It's nearly six. I'm dropping you at the back of the
house . . . then I'm going straight to a friend's house to wash up. Don't
expect to see me tonight or tomorrow. We must keep apart until we can
look at each other without the world seeing how we feel."

"It's no good, Drum, it's impossible." But she wasn't unhappy now.
With an almost motherly feeling, she realized he wasn't so experienced
after all. He thought their feelings could be switched on and off like
electric light bulbs, when in reality the feeling between them was like
electricity itself, always present in the atmosphere. In order to be fair,
she would have to tell Roger at the first opportunity, but she said
nothing to Drum. It was better not to worry him at this point, she
thought, because he obviously didn't want to be Roger's enemy.

She crept up to her room, hearing Drum's car gather speed as he
went off in the direction of St. Joseph. She was in luck. Only a minute
before, Roger had been in her room, pacing back and forth. He had
spent the last three hours looking for her everywhere. As it was, when
he returned to her door once again thirty minutes later, after both Rose
and he had tried to find Drum to announce that Alicia was missing, it
was to find it bolted. "Alicia, Alicia, are you in there?" he cried, hoarse
with anxiety.

"Yes, yes, I'm fine," she called out in a high hysterical voice.
"Please, don't worry. I promise to come and talk to you tomorrow, but I
must sleep now. Please understand."

Roger thundered at the door. "Let me in this instant or I'll break the
door down!" He gave a kick at the door that shook the old timber.

"All right, all right, you asked for it," Alicia said sulkily. She wrapped
her robe tightly around her and, her face scrubbed shiny like a child's,
opened the door.

Roger burst through. "Where have you been all afternoon? What are
you trying to do to me?"

"Nothing, Roger dear, nothing." Her calm composed voice startled
him. He had expected tears, hysterics, explanations, probably lies—but

not this. "Alicia, what on earth has got into you? You went off on horseback? Your horse was brought back and nobody knows where you've gone? Is this fair? Rose and I have been demented. . . ."

Alicia snorted with laughter. "I bet Rose was demented all right."

Roger shook her hard. "How dare you laugh. Do you know what you're doing to me? Where have you been?"

"With Drum."

He stepped back, closing his eyes, moving his head as if to avert a blow. He had been expecting it and . . . yet . . . he hadn't believed it could really be true. "With Drum? You mean . . . you mean . . ."

Alicia turned on her heel with an expression he remembered seeing at the Savoy the first time they'd met, a supercilious toss-of-the-head expression as if to say "Well, what of it . . ."

"We're in love. . . ."

Roger sat down heavily on the bed, shaking his head in disbelief. "In love?" As quickly as his strength had left him, fresh adrenaline poured through his body. "I'll kill him!" he screamed. "I'll kill the little bastard. I'll kill him."

Roger lumbered out of the room like an old man, but Alicia came running after him, screeching, "No, no, no, it's not Drum's fault! It's mine. I love him. We couldn't help it."

He turned on her with a look of such scorn that she cowered back on the staircase. "Has he laid his hands on you? Have his fingers done to you what you like so much? Has he stuck them in your aristocratic, precious little cunt?"

She was aware of someone watching them from the gallery above. It was Rose, who made no attempt to move away when Alicia looked up, flushing as she realized Rose must have heard everything. With a flash of temper, Alicia screamed, "So now you know, too! Yes, I love Drum and he loves me. . . . We'll always be together."

Rose never raised her voice, but her tone was threatening. "Over my dead body. My son will never do that to me."

Roger ran from the house and, jumping into the first car he saw, he drove off, tires screeching down the driveway.

Alicia was suddenly bent over with stomach cramps and, retching, started to crawl back to her room, not caring any longer that Rose was still watching every move.

As the night dragged on, Alicia's new-found confidence in Drum's love wore thin. She couldn't stop her hands from trembling or her teeth from chattering as she contemplated what kind of future lay in store.

Oh, how she loved him. It didn't matter if now he didn't love her quite so much. She would make his love grow, however long she had to wait.

Roger never came back to the house. Two days later he was to leave Trinidad, vowing never to return. When Rose made her first journey to Port of Spain in months to visit him at the Queen's Park Hotel, pleading with him to forgive Alicia and take her back, that the girl was just a spoiled child whose head had been turned by the sensuous air of the tropics, he had curtly told her she was wasting her breath.

It had given Roger no pleasure to see Rose groveling, something he'd once have given his all to see. She was no longer his foe. It was her son, Drum, the apple of his father's eye, the golden-haired boy who'd always come first and now was first again, stealing as he had always stolen the love that should have been his.

Even seeing the blood spurt out of Drum's nose when he'd finally caught up with him that early dawn, creeping out of his friend McMurtrey's place, hadn't been much of a solace. And Drum hadn't even attempted to fight back, only put up his wiry arms to protect himself as Roger had waded in, trying to punch the good looks away forever. He would have, too, if McMurtrey, guessing something was up when he didn't hear Drum drive away, hadn't come out to intervene.

It was only when Roger was airborne on his long way back to England and looking down at the silver sea as it stroked the gold Trinidad strands—so deceptively peaceful and idyllic—that he'd wished he'd stayed one more day so that he could have bloodied Drum's nose once more. But he'd had to get away before there was the slightest chance his aching for Alicia would reach critical proportions, remembering how Drum had cried, "But Roger, it's not true. We don't love each other. I was just fooling around. Believe me, I'm sorry. . . ."

Fooling around! Did that mean fucking around? Perhaps not, but it didn't matter. "We love each other," she'd said—and there'd been a note of truth in her voice, a note that had never been there for him.

Drum could hardly bear to look at Alicia now, let alone touch her. A look at her was a look at his innermost soul, a sign of his weakness, his betrayal of the man he honored, loved. Now he'd lost Roger's respect forever, and for what?

"What shall I do, Bill?" he blurted out after several rum and sodas one night, delaying his departure from McMurtrey's house, trying to avoid spending more time than he had to with Alicia. "I've told her I'm not interested in marriage—yet."

"That was your mistake, Drum. That's a very hopeful word to a lady. 'Yet' can be translated into 'soon,' even 'tomorrow,' if she puts her mind to it. You'd have been better off with 'never'—that is, if you mean 'never.' Do you?"

Drum nodded his head vehemently. "My God, I do mean it!"

The thought of marriage to anyone wasn't appealing, but the thought of marrying Alicia was appalling. The overwhelming "itch," as he described it to himself, had gone, wiped out by the enormous guilt he continued to feel over Roger. And besides, with the election following right after Roger's departure, he'd become so busy he really had no time to think about Alicia—or her enticing body parts.

Along with Jack Kelshall, Bill McMurtrey and others, he'd worked hard to bring about a coalition of as many of the "progressive" groups as possible under the United Front label, hoping to obtain all the nine decision-making seats on the Council. By far their biggest plum was Albert Gomes, who brought the trade unions with him and decisively beat Uriah Butler for Cipriani's Port of Spain seat.

Gomes's defection was a bitter blow to Roland, although initially he accepted Gomes's explanation that the United Front had just become too strong. Once in power, Gomes promised, he would see Roland was given more of a chance to play his own role. *Patience*, he'd told him silkily, have patience.

It had been bad enough to see Drum lionized in the press as a "young man of magnanimity," after he'd tried to uphold the family honor by turning down Drum's offer of reconciliation. Such an obvious "carrot" with the election coming up. Gomes had told Roland he'd been wrong to turn it down, but he just hadn't been able to summon up enough willpower to put his teeth together in a smile and go along with the rest of the family . . . even just to shake hands with his infidel of a sister and her snake-tongued son.

And where was Gomes now when Roland tried to get through to him? Up at Golden Hill more often than not, taking tea with Drum Pollard and this Lady from England, who was somehow still there, although Roger, her fiancé, was not.

It was a tea party at Golden Hill with Gomes as the honored guest that finally caused Alicia's downfall.

At first it had gone well, with Alicia showing her breeding in a way Drum could not help admiring. She knew what to order and how to serve it with no fuss, but as the afternoon went on and Gomes rumbled on about the deplorable lack of men of sufficiently high caliber on the island to be entrusted with greater political responsibility, Alicia began to take exception to "this pompous half caste," as she privately considered him.

"The talent displayed during the last election was much too fluid and unstable to earn us the right to more ample political opportunity. Before we can even dream of self-government, more young men must begin to think 'politically.' There must be more education and economic development. . . ." With a sly look, Gomes continued, "Something I must warn you, Drum, your young Uncle Roland is very much aware of. More perhaps than you realize."

Drum was not at all put out. He knew Roland wasn't an adversary to ignore, and he didn't take him lightly, but Alicia began to feel aggravated.

To cover it up, to Drum's embarrassment, she said in her baby voice, "Don't talk like that to my Drummy. Drummy is a very clever boy, aren't you Drummy?" The afternoon deteriorated rapidly to Drum's fury—as he was even beginning to like Gomes and wanted to gain his respect, in order to gain his confidence.

When Gomes left soon after the baby talk began, Drum turned on Alicia in front of his mother. "Don't you know when to shut up," he said icily. "Who told you to butt in? You sounded like a total lunatic." Alicia burst into noisy tears, but the sight of her shaking shoulders didn't move him. "What are you still doing here anyway?" he went on, now no longer caring what the outcome might be. "You don't belong here. My mother's right. You belong with Roger. Go back where you belong. I'll arrange a return ticket for you this week."

As Drum marched out of the room, Rose felt a surge of excitement welling inside her, a feeling she'd never expected to feel again.

Alicia rushed after Drum, no pride left, desperate not to be sent away. "Drum, Drum, don't send me back," she beseeched.

But he pushed her away, saying, "I'm not coming back to Golden Hill until I know you're on the way to England. You're an embarrassment. I wouldn't be surprised if Roger hadn't realized his lucky escape by now."

Later Alicia thought of suicide, trying to visualize how quickly she might die if she were to jump from the top window or tie some stones around her and jump into the deep pool. But as she recalled that mysterious green cavern and her afternoon there with Drum, her tears fell afresh until in the early hours of the morning she finally fell asleep on the windowseat.

Her ticket was on the breakfast tray in the morning, and when Obee, shame-faced, told her Maize had already been sent to her room to pack her things, Alicia realized Drum meant what he said.

It was the sort of dismissal one might present to an inefficient servant, and if a letter hadn't arrived that day from her uncle, the earl, who knows if Alicia mightn't have tried to accomplish a dramatic death, but his letter was a life raft, a signal that there *was* life after Drum and Golden Hill.

The letter was also a reprimand, telling her that Roger hadn't said much, but was obviously a broken-hearted man . . . that she'd better come back soon if she wanted to mend things. He was worried about her ". . . out there with all those golliwoggs. Don't you remember how you screamed when you were given a black doll one Christmas?"

The wry phrases were as British as marmalade, the old oaks in Chingford Park and the House of Lords. The letter made it easier for her to climb in the back of the Bentley, without looking back at the beautiful old house, to be driven to Piarco Airport, where Obee, who still found it difficult to look her in the face, gave her a letter from Drum.

There wasn't much to it. "You'll soon find out I was right. It's for the best. We were both too hasty. You're a lovely girl. The man who gets you will be a lucky chap. I'll always remember you and our time together, but it would never work out. Our lives are just too different. I'm too busy for marriage for years." Clipped, polite, final.

Relief washed over Drum when Obee reported to him, "De lady sh' be gone bac' through de air t' where sh' be from, Mastah. . . ." But there was nevertheless an emptiness about the place.

Without the tension and the sense of living on a high wire, uncomfortable though it had been, there was now a void, made even worse by Rose's obvious complacency—as if, with Alicia's removal, Rose now knew she never need fear any woman taking her place on the Hill.

Restless, frustrated, Drum started talking about leaving the island again. "Hell, I know it isn't a smart time to go," he told a group of oilmen gathered together for a late supper at Bill McMurtrey's one night, "but I've got to see how different groups live together in other parts of the world, before I can tell anyone how to do it here. . . ."

"Here, here, young fellah," said Josh Wilson, an oilman from Texas. "You're speaking a lot of sense. Communication, that's the key. If you don't know how the other half lives, you can't know how they think and it's their *thinking* that's half the trouble."

As they strolled in McMurtrey's garden, Wilson said, "Hey, Drum, what about you and me having a nightcap after this?" He winked. "I hear they've got some swell girls at this fancy place on the edge of town. What's it called—Le Plaisir Hotel?"

Drum looked stunned. "Oh, I don't think so, Josh. It's pretty trashy."

They were joined by a couple of other men, who along with Josh started to tease him, asking where "the action is, ol' boy?"

Reluctantly, Drum finally admitted that he'd heard Le Plaisir wasn't that bad. "I'll take you there, but if you don't mind, I'd rather not go in. It's a personal matter."

Was it ever! He knew Magdalen Finch had something to do with it, although from time to time he had also heard, even from the chief of police, that it wasn't really a brothel, more a high-class bar where you could meet a beautiful girl or two when your spirits needed cheering up. But Magdalen Finch! From what he'd heard of her, she was the devil incarnate, apart from what her baby-faced son had perpetrated as an accomplice to Jack Bracken.

By the time Drum drove Josh Wilson and one or two of the others to Le Plaisir, he'd had to put up with some good-natured ribbing. "If you haven't bedded anyone yet, young Drum, perhaps you're a backwoods boy, after all . . . in spite of your devil-may-care looks. Well, it's time you did, don't you think? I can promise you, there's nothing like a sweet pussy to give you sweet dreams. . . ."

Sweet pussy. It was a perfect description of Alicia's secret pink hole, and the more he thought about it, his fears lulled by McMurtrey's fine brandy, the more the idea of a nightcap and a little "action" at Le Plaisir didn't seem such a bad idea after all. However, there was still the problem of running into Magdalen Finch. He'd never set eyes on her, except in a newspaper photograph at the trial. Would she recognize him? Probably not, except also from newspaper pictures.

"All right, Josh," he said laughing, deciding to risk it. "I'll go in for a quick drink, but do me a favor first. See if the proprietress is in residence? I don't particularly want to run into her."

Josh winked and knocked on the ornate door. The shiny brass plate on which "Le Plaisir" was engraved slid back and Josh and the men beside him were inspected before the door was opened and they stepped inside. Minutes later Josh was back, beaming. "It's a swell joint, kid," he said, "and you're in luck. The proprietress—if you mean a Mistress Finch—is away for a couple of nights, but they assured me we will still be well taken care of."

Drum looked up and down the dark street furtively. No one about. Well, if the chief of police could go in without fear of blackmail, so could he.

Drum had to admit the place had charm. It wasn't gaudy. In fact it looked rather Oriental, with handsome jade ornaments and some good pieces of black carved furniture.

A girl with Chinese eyes and a full bosom asked the men if they'd enjoy the "specialty of the house—an unusual, Oriental massage treatment," and the Americans, winking at Drum, said they thought it might be very interesting. Drum shook his head and sat back, intending to wait for the men to return, when a demure little colored girl—she couldn't be more than twelve or thirteen Drum thought—came to sit at his feet.

Drum sat up stiffly. Surely, anyone this young couldn't be a prostitute? Trickles of perspiration started to run down his neck as she stroked his ankle with delicate hands, running her fingers lightly up and down his calf.

"Would yo' lik' more massage?" she whispered.

He was fascinated against his will. Everything about her was what he responded to most, the size of her wrists, the delicate neck, the tiny tendrils breaking on her glossy coffee-colored skin.

She led him up a small flight of stairs to the right of the drawing room. At the top was a room, in total contrast to the Oriental one he'd just left, dominated by an enormous white-lace-covered bed. The young girl was wearing a primrose-yellow dress that accentuated her coloring and slight, immature figure. To his amazement and before he could stop her, she had untied her sash and opened one fastener at the neck and stood before him totally naked, her skin shining, almost polished, her nipples painted vermilion.

"No, don't . . ." he said weakly. "You're too young. . . ."

"My name is Gloria," she said and jumped on the bed, patting it for him to lie beside her.

"You're too young," he began again, but already her deft fingers had unfastened his belt and his shirt and had begun to caress his penis with assured movements.

"Oh, no, no, no," he gasped as he realized with horror he was within seconds of coming.

"Not so quickly?" She stood on the bed, her feet on either side of his head so that her vagina was immediately over his face. He started to reach up, longing to insert himself inside her, but he hesitated, frightened.

Then his lust overcame everything. He pulled her down hard to sit on top of him, amazed to find his big rod pushed through her tiny vagina as if it were greased, every inch sucked by her flesh until he thought he was drowning.

How could he have thought making love to Alicia was the most marvelous experience in the world? This child, this girl-child, why he was already infatuated with her. To think what he'd been missing.

He stayed with her an hour, which passed all too quickly, making love. "Yo're a very beautif'l man," Gloria told him as she helped him back into his clothes.

"Gloria, I *must* see you again . . . but I can't come here. Will you see me somewhere else? You're very . . . special."

She looked at him soulfully. "Dere's dis rule. . . . I canna see any man away from dis house. Mistr'ss Magdal'n, sh' looks aft'r me."

"But I am not 'any man,'" Drum told her fiercely. "I will be your protector. Trust me. Do you know who I am?"

Gloria nodded simply. "I've seen yo' pictures in de paper. Yo're a wonderf'l man, I know. Yo're workin' for de people. I've read yo' articles. . . ."

There was a tap on the door. Gloria hastily stood up. "I mus' go now."

Drum looked at her longingly. "Please . . . is there a way?"

Gloria hesitated, then quickly wrote down an address in Barataria, adding, "Wednesday afternoon."

It was the beginning of many secret meetings at her mother's ramshackle house where Gloria came to give her part of her earnings and where Drum paid her an extra fifty, sometimes one hundred dollars— more money than Gloria's mother had ever seen—in order to keep her away all day.

Now Drum knew that although Gloria looked like a child, she was in fact sixteen and, as far as pleasing a man was concerned, had the experience of a woman twice her age. She told him with pride she had started her "apprenticeship" a year before when her mother, recognizing her beauty, had taken her to Le Plaisir, after learning it was a place where a talented, beautiful young girl could earn a fortune.

She was a born plaything, Drum told himself, and he loved her as he loved a puppy, a young rabbit or, more appropriately, a sleek, dark, young foal. He loved all young things, as he recoiled from the old and twisted and perishable. And he believed her when she told him he had been her first "real" client. Other men had been allowed to fondle and play with her, but she had allowed no one else to go further . . . yet.

Drum felt more relaxed than he'd ever felt in his life, more able to enjoy the beauty around him at Golden Hill, where everything he introduced was increasing profits just as everything he suggested to Gomes was also bearing fruit.

Not everyone congratulated him on his skillful maneuvers. As Drum well knew, one man above all others considered Gomes a traitor who had reneged on his promises to the masses and had become a tool of the "capitalist clique." That man was Roland Bracken, for Gomes was no longer "available" when Roland called, and Drum's privileged position at Gomes's side was an added insult to the incredible change that had come about in Roland's former colleague's attitude.

As Roland exploded to Uriah Butler, "Gomes will do anything now to bury the memory of his link to trade unions . . . and to his 'red past.'" It was the signal Butler needed, for he, too, rankled over the fact that although his party had managed to seat three members in the Council, he himself had been thoroughly defeated by Gomes when he'd fought him for Cipriani's seat. Headstrong and fearless, Butler stormed the Red House, Trinidad's Parliament Building, calling the people to join him in a massive new general strike.

The lull before the storm, Drum thought looking back, because the same week Uriah Butler went into action Gloria dropped a bombshell of her own.

It had been a particularly sensual afternoon, when their passion had grown to even greater intensity. At last sated and spent, Drum had lain back with his eyes closed, feeling a soaring sense of happiness as Gloria gently sponged and cleaned him, every touch still a caress. He had heard her speak, understood the words, yet for a few more seconds the world had retained its radiance . . . then reality.

"I'm expectin' yo' child."

He hadn't questioned her. The relationship was too honest for there to be any doubt, and in any case she had told him—and he believed her—he was still the only man whose semen she had allowed to enter her.

"You can't have the child," he'd said, explaining how an illegitimate child at this point would ruin his political future.

She hadn't argued. She hadn't challenged him or suggested the child need not be born illegitimately if he married her, but she had been adamant. "I mus' bear yo' child, Drum. I wan' yo' child. But no one will ev'r know it's yo'rs—on dat I giv' yo' mah solemn word."

During the next few weeks Drum tried to no avail to change her mind. When at last he began to see her trim young belly begin to swell, he knew he had to say goodbye.

It was too dangerous to go on seeing her. He couldn't marry her—there was no way he could explain her past in his future. She didn't ask for a penny, but through Josh Wilson, Drum invested a large sum in her name in a stock that he estimated should provide her and the child with a good income for life.

Uriah Butler was banned from the oil belt once more under the Emergency Ordinance Act because of his attempt to cause a major uprising. At the same time Roland Bracken set off on a speaking tour through the Caribbean ostensibly to preach West Indian unity. In reality he went on an important mission—to form a network of comrades, who thought as he increasingly did, comrades who would support him when the right time came to rise up against white domination.

Although after a month away he felt his trip had not been a total success, it did produce one notable achievement in the form of a wife—Emerald, a dazzling black girl he met and married in Barbados all in the space of three weeks—and who six weeks later announced she was pregnant.

At the same time Drum went with Gomes to Montego Bay, Jamaica, to attend a conference concerning the possibility one day of a Federation of the West Indies. While he was away, Gloria gave birth to his child, whom she called Naomi.

To Gloria's disappointment, although Naomi was a pretty baby, she gave no sign of her father's golden-skinned genes. Her skin was black.

How relieved Drum was when he finally heard the news. Aware of how close he had come to ruining any political future he might have, he stayed rigidly away. It wasn't easy. He loved Gloria in a way—and oh, how he missed the delights of her squirming delicious body. But after the Montego Bay conference, he realized more than ever how much power and influence the political life could offer—far more than his father had ever dreamed of.

Theo
1948

AREN'T you lonely?"

Magdalen knew the answer very well, but she felt impelled to ask the question, trying to get through to this stranger, who was her beloved son.

"Lonely?" Theo repeated the word as if it were a novel idea, something to be explored and assessed before an answer could be given.

There was a trace of pity in the smile he gave his mother. "I don't have time to be lonely, Mother, and"—he hesitated before saying what he felt he had to say—"except for . . . for . . . you, I have no one to miss."

As far as the eye could see, dense tropical forest stretched to the foothills of the Northern Range, which all but encircled the small plantation outside Arima that was now Theo's home and retreat from the world.

Even the palms immediately surrounding his simple whitewashed cottage were gru-gru palms, Magdalen noticed irritably, loaded with thorns, the only kind she couldn't help thinking that Theo probably felt able to tolerate, as he toiled from dawn to dusk, dedicated to carrying out his own form of penance.

How different she'd imagined it was all going to be that joyous day when, after months, years of trying to win his reprieve, the news had come through that prisoner 45772 Theo Finch was going to be released on parole for the remainder of his sentence. She'd known he couldn't live with her at Le Plaisir—that would scarcely have helped him stay on the straight and narrow path—but she hadn't expected him to want to turn into a monk either.

It was such a waste. As Magdalen looked at her son, at the gentle, yet almost always serious set of his mouth, the tousled thick dark hair touching his powerful shoulders, she felt like weeping, for she knew how much he disapproved of her, how repelled he was by the way she lived her life.

When she'd finally realized Theo was determined to be a hermit, to live by himself in the wilderness if it came to it, Magdalen had heard about a small property outside Arima, so remote it was almost being given away. She'd snapped it up, wanting to give it to Theo, telling herself that, after a few months of living a solitary life and thinking out his future, he would want to return to normality and live nearer to civilization . . . and to her. But Theo had been adamant that he couldn't accept the property in his name—knowing where his mother's now regular supply of money came from—and, after clearing what was necessary to get to the broken-down house in the center of the property, he'd become more, not less, of a recluse.

It was all because of the sanctimonious, interfering Jesuit. Magdalen shot a dark glance at the stocky Irish priest, Father O'Sullivan, who sat beside Theo on the rickety veranda, the man she knew Theo considered his best friend, responsible for saving his sanity while he'd been in prison.

As if reading her thoughts, as she sat smoldering, Father O'Sullivan yawned and slowly unwound his large frame out of the chair. "It's time we saw what young Theo has for us in his *canaree*, don't you think, Mistress Finch? I don't know about you, but I'm mighty famished after that journey in your fancy car. . . ."

She didn't like the way he called her Mistress Finch or the way he described her car as fancy. She didn't like the affectionate, familiar slap across the shoulders he gave to Theo either, but most of all, she decided, as Theo and he bowed their heads to say grace a few minutes later, she loathed the sneaky way he was always reminding Theo of God, of the differences between good and evil, almost linking them, she thought, to the difference between a life of poverty and prosperity. In some cunning way, by describing her proud new possession as a "fancy" car, she felt Father O'Sullivan was reinforcing Theo's contempt for the way she earned her money, whereas he positively beamed with approval at the sight of every new callus on Theo's hands.

From the moment they'd arrived, Magdalen had also been wondering how a man of God could drink so much rum . . . it didn't seem right. For a moment of happy daydreaming she wondered what would happen to Father O'Sullivan's soul if she were to lure him across the threshold at Le Plaisir? If he liked rum so much, did he like girls, too? Could she get him "undressed" and defrocked at the same time? The idea made her feel cheerful for the first time that day, but as she became aware of the Irishman's inscrutable eyes on her, she realized its futility.

Out of what the natives called a *canaree*—a huge earthenware pot blackened with age—came a delicious mixture of hot chicken, rabbit and vegetables, to be piled onto plates of steaming rice.

The *canaree* was a familiar sight in every plantation home, usually placed at lunchtime on a back veranda table to offer sustenance to anyone passing by, stranger, friend or workman. At this plantation home there was no back veranda and scarcely a front one, but Theo had revived the old country custom and there was a long table on which the old pot was placed daily, a table already known for miles around as "Mastah Finch's place for de poo' pussons."

As the afternoon went on, lulled by rum-and-milk cocktails and the soft, humid air, Magdalen found herself laughing along with Father O'Sullivan as he told the story of visiting a grand old plantation with a bishop from overseas. ". . . He approached the *canaree* with his nose just so"—the priest wrinkled his bulbous nose in an attempt to look fastidious—". . . plunged in the spoon and, on the Holy Father's name I swear, out came a tiny clenched fist."

Theo threw his head back and laughed until tears came into his eyes as O'Sullivan explained, "It took a devil of a time to convince His Grace that the fist belonged to a certain kind of monkey—a delicacy often eaten in the West Indies. . . ."

Although he'd enjoyed their visit, Theo heaved a sigh of relief when he saw the tail-lights of his mother's car finally disappear down the trail. For the last hour she had tried to persuade him to go back with them to Port of Spain . . . "for a rest." He shuddered at the thought.

"An owner's footsteps is a plantation's best fertilizer," he'd said light-heartedly at first, but as she'd become more insistent, he'd had to retreat behind straightforward refusals, until thankfully Joe O'Sullivan had come to his aid and insisted they leave before they were forced to risk their lives "negotiating the roads in the dark."

As he lit the kerosene lamps in the large shutterless room that passed for his living quarters, a swarm of flying cockroaches zoomed toward him. He smiled as he thought of his mother's squeals if she'd still been there. Once the insects might have troubled him, but not any more. After being incarcerated in that filthy dark prison, every evidence of nature in all its complex forms delighted him.

He had just settled down with Dylan Thomas's *Deaths and Entrances*, one of the books Father O'Sullivan had left him, when he heard a light tap on the screen door. Without looking up he said wearily, "Come in Zizi. . . ." It was an old Creole woman, one of his few regular companions, almost bent in two from years of carrying heavy loads on her back.

It was Zizi who'd helped reduce the swelling from a mosquito bite with a mixture of nutmeg, coconut oil and salt and it was Zizi who had taught him how to cure a number of ailments with natural potions, showing him how to use the bark of the cupre tree (princewood) to make bitters and leaves from soursop, lemon grass and benit to make teas for different purposes.

Now he knew she was bringing him samples of various plant oils he'd been experimenting with, using tonka beans to stabilize their fragrance . . . beans he shortly hoped to market as a key ingredient in the making of both perfume and pipe tobacco.

Long after the old woman shuffled out, Theo was still engrossed, testing his compositions, Dylan Thomas forgotten as he dipped long bamboo tapers into the different oils.

Lonely? His mother's question came back to him as, before he dived beneath his mosquito net, he stretched his arms up to the heavens outside, marveling at the magnificent southern constellation of stars. No, he wasn't lonely . . . or bored . . . or restless, or any of the things his mother expected him to be. She couldn't understand that he was only just learning how to live with himself, only now waking up without guilt tearing him apart . . . and it was only by driving himself relentlessly, using up every pound of his physical strength, that he'd been able to survive his freedom.

It was ironic. He'd spent the first year of his confinement planning to escape to "freedom," the second year, foiled in every attempt, slumped in despair. Then in the third, fourth and fifth years with Father O'Sullivan's arrival, he'd embarked on his voyage of self-discovery, beginning to see his participation in the crime for what it was . . . understanding his motive more clearly.

He didn't remember when remorse had first set in. It had been gradual, but one day he'd simply awakened to the fact that—although he still believed a miscarriage of justice had been perpetrated against his grandfather (and so his mother)—his way of righting that wrong had been much worse. His guilt had consumed him, even after his first confession when he'd expected to be miraculously relieved of the burden. . . .

When his mother had brought about his release and he'd learned for the first time how she'd been able to exert such influence—it was then that the ugliness of life had overshadowed everything else.

He'd climbed to the highest peak on the island and looked down to where the Northern Range unfolded itself in a myriad of mysterious ridges and craters to the flat central plain in the south, falling steeply into the white surf of the ocean in the north. He'd seriously contemplated jumping off into the yawning emptiness, but he hadn't, thinking of Father O'Sullivan's belief in him and of his mother's grief, although he could not condone the "compromises" she'd made on his behalf.

From then on he'd decided to use his body to the point of pain as a way to get rid of his guilt, using physical ordeal to subdue mental anguish.

And now at last he *was* beginning to live again, finding he loved to study long into the night, just as he'd enjoyed it as a little boy, but now studying the extraordinary, exotic flora, fauna and geological wonders of his own land, learning how to extract its treasures, hopefully for the benefit of others.

While Magdalen's driver negotiated the narrow twists and turns of the trail, Father O'Sullivan extolled Theo for his determination to turn such a tangled wilderness into a paying plantation. They could see the signs of his endeavors as one neat area devoted to coffee, the tender plants about two years away from bearing berries, gave way to a group of breadfruit trees, and then a grove of citrus, shaddocs, limes, lemons . . . every few yards came fresh evidence of Theo's backbreaking toil.

Magdalen said nothing. What good would it do to tell the priest she thought it was all a terrible waste. As her driver neared the main road and got up speed, she shut her eyes, hoping her companion would soon stop talking, but, just as if he could see her mind working away behind her closed eyelids, Father O'Sullivan didn't give up—harping on Theo's qualities, hoping she was proud of him, ". . . as I venture to say you should be, Mistress Finch. . . ."

It was too much. As they approached the city, passing the turn to Maracas Valley and Golden Hill, a low-slung sports car crossed in front of them and they could clearly see Drum Pollard's handsome golden head behind the wheel.

Father O'Sullivan turned as if to comfort her, even patting her shoulder as he said, "You need never worry about Theo and the Pollards again. He understands why he acted as he did. He will work out there in Arima until he feels he's done his penance and is ready to join the world as a first-class, God-fearing citizen."

Magdalen said sharply, "Penance! My son has already long ago paid his dues. He should never have been arrested in the first place. He was a child, even younger than Drum Pollard, and remember"—Joe O'Sullivan was startled by the harsh rasp of her voice—". . . remember the Pollards *did* steal my family home, Golden Hill, the place that Drum Pollard is heading to now, where *Theo* rightfully belongs."

"Now, now, Mistress Finch . . ." Father O'Sullivan interrupted hastily.

"I don't want a sermon. I've said my piece. I'm not saying any more . . . other than I consider it's more of a crime that my son should be slaving himself to death in the backwoods, than anything that ever happened to the Pollards!"

Thank God, thought Father O'Sullivan, as they neared his church, thank God Theo is so far away from his mother's influence. May he stay away from her as long as she lives!

The fact that Magdalen had seen Drum Pollard in the flesh for the first time that evening, instead of the likeness she'd grown used to seeing in print, was a lucky break for Roland Bracken, who'd been trying to talk to her for months.

At first Roland hadn't seen much significance in the fact that Drum's half brother Roger had rushed off the island, to be followed a couple of months later by his fiancée, but servants listen and talk and little by little some of the stories behind the departures had filtered back to Roland. The facts were interesting and possibly useful—as far as Roland was concerned, because not too many days after the Honorable Alicia's departure, according to a member of his brother James's steel band, the Sunbeams, Drum had been seen leaving Le Plaisir, not the kind of place usually patronized by a young political hopeful. . . .

Did it mean his nephew had a natural, but nevertheless potentially dangerous flaw? Roland had put all the pieces together and come up with zero, but he told James, who in turn told the Sunbeams to keep their eyes and ears open for any news about Drum Pollard's possible sexual weaknesses . . . and hopefully indiscretions. When nothing turned up, Roland had decided to approach Magdalen Finch herself, a woman he'd avoided since the events of 1941, but now, he'd reflected, possibly a woman who might be just as interested as he was in pulling a Pollard off his lofty pedestal.

She hadn't been easy to get to, but Roland had persevered, first with a letter, then with telephone calls and finally another letter.

It was strange, Magdalen thought, annoyed with herself, as she now sat uneasily in her private sitting room waiting for Roland Bracken to arrive, how just one glimpse of the golden-haired boy had so quickly crumbled her opposition to the idea of letting a Bracken come even within spitting distance. His name was anathema, despite her common sense nagging her with the irrefutable fact that Roland Bracken was rapidly becoming a force to be reckoned with in the black community—and one would have had to be an idiot or a nun in a closed order not to recognize the growing power and influence of the blacks.

However, none of that reasoning had made her answer the letters or phone calls. It was knowing Roland wanted to talk to her about Drum Pollard after seeing Drum so unexpectedly that day that had made her suddenly decide to find out what it was all about. Now, in her mind's eye she had two images: the sweating, calloused hands of her son, swiping away at the undergrowth, and the smooth, tanned hands of Drum Pollard on the wheel of an expensive car. . . .

Magdalen was impressed. Roland Bracken wasn't a good-looking man, but in minutes it was easy to forget his homely appearance and appreciate that here was a man of superior intelligence and of maturity beyond his years.

To Roland's disappointment, however, Magdalen told him that although Drum had indeed visited Le Plaisir she hadn't been there at the time and as far as she could establish, as she put it haughtily, "He didn't take advantage of any of our services. . . . I am sure he hasn't been back. I only wish I could be of more help."

Roland knew she meant it and looked at her reflectively. "Perhaps you can one day."

It hadn't taken him long to see beneath Magdalen's prim lady-of-the-manor exterior. Underneath, he suspected, she burned as he did, with a sense of injustice. Her reason was different, but their cause was the same.

She hated the Pollard name because it represented all that she had lost. When Magdalen spoke of Theo—the "rightful heir" as she called him that afternoon—tears came into her eyes. "He thinks he has to kill himself with work, doing penance for a crime Piper Pollard brought entirely on himself. . . ."

It was a relief to be able to show his emotions to this woman, so volatile beneath her "madam" role, but Roland's voice was icy rather than heated as he told her, "I hate Drum Pollard, too. He's a hypocrite, like his father always was. . . . His approach to my family—his offer of forgiveness, of a reconciliation—bah!" He almost shouted out the words. "Sheer hypocrisy . . . an attempt to crush my opposition . . . to convince the people of his impartiality to color . . . yet he managed to manipulate my refusal to acknowledge his hypocritical offer into a triumph for himself! He uses the landowning press, who instead of exposing him as an imposter, eulogize him . . . turning him into a young hero! It's contemptible."

Roland felt shaken when he left Magdalen. It was unusual for him to unleash his feelings, to show, let alone speak about, the deep loathing her felt for his sister and her son, who so far had managed continually to rub his nose in the dirt.

Grimly, Roland went to his next meeting with Luis Delorso, a new friend he'd met in Cuba during a Caribbean tour with Uriah Butler. Luis had introduced himself and congratulated Roland on his speech, which, he said, had made clear the many diabolical and cruel acts of the British in the colonies, carried out under the guise of leadership but against all humanitarian values. Roland knew now that Luis was a Communist, but what of it? At least he was not a hypocrite. He believed in what was really true democracy, in "share and share alike," and to Roland's gratification the more they met, the more Luis seemed to think he had it in him to lead the Trinidad people.

This afternoon Luis had grim news. In the South African elections the war hero Field Marshal Jan Smuts had been defeated by the Nationalist Afrikaaner bloc favoring apartheid, separation of the races. ". . . And you know what that means, my friend," said the silky voiced Cuban. "It's a deplorable state of affairs and there's even worse news. The Jews are in the ascendancy once more—despite all Hitler tried to do to get rid of them. The Jewish capitalists have again scored, getting just what they want—a State of Israel—and with a push and shove, out into the desert go thousands of our Arab brothers homeless, in despair. . . ."

Roland sat with his head in his hands. "It doesn't make sense. The majority lose, the minority win. How can we make sure the majority win *here* one day, Luis? And don't tell me 'have patience'! That's what Gomes said and look where that traitor is now, licking the boots of the capitalists, the white elite!"

"You're two years away from the next election, Rollo. You have two years to win a place in the next Legislative Council and that might well be as a member of Butler's party . . . but the people know you already as a more reasonable, shall we say . . ." Luis tweaked the cuffs of his shirt away from his sweating wrists and went on, ". . . more likely candidate. . . ."

As he spoke, the Cuban opened his wallet to take out several hundred-dollar bills. "You also have two years in which to discredit your old colleague Albert Gomes. It won't be easy, but remember he has a 'red past' to live down." Luis allowed himself a soft laugh. "I think you must make sure that he does not live it down. It's the one thing the capitalists are terrified of, and we know how to cause dissension among the trade unions, don't we? Because of Gomes, it's just one more step to start spreading the idea that other United Front members are 'Moscowphiles.'" Luis handed Roland the wad of bills. "This will help you spread that dissension and build your base at the same time. Count on me for more support as time goes by, and toward the end of the year you must return to Cuba with me to meet more people who think as we do."

Roland was smiling when he left Luis an hour later. His earlier feelings of helplessness had gone and even the unwelcome news Emerald gave him that against his advice his younger brother, James, had decided to marry an uneducated mulatto girl named Carmelita didn't dispel his optimism.

Luckily, he had enough brains for all the family. It meant he would simply have to watch them to make sure they caused him no embarrassment. And when the time came for him to assume power, he'd make sure James never went near a steel drum again and little April married the man of his choice not hers.

As Emerald held their baby son—whom Roland had perversely insisted on naming Jack—to her ample black breast, Roland visualized the life young Jack would have one day, so different from the one lived by his namesake uncle. It would be a life of the best schools, the best houses, travel, experience . . . and, if he wanted it, a job at his father's side, learning how to administrate and govern.

"For God's sake, Alicia, turn that infernal machine off. You're driving me barmy." The Earl of Chingford rustled the pages of the *Sunday Times* vigorously as if to shut out the sound of "Some Enchanted Evening," Alicia's current favorite song, which she'd been playing on the gramophone for the past hour.

The needle screeched across the record's surface as she abruptly shut off the gramophone and the phone started to ring. Shortly afterward Bins, the only family retainer left at Chingford Hall, knocked on the library door to announce, "A Mr. Roger Pollard on the telephone for Miss Alicia."

"Tell him, I'm not at . . ."

Her uncle cut across her with a note of rising temper. "Alicia, I must insist you face up to your obligations. I'm tired of you refusing to speak to him. Tell him what you've told me—that you don't want to see him again. Get it over with, girl!"

Alicia was defensive when she returned. "Unky, don't be cross. I got talked into meeting him tomorrow. Somehow he's managed to get two tickets to the Olympic Games. You know how I've longed to go . . . and anyway, he's talking about going to the States, so this will really be goodbye."

Robin Chingford heaved an exasperated sigh. "Well, as long as you don't go back to golliwogg land—but don't get talked into anything else, or I'll wash my hands of you and that means no more allowance—I mean it!"

I won't get talked into anything, Alicia thought as the next evening she sat with a demure expression facing Roger in the American Bar at the Savoy. Thank heavens, they hadn't been able to talk much at Wembley Stadium, where in the crush of thousands of bodies they'd watched the U.S. team win most of the medals.

After a half hour of desultory conversation Roger said desperately, "Alicia, can't we start again? I'm sure it was as much my fault as yours. . . ." His earnest, hangdog expression made her feel sick, but Roger didn't see the scornful look in her eyes. He leaned toward her. She wasn't withdrawing. Perhaps it was all going to be all right after all. "Now, you know what a bloody rotter that half brother of mine is—I should have beaten him into a pulp— We'll never go back to that crazy hothouse. Come with me to the States. I'm going to go after my original idea. . . ."

Words had started to rush out of him, but at the mention of Drum's name a flush crept up Alicia's neck to her face. "I won't have you speak of your brother like that," she almost hissed. "There's no way we can *ever* start again! Don't think I wanted to leave that . . . that 'hothouse' as you call it. I wanted to stay . . . to stay. . . ." Tears bubbled out of her eyes, and she didn't attempt to stop them, oblivious to the curious looks directed their way. "I love him and he loves me—get that into your thick, boring head!"

Roger went white. He pushed his way blindly out of the bar to the men's room. He wanted to be sick, but he was unable to get it up, just as he wouldn't be able to get the whole episode out of his head for days, weeks.

When he went back to the bar she'd gone. He walked until dawn, wrestling with his longing to go after her, to knock down the door of her flat, to push his way into her bedroom . . . into her—but finally defeated, broken, he went back to his rented flat and drank himself into a stupor.

What was he going to do with his life? Six weeks later General Foods in the States offered him his old job back—but there was nothing in that to take his mind off the disease that still afflicted him, the disease of Alicia.

He was tempted to see what was available in England, but he knew Alicia was his real reason for staying around—and he also knew he'd end up suffering, with the humiliation just getting worse. Then there was nothing about the British economy that gave one much hope for building a future: with the railroads being nationalized and national health . . . soon there'd be no private sector of investment left!

Roger was on his way to Thomas Cook to book a passage to New York when the postman stopped to give him a large packet sent on by the faithful Watkins at Golden Hill. Because of the packet's size, Roger decided to go back to his flat to go through the contents first, although even the sight of the Trinidad stamps on the envelope gave his stomach a twinge.

The first thing he took out was a newspaper clipping with the black face of Uriah Butler grinning out. "Butler lionized by the British Press, says he is looked upon as 'the man of the hour from the colonies' . . ." The foreman had scribbled across it, "God help us if it's true. . . ." Well, it wasn't true, Roger thought wearily, but he was too emotionally exhausted to write back and let Watkins know he didn't have to worry about Butler's influence.

Inside the clipping was a thick envelope with a Texas postmark addressed to him at Golden Hill. Texas? Who did he know in Texas? He slit open the envelope without much interest to read a letter from the United Texas Oil Group, signed by the chairman of the board, W. William Lovell, expressing interest in leasing land at Cedros, which they understood belonged to him free and clear, with the intention of commencing as soon as mutually satisfactory an oil drilling program there.

In dry concise terms the letter indicated the company had already found oil on the land immediately to the east of the Cedros property, which was producing "an average of 12,000 b/d from 60 wells (see full details attached)." Roger then saw a number of technical papers and geological surveys had been attached to the letter. Mr. W. William Lovell proposed a meeting "at the earliest possible opportunity to discuss a partnership arrangement we believe will be of interest to you."

In the last paragraph it was suggested Mr. Pollard call the head office in Dallas "collect" in order to make travel arrangements to bring him to the States, as due to Mr. W. William Lovell's disability he found it difficult to travel far.

Roger's head was reeling. Oil. Texas. It added up to money, big money, the kind his father had enjoyed from the moment he struck oil as a young man. Oil meant houses like Golden Hill, Bentleys, travel and any woman a man might want. He looked at his watch. It was too early to call America. What was it, six or seven hours behind—for all he knew Texas might be even further back in time.

He was about to call Alicia with the big news, but the memory of her sharp young voice scarred his mind. It wouldn't make any difference to her opinion of him. It would be years before the memory of her cruel words would fade.

Forty-eight hours later, United Texas had accomplished the impossible. Although every travel agent in London had told him all flights to the States were booked for weeks ahead, Roger found himself arriving at New York's new Idlewild International Airport, only dedicated by President Truman a few weeks before. Well, that was apparently the way oil money could influence the world.

The next day the longest car he'd ever seen was at Dallas Airport to meet him. When he inquired of the brawny chauffeur what kind of vehicle he was getting into, he had trouble interpreting the drawl, but

he finally managed to understand "a sixteen-cylinder Cadillac, sir. . . ."
The car pulled up outside a neat privet hedge about twelve feet high
with an iron gate set squarely in the center.

This, he was told, was Mr. W. William Lovell's office residence—
whatever that meant. Roger was disappointed. After the waving of
wands to get him the transatlantic ticket and the sixteen-cylinder Cadillac, he'd expected at least a house the size of Buckingham Palace, but
behind the gate was a squat two-story building with a small portico that
could have fitted into Golden Hill's massive entrance half a dozen
times.

He wasn't disappointed for long. When he entered through the brass-
studded front door he came face to face with elevator doors, and, when
he knew W. W. better, he understood why the "office residence" had
been built on top of a ridge, with all the major rooms spread down the
side of a hill at the back leaving only the entrance hall, secretary's office
and bedroom on top for the world to see.

W. W. had a mania for secrecy—especially where it concerned his
private life. As he had told Clare—his only child—from infancy,
"Never tell anyone anything they don't need to know . . . and only five
percent of the rest. No one can be trusted in this goddamn world,
Clare, and that goes for you and me, too."

From the minute Roger stepped into the elevator with its dark green
leather walls and gold push buttons to go down five floors to his bedroom, where two pretty Filipino girls in white uniforms unpacked his
one bag, he realized he was indeed in another world.

Even Hollywood can't be as luxurious as this, he thought an hour
later, as he stretched out in a whirlpool bath, a glass of his favorite
whisky on the side. He'd found his usual brand of cigarettes in an onyx
box on the desk, too and—he'd really gasped when he'd seen it—even a
day-old copy of the *Trinidad Guardian* with . . . yes, there he was
flashing his "film star" smile, a picture of Drum Pollard on the front
page shaking the hand of the British secretary for the colonies. Roger
received a certain amount of pleasure tearing the paper in two, so that it
severed Drum's head from his body.

Wrapped in a thick toweling robe with a large dark blue L on the
back, Roger looked moodily out across the Texas countryside, wondering what Alicia would think of it all. She'd probably turn up her snob-
bish little nose at the "flagrant ostentatious show!" The phone trilled in
a strange high-pitched way and a voice with a strong Texan accent said,
"Hi, there, Mistah Pollard. Glad you could come. Let's meet in my

study—on the third floor—in, say, thirty minutes? Does that suit you? It's the door to the left of the Renoir painting, young fellah."

Roger was amused. Did thirty minutes suit him? What other pressing appointments did W. W. think he might have? The door to the left of the Renoir, eh? Was that to tell him the Lovells were a cultured lot? Or was he being tested himself? If so, he wasn't sure he'd know a Renoir if he saw one, but he didn't have to worry. As the elevator doors opened on the third floor, a black-coated manservant led the way down a corridor lined with paintings of every kind and at the end a diminutive, darkly tanned man leaning on a silver cane extended his hand. "Welcome, Mistah Pollard. I hope you're rested from your journey. We've got a lot of talking to do. . . ."

That was an understatement. By the time twenty-four hours had passed Roger had never done more talking or more listening—not realizing the few facts W. W. Lovell let loose had been carefully calculated to bring about in the quickest possible time Roger's acquiescence to all W. W. wanted.

So Roger learned that the "gusher" W. W. had brought in back in the late thirties in eastern Texas had already produced more than a million barrels of oil—almost as much as that produced by the field in Rusk County purchased by his closest competitor, H. L. Hunt from wildcatter Columbus Joiner, which Roger learned had made Mr. Hunt the richest man in America.

"How would you like to be the richest man in the Caribbean?" Lovell asked suddenly in a deceptively soft voice. Seeing little reaction he went on, "In Britain? Does money interest you at all, Mr. Pollard?" He laughed without humor as Roger nodded in what he hoped was a casual way.

Where was all this leading? It was leading finally to the offer of a leasing arrangement of the Cedros land, to be renegotiated after five years, in which Roger would receive in the currency of his choice the equivalent of two thousand U.S. dollars a month, and—with United Texas bearing the cost of the expensive drilling operations they wished to commence—one-eighth of any emanating oil or gas royalties.

Roger didn't know what to say. He looked around the room as if seeking someone to ask for advice, but of course there was no one. Finally he said slowly, "It sounds fair . . . but . . . but I'd like to think about it." He really didn't know why he said what he said. With a five-year guaranteed two thousand a month, on top of the allowance he already received, he didn't need to be a mathematician to realize he

would be very comfortably off, although scarcely the richest man anywhere except in Laventille . . . but that was whether United Texas
struck oil or not. If they didn't, he knew the land could still eventually
be put back into shape for agricultural purposes. And if they *did* strike
oil . . .

The manservant appeared at the door, and although Lovell never said
a word Roger realized he was being dismissed.

The next morning when Roger went to the breakfast room on the first
floor at the foot of the hill, with a heart-shaped swimming pool outside,
there was a typed note, signed by W. W., beside his plate. "We haven't
any more time to waste," it stated. "My daughter Clare will show you
around this morning and we have to come to a decision this afternoon."

There was nothing for it but to go along, but Roger sighed aloud at
the prospect of the sightseeing trip ahead.

"Good morning." It was a Lauren Bacall slow drawl and he turned to
see a tall, golden-skinned blonde in a skimpy two-piece bathing suit
observing him from the breakfast-room door. "Daddy tells me you'd like
to see our town?"

If he closed his eyes he could make believe it really was Lauren
Bacall standing there, the voice was so amazingly similar, as soothing
and seductive as he'd heard it in *Key Largo*.

His spirits perked up. Daddy's daughter might turn out to be an interesting guide after all.

In another Cadillac—this one deep brown with CCL on the license
plate—they drove past the Lovell Foundation Medical School, the
Lovell Library, the W. W. Lovell Institute of Petroleum Studies . . .
and all the while in the same "take-it-or-leave-it" careful drawl, Clare
Cordelia Lovell made Roger realize that when Daddy Lovell thought oil
was in the ground, there always *was* oil in the ground and everybody got
rich. By the time they returned to the house he'd decided "what the
hell," he'd go along with Lovell's offer. What did he have to lose?

But for some convoluted reason—due perhaps to the part of his
character that had never forced the issue with Alicia—when Roger sat in
front of W. W. again, he didn't immediately sign the lengthy document
pushed toward him. How glad he was later that he hadn't.

And without realizing it, Roger won the grudging respect of the tough
old oil man by not signing right away. So he isn't the simple simon he
appears, W. W. thought, as he looked piercingly at the apparently self-
contained, neat-cropped product of Trinidad, an English public school
and the Canadian Air Force. He looks as if he doesn't quite grasp the

enormity of the project ahead, yet at the same time there isn't the semblance of greed about the man. Why was he dawdling?

W. W. did an unusual thing. He jumped to the wrong conclusion.
"All right, young fellah," he barked. "So you're wondering about the
seven-eighths-to-one-eighth arrangement after five years, eh?" Roger
said nothing, just stared out of the window behind Lovell's hunched
back to where, in the distance, he could see a puff of smoke from a train
disappearing into a tunnel.

Lovell barked into an intercom, "Come here, Miss Docker." An elderly woman, as tanned and wrinkled as her boss, came into the room
with notebook at the ready, and at breakneck speed Lovell dictated an
addendum to the lengthy arrangement. ". . . If oil is struck at Pollard's
Cedros field, at the end of five years the United Texas Oil Group will
have the option to buy the property owned by Roger P. Pollard at
Cedros, Trinidad, West Indies, for seven hundred thousand dollars
cash, fifty thousand dollars in short-term notes and a guarantee of one
million dollars from future production. In the event Roger Pollard is
unwilling to sell, a review will be made of the present one-eighth landowner's oil or gas royalties, the review to favor the owner, Roger P.
Pollard, with the United Texas Oil Group still to receive the larger
share."

Roger beamed with pleasure. He hadn't thought further than five
years, but now he realized if he'd signed the document before this addendum was added that after five years he might have had trouble receiving any oil or gas revenues at all, with W. W. Lovell easily proving
United Texas had put up all the money for the drilling—which Clare
had told him dryly could easily run into millions of dollars with 90
percent of most wells drilled coming up dry . . . "except for those
Daddy chooses to drill!"

Alicia read the news in the *Daily Express*, stifling a "Good God" as she
saw Roger's earnest expression looking out at her.

"In a joint statement issued today by the United Texas Oil Group and
Mr. Roger Pollard, a major oil discovery has been located on a coconut
plantation owned by Mr. Pollard in the southernmost part of Trinidad
known as Cedros. Mr. Pollard entered into a partnership agreement
with the United Texas Oil Group six months ago after being approached
by W. William Lovell, the American multimillionaire whose fortune is
said to be derived from successful oil exploration. From seismic studies

already carried out, Mr. Pollard intimated the Pollard/Cedros field will far exceed the production of anything found in Trinidad to date."

There was more, much more, putting Alicia in such a bad temper she had to have another steadying cup of tea. So Roger was going to marry an oil heiress, a woman apparently so special and so rich her ailing father had had to chase away numerous fortune hunters (the reason she was still unmarried at nearly thirty), until at last this noble, selfless colonial had come along to prove his worthiness! By the time she'd read the story two or three times Alicia felt so depressed she pushed aside the teapot and made herself a gin and tonic.

It had all happened so quickly. After Roger had signed the document with the addendum neatly typed at the bottom, there had been a celebration party at the Lovell Ranch, near Guthrie, where to his embarrassment, Roger had found he'd been expected to wear a ten-gallon hat and ride a bucking bronco.

Following a cutting horse display, a feast had appeared, liltingly described by Clare as a "real down-home Texas barbecue," complete with guacamole, chili beans, ribs, tostadas ("fried corn tortilla chips," Clare had explained), biscuits and handmade flour tortillas.

Roger and Clare had found themselves talking like old friends, and before the interminable night was over—Texans, Roger was sure, were too insecure to go to bed at any normal hour—he'd made plans to fly with her to Los Angeles for the weekend, where she'd told him with a trace of wistfulness, she'd once hoped "to make it as an actress." It was Daddy who'd stopped that little venture—just as he'd stopped her making so many wrong decisions, Clare had told him in a spare, flat voice.

A month later Clare went to her father's study to tell him she'd decided to marry the shy, yet strong man from the Caribbean. She saw without surprise that for once he didn't look as if he intended to oppose the idea.

She knew why . . . and it was a Clare Roger wouldn't have recognized who drawled sarcastically, "Are you really going to let your 'darlin' daughter' off the leash, Daddy darlin'? Do you trust this one at last? Are you beginning to realize time's running out . . . that your little gal hasn't many years left to get herself pregnant and present you with an heir?"

Her voice harshened as her father tried to will her with his eyes to shut up, but she was warming up to her subject. "Don't you wish now you'd let me have that bastard son when I was seventeen? It was a boy, you know, that you made those fucking doctors take out of me! So his father was only a 'no-good out-of-work actor after my money,' but that baby was a boy!" She started to laugh hysterically, as Lovell's face twitched with rage, and he picked up his cane as if to slash it across her face.

She stepped back toward the door. "D'you know you don't frighten me any more, Daddy. Even if I had your chauffeur's baby in my belly today, your raunchy ignorant cowhand chauffeur, I'd take so much care of it, I'd make sure you and your bunch of Nazis could never, never get near me to drug me and kill my baby. . . ." Her father slumped against his chair, all semblance of power out of him.

"I'm going to marry Roger Pollard." Now, she spoke in her usual languid drawl. "He's the gentleman you said you were saving me for. He's an innocent, but he's strong. He'll give me a son to fight you with—to pay you back for all"—her voice broke as she went on— ". . . all the rotten tricks you've played on me. . . . I'm going to marry so I can leave your torture chamber and live my own life. . . ."

"With your lesbian friend?" Self-possession had returned and her father barked out the words, not expecting the reaction he received.

Clare went over to his desk, leaning toward him with a thin smile. "You mean your devoted nurse? Well, Daddy darling, Victoria is a little tired of helping your sick old body. Yes, that's a good idea. Perhaps Victoria will make her home with us. . . ." She swung out of the room, her long skirt swirling around her thin ankles, elated she'd managed to get the better of the man she both adored and detested, who'd ruled her as he'd ruled her mother—with an unrelenting, totally selfish will. It had killed her mother's spirit and finally her body, too. She wasn't going to let that happen to her. Roger Pollard wasn't exciting, but he had a stoicism, guts, the kind she'd make sure he'd use to stand up against her father, until he became a force in the oil business himself. And he'd give her a son as strong and as stoic as he was—so she'd never have to worry again about her father's threats to throw her out penniless.

And Victoria? Clare ran her tongue across her lips. Her father had been wrong. Nothing had happened between them. When he'd come unexpectedly into Victoria's room that day the young nurse had simply been showing her the kind of embroidery she could do, lifting up the skirt of her uniform to show her the stitches that edged her cami-knickers. Yes, Clare had had her fingers on the cheap material, so her knuckles had touched the warm skin of the nurse's thigh, but that was all.

Did he love his wife? As he shaved in the elaborate marble bathroom of the Lovells' Eaton Square flat in London, Roger asked himself the question he'd been asking himself since he slipped his mother's ring onto Clare's finger. Sometimes he wondered if he'd been imbibing a slow-acting drug during the days he'd spent in Texas, because when he went over all that had happened, he still couldn't work out what had given Clare the idea he wanted to marry her.

He liked her. He admired her easy charm, the touch of Texan earthiness buried beneath her cool, reserved drawl, but love her?

If love was the destroying hunger he felt for Alicia (a hunger he'd pushed so deep inside him, with the fast-paced life he now lived, there were even days he forgot it was there) then, no he didn't love Clare. But he hoped that wasn't love—for now he realized most of the time it had only given him the kind of misery his love for his father had given him; unrequited, meant to cause pain.

He didn't long for Clare's touch, but she seemed to long for his . . . and that was all right, too. It was, in fact, quite wonderful to be wanted, instead of wanting. . . .

For once, even the thought of Drum's imminent arrival at their cocktail party didn't depress him. As a matter of fact, if he was honest, he was looking forward to showing Drum the kind of life he now lived, to impress on him how thankful he was not to be stuck in that colonial hellhole; instead to be independently wealthy—and getting wealthier every day—as well as universally respected, because he was in partnership with one of the most powerful men in the world.

Just as important, if not more so, Roger looked forward to showing Drum how his attractive sophisticated wife doted on him.

The Eaton Square party was the third Clare and Roger had given in the months following their Dallas wedding, with the two preceding parties given in two different capitals, Washington, D.C., and Paris.

"We have to do it, darlin'," Clare had told him with a light laugh. "Everyone wants to meet the man who finally got Daddy to let his lil' daughter go."

Although she'd laughed, Roger was already beginning to differentiate between the laughs that meant his wife was amused and the laughs that held quite a different meaning. He didn't pry. He realized he didn't want to dig into every crevice of Clare's mind, as he'd wanted to do with Alicia. If Clare wanted to tell him something, in time he knew she would.

Two hours later Drum felt distinctly ill at ease as he stood clutching a glass of champagne in a crush of strangers; the only faces he could recognize belonged to the rich and famous—like General Eisenhower, surrounded in one corner, and Gregory Peck in another. Even the airy way Clare had said to him, "How lucky we are to get Greg . . . he's in London for the opening of his new movie," had emphasized Drum's feeling of not belonging. He found he literally couldn't join in much of the conversation. He tried, but it was hopeless. No, he hadn't read *1984*, the book by George Orwell that apparently *everyone* in London had read . . . and no, he didn't know what to think about John Paul Getty obtaining the concession to drill for oil in the neutral zone between Saudi Arabia and Kuwait. He'd never heard of the neutral zone, let alone the man!

He tried to get near a pretty vivacious brunette waving a cigarette in a long holder, but every time he moved in her direction, he was blocked, and he gave up when he realized she was actually Princess Margaret, the sister of the heir to the British throne and so much prettier than her photographs.

To Drum's surprise, and growing irritation, he saw that Roger looked perfectly at ease as he moved from group to group, occasionally bringing someone over to introduce to Drum. He knows I don't fit in, Drum thought bitterly as people began to leave. When Clare asked him if he'd like to stay for a quiet supper—which Drum found still included notables like Charles Brannan, the U.S. secretary of agriculture, he made the excuse he had another appointment.

He cursed himself as he caught a taxi back to his hotel. He'd fallen headlong into the trap Roger had set, and it was obvious Roger had enjoyed every minute of his discomfiture, had reveled in the fact everyone he'd brought over to introduce to Drum had found him a "hick from the sticks," unable to talk about anything much—except the reason he was now in London so frequently, acting as a go-between for Gomes and the British Colonial Office. Who cared about Trinidad, or the West Indies for that matter?

As one languid English debutante had asked, "Where act-u-ally *is* Trinidad? Should one go there for one's holidays? I mean, ha ha ha, are the natives friendly?"

"No, they bite," he'd told her with satisfaction, disliking her as much for her affected accent as for the thick powder he could see layering her face.

What a fool he'd been; yet only that afternoon he'd been counting the hours until the party—thrilled to think Roger had forgiven him, when all Roger had wanted was an opportunity to show what a man of the world he was, a big fish in a big pond, whereas he, his little half brother, was only a big fish in a little pond.

Drum's jealousy grew as he read Clare and Roger's names in the *Times* a few days later among guests attending a private party at the American Embassy in honor of the king and queen of England.

It was then another name caught his attention in the obituary column farther down the page: "Lady Forrester, dead at 62. . . ." He skipped the details until he came to the name he was looking for, ". . . survived by her daughter the Honorable Alicia Forrester." Alicia. She would be able to help him negotiate the social hurdles. Drum decided he'd look her up, if only to take her out to dinner. With her he'd certainly know what to talk about—himself—and she'd love it!

He dashed off a note of condolence and mailed it to Chingford Park, Essex, before setting off for the Colonial Office, where he knew he faced the first of many long days, trying to get the British government to afford some protection to the island's sugar crop.

He got so caught up in meetings, it wasn't until he was on his way back to Trinidad with the beginning of a crack in the Colonial Office's hitherto stonewall attitude that he realized he hadn't followed up his letter with any attempt to see Alicia.

On his next trip to London before he even made contact with the officials he'd come to see, Drum looked in the London telephone book to see if Alicia was listed, and there she was . . . the Hon. A. F. Forrester in Curzon Mews.

"Oh, Drum. . . ." There was no mistaking the excitement in her voice. "What a lovely letter you wrote." She invited him for a drink the next evening. "But don't come before six. I've got a job, you know." She told him she was assistant features editor of *Harper's Bazaar*. "It's the kind of job that when you ask for a raise, they tell you to ask your family to increase your allowance."

The high-pitched, childlike voice that had scratched at his nerves in Trinidad seemed fresh and attractive here in London.

She belongs here, I was right, Drum thought the following evening, as, pert and pretty, Alicia mixed them both dry martinis, before showing him around her little mews house.

He saw her a couple of times after that, once for lunch and just before he left when she drove him out to Chingford Park, the ancestral home. She told him with no sign of regret that her uncle was selling.

"It's going to become a boarding school. Uncle Robin thinks he's very lucky to be able to sell it. I've never really liked it, you know—it's too gloomy. When you think about living here and living at Golden Hill . . . well, you know what I mean."

Drum looked at her affectionately. Perhaps she really had felt something for Golden Hill after all.

This time when Drum returned to Trinidad, it was with the promise he'd be back in three months and would certainly let her know the date.

He was forging ahead as Gomes's emissary, able to report that it looked as though for the first time since 1937 the government was about to give in to repeated demands to modify the colonial governing system, with a plan that would mean in the 1950 election five elected officials would run five key ministries, although the British governor would still retain ultimate responsibility.

It was a major step toward self-rule, but as Drum wrote in the *Trinidad Guardian* before returning to London once more in the new year, "Administrative and intellectual skills are needed more than ever now, for at last we are to have a much stronger say in our own affairs. But for that healthy situation to continue we must unite and not fight among ourselves." It was a hopeless plea and Drum knew it.

Already there were one hundred and forty-one candidates for the eighteen seats available on the Council, and of those, ninety were "independents" all at variance with each other, while the other fifty-one carried different kinds of party labels.

When Alicia learned Drum was back in London, she persuaded her uncle to give a small dinner for him at the House of Lords. Drum was immensely gratified, the Eaton Square scene flashing into his mind. Roger may be able to attract American film stars and generals—and yes, even royal princesses, too, with his "new" oil-fortune background, he told himself smugly, but he, Drum Pollard, was being listened to because of his *own* brains and determination to be somebody.

It was snowing when they left the House of Lords and, to Robin Chingford's fury, his car was nowhere to be seen. While he went back inside to phone his London flat, Drum and Alicia walked up Whitehall trying to find a taxi.

By the time they found one and reached Curzon Mews, Drum was shivering, his thin tropical blood unused to the rigors of an English winter.

He was still shivering even after two brandies, and, as Alicia lit the gas fire, he found himself falling asleep. He awoke with a start, his body throbbing and sweating. "My God, I must go." He stood up as he saw the clock on the mantelpiece pointed to almost one o'clock.

"Oh, you can't go, Drum . . ." Alicia said quickly. "You'll be really ill if you try to get back in this blizzard." As if to emphasize her words, a mixture of snow and hail rattled against the windows.

"I can't stay here . . ." he began half-heartedly, but, without much more persuasion, feeling completely exhausted, he followed her up the stairway to the bedroom, where he hardly remembered slipping off his shoes and trousers and climbing between the sheets.

It was pitch black when he opened his eyes, wondering where he was, trying to focus on a familiar object. Suddenly he felt Alicia's breath on his cheek and realized she was in bed with him.

"Oh, Drum, oh, Drum. . . ." She was naked, as she had been that day by the tropical pool, and now in the soft down of the bed, her body was even more inviting.

Drum sighed. He couldn't resist her, yet it was a terrible thing, for he felt sorry for her, sensing the great love waiting there, a love he didn't, couldn't reciprocate.

"Are you still a virgin?" he whispered.

Alicia shook her head vigorously. "No, no. . . ."

"Are you telling me the truth?"

She cried yes as she began to stroke his penis into life. The moment was electric. He wanted to possess her—to do to her what she'd been asking for ever since the day at the cocoa shed.

"Is it safe?" he asked. "Are you protected?"

Her yes was as vehement as her no had been.

"Turn on your side," he commanded.

She hesitated, then turned obediently, whimpering in a way that aroused him more as he brutally pushed her buttocks apart to insert his penis, pushing until it found its way through to her vagina, his fingers all the while probing into her from the front, forcing her back again and again onto his rod.

She was screaming, but he didn't care. He shut out the noise, intent only on the gratification he was receiving. He wasn't even aware that she must have lied to him about her virginity as his penis broke through her hymen and became engulfed in a warm flood, coinciding with his own orgasm, which rocked the bed as he let loose the pent-up desire of months. They clung together in the darkness, with very different thoughts.

At last, Alicia was thinking, he loves me . . . while . . . How can I get out of here was Drum's thought before he fell back into a feverish sleep.

Alicia tried to stay awake, reliving the most glorious moment of her life—Drum's fingers on her body, his penis inside her—but the sound of his heavy breathing was so soothing, so comforting, she closed her eyes and in minutes was asleep, too.

When she awoke to the sound of snow falling from the roof, Drum was gone.

She searched for a note, for something, anything to show the love she was sure he now felt for her, but there was nothing . . . and she heard nothing, not in the days or weeks that followed, when like a madwoman she went from place to place, from hotel to hotel, from the Colonial Office to airline offices, trying to find him.

Eight weeks after the night they'd spent together the doctor confirmed what she'd prayed for. She was pregnant, and whatever happened Alicia vowed she would give birth to Drum's child.

"I'm going to Trinidad," she announced to her uncle. "Drum and I are going to be married."

"Hmph! Back to golliwogg land! You're out of your mind, Alicia." The earl looked at her wearily, knowing there was nothing he could do to stop her. She had her own money now, inherited from her mother. Still, he made one more effort. "Why are you going to Trinidad to be married? Isn't that rather an extraordinary thing to do? Just because Chingford Hall has gone, doesn't mean I can't give you the right send-off here, you know . . . because don't think I'm going to venture out to that fool's paradise. You know I can't stand the heat, let alone golliwoggs."

Alicia put her arms around her uncle's neck. "I know, dinkums. Perhaps we'll come back to be married all over again here, but you know Drum's a very important person over there and Golden Hill is . . . well, like a palace . . . so it's almost like marrying a young prince."

The more she spoke about it, the more she convinced herself it was all going to take place just as she described. The pain of not hearing from him—the way he'd left her so abruptly—receded, and Alicia saw herself at the altar in the chapel at Golden Hill with Drum gazing at her with blazing eyes as they exchanged their vows, the way he'd looked at her the day she'd gone cocoa dancin'!

The earl of Chingford couldn't understand why Alicia cried so much at the small party he gave to bid her farewell.

It disturbed him greatly, but then, he'd never pretended to understand women . . . which, after dealing with his sister-in-law and niece,
was the reason he'd decided long ago to remain a bachelor.

Drum had never seen Obee so agitated. His stomach started to turn over
as Obee almost fell down the main steps in his rush to reach him as he
got out of his car.

"Is it . . . my mother?" Drum felt the blood draining out of him.

Obee tried to get the words out, shaking his head vigorously. "No,
sah, no, sah . . . it's . . ."

"It's me, Drum."

He couldn't believe his eyes. There was Alicia, looking down at him,
standing demurely on the top step.

"Alicia. . . ." Now the blood was racing back, flushing his skin,
while nervous perspiration soaked his shirt. "What on earth are you
doing here?"

He waved Obee away as he stared at Alicia as if willing her to
disappear.

"I had to speak to you, Drum." She was outwardly composed, the
only sign of her agitation was her hands twisting together behind her
back.

"They've invented the telephone for that purpose." His voice was
cold, unfriendly.

"Oh, Drum. . . ." Her composure wavered for a split second, but she
quickly reminded herself that to succeed she had to show Drum she was
no longer unstable, but a mature woman, capable of helping, not hin-
dering his political chances.

He slowly walked up the steps as if to pass her, but she caught his
arm. "I have to speak to you."

He knew what she was going to tell him. Ever since his return—since
that crazy night when for some inexplicable reason he'd given in to her
need for him—he'd had a premonition, strengthened by every overseas
phone call, every letter with an English stamp he'd received. The only
thing he hadn't expected was to receive the news from her in person.

Like a doomed man, Drum followed Alicia to the veranda swing that
faced Mount El Tucuche, its summit starkly silhouetted against the sky.
He stared at the vista, waiting for her words to collapse the security
around him.

Alicia stumbled over the sentence she'd been practicing for days,
weeks, but perhaps it was a good thing she did. Her confusion touched

him the way she'd often touched him when he'd least expected it, triggering the nerve that made him view her with pity instead of exasperation. "You . . . you must know, Drum . . . I love you," she began.

He shook his head quickly as if to brush away a fly, steadfastly staring ahead, trying to remain unfeeling, unheeding.

"I know you don't feel as much for me but . . . you . . . you do . . . do love me a little, I know you do." Her voice grew more timorous as still there was no response.

A yellow bird dived to sip water from the alabaster wall vase full of hibiscus. So free, thought Drum. So spirited, youthful and innocent, all the things life should be, but never can be for human beings.

Then came the reason for her visit, the premonition translated into hard, unavoidable fact: "I'm . . . I'm carrying your child, Drum, our love child. . . ."

In his mind he could hear Gloria's voice . . . could see Gloria's earnest little face mouthing the same truth.

He put his face in his hands, his shoulders shaking with some sudden ague, and he instantly felt Alicia's arms wrap around him—like a lasso, wiry, steely, tying him to her forever.

"No. . . ." He jumped away to grasp the veranda rail. "No, no, no!"

"Drum, I'll be a good wife. I'll help you. I promise you, you'll never regret it. . . ." There were those arms again, those cloying, clinging arms with hands that, before he knew it, would be old hands, like his mother's holding him in bondage. Alicia started to sob so hard he felt her tears soak through his already soaked shirt.

Drum felt suffocated, buried alive. He tore himself away from her grasp to run along the veranda, down the steps into his car to drive away . . . anywhere, it didn't matter where. Oh, how could he have been so weak, so stupid? He drove toward the mountains, cursing himself for acting like an animal. He hated himself, his body, for letting him down, hating the potency of his seed that took root with such immediacy.

In the early evening, Drum arrived at Bill McMurtrey's, half sobbing, half shouting Alicia's news, which, the more he thought about it, the more ruinous it became to all his dreams and plans.

Piper's wise old friend heard him calmly, then said, "First, Drum, get yourself under that shower, man. Cool off—then we'll talk."

After the shower, over a tall glass of rum and soda, Drum, ashamed at his lack of control, and McMurtrey, determined to rub home the fact that a politician has to display control at all times, no matter how great his burdens, discussed Alicia's arrival and the devastating news she'd brought with her.

By the time Drum left McMurtrey's house some three hours later, he was a different man, returning to Golden Hill with a sense of duty, and regarding marriage to Alicia not so much as inevitable as expedient.

"Look at it from a pragmatic point of view," McMurtrey had challenged him. "Look at it as a job to carry out for your future, not as something that's going to destroy you. The young woman is the niece of an earl, right? Her uncle, you tell me, has already been very helpful to you, so we're not talking about some tawdry affair with a second- or third-rate tart, are we? You're young, not exactly ugly. . . ." The older man winked. "In other words, a man in your position, with your aspirations, is bound to be talked about . . . talk about women, loose living. . . . That kind of gossip can be silenced by the right kind of marriage to, shall we say, a woman beyond reproach?"

Drum winced, catching McMurtrey's shrewd glance. Did Bill know about Gloria? Was it possible? Had there been talk? A cold wave passed through his body, but the moment passed as McMurtrey slapped him across the back. "Always look on the positive side, m'boy. The Honorable Miss Forrester can be an asset to you—and to us and our cause. New doors will open. You never know . . . and"—he cackled—". . . if I remember rightly she's an attractive young thing. It's not as if you have to go to bed blindfolded. Well, you already know more about that than I do!"

Despite Rose's shrieks and curses and weeks of tension when Drum expected hourly to hear his mother had either jumped out of the window or had attacked Alicia with a machete, Drum stood fast in his decision to marry.

It was already late. He could see Alicia's breasts were fuller, supported by a brassiere for the first time in her life, while even her behind and, of course, her stomach, seemed rounder, much to his embarrassment.

The elder statesmen rallied round; Bill McMurtrey, in particular, spent one long afternoon trying to get Rose to see the wisdom of the match. After her husband's old friend left, Rose walked through the arbor, fragrant with the scent of pale yellow roses, leading to the chapel where in only a few days the detestable Alicia would become her daughter-in-law!

From the back of the chapel, Rose watched the preparations going on for the wedding and suddenly remembered vividly the long-ago day when *she* had joined Piper at the altar rail in the svelte, close-fitting dress that had been the talk of Trinidad for months after. Where was that dress now? Would it still fit her?

Tears filled her eyes. Of course, the dress had gone in the fire, along with all her hopes, and dreams . . . and now there was going to be a new mistress of Golden Hill.

As Rose returned to the house, anger built inside her so strongly that it sent her hunting through the racks of clothes in her wardrobe, then searching for the right colored silk to thread through a needle for the first time since Piper's death.

The same anger revealed to her the extent to which she had neglected her skin and hair, and the wasted look of her body.

It was too late to stop the wedding but, she vowed, it wasn't too late to show this stuck-up Honorable Miss that Rose Pollard was still the lady of the house and intended to remain so. Rose Pollard had shown the gentry once she was as good as any of them and now she would show one of their kind again.

As her needle flashed in and out of the elegant silk dress she'd selected as the one best able to show her standing in the community, she warmed to the task, putting a tuck here, a flounce there. Soon it would look fashionable but—more important—would give her the look of curves she'd unfortunately allowed herself to lose. She lost track of time as her enthusiasm for putting on a bold new face grew or, perhaps, she laughed softly to herself, it was more accurate to describe what she was doing as reviving her old face! She would show *them!* She would show *her* what Rose Pollard was capable of. She washed, cut and straightened her hair in the methodical way she'd once always done. There were silver hairs among the black. She nipped some out, left others, thinking they gave her a look of dignity. She wasn't trying to look like the belle of the ball. She was *going* to look like the mistress of Golden Hill.

There were lines on Rose's face she couldn't nip out. But then there were new cosmetics she'd heard of that could give a more natural glow to skin than the old pot of rouge she'd used so carelessly on Drum's twenty-first birthday. She sent Obee out to buy as many new American magazines as he could find, magazines like Vogue, that showed one so cleverly how to apply colors the right way. She studied the pages excitedly—reminded of the days she'd worked so painstakingly with the tutor installed by Piper to correct her speech and teach her how to behave like a lady. Now, she was teaching herself how to *look* like a lady again, instead of some poor old ragbag, easily swept into the dust heap by someone as dangerous and determined as the Honorable Alicia Forrester! As she practiced using the cosmetics Obee bought at her direction, every stroke on her face was made for her son's sake, who would soon need her support, she told herself, living with such a stupid girl, who had no understanding of the tropics, who almost fainted at the sight of a lizard, who made scenes when the servants didn't understand her affected accent.

The day before the wedding Rose inspected herself from every angle. She had shortened the dress and decided to wear the gossamer silk stockings she'd found in the drawer . . . and the long white gloves . . . and the little gray hat, which was perfect now she'd added the pale pink rose that exactly matched the shade of the dress.

She noted with a proud flush that even if she didn't look so young any more, one could see once again why the great Piper Pollard had noticed little Rose.

It was true. With her brilliant needlework Rose had altered the pink dress, bought back in the late thirties, so radically that it now flattered and gave new shape to her too-thin form. The addition of the small velvet toque with its perky pink flower was a stroke of genius, hiding much of the gray in her hair, allowing the rest to fall in a graceful curve around her face, which, animated with success, sparkled like the old Rose with a special vitality.

When she walked through the arbor on Bill McMurtrey's arm, Rose felt a triumphant thrill fill her as she heard again the same kind of surprised gasp she had heard twenty-six years before—and again it was because of her appearance, a vision from the past.

"Why, it's Rose Pollard . . . how wonderful she looks . . . it's unbelievable. . . ." She heard the murmurs as, like a bride herself, she walked graciously down the aisle of the chapel.

Drum, white-faced, tense, gave her only one startled glance before he looked quickly away as if he'd seen a ghost.

It was all right, Rose told herself, smoothing the fingers of the beautiful white gloves with satisfaction. He didn't need to compliment her on her return to life. She could see how unhappy he was, knowing he was being trapped into a marriage he didn't want.

Rose couldn't remember feeling so pleased with herself in years, knowing she'd been right to work so hard, proving to Drum how much she was going to help him in the difficult times she was sure lay ahead . . . help him and make sure Alicia never usurped her position.

As Alicia, with Maize's help, stepped into the simple, ivory-colored

Hartnell dress, one she'd brought with her from London for the occasion, she was as excited and happy as if Drum were the most ardent suitor a girl could long for.

In the chapel she knew would be all the people Drum valued most highly, members of the leading families in the Caribbean, the decision makers, among them the governor appointed by the Crown and—most important—Albert Gomes, who Drum had already warned her meant a great deal to him. The warning had not gone unnoticed.

She knew he was referring to the last time she'd met Gomes, when according to Drum, she'd made a fool of herself with her ridiculous baby talk.

That Alicia was gone forever, she told herself as she stared at her reflection in the long cheval glass. If she couldn't win Drum's passionate love, she would win his respect and help him reach the pinnacle of success he'd set his heart on. . . . And when their son was born—Alicia patted the slight bulge beneath the ivory silk—Drum would be so proud, he'd never regret the wonderful night they'd spent together, a night, which little did she know then, would never be repeated.

9

Paulette
1950

THEY were as still as if they were in church, their elbows pushed
down hard against the wooden tabletop in front of them, keeping
their hands steady on the binoculars they held so tenaciously to
their eyes, even the clearing of a throat accompanied by a self-
deprecating little nod of the head.

To the uninitiated, it was a freakish sight. Breathing flesh and bone
deliberately immobilized, fingers turning white and numb from the
pressure of holding a heavy object in one position for long minutes at a
time, shoulders set in a rounded shape, it seemed, never to straighten
up again, profiles wearing similar earnest expressions—like children
playing "statues" at a party.

Suddenly, one of the two women at the screened window heaved a
noisy sigh, not of fatigue or boredom, but obviously of deep satisfaction
as at last the object of all their scrutiny came into her view. In the next
hour, other sighs and ohs followed, one melding with the other, sounding as if a soft breeze were brushing through the room.

They were ornithologists—birdwatchers—from Miami, Florida, the
Chinese innkeeper hoarsely whispered to Theo from the shadows. Theo
didn't need to be told what birds they had come to watch.

Decades ago the little inn in the northeast corner of Tobago had been named after the rare and exotic bird of paradise, found on the island of Little Tobago and clearly visible from the hotel's cliffside perch . . . and now the Bird of Paradise Inn was famous for birdwatching, and not much else, despite its idyllic location.

Like the birdwatchers, Theo had been up since before dawn from habit. As he sipped a cup of steaming black coffee, he saw each member of the silent group slowly lower his or her binoculars and stretch as the sun began to rise out of the glittering silver sea.

Light crept through the room, and the woman who had first spotted the elusive bird of paradise was now being patted on the back by her companions as she jotted down a few notes in the manual at her side. She walked, yawning, toward the breakfast buffet, twisting her shoulders from side to side, trying to release them from a cramp.

It was the same woman, Theo realized, whose looks had surprised him on his arrival at the inn the night before, when he'd seen, first from the back, a white-haired lady carrying what appeared to be a heavy bag full of twigs and plants up the inn's narrow staircase.

"Please, let me help you . . ." he'd called out.

The face that had turned, declining his assistance, had surprised him, because it didn't go with the elderly snow-white hair at all. It was a young, lively face, which he'd thought briefly then, couldn't be more than thirty years old if that.

This was his third visit to Tobago, and the more Theo saw of Trinidad's "little sister" island, the more he decided he liked it. He'd been thinking of leaving Trinidad for some time—to establish himself on a piece of property he could now afford to buy for himself, leaving the Arima property he still obstinately refused to consider as his, despite his mother's pleas.

Theo didn't acknowledge that, in choosing Tobago, he was giving in to a deep-seated longing to put at least a small stretch of water between himself and his mother; for his attempts to hide his disgust at the way she continued to live her life had become more difficult.

As he'd walked down to breakfast to find his favorite stopping place inundated with "American birdwatchers," he'd been going over in his mind the best way to break the news to his mother . . . that he hoped to be moving away from Arima and Trinidad before the year was out, leaving behind (he'd reflected with pride) a beautiful profit-producing estate that he'd dug out of the wilderness, an estate his mother could sell with ease and make a "bundle of money."

He was so immersed in thought, he wasn't even aware that the white-haired young/old woman sitting at the next table was directly in his line of vision.

Without warning, she looked up from the plate of pickled meats and cheeses she'd selected from the buffet and stared right at him, as if, like the bird she had been so painstakingly tracking, she was suddenly alerted, aware she was being studied herself.

Theo blushed, color pouring across his face all the way from his collarbone. Before he could look away, the woman said calmly, "Well, at least now I know why the birds try to stay out of sight! Do I have a smudge on my nose or something?"

He blushed all the more as he stammered, "Excuse me. I wasn't thinking. . . . I mean, I was thinking about something else. . . . I honestly didn't even realize you were there. . . ."

She laughed cheerfully. "You certainly know how to put a girl in her place."

This was dreadful. Theo went over to her and shook his head ruefully. "Please accept my apology for staring. It was—it was rude—but . . ."

She waved his words aside. "Don't give it another thought. . . ." As he began to move away, she said impulsively, "Wait a minute. Don't go. Do you know this place?"

He started to say, "Not that well," but she went on, waving her fork in the air to make him realize how important her request was to her. "Do you know by any chance where I might see the rufous-tailed guan?" In an excitable voice she began to describe the bird.

Theo laughed. "You mean the cocorico? Well, yes, I think I might."

She shot out a capable hand. "I'm Paulette Cobble, from Miami. Glad to meet you, Mr. . . ?" She looked up at him inquiringly, forcing him to give her his name.

An hour later, he sat beside Paulette as she drove an antiquated Ford, rented by the "Ornery Ornos" as she described her group, bumping over dirt tracks, in and out of coconut trees in search of the cocorico, as the natives called Tobago's national bird, not quite knowing how he'd got himself there.

Her knowledge of birds was extraordinary, Theo thought, as the day went on and between them they identified a Caribbean pewee, a roseate spoonbill and even a little blue heron, without seeing one cocorico. Theo was surprised to find how much he was enjoying himself.

By the end of the week, without even trying, he had learned a considerable amount about Paulette Cobble. She was a "hail-fellow-well-met"

kind of boisterous woman who, as he'd suspected, wasn't even thirty
. . . but still had "one more year to go!" as she put it with a grimace.

She had teased him into admitting his surprise, if not shock, the first
time he'd seen her. "Come on now, Theo ol' pal. How old did you
think I was?"

She'd roared with laughter when he'd confessed he'd rushed to her
aid, thinking at first she was a very old lady. "Then," he mumbled, "I
couldn't believe you were the same person when you turned around.
. . . Why, you don't even look . . ."

"Look what?" she'd asked quickly, a more guarded look on her face.

"Well, thirty . . ." he'd finished lamely.

She was obviously relieved by his answer and had then given him an
explanation for the pure white hair. "I'm afraid these snow-white granny
locks run in my family! I went this color when I was twenty-two! Can
you imagine! But I couldn't face using one of those newfangled chemical color jobs. . . . I *hate* that kind of stuff. I tried to change the color
once or twice with some natural methods . . . rhubarb stains, you
know, henna and all that jazz, but the only things that ever got colored
were my fingernails! Pink for weeks they were!"

There was no subterfuge about her, Theo thought admiringly, no
attempt to make an impression. Paulette openly told him about one or
two "important" broken romances and about the match she didn't want,
increasingly forced on her by a "very strong mother" until in desperation she had come to the West Indies on a birdwatching expedition,
". . . to show Mama I really meant it when I said no to Henry and
planned to start on my project. Mama hates the idea of my 'going into
business' . . . says it would make my father turn over in his grave.
Theo, you have no idea how difficult it can be to go against your
mother's wishes. . . ."

"Oh, don't I!" Even the fleeting thought he gave to Magdalen,
watching over her stable of young fillies back in Port of Spain, made his
palms sweat, but he said nothing.

And what was her project? This was what intrigued Theo the most
about his first female friend. The contents of the bag he had seen her
carrying that first evening could have given him a clue, for with a degree in chemistry "earned with blood, sweat and tears, my love, from
Duke University, class of 'forty-two" (Theo shuddered: that was the year
he had been sentenced to jail), Paulette told him she wanted more than
anything else to start her own cosmetics company. "Not any pie-in-the-
sky, you'll-look-luscious-tomorrow sort of stuff; packed full of rotten old

chemical doodads. . . . I'll leave that to those face-saving old monsters, Miss Arden and Madame Rubinstein. No, I've got a different idea. I can't say it's totally mine—wouldn't be true—but I've been working with an old darling of a German chemist in Miami for the past couple of years, extracting some of the active principles from plants for possible medicinal purposes. Boy, it's incredible what we've turned up . . . lavender, marigolds, cornflowers—they're loaded with goodies—'beneficent botanicals,' old Professor Guertermann calls them. . . . Well, I want to use 'em and thousands of others for beauty products that will be as natural as I can make 'em and since I've been down here in the tropics I realize the sky's the limit. Now I want to give the whole idea a lift with a touch of the old exotica . . . using tropical plants . . . herbs, barks. . . . What do you think?"

He had hardly been able to believe his ears as she went on, explaining how the professor was willing to help get her started, providing she raised half the money herself.

It was as if she'd been able to take stock of the ideas that had been in his own brain for so long! He told her, with eyes shining, about his own experiments, and about the amazing remedies he'd first learned from Zizi the old Creole woman who lived on his property. When he explained how he pulverized tonka beans to stabilize some of his fragrance compositions, Paulette was as excited and enthusiastic about the idea as he was.

"Can I come back with you and see everything you've been up to?" She didn't wait for an answer. "I can't believe my luck running into you, Theo. When can we leave, partner?"

She was running ahead too fast for him. And yet why not take her back with him to Arima? Theo smiled. Perhaps Paulette was pointing him in the direction he should really go? Perhaps it was fate? He didn't mind farming, but it was the analysis of nature that gave him the most pleasure, when late at night he worked creatively . . . on possible hybrids . . . on ways to improve and strengthen his crops as well as creating perfume compositions. It was incredible how in a few short days his enthusiasm for buying agricultural land in Tobago had completely diminished.

But what would Paulette think about him if she knew the truth about his past? That he had helped murder two innocent people?

Theo gripped the bamboo stick he had whittled for her until its rough edge cut through his skin. It was still agony to think about, let alone mention. He couldn't bring himself to tell her . . . perhaps she would never find out. . . . Anyway he had to risk it.

They crossed over the straits separating Tobago from Trinidad the next day, arriving at the Arima property under the light of a full yellow moon. Paulette was speechless for once as she sat on the old veranda looking up to where the stars almost seemed to touch the dark mountaintops, the air heavy with the scent of night-blooming jasmine, frangipani and tuberoses.

Her visit—originally planned for a week—stretched into a month and then longer, as like an excitable young girl Paulette followed Theo over every inch of his property. The two of them worked side by side at night in Theo's makeshift laboratory, exchanging formulas, exploring every new idea as it came up, plotting and planning the formation of what Paulette announced one day was going to be called the Tropica Natural Cosmetics Company.

For Theo, Paulette's mind was a revelation. It never occurred to him that the only woman he had ever really known was his mother; a woman he both loved and despised. He didn't see the look in Paulette's eyes when he stood with his arm casually around her shoulder as they looked to see what was happening in a dispensing jar; didn't respond to the warm squeeze she gave him just before sunrise when they were both eager to get up from breakfast and go out into the fields.

Theo could hardly believe his sense of loss when Paulette told him she had to return to the States, to start—as she put it—"on the nuts and bolts of the plan."

"Can't you wait until after Christmas?" he pleaded, his eyes moist at the thought of losing her. For the first time he realized what a solitary life he'd been leading. He knew he would never feel the same about living alone again. He cajoled and pleaded so eloquently that again she postponed her return. In exchange he opened up, telling her about his early life, carefully camouflaging the facts of what he looked back on as a poverty-stricken childhood, ironically talking more about a life he had never lived, and a house he had never lived in, describing Golden Hill, the house of his ancestors, built, he explained with a shy pride, by the heir of the island's first British governor Thomas Picton . . . "my great-great-great-great . . ."

Paulette interrupted him, flinging her arms around his neck, as she often did, crying, "Oh, you big snob," and depositing a wet smacking kiss on his cheek like a sister might do.

As they sat close together the night before Paulette had decided she *had* to make the fifteen-hour journey back to Miami, Theo was aware of her body for the first time. It wasn't even the fact it was Paulette's body. It was a woman's, moist with sweat, its feminine, slightly salty smell invading his nostrils, unlocking his control. He had read enough about sex to realize that it was the greatest force in the world; that was the trouble. He didn't trust himself. Once his sexuality was unleashed, who knew what might happen?

Days later he tried to explain how he'd felt to his confessor, a shy young priest who had only recently received his holy orders and been given the souls of Arima to guard over. "Bless me, Father, for I have sinned. . . . It is three weeks since my last confession . . . and . . ." Theo stopped.

"Go on, my son. The Lord our God is a merciful, forgiving God."

"I lusted after a woman, Father. I touched her . . . I . . ."

"You fornicated?" The word sounded quaint, unnatural, coming from the youthful, overanxious holy man.

"No, no . . . but I wanted . . . I . . ."

After the priest had given him absolution and he began to recite his penance, six Hail Marys and ten Our Fathers, Theo found himself continually having to tug his mind away from the last night of Paulette's stay.

He'd been distraught, despite her assurance that she would write "often" and return "as soon as I've got the finances worked out for Tropica."

It was already arranged that, to begin with, Theo would supply the tonka beans and certain other extracts, once they'd established the right channels of delivery, he from his end, she from hers, checking with the agricultural agencies that had to be consulted.

They'd strolled arm-in-arm to where the woods began, for Paulette to pick for the last time—"on this trip," as she kept trying to console him—a stalk or two of night-blooming jasmine to put by her bed.

As a screech owl let out its blood-curdling cry, Paulette had jumped back against him and the close proximity had suddenly affected him, although, goodness knows, they had been as close before, as he laboriously told the priest.

His arms had fastened around her and as she'd strained back, a button had popped off her shirt, allowing his fingers easy access to each one of her plump full breasts. He didn't tell the priest how Paulette had moaned and turned her body to his, opening her mouth to give him a very different kiss from the ones she'd dispensed before; how she, not he, had taken off her cotton skirt, when he'd carried her back to the old swing and was about to take off everything else if he hadn't stopped her.

In the garden, holding her in his arms, his penis had swelled, gorged with a rush of blood, and had stayed hard until she'd started to slip out of her cotton knickers, making whimpering noises as she'd tried to push his hand between her legs.

Just as suddenly as he had become hard, so his sexual organ had inexplicably become limp again, as if a hammer had knocked it insensible.

All the same he *had* touched her. Her distress, her need to be touched, had been too great to ignore—but he'd hated himself as he'd put his trembling fingers into her—and had hated the world for its ugliness as she'd rubbed violently up and down against his rough hand, acting as if she wanted him to mutilate her inside. Above all, he had hated the memory she had left on his skin—the heavy smell of her sex, which for days after she left, linked her in his mind for the first time with his mother's foul trade.

As Drum looked at his sleeping baby daughter, he half-heartedly tried to suppress the familiar feeling she was—and always would be—an irritating reminder that Alicia had tricked him into marriage . . . particularly if she grew up to look like her mother. Alicia had been a virgin— goddamn it—that night in London, and like an unsuspecting stallion being brought to a brood mare at precisely the right time he had well and truly "foaled in one."

It wasn't all bad. Drum had to admit Alicia tried. There was no more baby talk. No more stupid conversation and interruptions, and he had to give her credit for improving the running of the house. Not that it had ever lacked spit and polish with Obee in command, but Obee wouldn't have been able to mastermind the kind of entertaining they were up to their ears in now.

As he passed the newly decorated dining room with the set of Chinese Chippendale chairs just arrived from London and the impressive murals on the wall facing the wide veranda, Drum saw Alicia fussing over the place cards for the dinner party they were giving. A certain smug satisfaction made him go in to pat her neat little behind, knowing that even this affectionate pat could be dangerous, leading her to think that tonight he would be panting for her in bed. . . .

Let her hope, he thought casually, as he ran upstairs to his dressing room. It meant she would behave even more like a charming hostess and doting wife if she thought there was the least likelihood of his getting between her legs.

His half smile disappeared as he saw his mother waiting to greet him at the top of the stairs.

"Drum . . ."

"Yes, what is it, Mother? I'm running late."

"Drum, Alicia says there's no room for me tonight. I wanted to join you. I'm your mother, Drum. . . ." Rose started to sob and hiccup at the same time. "Tell her, Drum. Put her . . . her . . . her . . . in her place."

The dark rage that this kind of scene evoked in him these days gripped him by the throat.

One day, he thought, gritting his teeth, one day I won't be responsible for my actions. He clutched the balustrade as if to stop himself from falling, but it was a safety measure of a different kind. The cool wood acted like a brake on the hot temper waiting to break out. "Mother, if Alicia told you there is no room, there is no room. That's all there is to it. It's a political dinner. It would bore you—as you said the first dinner Alicia and I gave for Gomes on our return from England bored you. This one is no different."

Rose shook her head, her nose running, tears running, making her question so palpably absurd Drum even gave a short deprecating laugh as she cried, "But you and . . . need me to enter-ter-entertain your g-g-guests . . . I'm . . . I'm . . . Mrs. P-P-Pollard. . . . Can't I . . . can't I come down for c-c-cocktails?"

"For goodness sake, Mother, pull yourself together. We'll talk about this tomorrow."

Drum pushed her along the corridor, into her room, which was the one Alicia had occupied on her first visit with Roger, for since her marriage and the birth of Margaret six and a half months later, Alicia had gained control of Golden Hill in many more ways than Drum even realized.

It wasn't surprising he was unaware of all the changes she had made and was making, particularly when it came to putting Rose in her place, which as far as Alicia was concerned was very definitely in the background, out of sight.

It had been the most feverish year of Drum's life. Not only had he become a husband and a father; he had also been elected to Trinidad's Legislative Council in the 1950 election, "the youngest member of the chosen eighteen"—as the *Trinidad Guardian* had proudly announced.

Just as important, Drum was known throughout the Caribbean and all the way to Westminster as "Gomes's right-hand man," and Gomes had never been more powerful. Following the all-important election, true to their promise, the British government had allowed for the first time five elected officials out of the eighteen Council members to run five key ministries in the colony—with the British governor, Sir Hubert Rence, still retaining the ultimate responsibility. Gomes, who easily regained his Port of Spain seat, had become the most important of the five, controlling the vital areas of industry, labor and commerce.

"I *am* the government of Trinidad and Tobago," Gomes frequently boasted, and although Drum wished fervently his mentor would keep that fact to himself, he above all others knew it wasn't an idle boast, for he was up there with him in the driver's seat and knew he belonged there, just as his father's friends had predicted from the beginning.

So as long as Alicia continued to deliver her special stamp of breeding and charm to the many events and parties Drum now felt it was contingent to give, entertaining a never-ending stream of important visitors and government officials, she could make as many changes as she wanted to make, including the reallocation of rooms—moving Rose out of the master bedroom and moving Drum and herself in.

That Piper had left Golden Hill and half the acreage to Rose and not to Drum was of no consequence.

When Rose screamed, "It's my house, get out!" to the daughter-in-law she loathed more every day, Alicia merely turned up her aristocratic nose, for Rose's only life raft was Drum and Drum was too busy to be worried with "household details," and too often absent to act as a buffer between his mother and his wife.

The tragedy was that Rose's mammoth attempt to retrieve her looks, and the position in the community she'd reneged upon following her husband's death, had come far too late.

While others had marveled that day in the chapel and at the wedding reception at her "return to life"—her apparent renewed vitality and even beauty—Drum had had too much misery on his own mind to recognize and pay tribute to the major effort behind it. And without his support, his praise, his understanding that she had made the effort for him, it had been all too easy for Alicia to crush Rose's newborn spirit, to sneer away her attempts to look fashionable again, to show up her ignorance of current affairs and contemporary topics of conversation . . . for Rose was emerging from a past that had happened almost a decade before.

When she was sure both Drum and Alicia were out, Rose would

creep back to her old room, now "their" room, just as she had once gone to check Drum was still in the house when he'd threatened to leave to join the forces overseas.

Once there she'd go through drawers, shelves, pockets, searching like a jealous suspicious wife, not knowing what she was hoping to find, but always hoping to find *something* that would incriminate Alicia and force her out of the home that Piper, her beloved husband, had left to her and only her, Golden Hill, the home she longed to share with Drum and nobody else.

Instead of incriminating Alicia, however, it was Alicia who "incriminated" Rose, so that Drum always heard when she'd caused a scene or spilled sauce on her dress or hadn't bothered to change out of a soiled peignoir for breakfast, and Rose noted with increasing fear, as she saw herself excluded more and more, Drum was too preoccupied to notice any more how fiendishly clever Alicia could be. Rose would rock herself backward and forward for hours, trying to think of a way to break what appeared to be Alicia's hold on Drum, asking herself, What *can* he see in her sickening airs and graces?

Drum saw nothing, but he hid the fact well—except from Alicia. She knew she was no more attractive to him after their marriage than before. She tried everything . . . every kind of ruse to entice him, but she failed again and again. It wasn't that he was actively unkind, but . . .

At first Drum had been brilliant at avoiding the confrontation that he knew one day had to come. "Alicia, we must be careful. Wait until after the baby," he'd said at first, turning away from her burgeoning body, feeling physically sick upon seeing her protruding belly.

Then, "You're not strong enough," he said after Margaret's birth, which had been long and arduous with a few nerve-racking hours when the doctor had feared it might have to be a choice between life for the mother or the child.

Drum had tried to persuade the doctor to tell Alicia she should never have another child or even risk intercourse. It had appeared to be the perfect excuse to avoid the intimacy he dreaded, but the old idiot hadn't seen the point—in fact he had burbled on about the joys of motherhood, even exclaiming that next time it would probably be a whole lot easier.

The months had slipped by with Drum away whenever possible on Council business, still trying to bring about a major sugar agreement between Britain and her Commonwealth countries. He knew he would be met on his return by a wife playacting any number of roles to get him to make love to her, a wife whose entangling arms increasingly made him feel he was in bondage again, whose body he knew like an old toy he had discarded long ago, which would never again hold any interest for him.

Whether it was because she had tricked him—he, Drum Pollard, who was used to hearing how much smarter he was than everyone else—or whether it was because of her smothering love, which seemed to grow stronger as his attempts to hide his lack of interest grew less—his liking for his role of husband, let alone father, even decreased more as time went on. He had never been free, he told himself, and his spirit longed for freedom. His body ached for relief from the tension building up . . . relief with a similar free-thinking spirit, a young, unfettered body.

On occasions his penis even grew hard when he recalled Gloria, but then he would mentally castigate himself for even thinking of her, reminding himself of the danger she and their child represented. He would tether up his horse and ride into the mountains or drive into town on some pretext to discuss government business—anything to take his mind away from his sexual needs. On his next trip overseas Drum decided he'd risk taking a couple of days off to cross the channel and visit Paris where as an anonymous man about town he could find a place where, as he wryly put it to himself, he could "exercise the muscle that most needed exercise."

From the house on Harcourt Street in Port of Spain where Roland Bracken now lived in reasonable comfort with Emerald his wife and Jack their baby son, and from Le Plaisir Hotel, the Victorian mansion on the outskirts of town where Magdalen Finch conducted her business—the highly touted Pollard way of life up on Golden Hill looked altogether too perfect.

For Roland, his nephew's stunning success in the election had been a double blow. Despite outwardly favorable reactions from the crowd to his reasoned, clever oratory, and optimistic forecasts made even by journalists he knew suspected him, on voting day Roland had suffered a galling defeat at the polls.

Uriah Butler, his brother James and every member of his family had urged him to run as a member of Butler's party, but Luis, his Cuban adviser, had persuaded him with his financial backing to go it alone. "If rum-shop owners, tailors, moneylenders, butchers and schoolteachers can form their own parties, so can you," Luis had said pointedly. "It's your step out of Butler's shadow into your own place in the sun." But he had lost, and the more Roland thought about why he'd lost, the more he became convinced an editorial in the *Trinidad Guardian* had been responsible—and Drum Pollard, his vile nephew, had to have been behind it.

Roland had been forced to conclude there was still a stinking stigma attached to his name . . . and in case anyone had been foolish enough to forget why, the *Trinidad Guardian* had reminded the voting public in an unsigned sarcastic editorial a few days before the election, stating, without mentioning his name, that one of the independent candidates, a black member of a multicolored family, stood for government by force—riot, rabble-rousing and *arson!*

It was ironic and painful, as Roland reminded himself endlessly, that although Uriah Butler's party had actually won eight out of the eighteen seats, not one of his party had been nominated to the Executive Ministerial Council of Five.

"Political blasphemy!" Butler had screamed, vowing revenge and threatening "agitation surpassing anything ever seen before to make the new administration as rancid as ever. . . ." Roland sighed as he read in *The Bugle*, the newspaper Butler was trying to promote, of his speech to the crowds in Woodford Square the evening before, where he promised to come after every sitting of the Legislative Council to report to the people on "what is *really* transacted on your behalf!"

It was pathetic. Roland knew after the novelty of seeing Butler act like a jackass a few times, there would be no crowds around to listen. If *he*, Roland Bracken, had run on the Butler ticket, he might well have been one of the lucky eight who had a decision-making place now and perhaps he might even have been nominated as a "token black," knowing he was the blackest of them all, to the Council of Five.

"Bah!" Roland crashed his hand down on his desk in frustration. He didn't blame the Cuban for wrong advice. He was the one who had failed and until the day came when Drum Pollard was out of the running, out of sight and sound, he would probably *always* fail. That day *had* to come if there was any justice in the world.

He'd failed, but he was lucky that the Cuban apparently still felt he had the ability to achieve what he most wanted to achieve—for himself and for all their comrades: equality. It was being brought to bear in other parts of the world. On his shortwave radio Roland had learned even before the Cuban told him that the "share and share alike" comrades of North Korea had invaded the capitalist stronghold of South

Korea, that despite Truman having ordered U.S. air and naval support, the North Koreans were winning.

But how to unseat those in power in his own territory? How to topple his hypocritical nephew Drum Pollard, from his public pedestal? Drum, who despite one outward show of "forgiveness and friendship" repudiated the black genes in his white body, who scorned those with black skin just as his mother, Roland's own treacherous traitor of a sister Rose, had done before him?

Something had to change, but Roland knew it wasn't going to change through Uriah Butler, who so totally lacked the administrative and intellectual skills needed for the leadership role, much as he desired it. And, from the bitter experience of the last election, Roland doubted *he* could bring about the necessary changes himself—at least not on his own—not until he'd proved to the people how he could better their lot. And he *couldn't* prove it until he had the power. It was a classic case of the chicken and the egg . . . or of finding the right person's coattails to hang on to, someone who could sweep him into power as he was swept there himself . . . just as his nephew Drum Pollard had been on Gomes's coattails.

Magdalen hadn't thought of Monos and her trips there with the Middletons in years, but now—as she sorted through her clothes until she found the suit that had looked stylish on the shop's hanger but turned out to give her a rather matronly look—she realized her feeling of suppressed excitement was the way she'd felt so many years ago on learning she'd been invited for a holiday "down the islands."

Strange that an invitation from her own son should make her remember her adolescent years and how she'd counted the days until her departure on the old *Ant* steamer. Since Theo's letter arrived, Magdalen had been counting the *hours* until she would set eyes on him again. It had been a long time. She'd reread the letter so many times it now bore the traces of where she'd read it—a smear of yellow from the marmalade on her breakfast tray, a smudge of ink from holding it in her wet hands in the bathroom, even a smear of rouge from her make-up drawer.

Theo getting married! It had been such a thunderbolt she'd had to go quickly to find a bottle of smelling salts—an important and often necessary reviver present in every bedroom as a rule of the house.

Theo's letter, one of the few he had ever written to her, was brief and to the point. "My dear mother, I do hope it might be possible for you to visit me in Arima over Christmas this year. I have a very special request that I want to make in person before leaving in the new year for Miami, Florida, where I am to marry a lovely American lady named Paulette Cobble. Please be happy for me. I will tell you our future plans when you arrive here. Love, Theo."

"Love, Theo." Did her son love her? He was a saint. She was a sinner, Magdalen knew that. But now he was going to marry—and how on earth he'd ever managed to meet a "lovely lady" let alone an American one, was beyond her comprehension. Did that mean he now *knew* about love and passion? Would he now be more understanding of her life and the lives of those she catered to? Human beings whose needs were basic and simple, needs Magdalen knew how to satisfy?

She hadn't been back to Theo's property for over eight months, because on her last visit he'd told her he needed to be left alone; that when he was ready to see her again he would call. He'd been so loving, it had taken Magdalen all day to realize he meant what he said and so, although she thought about him constantly (and checked on his health through his nearest neighbor every so often) she'd respected his wishes.

Now, as she approached the house in the middle of the plantation she was astonished at its fresh spic-and-span look. Was Miss Cobble responsible for the transformation? If so, Magdalen heartily approved. There were gleaming coats of white paint inside and out, and even the veranda no longer squeaked and shook.

Theo showed his mother around with obvious pride, opening a door with a flourish to reveal a new room, her bedroom, he told her, which he had added on himself, the walls made of teak, its warm rich aroma adding to the scent of the apricot roses placed by the single bed.

Magdalen squeezed Theo's hand, tears in her eyes, as she saw that his hands were more calloused than ever. But there was a spirited look about his face she had never seen before, a look that said, "Life's exciting. I'm giving and taking all I can."

He was, as always, careful in his choice of words when he spoke to her. She longed to tell him to say what he liked, to get off his chest *all* she knew he really felt, but—also as always—just being with him filled her with such joy, she didn't dare risk upsetting him. Instead, a Magdalen few people ever saw, sat, listened and waited while outside a southeaster blew a light rain squall across the grass, shaking the small Christmas tree on the porch.

Theo was sure his mother would never understand a relationship that, based on friendship, had changed—a letter at a time—into a love affair, without even the benefit of a kiss to seal it. . . . Yet that was exactly what had happened. He didn't attempt to explain it that way. He told his mother the truth, because he always told the truth, but it was with many omissions.

"We met in Tobago. . . . Paulette returned with me to Arima because we share a mutual interest in the study of plants. She went back to America to start a small cosmetics business, using only natural extracts. . . . We have been corresponding ever since . . . and she has agreed to marry me."

He had no need or intention to reveal to his mother the extent of the paralyzing loneliness he had experienced when Paulette had finally gone away; his constant and unsatisfactory self-analysis as to why he had been so repulsed by her sexual need for him that last night together; how with every letter received and sent his need for *her*, not just as a companion, but as a woman to hold in his arms, had grown, and how as his letters began to reflect that, so all pretense of a platonic relationship had disappeared until the letters they exchanged were love letters, where each poured out deep-rooted feelings to the other.

He had thought of jumping on a plane to Florida to tell Paulette he couldn't bear to be without her, that he was meant to be joined to her in the deepest most spiritual *and* physical sense possible; but he'd been apprehensive, despite the increasing cry of and for love in her letters.

In the end he'd gone to the main post office in Port of Spain and had waited an agonizing two hours to get through to her on the telephone. He'd proposed there and then, three times in fact, as exasperatingly an operator announcing "Jacksonville" kept cutting in on the line. He'd only needed to hear her say once, "I thought you'd never ask. . . . Yes, darling, oh, yes," to let out a "Whoopee!" in the phone booth that even startled the passers-by.

After that momentous day, their plans were made by letter. He would arrive in Florida no later than the first week of January . . . to meet Mama. "And," Paulette wrote, "be prepared to be your most charming. She already thinks you must be a heathen, coming from such an outlandish place. . . ." They would marry the third week, come back to Arima for their honeymoon and then—and this was where Theo balked, but decided not to press the matter in a letter—Paulette had written it was essential she travel back and forth between Arima and Miami because Tropica "is just taking bud."

What did she mean, "travel back and forth"? "Three months in Miami . . . a month in Arima—when Professor Guertermann can look after the 'shop' for me, but when you can, you must come to the U.S.

with me, although it's important we develop the Arima end of *our* business, too."

By underlining the pronoun, Theo knew Paulette wanted him to feel he was a real partner, as he wanted to be, just as soon as he pulled his full weight. But he didn't think he could possibly do so without Paulette at his side at all times. The memory of his loneliness after her departure was too fresh in his mind.

Magdalen was told none of this. Only Theo's request—the culmination of many days and nights of deep thinking—reflected his long-term plan, a request he didn't expect his mother to accede to at first; but he had time and patience and above all a belief his prayers would be answered. If his mother only approved of his plans, it would not only solve his own dilemma, but could rescue and absolve her from her life of sin.

"Mother . . ."

Now, the reason for his letter, the *request* was going to be made. Magdalen unconsciously tensed.

"Mother," Theo began again, knowing he was beginning to blush as he always did whenever the subject of her business was raised, "I want the best for you, you know that." She remained silent, but slowly stroked his rough hand, which usually he would have quickly removed. "You also know how much I hate what you're doing, although I know you started it all for me. But now, you don't need to be involved with that vile trade any more. No, don't speak. Let me finish. Paulette believes we can work out an arrangement after our marriage, when she will—in effect—live between here and Miami, but it will never work. Absence may make the heart grow fonder for a short while, but God didn't create marriage for a man and a woman to live apart. You brought me up telling me how much you loved Golden Hill and life on the land, a life you lost. Now with your own eyes you can see I inherited that love. This plantation may not be in Golden Hill's class, but you must admit it's beautiful and it makes money—and it will make a lot more. Don't answer me now, but I want you to move here—to run the plantation for me while I'm away—because I know I'll have to make my main home with Paulette in America. I don't want us to live separate lives."

Magdalen drew her breath in sharply and removed her hand, but Theo quickly moved his to cover hers. "That's still a long way off, Mother, but there's more to it than that. We want to make use of Arima's produce, Paulette and I. Her new beauty business is called

Tropica, because the plant extracts she intends to use *are* tropical—from Arima as well as from other places. You can be part of it all!"

As Magdalen continued to look stunned, Theo tried to make her laugh. "Perhaps you'll become another Elizabeth Arden or Dorothy Gray. Paulette tells me those ladies didn't become famous until they were well into middle age. Please, Mother, *please*, think about it—for my sake and for yours. Join us in our venture . . . you'll never regret it. Please promise me you'll think about it."

She *had* thought about it; for days, weeks, months after her visit to Arima, and she would never forget the look of joy and gratitude on Theo's face when, six months after his marriage to Paulette, she arrived to tell him she had decided to try her hand at running the estate and, as he had asked, she was in the process of selling her Le Plaisir shares to her Chinese partner.

"Mother, this is the most wonderful day of my life!" Theo had cried, kissing and hugging her in a way he had never done before, not even as a small boy. "It's our greatest wedding present. You'll never regret it. Never!"

For Theo it was the answer to his prayers. It didn't mean he would stay away from Arima, far from it. He'd already entered into a profitable arrangement with an essential-oil house in the U.S. to supply them with plant and flower extracts apart from Tropica's small requirements, so he knew he'd need to come back often, but already, just as he'd expected, he didn't want to leave his wonderful wife, who, if God was really showering him with blessings, would tell him on his return to Florida that she was an expectant mother, too.

When Theo finally left the following week, telling his mother he would most probably be back in three months, he felt totally confident his mother would be able to handle everything.

He couldn't remember feeling so happy . . . so, it was worth telling a small lie, Magdalen consoled herself, as the car taking Theo to the airport disappeared around the bend, for she had no intention of selling her Le Plaisir shares or, for that matter, leaving a business she was proud she had built into such a flourishing success—at least not yet.

Some women were more capable than others. From the little she'd seen of Paulette Cobble, Magdalen had to admit that description would fit her . . . as it also fit Magdalen Finch. She had decided to devote a little less time to Le Plaisir in order to ensure the Arima plantation went from strength to strength . . . but she intended to run *both* and *better* than most people would be able to run one business. Of that she was sure, and she was right. She did.

On his next visit, Theo warmly congratulated his mother on the noticeable improvements she'd made in his absence. She had even introduced new crops, planting tobacco, castor seed and ginger near the slopes of the property where, Magdalen told him proudly, she'd learned the ground was continually being fertilized by lime from the overhanging mountains, which was then calcinated by the sun's powerful rays.

As they went over the books, Theo slung his arm around his mother's shoulders and praised her again for the speed with which she'd mastered the practical details of planting, producing and selling the produce, as well as for her imagination, for so often she had intuitively understood what they were looking for in a new formula.

Imagination! Magdalen smiled. Only a few nights before Theo's arrival from the States, she had heard that particular asset of hers praised at Le Plaisir for such a different reason, when she had dreamed up a *divertissement* for a particularly jaded French gentleman. She felt no guilt about deceiving Theo. In Magdalen's eyes her son was still a blessed innocent, and what he didn't have to know, he would never know.

Despite her "double life," she was beginning to love the time she spent at Arima. "And the strangest thing of all," she told Roland Bracken over a drink late one evening, "is the more I'm at Arima, the more it gripes me that the Pollards have control of Golden Hill. To think, the island's prime land—my family property—is in their hands! It makes me sick! You'd think I'd have enough to think about, wouldn't you, without fretting over 'what might have been!'"

Her tone was light, but that was all. Inside, thought Roland, she's still a fanatic about Golden Hill . . . for it takes one to know one. He wondered if only he would have noticed the way she clutched her drink tightly or the look of hatred that flared in her face when she mentioned the Pollard name?

Their friendship had developed and deepened since Roland's first visit to Le Plaisir four years before. Magdalen had been one of the first to agree with him that Drum Pollard in his own iniquitous way had to have been the hand that wrote the damaging editorial that had put an end to Roland's political aspirations, at least for the time being.

Now, Magdalen realized Roland wasn't just passing by on a courtesy call. "I've been babbling on. What's troubling you? Don't tell me Drum Pollard is after your head again?"

Roland showed his even white teeth in a tight smile. "Not him, but his 'trusted good friend,' the minister of works, is after my land. I received word from my sister, April, yesterday that our family property has been taken over in a shotgun sale."

"What do you mean?" Magdalen asked in alarm.

"They're going to run a road through our cocoa patch. They've been after it for months; not that it means that much to me, but it's where April decided she wanted to live when Mother died. Well, someone from the ministry called on April to offer her two hundred dollars for our ten acres. I ask you! Two hundred dollars! The land was given, you know, to my mother's ancestor over a hundred years ago! When April turned the offer down, he threatened to fine her for willful 'impediment' and lack of cooperation with the ministry of works. Yesterday she received a compulsory purchase order, telling her the bulldozers will be coming to knock everything down in a week. I'm going to take my hypocritical nephew at his word . . . and see if he still wants to 'help his poor black relations,'" Roland snapped out. "I'm going to ask him to intervene . . . to save what, after all, is part of his ancestry, too." He smiled a thin, bitter smile, as Magdalen shook her head. "I know . . . I know . . . he won't help, but at least, surely, the press will have to report the emptiness of the hypocrite's words."

Magdalen had a very important reason not to become linked in any way with what had been described in the press as the latest "Bracken-Pollard confrontation."

Just as she had predicted when Roland first broached the subject, Drum Pollard had not intervened as far as the Bracken cocoa patch was concerned. But, just as Roland had hoped, the press had whipped up a story out of his plea to his influential nephew, using it as an excuse to run a series of articles on what Gomes's "capitalist clique"—as those surrounding the minister were now called—were really trying to accomplish.

When Roland came to see her again to find out if there was any way she could help him in his crusade, he could see she wasn't really interested. Unlike the evening of a few months before, Magdalen didn't even want to pursue the tenor of the converation. He knew why.

She had a grandson. "Thomas Picton Finch," Theo had written, "named in honor of your father and our illustrious ancestor." It was the first time she'd cried, really cried as if her heart were breaking, since the day she'd gone down to the wharf to discover that Theo Bartrieve had sailed away without her.

"Her girls" at Le Plaisir at first thought that the letter she'd received from America must contain the most horrible news, for she'd shut herself up in her private quarters, making it clear she wasn't to be called for anything or anyone. When she'd finally appeared, her eyes red and sore, and ordered champagne all around, they had then thought she must be having a nervous breakdown—until, her voice hoarse with emotion, she told them the joyous news.

Now, preoccupied with her thoughts, Magdalen urged Roland—as Luis had been urging him—to go away for a while. "Have a good holiday, you deserve one," she told him.

Press interest was dwindling. Roland knew now that nothing and no one could prevent the road from being built. He decided to take Magdalen's advice—and what good advice it turned out to be, for if he hadn't taken Emerald and baby Jack to visit Emerald's family in Barbados, he might never have met Eric Williams, might never have had the opportunity to jump in and squash a persistent heckler as Williams delivered, in Roland's opinion, a mesmerizing speech on behalf of the Anglo-American Caribbean Economic Commission.

How Williams, employed by the Commission, could get away with his radical anticolonial stance Roland didn't know or care. The man was a genius! Roland had sensed it, even in the first half hour he'd sat listening to him. It was ironic, Roland thought, that although he'd often heard of Williams and the Political Education Group and Teachers' Economic and Cultural Association that he'd founded, he'd never given him much thought. How could he have been so stupid?

He'd automatically thought Williams *had* to be a stooge because of the research position he'd held since 1943 with the Commission, which was in reality a government agency, managed by the white governments on both sides of the Atlantic!

He'd been so wrong! Eric Williams was no stooge. He was a hero, again and again, despite all opposition, chronicling in his lectures the true story of black oppression in the Caribbean over hundreds of years. Why, Eric Williams could do more in one lecture than Uriah Butler could do in a thousand soapbox oratories. Suddenly it was clear to Roland, as clear as the black nose on his face, that Williams attracted *educated* blacks, admittedly only a handful, but what a handful it was! Because of their brains—and some luck—they'd all managed to attend universities abroad!

Williams didn't guess that there were differences between Roland's ideology and his own. He saw only an ardent young black man who had risked everything to bring about the changes that were so necessary for them all. Changes, Williams counseled Roland, that could only be achieved if he behaved with the utmost propriety and ran no risk of falling foul of the law.

Williams's words and voice of quiet authority rang in Roland's ears. There was no one, he decided, that he could really confide in. Williams was certainly the wisest man he'd met—a scholar, a visionary, but did he have the dynamism to be the leader the country needed?

Whether Williams did or didn't, Roland told himself, he now had to make a total break with Uriah Butler in order to convince Williams he was behind him every inch of the way.

He had no alternative. Nearer the time of the next election, when he hoped Williams would turn his full attention to ousting the British government's stooges—Drum Pollard among them—then perhaps would be the time to tell Williams how he *really* felt . . . about the only politics that seemed to make any sense in the world—the politics of Communism.

But now, with Joe McCarthy on the rampage in the States, Roland knew that to say anything would be death to his ambitions. Later, however, perhaps Williams would turn out to be just the comrade he'd been looking for . . . the one whose coattails he could cling to, sweeping them both into power. . . .

10

Rose
1955

THEY were away, hobnobbing in London with the new prime minister, Rose knew, although nobody had told her, certainly not Drum or Alicia. She had long ago learned how to find things out, as she told her reflection in the long mirror.

Nervously Rose checked the bolt on her door was locked before surreptitiously taking a copy of the morning paper from under the arm of her loose-sleeved jacket. "She can't hide anything from me . . . from me. . . ." The words came out half laughing, half sobbing, as with furtive movements she crept to the window to make sure she was not being spied upon, checked the lock on the door again, then went to her rocking chair, placed in the farthest corner so she could survey the entire room, to read the story below the picture of her son shaking hands with Sir Anthony Eden.

As she read the sentence, "Mr. Pollard was accompanied by his wife, the Honorable Alicia Pollard," her hand shook with anger, while tears of self-pity streamed down the once lovely face.

Bitch, bitch, bitch! Rose shook her thin fist in the air, the paper slipping to the floor where it would remain until she either stepped on it or one of the maids discovered what, until a minute ago, had been her latest secret possession.

To Rose anything from downstairs that she was able to bring upstairs was a special prize. It was a game of finders-keepers she played in deadly earnest, knowing that when her daughter-in-law, the Honorable Alicia, was at home even the morning newspaper was something to be fought over. In the last year, Rose had found even her presence at the breakfast table seemed to offend Alicia, often leading to a confrontation that she never won.

It wasn't that Drum necessarily agreed with his wife that his mother was someone who should now only be seen when absolutely necessary and never, ever heard . . . but he didn't disagree either.

The fact was that in the five years since their marriage, the once imperious, beautiful Rose was now the shunned one, treated like an unwanted servant, increasingly "sent" to her room by a daughter-in-law the newspapers described as "the perfect cohort for such a brilliant young man with a big future. . . ."

But now they were away. Rose laughed to herself again. She didn't know how long she had. With the speed of today's airplanes, you never knew, they could be gone one week, and back the next, but she was certain she had at least one day and perhaps even two days to go through Drum's things, to rummage through the drawers of his desk *and* to return to the cold cupboard at the back of the house.

She didn't bother looking through Alicia's things any more. It didn't make her feel any better to read letters from Alicia's uncle, the earl of Chingford, expressing his praise, his compliments on the way she'd settled down . . . to see the clippings Alicia carefully cut out from English and American magazines, reporting on her "Golden Hill salon . . . where world leaders and captains of industry know they are assured of a few hours or sometimes even days of undisturbed privacy in a home the Honorable Alicia Pollard runs with tremendous flair and charm, surrounded by the beauty of the tropics . . ." on Alicia Pollard's "imaginative interior decoration and ingenious ways with menus," or her "genuine interest in the underprivileged."

Bah! What unadulterated rubbish it all was! What a different story she, Rose Pollard, could tell the press, particularly about Alicia's "genuine interest in the underprivileged."

As the hall clock chimed the half-hour stanza Rose, with the stealth of a spy, crept to the top of the stairs, her ears straining for any sounds of servants. Only Obee was to be feared. He was the one who could steal up on her without making a sound, as he had two years before when she'd first found out about little Naomi. How she'd screamed until, a look of panic on his earnest face, he'd started to back away to run downstairs. But she'd run right after him, shaking her fist, yelling she'd make sure he was fired if he ever surprised her like that again.

Of course, they'd been away that time, too. Rose remembered well, because Drum had actually told her himself that Gomes had asked him to accompany him to the United States for a meeting with the new president, Eisenhower.

Rose also remembered how Alicia had pouted and sulked, until in the end Drum had had to take her along—with Gomes's permission.

It had upset Rose tremendously to see Alicia get her way but it had been a blessing in disguise. That first afternoon after their departure, going through Drum's desk, she'd found the old-fashioned key to the walk-in cold cupboard at the back of the house, where she'd suddenly remembered Piper had made her keep her new raccoon coat. It still had to be there! Although it was nearing ninety degrees, she'd had a longing to feel its silkiness around her, to recapture the feeling she'd had when she first put it on in New York back in the twenties. She'd been standing wearing it in the cold cupboard, almost in a trance, the letters in her hand, when the faintest squeak of the door made her whirl around to see Obee standing there staring at her.

He couldn't have told Drum or Alicia, she knew that, for when they returned, nothing was ever said about her wearing her coat in the cupboard. Everything went on as usual. She was still treated shamefully, never invited to dinner parties, ignored at breakfast and lunch except by little Margaret.

"Drum's child," Rose would say to herself, blocking out the thought that this dear little girl could ever have come out of Alicia's body.

After she'd found the letters the hurt hadn't been so bad for awhile.

Naomi . . . little Naomi . . . and Gloria—pretty, sweet Gloria! The fact that *she* knew about them and Alicia didn't, had made Rose feel she held a trump card she didn't know how to play. . . .

Now, satisfied the servants were nowhere in the vicinity, she slowly crept along the corridor to the cold cupboard to take the crumpled envelope from Drum's old overcoat pocket to read and reread the two letters inside, letters she had first read two years before.

"Dearest Drum," said the first one, dated February 4, 1949, "You are kind to us, but the money don't make up for not seeing you. You'd be proud of your little girl . . . Naomi sends you a big x." The second letter, written almost two years later—on December 22, 1950, said, ". . . All right, Drum. I understand. I won't write again. I hope you'll be very happy with your new smart wife and little girl. It's funny, but I wouldn't mind so much if it had bin a boy, then it wouldn't hurt so much." Both letters were signed, "Yours lovingly, Gloria."

Gloria. It had taken Rose months to work out who Gloria might be, but it was months of living again, of discovering her brain could still be stirred into action, as she slowly went through Drum's papers, checkbooks, statements, whenever he was away from the island and Alicia was either with him or away from the house. Methodically, she had examined old files, putting everything back as she'd found it, until she *did* find a copy of a stock purchase costing several thousand dollars bought early in 1947 in the name of Gloria Simpson.

Rose's discovery had been over a year ago and now she knew who Gloria Simpson was and where she lived—in her mother's house in Barataria with little Naomi . . . when she wasn't working for that dreadful Finch woman at her fancy hotel.

Rose had no idea what really went on at Le Plaisir. In the telephone book it was listed as Le Plaisir Hotel, with the owner's name and number listed immediately below—Mrs. Magdalen Finch.

It had upset Rose to discover Gloria worked as a manager for Magdalen, but although she despised herself whenever any bad thoughts came into her mind about her brilliant son, Rose supposed Drum's original investment on their behalf was no longer sufficient to support them, so Gloria had had to earn her living.

She'd begun to send them money with no note of explanation, mailing it to Gloria at the Barataria address, some note of caution making her write the checks out to "Cash," for, Rose reasoned, it was quite likely Alicia went through Rose's things when she was away from her room, just as Rose had once gone through Alicia's.

After she reread the old letters in the cold cupboard, Rose felt unusually restless. It was only two o'clock. The afternoon, hot and humid, stretched before her like a prison sentence. She suddenly had an exciting thought, dismissed it, then kept coming back to it like a bird to a morsel in the grass.

She couldn't, and yet . . . she longed to . . . go and meet Gloria in person, perhaps even to speak to her . . . and to Naomi. Tears came quickly to her eyes as she thought of her other little granddaughter, who probably didn't even know of her existence.

Who knew how much longer Alicia would allow Margaret to spend so much time with her? And when Margaret was sent away to boarding school in England, as Rose knew she would be one day (because Alicia had said so and everything to do with the family and the house now seemed to be Alicia's decision), how would Margaret treat her old granny then? Perhaps she would come back with her nose stuck up in the air just like her mother's?

Gasping for breath at her own daring, Rose combed her hair and hastily changed into one of the afternoon frocks she had made for herself so long ago, its old-fashioned cut with set-in sleeves and narrow long skirt adding to her look of eccentricity.

She worked everything out. She'd ask Obee to drive her to the Queen's Park Hotel, then ask him to come back in two hours. Her breath continued to come in short gasps when she thought of her audacity. Once Obee left her, she would order a taxi to take her to the Barataria address.

Rose hadn't been near the Queen's Park Hotel since she'd gone there to beg Roger to forgive Alicia and take her back to England with him. If only he had! When Obee asked her if she wanted him to accompany her inside, Rose hesitated, wondering for a second whether she should forget the whole idea and return home, but Obee's look of curiosity forced her to go on with her plan and she dismissed him curtly.

Her footsteps faltered as she neared the hotel's entrance, particularly as there was no doorman in sight and no taxis either. She went into the lobby, raising her eyes furtively from the ground to see if she could locate the doorman. As she saw him directing a porter to a pile of luggage, someone touched her arm. She jumped as if she'd been assaulted.

"It's Mrs. . . . Mrs. P-Piper Pollard, isn't it?"

Rose blinked her eyes nervously at the woman who seemed to tower over her, her hair, burnished like shiny mahogany, standing out around her handsome face in a well-coiffed halo. Rose didn't recognize her at first. She scrutinized the well-made-up face with its discreet pink lipstick, long lashes coated with mascara, looking for a clue as to her identity.

The woman still held her elbow and was now propelling her to a chair as she said, "Forgive me, Rose, but you don't look well. It's a scorcher today—perhaps the heat . . ."

Rose realized the woman was right. She didn't feel well. The room had begun to spin around her, but just as she thought she would fall, this kind woman held some smelling salts under her nose and the room righted itself again.

"You don't remember me, do you?"

Suddenly to Rose's horror, she did. It was the dreadful woman herself, Magdalen Finch, older, but still attractive, Rose had to admit.

Magdalen was shocked. Rose was a travesty of her old self. She could hardly believe her woebegone appearance, the once smooth skin sagged and creviced, the beautiful, curvaceous shape bent, the old-fashioned silk dress with its high neck and puffed sleeves emphasizing her frailty.

To her surprise, Magdalen felt the stirrings of a strange emotion for her—pity. Who would have thought she could ever have felt pity for a woman she had once loathed and envied with such passion?

Impulsively Magdalen leaned forward. "Would you like some tea? It's still not bad here and the cream cakes are delicious. If the fans are working it could be pleasant. . . ."

Rose felt as if her legs had turned to water. She didn't want to have tea with this woman she knew to be her enemy, and yet she had no more strength to locate the doorman to find the taxi to go to Barataria. For the first time an agonizing thought struck her: she had no idea whether Gloria and little Naomi would even be there if and when she arrived.

As usual, tears slipped easily down her worn cheeks and Magdalen, as if she were guiding a very old lady, tucked her arm through Rose's and carefully led her into the cool Palm Court Restaurant. Magdalen's look of sympathy, the way she so attentively poured her tea, asking her exactly how she liked it, her kind tone completely unnerved Rose.

It was all too much, coming from a woman she'd hated and feared for years. It was as if the world had turned upside down—her own family forcing her down, while her enemies now appeared as friends.

She broke down, pouring out stories of her treatment from Alicia, the continual slights she had to endure, being sent to her room in front of the servants, told to be quiet in front of her little granddaughter Margaret. Once the tap was turned on, nothing would stop the flood of revelations and as one cup of tea followed another, Magdalen's pats on the knee and persuasive murmurs of sympathy were all balm to Rose's wounded spirit. She stuttered in her anxiety to pour out the pent-up pain of years . . . about Drum trying to persuade her on Margaret's birth to sell to him Golden Hill and the acreage she owned, although, as she piteously pointed out, she'd told him years before she'd left everything to him in her will.

"It's all because of his witch of a wife. *She* wants me out of the way. . . ." As she spoke a piece of cake fell onto her dress. To Magdalen's horror, when Rose noticed it, her sobs grew louder. "If she were here, she'd send me to my room. . . ." Rose looked around wildly as if she expected Alicia to materialize from behind a potted palm.

The woman's crazy, Magdalen thought, completely out of control. She turned in embarrassment to see if there was anyone she might call on for help if Rose's hysterics got worse, but except for an elderly, gray-haired couple sitting quietly in a corner, there was no one in sight.

Magdalen couldn't believe her ears. Now what was Rose saying? Alert and tense, she heard Rose repeat, ". . . All because of Drum's little weakness. . . ."

What weakness? Magdalen grasped Rose's hands tightly, as a mother might take hold of a child. "Tell me, Rose," she said sweetly and softly. "Perhaps I can help you?"

To her surprise Rose's tears stopped immediately. She squeezed Magdalen's hands in return. "You can, you can. He doesn't know I know . . . but I've been sending her money. . . . That's why I'm here today. I was on my way to Barataria to see her. I long to see her—them—tell me about her. She works for you, doesn't she? Is she very beautiful?"

Works? Beautiful? Magdalen was dumfounded. What on earth was Rose talking about?

"Gloria . . . Gloria and little Naomi. They should be up at Golden Hill with Drum now, instead of that ugly, wicked bitch. . . ." Rose poured herself a fourth cup of tea, adding lump after lump of sugar like a greedy child.

Magdalen was so stupefied she had trouble holding her teacup without trembling.

Gloria! So Roland Bracken had been right after all. Drum Pollard had been "serviced" by the house that night . . . and after that first visit he'd obviously continued to see Gloria in private . . . and Naomi was the result! It all made sense. No wonder Gloria had always been so adamant about never revealing who was the father of her child.

Magdalen sat back, her eyes half-closed as her mind reeled with what Rose had just told her.

Rose looked at her pathetically, waiting for Magdalen to confirm that Gloria was beautiful, that she did belong at Golden Hill.

"You've never met Gloria?" Magdalen asked slowly, struggling to remain calm.

"No, no, no . . . she's only just begun to cash my checks. I expect she's frightened, but she doesn't need to be. I want her for my friend." The waterworks started again, but this time more quietly, as between the gulps and sobs Rose whispered, "What's she like—the girl who should be Drum's wife? Is she dark, fair, short, tall . . . and little Naomi? Is she beautiful, too? She must be."

Magdalen hesitated. Didn't Rose know that Gloria was black, well, light black, she supposed she could be called, while little Naomi had even darker skin than her mother? Magdalen decided not to answer Rose's questions directly as a plan began to form in her quicksilver mind. She drew her chair closer to Rose.

"They're lovely, perfectly lovely," she said. "And of course, I agree with you. Gloria *should* be living as Drum's wife at Golden Hill . . . but then Drum would have to admit his paternity." She looked at Rose carefully. "I think I know a way this may be able to happen. . . ."

"You mean Alicia would go away and Gloria would come in her place?" Rose looked at Magdalen as if she were her savior.

"Yes." Magdalen sounded thoughtful. ". . . If you promise me that you will do *exactly* what I say. If you follow my instructions *precisely.* . . ."

"Oh, yes, yes." Rose clapped her hands together excitedly, her tears gone, a pale version of her past beauty showing through in the wide smile she gave Magdalen. "Anything, anything."

As if addressing a child, Magdalen then slowly told Rose what she had to do, asking her to repeat everything she said.

"I must tell Drum as soon as possible that I know all about Gloria and their child Naomi . . . that I have been sending them money. . . ." Rose stopped, a look of terror on her face. "But he'll beat me—he'll—he'll. . . ."

Magdalen was horror-struck at Rose's words, but gave no sign, saying hastily, "Of course, he won't be angry when he hears *why.* You must tell him you've been trying to help, because you've learned Gloria is threatening to sue him for paternity. . . ."

"Sue him for paternity?" Rose's face was a picture of confusion. "Is it true?"

"No, of course, it isn't true. Gloria would never do anything like that. She is a *lovely* person," Magdalen emphasized, watching Rose's face intently for every reaction. "Remember Drum hasn't seen her for years. . . . You told me yourself that in her last letter Gloria was saying good-bye, but I know she has never loved anyone else. . . . She's always told me, in fact, she would never, never marry. . . ." Magdalen embellished the facts, for Gloria had never discussed her private life with her.

"So I pretend that she's going to sue . . . because she has been advised to do so by Drum's enemies. . . ." Rose repeated Magdalen's sentence parrot-fashion, but she understood clearly what was expected of her. "And then?"

"You mark my words." Magdalen stared into Rose's eyes. "Drum will come calling on Gloria—and if what I believe is true, he will fall under her spell all over again."

"But how will that make Alicia leave?"

"Be patient, dear Rose." Magdalen smiled serenely. "When Drum starts calling on Gloria again, between us we must make sure Alicia knows all about it, mustn't we?"

So the worm—even that luscious little worm—had turned.

Drum, his hands still shaking from the encounter with his mother, stared at himself in the mirror, seeing nothing, not the strange pallor of his skin, or his trembling lips and bowed shoulders.

He couldn't believe it, yet he couldn't afford *not* to believe it.

He felt no remorse for the bruises he knew he must have inflicted on his mother's thin arms. He hadn't been aware of gripping her so tightly at first, as he'd tried to shake more words out of her, incensed at his own stupidity for holding on to Gloria's pathetic letters—letters he'd known were in that pocket, letters he'd never read again, yet for some inexplicable reason had never been able to throw away. And all the time his own mother had been sniffing around like one of Roland Bracken's bloodhounds, tracking him down like a criminal.

Later, as he sat at his desk in the study, a pile of documents in front of him, Alicia came in to tell him dinner would be in half an hour, but he pleaded he had too much work after their trip abroad to stop for dinner.

"Do you mind? I'd like to skip it. Just get Em to make me a sandwich. . . ." He tried to make his voice sound friendly, but it was an effort.

There he was in one of the finest houses in the world, surrounded by luxury and beauty, living with two women he was now beginning to loathe.

Alicia tossed her head and walked out, slamming the study door without saying a word. "Good riddance," he muttered, swiftly going over to lock the door, coming back to stretch out on his father's old chesterfield.

So Gloria was thinking of suing him for paternity, the little witch. . . .

It was strange he didn't hate *her*. Even as he sweated at the thought of her threat, in a peculiar way his longing for her was still there deep down inside him. But, my God, it would ruin him. Ruin him! She had to be stopped, but how?

There was only one way. He would have to see her, talk sense into her, review her financial situation. . . . Yes, that was it . . . it had to be money . . . but why hadn't she come to him instead of gossiping and letting the situation get out of hand?

It was his mother's fault, he decided grimly. If she hadn't started sending Gloria dribs and drabs of money, Gloria would never have dreamed of trying to hold him up for ransom.

Oh, if only his mother had been taken in the fire and not his father. Drum dug his nails into his hands at the treacherous thought, trying to summon up some vestige of feeling for her, torn between hate and an agonizing pity.

He looked at his watch: 7:00 P.M. Where was Gloria likely to be now? At Le Plaisir? He doubted it, but he also doubted there was a telephone in her mother's house in Barataria.

There was nothing for it. He'd have to wait the long agonizing hours until morning. Should he seek McMurtrey's help? Should he ask the old warrior to act as an intermediary?

Drum dismissed the idea before it was even formed. That would mean McMurtrey would have to know about Naomi and after running to him for help when Alicia had suddenly arrived to announce she was pregnant, who knew what he might think of him . . . that he was some kind of sex fiend!

Drum threw his hands up in the air as if in supplication. He wasn't a fiend. He was a normal, full-blooded male, who'd never been free, who'd been born to have a noose around his neck and who'd been tricked into a marriage he didn't want just as he was beginning to escape.

The next morning, after a miserable, sleepless night, Drum drove into Port of Spain and after spending a couple of hours at the Pollard Oil Company office, sent his secretary out to lunch early. Attempting to disguise his voice he then phoned Le Plaisir and asked to speak to Gloria Simpson.

He was told she didn't report for work until five in the afternoon and, just as he'd imagined, in response to his inquiry, he was told there was no phone at her Barataria home.

He was too tense to eat lunch. He spread numerous papers and press clippings out on his desk, all of which concerned the British Colonial Office's recent approval of a controversial motion proposed by the Legislative Council to postpone the September elections until the following year—"in order to allow more time to debate the recommendations of the Sinanan Constitutional Committee."

Despite the feeling he was on the edge of a precipice—for the second time in five years—Drum forced himself to study the press reactions, which, just as he'd predicted to Gomes, were highly critical, both of the Council's motion and the Colonial Office's sanction.

As Drum saw clearly every day, since his election in 1950 Gomes had pushed for more and still more power, not content with his leap almost to the top of the totem pole. It was ironic, Drum thought, that from the beginning the fat Portuguese had run the show as if he really *was* at the top and had the power to do what he liked, when in fact he did not. The British governor, Sir Edward Beetham, was supposed to approve or disapprove every piece of legislation . . . but in his insidious way, Gomes just glided on and on.

And yet it still wasn't enough for him. He wanted the world to know he *was* the chief minister in name, not just in practice . . . and that was exactly what was going to happen, thanks to him . . . and Gomes knew it, although he never said so.

Hadn't he been lobbying all these past months for the Colonial Office to appoint a group of men to study the situation, bringing the Sinanan Committee—named after the leader of the group—into existence to see if Trinidad was ready for another big step away from the mother country's apron strings?

Americans called a spade a spade, Drum often reflected. There, lobbying was a respected part of political life, but the British—and even Gomes—turned up their noses disparagingly whenever Drum dropped the word to ensure that his colleagues, and especially Gomes, knew how much "lobbying" of the British Colonial Office's stuffed shirts he'd carried out during the past six years . . . ostensibly on Gomes's behalf, but with a very definite eye on what could be ahead for himself.

And now, almost word for word, the Sinanan Committee had recommended what Drum had been recommending for so long—an enlarged Executive Committee, with one person designated as chief minister, Governor Beetham merely to remain as "overseer." Drum would never forget the look of unadulterated joy on Gomes's face when he'd learned of the recommendation. It was almost indecent, Drum had decided, for a man to show his greed for power so publicly.

And now, except for the outcry from the public over the postponement of the 1955 election—exaggerated and inflamed by the press—it was going to be plain sailing all the way.

Drum groaned as reality hit him a sledgehammer blow. Unless he could put a stop to Gloria's paternity suit, it was going to be plain sailing for everyone but him. He doubted it was legal for Gloria to pursue her rights and the rights of little Naomi after so many years, but the adverse publicity would wipe him out completely. There would be no chance for any position on the newly powerful Council for him . . . and worse, the publicity would wreck any hopes he might have in the future for a decision-making role with the West Indian Federation, no longer just a pipe dream but a real possibility.

"REAL REASON BEHIND THE DELAY," screamed one headline. "The British government wants to hold all the aces . . . wants to ensure the West Indian Federation comes into being before making any changes in Trinidad's Legislature."

Drum pushed the papers away and put his head in his hands in despair, noticing as he did so the time by his watch: two-thirty. Another two and a half hours of hell. It was probably just the beginning of many of them . . . and all because of his "itch" for sex, bloody sex. How did other men get away with it? Life was so blastedly unfair.

Magdalen had given strict instructions to the Le Plaisir telephone operator to report to her immediately anyone trying to contact "young Miss Gloria." And so, when Drum again ineptly tried to disguise his voice around five o'clock that afternoon, it wasn't only Gloria who heard him. As she was brought to the booth at the back of the downstairs drawing room, Magdalen was listening on the line upstairs.

Gloria couldn't believe she was actually hearing Drum's voice, but after a second of soaring happiness, she slumped back as he began to shout, "How could you, Gloria? I kept my side of the bargain. Why do you want to destroy me like this?"

Magdalen smiled grimly as she heard the note of torment in Drum's voice. The fish was well and truly on the hook, just a little tug here and there. . . .

She waited for Gloria's response, hardly daring to breathe.

Gloria's voice was hard, cold. "I don' know what yo're talkin' about, Drum." Her joy dead at hearing the voice of the father of her child, she hardly listened as he ranted and raved with never a word about Naomi, not one solitary word about his own little girl.

Tears of anger splashed onto her lap as she clutched the receiver. He sounded like a madman, but then he *was* a madman . . . and she was a madwoman ever to have loved him, trusted him.

". . . Sue for paternity, but I'll ruin you. I'll run you off the island."

The reason for his call penetrated. She grew hot with indignation. "Don' yo' threaten *me*, Drum," she said icily. "Dere's nothin' yo' can do t' me dat yo' haven' done already."

A resentment long buried—of his marriage, his new child, the endless publicity about the lovely, lofty life he lived with his titled wife and daughter (that was a very deep hurt)—surfaced. As if it were somebody else speaking, Gloria heard herself say coolly, "Well, now yo've suggested it, it be a very good idea, Drum. I've wanted t' leave dis place for years an' set up somewhere on mah own away from readin' every day 'bout dat grand Mr. an' Mrs. Drum Pollard an' dere loverly life and their loverly little girlee. Yes, it be a great idea. . . . Thank you very much, Drum. . . ." Her voice broke.

In a flash Drum realized he'd been wrong. His mother had obviously been misinformed. Whatever story was behind it, he didn't know, but Gloria had been loyal and was *still* loyal, of that he was suddenly sure. Oh, God, what had he done? He tried to apologize, hearing Gloria weep at the other end of the line. He pleaded to see her, to help her. He'd never felt such a villain, realizing how callous and unfeeling he must have sounded to the only woman he'd ever really cared about, who'd never given him any trouble, who'd never asked for anything.

"Gloria, goddamn it, what a fool I've been . . . listening to gossip. . . ."

She dried her eyes with her sleeve. "What gossip?"

"Look, don't let's say any more now. I don't like talking to you at this place. Can't I come to . . . to Barataria . . . to your mother's house to settle what has to be settled for your future once and for all . . . and for Naomi."

It was the first time he'd ever said his daughter's name and, hearing Gloria start to sob again, he said quickly, only wishing he meant it, "I'd love to see little Naomi . . . even if it's for the first and last time. Please, please, Gloria. . . ."

To Magdalen's relief she heard Gloria agree to meet Drum the following week, her pleasure at his request to see their daughter overwhelming all her other emotions. Gloria was too practical to expect it could possibly mean any renewal of their relationship. She'd never expected anything—except, she now realized, a word, a gesture from

Drum to show their child had come into the world because of their love and not only because of his sexual needs.

Drum didn't bother to confront his mother with Gloria's response to his accusations. What was the good? He was still shaken she'd found the damaging letters, now burned, but what did it matter if she babbled on about them? Nobody, least of all Alicia, would take her seriously.

He might have reached a different conclusion had he seen the amount of preparation that went into the day Rose had been longing for for over five years, a day when, as Magdalen (her new ally) assured her, Alicia would meet her downfall.

Magdalen and Rose were trying to accomplish two different things. Magdalen wanted above all to discredit Drum Pollard, to humble him once and for all, and, if he happened to lose his honorable wife along the way, so much the better—but of course Rose didn't know any of this.

When Magdalen relayed to Rose her new instructions, knowing now the time and date set for Drum and Gloria's reunion, in Rose's muddled mind she thought they had one common goal—for Alicia to be replaced by Gloria as mistress of Golden Hill, an exchange that would immediately bring about a wonderful elevation in her own position, for Gloria, she knew, would be everlastingly "grateful."

As Magdalen expected, Drum went home from the office to change and freshen up before driving over to Barataria by nightfall. She had no fears about his ability to give Alicia a plausible excuse for his absence at dinner that night. She could almost hear him saying, "Something's come up, sorry, darling. . . ."

From the third-floor-landing window, Rose watched Drum drive away. *Now* was the moment. With confidence built on her overwhelming desire to extinguish the sneering, disparaging, high-and-mighty Alicia once and for all, Rose swept into the library, where as she expected, the "honorable one" was making herself a drink at the bar trolley.

"And what do you think you're doing here?" Alicia asked imperiously, looking Rose up and down as if she were an impertinent servant.

Rose was flushed with happiness as she faced her loathed adversary.

Alicia clutched her throat. Had the woman gone mad?

Before she could speak, Rose started to laugh, swaying backward and forward, hands akimbo on her hips, looking as if she were about to start a macabre tribal dance.

Alicia moved toward the onyx bell wired to the servants' quarters to summon Obee, but she didn't touch it once Rose, in a surprisingly calm voice, began to speak. "You've lost him, Alicia. You've lost him. . . ."

"What are you talking about, you dreadful old woman?"

"You lost him a long time ago. You think he's gone to a business meeting tonight?" Again Rose laughed, a high cackling laugh. "Oh, no, he's gone—as he's gone so many times before—to see his long-time love and the little daughter she bore him. . . ."

Alicia went white. "How dare you!" She tried to shout but the words came out in a hoarse whisper. "How dare you!"

Rose felt like the mistress of Golden Hill again, in complete command, as she continued, ". . . Yes, but now tonight is different. He knows that at last I know. I should have told him years ago. But now Drum knows I want Gloria here with their child at Golden Hill, that I'm willing for him to recognize his responsibilities. . . ."

Magdalen would have been proud of Rose as, encouraged by Alicia's look—a mixture of fear and confusion, but mostly of fear—Rose kept to the script Magdalen had prepared. It was easy. Rose meant every word. She didn't have to lie about any paternity suit as she'd had to lie to the son she loved so deeply.

"I hate you," she said with a radiant smile. "And Drum knows I hate you. Now, he can hate you, too, because he knows I want Gloria and their little daughter here . . . oh, yes." Rose paused for a moment, racking her brains as if she'd forgotten something very important. "Of course, I want little Margaret here too. It's only you . . . I—we—want to be rid of. . . ."

Alicia had had enough. She rushed over to Rose, trying to push her out of the room, but Rose's new-found sense of power had given her new strength.

They struggled together, perspiration pouring down their faces, until Rose managed to break away, waving a piece of paper in the air as Magdalen had told her to do. "He's with her now . . . in Barataria . . . where she lives in her mother's house—but not for long, not for long!"

Alicia snatched the paper out of Rose's hands, just as Magdalen had predicted she would.

It was all working perfectly, but now came a change of plan. As Rose relaxed with a sense of accomplishment, Alicia leapt on her like a tigress, scratching, beating, biting, pinching, propelling her out of the door as she screeched, "I'll make you eat your words. You'll come with me now to Barataria. I'll prove to the world what a crazy old woman you are. This is the last straw! Now, at last, Drum will *have* to consign you to a mental home. You're not fit to be in the same house with my daughter. You're insane, senile. You'll pay for this, you disgusting, foul-mouthed fiend!"

She held Rose's arm in a pincerlike grip as she forced her into her car and sped toward Port of Spain, Rose alternately crying and laughing hysterically.

As Alicia turned at the signpost to Barataria, she slowed down to slap Rose viciously across the mouth. "You'll pay for this, you wicked woman!" she cried. "You're on your way to the asylum and don't think you're not." She peered out in the badly lit street to find the street sign she was looking for, finally pulling up outside a dilapidated house, the porch broken and sagging, a child's swing hanging forlornly from an almond tree by only one rope.

"Get out," Alicia hissed.

Rose, her hand white from gripping the door handle, refused. "I won't! I won't!" she cried hysterically.

Alicia was beginning to feel embarrassed. She realized too late that first she should have gone to Drum's office, where, although she knew how much he hated scenes, she would have insisted he listen to the incredible, horrific story of his mother's accusations. Now, looking at the dismal house, Alicia thought she was going to make a complete fool of herself.

She tried to yank Rose's hand away from the handle to pull her across the driver's seat and out of the car, but Rose held on with grim tenacity.

Alicia then decided to get out and at least knock on the decrepit door, although she grimaced at the thought of even *touching* the knocker.

She would ask whoever the occupant was (Gloria? She pushed the paralyzing thought away that anyone living in such a slum could have anything to do with Drum and Golden Hill and their life) to come outside to witness the total collapse of her mother-in-law. Just looking at Rose, Alicia reflected, anyone could see she wasn't normal, and she would need a witness when it came to making the arrangements to put Rose away.

With more resolve, Alicia left Rose inside the car and approached the front door.

From inside she could hear the faint murmur of voices, but as far as she could see, there was no knocker with which to knock. From a side window she saw a shaft of light illuminating a giant hibiscus bush, and as she didn't want to touch the peeling paint of the door with her knuckles, she went toward the light, coming from a room in which a table was set for dinner with glasses, plates and napkins, each one—to her surprise—neatly pleated into the shape of a fan.

Alicia frowned, wondering what to do next. She continued around to the back of the house where again she could hear voices.

Making up her mind that as Mrs. Pollard she need fear nothing or nobody—that she had a job to do that Drum would thank her for later—Alicia turned the back door handle to find the door opened easily.

At the end of a short hallway there was a chink of light and she realized the voices were coming from there. She looked at her watch hastily. Its illuminated hands gave the time as eight-twenty. Well, there was nothing for it. She needed help. She would be mildly apologetic for disturbing them, but authoritative, too, particularly if there *was* a Gloria in residence, who might have some explaining to do in any case.

Her heart pumped faster as she approached and, lightly knocking on the door, pushed it open. The sight she saw inside would never leave Alicia's mind for as long as she lived. She would dream of it at night and think of it during the day, the same sick vomit rising in her throat that rose then to fill her mouth.

Drum, his eyes half-closed, a beatific look on his face, lay on his back on a large bed that filled most of the shabby room, one arm possessively encircling a naked little black girl who, fast asleep, rested her tight black curls on his shoulder, while a slender, beautiful colored girl had her mouth fastened to his nipple as he fondled her full dark breast with his free hand.

Alicia screamed, one long piercing scream of agony, forced out of her by a torture as devastating and destroying as any physical thing could have been.

Although she was aware of whirling forms, of Drum leaping up, of the little girl wailing, it was all a blur as she stumbled out of the house to the car, where, seeing Alicia's total disarray, Rose's face lit up in a smile that for a few haunting seconds took away all her years.

Alicia couldn't speak; her teeth were chattering and her whole body ached as if she'd been on the rack. As she got into the car, she saw Rose's look of delight. Before Rose knew what was happening, Alicia leaned across to open her door savagely, pushing Rose out onto the road, before starting up the engine to zigzag wildly down the road with the passenger door still swinging open.

Drum rewrote the letter he'd just written, enclosed the check and on sealing the envelope, leaned back in the study chair with a feeling of relief. So far, so good . . . but how long could it last?

This was the third letter he'd written to Alicia in six weeks, the third fat check sent and still no answer from London.

Was she going to start divorce proceedings, and, if so, on what grounds?

Knowing her as well as he did, Drum could just imagine the mental somersaults Alicia was going through as she weighed up the endless pros and cons.

On the one hand she probably now faced the truth: that he didn't love her, that their marriage was a travesty that had to end . . . yet on the other hand, she realized the publicity that would inevitably follow from a divorce would mean the world would learn the facts—facts, which any way you looked at them meant the Honorable Alicia Pollard had lost out, not only to a colored girl, but a colored prostitute, who had given birth to a child, fathered by her husband.

It was an ugly story, Drum reflected—almost as if it were about somebody else—and for that reason he doubted Alicia would do anything. With his father's gambling instinct, he betted that far more likely a course of action would be for her to insist on a legal separation, holding the facts over his head like a sword of Damocles unless he paid and paid and paid. . . . Well, he didn't mind paying for the privilege of encouraging Alicia to stay in England. He missed little Margaret, but it was only after she'd gone that he'd realized he'd begun to grow fond of his pretty, shy daughter. But she'd been snatched up by a half-crazed Alicia that night and they'd both flown out of Trinidad on the last plane that happened to be going to Barbados—not that she'd apparently cared where it was going.

Drum could still remember the relief that had swept over him when he'd finally returned to Golden Hill with his mother—acting as if it were the happiest day of her life—to find Alicia and Margaret gone.

It had been hard for him not to smile almost as idiotically as his mother, a smile he'd been pleased to wipe off her face, when he'd snapped she must really be out of her mind if she expected to see Gloria and Naomi now move into Golden Hill in place of Alicia and Margaret.

By then he'd learned to his amazement that his mother had never even seen either of them, so again it had given him great satisfaction to say casually, "Mother, would you *really* like to see a colored girl as my wife? And Naomi, well, yes, she's pretty, like her mother . . . but, of course, you'd think she'd be even prettier if she wasn't so black. Yes, coal black, mother . . . all the way from Louisa Calderon. Funny things, genes, eh?"

Rose had covered her face, bleating, "It's not true, not true. Magdalen never told me. Magdalen never . . . " It had slipped out.

Magdalen Finch! So *she* had been behind the whole sorry mess from the start. And if *she* was involved, Drum was 100 percent sure his Uncle Roland had to be involved, too. It was natural for Roland to link up with Magdalen Finch; they were natural comrades . . . happy to be back in the Pollard-baiting business!

For hours that night, Drum wrote and ruminated, planning, as his father had once planned, a campaign of action that seemed as foolproof as his father's once had, when Piper had decided to marry the girl he adored, a girl with colored blood, proving to the people his commitment to improving their miserable lives.

Drum didn't have marriage on his mind. Far from it. Marriage, love and sex had always been his undoing, and he was determined to stay as far away from all of it as he humanly could. Instead he had affairs of state to attend to. . . .

He had immediately taken care of the "problem" of Gloria and Naomi, determined to avoid ever succumbing again to a passion that had so surprisingly overwhelmed all thought of caution, a passion incited still more by the docile child who was his, the silky, naked child who, at Gloria's request, had nestled to sleep beside him while her mother's mouth stirred him to ecstasy. No, never again, he vowed—and Gloria, seeming to understand him better than he understood himself, had given him her word she would stay in Martinique, in the house he then bought for her, never again to return to live in Trinidad.

With temptation behind him, Drum was now ready to take on his Uncle Roland who, together with Magdalen Finch, obviously hadn't learned any lessons from the past.

From that moment on, Roland Bracken was a marked man, and so was that "educated snake" as Gomes referred to Eric Williams, the man Roland now openly supported.

As Drum pointed out in a letter to the *Trinidad Guardian*, "How is it possible that for the past thirteen years Eric Williams has been allowed to 'bite the Anglo-American hand that feeds him'?" Drum then listed in detail Williams's endless anticolonial interpretations of Caribbean history and politics.

It was the beginning of a crusade against Eric Williams and Roland Bracken, one that Roy Joseph, the minister of education, who'd granted Williams the use of government buildings for his lectures, soon joined in at the instigation of Gomes.

When Roland appeared on a platform with Eric Williams one evening, it was the opportunity Drum had been waiting for. In twenty-four hours Roy Joseph gave Williams an eviction notice: "You can no longer use any government buildings for your defamatory, undermining remarks. . . ."

Eric Williams was undeterred. The next week, with Roland and members of his Teachers' Economic and Cultural Association beside him, he addressed a growing crowd in the open air, announcing his platform from then on would be known as "The University of Woodford Square."

"It's open hostility," Drum said heatedly to the five ministers, as they finished a late supper at Golden Hill one summer evening. With Alicia gone, the parties had gone, too, although the same tightly knit influential group still gathered "up on the hill" to discuss in private the many machinations of politics, and (to Magdalen's disappointment) with no divorce pending or any sordid details emerging from Drum's reunion with Gloria, there had been no noticeable decline in either Drum's influence or arrogance.

Gomes yawned, not convinced that Eric Williams was really worth worrying about, but humoring Drum because he knew, although Drum didn't know that he knew, how much trouble Roland Bracken, evidently Williams's latest supporter, continued to cause him. Pity he couldn't think of a way to deport the man who had once been his own colleague. Gomes sniffed some snuff and decided it was time to stop Drum worrying once and for all.

"Eric Williams wants to become secretary general of the Commission," Gomes began ponderously. "This is obviously out of the question. On the contrary, the man has to be taught a lesson. I suggest from now on we insist on receiving advance knowledge of his speeches and any written statements on the Caribbean that he intends to make. If he refuses"—Gomes yawned again affectedly—"we will, of course, accept his resignation."

"Do you mean it?" Drum asked with obvious delight.

"Of course, I mean it, dear boy. . . ."

Roy Joseph coughed to remind Gomes that this was his territory. "It's the obvious thing to do. . . . We can't put up with this . . . this disobedience," Joseph finished lamely.

It was a huge error, compounded by the delay in the 1955 election that the five ministers had requested and that had been agreed to by the British Colonial Office.

As the five dispersed that hot summer evening with a roll of thunder echoing through the mountains, no one gave more than a fleeting thought to the decision Gomes had just made.

Who was Eric Williams anyway? An educated upstart who had had the luck to win a scholarship to Oxford, to go to Howard University and then to hold an important research position with the Caribbean Commission. "Luck" he'd then "repaid" by criticizing the men in power who'd helped him develop his brains! Who would take a history professor seriously? Most of the population probably couldn't understand a word he said.

Perhaps because he didn't want to acknowledge how wrong he had been to initiate the campaign against Williams . . . perhaps because he couldn't really accept that Williams's dry and somewhat pedagogic manner could affect the masses, Drum for once didn't see what was happening on his own doorstep until it was too late.

The steps he'd urged be taken against Williams—his eviction from government buildings, the push to obtain his resignation from the Caribbean Commission as more and more obstacles were put in his way—together with the year's delay in the important new election, by which a chief minister would have real power for the first time, all this gave "the new name in Trinidad politics," as Williams was beginning to be called, the necessary time to consolidate a totally new political party.

The People's National Movement (PNM) founded and led by Williams was a party composed of educated and professional colored people who, like Roland Bracken, had been ceaselessly working with Williams since the day they first met him.

Now they worked harder day and night, touring the island, airing major issues—education through denominational or government schools, the role of the press (with many critical references to those like Drum Pollard with vested interests behind the scenes), the necessity for family planning, morality in public life and the true position of ethnic groups in Trinidad's society.

If Drum was one of the last to see Eric Williams as an enormous threat to all he'd worked for, Magdalen Finch was one of the first.

Slowly she started to realize that perhaps she wouldn't need to worry much longer about toppling Drum Pollard from his perch, that fate was taking matters into its own hands . . . for as the weeks went by she was becoming more and more aware of Eric Williams, the "new hero of the masses," unanimously accepted by Indian, Chinese, colored and Negro alike, as well as—to her astonishment—many influential whites. All over Port of Spain she began to see the slogan, "Eric Williams is our man, a man of the people. . . ." and frequently she saw Roland Bracken's name, too, stating his support for Williams and all he stood for.

She hadn't seen or been in touch with Roland for ages, she realized, cursing her lack of foresight. On impulse she called him to wish him and the "new hope for Trinidad" good luck.

To her relief Roland didn't say anything about her lack of contact. But when she invited him for a drink, he demurred.

It wouldn't help him or his illustrious colleague to be seen anywhere near Magdalen's establishment; that it was patronized by those in power—the police, the judges, the "elite" white group—was all part of the corruption that had to go. But Roland never said anything of this to Magdalen. She could still be useful, he considered, so he invited her to tea with Emerald and himself to tell her, "If it hadn't been for Gomes and his group of puppets forcing Williams out of his job with the Commission, we probably wouldn't be in the position we're in today."

He looked at the attractive woman listening so intently, wondering if she could comprehend what he was trying to convey. "You see, Williams doesn't really care for the political cut-throat mentality. . . . He's been making excuses to stay out of the fray for years, while pointing out, as no one else ever managed to do, the facts of our dire situation at the hands of the British despots. When the imperialists he criticized for so long tried to cut his feet from under him, he had no more excuses for staying out. For some reason Williams seems to believe in me. . . . I've been able to keep his mind set on running for office." Roland stretched back, deceptively languid. "Magdalen, I'd say we've definitely got a chance at last!"

At the Inaugural Conference of the People's National Movement on January 15, 1956, Eric Williams, with Roland sitting proudly among his other confidants on the platform, attacked Gomes and the Legislative Council openly for the first time.

In the audience, even Magdalen, used to fierce rhetoric and oratory, found herself moved as Williams brilliantly told a terrifying horror story from the past to the present of slavery, capitalism and continued colo-

nialism. All around her she could see the influence he was having—
and, she thought, totally impressed, what a profound influence he has
already had on Roland Bracken, who'd told her that, since meeting
Williams three years before, he had resumed his legal studies and would
shortly be able to practice law. As he'd put it, ". . . working for Eric
Williams in his administration!"

"You really think there's a chance?" Magdalen had asked him again.

On September 23, 1956, Eric Williams showed Magdalen and the
whole of the West Indies what a chance he had, making history when
the PNM beat eight other parties and thirty-nine independents to win
thirteen out of the twenty-four seats available, the first party to achieve a
majority since universal suffrage had first been introduced after the war.

The governor, on instructions from London, followed Williams's victory with an unusual step. He filled the other nominated seats with
candidates acceptable to Williams's majority party, rather than from
representatives of the special-interest groups, so increasing Williams's
power. Although the governor was still the "overseer," Williams was
elected without delay as chief minister, the outcome Drum had "lob-
bied" the Colonial Office so hard for on Gomes's behalf.

And Gomes? Not only was he *not* to be chief minister, he was out in
the cold, having lost his seat in Port of Spain North.

Drum stared out at his land, at the wealth of agriculture that
stretched uninterruptedly as it had in his father's time all the way to the
foothills of the Northern Range.

Everywhere he looked he could see workers, most of whom he knew
by name, working away in the fields. Downstairs, he knew the silver
and the beautiful furniture would be shining, the cellar would be
packed with fine wines, the servants industriously polishing, cleaning,
washing, cooking. And from the upper windows looking south, with a
stretch of imagination, he could visualize the Pollard oil wells pumping
out the black gold that had helped first his father and then himself
become decision makers on the island . . . but now, what was going to
happen?

Drum shivered, a sense of foreboding clouding everything. As if to
match his mood, a single black cloud smothered the summit of Mount
El Tucuche. What hope was there for him now with Eric Williams in
power and his detestable Uncle Roland beside him?

The only path left for him to follow was the one leading to a West
Indian Federation, where Trinidad would be but a slice, albeit an important slice, of the whole cake. Drum decided he would seek the ad-

vice of Grantley Adams, the prime minister of Barbados, who was one of the Federation's staunchest supporters and a man who'd been to Golden Hill to ask Drum a favor or two in the past. Now, Drum thought grimly, he didn't want any favors, but he *did* want Adams's support, so Adams needed to be told as soon as possible Drum was with him all the way on the Federation issue.

As he deliberated, Drum began to feel better. What did Williams's victory really mean to him? That he could concentrate on becoming part of the Federation, that was what it meant.

Quickly he ran downstairs to pick up the estate office phone to ask his secretary to book him a seat on the next plane to Barbados.

11

Clare
1956

DAY by day, from where Roger Pollard sat in his austere, but expensive suite of offices, he could clearly see a series of steel spires moving upward into view from the deep pit that would become the basement of the new Dallas Memorial Auditorium when the building was completed in 1957. The completion date was the same as that scheduled for the new Love Field air terminal, his father-in-law, W. W. Lovell, had told him sometime back. Perhaps he ought to set the date in marble, Roger had thought caustically, because the terminal was being built on land bought "for peanuts" by W. W. back in the thirties, then sold he'd been told for a figure so astronomical that even W. W.'s personal secretary had made a mistake when first typing the zeros.

As the intercom buzzed twice, Roger sighed. Twice meant Clare was on the line. Remembering her parting shot that morning, he didn't feel up to listening to any more barbs or sneers.

The intercom buzzed again like an angry wasp and, mentally trying to stiffen his resolve to be impervious, Roger lifted the receiver and said quietly, "Yes, Clare?"

Clare's tone was distinctly chilly. "I can't get out of this farce. Daddy insists on giving us—you—this anniversary party. I don't want it. I told

him seven years of marriage isn't the kind of anniversary *anyone* cele-
brates, but he says he feels like celebrating . . . and now he's talking
about inviting Shivers. . . ." Abruptly, almost as if she'd forgotten who
she was talking to, Clare's voice became more thoughtful, even softer.
"I wonder what he's got up his sleeve?"

"Governor Shivers?"

"Oh, don't be more stupid than you can help, Roger!" The cold,
clipped tone was back. "Daddy, of course. He's up to something, that's
for sure. Why don't *you* call him. Tell him the truth . . . that we're
talking about a brand new divorce, not a seven-year-old marriage. Krick!
Krick! Krick!" She slammed the phone down before he could reply.

Krick! The name cut through his mind like an electric saw. The
celebrated "rainmaker" Dr. Irving P. Krick, brought from Denver with
great hullabaloo to break the terrible Texas drought, was probably the
most ridiculed name in Dallas at that moment, as his cloud-seeding
contract to bring rain to the stricken soil had run into its third year with
little results.

Only that morning Clare had scornfully read to Roger that Dr.
Krick's controversial contract was finally going to be canceled, ". . . although Dr. Krick maintains"—she insisted on reading aloud despite his
attempts to get her to stop—"he would have the greatest chance to prove
the worth of his silver-iodine-crystals theories when conditions will be
right during November." Clare had thrown the paper down, almost
snarling. "It sounds so very much like one of your excuses, darlin',
'when conditions will be right . . . let's go on another honeymoon. . . .
You need to relax a little more . . . then perhaps you'll conceive!'"
she'd mimicked.

To compare the long, hard Texas drought with their inability to conceive a child was ridiculous but, as Roger knew now, it was typical of
the way Clare's mind worked, so that whenever she heard or read
Krick's name it sent her off on a painfully familiar harangue.

The doctors they'd seen all over the world! The bills they'd paid! The
rhythms and "programs" they'd followed! Roger shuddered as he looked
out at the builders working in the broiling sun. At first she'd blamed
herself—having her tubes blown, going through curettage after curettage, assured by a number of leading doctors that although she was in
her mid-thirties there was still a chance.

Although he'd been so full of compassion, willing to go along with
every idea she came up with to help make her pregnant, suddenly she'd

decided it was *his* fault, that despite what the doctors said, *he* was impotent, unable to produce, as she now loved to say, "a childbearing seed."

Their marriage had slid downhill fast.

Well, if she wanted a divorce, all right, Roger thought now fiercely. Let's get it over with. He'd tried, God, how he'd tried to make her happy, but one thing he knew with certainty: money couldn't do it. She'd always had so much anyway, so that although now he could buy her anything, take her anywhere, nothing had worked.

The lack of love in her face these days had ironically reminded him of seeing Rose again after the war, when the thought had hit with such force that Rose must have loved his father after all, because every vestige of the lovely Rose had disappeared, gone because his father had gone. When he was gone, the reverse might happen, he reflected bitterly. Clare might suddenly bloom!

It was only in the last year Clare had started to threaten divorce. He hadn't taken her seriously, knowing that while she might mention it in the morning, he might easily end up rocking her to sleep at night, after she'd stormed into his bed, demanding he make love to her, trying to hit him in frustration, as she aroused him less and less with her hysterical accusations, finally collapsing into a torment of tears, asking him to forgive her. He was sick of it. If she threatened divorce again, he would tell her that was exactly what he wanted, too.

What would old man Lovell think about it? Since the review of their original agreement, Roger knew the old Texan liked him, as much as he was capable of liking anyone.

Roger had had nothing to lose and everything to gain, with the addendum so clearly spelling out that, at the end of five years, if oil had been found on the Cedros property there had to be a new agreement "benefiting the owner of the property, Roger Pollard."

The increase from seven-eighths to United Texas Oil and one-eighth to himself to three-quarters to one-quarter in perpetuity on all Cedros gas or oil royalties suited him, for he knew, as the old oilman knew, that the coconut plantation at Cedros was likely to be awash in oil for many more years than they'd both still be on earth.

What could he do with all the money? Another private plane? Another ranch? A yacht? A castle in Spain? What was the use of any of it without the right companion? Clare could have been. Until recently he had still thought she could be . . . but things were going from bad to worse.

To take his mind off Clare and the intercom, which every so often emitted sets of staccato buzzes, Roger went into his private dining room to reread the letter he'd just received from Drum.

Here was another case of somebody who wouldn't listen to reason, wouldn't learn from the facts. At the same time, he reflected sardonically, it was another lesson for himself. Why on earth should he *care* whether his half brother listened or learned, the half brother who'd ruined the only chance he'd ever had for any real happiness with a woman?

Roger looked at Drum's bold scrawl, wondering why he was thinking that way, for, to be honest, he hadn't thought of Alicia in months.

At first it had been deliberate; then it had become natural not to think of her, and slowly the memory hadn't twisted his guts any more. Perhaps because of that great hurt, Clare had never been able to hurt him to such an extent either.

Roger poured himself a scotch and soda from the bar behind a false wall of vellum-bound books. ". . . After all, my knowledge of Trinidad and its people has to be greater than yours, but I appreciate . . ."

Roger didn't bother turning the page. After reading the letter only twice, he could almost remember it word for word—particularly its pompous mind-your-own-business tone.

Roger had written to Drum a few weeks back, trying to tell him to be on his guard regarding Roland Bracken. It had been a tremendous effort and he'd put off writing the letter for weeks, but then, when the news came that there was a new force in Trinidad politics, and according to the United Texas Oil people working out at Cedros, Roland Bracken was definitely an important part of it, Roger had known he had to act. He was first and foremost a Pollard and the Pollard name, and more important the Golden Hill estate, had to be protected, even if it also meant protecting his treacherous half brother.

Two disquieting, seemingly unrelated things had occurred, causing his uneasiness in the first place. First, some months before, he'd seen Roland Bracken, newly affluent, totally assured, in the Nacional Hotel in Havana. When he'd asked his Cuban business colleague who Roland was with, he'd been told it was a man with strong links to the Mafia. Later, when he'd returned to the hotel, he'd seen Roland again—this time apparently hanging on the words of a tall, rugged bearded man.

Rushing to another appointment, Roger had been unable to find out who Roland's companion was. He hadn't thought about the incident again until six or seven weeks later, when a business contact sent him a

strange article in which Roland Bracken, interviewed during a Caribbean lecture tour, had made pointed references to a young "Moscow-
phile" with considerable influence in the Caribbean, masquerading as a
white, Western-loving landowner and occasional columnist. Roland's
remarks had clearly indicated he was referring to Drum.

Roger had sent Drum a copy of the article, pointing out that it was an
obvious attempt to discredit him, ridiculous though the accusations
were. He'd also told him about Roland's apparent meeting with a member of the Mafia in Cuba, and warned him to be on the alert, particularly now that Roland was Eric Williams's close aide, but Drum
obviously thought he knew better.

He knew how to handle men like Bracken, he'd written, admitting,
however, that with Williams's help, Roland had already opened his own
law office and had been given a great deal of government work to get
started.

"However, it's chicken feed," Drum had continued. "I'm working
closely with Grantley Adams and, although you may have read Trinidad
has been rejected as the seat of the Federation, because of the 'corrupti-
bility of its politics,' don't think that's by any means the last word. The
Colonial Office listens to me as much as ever and don't doubt it. Williams and Bracken may be powerful today, but when the Federation
comes into being, just see what happens to them tomorrow!"

Roger sighed as his secretary tapped at the door and came in, a concerned look on her face. Before she spoke, he knew what she was going
to say. "Mrs. Pollard says it . . ."

"Yes, I know," he interrupted, "it's very urgent she speak to me. I
know. . . ."

They were all there, the Texas kingmakers and what stood for kings in
the state—the enormously rich and powerful. In front sat Governor Allen Shivers, who was vacating that role in order to fight Senator Lyndon
B. Johnson for his seat in the Senate. Not easy, Roger thought, amusing
himself by wondering how a man who had left the Democratic Party to
help elect Eisenhower in 1952, now intended to gain the Democratic
votes he needed to beat Johnson.

Although it was ostensibly a party in their honor—with the Dallas
Symphony orchestra performing before a splendid banquet—W. William Lovell, the host, was the star, a magnet attracting the attention of
anyone he wanted to attract, even if he happened to be far away at the

end of the Statler Hilton ballroom, where he'd decided to hold the soirée.

As the orchestra finished Stravinsky's *The Rite of Spring*, W. W. limped to the rostrum to shake director Walter Hendl's hand, before raising his glass of champagne to toast the orchestra, which had been under Hendl's direction for the past seven years. Applause echoed around the ballroom. There was a clash of cymbals. A pause.

What's coming now? An alien anxiety gripped Roger's stomach. There was something about W. W.'s unusual jauntiness that was alarming.

Looking around the ballroom, packed with expectant, obedient faces, silent as they waited for what they also sensed had to be portentous news, Roger saw Clare looking at him from a doorway. She'd left her seat beside him shortly after the symphony began. She indicated she'd like him to join her there. It was as well he did.

Her father started to speak, asking his guests to be ready to join him in another toast. To Roger's surprise Clare slipped her arm through his, clutching on to him as if he were a life raft in a bumpy sea. Outwardly she looked the usual composed, sophisticated Clare of the international set, but Roger could feel the fast beat of her heart, could see the pallor beneath her make-up.

". . . And so a very good reason for my party, my friends, the second party ever to be held in the ballroom since the hotel's inauguration." W. W. nodded toward Conrad Hilton sitting proudly in the front row. "To Clare and Roger!"

W. W. raised his champagne glass. "Come up here. Come on, don't be shy." He gestured toward Clare and Roger, but Clare charmingly waved her hand, shaking her head at the same time, "No, Daddy, no, go on. You have more to announce, haven't you?"

Roger looked at his wife searchingly. If anything, she was now even paler.

What was going on? Was this some kind of bizarre joke the Lovells were playing? Was W. W. now going to announce their impending divorce?

As if to reassure him, Clare squeezed his arm even more tightly, her long nails digging painfully into his wrist.

Lovell, leaning heavily on his silver-topped cane, gave his usual humorless laugh. "Yes, Clare, you're right. I do have more to announce, but I wasn't aware you knew that." The crowd laughed along with him, as curious as Roger was.

The cymbals clashed again . . . as W. W., turning to the right, said gruffly, "I want you to meet my bride . . ." and Victoria, the nurse Roger had always considered so perfect in her job, so dependable and retiring, came onto the stage to kiss the old man's weathered cheek.

As the crowd roared "hooray," whistled and applauded and the new Mrs. W. W. Lovell put her arm demurely through her husband's, Clare slumped heavily against the wall. For a moment Roger thought she was going to faint, but in a second she recovered, quickly shooting out a hand to grab a glass of champagne from a passing waiter.

Before Roger knew what was happening Clare had left his side to stride up to the stage where both her father and Victoria started to smile as she approached.

Clare turned to face the crowd that was still roaring with excitement over the amazing news. As she raised her glass, like well-trained seals the majority of onlookers raised theirs, too, their smiles still stupidly on their faces as she said, her old drawl coming back as she spoke, "To the cleverest little gold digger in the good ol' U.S.A., folks!" She swung around and threw the contents of the glass in Victoria's face, striding back down to the ballroom floor with a look of satisfaction.

In seconds the scene was one of chaos, as Lovell's underlings scrambled to help Victoria and W. W. make as dignified an exit as possible.

Victoria never showed the slightest trace of embarrassment, and, as Roger left to go in search of Clare, whom he was now sure had to be seriously unhinged, he saw the ex-nurse calmly use her new husband's handkerchief to wipe champagne away from her face and splattered shoulders.

Just as Victoria never showed any signs of discomfort, neither did Clare. As the Pollard chauffeur was nowhere in sight, Clare hailed a cab easily, calmly.

It was only when she sat back, eyes closed, that the enormity of what she had just done swept over her. Oh, but she would do it again and again . . . as one day she had thrown a glass of champagne over Victoria's bare, beautiful breasts, playfully licking and sucking away every bubble until Victoria had been ready to do anything she'd asked her to do. The lying wretch.

Clare forced back the tears. She wasn't going to cry over that tramp. She wouldn't. She couldn't.

Right up until that terrible agonizing moment in the ballroom, she hadn't wanted to believe, had still clung to the foolish hope that Victoria hadn't returned her phone calls, hadn't been to see her in almost a month, because she really was still away with her sick mother.

That her father had also been away for the past two weeks had forced her to be suspicious, yet, when she'd gone over everything in her mind, trying to think of something that might have appeared different in their relationship, she hadn't been able to remember a thing. Not a look, a word or a touch.

Even Victoria's "sick mother" had to have been part of the plot. "She'll be back with Mr. Lovell by the end of the month," was all she'd been told, and that was certainly true. Victoria had come back to be introduced to the world as her father's wife, as her stepmother!

The tears wouldn't be stemmed. They rushed, crashed down her face, streaking her make-up, breaking through the composure she'd built up so steadily through the years.

By the time Roger found her, Clare was comatose, on the way to oblivion and death, a bottle of empty sleeping tablets on the bedside table beside her. She would have achieved her objective but for Roger's intervention, something she told him, on her recovery in the private clinic, that she didn't feel she should thank him for.

Nevertheless, as she recovered she became a different Clare. Neither the old Clare nor the one who had started to threaten divorce during the past year.

To outside observers, although a major rift in the family was expected, it was as if nothing had happened. No threats of "never darken my doorstep again," no more glasses or even epithets thrown in public.

There was a coolness between father and daughter that most of the outside world never saw, and Roger suspected the old man had, in fact, probably received a vicarious thrill from the jealous scene played out at the Statler Hilton . . . because as far as Roger was concerned that was what it had all been about. Clare had obviously become obsessed with having a child. She had momentarily "lost her balance," and, as Roger evaluated it, it was as if W. W. had announced the arrival of a new child, as Victoria certainly could be as far as her age was concerned.

It was a case of "mistaken identity," and the psychiatrist that he and Clare visited together after her attempted suicide seemed to concur.

Although it had been a traumatic time of tension and anxiety, perhaps it all had to happen in order for the new Clare to emerge . . . she was more subdued, less abrasive and aggressive in her demands . . . a reflective Clare, who, two months after her discharge from the clinic, agreed to Roger's suggestion that they take the new yacht down to the Caribbean, and perhaps even look in on Golden Hill.

The day before they were to leave, Roger was dictating to his secretary when the intercom buzzed twice, but now he no longer dreaded to hear Clare's voice.

"Darlin', I have some exciting news for you, for us. . . ." The careful slow enunciation, the deliberate placing of each syllable all meant she wanted his total attention.

Even so, Roger was unprepared when she began to cry softly, telling him, "We can't go on the cruise, darlin'. The doctor has just told me I'm . . . I'm pregnant. Oh, Roger, come home quickly."

There's something about French perfume . . . about Fr-French women . . ." Paulette said drowsily, oblivious to the hiccups that neatly punctuated every few words.

Theo sat back relaxed, in no way embarrassed by the knowledge that had come to him a few minutes earlier that his wife was getting tipsy.

It was such a rare occurrence to see Paulette take a drink, let alone two or three drinks, he found himself amused to note the glazed look on the French perfumer's face, as he tried to look interested, even fascinated by his important new customer's platitudes.

Theo couldn't let the man suffer for long. He interrupted Paulette's monologue to ask the perfumer an ego-building question about his most recent fragrance composition, and the glazed look disappeared immediately.

The size of their first order had been impressive, even to a company used to supplying the giant cosmetic companies of the world, Theo knew that. As he had casually dropped the figure, a ripple of satisfaction had crossed the generally impassive face of Henri d'Arabées, head of the old, established, essential-oil house, who only the year before had decided to take an unprecedented step and open a subsidiary in the United States. It was a step that, according to the other French suppliers, was destined to be the first mistake of his long acclaimed career, for as the Frenchmen remarked between themselves, d'Arabées actually believed one day American women would buy perfume for themselves in the same quantities as did European women, buy it and then wear it on a day-to-day basis, not just a touch behind the ears three or four times a year on "special occasions" as they were in the habit of doing now.

As lush, pale gold Viennese pears, floating on a foam of champagne, were put in front of them, and more Dom Perignon was poured into glasses so finely cut that, at the first sip, Theo had been alarmed he might accidentally drink the glass, too, fireworks far below illuminated the summer night sky, coloring the Mediterranean shimmering silver.

Paulette was in ecstasy. To come to the South of France and particularly to Grasse had been a lifetime dream come true. She hiccuped again as she stared at the ribbons of lights hundreds of feet below, lights that from the celebrated restaurant built halfway up the mountainside stretched in one direction all the way to the Italian border and in the other across the hills to Antibes and Cannes.

As her gaze returned to the beautiful restaurant terrace where they were seated at one of the best tables, she gasped. Could it be possible?

The French perfumer followed her gaze and, with an air of satisfaction—as if he had personally arranged the surprise just for her—answered her unspoken question. "Yes, Madame Finch. It is indeed Winston Churchill. He is very fond of the Château de Madrid. He is almost certainly here with his host, on his yacht, the *Christina*, in Monte Carlo. Ah yes, see he is right behind him, Monsieur Onassis with . . ." The Frenchman sniggered suggestively, "Maria Callas . . . and, well, yes amazing, tonight also Greta Garbo is with them. . . ."

As he heard Paulette gasp again, although he knew he should ridicule this American woman's passionate interest in the powerful, famous and rich, he was at the same time elated, congratulating himself that he had chosen to bring the Finches to the Château de Madrid on such a perfect night for "stargazing." He complimented himself on his appropriate pun—his English was improving, the term "stargazing" had come so quickly into his mind—as waiters bowed and fawned around the illustrious group as they moved slowly to a tucked-away corner table.

"Did I drink too much at the Château de Madrid?" Paulette asked Theo with a worried frown, as a few days later she clipped her safety belt into place on the plane taking them back to New York, via Paris.

"Not one drop too much." Theo patted her knee. "Happy?"

"Ecstatic. Oh, Theo, can you believe it? I can't. . . ."

"We've worked for it, darling, and we deserve it. But you know this French division means I'm going to be away more than ever . . . but . . ."

"Oh, I don't mean that!" she interrupted. "I mean seeing Winston Churchill that night and . . . oh, I'll never forget this trip, never!" As quickly as she had looked excited, she suddenly looked wistful, forlorn. "I wish it could go on forever."

Theo laughed. "But it can! It will . . . it's going to. It won't be long before people will feel the same way about meeting you as you feel now about meeting the famous. You're going to be a star, Paulette, just like Helena Rubinstein and Elizabeth Arden, only much much younger!"

She pinched his arm. "Stop teasing me, Theo! You know I'm not up to that. You'll be the star, not me. You're the one with the looks, the charm. . . . I'm just a back-room girl. . . ."

It was a familiar conversation and Theo sighed, before beginning his usual half-scolding, half-loving lecture to build his ·wife's self-confidence.

By the time they were halfway across the Atlantic, the star-studded visit to the South of France was already part of Paulette's memories, as she worked with Theo on the plans for the Tropica opening at Bloomingdale's, cleverly worked out by Theo to coincide with the opening of New York's most spectacular new restaurant in years, the Forum of the Twelve Caesars.

"Joe Baum plans to have toga-clad waiters," Theo told her, as the long journey went on, ". . . the wine will be served in buckets made out of centurion helmets . . . and at each table it's agreed will be special favors from Tropica—the Milk and Honey Skin Treasures in the new Cleopatra packaging."

"And the next night Bloomingdale's is really giving *us* a party to celebrate our opening at the store?" Paulette's voice was shrill with excitement.

"Paulette, it's the least they can do. They're really giving *themselves* a party . . . to congratulate *themselves* on winning out against Lord & Taylor and Saks."

In forty-eight hours Theo could hardly remember he had ever been away to complete the lengthy but satisfactory deal with one of France's most eminent essential-oil houses . . . commissioning a totally "different" kind of French perfume to capture and hold the attention of the American consumer, who, he agreed with d'Arabées, could be an enormous fragrance user . . . once the right formula was found.

He hardly had time to go home any more, he thought as he shaved in the simple tiled bathroom attached to his New York office. Whatever happened, he had to talk to Tommy before he was put to bed and he *had* to finish the letter to his mother.

As Theo slapped a new submission scent around his chest and neck, he grimaced. It still wasn't right. A man wasn't going to wear anything with a fruity note, goddamn it. To think of the time he'd wasted with that young ass of a perfumer, who had the audacity to think he knew more than God. Theo threw the small unlabeled bottle into the waste-paper basket and picked up the phone.

"Is Tommy there, Babette?" He smiled as he heard the singsong Trinidadian voice of his son's nurse . . . and probably Tommy's best friend by now, he thought ruefully.

"Tommy? Well, old man, and what have you been up to today? A sailing lesson? That sounds great. You got wet? Well, sailors always get wet—that's half the fun."

As he talked to his small son, Theo's eyes searched for the letter he'd started to write to his mother. It had to be somewhere on his desk . . . in the pending file probably, as he now remembered he'd started it the day he'd left for London, Paris and Nice.

"Don't forget to say your prayers. Yes, God bless Granny Mags, too, that's right. No, I know you don't remember what she looks like—but God does. He won't make a mistake, I promise you. He'll know who you mean."

By the time he put the phone down, Theo had renewed his deter-mination to finish and mail the letter the next day, even if it meant he had to stay up all night. It was terrible, he told himself, that his mother had only seen her grandchild once, and that was three years ago, the only time they'd ever taken Tommy down to Trinidad. It was a ridiculous situation altogether that his mother was still living in the Caribbean, when they could now offer her such a comfortable life in the United States . . . a life, Theo reflected, she couldn't comprehend because, despite her amazing grasp of things, she had never once set foot off the island.

It was still dark at six the next morning when Theo arrived at his office and switched on the study lamp to reread the letter he had started to his mother almost three weeks before. He grunted with satisfaction at the way it still seemed to flow ". . . From what I read in the papers and what you yourself have written to tell me about Williams's five-year plan and his mandate to produce a welfare state with free health, educa-tion and cheap houses for all who can't afford to buy them, subsidies to small farmers, a bigger harbor, etc., it sounds to me as if it's time you started to think about leaving! For who's going to pay for it all? You know he can't raise sufficient loans, so now there are all these rumblings about increased taxation of the rich. It's obvious to me, Mother, it's only a matter of time before the white landowners will be driven out and their land becomes 'nationalized.'"

Theo wrinkled his forehead as he picked up his pen. "All this means I really believe the time has come when you must consider selling the property at Arima. You obviously can make a large profit, but that isn't the main reason I'd like you to sell. Paulette and I recently returned from France, where we signed a very advantageous arrangement to import certain essential oils—jasmine, tuberose, carnation—lovely oils. It means we will be taking less from the Caribbean, where already irritating restrictions are being put into force."

Theo leaned back. Now he was getting to the part of the letter he looked forward to writing. "The most important point of this letter is that a few years back Paulette and I opened a nest-egg account in your name in a Miami bank, looking forward to the day when we could tell you there were sufficient funds there for you to be able to join us here and buy a house near ours. That day has now arrived. We're waiting with outstretched arms to welcome you to a life, I can promise, you will be able to live very comfortably and 'happily ever after' and"—Theo smiled as he imagined his mother's tearful face as she read the last line—"Tommy can't wait to get to know his Granny Mags. . . ."

As Theo imagined, Magdalen was tearful as she read the last sentence of his letter.

Tommy! How she yearned to get to know her little grandson, too, but Theo was quite wrong about Williams, she told herself. Williams was a uniquely fair man; he'd even invited a white man to join his first cabinet! He might well bring about a welfare state, but there was nothing wrong with that, Magdalen reflected, remembering her own galling growing up and the way she'd had to pinch and scrape to give Theo any kind of education.

Nationalized land? That was something else again. She doubted it would ever happen. There was one way to find out. She would call up her old friend Roland Bracken and ask him outright.

It wasn't that easy, however, to get through to Roland any more. He eventually returned her call but then only to say he was far too busy to make an appointment to see her.

It was not a lie. He was busier than he had ever been, not only working for Eric Williams, but increasingly now for the nameless ones behind Luis, who supplied him with an endless stream of money. This he was directed to use in a number of subversive ways, above all to implant seeds of discontent in Williams's mind—to move on his pledge to get the British out of Trinidad, and to show both the U.S. *and* Britain that if they wanted to continue to get their greedy hands on Trinidad's oil, they would now have to pay the proper price.

With careful prompting, as the weeks passed, Williams gave Roland the go-ahead to start renegotiating the tax arrangements made years earlier with the major British and American oil companies, at the same time warning him to move warily. "This is a crucial time. We need the support of the leaders of the white community," the chief minister stressed.

It didn't help Roland's frame of mind to see a photograph of his nephew on the front page of England's *Sunday Times*—in London on the occasion of the birth of the West Indian Federation. "A Federation," said the caption, "governing three million people scattered in islands covering over seventy-seven thousand square miles." It was painful to swallow the news that Drum Pollard was now considered "Grantley Adams's most able lieutenant . . . and a rising star to watch in the Caribbean." It was all the more painful that for the time being, having agreed not to "antagonize" Drum, Roland knew his hands were tied, for to Eric Williams that same newspaper report was a forcible reminder that Drum and others like him still had considerable influence.

To Roland's dismay in April at the first elections for the Parliament of the West Indian Federation, the opposition Democratic Labor Party won six out of the ten seats allotted to Trinidad, totally defeating Williams's People's National Movement. What was worse, Drum Pollard actually won one of the seats as an independent. "The rising star has risen," screamed the *Trinidad Guardian*.

Luis was swiftly on the scene, as if he sensed that for all his careful training Roland might easily be tempted to do something stupid. He outlined a plan of action, one that could not only knock Drum Pollard off his public pedestal, but could seriously undermine the life of the Federation itself . . . and the plan started with Roland planting suspicions in Williams's mind about the intentions of the other West Indian leaders.

There was also another way to achieve their objectives. Luis instructed him, "When you start to renegotiate the oil contracts, start with the company where there's a Pollard involved—United Texas Oil. Get Roger Pollard down here at your beck and call. By the time you've 'renegotiated' with Pollard, Eric Williams will be ready for you to start a different campaign against Drum, your real adversary . . . a 'smear' campaign that will make McCarthy's in the States look like child's play."

"It happened in Venezuela. It's happening with Sukarno's ban on Shell Oil's operations in Indonesia. It's going to happen in Trinidad. They'll steal the oil we've spent millions of dollars to get out of the ground. They're thieves!" As usual, W. W. never raised his voice, but he sounded unusually hoarse, Roger thought, as they breakfasted together.

"D'you really think I need to go down there?" Roger interrupted irritably. "I don't like leaving Clare. You know, she's very . . . well, edgy, nervous. The doctors say everything is going well, but obviously she's not a twenty-year-old going through her first pregnancy. I'm not sure. Why not send Ballantine? He's a tough negotiator."

W. W. Lovell watched Roger through narrowed eyes. "He's tough all right, and he's a better negotiator than you'll ever be, Roger, but you're missing the whole point. It isn't a case of negotiation. This is a confrontation." He leaned back as if he were suddenly fatigued. "The only way we're going to do business with these black bastards is for them to think we're giving 'em what they want . . . and they want a Pollard. Don't you see? They want to show off to a Pollard . . . to prove they're the guys on top now, not the Pollards of Golden Hill. They've asked for a Pollard and that means *you*. If you want to please me, you'll agree to go and let 'em think you know when it's smart to eat humble pie."

Roger was silent, annoyed at himself, knowing his father-in-law was right on target as usual, knowing he was going to do exactly what he wanted him to do . . . not because by "eating humble pie," as W. W. put it, he felt he could ameliorate the situation. What did it matter if United Texas Oil's share of the Trinidad cake was going to be less? It was still a mighty thick slice. No, he would go to Trinidad because if he could do something to please the old man, then he knew he wanted to do it.

As Roger drove down the long drive of his magnificent home on the outskirts of Dallas, he wondered how he'd break the news to Clare that he had to make a quick trip to Trinidad, for he'd promised her that wonderful day she'd told him the news that he would never leave her until their baby was safely delivered, and the last three months had been the happiest they'd ever spent together.

To his surprise, Clare hardly demurred when he explained the situation. "Oh, Clare, I'm so happy you're not upset. I hate leaving you even for a few days." He hugged her to him, feeling her tremble, hoping she was feeling the same surge of warmth for him as he was for her.

She moved away so imperceptibly he wasn't even sure who'd moved first.

She seemed different even from the Clare of only that morning, but he put it down to tiredness. "Did you take your pills, baby?" he asked concerned. "I hope you haven't been overdoing that fund raising? Has Fred Florence been driving you too hard?"

Clare put her arms loosely around his neck, looking at him mischievously. "Looks like we'll reach the four-million mark. . . . In fact Fred says we're going to get more . . . enough for two new hospitals on Hines Boulevard if we want them, not just one, sweetie pie. . . ."

Roger kissed her. "Oh, you're too hard to resist. No one can resist giving you whatever you ask for. . . ."

Is it true, Clare asked herself, as she lay awake hours later. Roger's heavy breathing was telling her that he'd fallen into his usual healthy deep sleep. Am I irresistible? Is that why Victoria called me today? "For old times' sake," she'd said. What did that mean? Which "old times" did she want to remember?

Clare turned her body carefully to one side, feeling her abdomen with delicate hands. No sign of life yet . . . but the doctor had said everything was going according to plan. Was she really going to get everything she wanted after all? A child—perhaps even a healthy robust son that her father wouldn't be able to ignore, a grandson to inherit the millions not already bequeathed to the Lovell Foundation? Was she actually going to bear a son . . . and . . . the thought made her sigh aloud . . . also enjoy Victoria again?

She went over Victoria's words. It had been a one-sided conversation. She just hadn't known what to say. The call had been so unexpected.

"Clare?" Even the familiar slightly mocking note in Victoria's voice had made her feel weak.

"Yes." No more, no less.

"Clare, why can't we meet?" She hadn't replied.

"For old times' sake. . . ." Still Clare hadn't replied.

"Can't you speak freely now?" Without waiting for an answer Victoria had gone on quickly. "Clare, please call me tonight at my mother's number." Click. She had put the receiver down.

Now, although from the bedside clock Clare could see it was nearly eleven-thirty, she longed to make the call. She held her breath as Roger stirred, muttered something in his sleep, then resumed his heavy breathing.

Slowly, she slithered out of bed, sure Roger wouldn't wake, yet every one of her nerve endings alert, anxious not to change even a crease in the sheets.

She went into her dressing room, seeing herself reflected a dozen times in the mirrored walls, her cream-colored silk nightgown merging with the cream suede chaise longue, the cream-colored antique silk pleated drapes.

Even the phone took on new dimensions as she stared at it . . . an instrument of torture, she knew that already.

She lifted the receiver. She put it down. She lit a forbidden cigarette and lay back on the chaise longue, flexing her long legs, willing herself to go back to bed, telling herself fiercely the whole idea of Victoria waiting for her call so late at night was ridiculous.

She was dialing before she knew what she was doing. She might have been somebody else fumbling to find the right digits: 8824. Even before it began to ring, she put the receiver down as if it burned her fingers. She got up to go back to the bedroom. . . . Oh, what the hell!

Clare stubbed out her cigarette and this time dialed with steady fingers. It rang once, twice. . . . She was about to put the receiver down when Victoria's voice came on the line as clear as if she were in the same room. "I was giving you until midnight, Clare. I thought you'd call. When can we meet?"

"You witch . . ." she whispered, her body shaking with a mixture of anger and longing. "Why aren't you home with my father?"

"That's a good question, but I don't have to answer it. It's all right, he thinks I'm doing good works"—she paused—"When, Clare, oh, when. . . ." There was a note of pleading, turning Clare's insides to pulp.

It was as if somebody else were speaking. "Roger's going away next week. . . . I don't know which day. I don't know anything. . . . This is insane!"

"I'll come to see you the day he leaves. I'll know when you know. I have something important to tell you." Click. Victoria had put the phone down, again before Clare had a chance to reply, something she would never have dared to do once.

Clare frowned. This was a new Victoria. She looked at her reflections, sinuous, graceful. As she lay back the skirt of her nightgown slipped open to reveal one leg all the way up to her thigh and she smiled, a slow smile at the many Clares in the mirrors.

Perhaps there was a more assured, new Victoria—not surprising as she was now the wife of one of the country's richest men—but that one give-away note of pleading Clare had heard in her voice meant the Victoria she knew so well was still alive—and in need.

Roger had frequently vowed never to set foot in Trinidad again, fearing he wouldn't be able to bear the pain if the wound Alicia had caused reopened as soon as he stepped out into the sensuous, tropical air.

But it was going to be all right, he told himself with relief, as he looked out at the familiar street scene. There was no pain; no agonizing thoughts of the past. He was cured. Alicia could never hurt him again. Instead, as the chauffeur-driven car neared Port of Spain, Roger found his thoughts returning to Clare—and a wonderful feeling of contentment filled him as he recalled that, although he'd only just arrived, he was already counting the hours until his return to Texas, to his lovely home and wife.

He'd decided before leaving the States not to stay at Golden Hill. He hadn't wanted to put himself in the position of having to ask Drum for anything, least of all "room and board," and he knew he'd feel uncomfortable, however welcoming Drum set out to be, especially having to encounter Rose who had last seen him so out of control the day she'd come to beg him to forgive Alicia and take her back with him to England.

And now, he'd been told, that's where Alicia was again. It hadn't given him any satisfaction to learn the marriage hadn't worked; he'd been too taken up with his own problems with Clare to give it much thought—problems, thank God, that were now behind them.

It was difficult to believe, he reflected now, that he'd once hated Drum so passionately he'd wanted to knock him senseless, perhaps even kill him, when now a deep-rooted feeling made him want to watch over his younger, wild half brother . . . to warn him there were dangerous winds of change in Trinidad that could sweep him and his assets, including Golden Hill, onto the dust pile.

The next day, as Roger sat facing Roland Bracken in his large air-conditioned office, he felt the same uneasiness he'd felt in Havana, seeing Roland so engrossed, first with a member of the Mafia and then with the hypnotic, bearded stranger.

As the meeting progressed, Roger's uneasiness grew, not so much because of what Bracken said—Roger had been prepared for demands to increase the island's participation in oil profits. It was more because Roland acted as if it went without saying that the glaring inequities of an arrangement made at an unenlightened time had to be rectified.

He left Roland's office dispirited, feeling he'd been at his least effectual, not even sure what to report back to W. W. Nothing had been signed, no specific figures given; only one word had dominated Roland Bracken's half of the conversation: *change.*

It was beginning to dominate the Trinidad headlines too, Roger noted the next morning, when his nameless fears took on fresh meaning as he read the lead story about Eric Williams's just-announced proposals to eliminate the power of the British governor and the Crown.

Roger could hardly believe his eyes. At the same time he cynically reminded himself that what was of such shattering importance to the Trinidad white population, probably hadn't even rated a line in the *Dallas Morning News,* if indeed in the *New York Times.*

To Roger's annoyance, immediately beneath the main story was a brief mention of his own arrival in Trinidad "for the first time in twelve years—a visit, we are told by a reliable source, necessitated by the chief minister's long-term plan to nationalize the Trinidad oil industry."

Everywhere he went he heard fears expressed that Williams and his People's National Movement were looking for support from the Eastern Communist bloc to replace that given over the past one hundred and fifty years by the British. Just where did Roland Bracken's real sentiments lie, Roger wondered, remembering the article he'd been sent containing Roland's ambiguous remarks about Drum being a "secret sympathizer with the reds."

It was too complex to think about. To his relief, he'd discovered Drum was away in London, while Rose was "indisposed and unable to see anybody." It was time to leave. He'd carried out his father-in-law's wishes. He'd put forward the United Texas Oil Group's position, pointing out the company's colossal expenditure in drilling for oil on the island, and there hadn't been any reaction.

He'd been away four days. It was four days too long away from Clare. As he told the United Texas Oil office to get busy working on his return ticket on the next available flight, the uneasiness his meeting with Roland Bracken had provoked gripped him by the throat. Clare. He had to get back to Clare.

There hadn't been a moment's embarrassment, no opening sentences, no apologies or explanations.

As soon as the maid closed the door behind them—"I don't want to be disturbed," Clare had instructed—they had had their hands on each other. Clare feeling Victoria's sharp shoulder blades as she held her at arm's length. Victoria squeezing Clare's waist.

"Champagne?"

Victoria nodded, her eyes never leaving Clare's face as she deftly opened the bottle waiting in the ice bucket.

"To us." Victoria raised her glass.

Clare didn't respond, sipping the champagne, aware Victoria was still watching, almost studying her.

Did she think she was going to throw another glass of bubbly over her? And spoil her obviously expensive silk dress? Clare laughed at what she took to be an apprehensive look on the girl's face.

"Come here." It was a command she had often given, obeyed in the past too quickly—or so she'd teased Victoria. ". . . Your nurse's training is useful, my darlin' . . . but I'm not dying. Take your time. Let's savor every moment." But Victoria was no longer a nurse. She was a rich man's wife, already used to giving commands herself and, as if to emphasize that fact she sauntered over to the sofa to sink back leisurely against the deep cushions.

It was a game they were playing, Clare thought, half amused, half angry, where each thought they knew the moves the other was going to make. Well, she wasn't going to give Victoria the satisfaction of behaving as she'd behaved before. Nevertheless her heartbeat quickened as Victoria languidly leaned forward to put her glass down, her decolleté neckline opening wide to expose her bare breasts, her full pink nipples. Clare could already feel them in her mouth as she sat beside her on the sofa.

Her voice throaty with the strain of holding back, she quickly said, "To what do I owe the honor of Mrs. W. W. Lovell's presence? What's so important that couldn't be said on the phone?" She began to feel faint as Victoria moved toward her, her face so close now that Clare could smell faint acidity from the champagne on her breath, while her fingers—God, she'd forgotten what wonderful, crazy-making fingers the girl had—slowly traced the shape of her belly.

"You're more beautiful than ever, Clare," she murmured. "Your belly's rounder, softer. Pregnancy suits you. D'you think it suits me?"

"Suits y-you? What d'you . . . you mean?" The room was swinging around as Victoria came closer . . . closer, one hand pinioning her back against the cushions, as the other insolently continued its caress.

"Yes, isn't it ironic,"—Victoria was almost hissing—"both of us pregnant at the same time. Your father's beside himself with joy at the thought of having a son and heir at last. . . ."

Clare tried to scream, but no sound came out. Victoria pregnant! An heir for the Lovell millions. Victoria was smiling, a peculiar, gloating smile. It was the last thought Clare had before she fell into a dark, deep chasm.

It wasn't the brilliant light flooding through the room that returned her to consciousness. It was the pain, crashing through her body as if a sword were sawing its way through. A man in a white coat was standing over her, a syringe in his hand.

As pain engulfed her, she screamed—and this time she could hear her high-pitched hysterical scream of fear. "No, no, no. . . ." She was drowning. Her body was drowning. Her baby was drowning. She could hear Victoria's voice: ". . . beside himself with joy . . . a son and heir at last!"

When she awoke, her head and heart pounding, she could hear voices—a man's and a woman's. Victoria's?

She heard a door close and carefully tried to peep through her lashes without totally opening her eyes.

A familiar hand was on her arm—and now came the man's voice again. Roger's voice.

"Clare, my darling, my angel, don't . . . don't move. Everything is going to be all right. Oh, my darling. . . ."

There were tears in Roger's eyes. Idiot, Clare thought petulantly. Men always cry when women have babies. Well, what kind of baby had she had? A boy or a girl? It had to be a boy.

"Where is he?" The voice didn't sound like hers.

To her horror Clare saw tears coursing down Roger's cheeks.

"I blame myself," he sobbed. "I should never have left you . . . never, never! I'll never forgive myself!"

Blame himself? What on earth was he talking about?

She began to shake . . . she couldn't stop shaking. Had they taken another baby away from her? They couldn't have—there was no reason. Roger, the father, was the husband almost hand-picked by her father.

The bitter realization that she'd lost the baby hit her at the same time as she remembered the scene in the drawing room. "The shock . . . the shock . . ." she began to moan as Victoria, an anxious look on her face, came into the room.

"Oh, Clare, your father and I are so sorry . . . so very sorry. . . ."

"Go away," Clare screamed. "Go away! You're responsible. If it weren't for you. . . ."

Roger tried to calm her, saying "Clare, Clare, everyone wants you to be well. You don't know what you're saying. . . ."

"Oh, don't I! If she hadn't told me she was pregnant . . . that my father was beside himself with joy at the thought of having a son and heir at last. . . ."

Victoria backed against the wall nervously. "Clare, what on earth d'you mean? How could you ever have got that idea? I'm not pregnant or ever likely to be. Oh, Clare, poor darling, you're imagining things. . . ."

As the months passed, Clare gave up trying to make Roger believe Victoria had deliberately lied, "inventing" a pregnancy because she'd known how much it would upset her.

It didn't matter how many times Clare tried to impress upon him that Victoria *knew* she would lose the bulk of the Lovell fortune if she— Clare—gave birth to a son, because Victoria *knew* her father had promised her, his only daughter, that if she settled down and married "the right man," then had a son christened to carry on the Lovell name, by far the largest part of the Lovell fortune would be left to him. But Roger refused to believe anyone could behave as Clare accused Victoria of behaving. It was unconscionable, he said, inconceivable.

Would no one ever believe her? Clare felt trapped, powerless to stop what she could see happening in the future—when Victoria, that evil, seducing witch would walk away with everything!

She started to pick up the pieces of her old life, going to the Paris collections, New York and London first nights, making new "friends," artists, designers, dancers, jockeys, racehorse trainers. If Roger didn't like the fact she no longer even made excuses about going out without him, then he knew what he could do!

Unlike Roger, Drum hadn't hesitated to ask his brother for "room and board" when he came up to New York in the spring. No hotel room could compete with United Texas Oil's luxurious apartment on Fifth Avenue. Drum knew that, and he also knew staying there could only increase his standing with Grantley Adams and the other West Indian leaders, en route to an economic conference in Washington.

Only Eric Williams was missing. It was typical of the man, Drum thought, that he would never miss an opportunity to show he considered he had nothing to learn from either the U.S. or the U.K. Not that his go-it-alone stance was getting him anywhere as far as the Federation was concerned.

Drum couldn't wait for Roger's arrival so that he could tell him it had been proposed that the best site for the federal capital of an independent West Indies was the Chaguaramas Base in Trinidad. This would mean that with his own headquarters at Golden Hill—the most beautiful private home on the island—he would be in the best position to increase his influence, entertaining every world leader who came to call.

Drum frowned as he picked up the letter and clipping delivered by hand an hour before. Roger was trying to be helpful, but really his half brother had a buzzing bee in his bonnet about undercover Communist activities in the Caribbean. Like many Americans, Drum thought cynically, Roger was caught up in the atmosphere of suspicion generated by the McCarthy era, and saw a "Commie under every chair!"

On Roger's arrival Drum started to tease him about his "Commie paranoia" but Roger interrupted him sharply. "I assure you, Drum, the man I saw in Havana with Roland Bracken back in the early fifties was Fidel Castro. It gave me quite a shock when I saw Castro's picture in the *New York Times*. I don't like the Bracken connection one bit, and I might say neither does the State Department. Why do you think Washington is suddenly so interested in courting the West Indian leaders. They can see the dangers. Think of the influence Cuba can have on the rest of the Caribbean now. . . ."

"There you go, Roger, always looking on the black side. This conference was arranged months ago, long before anyone dreamed Castro had a chance of taking over. . . ."

Roger interrupted him. "Drum, for once you're going to listen to me. I *know* there's a great deal of undermining going on to scuttle the Federation. Until I set eyes on this picture of Castro and realized Bracken must have been in cahoots with him for years, I believed Eric Williams and his declared preference for a Western alliance. I've never accepted he's totally anti-Communist, but I never believed he was particularly pro the reds either. Now I'm not sure any more, and believe me this isn't 'paranoia,' as you put it. There's definitely this undercurrent, this attempt to cause dissension between the different leaders, to build suspicion of Williams and to increase Williams's own already suspicious attitude of them. You must have noticed it?"

Drum nodded abruptly. "I know. I know, but there's no chance. The Federation is here to stay and Williams knows it!"

Roger's warning came into Drum's mind a few times over the next few days as he noted uneasily the West Indian leaders' apparent inability to deal with each other as equals and colleagues.

He shook off his fears when he went back to Trinidad, determined to do everything in his power to strengthen the infant Federation, but every day came a new shock, as Williams's power and influence grew, with constant reminders that Roland Bracken, always at his side, was also growing more powerful.

Later that year the bomb dropped. The Colonial Office announced it had agreed to all of Williams's proposals. The British governor would no longer preside over the Legislative Council; the offices of council and chief minister were to be renamed cabinet and premier respectively, and the new premier, Eric Williams, would now be empowered to appoint and dismiss ministers and parliamentary secretaries. All this in exchange for an extension of the Chaguaramas Base lease to the Americans.

"It makes me sick to see the way the British government is kowtowing to Williams," Drum exploded to Bill McMurtrey. "It's obviously at the behest of the Yanks that they're giving him whatever he asks for in case he turns to the East for help. I ask you, Bill, where's their reasoning? The more they give, the more he'll ask for—and when they've given him everything, what hope is there for us?"

McMurtrey reminded him of his own position in the Parliament of the West Indian Federation. "Isn't that the future, Drum? Don't kick up your heels over Williams and Bracken. You told me yourself they're only small potatoes now. Then this Chaguaramas extension the Colonial Office is asking for, didn't you tell me Adams and Manley have been egging Williams on to resist it? If you ask me, Williams isn't about to give in on that score either. He'd like the federal capital here, too, to keep an eye on everything at first-hand . . . and so would you!"

As Roland told Luis at their now-regular meeting, although he could take some credit for helping stir up the storms erupting between the West Indian leaders and Eric Williams, not even he could have predicted that Grantley Adams would suddenly change his mind about Chaguaramas and agree with the British and U.S. technical experts that in view of Chaguaramas's strategic importance, it should remain an American base for a further ten years.

"Williams is *hopping* mad!" Roland said gleefully. "I hardly need to say a word to persuade him it's a case of malice directed toward him personally." Roland winked at Luis. "But of course, I have pointed out to the premier that Grantley Adams's statement is a flagrant betrayal, considering he and Manley urged him to get the Americans out in the first place."

"Excellent," Luis purred. "Excellent. A breach of this magnitude is hardly likely to be repaired. More likely it will widen."

And widen it did; communication between the government in Trinidad and the other West Indian leaders was virtually breaking down as Williams and Adams hurled public insults at each other.

At the convention of the People's National Movement in March 1960, Williams urged everyone to make a public protest over the Americans' "continued and illegal occupancy of the Chaguaramas Base." On April 22, it was estimated about thirty-five thousand marched in pouring rain with Eric Williams at their head to deliver their protest to the U.S. Consulate. A great roar went up all the way to Westminster and Washington that Williams was definitely pro-Communist and anti- the West.

To Drum's dismay, soon after the marathon march on the U.S. Consulate he learned the colonial secretary was thinking of calling on Williams personally—in order to come to "honorable terms with the chief minister and his party over Chaguaramas, and to concede internal self-government."

It was the worst news Drum had ever received. But sure enough, Ian Macleod's visit took place in May. Drum was further chilled when he was told the colonial secretary was "unable to visit Mr. Pollard at Golden Hill." It was the first time he'd ever been snubbed, the first time Golden Hill hadn't been the setting for "history in the making."

Now, when Drum wandered through the wide and handsome reception rooms, he saw how unlived-in, how empty and soulless they'd become. Suddenly, all he could remember were the glamorous parties, the endless social activities Alicia had created and handled so well, her sly suggestions about whom to invite, the articles about her "salon," her "unique way of entertaining" the great and famous.

He started to kick himself for letting Alicia go. How often had he been to the House of Lords since her departure? Obviously not once. And had his sphere of influence really grown since he'd joined forces with Grantley Adams? Analyzing the situation seriously, he realized that, if anything, it had shrunk.

He thanked his lucky stars that, as he'd predicted, Alicia hadn't asked him for a divorce. Instead she'd obtained a legal separation, the lawyers coming to an agreement over financial support.

Drum decided to talk things over with Bill McMurtrey, who, more than anyone else, always seemed to be able to steer him in the right direction. "D'you think I'm making any sense, Bill?" he asked anxiously, mopping his brow on an unusually hot and humid night. "D'you think I ought to go to London to see if Alicia will give me another chance?"

McMurtrey looked at Drum serenely. "It all depends on your motives, Drum. You can't play around with a woman's emotions forever, you know. If you want her back because you finally realize you need a woman in that mausoleum up there, that you miss her—and surely you must miss your little daughter—then I say go after her and Godspeed. But if you have one of your usual Machiavellian reasons up your sleeve, then I say, damn you, leave the woman alone."

Drum crouched forward morosely. He couldn't truthfully say he felt any more love for Alicia now than he had in the past. But goddamn it, did it always have to be *love* that brought two people together? Couldn't a relationship be based on respect, friendship, admiration? Being a wife was a job after all and as *his* wife it was an important job—with Golden Hill to look after. . . .

So Alicia would obviously want him to sleep with her—that he couldn't get out of—but perhaps it wouldn't be so bad. Perhaps he'd become more mature—and he admitted to himself it was about time—because he hadn't fancied any young piece of fluff in months. The more he thought about Alicia, the more he remembered her many talents—and none of her flaws.

It was the first time he had ever traveled to London without having a definite government job to do. He felt strange checking into the Dorchester, knowing there would be no "urgent phone messages" from the Colonial Office waiting for him and no letters coming in by courier. He felt apprehensive, lonely.

In the morning he didn't feel any more confident, but after checking Alicia's address with the London bank who sent off her quarterly checks, he went to Constance Spry's flower shop to send her three dozen white rosebuds. He deliberated for a few minutes over what to say on the card, then wrote "Miss you" without signing his name. He then went to Harrods to the toy department and found himself enjoying choosing a large doll from hundreds of all shapes and sizes. He was just about to buy a large black doll—which had the prettiest face by far—when he removed his hand as if it had been stung. The last thing Alicia needed to be reminded of was a black pickaninny. God, what a fool he could be at times . . . perhaps all the time.

When he showered and dressed later for the evening, the thought hit him, for the first time, that he knew practically nothing about Alicia's life. For all he knew, she might have a live-in lover, but somehow he doubted it.

He grimaced as the taxi sped by the Garrick Theatre. *Fings Ain't Wot They Used T'be*. What an extraordinary title for a show—one he promised himself he'd miss, because "things certainly weren't what they used to be" for him, either!

At thirty-five what had he to show for all his early years of training by those in power? He'd been a "rising star" for so long, the Trinidad population probably thought he was ancient history by now. All the racing about the world he'd done for Gomes, back and forth between Trinidad and the Colonial Office, lobbying for the power that had finally been given to Eric Williams. And Williams was supported by his worst enemy, his own Uncle Roland, who, he was sure, wouldn't rest until he saw him snuffed out like a match.

By the time the taxi reached St. Giles Circus and turned into the cul-de-sac where Alicia now had a new flat, Drum was beginning to wish he'd never had the idea in the first place. Apart from the unnerving thought of seeing Alicia again, the thought of actually seeing Margaret, instead of merely speaking to her a few times a year, began to terrify him.

What a monster she probably thinks I am, he thought despondently, and rightly so. I *am* a monster. Why do I feel so little for her? Why do I yearn for Gloria if I ever yearn for anyone . . . for Gloria and little Naomi?

It was twenty past six. He noticed an attractive-looking couple outside Number 17, Alicia's address, but when he turned to join them, they'd already gone inside, leaving the door slightly ajar. As he stood hesitantly wondering whether to knock or go inside, another couple came up behind him.

"It's all right, old chap," said a portly young man in a city pinstripe. "Alicia told us to go right up. We don't have to announce ourselves. I'm Toby Plugge. This is my wife, Viv. . . ."

Drum shook hands self-consciously. What was going on? It looked as if Alicia was giving a cocktail party. Well, at least that meant she was home, and perhaps with other people around their first meeting in nearly five years wouldn't be so traumatic.

The first thing he saw as he went in behind the Plugges was a cut-glass vase full of the white rosebuds on the hall table. There was a roar of voices coming from a room on the right, so rather than trying to fight his way in, Drum stayed in the hall, realizing after a moment the bar was located in a room to the left. Every so often an agitated young waiter would rush inside to emerge a few minutes later with a re-plenished tray. Drum went to the bar to pour himself a gin and tonic, wondering why more people didn't try to help themselves.

"What are you doing here, Drum?" Alicia was in the doorway, her hands on her hips, trying to look furious but not quite succeeding.

Immediately upon seeing her, his apprehension disappeared. She still cares, was the jubilant thought that flashed across his mind as he noted her eyes suspiciously bright with unshed tears, her hands twisting a handkerchief into knots.

"You look very pretty," Drum said with his warmest smile—and he meant it. She did look pretty, with her hair in a new style as far as he was concerned, fluffed up so that it stood around her head in a curly halo, wearing the kind of tailored dress that had always suited her small proportions best.

"I don't want you here, Drum." Her voice was low, shaking. "I didn't think I'd ever have to see you again. Why have you come tonight of all nights, when I'm . . ." Her voice broke but she struggled on. ". . . I'm trying to give a party for two good friends of mine who are getting married . . . trying to act like a normal person for once. Why?" Her voice trailed away.

Drum put the gin and tonic into her shaking hand.

"You arrived to see me once out of the blue, don't you remember?" He tried to make his voice soft, kind, even a little unsure. "I'm sorry. I don't want to spoil your fun, but I do want to see you. Can I come back later?" At that moment, before she could answer, the bartender dashed in, accidentally pushing Alicia toward Drum so they collided in the doorway. She flushed as Drum looked down at her steadily, holding her arm with strong, firm fingers. As she tried to wrestle her arm away, he said, "I see you received my roses. . . ."

"*Your* roses?" She blushed even more. "I had no idea they were from you."

"Well, who else misses you?" He laughed lightly. He wasn't jealous, but he was curious. Did he have a rival? That would make the "courtship" even more interesting, because, as Alicia's familiar flowery scent filled his nostrils, he made up his mind that Alicia and, yes, of course, Margaret, too (he hoped she wasn't wearing braces on her teeth; he loathed looking at braces), must definitely come back with him to Golden Hill.

Golden Hill needed a woman's touch and a charming hostess again— a hostess like the Honorable Mrs. Drum Pollard.

A tear trembled on her lashes. He took it on the tip of his finger, then deliberately, his eyes never leaving hers, slowly licked the tear away as with his other hand he stroked her bare arm. She stiffened as he moved even closer to her.

"Shall I come back later?"

"No, no, no," she whispered, looking over his shoulder to where the waiter was obviously now taking his time over the refills. "Albert." She tried to sound her usual imperious self. "I know Lady Hobson is dying for her martini. . . . Have you had time to mix it yet?"

"I'll mix it." Drum released her to go to the bar.

"Never mind!" Alicia said stonily. "Albert will do it. . . ." But with a woebegone look, Albert was already on his way back in to the throng.

Alicia turned to follow him, saying over her shoulder in an exasperated tone, "Oh, stay if you must. I know whatever I say you'll still do exactly what suits you. . . ." She hardly knew what she said to any of her guests, as she went around the room, drinking whatever came by on the tray, aware that Drum hardly took his eyes away from her, watching her with that . . . that blazing look. Oh, God, please let me hate him, please, *please* make me want to send him away. Her prayers were useless, she knew it.

Every movement Drum made attracted her. He was so relaxed, exuding a kind of natural animal grace that she'd never seen in anyone else. . . .

If anything, he was even more attractive than before, she agonized, noticing how her girlfriends chatted him up, obviously impressed by his glowing vitality, his tanned good looks, emphasized by the crisp whiteness of his shirt, the dark gray of his suit.

Alicia groaned inwardly. What had he come back for? There had to be an ulterior motive. She wasn't a fool any longer. Margaret! That was it. He'd come to take Margaret away to that blasted island in the sun. Uncle Robin had warned her it could happen if she didn't make a proper arrangement over their daughter, but she hadn't listened. She could hear herself screaming inside as she went around the room, trying to behave like the perfect hostess, toasting the about-to-be newlyweds, longing for everyone to leave so that she could collapse and cry for a week.

With a lurch she saw the time and realized Margaret would soon be home from her piano lesson. Would Miss Gibb take her straight upstairs to bed or would Margaret plead to come in to say hello to her friends as she usually liked to do?

Alicia rushed out to the hall, sure she could hear steps on the stairs, and a few seconds later Margaret came racing up, crying, "Mummy, Mummy, I can play 'On the Road to Mandalay'!"

"Oh, darling." Alicia squeezed her so hard Margaret protested.

"You're hurting me, Mummy. What's wrong? What is it? Didn't Albert come to help?"

At that moment Drum came into the hall looking for Alicia. He stopped, startled, the color draining from him, a surge of emotion flooding his body. He bent down. "Margaret, hello, little Margaret." The feeling of excitement, of happiness, was so unexpected, it made his voice sound cracked, unnatural.

The child backed away in alarm, searching for the comfort of Nanny Gibb.

"Don't be frightened, Margaret. Don't you remember me?"

Margaret fixed solemn eyes on her father as she shook her head determinedly. Alicia quickly intervened. "Don't rush her, Drum. She's tired. Nanny, she should be in bed."

For once without a word Margaret followed Miss Gibb demurely up the stairs, glancing back at the handsome man who stood looking up at her so strangely. She was both glad and sorry to leave him.

Who was he, she wondered? She knew him and yet. . . . She could hear his voice again . . . hear it and recognize it. Why, it was . . . it had to be her father, her very own daddy.

Margaret clutched her old teddy bear, wondering if he had come to take her away somewhere . . . wondering if she was going to be able to show teddy bear the place where she dimly remembered oranges really grew on trees. . . .

Margaret
1963

S HE watched a lizard defy gravity, half on the ceiling, half on the wall, wondering as she often did whether it was watching her with the same intensity, waiting for her to make a move as she was waiting for it to make a move . . . toward her.

Although Em the cook kept telling her she ought to like lizards because they ate up all the "pesky buzzin' an' flyin' critters," she knew she never would. She kept her eyes fixed on the lithe articulated creature, knowing she only had a few minutes left of being able to see anything before the sun dipped behind Mount El Tucuche and her room would be left as dark and as unfathomable as the cave on the highest part of the estate.

She never went all the way into the cave, because she hated the dark even more than she hated lizards, particularly the inscrutable dark of Trinidad, which descended so rapidly and thoroughly it was like having a hood thrown over your head.

Margaret no longer cried out for her mother as she had cried two years before when they'd first returned to Golden Hill. Her mother had told her too often to stop being a baby, and after a while she had realized it was hopeless. She was too far away from the main wing for her mother even to hear her scream. Before, her bedroom had been near her parents' room, but now her mother had made it clear that as she no longer shared it with a nurse—"as you did when you were a baby"—that bedroom, along with all the others with the best views in the main wing, had to be kept for guests, important guests whose names were regularly in the papers. As her mother put it, "guests who regard an invitation to stay with the Pollards at Golden Hill as either an honor or as their due—depending on how high up the ladder they really are!"

Margaret had never yet been able to understand what she meant, wondering where the important guests kept their ladders and why they needed to climb them anyway. Growing up was full of confusing, often inexplicable details.

As the crickets added their wistful chirp to the usual night music the little girl closed her eyes to try to concentrate on something cheerful. She told herself, as she told herself every night, that Em was only about a hundred steps away in the kitchen, humming with her usual tuneless hum as she chopped calaloo leaves to make her special calaloo crab soup for the dinner party taking place that night.

In her mind Margaret climbed the curving staircase to where Alicia, her mother, was probably changing or perhaps bathing in her dark green marble tub full of soapy bubbles that filled the room with the scent of lily of the valley.

Since their return to Trinidad from London Margaret knew her relationship with her mother had changed—much to her relief. Although she had never known and still didn't know from one day to the next how her mother might react to anything, she no longer felt her mother "depended on her," bursting into frightening floods of tears as she'd once done in London, tears that had only been dammed up when she'd given her mother a required number of hugs, told her how much she loved her, how pretty she was, and had gone to ask Nanny Gibb to make her mother a pot of tea.

Since her father had persuaded her mother to give him "one more chance"—as her mother had explained it to her—and they'd all returned to where she had been born, Margaret imagined her mother was now too busy to have a good cry about life's injustices . . . yet Margaret felt uneasily her mother's tears had only been put away temporarily. She hoped not, yet there were times when, looking at her mother's face, she was sure she was about to break down, but so far, and Margaret would cross her fingers about this, it hadn't happened.

The problem was she no longer knew when she might be displeasing her mother. She didn't know what her mother—until now the greatest influence on her life—really thought about her and, for the moment, she didn't care.

There was a new and growing influence in her life, one she hadn't yet understood or acknowledged, but as she grew sleepy, she wondered if her father would come to say goodnight as he had come for the first time the week before.

It had happened as the frogs began to croak and her mind was just starting out on its nightly meander through the house, out to the plantation and sometimes even back to her other life in London that now seemed so remote.

She had cried out in terror, when the wicker lamp beside the door had suddenly been switched on and she'd seen a tall figure leaning in the doorway watching her. It had taken her at least a minute to realize it was her father, who had put a warning finger over his mouth and whispered, "Don't be frightened, Margaret. It's only me. It's time I came to kiss my lovely little girl goodnight, don't you think?"

She hadn't known what to say, so she hadn't said anything, as he'd sat on the edge of the bed and stroked her dark blond fringe away from her damp forehead and traced his finger lightly down her cheek. After the first nervous shock she'd felt a warm surge of happiness that the father she was only just getting to know should come to kiss her goodnight like other fathers kissed their children.

In the soft bedroom light his face had looked younger, less strained than it did during the day and because he was smiling, which he didn't do very often, she hadn't felt her usual sense of apprehension. She had enjoyed his closeness, the faint smell of lemony cologne, far preferable to the rum smell she sometimes recognized on her mother's breath.

He had slipped his arm around her shoulders, so her face came into contact with his soft silk shirt and through the silk she'd felt unexpected prickly hairs. He'd asked her almost shyly if she would like him to tell her a story and dutifully she'd nodded, half amused, half touched that her father knew fathers told stories at bedtime to their children. But it hadn't been a made-up story.

He'd told her about Golden Hill, the plantation with its magnificent plantings of cocoa and citrus and about his father, the grandfather she'd never known, Captain Piper Pollard, who'd come from America so many years before to strike oil on land he'd bought in the south of the island—oil that had made him and the family rich. He'd smiled and gone on to tell her about all the good things his father had done for the poor black people and how loved he had been. He'd told her how the

British had routed the Spanish after three centuries of Spanish rule, and about the first British governor, Thomas Picton, whose descendant had built Golden Hill in the first place. A stern look had crossed his face and she'd held her breath, wondering what he was going to say, but it had only been about Eric Williams, Trinidad's black prime minister, who last year had apparently cut all ties with the British Empire after one hundred and sixty-five years.

She'd begged him to go on about his father's early days building up the great estate, because he'd made it sound so romantic, igniting her imagination and, as he'd talked so quietly he'd begun to stroke first her arm, then her hair, her shoulders, moving down to trace her un-developed body through the sheet. The stroking and gentle tone of his voice had been soothing and exciting at the same time and it wasn't until Luralene, one of the maids, had thrown open the louvered shut-ters the next morning that Margaret had realized she must have fallen asleep while her father was still telling the story.

She'd felt shy, even apprehensive when he'd returned home for lunch that day on horseback, "still my favorite form of transport," he often said . . . but everything had been as it always was.

Her mother had complained about the heat, the servants, the lack of anything to do, to read, to see, the dullness of her father's friends and how she missed the sharp wit of her own friends in London, and, as usual, her father had hardly responded, reading papers, writing notes, looking preoccupied and serious, hardly acknowledging her Grand-mother Rose when she'd shuffled out onto the terrace and they'd all gone into lunch.

It was hard for Margaret to reconcile the fact that Grandmother Rose had been married to dashing Piper Pollard, the man her father had described so eloquently. After the night her father told her about Golden Hill and her grandfather's early days, she would steal a look at her grandmother, trying to see something in the old, tremulous lady that linked her to those wonderful days of the past.

If Margaret was in doubt about her mother's opinion of *her* behavior, she knew positively her mother hated Grandmother Rose. She was only a shade away from being insulting whenever she addressed her, which was rarely, while Rose—who Margaret thought had to be at least a hun-dred years old—ate so quickly, it always appeared she was frightened her plate might be taken away before she'd finished.

It was only today there had been any noticeable change in the atmosphere.

Her parents had quarreled in front of her about a subject often brought up, but just as often dropped whenever she was present.

Her father wanted her to continue her studies at the local convent school. ". . . At least for a time. Remember I was without my daughter for five years."

At this point Margaret knew her mother's eyebrows would arch in a particularly imperious way and her voice would grow icy as she interrupted to say, "And whose fault was that?" when the subject was dropped or changed.

Today it had not been dropped and Alicia, obviously determined to conclude the matter once and for all, had announced she had enrolled Margaret in an English boarding school ". . . to start just after her thirteenth birthday in the autumn term."

"That's impossible!" her father had cried stormily. "Margaret is going to stay at home until she goes to finishing school in Switzerland when she's seventeen or eighteen. . . ."

"Absolutely not!" her mother had clipped as if there were nothing more to be said. Their voices had risen until they were screaming at each other, while Margaret had sat white-faced, tears running down her cheeks, not knowing whether to run away, as her grandmother had done at the first signs of dissension, or stay sitting there.

If Obee hadn't come to announce a Mr. Jamandar wanted to speak to her father urgently on the phone, Margaret wondered how it would have ended, but she knew he was one of the important guests expected that night and her father had left the table, looking in her direction with a curt, "You see what you've done to Margaret! We'll discuss this later. Margaret is not, I repeat, *not* going away this year!"

Now, as she lay under the white linen sheet with the fan whirring lazily above her, Margaret reflected that England no longer seemed like home, yet only a few months ago she'd hated everything about Golden Hill, where she'd been born.

She hadn't remembered much about the house, except it was very grand at the end of a straight white road. She'd hardly remembered her father either, when he'd appeared that evening in their London flat. It was his voice she'd remembered later, lying upstairs in bed, because after all it was only his voice she *could* remember, having not set eyes on him during the years they'd been away, although as her mother had pointed out he had never once forgotten her birthday or Christmas. There had always been presents to unwrap from Daddy.

Her thoughts went back to the day her mother had told her melodramatically, "I've forgiven your father. We're going back to Trinidad to live at Golden Hill. . . ."

It had been a terrible shock and she'd cried buckets, having to leave all her friends and Nanny Gibb, who'd cried buckets, too, explaining she was too old to move so far away.

The distance had seemed all the greater because in just a few hours they had moved from the depths of an English winter to a boiling hot summer day.

It had been snowing the morning her father had come to help her mother pack up and arrange things and it was still snowing two weeks later, when they'd arrived at London Airport to find all the planes grounded.

During the long hours waiting at the airport she had had plenty of time to study her father's still unfamiliar face. He was so much browner and healthier looking than all the people around him, with strange eyes, blue yet with gold flecks in them, except in different lights when they darkened and looked foreign and . . . almost frightening.

When her father had left the table at lunchtime, she'd quickly scraped her chair back and run, run, run—anywhere to hide from her mother, who she knew would definitely want her to say to her father how much she wanted to go to boarding school, but now she didn't.

She wanted to stay home to be near him, just as he wanted to be near her. She knew deep down, whatever she'd said, her mother was going to win the argument. Not that she got her own way that often—Margaret knew that was another reason for her mother's bad temper—but on certain subjects, particularly anything concerning her, her mother's decisions so far had always been final.

She didn't need to hear the servants saying her mother was clever or listen to the compliments paid to her by flocks of people who were always in and out of Golden Hill, which apparently since their return was considered an "open house for any political hopeful" . . . whatever that meant.

She knew her mother was clever, but now she was beginning to realize that perhaps her father was cleverer. . . .

Later as she'd nibbled on a stick of sugarcane in the kitchen, her mother had come rushing in. "What are you doing here after your disgraceful behavior at lunch? Sniveling, then rushing away like a hooligan! Have you done your homework?"

The questions had come out rat-a-tat-tat as her mother had gripped her shoulder and marched her down the flagstone passageway to her bedroom. "You know we have Prime Minister Barrow of Barbados coming for dinner tonight *and* Mr. Jamandar *and* Mr. Gairey of Grenada *and* Mr. Bradshaw of St. Kitts. I don't want your father worried about you. You stay here out of sight until tomorrow. Do your homework and I'll send your supper in on a tray. I shall want to see that English essay tomorrow morning before you leave for school." Margaret had known from long experience it was useless to argue. As her mother had swung out of the door on high-heeled red sandals she'd cried aloud, "Thank goodness Drum has listened to me on this subject. If she stays here much longer she'll end up with the brains of a nigger!"

Margaret didn't know whether the remark had been addressed to her or not, but an angry knot had twisted in her stomach, and she'd sat at the heavy old-fashioned desk that had been in the house since her grandfather's day, fidgeting back and forth beneath the fan, daydreaming, not writing, watching the soft clouds float past the San Fernando Hill, faintly visible in the distance. It's like a tide in the sky, she'd thought, longing to immerse her body in the cool drink of the sea. The mist retreated and returned to cover the hill again and again, while Margaret daydreamed on about swimming in the deep, incredibly blue waters of Maracas Bay.

She only had half a page written when Em came in to remind her to take her bath and to say her supper "will be alon'" in her high, singsong voice. When she waddled in again half an hour later, a surprise was on the tray: a large scoop of the special honey and almond nut ice cream, which Margaret knew was to be served later to the guests in scooped-out pineapples she'd seen being gathered only that morning.

Lying in bed in the dark she imagined the guests soon driving up the straight white road to the impressive colonnaded entrance, where Obee would be waiting, dressed in a blue waistcoat with matching cummerbund to act as butler with Luralene and Maize, their hair newly plaited, directing the ladies to the powder room if they wanted to repowder their perspiring noses before joining everyone on the terrace.

Her grandmother would not be there, that Margaret knew. Once, soon after their return, she remembered she had crept out to peep at Harold Macmillan, the prime minister of England. Her mother had been impossible for days before *that* dinner party! As she'd heard him announce in a toast that "Trinidad is the Athens of the Caribbean," she had been overcome with a mixture of fear and pity as she'd seen Grandmother Rose peering down from the top landing.

It had been the first time she'd realized her mother was in total charge of the house, that anything she said seemed to be law, for Margaret had heard her say forcibly she wouldn't have Rose at any dinner at any price, so, as Margaret knew, tonight Grandmother Rose would be having dinner in her room as usual.

Tonight's dinner had to be almost as important as the one her parents had given for Prime Minister Macmillan, for during the past few days her mother had been fidgety, screaming at the maids, telling them over and over again she wanted to inspect every one of their fingernails before the guests arrived.

It was something to do with her father fighting Eric Williams, and Vernon Jamandar was the man who was going to help him, although no one was supposed to know. Margaret sighed at the complexity of it all. Already so many people knew, how could her father expect to keep it a secret?

All last year there had been endless gossip in the kitchen and in the fields about the fight her father was putting up to save something called the Federation.

There'd even been a calypso on the radio, written and sung by Little Sparrow, the most famous calypso singer in the Caribbean. . . . Margaret hummed it under her breath: "This ain't no time to say we ain't federatin' any more."

She didn't know what it meant. She only knew her father had lost, that the Federation was no more, because Eric Williams and a very bad man called Roland Bracken (incredibly she'd recently discovered he was a member of her grandmother's own family) had managed to destroy it. As she'd heard Em say once, "Now de people o'Jamaica has said dey wan' no part in any ol' feder'tion, I say we all don' wan' no part if de udder islands dey don' wan' t' be wid us. . . . No matter wot de Mastah he say. . . ."

No wonder her father had looked so upset when even his own servants weren't really on his side! He'd gone away for two or three months "to try to whip up support for union between the remaining nine islands," was how her mother had explained it, looking as sad and as lonely as she'd ever looked in London.

Margaret squirmed restlessly, feeling angry as she contemplated that, just like her grandmother, she'd been put away like the dogs who got overexcited when more than two or three cars arrived at one time.

Now that she was nearing her thirteenth birthday it was time she was allowed to stay up to meet the guests, she decided. Why would the prime ministers of Barbados, Grenada and St. Kitts be so important anyway? If you believed the servants, only one man counted in the Caribbean—apart from "de Mastah," her father—and that was Eric Williams, Trinidad's prime minister, who Margaret had heard Em say giggling, "sure ran rings roun' dose federatin' people bac' in June. . . ."

She yawned and stretched her toes down in the bed trying to find a cool spot. She couldn't understand why her mother fussed and fretted herself into a nervous attack over giving a dinner for these prime ministers, because she was sure they were black men and her mother's poor opinion of black people was frequently expressed. Her mother often used the word *nigger*, though not in front of her father, who Margaret knew with a certain sense of pride had beaten a man who used the word to describe one of the workers.

As she mentally sorted out the black people she knew—friends and workers, who might be considered important and unimportant, she heard her door open.

This time, although her heart sounded as if it were suddenly banging out of her chest and her body tensed under the sheet, she didn't cry out. The light clicked on and there was her father, smiling again like the last time, but dressed as she had never seen him dressed before . . . in a black suit with a black bow tie and white ruffled shirt . . . the way some of the men who'd come to pick her mother up in London had often been dressed, but—her legs felt trembly—none of them had ever looked as handsome as her father.

Drum carefully hung his jacket on the back of a chair. "Little Margaret, I'm sorry you were so unhappy today," he whispered. "I don't want you to go so far away from me . . . now that we're just getting to know each other." He turned her sheet down slightly, leaning forward to kiss her shoulder, saying close to her ear, "Your skin is as white as our sugar. You must never let it be burned by the sun. Keep it white like sugar. . . ."

She giggled self-consciously, now hardly listening to what he was saying, because as he spoke he was slowly unbuttoning the small buttons of her nightdress until he could see the slight swell of her just-developing breasts—and her nipples. He drew in his breath.

Although she was tense with a kind of strange excitement that was terrifying at the same time, not knowing what was going to happen, she also agonized, knowing he could see something that set her apart from the other girls at the local convent school. It wasn't only that most of the girls were flat like boys, while she was already swelling. No, that wasn't the worst of it. Her nipples weren't pink like the other girls'.

They were dark, dark brown, almost black. She longed for them to be pink because then they wouldn't show up so much against the whiteness everywhere else, but instead, however much she washed them with soap, they seemed to grow darker all the time.

Margaret felt she would die from embarrassment as her father didn't take his strange blue-brown eyes away from her breasts. Then, as one hand again stroked back her fringe, he bent his head to run his tongue slowly, languorously back and forth across her nipples. A tremor ran through her body. She felt weak, and an unaccustomed thick wetness came between her legs. His tongue wasn't rough yet it wasn't quite smooth. She longed for him to stop . . . and yet go on at the same time. It was the most delirious yet dangerous feeling she had ever imagined anyone could have.

Then, just as carefully as he had unbuttoned her nightdress, he started to rebutton it, stopping to circle each nipple with a long tanned finger one more time before continuing to the top button, when he pulled the sheet up over her shoulders.

"Beautiful," he said softly, "beautiful buds that don't need the sun in order to ripen." His words made her feel weaker still, yet she longed to mention how worried she was that she was different from the other girls, but she was too shaken to speak.

As he got up to put on his jacket, her overwhelming feeling was that she couldn't bear him to leave.

He came back to the bedside once more but didn't sit down. Instead, he ran both hands lightly over the sheet, feeling her body, fiercely cupping her small breasts, pushing the sheet between her legs to feel her wetness through the fine linen.

"Sweet dreams, my little bud. How lovely it will be to watch you flower. . . ."

He was gone, leaving her throbbing, afraid, yet with a growing sense of happiness. She turned to bury her face in her pillow, not understanding in any way the tumult of her feelings, her yearning for something . . . for what?

She felt the need to put her fingers between her legs and pushed them deep into the wetness there, moving them back and forth, trying to comfort herself until she finally fell asleep.

"We have three years of hard work ahead of us," Vernon Jamandar was saying, his intelligent Indian face momentarily obscured by a cloud of cigar smoke.

Drum realized the message was being directed at him and he mentally shook himself out of the reverie in which he'd been lost for the last minute. He'd been lost to reality so many times during the long dinner, as he'd relived the overwhelming sensuous shock he'd received as he'd gazed on his daughter's pale breasts with dark—unbelievably dark and large—nipples.

As he fought to concentrate at his own dinner table—at the all-important dinner he was giving to make his alliance with Jamandar—he was still shaken by the feeling of desire the visit to his daughter's room that evening had unleashed. It was a desire different from any he had ever experienced, coupled with a feeling of compassion so encompassing that, even as he sat there, he vowed to himself he would do everything in his power to protect her from what he was forced to admit was his own terrible weakness—as well as from *any* man's desire.

Barrow was talking; Gairey was interrupting. Drum pressed his nails into his palm before swallowing down the rest of his port to drag his mind back to the present. Not that they were saying anything new. He'd heard it all over and over again during the past year, and inwardly he groaned. He'd obviously have to go on hearing it for months to come as they rehashed the events of the past few months.

As the long night went on, Drum went over the events that had brought this particular group together with one common cause. It was painful, but it had to be faced. Eric Williams and his cohort Roland Bracken had defeated him—and everyone present. As Grantley Adams had finally summed it up, it had all been relatively easy to do. "It's amazing that the Federation ever came into being in the first place. . . ." Adams had put his finger on the real reason behind the other leaders' last-minute reluctance to join together in a union and sever their ties forever with Britain. "In theory, you see, it's all well and good . . . but in practice the Federation doesn't only mean *political* independence. It means economic independence. Trinidad can afford it—it has oil. The other islands don't and can't."

That was the reason, Drum knew now, that Adams and Manley had so unexpectedly backed down from their support of Williams over the Chaguaramas issue, to go along with whatever the British and American authorities wanted. Chaguaramas wasn't worth fighting over if it cost Barbados and Jamaica any economic support, not to mention upsetting the Yanks! From then on it had been all downhill, and once Jamaica voted no to joining the Federation in a people's referendum, Drum had known the battle was over and they had lost.

And that's just how it had all turned out, despite his backbreaking work around the islands of the southern and eastern Caribbean. It was galling to think Roger had been right and he had been so wrong, that there had indeed been evil forces at work to scuttle the Federation as far back as 1958—and scuttle it they had!

Drum looked down the long table gleaming with silver and crystal. Well, now he was in the same boat with his "federatin' friends," as the local press called the leaders of the other islands.

At that moment Drum heard Bradshaw, the chief minister of St. Kitts, mimic Williams: ". . . They prefer to remain colonies and be tuppenny rulers in their own little bivouacs, rather than be led by the People's National Movement, the undisputed intellectual leaders in this part of the world!" Bradshaw snorted derisively.

But before the other leaders could follow suit and quote any more of Williams's often derogatory remarks, Drum quickly intervened. "All right, all right, so we know the man's head is bigger than a dinosaur's egg. Now we have to crack it! As Trinidad is an independent parliamentary democracy with a two-party system, we must work through the proper electoral procedures to ensure the other party offers a strong alternative in 'sixty-six . . . and I say the only way that can happen is to elect a new leader for that other party. . . . And that leader is sitting here tonight—Vernon Jamandar, who *must* replace Rudranath Capildeo and lead the Democratic Labor Party to victory! The party, let no one forget it, that soundly beat Williams in 'fifty-eight at the time of the federal elections."

His rhetoric was impressive, but although they listened attentively and pledged to help Drum and V.J.—as Jamandar was being called by the end of the evening—they all knew the odds were against toppling Williams. He was now very much in control.

As Drum undressed that night in his dressing room, he faced the harsh truth, remembering the heart-sinking moment at Marlborough House the year before, when at the ceremony marking Trinidad's severance from Britain after a hundred and sixty-five years, he'd heard Reginald Maudling, the British colonial secretary, make the dramatic statement, "The last vestiges of external control are about to be removed . . . and a heavy responsibility therefore lies upon those attending. . . ." Drum had described the occasion in an article in the *Trinidad Guardian* as "the last pilgrimage to London." It certainly had been for himself as well as for Trinidad . . . a pilgrimage he once would never have dreamed possible.

As he brushed his teeth, he wondered what Williams and Bracken might be thinking about the dinner he'd just held up on the Hill. He knew they knew all about it. They knew everything he did, although since that historic day at Marlborough House when Drum had felt Williams's and Bracken's eyes on him from across the room they had behaved extremely civilly toward him . . . but they *knew* he was still holding the torch that Gomes had lit years before, bringing together a coalition of the three leading political parties to form a European and Hindu-based Democratic Labor Party, the only political opposition Williams now had.

Drum turned off the light, determined to sleep in his dressing room, much as he knew it annoyed Alicia. He couldn't bear to get into her bed tonight. He had to be alone in the dark . . . to savor just once more the thought of his daughter's delicate breasts with their astonishing dark areolas and sweet pointed nipples. He shut his eyes . . . just one more heart-aching time alone with that sensuous memory before he vowed to dedicate *all* his thoughts and energies to getting Williams out—in order to regain his own sphere of influence.

In April it was a luxury—Magdalen smiled to herself that she could still consider it as such—to sit beside a cool mountain stream as it made its way through the woods and valleys. It was a pity in one way that Theo and Paulette couldn't wait until late May to arrive, when at least there was the chance of a shower or two.

Magdalen stretched and slowly got to her feet. She was tired, but then perhaps one was always tired after sixty? She tried not to think about it, because it seemed ridiculous that she could be anywhere near sixty when her mind kept telling her how young she was, that she still had a lot of "living" to do. According to Theo that "living" was all ahead of her when she moved to the States . . . *if* she ever moved to the States.

As usual the thought of her son softened her face as she strolled back along the trail heavy with the scent of roses. It was hard to believe the charming, low-slung house she could see in the distance, surrounded by well-kept smooth green lawns, could have emerged from the almost derelict one-room place where Theo had first lived as a bachelor. In fifteen years, both the house and the property had changed so dramatically that neither bore any resemblance to the secluded Arima plantation she had bought originally with the hope Theo would tire of "doing penance" in seclusion and move back to Port of Spain to be near her.

How ironic it all was. Instead, his love of nature had taken him far-

ther and farther away from her, not only in distance, but into a sophisticated world she knew little about at first hand, although privately she
was sure the people who inhabited it had the same needs and desires as
those who had patronized Le Plaisir over the years. Well, she was well
out of *that!* Only that morning she'd read in the *Trinidad Guardian*
that Le Plaisir had been fined for the second time for breaking the new
"moral" code, that it was now under notice that should there be any
more "irregularities" on the premises it would be closed down.

Phew! That was really something! Thank goodness she'd acted so
promptly on Roland Bracken's advice, given on the day she had finally
managed to get an appointment to see him.

He'd been so hard to get to that, as the prime minister's closest adviser, she'd expected a different, pompous kind of Roland, but he'd
been just the same, despite the impressive office and number of minions
around to do his bidding. He'd asked her to meet him at his office,
then—she imagined on the spur of the moment—he had suggested they
have a drink at the Country Club together.

She'd tried to hide her look of surprise, but he'd said sarcastically,
"Yes, I can be a member now. Didn't you know that? No more 'color
bar' here, now that Eric Williams is in command."

It had taken her a while to get around to her objective—to find out
once and for all whether there was any substance to Theo's constant
warning about land becoming nationalized. It was only when she was
back at Le Plaisir she'd realized she'd never brought the subject up, but
instead had come away with a very definite and different warning from
Roland, that "Socrates" (as Roland jokingly referred to the prime minister) was now ready to act on his 1961 election pledge . . . "to clean up
and clamp down on all corrupt establishments: to throw out all feckless
money wasters, no matter what their color or creed, in order to show
Trinidad to the world as a shining example of how the noblest thinking
can lead to the highest productivity and standard of living for its
people. . . ."

Magdalen had remembered Williams making that vow before the
election, but as Roland repeated his words, she'd felt a cold chill as
she'd realized Roland was telling her she was very definitely a target.

"If you're still involved with . . . hmm . . . the establishment Le
Plaisir, I advise you to extricate yourself immediately. You could be
used as an example—of a white woman who for nearly twenty years has
made money from the weak and spineless. . . ." Roland had winked at
her, but she found it hard to wink back. So it didn't matter she'd sup-

ported Williams in his early days, had given money endlessly to his party, for, of course, Roland knew, just as Eric Williams knew, that she was still involved. This was a definite threat, based on knowledge of what was to come.

The next day she'd decided she would sell out and it would all be for the best. She was surprised to find she was even relieved that at last she would no longer have to deceive Theo, who believed she had relinquished all interest in the brothel years ago.

Tong-Li hadn't been surprised or apparently even sorry when she'd told him she finally wanted to sell out her participation. "I want to die without my son ever knowing I lied to him," she'd told him simply.

"Well, Magdalen, I don't think you're ready to die." Tong-Li had given her his usual searching look. "You still look remarkably healthy to me . . . but with this new wave of morality, this fresh clean air that Eric Williams wants to blow through the streets of Port of Spain, perhaps you are wise, my old friend. . . ."

He was more than generous when it came to the final settlement between them—so generous, Magdalen thought with amusement, she was now a comparatively rich woman, who didn't even need that "growing nest egg" that Theo referred to in his infrequent letters. Little did her darling son know that over the years, settlement or no settlement, she had amassed quite a sizable fortune that he and Tommy would inherit.

Well, she had to start making preparations for their visit and stop thinking about old age and death.

As she inspected the cache of cascadura in the kitchen, captured early that morning in baskets and hand nets as the muddy water in the nearby creek subsided, she whistled through her teeth, wondering what Theo was going to say when he heard Roland Bracken was actually coming to dinner . . . and what a grand, decision-making dinner she was determined it was going to be.

Retire to the States? Live a mollycoddled, boring life in Florida, "babysitting" for her fast-growing-up grandson? "Over my dead body. . . . Oops . . . here I go again," Magdalen told a yellow bird that flashed in and out of shiny copper pans over the new kitchen range. "I'm not dead yet and I don't intend to 'bury' myself in Miami Beach either!"

"Isn't my mother an amazing woman?" Theo asked for the second time that evening, not expecting or even wanting an answer as he leaned back in the veranda swing, idly watching the moths as they beat their delicate wings against the lamps.

"You don't need to ask me that, Theo," said Roland dryly. "I've known it since the first day I ever laid eyes on her. We've shared a lot, you know. . . ."

"If anyone had told me forty-eight hours ago that I might seriously consider opening a business—an essential-oil house in Trinidad—I'd have asked him to have his head examined, not mine." Theo smiled, not realizing how it transformed his usually serious, set expression, making his vivid eyes sparkle with sharp intensity.

My God, he's a handsome man, Roland thought, as he'd been thinking ever since he'd shaken Theo's hand hours before. What's more, I don't think he's even aware of his God-given looks. It still twisted his guts to realize this earnest, sophisticated man—what must he be now, Roland thought, thirty-six, -seven?—had actually been his poor, luckless brother's accomplice in the great Pollard fire so many years ago. And now he was the owner of a rapidly growing U.S. cosmetics company, getting richer and more famous by the minute, while his brother's bones had long ago disintegrated in a prison cemetery plot.

Roland felt no bitterness, just a profound sadness as he looked at the beauty around him. He had survived, triumphed, and one day—perhaps a day now not that far off—he would lead all the others on this particular patch of earth called Trinidad.

Against his will, Roland thought of his sister Rose. The memory of her great beauty was so faded, it was hard to believe it had ever existed except in his imagination, but it *had* existed—to cause their brother's death and probably their mother's too—from a broken heart, while the living result of that beauty was his treacherous nephew Drum Pollard, who still posed far more of a threat than Eric Williams seemed to realize.

With an effort Roland pulled his thoughts back to the business at hand. He was glad he'd accepted Magdalen's invitation. He'd done so out of a mixture of curiosity to see once again the boy who'd climbed the saman tree to render such vengeance on his sister's family—curiosity and an acknowledgment that Magdalen's idea made good business sense.

And now he could see her idea had taken root much faster than either of them had ever dreamed possible.

"There's another valid reason for you to think of forming a company here." Roland waved his arms expansively as the moon climbed high to illuminate the tall trees all around. "I'm looking to the future—to the day when your son will inherit all this. . . ."

Theo interrupted him. "But this isn't my property. It's my mother's."

"Tut, tut, Theo," Magdalen said crossly. "I had the deeds made out in your name years ago. Don't think I took any notice of your obstinacy. . . . I didn't have to have your permission, you know. I just banked on you coming to your senses one day to realize what a wonderful property you had created that you *deserved* to own! I didn't expect you to fall in love with an American girl, who'd take you so far away. . . ."

Paulette's eyes were moist as she looked at her husband. She hoped he loved her as much as she loved him. With their busy lives she often wanted to cry out, "Don't go on building the business even bigger! Let's escape. Go around the world in a kayak made for two . . . go back to the woods . . . to the jungle . . . make love to me!" Just once in her life Paulette hoped she could make Theo show some sign of passion for her. . . . If only he weren't so busy . . . if only she weren't so tired. Perhaps this new business would be the answer. Perhaps spending more time in the tropics would put some romance back into their marriage—a wonderful marriage, but just rather . . . well, dull.

She realized Theo was looking at her with a searching look that melted her right down to her toes. He doesn't know what he does to me, she thought. He just doesn't realize the sheer sexuality he exudes. One day, she told herself, we'll be here alone together as we were once and I'll make sure he realizes he isn't all soul, all spirit, that God gave him a magnificent physical presence that He meant him to make *use* of.

"Oh, lovely, lovely, Arima," Paulette cried, lifting her arms up as if to embrace the sky. "I love you. I love you."

"Paulette. . . ." Theo laughed. "What's got into you? Not too much poncha crema I hope. . . ."

She made a face. "Why not? I feel I'm living again. This place does something to me—that's why I know your mama is right. It's a brilliant idea to start a small business here. . . ."

"Not so small," Roland interjected lightly. "As I was saying, and I will rephrase my sentence . . . if either you or your mother wishes your son to inherit this property one day, your own absenteeism from the island for all these years could make it difficult, particularly as I believe Tommy . . . isn't he named Tommy?"—Paulette nodded her head eagerly—". . . Tommy was born in the United States. If you commence an operation here now, bringing in American money and expertise to train our people—providing you have Trinidadian partners—this will ensure this property stays in your family."

"Well, that wouldn't be a good reason for setting anything up," Theo said abruptly. "America's a *free* country. . . . If American money comes in, it must be 'free' to come out too. Are you trying to say land will be nationalized?"

Magdalen tensed. At last the question had been asked. She relaxed as Roland leaned forward anxiously. "No, no, no, but all the same the prime minister wants to imbue his people with a sense of nationalism . . . to encourage those born in the island . . . with roots here—and yours are unique—to want to live here and contribute to the general good."

Theo smiled enigmatically, thinking what a good politician Roland Bracken had turned out to be. "Well, that makes sense . . . and the more I see and smell the plantings here, the more I realize I've probably been making a mistake, turning my back on what inspired me about the beauty business in the first place." Theo looked at his mother. "Remember Zizi, Mother, the old Creole who taught me so much?" He turned to Paulette. ". . . And remember the first experiments we carried out together here in the little shed?" As he spoke, he felt excited, realizing how far they had traveled since those early days, achieving success, yet losing the joy of working with nature. He couldn't remember feeling so enthusiastic about anything in years.

Was it possible, Roland thought, that his hypocritical, sly nephew was actually swallowing the bait, believing in the offer of cooperation that Eric Williams had asked him to proffer?

It still gave Roland pleasure to invite white people to the Country Club, their stronghold for so long, where until 1961 no black had ever dared attempt entry except as a servant.

He ordered another round of drinks and sat back, observing Drum as he'd once observed Commander Brett, not missing a single inflection or a single muscle moving in his nephew's face as Drum received the unexpected overture from his long-time adversary.

"You don't know how much I've longed for this day," Drum said earnestly. "When I received your secretary's call . . . well, it had to be the best damned news I've had in months."

"Yes, you haven't had much good news, I agree."

Drum shot Roland a sharp glance. Was he getting in a sarcastic crack? There was no need to rub that fact in. He decided to overlook it.

"We know you're in close contact with Jamandar," Roland said smoothly. "The prime minister has great respect for him, you know. . . ."

"He is a good fellow but, well, let's face it, no one can measure up to Williams. It's astonishing how much he's achieved in so short a time."

Sycophantic bastard! Roland's antipathy for his "passing for white" nephew grew as the afternoon turned rapidly into evening and the lights went on around the Olympic-sized Country Club pool. Remembering Williams's admonition to appear to offer a truce, he had to summon up all his willpower to act as if at last the time had come for them to settle their differences.

"We still have a hard row to hoe. We have to work ten times harder to prove we were right and our enemies wrong, now that the Federation has finally been abandoned."

As Roland appeared to listen attentively to Drum and consider his point of view, Williams's words rang in his head: "Remember, the less visible and influential enemies the better. Mend fences, particularly with your nephew Drum Pollard. His column in the *Guardian* is widely followed and quoted. He has strong friendships with the leaders of the other islands, all with their noses out of joint since we opted against forming a Southern and Eastern Caribbean Federation. If Drum Pollard offers you another olive branch—and I guarantee with no Federation post it won't be long in coming—I want you to appear to accept it."

Williams's reference to Drum's column had particularly nauseated Roland, who only that morning had allowed himself to give in to an outburst of temper, shredding the newspaper containing Drum's article lauding Martin Luther King, Jr.'s speech commemorating the centennial of the Emancipation Proclamation. How dare Drum Pollard write of his support of King's intoxicating words: "I have a dream that one day sons of former slaves and sons of former slave owners will be able to sit down together at the table of brotherhood. . . ." How did Drum Pollard consider himself? As the son of a slave . . . or of a slave owner? Condescending bastard! Yet now Roland could hear himself saying with an amazing ring of sincerity, "Perhaps you'd like to meet one day—unofficially, of course—with the prime minister and myself? Who knows, perhaps you may have a role to play as Cyril Merry did. . . ."

Drum was elated. Cyril Merry indeed! To everyone's surprise, Merry, a white landowner, had been chosen by Williams in 1956 to join his first cabinet. Merry!

As Drum wrote to Roger later that week, ". . . It's probably hard for

you to believe but at long last after all these years of ups and downs it
may well be that Roland Bracken and I will be colleagues after all. He
wants me to sit down with Williams . . . has intimated there could even
be a job for me."

Roger read Drum's letter twice before throwing it into his briefcase. Was
his half brother totally asinine? Or had he become so egotistical he
couldn't see a frame-up when it was right under his nose?

Roger stared unseeingly out of his office window. He wondered if he
hadn't seen Roland Bracken with Castro that evening in Havana
whether he would ever have suspected the man? Probably not . . . and
the irony was that nobody was sure, not even the experts in the State
Department, whether Williams was also an active Marxist beneath his
philosopher's mantle.

Since Castro had declared himself to be a Marxist-Leninist, forming a
party to introduce Communism to Cuba in 1961, Roger had taken it
upon himself to follow up every lead to link Roland with Castro's
avowed intentions to spread Communism throughout the Caribbean.
He'd spent thousands of dollars employing a crack investigative team,
never learning anything, until the day Roland Bracken had turned up in
New Orleans. Roland had been trailed and secretly photographed with
one of Castro's ablest lieutenants, the same day another man had been
in New Orleans handing out "fair play for Cuba" literature in the
streets, a man whose name would later go down in history for his assassination of a president riding in a motorcade along a Dallas street.

The State Department official had confirmed that Roger was certainly
on to something when, as usual, he had passed the information on.
However, from then on, he was to leave the surveillance strictly to the
government. If he came across anything by accident he knew how to
reach the right man, but, "Sir," said the fresh-faced young man, who
scarcely looked long out of high school, "this can be a nasty business.
You don't want to get yourself killed, do you, sir? You're too important
to the economy . . . to the oil business, I reckon."

Important? Roger realized he was still staring out of the window without registering anything. If he weren't married to Clare, perhaps he
would have begun to feel important by now. He sighed. It looked as if
they were headed for divorce after all, and looking back over the past
couple of empty years when he had really been too busy to be hurt by
her many disappearing acts, he realized if she had time to sit down with
the lawyers, that was really all there was to it. He'd find the time to sit

down, too, and who knew, perhaps, somewhere out there in the harsh, unfriendly world, was a woman who wouldn't think he was a bore. A woman who would love him even if he didn't give her a child.

He looked at his watch. For some reason he didn't feel like staying at the office today. Drum's letter had given him the jitters. He had the uneasy feeling in the pit of his stomach again. It was early, but he decided he'd go home, where he'd swim a hundred lengths to let his muscles knock the queasiness right out of him.

Victoria's car was in the driveway when he pulled up outside the poolhouse. Strange. She wasn't in the habit of calling, and why wasn't she up at the main house? Roger's uneasiness grew. What did her unusual visit mean? Was the old man. . . ? He rushed through the side gate that led to the garden surrounding the pool, once one of his proudest possessions. He had designed it himself to look "natural," directing the builder to create a waterfall, that cascaded down from rocks into first one pool, then another and finally into the Olympic-sized main pool below. Now, none of his possessions gave him any pleasure. Possessions were lifeless, sterile.

He could feel his heart thumping against his chest as he went toward the women's changing room and showers, defined by a stylish mermaid with long-flowing locks painted on the lattice doors. Voices were coming from there. He hesitated and knocked.

The door was opened immediately by Victoria. The same cool-mannered, efficient Victoria he was used to, while Clare, his usually assured wife, stood back against the wall, her hands clasped protectively over, her bare breasts, water still trickling down from her wet hair onto her shoulders. As he stood there alarmed, Victoria clutched his arm. "I must talk to you. It's . . . it's Clare's father. I came to tell Clare, but she became hysterical. She . . ."

Before Roger knew what was happening, Clare had thrown herself at Victoria, clawing, scratching, screaming, "You liar! You evil bitch! Don't you dare lie again. You know why you came. You lying murderess. . ."

Roger could hardly believe his wife's strength as he wrested her away, seeing the vivid scratch marks she inflicted on Victoria's cheeks. It was all over in minutes, yet it seemed like hours as Victoria hurriedly left them with the ominous message that her husband had been taken ill and was in bed, that she was worried about him . . . W. W. Lovell, who never took to his bed.

As Clare curtly asked him to make her a drink, Roger's thoughts were in turmoil. Could it have been a look of terror he'd seen on his wife's face until Victoria started to speak, when she'd changed into a screaming virago?

As if she could read his thoughts, Clare suddenly sat up to say in her usual mocking tone, "Darlin', don't let it concern you. It's a little private matter between Mrs. W. W. Lovell and Mr. W. W. Lovell's little ol' daughter. . . . And do you know something, sweet?" Clare leaned forward to give him a dazzling smile. "I think it's time you and I parted company. We've got nothing to say to each other any more, have we, darlin'?" She stretched herself lazily, then stood up and shook out her still-wet hair. "I'm just going upstairs to phone my daddy to see if his loving, tender wife is telling the truth for once—and if she is, I'm going to make sure she isn't in the vicinity when I go to his bedside. Then I'm going to phone my lawyer about us getting a divorce. . . . Don't you think that's a good idea?"

She didn't look at him and didn't wait for an answer as she walked, trailing the towel behind her like a train, toward the steps leading up to the main house.

He felt washed out as he went out to his car. He didn't care that Clare had finally said the words he'd been expecting for months. It was inevitable.

He looked at his watch two or three times to convince himself that only an hour had elapsed since his arrival at the poolhouse. Then suddenly he wondered why on earth he was wasting time.

If W. W. really was in bed, it meant something was very wrong. He had to get over there, even if he arrived only to be shown the door by the old oil man, complaining it was time Roger knew how to keep his crazy wife under control.

But Victoria hadn't lied. The old man was ill, very ill. He looked shrunken, dwarfed by the pillows that propped him up.

"How long have you been like this?" Roger asked, realizing with a pang that weeks had passed since he'd seen or even spoken to his father-in-law.

Lovell's voice, never very powerful, was now so low Roger had to lean over the bed in order to catch what the old man was saying. "Who cares? It's how long I am going to be around that's been worrying me. . . ."

The door opened and Victoria came in with a nurse. It was the only time Roger had ever seen his father-in-law emotionally upset. Tears came to the old man's eyes and Roger got up to vacate his seat, intending to let Victoria take his place, but the old man's fingers clung to Roger's hand, squeezing it as if to implore him not to go. With his other hand he gestured violently toward the door. "Leave us alone," he growled. "Leave us. . ." As calmly as she had greeted Roger thirty minutes before, fresh make-up barely concealing her scratches, Victoria now walked out without a backward glance. The nurse left too, after giving her patient some pills.

W. W. continued to hold Roger's fingers fast. With an obvious effort he started to speak again. "Promise me, Roger, promise me, you'll look after her. . . ."

Roger was startled. "Victoria?"

The old man's eyes filled with tears again. He shook his head as vehemently as he could from side to side. "No, no, no. Clare. She needs you. She loves you."

If the old man only knew. Roger swallowed hard and tried to smile.

W. W. went on slowly, "She doesn't know what love means. Protect her . . . from . . ." Again the voice was fading.

Roger leaned nearer to whisper, "Don't worry, W. W., I'll take care of her."

He didn't seem to hear as he struggled to say, "I've made you my heir. . . ."

The words didn't penetrate. To Roger's horror, he saw blood start to ooze from Lovell's mouth. He tried to disengage his fingers. "I must get your nurse. . . ."

W. W. shook his head, gasping now for breath.

"Promise me, you'll . . . never . . . never . . . leave Clare. Promise me. Save her from herself. . . . Don't let my . . . my . . . wife . . . near . . ."

A strangled sound broke from the old man's throat as blood gushed out in a flood and Roger found his fingers free.

Drum
1965

T HE Santo Domingo takeover had gone wrong. As Luis informed
him icily, all his carefully laid plans of eighteen months' duration
were useless.

There had been a tip-off. Luis handed Roland a press announcement from the U.S. State Department that stated, "Peace-keeping forces of U.S. Marines have landed in the Dominican Republic to
protect U.S. citizens and prevent an alleged imminent Communist
takeover of the Santo Domingo government. An Inter-American Peace
Force from the Organization of American States (OAS) will take over
peace-keeping operations on May 23."

"You're being watched, Roland. Somebody in the State Department
has been tipped off, and our contact tells us the Pollard name is involved. You must mend the breach with the Pollard family once and for
all. You are to lie low until the 1966 elections."

It wasn't only Luis's words that made Roland feel he was a doomed
man; it was his tone. Cold, clipped, emotionless. It was the worst moment of his life since his brother Jack had been sentenced to hang.

Like a wounded animal he went to ground, staying home for two
weeks with the excuse to the prime minister that he had a slipped disc.
But, as he constantly reminded himself, it was his mind that had

"slipped," not his disc, and that was a far more serious predicament. Somewhere along the way he'd made a crucial mistake and, fast as a rattlesnake, Drum Pollard had been onto it.

He thought back to Drum's eager face as they'd sat together that first time at the Country Club, when he'd been fool enough to think his nephew believed all he'd been telling him about wanting a truce. All the time the yellow-livered rat had been plotting behind his back. He could hardly believe it, but the facts in the Dominican Republic spoke for themselves.

Now it wasn't just a question of waiting for the next chance to work for the cause; it was a question of regaining the confidence of those nameless ones for whom he'd been working for so many years.

To *survive* he had to follow Luis's instructions *to the letter* . . . which was why the news of cousin Sam Bracken's impending marriage to Gloria Simpson had been manna from heaven. It gave him a perfect excuse for a public showing of unity, a reason for celebration and a reconciliation party that would be seen by Luis and, more important, his comrades, as immediate acquiescence to their orders—and by Eric Williams as either a common-sensical way to solve a problem already hoary with age or as just one more move in the complicated chess game they continued to play.

What would his family think if they knew the *real* reason behind the invitations to his party hand-delivered to Golden Hill a few weeks later?

As Roland shaved that morning he could just imagine the heated arguments that were bound to ensue when he broke the news to his brother James, who would then scream it down the phone to April. But how would they react to the truth—that their "estimable, important elder brother," was a confirmed Marxist, at a crucial stage in his life, who had to "appear to mend fences," not because of the past, but in order to have a future?

Drum stared at the handsome white envelopes sealed with the Trinidad government seal.

He was sure they contained invitations; he could feel the firm cards inside, and the envelopes had been carefully scripted by an expert in calligraphy. "Mr. Arthur Donald Pollard and the Honorable Mrs. Arthur Donald Pollard" . . . "Mrs. Peter Pollard." How strange it was to read his father's real name after all these years. Drum strained to capture his father's striking face in his mind, but it was gone. He could

only think of him as the photographs on the library table showed him—
stiff, unnatural, revealing none of his happy-go-lucky smile, the love
that had shone out of his eyes like a beacon, always offering him support and guidance whenever he'd needed it.

"What is it, Drum?" He was startled, lost in the past, not aware
Alicia had come into the study.

"Oh, nothing much," he muttered, putting the envelopes aside.

"You look as if you've seen a ghost. . . ." Alicia hiccuped loudly,
covering her mouth with an exaggerated, "Excuse me!"

"Are you drunk already, Alicia? Isn't it a little early in the day?"
Drum feigned a bored expression, but in fact Alicia's attachment to the
rum bottle disturbed him more than he was prepared to admit.

"I haven't . . . haven't . . . "—she hiccuped again—". . . had a
dwink . . . drinkie for days, but what if I have? You don't care. You
don't care about anyone, except yourself and Margaret."

He snapped back, "Just as well somebody cares for Margaret. You
don't call yourself a mother, do you? The only reason I'm glad you got
your way and sent her away to school is that she's well out of your
clutches."

Increasingly unpredictable, now to his surprise Alicia started to giggle, leaning over the desk to try to reach one of the envelopes. "I happen to know . . . that . . . one of those envelopes is addressed to me. I
happen to know . . . "Drum snatched it out of her reach and opened it
irritably, intending to read the contents aloud and then go on to the
estate office, but as he glanced at the engraved words, he paled, whispering, "Good God!"

"What is it? I want to see . . . gimmee . . . gimmee!" Drum handed
her the elaborate card without a word, sitting down heavily at the desk.
As she read she screamed, "How dare they! How dare they insult me
like this? Bloody black bastards, I'll get them for this!" She picked up a
paper knife and started to jab it furiously through the stiff card before
Drum snatched it away.

"You won't do anything of the sort, you crazy woman. Sit down. Let
me think. There's more to this than meets the eye. Calm down, will
you!" He pushed her rudely down into an armchair. "They've invited
my mother, too. It's the full-scale 'reconciliation' attempt . . . or is it?"
As he paced up and down and Alicia rocked herself moodily backward
and forward on the chair, the phone rang.

"Yes. . . ." Drum put a hand over the mouthpiece. "It's Bracken's
secretary." He sat down as if to steady himself. "Yes, Roland, I've just

received it. Very good of you. . . . I'm not sure. Williams? Oh, yes, and members of the cabinet, too? Well, quite a full-scale turnout. Congratulations. I'm not surprised. No, I don't know him . . . never heard of him . . . your second cousin? So what does that make him as far as I'm concerned? My third cousin?"

Drum listened, silent for awhile, then said hesitantly, "I'm not sure. I don't think so, though her name is familiar. . . ."

"Bitch!" Alicia spat out. "She's familiar all right. You want me to tell your precious uncle what I know about Gloria Simpson?" She tried to wrest the phone away, but he quickly moved out of her reach, holding his hand up, a look on his face that stopped her in her tracks.

"Well, it sounds like a very happy occasion. I'm sure we will be able to make it. Yes, it's long overdue." Drum tried to inject a note of light-heartedness into his voice. "I tried, remember . . . on my twenty-first birthday. No, I don't even like to think how long ago that is! Water under the bridge. . . . Well, I'm glad the prime minister thinks so, too. Yes, that's all behind us. We have to work together, I agree. . . ."

As he put the phone down, Alicia walked to the study door, making sure there was enough distance between them before she cried again, "Bitch! Don't think I'm going to dance at any party being given for *her*. I'll only dance at her funeral!" She slammed the door behind her so hard that a Dresden figurine fell from its stand, its fragile arm breaking on the marble floor.

"You're a bitch all right," Drum muttered, as he bent to pick up the broken pieces.

His uncle's call had unnerved him further. He was trapped, hoisted by his own petard, he reflected, as he read the invitation again. After my protestations of wanting to forget and forgive the past, how can I stay away from this all-important party? Drum racked his brains, realizing, as he often did, how much he missed the wise counsel of his recently deceased old friend and adviser, Bill McMurtrey.

And if he stayed away, wouldn't it also add fuel to the rumor that Gloria Simpson had once been his mistress, that he was the father of her daughter, Naomi?

He did what he always did when he felt desperate. He had a cold shower, a long, cool drink of homemade lime juice, then got on his favorite horse, Cameron, a feisty black devil of a stallion that needed his full attention.

By the time he returned to Golden Hill, dripping with perspiration, his head was clearer. Perhaps he was overreacting. Perhaps this was a genuine olive branch stretched out, albeit for public-relations reasons, but genuine nonetheless. And why should he think Roland and the rest of the Brackens knew about his relationship with Gloria?

She had never talked, of that he was certain. Although it was ironic she should fall into the hands of a Bracken, no matter how many cousins removed, it was all for the best, he supposed, even relieving him of any further responsibility. He had given her a home, an income for life. His conscience need never bother him again.

Only Alicia was a problem. He decided there and then he would take his mother—who would also be a problem, but much less of one, and one he knew how to handle—but he would make sure Alicia stayed home. It would be easy. All he had to do was pretend she could accompany him and say whatever she liked to Gloria, then, at lunchtime that day, suggest she "stoke up her courage" with a few rounds of martinis, followed by her favorite rum punches, ones he would make personally. He knew from past experience that by six o'clock she would be so inebriated she would have to be carried upstairs to bed.

But things didn't go entirely according to plan.

Drum cursed his mother under his breath as he drove his new Jaguar toward Port of Spain. Obviously, her absence was going to cause comment. He was sure his excuse about his wife having had to take to her bed with heat exhaustion would be accepted without question—although regretfully—but now here he was, all spruced up for the inevitable "truce" pictures he expected would be taken, without the key figure in the drama. Rose, his mother, the woman who had caused all the trouble in the first place.

The irony was that Rose really wasn't well. This time it wasn't her dog-in-the-manger obstinacy that had forced him to accept she wouldn't be able to accompany him. It was a fever—one hundred and two degrees, the doctor had said. Drum almost laughed out loud at the lunacy of his thoughts, wondering if he should have asked the old doc to write a letter testifying that in his opinion it would be foolhardy for Mrs. Peter Pollard to be present on such a demanding occasion. It was droll!

What would his father have thought about the evening about to take place? Drum felt certain that he would have approved—that perhaps his father had always wanted to acknowledge his wife's family. His father had been right about everything, so, Drum reasoned, surely he would have had the right instincts—if not the right reasons, for going along with Roland Bracken's "reconciliation" attempt, knowing that one day the minority would have to take a back seat and let the black majority take over their lives.

Well, he would never know what his father had really thought about his wife's motley colored family. For years he hadn't even known they existed, for his mother would never discuss it; not that he'd have believed a word she said anyway.

He could hear music—seductive, swaying music—and he saw blazing torches fluttering in the soft evening breeze as he slowed down to join a line of cars edging along to the entrance of the hotel where the party was to take place.

Suddenly there was a wail of sirens and the scream of motorbikes, and Drum could see a motorcycle escort followed by two or three limousines coming against the traffic on the wrong side of the road. He looked at his watch: 6:57 P.M. The guest of honor, the prime minister, was exactly on time as his British predecessors had always been.

As the rhythm of the music invaded the car and his hand began to tap to its time, Drum decided, what the hell, he would try to enjoy himself! He might even have the chance to dance with Gloria. He realized' he was looking forward to seeing her and he hoped she was also looking forward to seeing him.

As Obee took over in the driver's seat to park the car and Drum walked through an arbor planted only that afternoon with tuberoses and dark rich ferns, he reflected he wasn't even sure how old Gloria was, although little Naomi (as he always referred to her in his mind—when he allowed himself to think about her at all) little Naomi . . . my God, it was a shattering thought . . . had to be nearing nineteen!

How could he have been so consumed by his plot to keep Alicia at home and ensure his mother's presence at the party that he hadn't given any thought to seeing Naomi, a grown-up probably very beautiful Naomi. Would she know he was her father?

His palms were sweating, and no matter how many times he wiped the sweat away, back it came, pouring out of his pores as fast as his decision to enjoy himself evaporated and the possibility of a public announcement of his paternity came into his mind. Was that the real reason for the party? Was it a plot to trap him after all?

There was the receiving line. Roland, looking stern, stiff and not at all relaxed, stood beside his roly-poly wife, Emerald, who was squeezed into a sequined gown that looked expensive, but totally inappropriate for the tropics.

Drum inwardly shuddered at the thought of his sweaty palm squeezing hers . . . and then he saw Gloria, with a coffee-colored man who
had to be her new husband beaming broadly beside her and . . . Drum
relaxed imperceptibly. There was no lissome, supple black girl beside
them, no sign of *anyone* in the receiving line who could be an eighteen-
year-old Naomi, who perhaps was not at the party at all. A girl of eighteen could be almost anywhere, Drum told himself. She didn't have to
be at her mother's party.

He looked down into Gloria's sweet face, almost unlined, her candid,
clear glance reassuring him, telling him without words that there wasn't
going to be any embarrassing announcement, that it was all right, she
had kept her vow of silence. If other people had talked, she hadn't—and
only she and he knew the truth for certain.

Flashbulbs popped, as Roland gripped his shoulder and gave him—
Drum thought—an unnecessarily effusive hug, followed by a wet
(ghastly!) kiss from Emerald.

Roland then insisted on making a telephone call to Golden Hill with
Drum at his side, hoping, he said with a poignant catch in his voice—
directed to everyone within listening distance—to speak to his sister
Rose after all the years gone by.

It was no good telling Roland it was useless. Whether he spoke to
Rose or not, Drum realized, was entirely beside the point. It made a
good picture, and so did the show put on with James Bracken—although Drum didn't feel the greeting from that quarter was too genuine.
The thought flashed across his mind that James would probably have
preferred to be photographed using Drum's head, or better still, his
skull, for a drum!

It wasn't until ten o'clock, when, lulled with wine—that he had to
acknowledge had been amazingly well chosen—Drum went over to
Gloria's table to ask her to dance.

It was the last dance before the "entertainment," when a bevy of
beautiful girls in minuscule flashing costumes shimmied and shook,
their breasts and buttocks bouncing in erotic unison.

Whether it was having had Gloria in his arms after so long, Drum
didn't know, but suddenly he longed to penetrate the whirling flesh on
the dance floor. As each dancer arched, spun and proudly presented her
body to the audience, he could feel his penis throb. Although he tried
to wrest his mind away, his thoughts kept straying to his beautiful
daughter with the soft, silk lashes and bold, dark nipples—nipples that
asked to be sucked, that one day another man would suck and feel and

pull. Drum pushed his feet against the floor as if to trample that man to death, agonized to think one day Margaret would be in another man's arms.

Every term when Margaret was away at her English boarding school seemed like an eternity, yet he didn't know whether he suffered more when she was away or when she was home for the holidays.

When she was in the house, he wanted to stay close to her, to touch her as he allowed himself to touch her when he went to her room to kiss her goodnight.

Innocent Margaret, with her eyes like soft moths loving him from across the room—if she only knew what agony it was for him not to be with her every second she was home. Instead he forced himself to make business trips to the other islands, lying awake in strange bedrooms thinking about her . . . her developing shape, more evident every holiday, the creamy, pendulous perfection of each breast that he knew she loved him to uncover. He could hear her softly whisper, "Darling Daddy. . . ."

Oh, Margaret. He shook himself, startled, not totally sure he hadn't murmured her name. He was a cursed man, destined never to experience the rapture of other men, who could become one with the woman they loved in mind and body.

People were standing up to applaud. The prime minister was leaving, followed sheepishly by members of his cabinet.

Drum downed the last sip of his wine and went over to shake Eric Williams's hand. Then he looked at his watch. Ten forty-five. The evening hadn't been so bad after all. Soon he would leave and let an icy shower freeze the desire out of him.

As he turned to go to the bar for one last drink before looking for Obee outside, a heavyset colored woman whom he knew he had been introduced to—as he had been introduced to so many during the last four hours—stood blocking his way. She giggled nervously. "It's a ladies' invitation. Won't yo' dance wid me?" The idea nauseated him, but, bowing gallantly, Drum offered the woman his arm.

As the lights dimmed and the Sunbeams hotted up the rhythm, Drum realized from the woman's reference to what she called "Jim's terrif'c music . . ." that he had to be dancing with James's wife, Carmelita. Well, it was all part of the job.

If Eric Williams meant what he said and Roland was going to call him to set up a meeting, he told himself, then he was willing to put up

with dancing with this heavyweight lady. He winced as she placed a
solid foot down on his toe.

With the officials gone, the party was starting to loosen up and Drum
felt light-hearted again, as he saw people start to dance with the sort of
abandon only a mixture of many races like the Trinidadians could produce. After that one false step, he found Carmelita wasn't such a bad
dancer after all and, providing he didn't have to look at her, he realized
he was enjoying dancing, something he had done little of over the
years.

The Sunbeams launched into a version of the Paul Jones "face your
partner" and Drum found himself propelled to join a large circle of men
dancing around a swaying inner circle of women.

He shrugged his shoulders at the innocent absurdity of it all, allowing
himself to be pulled around as the music went faster and faster. It
stopped abruptly and, as he was about to try to break away and leave, he
felt a timid tap on his elbow. Before he could demur, a pretty colored
girl with laughing, mischievous eyes nestled into his arms, pushing her
thighs tight against his. As the Sunbeams played one sultry number after
another, the young girl moved closer . . . and closer.

Her young breasts, which had already given milk to a baby she'd
borne two weeks before her fourteenth birthday, were full, motherly
breasts on so slight a body, brushing Drum's chest, soothing the ache he
felt for Margaret.

He looked around. Everyone was dancing closer and the lights were
getting dimmer, darker. Nobody could see that this exquisite dusky-
skinned child was actually rubbing herself against his prick. It was an
irresistible sweet torture, one that was getting at once better and worse as
the minutes went by.

What was she whispering? Was it possible? Was it safe?

Again Drum's eyes scanned the crowded floor of happy laughing
dancers, nibbling each other's ears, rubbing against each other, releasing their libidos, dancers who probably would soon be going home to
make love to each other like normal healthy people.

Now this girl-child with the big soft breasts was gently motioning with
her body, prodding, pushing, directing him toward the darkest corner of
the ballroom, behind which, she whispered, there was a first-aid station.

First-aid! The thought of this pulsating, velvet body delivering the
remedial treatment he suddenly felt he desperately needed made him
feel dizzy. She would slip out. He would follow.

No one was watching them he thought; everyone was lost in their own dreams, the music sweeter now, more insistent. He looked around carefully one more time before following the swaying behind.

How long had he practiced self-control? How long was it since the last time? Weeks, months—it felt like years, as his love and longing for Margaret had grown, and he'd forced that longing deep down into his body, looking away from its reflection in Margaret's eyes, a longing he knew she scarcely comprehended.

As he entered the fluorescent-lit first-aid station, the girl was taking off her flimsy dress. She lay down on a trestle bed, naked except for skimpy panties that Drum knew had to be wet but not from the heat.

She giggled as she quickly pulled her panties down to her ankles, revealing a surprising mound of black curly hair.

His head was spinning—whether with wine, lust or a combination of both he didn't know—and he hardly knew where he was as she arched back, sticking out her large breasts, opening her mouth, flicking a pink tongue in and out. Almost moaning, Drum opened his trousers to let her experienced little hands take out his throbbing penis. She fastened her mouth hungrily around it, licking, sucking him into delirium as he stood over her, his eyes closed, hardly aware he was clamping her down onto the bed with one hand while his other hand squeezed and pulled first one then the other fat teat.

As he felt himself coming, he heard a series of clicks. He opened his eyes to see a ring of light, soft, not bright or harsh, like the light from a photographer's flash. Even as he tensed, sensing danger, he couldn't, wouldn't withdraw. He had to be released, purged. As the orgasm passed, he felt violently sick, faint, while the girl sucked her thumb and gyrated backward and forward as if she would never be able to stop.

He didn't know how he stumbled out to where Obee was waiting. The only thing he knew for sure was he hadn't said goodnight to any-one—and he only knew that because Roland telephoned the next morn-ing, concerned something had happened to him, wondering why he'd disappeared so suddenly, wondering if anything had offended him?

What could he say? His own hesitant explanation—a sudden extraor-dinary wave of nausea . . . not wanting to break up the wonderful party—had sounded hollow and forced, but Roland's call had relieved him.

He had obviously overreacted. His nerves were on edge. He hadn't heard clicks. He hadn't seen flashes. Perhaps, he even thought, he'd caught his mother's flu. He must have gone to the party with a slight temperature and the events of the evening had raised it still higher. No wonder! A familiar mixture of shame and erotic excitement sent his head reeling as he thought of the fierce young mouth, the sperm that had covered the velvet skin, the amazing full breasts on one so young . . . but he couldn't remember anything else, not even her face.

Another day passed before the appalling truth confronted him in sharp focus.

Marked "Strictly Personal and Confidential," in a manila envelope with the Trinidad government seal on the back, came two photographs, one in which the girl lay looking up at him—unmistakably him—with imploring, dark eyes as he appeared to force his penis into her mouth, one hand forcing her down, the other pulling hard at her nipple, while her hands, which, even as he looked at the dreadful scene, Drum remembered had moved with such ease to draw him into her sucking orifice, appeared to be trying to push his away in vain. He shuddered. The other picture showed the girl's crumpled dress on the floor, while she lay naked, her panties appearing to link her ankles together as if she were in bondage, while he towered over her like a Nazi guard about to rape a child prisoner.

Accompanying the pictures was a simple sheet of paper bearing the typewritten message: "Child Molester: Your vile acts will be known to the world unless you send ten thousand American dollars to the Royal Society for the Prevention of Cruelty to Children." The note was unsigned.

Who had sent it? Who had nailed him to the wall with photographs so obscene that they sent him reeling to the bathroom to try to vomit his self-loathing away. This time no cold shower could take the sickness out of him.

He tore the photographs into shreds, flushing them out of sight, but not out of mind. He was going mad. He didn't know where he was going when he left the house to ride for hours, to walk, to stare down at the ocean torrents, screaming inside for help.

It was the end. What help was there for him now? Every good thing he had ever done could never wipe out the evil dominating him, evil the photographs had documented, as nothing else could.

The truth about his weakness taunted him at every step, as he wrestled with the question, who could the blackmailer be?

It seemed obvious it was Roland Bracken—from the careful arrangement of the party, to the government envelope containing the foul photos—yet something wasn't right. Roland Bracken didn't *need* to destroy him now that he was at the height of his career, with, it was said, an ambassadorship in the offing.

A day later, a second manila envelope arrived with another photograph of the girl and himself. This time the message was shorter. "You have one week to pay before the pictures are released."

Now Drum was terrified to leave the house. What if another envelope should arrive and someone opened it by accident? If Alicia should see the photographs, God forbid, in her alcoholic state, what might she do with them?

He sent the money to the RSPCC by messenger. Then he locked himself in his dressing room, unable to stop his body from trembling as the hours went by and he waited for the judgment inexorably moving toward him.

The day and night passed. Then came a flood of thank-yous from the president of the Society and other members of the committee, each one sounding more surprised than the one before. Phone calls were followed by letters, eulogizing his incredible generosity, his thought for others, his "inspiring citizenship." Every call, every thank-you letter was like a sword cutting through his flesh, for where was the hidden threat? When would these God-fearing, selfless citizens, having received the money— the *proof* of his guilt and shame—turn into menacing judges, arriving en masse to denounce and condemn him? As the election came closer, and Vernon Jamandar was *not* elected leader of the opposition party, despite the fact the present leader, Rudranath Capildeo, continued to live more in London than in Port of Spain, Drum became convinced someone was using the long conflict between Roland and himself as a cover to conceal his own identity, for without Jamandar, Williams simply had no opposition of any kind. As Williams told him himself, he was "happy" Roland had made "peace" with Drum, hoping, as Drum knew, if he went along with his party, other influential whites would follow.

One sleepless night followed another. Drum grew haggard, forgetful, only just avoiding a fatal accident as he drove out of Golden Hill's gates at breakneck speed, without looking to the left or right.

Did he have a death wish? If he did, he wanted to see his daughter, his flawless, innocent daughter once again before he died. He looked at the calendar, counting the days to her return, still almost two months away.

He *had* to discover the truth before her arrival. It was better to face it than never know it. He contemplated a showdown with Roland Bracken, but what would it accomplish? If Roland Bracken was, for some inexplicable reason, really behind the blackmail—and everything happening around him continued to throw doubt on that likelihood—then he was trapped as completely as if he were bound hand and foot.

Drum received a new demand, accompanying a smaller photograph, but one just as explicit and searing to his senses. This was followed a couple of weeks later by yet another demand to yet another beneficiary—the Royal Society for the Prevention of Cruelty to Animals—with a close-up shot of his penis as it neared the small open mouth.

He paid the money, then went personally to every committee member of the RSPCA to ask each one a simple question.

The idea had come to him as he'd tried to assess the reasoning behind the demands.

How did the blackmailer *know* he'd paid what he'd been asked to pay? The last demands had stated he was to make one request of the recipients: no publicity, no announcements of his gifts of any kind, and he'd been only too anxious to comply. But with all the secrecy involved, how did the blackmailer know he had complied, *unless* he or she was a member of both committees?

Suddenly he learned the truth—and the name of the person who'd aged him more in two months than he'd aged in twenty years. He should have guessed from the beginning who it was.

"Has anyone called you about my donation?" he'd asked. Committee members had shaken their heads, puzzled, reminding him that he himself had asked for anonymity, no publicity of any kind, which they told him with respect had made his gift seem even more special!

On the day Margaret was arriving home from school for the summer holidays, Drum called on Mrs. Destano, an elderly, infirm lady, who'd been one of the first to set up a branch of the RSPCA on the island.

She offered him a milk-and-rum cocktail, something she reminisced his father used to make and like.

"What a handsome man he was." She looked piercingly at Drum. "And his son is handsome, too, in a different way. But something is troubling you? What is it?"

He was shocked she could see his torment so clearly, but he laughed, dismissing her question, asking casually, "Has anyone asked you recently if I've made a large donation to your cause?"

Mrs. Destano was about to say no: then she muttered, "I did receive a telephone call before we received your most generous check, but it wasn't to ask if *you* had made a donation. Rather, it was to ask if we were in need of funds. At first I *thought* the two events had to be connected."

"Who asked you?" His voice sounded unnaturally shrill, as if his vocal cords were strung up tight.

"She told me not to say anything, but not very forcibly. I expected to receive some money from her—that perhaps it was her way of doing penance for the way she lived her life for so long, but when she didn't send anything herself, I dismissed it as fanciful."

Mrs. Destano seemed to fall into a doze, opening her eyes only to nod absent-mindedly as Drum asked sharply, "Her? You mean . . ."

"Magdalen Finch," Mrs. Destano mumbled. "You know her."

He felt there was extra power in his hands on the wheel as he drove toward Orange Grove, where he'd heard Magdalen Finch now spent most of her time in a new house, supervising the setting up of her son's first investment in Trinidad, the Tropica essential-oil plant.

It wasn't until he located the plant, seen in the distance across a sugarcane field, that Drum realized in his anger—and anguish—he'd completely forgotten about meeting Margaret at the airport.

Obee would be there with the station wagon, but he could physically feel Margaret's disappointment, as she would scan the waiting faces to find no sign of him.

His hatred of Magdalen Finch intensified. Now the persecutor was about to be persecuted.

As he approached a wide front veranda, he glanced at his watch. If the plane was on time, Margaret would just about be coming down the ramp, smiling, waving to Obee, her golden mane of hair released from the school's pigtails and flowing down her back.

The thought of her strengthened Drum's resolve. He was going to get those negatives . . . or else!

He didn't ring the bell. He turned the handle and walked straight into a large airy hall, surprising a maid who was polishing an antique library table in the center.

"Where is Magdalen Finch?" He made no attempt to hide the anger in his voice.

The maid backed away in alarm. "I don' . . . don' know, sir . . . I'se . . ."

"It's all right, Susie." Magdalen had come out of a side door, apparently in no way nonplussed by Drum's appearance for the first time in her house.

The maid scuttled away as Magdalen went on coolly, "Mr. Pollard will want to be alone for our conversation. Make sure we are not disturbed." She turned haughtily, saying over her shoulder, "I've been expecting you, Drum. It took you longer than I thought it would."

The insolence of the woman. Drum felt his temper rising.

As they stood face to face, Drum noticed with an added burst of irritation that, despite her age, Magdalen Finch was still a remarkably good-looking woman, silver glints in her dark red hair giving a needed softness to the effect of her angular cheekbones, the proud tilt of her head.

What had he ever done to this woman that she should hate him so much? She had lied to his mother that Gloria was going to sue him for paternity, ruining any chance of making a good marriage with Alicia, almost losing for him the only person he cared about, his daughter Margaret—and now she'd perpetrated vile, ugly blackmail, exposing his weakness, playing on it, driving him almost to suicide.

She hadn't spoken, but was watching him, a strange half smile on her coral-painted lips.

There was no point in beating around the bush. She'd said she'd been expecting him. "What do you want for the negatives?" His voice shocked him. It was hard, ugly, snarling with desperation.

"Negatives?" Magdalen picked up the needlepoint she had been working on. She wasn't as cool as she looked, he was glad to see. Her fingers were trembling.

He stood over her. "You know what negatives, you bitch. What do you want for them?" He shook her, beside himself, hardly knowing what he was doing. If anything, his action steadied her. She slowly took the needle from the canvas and deliberately pushed it into his hand.

Blood spurted out before he clasped his hand to his mouth. "Perhaps that will calm you," she said in an even tone. "I don't know what you're talking about."

"Why did you say you were expecting me then?"

"Did I say that?" Magdalen started to laugh, a humorless, low laugh that sent blood racing to his head. He longed to squeeze every molecule of life out of her long pale neck.

"If you don't destroy those filthy negatives in my presence, I promise you, Magdalen Finch, I'll kill you if it's the last thing I do." He placed his hands around her neck. "I'll kill you!"

She stared up at him with large, expressive eyes, and he could see she wasn't frightened.

"You *can't* frighten me, Drum Pollard. Death holds no fear for me. But I should tell you if anything does happen to me, perhaps something will then happen to you—or should I say to your 'flawless' reputation!" She didn't bother to hide the sarcasm in her voice.

"You wicked witch! Everything everyone has ever said about you is true," Drum cried.

"And everything everyone has ever said about you has been untrue!" Magdalen screamed back.

They yelled at each other, old stories hurtling through the air, names, insults. In the back of his mind, Drum was aware of time ticking by, of Margaret wondering where her father was on this all-important day of her homecoming.

He sat down wearily on a large chintz armchair, struggling for composure. "All right, you want something. What is it? I'm willing to consider it if we can put an end to this terrible situation. What is more, there will never, *never* be any likelihood of this happening again."

He hadn't meant to express his resolve to a woman he considered to be lower than a rattlesnake in the sugarcane, but saying the words aloud became a step toward his salvation. "Well," he barked. "What do you want?"

Magdalen looked at him levelly. "You know what I want."

He was mystified. "I know?"

"Oh, yes, you know! I don't want what is rightfully mine for myself any more. I want it for my son—and even more for my grandson."

Drum looked at her as if she'd taken leave of her senses. He laughed a short, sarcastic laugh. "If you mean what I think you mean. . . ."

Now it was Magdalen's turn to lose control. She threw her needlepoint down to come at him, arms flying, pummeling, screaming, "Yes, I want back what is rightfully mine, mine, mine! Golden Hill. Promise me you will leave it to my son or my grandson to inherit! Promise me, promise me!"

Drum pushed her away as she clung to his arm. "You're insane, woman. Golden Hill yours? Don't make me laugh. You're mentally sick or you wouldn't have had those pictures taken, which you know as well as I do don't illustrate the whole truth. Who was the little creature? One of your midget prostitutes? How many years did you spend training her? You're insane. It's time Eric Williams deported vermin like you. I'm going straight to Williams, to Bracken. . . ."

"I wouldn't do that if I were you." Magdalen lay sprawled on the floor where Drum had sent her flying with one fierce push. "You don't

think I was in this alone, do you? Why do you think I wasn't invited to
the Bracken party? Because *they* knew if you saw me there, you might
become suspicious . . . and above all they didn't want you to be suspicious that night. Do you get my point?"

Suddenly the fire went out of her. She stretched up her hand im-
ploringly. "For the last time I implore you, do the decent thing. Give
Golden Hill back to the family who created it. I don't want the Pollard
land—only the few original Picton acres surrounding the house. . . ."

Drum could bear it no longer. He rushed out of the room crying,
"You're sick . . . sick! You haven't heard the last of this!"

"And neither have you, you child molester!" Magdalen screamed at
the top of her voice, tears choking in her throat. "The world is going to
know . . . to know what you're really like!"

Drum tried his best at dinner to act normal, to ask Margaret about
school, about the abominable Miss Potts who taught algebra in French
instead of in English, about school food, snobs, brats—all the things
they had laughed and joked about during the last holidays, but Magdalen Finch's voice rang in his head as he mentally went over his
options.

Margaret looked at her father, longing for him to change his expression, to soften as he always softened whenever he looked at her . . . and
only when he looked at her, but he was deliberately looking away. What
was wrong? What had happened to change him in the short months
she'd been away? What terrible thing had happened? The house seemed
full of it.

Margaret blinked back the tears that had threatened since she'd come
rushing down the plane ramp, longing to see her adored, handsome
father, hoping he would like her new short bob, which all the girls were
wearing, the higher heels that emphasized the slimness of her calves.
But he hadn't been at the airport. Only Obee had been there—sweet,
dear old Obee, who'd tried to explain what a busy man her father was
these days, ever since the prime minister had had to ask for his help
after all.

She knew how busy her father was, but he'd always made time for her
ever since the wonderful night he'd first come to her room. As she
thought about the visit she was sure would come later, a flush spread
over her face. She shouldn't look forward to it so much, but other people just didn't understand. She'd tried to explain to Deidre, her best
friend at Heathfield, how special her father was. But Deidre had be-

come upset, not able to accept there was nothing wrong with her father seeing her body or some of it, only her top half really, even though it was such a strange top half with her awful dark nipples. In the end, she'd had to say she'd only been joking, that she'd made up the story to take Deidre's mind off the horrible childbirth film the headmistress had insisted they see. But *she* still didn't see what was so wrong. Her father loved her and she loved him . . . more and more.

Now, as she saw traces of perspiration on his face, the way he clenched and unclenched his hands, she *knew* something was terribly wrong. She promised herself she would *make* him tell her what it was all about when he came to her room for their usual secret talk.

She had a surprise for him, too. She would be wearing her first negligee, a beautiful one, given to her by a new boarder, a Moroccan princess, whom she'd helped during the term with her English lit.

The princess had explained that you wore a negligee *sitting* in your bedroom, as opposed to lying in bed—and *she* intended to be sitting in the chair by the lamp in *her* bedroom when her father arrived, instead of lying in the dark like a little girl.

As she thought of her father touching her, she tried to stop it, but it was too late. She could feel wetness coming between her legs. It was a lovely yet frightening feeling, because she knew she wanted him to touch her where the wetness was and that was really bad—something she could understand Deidre getting upset about if she ever knew. That was where her curse came from—where babies came out and where men put their . . . She didn't want to think about that! She particularly didn't want to think her father and mother had ever . . . It was too awful!

Margaret sighed aloud without meaning to, and both her parents looked at her at the same time, but in such different ways.

Alicia stared at her as if she were a stranger she didn't particularly want to entertain. She knew it was her little daughter Margaret, yet she could hardly recognize this shapely young woman, so much taller than she'd been only three or four months before.

"Go to bed, Margaret . . ." Alicia slurred. "You must be exhausted after that . . . flight from New York."

"From New York, Mother?" Margaret laughed. "I came from dear old London, but you're right. I am tired. I'll go to bed early tonight, even though it's my first night home."

Margaret looked meaningfully at her father, hoping for the small sign he always gave her that meant "I won't be long. Don't go to sleep before I've come to say goodnight," but he was frowning down at his plate.

"Goodnight, Daddy," she said unhappily.

"Goodnight, darling. It's wonderful to have you home. Get a good night's rest. We'll go riding tomorrow—if it's not too hot, and if it is, we'll take a picnic and swim at Maracas."

"Too many sharks," Alicia snapped moodily, leaning across the polished wood of the table as if she were going to collapse there.

"Rubbish!" Drum attempted to smile at Margaret. "Whatever we do, it will be fun, won't it, precious?"

"Oh, yes, Daddy. I'm so happy to be back. In a way I'm glad we're not in Europe this summer." Margaret sang her favorite song, "Alfie," all the way to the kitchen, depositing a kiss on Em's hot cheek. "You're glad I'm home, aren't you, Em? Oh, you're so good!" she exclaimed, looking at the neat kitchen. "Already washed up and we've only just finished that de-lic-ious coconut and banana pie, my absolute favorite!" She whirled out excited, yet apprehensive, wondering what her father was going to say when he saw her sitting in the negligee, which barely concealed her breasts with skin-colored lace, while the matching nightdress that he would see if he unlaced the negligee's long silk ribbons—and she hoped fervently he *would* unlace them—was so low cut, she only had to bend forward slightly for her nipples to pop right out.

It was very naughty, but it was so exciting.

Drum promised himself he'd make up for his silence at dinner by taking Margaret for a long drive by herself the next day, whatever Alicia had to say about it. He followed his wife, who lurched unsteadily from side to side, out of the dining room.

As he was about to go to his study, Alicia turned to clutch at his sleeve, her fingers holding on so tenaciously as he moved back he heard the material rip.

"What the hell!" he bellowed.

Still Alicia clutched him, her alcoholic breath foul on his cheek. "Why don't you ever call me . . . me . . . mmmeee darling? Why is it always 'darling Margaret' . . . 'my precious' . . . 'my love'?" she mimicked. "Is she your darling now, Drum? Am I too old for you? 'Yes, darling Daddy, no, darling Daddy,'" she went on, trying to imitate Margaret's breathless voice.

"Get away! You're disgusting. The Honorable Alicia Pollard! What a joke." Drum looked at her with loathing. "Honorable, my foot. You're just a soak, nothing but a rum-soaked, selfish, jealous woman who's never had a decent emotion in her life."

Alicia ran ahead to the study, closing the door, attempting to lock it, but Drum was too fast for her.

As he entered, she picked up the sherry decanter and hurled it at him. He ducked just in time, the heavy glass hitting the paneled wall, where miraculously it didn't break, until it fell to smash to pieces on the marble below, the golden liquid spreading in silky rivulets across the floor.

He slapped her so hard she fell backward into a chair, her expression a mixture of cunning, hatred and fear. He was about to slap her again when he heard the dining room doors closing. It had to be Obee checking up. Obee, the faithful one.

Drum ran out of the room and up the stairs, tears streaking his face. Twice in one day he'd let his inner rage boil over. He couldn't stand this life any more. He had to get away, far away and start all over again.

Without Margaret? asked an inner voice. It was unthinkable. Yet what else?

With Margaret? Yes, yes, yes, said another voice. He would protect her—from all men, all of whom had a bestial side. They would live as father and daughter should live. . . . He would conquer his terrible weakness, but first he had to deal with Magdalen Finch.

He locked his dressing-room door and paced up and down, going over the events of the afternoon. Magdalen Finch had said he couldn't frighten her, but she could probably be frightened if threats were made on the life of her son—or better still her grandson! That was it! Her grandson! Why, she'd even begged him for the return of Golden Hill for him, not for herself or her son!

What was his name? Tommy?

He would find out *everything* there was to know about Tommy. He'd put a private detective on the job in Florida and then he'd start on his campaign of fear—a hint here, a hint there.

He went over to his safe to get out the 32-caliber gun he'd bought because his father's old guns had been so heavy he'd always had trouble managing them. He hated guns. They had been a necessity in his father's time. He could remember his father showing him how to use one if he were ever in trouble. Now, as he felt the cold handle in his hand, he remembered, as if in a trance, the talk of black men marching, of threats made on his father's life—and then he'd died of smoke inhalation. Smoke. Everything was going up in smoke once again.

He pulled the trigger. It was easy, child's play. He loaded the gun, tempted to pull the trigger again to see what kind of hole a shot would make in the wall . . . to visualize one shot through Magdalen Finch's head.

The thought of the hideous photographs again festered in his mind. When would the fiendish woman send others?

She *had* to be stopped. Now! There was no time to find out about young Tommy Finch. He would have to make her think he already had her grandson under surveillance. . . .

Drum decided he would keep going back to Orange Grove when she least expected him, arriving out of the blue to inform her he now knew exactly what he had to do to make her more "cooperative." In a couple of days he would let her know he'd made contact with friends in Miami, who knew where Tommy lived . . . played . . . went to school. He would play on her nerves, just as she had been playing on his for years. What he would actually *do* in the end, as far as Tommy was concerned, he hadn't worked out—but he would think of *something!* Already his mind raced ahead. Now he had *something* to start work on.

From downstairs he heard the sweet stanza of the old clock striking the full hour. Midnight! Where had the day gone! Drum sighed, feeling old and beaten, but he knew there would be little sleep for him.

There was nothing else for it. He would return to Orange Grove before dawn to have another confrontation with Mistress Finch! If she were fast asleep, perhaps he would even have an opportunity to search for the negatives first. It was a forlorn hope, but he had to leave no stone unturned, no drawer or closet unopened.

Midnight! Margaret looked at her watch. She couldn't believe it.

Was it possible her father wasn't coming to say goodnight on this her first night home?

Tears streamed down her face. She had done something wrong. He was displeased with her: that had to be the reason he hadn't met her at the airport, had been so silent at dinner, refusing to meet her eyes.

There was no way she could sleep without finding out what it was she was supposed to have done.

She opened the door onto the loggia, the eerie croak of the frogs breaking more loudly into the room like a melancholy tangible echo of her unhappiness. She crept along the passageway, then through the door to the main wing just as the clock finished chiming the full hour.

She looked in the study and quickly looked away. Her mother was slumped, apparently asleep, at her father's desk with an overturned glass and empty bottle in front of her.

She trembled with fear, with anticipation, as she climbed the stairs, each creak of her footsteps making her pause, waiting—she didn't know what she was waiting for. It was as if the old house were trying to tell her something.

She clutched the flimsy negligee around her, feeling an inner chill the temperature did nothing to dispel.

Why should she be frightened going to see her father, who loved her as much as she loved him? Yet she *was* frightened, because the father at dinner had been so different, so remote.

With more resolve, Margaret continued up the long stairway to her father's dressing room, praying he would still be awake, longing for him to reassure her even with a word, if not a touch, that everything was as it had been before.

The door was locked. She tapped on it timidly, hearing him walking about inside.

"Go away," he growled.

She started to cry. "It's me, Margaret." Silence.

She tapped again. Suddenly he unlocked the door, standing there with a grim expression and, to her amazement, holding a revolver in his hand.

He turned away, saying sternly, "What are you doing here, Margaret? Don't you know how late it is? You shouldn't be here. Go back to bed, darling. We'll talk in the morning."

Tears fell uncontrollably down her cheeks as she followed him, moving closer, closer. She didn't even realize she was untying her own ribbons, letting the negligee fall open to reveal the daring nightdress, the beautiful swell of her breasts gleaming in the soft light from the lamps, her dark areolas so dramatically apparent through the lace.

"Oh, Daddy, I've missed you so," she cried. "Don't you love me any more?" She stood on tiptoe to put her arms around his neck, not caring that the movement exposed the full black nipples, desperate for him to comfort her, to kiss and caress her. She felt her father's body stiffen and tried to hold on to him, not knowing why he was backing away until she heard her mother's voice screaming behind them. "No, no, no! You won't, you won't, not again, you . . . you . . ."

The room spun around as her father pushed her violently away. She saw the gun fall from his hand as her mother ran toward him with a terrifying look of hatred. Margaret covered her face with her hands.

There was a sharp crack, crack, crack.

She saw her father crouch over, his hands clutching his chest, slowly falling, falling—but as she stretched out her arms to help him, everything went black.

There were a lot of people in her room. Too many for them all to be seated, she thought carefully, because she only had two chairs unless you counted the footstool. Why were they there anyway? In her bedroom? Only her father had the right to be in her room. Others might come and go like Em . . . and her mother . . . and Maize and Luralene, but they didn't count. These people were strangers. Who were they?

The doctor smiled at her. "Margaret, don't be alarmed. I am Dr. Fanjo, an old friend of the family. This is Detective Brewster and Sergeant Marristen. They would like to ask you a few questions. It won't take long."

She wanted to dive under the bedclothes as she'd done as a little girl, hiding from the world, from her mother—her mother?

Something to do with her mother? There was something wrong. She started to cry silently.

"Dere, dere, don' yo' cry, Miss Margaret. Ol' Em's here. . . ." Em was on the other side of the bed, tears streaming down her old cheeks, too, and then Margaret saw with surprise Grandmother Rose was crouched over in one of the chairs.

"Your Uncle Roger will soon be here," the doctor told her with a sad look.

"Uncle Roger?" Her father's brother? Why was he coming? She wasn't sure her parents even liked him that much.

"Where's my mother?" She finally asked the question.

Something told her not to mention her father. She would tell him all about it later. She had to keep his secret. She couldn't quite remember what his big problem had been, but it would come back—and something told her not to mention her father to the detectives.

Rose was leaving the room with Em, at the request of the doctor.

Now the policemen came closer, smiling, asking her politely and calmly what she could remember about the events of the previous night.

She closed her eyes trying to think hard. Her father had been desperately worried about something. He'd been cross with her. She'd done something wrong, but she hadn't known what it was, and he hadn't come to kiss her goodnight.

Her breath came in short gasps. She felt trapped, hunted down. What had she done?

It was seeing her watch on her wrist that brought the scene back into her mind. Her mother's angry, scolding face, her screaming abuse, the crack of gunfire . . . and then she remembered being on the floor, looking across at her father who was groaning, lying just out of her reach.

There had been blood all over his beautiful shirt. She had been trying to get up to go to him . . . and she'd heard the angry neigh of a horse outside. . . . it had sounded like her father's horse.

Margaret told this to the policemen in quick little whispers, sure they knew it anyway—except perhaps about the horse.

Why had she heard Cameron neigh at that time of night? She asked the question with huge, frightened eyes. The men looked at each other strangely, but they didn't answer her.

Now only the doctor was left in her room. At last she felt safe to mention her father. He'd been hurt, she knew that. "Can I see my father now? I know he's been hurt," she said timidly.

The doctor looked helpless, lost.

She started to sit up but suddenly remembered, with a sense of shame, that she was wearing the naughty nightdress.

She looked at her arms, but they weren't bare. They were covered in cotton, her pink pajama top. So Em had made her decent! Margaret surreptitiously ran her hand down to feel her legs. She was wearing her pajama bottoms, too!

She could get up and put her slippers on, and the doctor would take her to her father's room where he would smile and tell her everything was all right now—that she hadn't been bad after all, she'd been imagining things.

But the doctor was telling her something quietly, carefully choosing his words as if he were speaking a foreign language.

Who was screaming? That wasn't her. It couldn't be. She was too well brought up to scream like that.

Her father *dead?* No, no, no!

What had she done?

Why had she done it?

Magdalen
1966

As was usual at this time of year, Magdalen heard the heavy downpour start a half hour before sunrise and she knew it was likely to last until at least ten o'clock, when, like a signal from heaven, the sun would suddenly command the sky, and in minutes the earth would be baked dry into submission, only to be soaked just as suddenly an hour or so later.

Well, rain or shine, it didn't matter today. She had much more to worry about than how the crops were faring or how the plants were holding up in the special area reserved for Tropica.

She was on her way to Golden Hill, come hailstorm or heatwave, to pay her last respects to the dead and to receive from the living the signatures that would mean she could go to her own grave a contented, happy women, knowing she had been able to right the wrongs of the past. The signatures that would mean at last her descendants would inherit their birthright.

Although she hummed as she brushed her strong wavy hair, she could never remember feeling so tense, not even on her dreadful "honeymoon" night when she'd waited for her loathsome bridegroom to return from "punishing" his errant workers.

It wasn't surprising. She'd nearly fainted when she'd first heard the incredible news of Drum and Alicia Pollard's deaths. *And* the facts behind them that only a select handful were ever going to know, for she'd discovered that, through Roland Bracken's intervention, the true story was going to be hushed up.

The fingerprints had been as clear as any fingerprints could be on the gun that had killed Drum, but the newspaper and radio reports simply stated Drum Pollard had been found fatally shot shortly after his wife's body had been discovered in a deep gully, with her neck broken, apparently having been thrown by Drum's stallion, Cameron, who'd stood snorting and scuffing at the earth nearby.

The implication was suicide, not murder, but what had it mattered to her that the public would draw the erroneous conclusion that Drum Pollard, grief-stricken over his wife's death, had killed himself? What had it mattered that Alicia must have found the loathsome photographs and at last killed the man who'd treated her so appallingly over the years? Only one thing had burned in her brain. Drum Pollard had cheated her again, escaping from her clutches just when she had seen the possibility of retrieving Golden Hill at last.

She had tortured herself, letting her thoughts switch back to the day before, seeing Drum's desperate face as clearly as if he'd still been sitting across from her, knowing he no longer had any "friends at court" to help him—and even if he had, who could he go to with such a seamy story, dirtying the hands of anyone who tried to intercede on his behalf? She'd even convinced herself it wouldn't be too long before she saw Drum again, willing to *discuss* the return of the family seat built by her ancestors.

She had been so complacent . . . so sure . . . and then to have victory snatched out of her hands! It had been impossible to accept.

She had no idea how long she'd sat there brooding, seeing ghosts from her past reflected in the relentless torrents . . . her mother as she'd run from the drawing room at Golden Hill to escape the giant insects as they flapped their wings in her tormented face . . . the stern, humorless figure of her grandfather, whose only vision of God had been of such an unforgiving, punishing God . . . her drunken father, pushing her into the arms of vicious Joseph Accera . . . and Theo, her demented lover, who'd first made her aware of her fierce sexual appetite. One by one they'd filed past in the rain, filling her with melancholy until she'd realized the rain had stopped and the garden was flooded with brilliant light burning the puddles away, penetrating the mist in her mind. Her mind had started to clear just like the sky and she'd told herself she hadn't spent her long life scheming for justice to be done to be thwarted now.

Until Drum's visit, she told herself, she hadn't appreciated the strength of the weapon she'd held over his head. It had been as much the defeated slump of his shoulders as he'd sat in her chintz armchair as any of his words that had given her this precious piece of information.

She remembered the exhilarating warmth that had grown as the knowledge became confirmed that Drum Pollard thought he was power-less to extricate himself from a situation that spelled his ruin. She'd hardly been able to contain her new-found sense of triumph as he'd repeated, "What do you *really* want?"

And then she'd heard Drum's mother's voice as it had quavered that afternoon at the Queen's Park Hotel when Rose told her Drum was her only heir, that Drum would be the owner of Golden Hill when she died. . . . Yesterday, Magdalen brooded bitterly, she had thought only of the future, when she'd told Drum she wanted Golden Hill back for her descendants—that he could save himself only if *he* gave her that guarantee; for yesterday it had been natural to assume Rose would die long before her son, yet now unnaturally Drum was dead and Rose was still alive to rewrite her will and leave Golden Hill to somebody else. Rose! There hadn't been a moment to lose.

There had been such confusion at Golden Hill that morning, the house crawling with people, it had been easy for one of Magdalen's men to call at the back veranda and send a maid upstairs to tell Rose to come with him at once. There was a matter of great urgency she had to attend to. Nobody was going to miss Rose for an hour . . . for a day for that matter, and it had been child's play to convince her once they'd met that she, Magdalen, was doing her the greatest favor one mother could do another.

Rose was doddering, almost senile, one moment telling Magdalen she didn't know what the commotion at Golden Hill was all about, the next, as a burst of sanity illuminated her brain, bursting into noisy sobs, crying, "Drum, Drum, my little boy. Oh, come back, please come back. . . ."

At first Magdalen had cooed in her sweetest, most dulcet tones that she knew, as Rose knew, that Drum had had a terrible weakness.

In quick succession she had shown Rose one, two, three of the photo-graphs. Rose had cringed back against the car seat, as if they were alive, trying in vain to escape from their evil message, but Magdalen had gone on relentlessly. "Your brothers are responsible for these disgusting pictures," she had hissed. "They arranged that party to trap Drum. Alicia must have found the pictures." Rose had clapped her hand to her mouth to prevent a scream from escaping. "They plotted to lure him into behaving . . ."—Magdalen had tried to think of an appropriate word—". . . indiscreetly with that stupid little brat, playing on his weakness. They have been trying to trap him for years."

Rose had clutched her so tightly Magdalen had felt her nails penetrate her skin. "I told him not to go," Rose had cried. "I begged him, but he wouldn't listen. He would never listen to me and I was too . . . too ill to go with him. To watch over him. Oh, oh, oh. . . ." Sobs had wracked her body. "I warned him. I warned him!"

Magdalen had ignored her sobs, her anguish. "They've been blackmailing him, but I know where the negatives are. The negatives of these terrible pictures. . . ."

She had tried to look like an avenging angel, drawing herself up to her full height, lowering her voice menacingly. "I know how your brothers intend to use these terrible photographs to destroy Drum's memory, his reputation—because they want to destroy *you* and everything you and the Pollard name stands for. They'll stop at nothing, even though they have achieved one of their objectives. Drum is gone. Soon *you'll* be gone and Margaret, well, she's a little girl whose roots are more in England and always will be. She won't want to stay here without her mother and father. Who will be left to look after Golden Hill— the house that meant so much to Drum and to his father—when you're gone?" She hadn't waited for Rose to answer. "Your brothers," she'd snarled. "This is all part of the plot. They want vengeance for the past. They want Golden Hill, and when you're gone it will all be easy. Roland will move in and rule the roost from the house you never allowed him to enter, the house on the hill where you reigned and spat down on your black brothers and sisters and your old black mother and father. . . ."

Rose had cringed back into the corner, hands over her ears, trying to block out the words, but Magdalen had persisted, leaning closer, warming to her story, adding to it piece by piece like an aria in an opera. "Only you, Rose, hold the key to stopping that desecration. Only you can stop your powerful black brother from taking over the house Piper loved so much! Only you can stop the destruction of the Pollard name."

Magdalen had paused dramatically, her silence as threatening as her words, waiting, expecting Rose to say what she then said piteously.

"What . . . what . . . can I do? I haven't any strength left to fight them!"

Again Magdalen had cooed softly, suggesting everything would be as Rose wanted, if only she would put everything in Magdalen's hands. "Do the just thing, Rose," she'd whispered, every syllable sounding now as if she were praying. "I know where the negatives are. I will make sure they are destroyed, if you do the just, honorable thing and sign a document unconditionally returning Golden Hill and the original Picton acres on your death to Theo Finch, the great-grandson of the original owner, to hold in trust for his son Thomas Finch and his heirs."

Rose had looked at her in bewilderment. "But he is my enemy, too. He killed my husband."

Magdalen had looked at her pityingly. "He was a little boy, don't you remember? Just a little boy. It was your own brother Jack who lit the torch that . . ."

Rose had put her hands over her ears again. "Don't say it. Don't say it. Yes, you're right. I remember now. I remember . . . my brother." Her lip had curled viciously. "Oh, how I hate them. I hate them all." She had suddenly sat upright, looking suspiciously at Magdalen. "You mean, if I do this you will be able to stop my brothers from moving into Golden Hill as well as getting rid of those hateful . . . hateful . . ." She couldn't say any more.

Magdalen had put her arms around the woman's shaking shoulders. "You will read the document and a clause signed by my lawyer swearing that the negatives will be destroyed on receipt of your signature." She had looked at Rose steadily. "We neither of us have much time left on this earth, Rose. With your signature, so much will be resolved. The house will be saved, treasured by the descendants of the man who first built it."

Magdalen played her master stroke. "You have already avenged your ancestor Louisa Calderon's memory. You lived and will die as the mistress of Golden Hill, the house built by Picton's heir. Don't let it fall into your brothers' evil hands. Who knows if they wouldn't burn it down to show their disrespect for all the Pollard name stood for. Let it stand as a proud monument to the past—the man who built it, the present—the Pollards who came after to treasure and maintain its beauty—and the future—"

Another thought had struck her, and she'd cried it out—amazed even herself at the turn her thoughts had taken: "By your signing this document you don't only safeguard the future of the house and protect your own son's memory. Young Margaret will surely inherit all her father's Golden Hill property and probably that left to you by Piper, too. Don't you see, it will mean she and my grandson Tommy will have a mutual interest in Golden Hill—a proper ending to an old feud—a new beginning for a new generation, and who knows where that might lead one day. . . ."

It had been a close thing, Magdalen reflected, as her driver opened the door of the car and she slowly climbed the steps to the Orange Grove house.

She felt she'd aged at least ten years since she'd left the house at nine that morning in the heavy downpour. However, safe and sound in her crocodile handbag was a new addendum to Rose Pollard's will, signed not only by Rose but by her granddaughter Margaret too.

It had been a terrible nerve-racking day from the moment she'd been driven up the long straight drive to Golden Hill until she'd stood, every nerve in her body strained and alert, in the young girl's bedroom, while Rose directed Margaret to put her signature at the bottom of every vellum page.

Just as Magdalen had expected, Margaret hadn't asked what she was signing. It could have been her own death warrant, Magdalen had thought more than once, for the girl had looked in such a daze, almost as if she were sleepwalking. But she *had* signed and the signature wasn't shaky in any way. It was legible, strong, which meant there could be no way the law could intervene after Rose's death to say she must have been demented, that she didn't know what she was doing at the time.

It had suddenly hit Magdalen with brute force an hour after her meeting with Rose that she had overlooked something terribly important, for unless Margaret, as Rose's only surviving descendant, appeared to acquiesce to her grandmother's decision and "true intent"—signature or no signature—the bequest returning Golden Hill to the Finch family might easily be torn to pieces by a lawyer acting on Margaret's behalf.

It hadn't been easy to find Rose in the sea of people flooding into the house after the funeral. But then she had looked up to see her, like a ghost, looking down from the top stairwell.

They had gone together to Rose's room, where, although Magdalen was quite prepared to wait while Rose read every word thoroughly, to her surprise she'd only wanted to see the lawyer's signature attached to the clause about the destruction of the negatives.

Once she had satisfied herself about that, Rose had taken out an old-fashioned fountain pen to write "Rose Pollard" laboriously on every page, not even querying Magdalen when she'd insisted Margaret had to sign too, in order to "tie up all loose ends."

Ironically, Rose had urged, "We have to hurry . . . have to hurry," as she'd led the way down three flights of stairs at the back of the house, through a long trellised walk, the air fragrant with lilies and roses, to Margaret's room.

"She's leaving already. Just like you said. She wants to leave," Rose had muttered. "She's packing her suitcase, but I'm not worried now. I keep thinking about what you said—about the new generation, about the Pollards—and the Finches. I like it." Magdalen hadn't corrected her.

In Rose's mind, Magdalen realized with a twinge of pity, she was already marrying a descendant of Louisa Calderon to a descendant of Governor Picton, justifying her signature on the document that returned Golden Hill to the Finch family. If that possibility made Rose feel any better, Magdalen smiled, then let her dream about it. However, the thought of *her* grandson ever uniting with the Pollard girl was something she would never tolerate! There would be no hanging on to the old world for *her* grandson.

Magdalen congratulated herself. She had thought of everything, for knowing her son as well as she did, with his strong sense of what was right and wrong, she knew Theo would *never* accept Golden Hill for himself on Rose's death when the bequest became known.

And that was the reason she had made sure the document read the bequest was to Tommy—with Theo only to act as custodian during his lifetime. This meant that in no way could Theo refuse to follow Rose's intentions.

Margaret had indeed been packing when Rose first knocked on her door. Watching Margaret's arm lift slowly inch by inch, as she signed the pages her grandmother gave her without a word, Magdalen was reminded of a clockwork doll that needed rewinding. As the minutes ticked by like hours, Magdalen had heard her own heart pounding as she'd kept an apprehensive eye on the door, willing no one to enter to disturb them, and ask awkward questions, to discover why Margaret Pollard was signing away the right to her own home.

Roger didn't know what to do or say to this beautiful, slender young girl who on the long trip back to New York answered everything he said so politely, so quietly, but never asked him anything at all. He had come to take her away, he'd told her on his arrival, away from the terrible experience she'd been through at Golden Hill, which seemed alien, full of ghosts even to him. He was going to take her to Southampton on the Atlantic Ocean, where, he'd found himself explaining, he kept a house open only for the summer, using it on occasional weekends to avoid the heat in Dallas and New York.

Her obedient responses to everything were far more unnerving than the tears and screams he'd expected. It was natural—he stole a surreptitious look at the niece he hardly knew—that she should be shy and reserved, but this oppressive silence, as if somewhere deep inside her she were living another life of her own—that wasn't natural, or was it? He knew so little about young people. He felt out of his depth, nervous, depressed.

Thank God, he told himself, that Clare wouldn't be in Southampton when they arrived. . . . She might hate the heat of Dallas, but she hadn't been about to pass up an invitation to a private lunch with the husband of the queen of England, in and out of Texas on a two-day visit.

Had Clare received his message about Margaret before her departure? He hoped she had. He could just imagine the kind of reception Margaret would receive from Clare if her appearance was "unexpected."

For the past two years their relationship had developed into one that he described to himself as a "wary truce." Clare went her way and he went his—with the unspoken understanding she wouldn't do anything "foolish," anything that might hit the headlines to embarrass him. The only conversation they had ever had on that subject had come two days after the reading of W. W. Lovell's will—the will that had so successfully harnessed emotions and brought about a number of decisions based solely on practicality.

"You see, I was right, darlin', wasn't I?" He could still see Clare as she leaned back that evening in her cream-colored boudoir, smoking what he'd realized had to be marijuana. "You did become Daddy's little darlin', and, even without giving him the grandson he wanted, he decided good ol' Roger was the man to take good care of his money after he'd gone!" He hadn't listened, snatching the joint out of her hand, flushing it away, telling her firmly, either there had to be a new understanding or he was finished with her for good.

As he'd spoken he'd appreciated all the more the power W. W. had entrusted him with. He held the reins and, as he'd told an amazingly chastened Clare at dinner an hour later, they would be slack reins *provided* she never saw Victoria again and provided she ensured her private life *remained* private, never causing either of them a second's embarrassment.

What alternative did she have? W. W. Lovell's last will and testament, filed for probate the day after the funeral, included a challenge clause that said anyone who disputed the will would automatically "lose and forfeit all right to any benefit and all right and title to any property" that might be due them under the will.

It had certainly stopped Victoria in her tracks, Clare had thought that night, remembering the brief flicker of hatred in Victoria's eyes as she'd learned she'd been passed over as the main beneficiary; that as W. W.'s widow (but his wife for less than ten years) she'd been left a generous, but hardly overwhelming annual allowance.

And Daddy had stopped her in *her* tracks, too . . . in a way that perhaps he hadn't even realized . . . or had he?

Clare had looked at Roger with grudging new respect. Had her father known she had been on the verge of leaving Roger, of moving to Europe where she'd been determined to live the unfettered bohemian life that fascinated, yet in many ways terrified her?

Her father had outfoxed them all, making Roger his primary heir, leaving him the major part of his stock in United Texas Oil, leaving her a guaranteed seven-figure annual income . . . *provided* she remain Roger's wife! What an upset—passing over his own flesh and blood, and even his own wife, for the "colonial"!

Looking at Roger's tight-lipped expression that night, when she'd at first thought she could get away with anything and everything, Clare had acknowledged her father had been right yet again. Roger *was* going to keep Daddy's little daughter in check, that is, if she wanted the money.

Cutting Victoria out of her life hadn't been difficult. Ever since she had lost the baby, Victoria had alternately terrified and tantalized her. It would be a good loss she'd told herself fiercely, and as for leading an "outward" life of propriety, well, what else had she been doing for all of her forty-three years?

Again Clare had looked at Roger as if seeing him for the first time, telling herself, this husband of mine means what he says. . . . Unless you toe the line, my girl, you're out in the cold because there's nothing in darling Daddy's will to stop *him* from divorcing *you!*

She hated to admit even to herself that deep down she was relieved.

Her father had always understood her better than she understood herself. He had left her with the safety belt she so sorely needed. . . .

The flag was fluttering proudly in the breeze; the people were lining the
street, applauding as she rode in an open carriage with her father. Every
so often a wonderful warmth thrilled her as she felt his dazzling blue-
brown eyes turn to look at her with obvious pride as she threw her head
back, so that her long gold hair flowed out over the dark leather.

In the distance she could see the Arc de Triomphe, where her father
was going to be honored—but as the carriage moved up the Champs
Elysées, suddenly, instead of the Arc de Triomphe, she could see the
colonnaded entrance of Golden Hill, and the horses started to race
faster and faster until she cried out for them to stop, turning to her
father for help, only to discover the carriage door swinging open with no
one beside her.

Margaret sat upright covered with perspiration. The flag had turned
into an unfamiliar blue-and-white curtain billowing out into the bedroom with a sudden ocean breeze. She ran to close the window, shivering in the early-morning air, the ocean outside as gray as the slate roofs
she remembered at school.

She preferred the gray mornings, for when the sun caught the water,
turning it silver blue to match the sky, it was too reminiscent of the
Caribbean. When the sun came out, so did the bikini-clad golden girls
and muscular, tanned young men who ran, jumped and surfed from the
beach just below her window, a beach that stretched as far as she could
see to the east and the west. She hated to see them and their obvious
healthy enjoyment of each other and the elements; their sheer physical
presence was painful to observe.

Only when it rained did she go to the beach to run there, until she
could feel her heart trying to burst through her chest, her breaths coming in short, damp gasps. Then and only then could she let go the tears
which were always just behind her eyes, releasing them, it seemed, to
make room for others waiting, pushing from behind.

As the weeks had passed since her arrival in the palatial Southampton
house, Margaret had waited for her mind to clear, to remember exactly
what had happened, but whenever she promised herself she would take
a deep breath and examine every hour of that terrible day and night
from the moment she'd stepped off the London plane until the moment

she'd found herself sprawled on her father's dressing room floor, some-thing happened.

Terror sprang from an unknown source, freezing her until her teeth actually chattered while more, not less of a cloud seemed to cover events, so that she could hardly remember whether she'd had dinner with her parents that last evening of their lives or not.

She prided herself that only once had she really broken down. She'd been making her usual effort to act as though she were no different from anybody else . . . but then she hadn't known what her aunt had meant when she'd said they were taking her to the East Hampton Show. As they'd driven through wooden gates and she'd heard the nervous neigh-ing of horses, the terror that she only exposed herself to when she was alone in her bedroom at night had descended so suddenly she hadn't even realized it was she who was screaming, and trying to get out of the limousine, she who had had to be held down by her uncle—she whom her aunt had described so scathingly as behaving like someone escaped from a mental home. After that the situation between her aunt and herself had grown much worse.

Margaret had realized from the first day they met that her aunt had no intention of trying to get to know her, let alone like her; that when-ever her uncle was away, which was a great deal, her aunt wanted her to realize that she was an unfortunate nuisance who should stay out of her sight as much as possible. If her aunt thought she minded, she was very, very wrong.

Ironically, as much as Margaret had warmed to her uncle and was wary of her aunt, it was only when her Uncle Roger was home that she knew she would really have to suffer . . . being taken to "so-and-so's dance" . . . being told that "such-and-such are coming for dinner." "Young people I think you'll really like" was her uncle's favorite expres-sion. Like? She didn't even know how to like. She was . . . well, disin-terested, the void inside her growing bigger every day, like the reverse of a tumor, a hollow growing bigger, an emptiness, a loss.

In the middle of August, Margaret learned with mixed feelings she wasn't going back to Heathfield. It had been decided it would be better for the time being if she went to school in America.

"Your mother's uncle—your great-uncle . . ."

"Robin . . . " she'd interjected listlessly.

"Yes, Robin. He's not a very well man. . . . He feels if you were so many miles away from me he would have to accept you as his total responsibility, and he's not up to it."

"Why do I have to be anyone's responsibility?"

"Well, I'm not putting this well at all." Her uncle's face had been a picture of consternation, so she'd squeezed his arm reassuringly.

"Oh, Uncle, of course, you are. I know I'm underage—but you know no one has to worry about me. I don't care what happens to me."

"That's just the trouble, young lady. It's time you *did* start to care. I'm worried about you. . . ." He'd looked at her searchingly. "I've . . . I've always wanted a daughter. I want you to feel you can rely on me, and as we get to know each other I want you to confide in me. Let me help you, Margaret. No one should try to go through what you've been through alone. Don't think I don't understand your feelings—your loneliness, emptiness."

She'd shut her eyes tightly, moaning, "Don't, Uncle, don't talk about it. I don't want to. I can't. I'll be all right, but just don't talk about it."

Roger had put his arm around her shoulders. "Whatever you want, Margaret. Whatever you want. Even if you tell me you long to go back to your English school, I'll think of something."

As he'd spoken, her thoughts had gone to Heathfield and to Deidre. How could she face Deidre? How could she answer all the questions that were bound to come? She couldn't. She'd shaken her head. As she'd been about to tell her uncle she definitely did *not* want to return to Heathfield, she'd realized he was still speaking and there was no need for her to say anything.

"Well, if you really *don't* care one way or the other, I think your life is going to be here. Have you thought what you want to do? All you girls seem to have such definite ideas these days. And of course you realize you're quite a wealthy young woman."

He had tried to bring up the subject of her inheritance before, but Margaret had for once been adamant, saying with a white strained face, "Don't, Uncle, don't. Not now. Look after everything for me. Whatever you do will be all right, I know that." She'd stared out at the ocean, crying stormily, "I don't know where my life is going to be, Uncle. I only know where it's *not* going to be."

The vehemence of her tone had surprised and in one way relieved him. It was the first indication she'd shown how she felt about anything.

"Trinidad," she'd said heatedly. "I never want to set foot there again."

"Oh, you'll change. . . ."

She'd interrupted. "I'll *never* change. I hate the place. I'll never go back to Golden Hill. I'd rather die."

Roger's eyes had pricked with unexpected tears as Margaret had let down her defenses. Instead of the remote teenager he was used to, he'd seen the frightened, lost little girl she really was, her face contorted as she'd tried not to cry, pulling her handkerchief to shreds in her lap.

He'd hugged her to him, feeling his own heart ache as he'd caught a sudden glimpse of Alicia's small features in her face, remembering as he hadn't remembered in years the tracing of freckles over the small nose, the quick sparrowlike grace, the Peter Pan collars her mother had liked to wear. This girl *should* have been his own daughter, Roger had thought with a sense of melancholy, at the same time praying it would be in his power to erase the girl's suffering, to help her escape from the past as he had once had to escape.

Theo put his mother's letter down with a sigh. It was increasingly difficult for him to feel any real emotion about what was going on in Trinidad. His mother didn't understand.

Every day, wherever he happened to be in the United States, he, in common with everyone else, was bombarded with news, views, discussions, arguments about the country's involvement in Vietnam. As more troops were shipped overseas and casualties mounted, Theo thought now, looking out with sadness at the soaring New York skyline, so people everywhere felt they were no longer in control of their own destiny.

It hadn't affected business. If anything, Tropica's sales were going to hit an all-time high. Nevertheless, there were dangerous currents in the air, throwing off sparks on the country's campuses in numerous antiwar demonstrations.

He glanced at the headlines in the *New York Times*: ONE HUNDRED THOUSAND MARCH ON NEW YORK, FIFTY THOUSAND MARCH IN SAN FRANCISCO, MARTIN LUTHER KING ENCOURAGES DRAFT EVASION— PROPOSES A MERGER BETWEEN THE ANTI-WAR AND CIVIL RIGHTS MOVEMENTS, CALLS U.S. GOVERNMENT "THE GREATEST PURVEYOR OF VIOLENCE IN THE WORLD." And his mother was worried about Tommy getting dual citizenship in Trinidad!

Theo tried to deal with the matter as he always dealt with everything—efficiently, quickly, finally—but today he felt too tired.

His old sense of purposelessness was back, something that had begun to taunt him during the past year. What was life all about? Why bother doing anything? His usual sanctuary, the church, hadn't been able to offer him solace. Life was as meaningless as the empty bowls of rice facing the Vietnamese refugees he saw on the TV news.

He read his mother's letter again. Well, at least one thing never changed! Life in the tropics kept one woman constantly in love with life, if his mother was any example.

" . . . Once the new laws come into effect," Magdalen had written, " . . . no foreigner will be allowed to own land in Trinidad, only lease it. This means it's essential you apply for dual citizenship for Tommy at once. I'm sure there won't be any trouble in the future, but you can never be *sure*." She had underlined the word "sure" three times in case he happened to miss it, he thought, amused, before going on as she had in so many letters, " . . . A certificate of land ownership can be obtained for a citizen if evidence is shown the land has been in the family for forty years."

Land, land land! Once upon a time he'd also thought land was the "be all and end all" of life and he only had to be back in Arima for an hour and even his own body responded to the sensuousness of it all. He could make love in Arima with joy, not with the shame that, however much he tried to fight it, usually accompanied the physical act of sex with a woman, even though that woman was his wife.

It was time they made a trip back to Trinidad. On the spur of the moment he buzzed his secretary to ask her how the next month looked. "Is there a space when Mrs. Finch and I can take off for the island?"

It would be tight, but it looked as if they might manage four or five days. How Paulette would squeal with delight when he told her, remembering their last visit eight or nine months ago when that fertile, rich place had released his inhibitions and for the first time in months their minds and bodies had climaxed together.

Theo told his secretary to look into flights. "I'll confirm it tomorrow, after the new packaging meeting."

It was time they went down to Orange Grove, he told himself. Quite apart from giving Paulette an unexpected surprise, there was something about the tone of the Orange Grove reports he hadn't liked lately. Something was biting the manager there, and Theo didn't think it was due to his usual complaint of too many mosquitoes.

He pulled out the report and scanned it briefly. The figures were all right, a neat balance of payments, with exports of essential oils flowing out and Tropica products going in to sell throughout the Caribbean. Nevertheless, there was something disquieting about the increase in pilfering and—what was it—a general tone of discontent. Yes, he decided, it was definitely time for him to make a thorough inspection.

It had taken almost a year for Roland to learn that Magdalen Finch had actually been Machiavellian enough to trap Drum Pollard at the party he'd given with such outward good grace, where he'd proved with every dollar spent he was following Luis's and the party's dictates to the letter, acting positively on action every word Eric Williams uttered. And what had been the outcome? Drum and Alicia Pollard's deaths, throwing the community into shock for days, weeks, even months.

How he'd thanked his lucky stars he'd had nothing to do with it. How he'd racked his brains wondering what on earth could have caused a tragedy of such proportion, never guessing that Drum Pollard was actually being blackmailed by that fanatical woman, trapped at the party *he'd* given—in a compromising position with a child, who, from the sound of her, should have been in reform school from birth.

If Luis ever knew that Magdalen had been involved in the Pollards' deaths, would he ever believe that Roland had not? Never! It would be the end of him, but Luis wasn't acting as if he knew, thank God. On the contrary, he was bringing him back into the inner circle for the first time since the Santo Domingo fiasco, delighted with his protégé (as he'd jokingly begun to describe him) when Roland told him that following Williams's landslide victory in the 1966 elections, with the opposition receiving only 34 percent of the votes, the ambassadorship he had been promised was imminent.

There was a great deal of progress all over, Luis told him, and now, with American setbacks in Vietnam, it was felt Roland could once again be helpful, encouraging the coalition of militant black groups springing up across the United States under the leadership of Martin Luther King, Jr., who, said Luis with a knowing smile, was proving every day he could not only unify, but *electrify* the black masses "as a born Messiah."

On his next visit to the States, Luis told him, he was to meet with King, and it would be the first of many fruitful meetings "when you will be the bearer of good news from thousands of your black brothers throughout the Caribbean."

Roland's increasing power and influence in Trinidad and now, it seemed, overseas as well, would have been something for his brother James to boast about, if James hadn't had to put up with his wife's endless jealous carping on the subject. As if that wasn't hard enough to bear, James also had to endure continual sneers and slights from another member of his family, his sour-faced malcontent of a son, Matthew, the elder of James's twins " . . . by five minutes, though he don' ev'r show it! Freddy, his brudder, be much clever'r by far," as Carmelita regularly told the world at large, whether Matthew was listening or not.

It was true that while from childhood Frederick had sat with his nose buried in a book, Matthew had regularly played truant from school, getting into numerous scrapes, and had given his parents nothing but problems. He despised both of them and never bothered to hide it, recently to James's despair, igniting and often stoking his mother's fury over Roland and Emerald's success.

Now Matthew scratched his tightly curled head as he stood up to stretch to his full six feet, saying, "Dat ol' uncle o' mine's off t' 'merica agin, Ma. See, here's his pikture in de pap'r. . . ." He waved the *Trinidad Guardian* at his mother's back as she peeled potatoes at the kitchen sink. "Yo' sur' married de wrong brudder, Ma. . . ."

As a veteran of past battles, Frederick, book under his arm, ducked out, soon followed by Carmelita, scooping up the two youngest children, knowing soon words and then things would be flying through the air, ending as it always did with James trying to push Matthew out into the street, yelling, "Get out an' don' yo' show yo' ugly face roun' 'ere again!" This time, when Matthew contemptuously slouched out of the door, he didn't come back the next day or the next. At first neither James nor Carmelita worried, but after a week when Matthew still hadn't returned, Carmelita talked forlornly about calling the police, while James wondered if he should attempt to call Roland's office and ask for help in locating the missing boy.

Frederick, always the intense one, who stammered whenever he had to be the bearer of any news, good or bad, blurted out, "Don't, D-D-Dad. It ain't . . ."—he corrected himself, for he knew better—"it isn't necessary. Matthew, he's . . . he's g-g-g-goin' to be all right. It's better he st-st-stays where he is."

His parents turned on him. They should have known his twin would know where he was. "Speak up, boy! Where's dat good-fer-nuttin' brudder o' yo'rs?" James yelled, knowing he was going to hate whatever Frederick had to say.

The boy scuffled his feet, the bare bulb in the kitchen spotlighting his face like a highly glossed moon. "He's gone t' Orange Grove."

"T' Orange Grove!" his parents hissed in unison. James looked at his wife in fear. "Oh, Gawd. I 'ope he ain' gone t' aggravate Mistress Finch!"

"No, no, Dad. . . ." The boy giggled nervously in his embarrassment—for how could he repeat to his parents what his twin brother had told him in fits of drunken laughter only two nights before?There was only one thing for it. He had to pretend not to know what it all really meant. "He's gone t' work at de perfume fact'ry." Frederick tried to slink out of the kitchen, but his mother's voice rooted him to the spot.

"What d' yo' mean, gone t' work dere? Doin' wha'?"

This time he wasn't going to answer, for how could he explain what Matthew had told him, showing off a wad of dollar bills and a new gold chain around his neck. "I'se got a great new cont'ct, man. I'se in de receivin' an' sellin' business, movin' de goods dat dis guy gets from Orange Grove. I tell yo', man, dere's nobody t' stop yo' takin' anyt'ing from dat place. Dere's only dat ol' white whore up dere at night!"

Frederick had been shocked. "That's stealin', Matt!" he'd shouted. "Yo'll get caught, dat's fer sure. I bet yo' wouldn't wan' cousin Jack t' know 'bout dat!"

Matthew had flung an arm drunkenly around his twin's shoulders. "I won' get caught, Fred. Why don' yo' com' in wid me? It's easy money, man."

Suddenly he'd removed his arm, looking at Frederick suspiciously. "Don' tell Jack. Promise me, Freddy, yo' won'. Jest tell him dat I'm savin' up fer de uprisin', 'gainst dis fuckin' white-lover Eric Williams. I'm bein' a good boy, workin' an' savin' hard for dat big day!"

Jack
1969

THIS is the proudest moment of my life." For once Roland meant every word he said as he raised his glass to toast his son. There was a noticeable break in his voice as he continued against a background of "Hear, hear!"

"You are the future, Jack! You *and* Frederick are the future. Trinidad is going to need the finest and I don't care if I am your father. . . ." He paused to look down the long table to where Frederick sat, sandwiched uncomfortably between two fat black men. ". . . And Frederick,"—Roland lifted his glass in his direction—"I don't care if I am accused of nepotism because, Freddie, I'm also your uncle, but you are both the finest young men I know, which means Trinidad's future looks very bright indeed!"

He sat down to a burst of happy laughter and applause, while Jack smiled easily and without a word lifted his glass to his father as if to say he totally approved, downing the champagne with one fast swallow.

If his father only knew! Jack sighed inwardly. If his father only had the *vision* to see what he, Freddie and others of his age and vitality, saw so clearly—that the Trinidad of the future was going to be a very different place from the one his father envisaged, that the *only* Trinidad worth living in was one without Eric Williams, a Trinidad where black dignity was the *only* thing that mattered and where white faces were the exception, and a subservient exception at that. That day wasn't far off if everything continued to go according to plan.

Jack looked with barely concealed disdain at the noisy, raucous men around him, all long-time cronies of his father's, black men who, like his father, he was sure, were still congratulating themselves that they could actually be swigging champagne in the Union Club, once a proud "whites only" enclave; men who preened and patted each other on the back because they were now allowed—allowed!—to walk and sit and fart where once only white men had been admitted.

It was hard for Jack to understand but he tried, if only for the sake of his father, whose life he was determined to make others spare when the revolution came.

He tried to rationalize that for all the men around him—twenty, thirty years older than Freddie and himself—it had taken all this time just to learn how to live as though they were *equal* to the whites, so it was an impossible task for them to believe they were actually capable of being *superior*—as he'd proved himself to be with a little, but not much, work, doing in two years what everyone else, white or black, had taken three years to accomplish, graduating with honors from the University of the West Indies, top of his class, and about to commence postgraduate studies in the States.

He winked at Freddie as he saw him try to maneuver his knife and fork in the limited space available. Good old Freddie. It was perfect timing that his cousin still had a couple of years to go before graduating himself. As a recently enrolled member of the National Joint Action Commiteee, Freddie would be able to continue the militant work he himself had been doing with NJAC's leader, Geddes Granger, and the other student activists, as well as encouraging the malcontents in the army to feel as they should feel—betrayed by Eric Williams, who had betrayed so many with his diabolically clever speeches.

Again Jack found himself thinking in a resigned, pitying kind of way about his father. . . . If he only knew his beloved son and favorite nephew were actually the leading members of an organization dedicated to ridding Trinidad of his boss Eric Williams, the one group it was said Williams actually feared. Perhaps, Jack thought, his father feared it, too, although he never said much. Again Jack silently pledged he would do everything in his power to protect his father when that jolt was delivered.

From the moment Jack had arrived on the St. Augustine campus two years before, as a cocky, "privileged" freshman, son of the illustrious Roland Bracken, right-hand man of the prime minister, he'd wasted no time making his true convictions known to Geddes Granger, who that same year had organized a loose but active federation of radical students, out-of-work dissidents and some older radicals who'd been in the forefront of opposition to Williams's leadership from the beginning.

He wasn't going to be a "spy" for his father, Jack had told an astonished Granger; not him! Not only was he with Granger in his avowed pledge to rid the country of Williams, he was ahead of him! As Jack had explained loftily, NJAC was but a spoke in the Black Power wheel. If NJAC was to spin with the other spokes and achieve its objectives, it would have to forge an alliance with other black militant organizations. "Go ahead," Granger had said cynically . . . and he had gone ahead, to Granger's initial amazement, first linking up with the influential Tapia House group in Trinidad, whose leader, Lloyd Best, a lecturer at the university, was one of the few men Jack respected, then with the Black Panthers in the U.S. and England.

Looking back on his two years at the university, Jack realized how far he'd traveled. It seemed another lifetime ago when he'd first accompanied his father on an overseas trip to New York, where Roland had been frantic one day, thinking his "little boy" was lost in the "big city."

Lost! What a joke! Jack had been meeting with black militants in the city, hearing from one of the most influential, Stokely Carmichael, about the week-long sit-in at Columbia University—a takeover planned by members of a radical student group that had gone entirely according to plan, halting the proposed building of a university gymnasium in an area the students believed should be used for low-cost housing for their people. It had ended with the New York police making arrests, but what did that matter when they'd achieved what they'd wanted to achieve— such chaos that a month later all formal classes had had to be suspended.

And now he was on his way to hanky-panky Yankee land for a couple of work-intensive years, where *he* would be a major influence, guiding even the clever but unstable Stokely Carmichael in the acts of anarchy planned for the next stage of the major plan, acts that would no longer run the risk of failing through the efforts of that God-fearing "obedient-to-white-liberal-doctrine," nonviolent shit Martin Luther King.

Whoever had pulled the trigger on him had given the Black Power movement a wonderful, unexpected bonus, for in Jack's opinion King had been a huge obstacle to everything the movement sought to achieve. He was a man Jack had more than once compared to the man he loathed most, the biggest hypocritical humbug living on earth, Eric Williams, who would one day, he hoped, meet the same fate.

Jack didn't need to drink champagne to feel high. He was high, riding high, knowing everything was ahead of him and it was all going to be good. His father was right. He *was* the finest, and Trinidad *was* lucky that one of its own native sons was going to lead the blacks to victory worldwide!

Far away on a euphoric cloud, Jack realized his father must have asked him something. "Speech! Me?" His father wanted him to say a few words "to leave in people's minds"?

Well, why not? He was a good speaker and he longed for the day when he could *really* let go and tell *his* people what was in store for them.

Now at the lunch his father was giving to send him off to the States with the gratifying feeling he was appreciated by his own people—and always would be—far more than by any of the new people he might meet overseas—Jack talked glibly about the progress black people were making all over the world . . . "in commerce and politics—increasing in influence as more civil-rights bills are signed into law in the U.S. and a more liberal immigration policy is at work in the U.K."

He concluded on a note he knew his father would appreciate: ". . . All I learn in the years ahead will be put to good use here, just as all I've learned here from my beloved father, my teachers, my colleagues—will be put to good use over there." Jack smiled, knowing a smile softened his features, without in any way lessening his look of sincerity. "I'll end with a saying made by a famous white man, a saying that's just as applicable, if not more applicable when a black man says it. Winston Churchill once said, 'We're all worms . . . but I do believe I'm a glow worm!'"

On the drive to Piarco Airport, Jack sat between his parents, holding his father's, not his mother's hand. It was his father he cared about, his father who was going to need help and support in the days he saw coming. Women were expendable. He loved his mother—as mothers went, she was all right—but she was still a stupid woman, with less than half the brains of his father.

Was there any way he could get through to him—even at this late date—to convince him of the tragic mistake he had made and was continuing to make in staying so close to Eric Williams that he was always identified with him? If you said "Williams" thought Jack despairingly, you said "Roland Bracken" in the next breath.

The next sentence from his father satisfied him there was no point in even trying. They were poles apart, because they'd been born in such very different times. "I'm heartsick Martin Luther King isn't going to be there to greet you. What a great leader. What an example to us all. What a loss. I can still hardly get over it. . . ." His father sounded genuinely sorrowful.

Jack couldn't resist saying something. He was leaving in less than two hours. He had no more time to lose. He had to put another point of view into his father's head. "I'm not sorry, Dad," Jack said curtly.

Roland shot a look at him. "What on earth is that remark meant to mean?" As he spoke, Roland pushed a button to close the glass partition that divided them from the driver.

"He was no hero." Jack allowed a trace of bitterness to creep into his voice as his mother screeched almost simultaneously, "Jack! What *are* you sayin', love?" He ignored her, waiting for his father's response, but Roland stared ahead, his face an inscrutable black mask.

Jack had to hand it to the old man. He was never predictable. He still never knew how his father might react to anything, and he also noted with a certain sense of satisfaction that his father's hand never stopped gripping his own as the limousine pulled up outside the departure gate.

As he flew westward, Jack little realized how great an impression his remark about Martin Luther King had made on his father.

As Roland waited patiently with Emerald in the public viewing area to watch the jet taking his son so far away from him soar into a brilliantly blue sky, he tried—without much success—to assess Jack dispassionately, to view him as a stranger—as Luis Delorso might view him.

Beneath Jack's fevered, nationalistic phrases, his obvious love of Trinidad, the importance he always put on "black dignity" (even as 'a teenager Jack had always taken almost unnecessary pride in the deep, dark color of his skin)—Roland realized with a jolt he didn't know if his son was for the present government or against it.

One thing he did know. Jack did not like Williams's cool, intellectual delivery of speeches or the way he often seemed only to half listen to anything anyone else said . . . but was there more to it than that? Was Jack a budding revolutionary himself? Had he been raising a son who all along thought as he thought: that Williams was hopelessly inept at countering the white elitist movement, that the black majority were hardly any better off than they had been in the bad old days of British rule?

Roland chastised himself. He had to be getting paranoiac, suspecting Jack, his own son, of being a revolutionary. It had to be because of the confusing times they were all living through. As Luis had told Roland at their last meeting, with race riots erupting in every major U.S. city, the

Black Power movement by "acting so independently," was beginning to hinder, not help the cause.

Luis had then described to Roland what had just happened in France as a result of "*unauthorized* activities carried out by a French-born German student known as Danny the Red." Through Danny's acts of violence and agitation, French universities had been forced to close down in May, during which time Danny had been exiled as a threat to public order. But, Luis had told him, ". . . As a result of the agitation, our Communist comrades lost their seats in the French election in June!" He'd banged his hand down on the tabletop. "Efforts have to be *coordinated* or disaster will invariably be the result."

"How do our comrades feel about the situation here?" Roland had asked, hoping for a clear answer. As usual he had been disappointed by Luis's optimistic reply, for there were many "uncoordinated" influences at work in Trinidad, all trying to topple Williams, which meant toppling him, too!

Roland couldn't understand why Luis couldn't see what was likely to happen. To him it was so obvious that there was a chance Williams could be thrown out and he along with him for being "too lenient."

The worst irony was the Black Power groups were right. They were after what Roland had always been after: "black domination with white elitism crushed forever"—but he had a secret master, who'd continued to want him to support Williams, cautioning "patience" year after bloody year.

As quickly as Roland contemplated Jack's possible connection to a revolutionary movement, he dismissed the idea. Jack was too much of a bookworm, as was his cousin Frederick.

Now Matthew, the bad egg of the family, was a different matter. He was up to all kinds of tricks. Roland grimaced as he thought of Frederick's twin, leading a lazy layabout life, and probably already on the wrong side of the law.

It was Emerald who'd first told him what she'd learned from Carmelita. "I feel so sorry for them," she'd said, her soulful eyes blinking back tears. "If t'was a son o' mine, I don't know what I'd do. Carmelita tells me young Matt's over at Orange Grove, keepin' bad company."

Roland's contemptuous reply had been that it was a miracle any of James's children had turned out well—as undoubtedly Frederick had, studious and hardworking, in his first year at the university. As Roland bitingly pointed out, while James's family had been growing up, James had been "like a child himself playing with his drumsticks!"

If he was considered the stupid one of the family, Matthew often thought, knowing well the kind of talk he was causing, it was damned funny he was the only one of the young group who ever had any real money.

How much did the "clever" one, his twin brother Frederick, ever have in his pocket for all his talk of Black Power? A few cents or dollars at most, unless *he* felt sorry for him and gave him a handout.

And what was cousin Jack going to accomplish for them all in the U.S. of A.? Sweet Fanny Adams!

Matthew would pat the clot of earth that concealed a steel box containing what he called his "loot." As he told himself smugly, he might not be such a hot shot at "learnin'," but he certainly knew how to get what he wanted from people. He'd even been able to make the old whore think he was a "nice, well brought up young man." In fact, he may have gone too far . . . if he didn't watch out, after teaching him how to use a knife and fork, she'd soon be trying to send him back to Sunday school. Well, he might even put up with that—if the price was right.

When Magdalen returned from Arima the next day Matthew was waiting on the veranda with a jug of freshly squeezed lime and lemon juice sweetened with honey from Tropica's own apiaries. "Just the way I like it," she exclaimed, fanning herself in the hot, humid air and thinking, What a thoroughly nice boy he is. She hoped his twin Frederick had turned out half so well.

Out of a raffia basket she brought two slim books. "I know Theo wouldn't mind you borrowing these, Matt." She handed the books to the boy. "I wish I could give them to you, but I can't. They're too precious, but they'll help you understand the active principles in plants, principles that can be applied very effectively in all kinds of treatments, even medicines." She went on earnestly. "Did you know in the old days they bound wounds with cobwebs?"

Matthew laughed, as he thought she expected him to, wishing she'd shut up and go inside to see what he'd planned for her. He couldn't wait for her reaction. It was his own revenge against the whites, his own way to show he was just as much behind the cause for Black Power as his brother and cousin ever were . . . for, only the day before, Matthew had read of a police shootout in Chicago in which two leading Black Panthers had been killed—with eighty-two shots to the Panthers' one!

The news had burned in his brain all day, when a great idea had come to him. He would prepare a surprise for Magdalen's return to Orange Grove, one that would give her a glimpse of the future to come.

He picked up Magdalen's raffia bag as she started to go inside the house. "Why, thank you, Matt. Aren't you in the packing shed today?"

"It's Sat'rd'y, ma'am," he said as courteously as he could. "Is dere anythin' yo'd lik' me t' do?" Although he sounded calm, his heart beat fast as they approached the hallway.

"Oh, goodness no." Magdalen laughed. "There aren't any slave drivers here, Matt my boy. If indeed there are *any* left in Trinidad today. . . ." As she uttered the last syllable, Matthew heard her swift intake of breath as she recoiled in the doorway.

"What is 't, Mistr'ss Finch?" He was pleased at the note of solicitude in his voice, and he dropped her bag to clutch her arm.

"What is 't?" he asked again, as if he didn't know, noting with satisfaction that in the strong afternoon light his handiwork was even more effective. For now the calm faces of the angels in the large religious painting hanging in the hallway were no longer pale. They were black, painted with a paint as black and impenetrable as tar, destroying the serenity of a painting Magdalen loved, a black ugly scar across the canvas.

"Mah God!" Matthew let out a wail. "Mah God, who could 'ave done such a t'ing?" He led a shaken Magdalen to the large chesterfield couch, bringing her smelling salts, alternately patting and clumsily stroking her arm, saying he wanted to call the police, but Magdalen demurred.

"What can *they* do?" she muttered as if to herself. "If any of this gets in the papers, everyone will think we're not giving the locals enough money or giving them too much work or something equally bad. . . ." She straightened up defiantly. "I shall have to interrogate every one of the staff; then if I can't find out who has done this cowardly thing, I'll call . . ."—she beamed in Matthew's direction—"your Uncle Roland. He'll know what to do. In any case, in these troubled times it's important someone as close to the prime minister as your uncle is, knows about this. It could have a deeper meaning. It could be a warning of something about to happen."

Every time Paulette heard Simon and Garfunkel's "Bridge Over Troubled Waters" she felt depressed, a loser—yet she had the cassette in her car and, more often than not, on the monotonous drive up to their new country place outside Woodstock, New York, she'd listen to it over and over again.

Masochist! Paulette told herself fiercely. I like hurting myself with thoughts that I invent more often than not.

The day she'd flown into La Guardia from Florida had been one of those "troubled waters" days. On the flight up she'd decided to check on what she'd been reading in one of *Vogue*'s beauty articles.

"The truth light," it said, "is above the clouds. Check out your real deficiencies when you're up in a plane. Make a list, then once you're on the ground, go about correcting them." As far as she was concerned, the "truth light" had been truthful, all right—in her compact mirror she'd seen the little wrinkles—"laugh lines," French magazines called them, "crow's feet," said the American ones—that the high-altitude light showed clearly around her eyes.

No wonder she could no longer lure Theo into a romantic sexy night together. If she was honest with herself, she'd hardly *ever* been able to manage it even when they were much younger—except when they were in Arima.

That was when she'd switched on the Simon and Garfunkel tape to depress herself still further, until nearly three hours later as she turned across the old bridge that led to their property and saw the pretty clapboard house high up on the hill surrounded by smoky trees and soft pale mists, she'd felt actual tears on her cheeks.

Was she going through the change of life? If so it was too soon. She wasn't ready. Her corpuscles were still throbbing with life, and sex—sex that she felt she'd never had enough of.

The phone had been ringing as she'd stood on the step waiting for Mrs. Evans, their wonderful new housekeeper, to let her in. She'd never been able to remember to bring the right keys for the right house, and now they owned three or was it four—of course it was four—five if you counted Orange Grove—it was next to impossible.

"Can I come with you?" she'd asked plaintively when the phone call turned out to be from Theo.

"Well, I'm not even sure I'm going myself yet. It couldn't be more inconvenient. I'm supposed to be in London on Monday. Remember we're opening at Harrods, and with the Conservatives in power everyone's getting optimistic that there'll be a business boom, at least until the euphoria of a new government wears off."

"Oh, let's go down to Arima, Theo, darling." There had been a note of longing in her voice. "It's been *so* long . . . and now Tommy's away with the d'Arbarées people in Grasse, there's no reason why we shouldn't take off."

For once Theo had sounded exasperated. "Paulette, it's only a few weeks since we had a break for Christmas and New Year's down in the Keys. D'you want to ignore the business opportunity of a lifetime? D'you want Tropica to be a worldwide operation or not?"

"What you're really telling me is you're not going down to Trinidad, even though the manager's left and your mother's worried. That's what you mean, isn't it? Why did you even bother to phone to tell me if it matters to you so little?" She hadn't meant to let the tears sound in her voice, but they broke through.

Theo's voice had softened. He hated to hear Paulette upset, but it was a familiar struggle. He continually told himself he would make his long and frequent absences up to her one day. He would make love to her as she wanted to be made love to then, but now there was no time. "Darling, I called my mother and, although the line was as terrible as ever, she insisted she was all right. The new fields are taking on well, the extracts are up to scratch . . . the warehouse is filling the orders. She says the only thing she'll miss is the manager's own concoction for fighting off the mosquitoes, which, since his departure, have returned in swarms. . . ." As so often happened, Theo was humoring her as he went on, "In any case she says she has a bright young boy with her. Can you believe it, yet another Bracken! He apparently was the manager's protégé, who's now staying at the house to look after her."

Paulette had sighed. "Well, I've got to go to the West Coast to solve that training director problem out there. As usual I suppose we'll meet like business partners at our monthly meeting. Are you coming up this weekend—before you go to London? I thought that was the whole idea. That we'd at least have a place to escape to—where we could meet as husband and wife on weekends. . . ."

"I'll try, darling, I'll really try." But already Theo's thoughts had been elsewhere.

The manager's letter of resignation had disturbed him more than he wanted to intimate to Paulette. He took it out to read again and was about to light a cigarette, when he remembered he'd promised to give up smoking for Lent.

As it was he put the unlit cigarette in his mouth, intending to discard it in a few moments, but as he perused the exact sentences, without thinking he struck a match and started to smoke. ". . . I fear for the future and now I'm beginning to fear for the safety of your mother. . . ." The manager related in detail the painting's desecration. "Your mother has faith in this Matthew Bracken, whom I believe to be worthless. If you want to safeguard your property and look after your mother, who, despite her formidable energy, is after all no longer a

young lady, I suggest you come here immediately and insist she return
with you to the safety of America. For me, I cannot endure it any
longer. There is going to be a black revolution here. I can smell
it. . . ."

Theo didn't know what to think. His mother hadn't even mentioned
to him what had happened to her painting, and, to his annoyance, the
phone had gone dead just as he'd been about to bring up the subject—
and after trying for forty exasperating minutes he hadn't been able to get
through again.

He decided he would "let the dust settle" for a couple of weeks, carry
out his business priorities, then think about going down to Trinidad
later—perhaps in April.

He penciled the world "Trinidad" with a question mark in his diary
in the first week, which he noticed resignedly already had a few dates
neatly penciled in by his secretary, with a star beside one or two that
meant "must do."

Since the unexpected deaths of the Black Panthers in the police
shootout in Chicago, Jack had been vigilant to make sure there were no
clues to link him to Black Power activities.

As he had been at the University of the West Indies, he was at the
University of California a model student, sailing with ease through business administration courses, then plunging into law.

With his ready smile, quick wit and "fantastic sense of rhythm," Jack
was also as popular on the UCLA campus as he'd always been at St.
Augustine. Having Jack Bracken as a speaker brought a full house at a
lively student debate on the question "Does the term 'benign neglect'
have any valid meaning in a civil-rights context and if so illustrate and
document." In the beginning Jack listened with only half his attention
as an intense-looking girl wearing the huge "Jackie O" dark glasses just
in fashion was introduced and started to speak from a prepared text.

It wasn't what she was saying—after the first sentence Jack dismissed
it as rubbish—that riveted his attention. What had Janet Szu said her
name was? Margaret Pollard? What an incredible coincidence that there
should be a student with that name at UCLA, the same name as the
daughter of that infidel relative of his, a name he'd heard all his life.

"Trinidad. . . ." She was actually mentioning Trinidad. It *was* Drum
Pollard's daughter, it had to be.

He started to listen in earnest. What absolute garbage she was saying.
Who'd brainwashed her? Her father? What had he ever known about
men like George Wallace of Alabama, who even now in the year 1970

still defied federal integration orders, thumbing his nose at government mandates because he knew, as Jack knew, that they all emanated from a bunch of lousy, lying hypocrites. Jack was on his feet, bowing politely, knowing how dazzling his teeth would look as he bared them in a brief smile in her direction.

He destroyed her argument in about five minutes, if that. He only had to quote a few who *did* know . . . Senator Abraham Ribicoff of Connecticut, who only a few days ago had said, "Northern liberals should drop their monumental hypocrisy and concede that de facto segregation exists in the North, by no means just the South" . . . and that monstrosity of a presidential adviser Daniel Patrick Moynihan, whose policy was one that again and again "amply demonstrates 'benign neglect' toward blacks." Jack chose the moment to let his voice rise in a crescendo, ". . . It's all part of a calculated and systematic effort by the administration to wipe out gains made by the civil-rights movement. . . ."

As he expected, he received loud cheers, pats on the back.

It was the underdog's time in history; he knew that. Campuses all over the world were in revolt. In the U.S. over the war in Vietnam. In London over "snooping in students' affairs." In Paris over prison sentences handed out to Maoist supporters. Everywhere students were on the march.

He saw the young woman hurry out, her shoulders hunched as she tried to keep books she had under her arm from falling. This was going to be interesting, fascinating. If this was *the* Margaret Pollard—and he was sure it had to be—what on earth was she doing so far from home? Until that moment he'd forgotten she even existed. Suddenly he remembered the fulsome obituaries about her father, the mysterious way in which both her parents had died the same night—and the papers reporting Margaret Pollard as "an heiress overnight," inheriting not only everything from her father, which was considerable, but property and money from her mother, too.

By the time he extricated himself from groups of admirers, the girl was already far away in the distance, heading for one of the chemistry buildings. He'd have to sprint. He didn't want to arrive at her side out of breath and sweaty—in Jack's eyes that appeared overanxious—but he wanted to keep up the momentum. There was nothing else for it. As he ran he asked himself, what do I need to know a Pollard for? The answer came back immediately. Because a rich Pollard can be immensely useful.

As it was, Jack struck the only chord to attract Margaret's attention.

He looked so uncomfortable, so out of breath, she wanted to put him at ease.

"Are you Margaret Pollard from Golden Hill?" Jack panted, his chest still heaving.

If he wasn't sure who *she* was, she certainly knew who the brilliant Jack Bracken was, not because he was from the island, but because he was the talk of her freshman year. "Sexy. . . ." "Have you seen the way he can dance . . . ?" "Boy, oh, boy, I wonder if it's true that black men are bigger? Can you imagine? And to think he has brains to match." She'd heard it all said, but she'd never joined in.

As she'd gone through three years at one of the best prep schools in the country as a naturally striving student, neither encouraging nor discouraging friendships—so she had slotted into her freshman year at the university, finding it easier in the less structured atmosphere to retreat into her own world.

Now, with this tall, black man looming over her, the one who minutes before had annihilated her at the debate, she was unusually flustered. "Yes . . . but I don't live there any more."

Jack tried to sound casual. "You know you're my . . . my . . ."

Margaret said abruptly, "Second cousin."

"Whew!" Jack wiped his face with a flamboyant gesture. "So you *do* know, yet you've never called to say hello to your long-lost relation." He smiled one of his best, most warming smiles, but Margaret didn't respond.

"You didn't exactly put out the welcome mat yourself."

Margaret began to walk on, but Jack put a restraining hand on her arm. "D'you have to go? Can't we talk?"

"What about?" He was unprepared for the flat, unemotional tone.

He tensed, sensing a racial slur in the brush-off he now expected. But he would not be brushed off—especially not by a Pollard! He would give her one more chance before cutting her down to her right midget size. "We can talk about men walking on the moon for the first time . . . or Teddy Kennedy's memory lapse at Chappaquidick or 'benign neglect' . . . or . . ."—his fingers on her arm tightened—". . . what about a little reminiscing about the Brackens and the Pollards, about the amazing ways human beings out of the same womb can behave—one black, one white."

Margaret wrenched her arm away indignantly. "I don't want to talk about it. It's nothing to do with me. Leave me alone."

"So you're a racist just as your father was . . ." Jack cried. "A hypo-

critical white-coated racist, making sounds about civil rights that you
don't know the first thing about."

Margaret was blushing, but she looked at him levelly. "I'm not a
racist! Really I'm not. It's just that . . ." Margaret looked at her watch
agitatedly, "I'm late for a chemistry class. I've got to go."

"That's not the real reason," he snarled. "You don't want to be seen
talking to me, do you?"

"Oh, Jack, you're wrong."

Again he'd struck the right chord. Anxious to prove how wrong he
was, now she touched *his* arm. "I really am late, but if you . . . you like
we could meet for a coffee later."

"In the cafeteria?" he asked sarcastically, choosing the place that was
always packed with people.

"In the cafeteria," she repeated slowly, again giving him the level
glance that he sensed hid a great deal of feeling.

And so they began to meet every other day or so for a coffee or a stroll
between classes. He was irritated that she took so much for granted, and
he began to lecture her on her easy acceptance of everything she had
and could have without lifting a finger, pointing out she was just as
guilty by default as those in government, who by their positive actions
propagated the world of "haves and have-nots."

It was during one of his harangues he realized how sensitive she was,
that he could easily bring tears to her eyes with a few well-chosen
words, accusing her of a racist remark or action. From that point on, it
became as easy as picking oranges from her Golden Hill trees to get her
to write out a check or two to "subscribe" to the causes he told her were
particularly effective in helping the underprivileged.

At first he asked for small donations, something telling him Margaret
Pollard's name on a check could be useful one day. As their "friendship" grew he found it was just as easy to get larger and still larger
"donations."

Everything started to go according to plan. In February, West Indian
students at the Sir George Williams University in Montreal totally
wrecked the university's computer center and were brought to trial.

A week later, acting on Freddie's orders, students from the University
of the West Indies led an orderly but effective protest march against the
trial to the Canadian High Commissioner and the Royal Bank of Canada, culminating in a takeover of the Port of Spain Roman Catholic
Cathedral that lasted several hours, during which time the agitators—

acting on what Jack had to admit was a brilliant idea of his wild cousin Matthew's—painted all the religious figurines in the church black!

Freddie reported that, just as Jack had predicted, several students had been arrested and Jack's advice had been absolutely right. Neither Matthew nor he had joined the march, much as they'd wanted to. As Jack had suggested—no, ordered!—they were saving themselves for the big day ahead.

On March 4, a Black Power march of ten thousand surged through the streets of Port of Spain, followed a week later by what Jack described to Black Power militants in the States as the first "meaningful" march, when thousands went from Port of Spain to the sugar belt at Couva, marching under the banner INDIANS AND AFRICANS UNITE NOW.

If he'd planned it himself Jack couldn't have been more pleased at what happened next. The day before he flew to Miami to make final arrangements for the general strike and major demonstrations planned to take place later that month, a police officer in an excess of zeal shot and killed a young student member of NJAC.

Spending feverish hours on the phone, Jack, with the support of Geddes Granger's men, arranged for the student's funeral to provide the perfect prelude for what was in store for Williams and his government at the end of April.

Sixty-five thousand mourners in every kind of African raiment—agbadas, kentees, dashikis—marched behind the coffin yelling, "Power to the people!" It was the largest and most awesome crowd ever assembled in Port of Spain. Although the march thrilled and encouraged him, there was another change of plan Jack didn't bargain on.

From the beginning of his command, Jack had always given his cousins strict instructions that if they were to succeed in toppling Williams and achieve what they wanted to achieve in the island and throughout the Caribbean, they were to mastermind the operations but *never* take part in them. "Stay out of sight and out of trouble," he'd counseled again and again.

He had already set in motion the most daring part of the anarchy, a liaison between officers who wanted to defect from the tiny Trinidad army and a huge working force of peasants from the fields. It was a fragile unity at best, one that needed constant "stroking" and an endless supply of money to nourish. So it was essential, Jack told Frederick in particular, that he stay out of trouble, strengthening the liaison and building unity until the major coup could take place.

Matthew, however, was not trusted with all the facts of the plot, and since the marches began in February he'd found Jack's orders increasingly difficult to obey.

When the NJAC student was killed by the police officer, Matthew felt as bereaved as if it had been his own brother. "Why should Jack call all de shots?" Matthew whined to Frederick. "Just 'cause he can' be part o' anyt'in' 'cos he's in de States, why should we miss all de fun? I wanna be part o' it all, 'specially when dey shoot up de Red House an' get ol' Williams t' tie 'im up by de neck. . . ."

Frederick thought he'd managed to convince his twin to be sensible, warning him that the *real* action was now only weeks away. "We won't be part of anything if we get locked up *now*, will we?" he kept repeating, hoping to calm his volatile brother.

But Frederick failed to stop him from joining in the student's funeral march, and as he strode along in a brilliantly colored African tribal cape, swigging from a bottle of rum passed among his fellow marchers, the idea he'd been thinking about for some time started to block out everything else. He knew the major uprising against the government was only weeks away. What was he waiting for? Nothing. He should exact his own personal revenge against the whites, this day of the funeral, a day when all his black brothers felt the same way. Matthew looked along the line of sweltering marchers, sweat dripping down their faces, their voices hoarse with singing, shouting, "Power . . . power . . . power!" It *had* to be today!

He thumbed a lift to about a half mile away from Tropica's estate at Orange Grove, where he scooped out the earth to take out the vials of oils from his hiding place together with the panga he'd sharpened the day before.

Now, Mistress Finch, he laughed, as he imagined the look on her face when she saw him in his African finery, now you'll see I know what to do with a knife, old lady.

"EEEEeeee," he screamed, bursting through the door of the living room.

Magdalen sat transfixed, a pen held in midair as Matthew whirled toward her, a sinister look on his face. She forced herself to make light of it. "Glory me, Matt, it's you. With all the goings on in Port of Spain today, goodness knows who I thought you might be. Why are *you* trying to frighten me, silly boy?" Before she could say another word, he hit her so violently that the ring on his finger sliced open her temple.

"EEEEE!" Matthew screamed again. "Now yo' know, yo' ol' whore, yo' days are number'd, an' yo' white cocksuckin' friend, dat prime minister, yessir! 'Well, Mistress Finch'"—he tried to imitate Eric Williams's educated voice—"I t'ink it's time, m'dear, dat yo' saw de light. . . ." As he spoke Matthew took out the vials of oils and poured them over her, saturating her hair, her skin, causing the wound in her head to burn fiercely.

He grew more excited, screaming, "De Black Power is a comin'. Williams will be dead, man, dead! We'll be de bosses. No more cocksuckin' de whites . . . no more. De army's wid us. Nothin' can stop us now!" He tried to strike a match, attempting to set her and the room alight, but he was so drunk and his hands so damp he couldn't get the match to light.

Magdalen, at first frozen with terror, found her resolve stiffening. She sat up. For a second her apparent return to life and vigor deflated Matthew, as she said in an icy voice, "Matthew, at nearly seventy years old I am sure my days *are* numbered. *All* our days are numbered, *yours* too. Why don't you act like the good boy you really are and calm down."

To her horror, her calm words made him scream with renewed hatred. As he turned to pick up the gleaming panga from the table, a door opened and, to her relief and amazement, she saw Matthew's father, James, with two or three policemen, rush into the room.

Later she was to tell Theo it all seemed to happen in ghastly slow motion. Whether it was deliberate or not, Magdalen would never know, for Matthew on seeing his father seemed to swing the panga down straight at him, almost severing his arm from his body, before running straight through the glass doors at the end of the room with the police in hot pursuit.

Roland had warned Luis, and Luis had appeared to take no notice. Now the revolution Roland had suspected was imminent had not taken place after all.

For all his prying, ferreting and knowledge of men in high places, Roland still hadn't been able to find out exactly how catastrophe had been averted. To him there was something ominous about the whole affair, not because his two nephews had been implicated and arrested, with Frederick released after cursory questioning, while Matthew, charged with molestation and threatening behavior to human life, had been imprisoned.

No, the ominous feeling he had was for his own safety.

Could it be he was *still* being held responsible for the Dominican Republic debacle? Could it be that all along Luis had known Magdalen Finch had been blackmailing Drum Pollard, so believed he had also been part of the plot?

Roland went over the facts he knew for sure—information that had come into his possession shortly after the mass demonstration following the student's funeral—that a mutiny against Williams and the government had been planned by the army: He'd rushed to warn Luis who'd told him not to worry! Worry! It was an incredible reaction. He'd then told the prime minister, because Luis had said he could tell him if he wanted to . . . yet neither of them seemed unduly perturbed. *That* was the ominous part.

When it was all over, Roland had discovered the proposed "revolution" had gone ahead as he'd been told it would: the commander of the army had telephoned his deputy at the Teteron Bay headquarters, warning him that he'd discovered two lieutenants were sympathetic to the Black Power movement, and that there was a plan for the army to link up with student activists to stage a mutiny.

The deputy had confined the two suspects to the guardhouse, causing considerable resentment among the enlisted men. The next day another disloyal lieutenant, with the aid of soldiers, had broken into the guardhouse to free the prisoners, take over the headquarters and "capture" the deputy commander, intending to march on Port of Spain, uniting with Black Power leaders on the way.

But *someone*—and Roland could not find out *who*, no matter how many questions he asked—had already alerted the coast guard, who sailed close inshore, training their guns on the shore road, preventing the marchers from taking one step. It had appeared as if Williams and Luis had known about everything before he did.

As the ensuing trials failed to establish whether the soldiers, as they claimed, were simply trying to improve conditions in the regiment or were really mutineers attempting to take over the Trinidad government with other Black Power leaders, Roland knew he wouldn't be able to hold back his contempt much longer for what Williams was allowing to happen on the island.

Whether Luis backed him or not, he decided, he now had to act for himself. Being patient for over fifteen years hadn't moved him one step further ahead in his ambition to be Trinidad's leader. Even his son, Jack, he sensed, despised him for so thoroughly subjugating his own personality to Eric Williams.

Between April and November, eighty-seven soldiers and fifty-four civilian militants were arrested, charged with treason, sedition or mutiny, while the two disloyal lieutenants who'd led the so-called mutiny received sentences, which curiously—ominously to Roland—were later set aside by the court of appeal.

Roland attempted to thrash it out with Luis to no avail. There was a far-away look in his eyes, that said, "Don't meddle—it's no longer any concern of yours."

Had Williams struck a bargain with the reds? Was he, in fact, no longer the "heir-apparent," so carefully groomed all these years to take over from Williams when the reds gave the word? Was Williams not going to be displaced after all?

Roland agonized over the situation, finding no joy, only more suspicion when he was called to the chief minister's office to be told the role of ambassador was to be his.

It was ironic, he thought, on the drive home to give the news to Emerald, that they would be leaving Trinidad—because he had the plum position he'd wanted for so long—just when he most wanted to stay. He became increasingly suspicious it was a plot to get him off the island, while Luis and Eric Williams conspired together.

Who knew what he would find when he came back? *If* he came back.

For one crazy moment Roland entertained the idea of discussing everything with Jack, the son who had more brains than most of the cabinet put together, and who, thank God, had not been mixed up in the Black Power mess that had just transpired.

He could never tell Jack he had led a double life all these years, but perhaps he could find out how Jack saw the situation in Trinidad? He'd been in the States for over a year now. What did he hear at the university, a known breeding ground for spies, as covert operations increasingly needed the best brains to operate in the world of plots and counterplots.

Roland thought of flying over to see Jack before he took up his ambassadorial post, but he finally dismissed the idea. Why should he burden his son with his worries, when Jack was taking his law exams a year early? He couldn't worry the son who, if he himself couldn't pull off the coup so sorely needed in Trinidad, might one day do it for him.

What a bloody mess! With every jab of his boxing gloves, Jack punched out his frustration in the gym, seeing Eric Williams's face with every hit he made at the punching bag, clenching his teeth as he mentally recited, "State of emergency . . . reintroduction of flogging . . . arrest of radical black leaders . . . a proposed National Security Act . . . no more freedom . . . the right to search *anyone, anywhere, anyplace* . . . detention . . . regulation of public meetings."

It was an outrage, and there was more to come according to an old friend from Trinidad, who had been to see him with the news, in fear of arrest himself as on more than one occasion he'd openly said, "Eric Williams can only reign by terror now." He had further reported a ban was about to be put into force of any report considered derogatory to Williams. No "anti" pictures, no "anti" words—only the smiling shit face of Williams was going to be allowed in the papers. There was even going to be a curfew!

"Will you go back?" Jack had asked his friend.

"Of course, I'm going back, man. What a thing to ask me. Come back yourself, Jack, and put some sense into that island of ours when you're qualified. Look at the scorecard: fifteen years after the brave new world of Williams was first ushered in fifty-three percent of the business elite is still white, twenty-four percent Creole–off white, ten percent mixed, nine percent Indian and black . . . bah!" The Trinidadian almost spat out the words "the black man—the majority of our population—has a measly four percent business interest in the island!"

The injustice of everything he'd been told rankled him all day. Jack couldn't eat. He moodily leafed through the lawbooks, looking at cases that had changed the course of the law. The law! He had to *use* the law on his home ground, to uproot the rot destroying his own people.

But first, he had to have *influence*.

It was ironic Jack was learning the lesson his father had learned from Commander Brett years before, but learning it in such a different way because—Jack hit the bag so that for a split second it seemed to stand on end—to gain influence, violence somehow had to be used, because it was the only thing people who already had influence understood. Violence meant guns, bombs . . . and that costs money.

There was this plan to protest the University of Wisconsin's participation in government war research. They needed money he'd been told, to blow up the laboratory where the research was taking place.

It was time, Jack decided, he paid another call on Margaret Pollard to bolster his funds for the "underprivileged."

As he showered, he started to whistle. As usual his optimistic nature was wiping out the feeling that one defeat had to mean defeat all around. Margaret Pollard would pay for the Wisconsin job, and her signature on the check would be enough to incriminate her.

From the moment Margaret mentioned Jack Bracken's name, Roger hadn't been able to concentrate on anything else. It had upset him so much that the fact that the weather had cleared and from all accounts his horse had an excellent chance in Ascot's Gold Cup, suddenly hadn't meant a thing.

Jack Bracken! The very name made his blood run cold. Of all terrible coincidences that his beautiful, innocent niece should meet up with the namesake of the boy who had been hanged for the murder of his own father, her grandfather. It was macabre.

Between races Margaret told him cheerily, "Jack isn't like the other members of his family. . . . He really believes in and works for a number of causes for the underprivileged." A warning bell rang in Roger's head.

As casually as he could he asked, "Have you helped him with any of them?"

"Oh, yes, of course, Uncle . . . well, only with money—which I suppose is a lazy way, but Jack's very grateful. . . ."

"Money?" Roger repeated weakly. "You mean checks, or cash?"

Margaret looked at him in surprise. "Checks, of course. You can't give anyone lots of cash to carry about in Los Angeles—it would be far too dangerous. Anyway, I like to keep a record of how much I give."

Checks! Signatures! Roger shuddered. From the sound of it, just like his uncle, Jack Bracken already had his own plan mapped out to harm the Pollard name.

He excused himself before the race to make a phone call to London. It was vital he find out as much as possible about Mr. Jack Bracken before Margaret returned to the States and met him again. If Jack Bracken turned out to be the one redeeming member of the whole clan, then Roger promised he would kick himself for being such a suspicious busybody!

Later as an equerry led them to the Royal Box where Her Majesty Queen Elizabeth II graciously extended her commiserations on Golden Hill's bad luck—"beaten by a head"—Roger found it hard to concentrate on anything, except how to prevent his beloved niece from any further entanglement with a Bracken. Even if the report came back "clean," he still felt there had to be a plot in the relationship to ruin Margaret's young life.

As they flew home, Roger tried to reason with Margaret one more time. "Darling, you know I trust your instincts, but people aren't always what they seem. You'd make me so happy if you'd consider seeing less of Jack—Jack Bracken. Would you at least promise not to support the causes he proposes, until I've looked into them?"

Margaret gave him her usual candid glance. "Uncle Roger, I know how even his name must make you feel sick, but please understand, that's one of the reasons I went out of my way to be Jack's friend, to try in a small way to make up for the past, which is after all so very long ago. Believe me, Jack does have my best interests at heart, but I promise I'll be careful."

Jack knew Margaret had returned from London and was staying in New York (he was in New York himself, on Black Power business) and Southampton for what remained of her summer vacation with her aunt and uncle, but he decided he wouldn't rush to call her. He would let her wait a while before setting up the meeting where he planned to get a big check for the Wisconsin job.

He looked at his watch. He'd been invited to a party out'on the island. He couldn't make up his mind whether to go or not, but for once he had a free evening. It was damnably humid and he'd been promised an ice-cold limo would take him to this fabulous house on the beach, only about forty minutes out of the city where the waves would be high and so would the girls, high and wanting.

In fact, it wasn't such a fabulous house, but the air was cooler and the ocean looked inviting. So did the girls, expecially one girl. He saw her as soon as he was ushered into the room as Mr. Big Shot. She was as tall as he was and just as black and skinny, but that was where the similarity ended. There was something wild and electric about her skinny body with nipples grazing her transparent chiffon shirt, and, when he was casually introduced, a peculiar thrill shot through his body, so unexpected that he held on to her hand for moments longer than he meant to.

"Okay, okay, so you're a top New York model, are you?" he asked, trying to remain cool and unaffected as she snatched her hand away. "Does that mean you charge for a handshake, lady?" Man, but she was nervous. Her huge brown eyes glittered, flashed, and chased shadows around the room, while her foot tapped time to Janis Joplin on the hi-fi.

For the first time in his life Jack wanted to be alone with this dizzy, nervous broad, not to make love to her, although that had to be part of the plan, but to talk to her. Of all things—talk! He didn't even know if she could put two or three words together. He doubted any model could, even one classified as "top."

He wanted to stop her eyes from darting around the room, looking at other people, to have her give him and nobody else her full attention. Had the crazy New York heat affected him; the heat that made even cats and dogs act as if the pavements were out to burn them to death?

She laughed too shrilly and for too long. She turned her back on him in the middle of his sentence, so he could see shoulder blades jutting out. She was totally indifferent, and it incensed him as the evening went on.

"Let's get out of here," he almost shouted, finding her alone for a second staring out at the big rollers as they crashed on the beach.

"Are you cr-cr-azy or something? Let me alone." She backed away as if he were a madman.

"Look, you may be Ms. Famous *Vogue* Cover Nanette Henry, but you're nothing but a spoiled brat to me. I'm taking you home—if you have one—whether you like it or not."

A look of terror crossed her face. "Leave me alone, d'you hear? You're heading for trouble, man. I'm not free. My man's coming to pick me up."

Jack put a hand across her mouth and backed her up against the terrace wall. "Just listen to me. . . ." He tried to pinion her with his body, but quick as a flash her teeth were in his hand and she ran inside.

He stood watching her from the dark, not caring about his throbbing hand, more fascinated by this gawky, glossy creature than ever. She was now dancing like a dervish, her short skirt flipping up to show a black velvet behind. Jack's crotch grew hot. He had to have her. He was suddenly wild about this gypsy who, he'd been told by his host, was one of the first black girls ever to be on the cover of *Vogue*.

But it wasn't a collector's item he was after. It was her squirming vital body . . . and he could take care of any pipsqueak of a boyfriend. Nobody could stand in his way if he wanted a woman badly enough, and he wanted this one so badly that he couldn't believe himself. It was as if he'd been infected by a disease that was fast taking over his whole body, making his hands shake, his body sweat, and his penis grow so that it bulged indecently beneath his jeans. She seemed to disappear. He felt frantic. He went over to the host. "Where is she, Will?"

Will Tollor shrugged. "Up there. . . ." Jack ran up a short flight of stairs to find a huge gorilla of a man blocking his way. "Can I help you, sonny?" he said with a leer.

Jack looked into the most ferocious face he'd ever seen, with dead, dull eyes and a nose that looked as if a baseball bat had slammed it back into its pockmarked flesh.

"I'm looking for Nan Henry," he said as boldly as he could, trying to ignore the wash of pain as thick fingers clamped his arm behind him.

"Off you go, sonny." He was being pushed around, down the steps again. The gorilla's strength was such that he had no option.

Moodily, Jack backed into a corner, gulping down a bottle of ice-cold beer to try to wipe out the burning feeling in his arm. He wondered whether it was broken.

Suddenly he could see Nanette again. She was out in the middle of the floor, dancing like a puppet, jerking her legs and arms in quick staccato movements as the music sped up and Jack saw a heavy, perspiring black man in a tight white suit leaning against the stair rail watching her through narrowed eyes. As she lifted up her skirt to show again the smooth folds of her behind, the man beckoned to the gorilla who was now by the bar. He ambled over to where the girl was dancing and threw her over his shoulder like a sack of potatoes.

To his surprise Jack saw the girl go limp. It was as if the giant man had pulled out the key from a dancing doll. Jack quickly ran onto the terrace, in time to see the gorilla emerge to throw her into the back seat of a long dark Cadillac. He then got into the driver's seat while the hefty black guy climbed in the back with the girl. Jack was aware of a shattering sense of loss as he saw curtains being pulled at the car windows as it sped away from the curb.

He was like a man possessed. He needed to see her again, had to find out what it was all about.

Although Jack's reputation was high, it took time, trouble and money before he found out from his Black Power contacts what he'd half guessed already . . . that Nanette Henry was a big-time model all right, but, more important, she was "the property" of Big Man, the hefty one Jack had seen watching her; Big Man, the simplistic name given to one of the biggest drug dealers in the city and someone who even the most daring and dangerous of Jack's contacts warned him to stay away from . . . "unless you want to end up in a concrete block on some new highway!"

He didn't care. Disproving all his own notions about female-male relationships, crazy as it seemed—and he looked helplessly in the mirror for signs of his impending lunacy—he was possessed by this girl.

He *had* to see her again, one more time. That Margaret Pollard had called to say she was back in the U.S. didn't break through his obsession. He'd catch up with her when he was ready. The Wisconsin job was still another month away. He had time to get the check he needed, but did he have time to find Nanette before she was totally destroyed?

He found out she would be at a photographer's studio on a test sitting for an important cosmetics commercial, but when he arrived to pick her up, the dark Cadillac was waiting at the curb.

He even managed to get through to her on the phone, but she slammed the receiver down as soon as she heard his voice and when he called back, there was no answer. The next day the number had been disconnected.

Jack went back to the house on the island a week after he'd first set eyes on her. "Will, I've got to see Nanette again. Tell me what you know about her, not about Big Man, I've heard all I want to hear about him. Is she too far gone? Is she on coke?"

Will stared moodily out at the ocean. "Maybe not, but it won't be long, though Big Man likes the idea of having a fancy live-in cover girl—and those top jobs don't go to girls snorting coke."

"Well, what's she doing with him? Tell me anything you know about her, *please.*" Will had never heard such a note in Jack Bracken's voice. He was amazed. You never knew, from one day to the next, how people could change.

"She came from France, I know that. She was Tony Basser's girl—he used to be one of the biggest photographers around. She was always kind of docile." Will looked at Jack craftily. "Well, Tony, you know, he's a Puerto Rican—a white guy—and he, well, he used to call Nanette his black slave. Goddamn it, man, he made her serve us dinner starko. Yes, that's right, not a stitch on that goddamn beautiful body of hers. Most exciting dinner I ever ate. We all wanted a piece of her!"

"Shut up." Jack walked up and down the terrace agitatedly. "She must be a bloody moron. I shouldn't even think about her."

"That's what I'm trying to tell you, Jack—forget her. She's too mixed up already. A sweet kid, but too mixed up, particularly for anyone with a future like yours."

Before Jack left, he found out the rest of the story: that Tony Basser had developed a drug habit that had "taken him over," so that he ended up owing Big Man so much "he arranged a deal—an exchange arrangement—Nanette for Big Man to forget what Tony owed him." Will sounded bored . . . "with some heroin thrown in for good luck."

When Jack woke up next morning he told himself he wasn't going to think about Nanette Henry again, that he'd wasted valuable time and had to get back on course.

He set up a meeting to discuss the Wisconsin job, then telephoned Margaret at her aunt and uncle's townhouse.

They met in the Palm Court of the Plaza Hotel and after Jack lambasted her for wasting time on something as archaic as the English social season, he sarcastically told her about *his* "summer vacation," working mostly in the city to raise funds for Edwin Reister's Social Service Organization started at the University of Wisconsin to help Americans, mostly black and living below the poverty line. He went on to explain with easy rhetoric the dramatic difference in terms of food and medical help "only ten thousand dollars can make." As he expected, it didn't take long before Margaret started to write out a check to Reister, actually one of the key figures in the Wisconsin bomb plot.

As he spoke he was looking over Margaret's shoulder, not believing his eyes, for sitting directly in his line of vision was . . . the girl of his dreams (and nightmares) . . . Nanette, who appeared to be sobbing on the shoulder of a beautiful young blonde.

In a daze, Jack got to his feet, taking the check out of Margaret's hand to stuff in his pocket. "You'll have to excuse me," he said unusually courteously as Margaret looked at him in bewilderment. He didn't care. All his resolutions disappeared as he looked at Nanette's strange, frightened face, all cheekbones and huge eyes, the tiny points of her bosom— as flat as a boy's—showing through a light colored shirt.

Margaret didn't know what to do. Jack stood awkwardly over two beautiful girls, one black, one white. They looked like models. They also looked furious. She saw the black girl cower into a corner. Jack sat down, talking fast, looking unlike himself, unsure, gesticulating, while the blond girl listened intently, but the black girl clapped her hands over her ears as if she didn't want to hear a word.

Margaret paid the check and left as she saw Jack begin to wave his finger, obviously lecturing the black girl, as he so often lectured her— but Margaret felt sure it wasn't about the number of people living below the poverty line!

She was furious, but glad he hadn't given her an opportunity to sign the check before snatching it out of her hand. When he called to ask why she hadn't signed it, then *she* would demand an explanation for his rude behavior.

From the minute Jack saw Nanette at the Plaza with her closest friend, model Becky Dermott, he knew there was no way he could dismiss her from his life.

For some reason, he learned from Becky—as talkative as Nanette was silent—Big Man trusted her and so allowed Nanette to see her, but she was the only one. "She's virtually a prisoner, Jack. He terrifies everyone, yet somehow he stays in the clear."

Jack could feel his flesh go cold, as despite Nanette's increasing protests, Becky insisted on delivering detail after detail about Nanette's incredible life, sensing in Jack an ally, and possibly, someone who might be able to help her bring about Nanette's escape.

Scorpio, as Big Man's "gorilla" was called, delivered and fetched Nanette from every modeling assignment, every beauty appointment, taking her "home" afterward to any number of different addresses Big Man had scattered throughout the five boroughs.

For days after their unexpected meeting at the Plaza, Jack shadowed Nanette with the help of the Black Panthers, learning more about the shady world of violence and fear she inhabited, where drugs, that Big Man seemed to have a monopoly on, dominated the action. How did he get away with it? Why wasn't Big Man under lock and key? There was no explanation.

The day Nanette called him for help was the day Jack found Margaret Pollard's unsigned check in his pocket.

He cursed himself for his stupidity. She'd been calling him, he knew, but for the last few days there had been no more messages.

What the hell! It was too late for the Wisconsin job now. There would be others to involve her in, but first he had to get Nanette either out of his system or out of danger.

He hadn't seen her in almost two weeks, when, desperate for news, he learned from Becky that after her last sitting she hadn't emerged from a West Side address.

"I'm off to Paris for *Harper's Bazaar*. I can't stop to find out more now, but don't worry. She'll be all right . . ." Becky added lamely.

So much for her support, Jack thought bitterly.

He had been trying to make up his mind whether to attempt to break into the West Side apartment when the phone rang about 10:00 A.M. At first he thought it was a freak phone call; then he could hear a squeal of pain, a cry for help, incoherent, Nanette pleading for him to come. . . .

His hands were trembling as he urged the taxi to rush to West 72nd Street. He knew it was bad. He fingered the revolver in his pocket. If Scorpio or Big Man were there, he had no alternative. He had to give it to them—fast—before they got him.

Telling the taxi to wait, Jack went up to the second-floor apartment. The door was off the latch. Revolver in hand, he crept down a long dark corridor, calling out Nanette's name as loudly as he dared.

At first there was silence; then he heard weeping. He pushed open a door to find himself in a mirrored room, brilliantly lit by fluorescent tubes.

There was Nanette sprawled naked, lying in the middle of what looked like a boxing ring, surrounded on all sides by cushions, chaise longues and the debris of what must have been an all-night party. The air was oppressive with cigar smoke, sweat . . . and blood.

Nanette had been badly beaten up, her eye half closed, her nose bloodied, deep clawlike scratches etched in her skin from her bosom down to her thighs, made, she told him between choked sobs, by a "new girlfriend" of Big Man's. He had recently introduced female fights to his program of entertainment for his clients, and Nanette murmured that on the two occasions she had been forced to take part she'd been the loser.

Jack had never moved so fast. He bathed her wounds, helped her into slacks and a shirt. Luckily it took her only a few minutes to find her passport before they took the taxi back to his place. In an hour, they were on the way to Kennedy Airport, to catch the first plane going to the Caribbean, hopefully to Trinidad. It was a lucky omen, Jack thought, that they were able to get two seats on a plane to Port of Spain.

All the long way down, as overcast clouds gave way to gray mist, then to the ethereal blue of Caribbean skies, Jack reflected on the incredible change of events in his life.

After the debacle of the black revolution, he'd wondered what direction his life should take—and one hot summer evening Nanette had unwittingly provided the answer. He would use his brains and legal degree in Trinidad after all—to get where he was undoubtedly going, to the top, with the first woman he had ever loved by his side. It was a love he had never thought he could experience, one he'd never believed existed outside of stupid magazines and movies.

He glanced at the fragile girl sleeping at his side. Beneath the dark shadows, misshapen mouth and bruised skin, there was an innocence despite the horrendous life she had lived. He knew very little about her, but something told him she was a good person, probably far better than he would ever be.

As for Margaret Pollard, he wasn't finished with her yet, but why should he let a Pollard spoil his life? She was already a mixed-up girl. She probably didn't need his machinations to make her come apart even further.

Nanette moaned in her sleep and he raised her fingers to his lips. "Don't worry, darling," he murmured. "Trinidad isn't expecting us, but they're going to have to get used to the idea. I think we may be returning at just the right time."

Tommy
1971

s Margaret came into the sunlit room, Roger grasped the arm of his chair. He couldn't believe his eyes. If she wasn't living, walking proof that his prejudice was ill founded and anachronistic, then he deserved to be lying on a psychiatrist's couch himself. He'd never said it—how could anyone say it in America—that he had always thought psychiatry was overrated; that Americans rushed to the psychiatrist, paying for the privilege to share confidences and talk out problems that in Europe were "sorted out" by being talked over with a reliable good friend.

But there hadn't been any alternative six months ago when he'd received a call from Los Angeles to say Margaret hadn't been turning up for class, that the last time she'd been seen she'd appeared disoriented, rambling, confused.

Now it was hard to believe that the radiant girl standing before him was the same Margaret he'd found disheveled and emaciated from lack of food in her apartment off campus. Of course she wasn't the "same Margaret Pollard." She was well and truly on the mend, not just different from the girl of six months ago, but different from the girl who had had to endure the trauma of all that had happened in 1966.

Roger looked with gratitude at Daniel Siden, the bearded young psychiatrist, who'd been recommended to him as a doctor who got results through a new and unusual method of direct patient therapist dialogue called "biofeedback." Roger didn't understand it and didn't want to. All he cared about was the end result, and he was looking at it with his own eyes.

It was ironic that he had to thank that blackguard, Jack Bracken, for the beautiful, assured Margaret who now stood before him. If he hadn't had the painful job of telling her he'd learned Jack was out to ruin her, linking her with some very dangerous militant activities, it was possible she wouldn't have collapsed the way she had, giving in to the nervous breakdown that had been pending for years.

He remembered how she'd stared at the name, "Edwin Reister," the name of a wanted criminal, responsible for blowing up a Wisconsin University laboratory, killing a research graduate, injuring others, and destroying a 1.5-million-dollar computer. The name had provided the last piece of missing evidence in the puzzle, and he'd proved to her there and then that Edwin Reister was no philanthropist, but an anarchist, and murderer, as so many of the people involved in Jack's "causes" had been. There was also strong evidence, he'd pointed out, that she'd been lucky not to be implicated in a number of student demonstrations that had caused damage and death.

That was all behind them. She was on the road to recovery and the most amazing thing was her request—that Dan Siden thought ought to be granted—to go with him to Trinidad and Golden Hill, to decide what to do about her land, to reevaluate her feelings about what was, after all, the family business.

Dan Siden, lanky, looking much younger than the forty-odd years Roger knew him to be, walked out with them to the clinic entrance, an arm familiarly slung around Margaret's shoulder. "Let's see, our next appointment is just before Labor Day. Right?"

"Right!"

"Remember to keep the diary as we discussed and do the breathing techniques whenever you feel you need to."

They're grinning at each other like two naughty children, Roger thought, astonished at the doctor's informal manner that had only surfaced for him to see that day. Obviously this casual manner was the way he'd been able to bring out the best in Margaret, and that was fine by him.

Roger had interrogated Siden closely when the doctor had told him Margaret was talking about returning to Golden Hill. "Are you sure it's nothing to do with the Bracken boy?" he'd asked anxiously. "It's all too much of a coincidence for me to swallow. You know he's down in the island now with his black-model friend. D'you think Margaret knows this? D'you think it was the culminating blow making her collapse? D'you think she wants to go down there in the hopes of seeing him again?"

The doctor looked pensive. "We can't be the judge of her motives, Mr. Pollard," he said finally. "However, I think I can put your mind at rest on one point. I'm convinced Margaret was never in love with Jack Bracken, if that's your interpretation of the reasons behind her support of him and his suspicious causes. Subconsciously, every check given, every attempt to please this man was an attempt on her part to 'make peace' with the past. She's quite a little peacemaker, you know."

Now, Margaret gave the doctor a shy peck on the cheek and ran to the waiting car. Roger looked at the doctor anxiously once more. "You're sure it's all right to take her down there? There won't be any—any relapse?"

"Not a relapse. Perhaps the return of full memory. You must realize, Mr. Pollard, Margaret still has no full recollection of what happened the night of her parents' deaths. She knows there's a discrepancy between what she read in the papers and what took place, but she doesn't know what the discrepancy is. It could well be returning to Golden Hill will jolt her memory, and that can only be one more step toward regaining full health. Margaret *is* better, but we have a way to go. Make her laugh, Mr. Pollard, it's good therapy. Above all, help her to enjoy her island in the sun." The doctor turned and walked vigorously down the corridor.

"That's absolutely what I intend to do," Roger was still saying three days later as he arrived with Margaret to catch the morning flight to Port of Spain.

Although Clare had been her usual unwelcoming self, if anything more acerbic than usual, it hadn't seemed to daunt Margaret. She'd been shy as she always was when Clare was around, but when Clare was out, it had delighted Roger to hear Margaret chat excitedly about the forthcoming trip and to his surprise she'd even brought up her parents' deaths, a subject that had been taboo for five years.

There was a loquacious acquaintance of Roger's in the departure lounge. Roger wished he'd go away or shut up. He tried to be polite as the man hemmed and hawed about his business difficulties "down the islands." He had to be polite. He knew how quickly he would be labeled "impossibly conceited . . . all that money has gone to his head . . ." if he moved away too abruptly. A few minutes before the hostess announced the flight's departure, a striking white-haired woman came rushing into the lounge, followed by a bespectacled serious-looking young man.

To Roger's relief the acquaintance left Margaret and him alone to go over to them—but his relief was short-lived. He was back almost instantly, propelling the late arrivals over to introduce them. "You *must* know each other, the celebrated always do know each other . . ." he said obsequiously. "The most famous name in oil in Trinidad, if not in the world, Mr. Roger Pollard and his niece Margaret Pollard . . . and the most famous name in the beauty business, Mrs. Theo Finch of Tropica Cosmetics and her son, young Thomas Finch. . . . You've never met? How amazing!" He brays like a donkey, Roger thought, irritated, but nevertheless he was pleased the introductions had taken place. There were only twelve seats in the first-class section, and Roger was also pleased to see Tommy Finch was just across the aisle from Margaret.

What a coincidence that we should all be on the same plane, Roger reflected—on such an important day for Margaret too, returning to Trinidad for the first time since the tragedy that took her parents' lives. A new generation of Pollards. A new generation of Finches—meeting for the first time. . . . Roger sneaked a quick glance at the youth, whose nose was buried in a sports magazine. He looked nice enough, this great-grandson of the man who'd let the great estate and house, Golden Hill, slip through his fingers into the hands of his own father, Piper Pollard.

As the plane flew toward the sun, Roger reminded Margaret that Golden Hill had once belonged to the Finch family, built by the descendant of Governor Thomas Picton, whose reputation had been ruined when he'd ordered the torture of Louisa Calderon.

Roger looked at Margaret and winked, remembering Siden's instructions to "make her laugh." "Your grandmother's very proud that she's a descendant of Louisa's. I can remember now how she boasted she was getting justice for Louisa at long last the day she moved into Golden Hill! The funny thing is, Rose always saw Louisa as Joan of Arc, when in reality the little lady was definitely found with her hand in the till. . . ."

Margaret did laugh, much to Roger's relief. "Oh, do go on, Uncle Roger. It's so fascinating. Now I understand more the reason for the Finches' resentment. . . ."

". . . It was more than resentment. It was bitter hatred," Roger interrupted, "passed down from father to daughter, then down to her son, Theo, the father of the young man sitting there . . ."—Roger indicated

Thomas across the aisle—"Theo, as you know, was much, much younger than his son is today when he was involved in the fire that killed my father, your grandfather, Rose's husband."

"What about today, Uncle Roger? That was all years ago. How do the Finches feel now?"

"Oh, I'm quite sure none of them even think about it. Theo Finch has built this great cosmetics empire with his wife—the lady over there sitting next to her son—and I imagine Tommy will go into the business, if he isn't in it already." This time Roger caught the slim youth's eye and smiled at him broadly. Who knows, he suddenly thought, if Tommy Finch won't be the one to make full amends to the Pollards one day.

As they talked desultorily during the interminable wait for their luggage at Piarco Airport, Margaret warmed to Paulette's easy charm, but she retreated back into her shell whenever Tommy spoke to her.

A couple of shy kids, Paulette thought, an idea forming. Why not bring them together? It would be a match made in heaven, a bringing together of two long-time warring families. She laughed, imagining Theo's reaction or—worse yet—Magdalen's. Well, she'd let nature take its course; first the kids had to get to know each other.

"As I told you before we boarded, we've been 'commuting' since Theo's mother had a stroke last year, following the terrible disturbances here. We had big trouble over at Orange Grove following the student's funeral—so now, what with all the upheavals, my husband and I take turns visiting. Actually he's here at the moment, too, because we have a lot of work to do with our essential-oils business. It isn't easy to get the right management. . . ." Paulette chatted on, easy, amiable, relaxed.

When they were finally outside the terminal looking for their cars, Paulette called over to Roger, "From what my husband tells me, my mother-in-law's making a good recovery. Perhaps Margaret would like to come over and visit us in Arima one day. We'll have a barbecue—a cookout—get the young folks together. . . ."

To Roger's surprise, Margaret answered for him. "I'd appreciate that, Mrs. Finch, and most of all I'd love to see your Orange Grove plant. I'm very interested in that kind of business. I hope to get my chemistry degree at UCLA when I get back. . . ."

Paulette beamed. "How exciting. Of course, we'd *love* to show you around. You may be able to give us some ideas! Are you staying at Golden Hill? Good. I'll call you early next week to make a date. . . ."

So Margaret Pollard had returned to Golden Hill after all. Jack Bracken put down the newspaper containing the story of her arrival and picked up his pipe for his usual after-breakfast smoke.

Many of his best ideas came when he was smoking a pipe. It soothed him, as he supposed the pipe of peace had soothed the old-time warriors, putting him in a tranquil frame of mind to face the day ahead, which was likely to be turbulent, the day on which his father had told him Eric Williams intended to announce his retirement.

From the terrace of his apartment, Port of Spain looked like a dream city, rich, prosperous, full of potential. You can't see the slum buildings, the broken roads from up here, Jack thought bitterly, but they're there all right, ugly proof of Williams's incompetence, exchanging a dependence on Great Britian as he had for an even greater one on the United States. His father had told him only the day before that, with a population of little over a million, U.S. investment in the island already stood at 1.2 billion dollars—twelve hundred dollars a head, but where was it all going? Why weren't lives improved, even in some small but at least visible way?

Well, if Williams kept his word, he had nothing to be upset about today! Not only was there Williams's retirement to look forward to, but his glorious bird, Nanette, would be arriving back before lunchtime from a modeling assignment in Venezuela. He could hardly wait, and he'd decided during her brief absence that he was going to tell her that there were not going to be any more modeling assignments overseas. No, siree. He had decided he would marry the girl and keep her pregnant every year for the next four or five years.

It was amazing how well he'd settled down; everyone agreed on that.

His father, after the initial shock of his return, had been so thrilled, there'd even been tears in the old boy's eyes. And now that he was back from his ambassadorial post on this new commission of Williams's— Jack took a satisfying draw on his pipe—he had to admit he liked the idea of having his pa around, especially now that he was qualified and could really get things moving.

Jack hadn't been back in Trinidad for more than a month before he'd started to rev up the sadly sagging Black Dignity Movement. He'd called Professor Lloyd Braithewaite, the vice chancellor of the University of the West Indies, encouraging him to chair a commission of inquiry into a case of racial discrimination, following an incident at the Trinidad Country Club, where two black overseas visitors had been refused use of the tennis facilities, which they were entitled to as guests of the Hilton Hotel.

Jack had been shocked at how the Black Dignity cause had slipped since the "revolution that never was." He'd decided it was time to "make waves," pushing a "Black Is Beautiful" campaign just before Carnival when for the first time in its history, both the Carnival queen and her runner-up were black. It wasn't surprising two black girls won. Jack saw to it that there were no white entrants.

Now with an election almost on top of them, Jack saw many opportunities for improvement. That is, if Williams really kept his word and retired. Although his father continued to believe the cunning, conniving chief minister, Jack doubted in his heart that he would go through with it.

Either way, whether Williams ran again or not, as Jack told his father, it wouldn't be long before the man toppled himself. Since his return he'd seen an enormous difference in the people's attitude. The fervor and zeal that had followed Williams's early triumph was flagging, broken by lack of organization, by the realization that despite their "positions of authority under the inspiring leadership of Dr. Williams," their own lives hadn't improved one iota.

On the contrary, most of them were making enormous sacrifices, working long hours for little pay, trying to get "out" of government and into the private sector in order to make enough to live on. The dream was well on the way to turning sour, and to Jack's surprise he'd found there really hadn't been any need for the attempted revolution! "Williams's own inefficiency will do him in . . ." Jack continually told his father. "It's time you got out from under, Pa. You may have the title of ambassador but what else? You don't have much money. You don't even have a car of your own!"

Roland hadn't answered—lost, Jack thought, in idealistic dreams of what still might be accomplished . . . but that was where he was so wrong. As Roland listened to his son's outpourings, he thought how ironic it was that everything Jack was saying he had been thinking himself for years—for every word Jack said was true.

Over the past few months, seeing a kind of malaise settle over Eric Williams, Roland had been capitalizing on his leader's often repeated weary phrase, "I'm not appreciated."

"No, you're not appreciated," Roland had told the prime minister only two hours before Jack's last harangue. It was all too easy to bring the people's criticism to Williams's notice. It was only too apparent, especially since Williams had had to take the unpopular step of penalizing any government official who tried to leave to find work in industry.

"Should I resign now—before the election?" Williams had started to ask Roland, whose quick response in the negative was subtly, craftily "tinged with regret" . . . with phrases like "It's a pity the people don't understand . . ." and "How can we get the people to realize your own sacrifices. . . ?"

Roland noted with satisfaction that every day sniping against Williams increased in the press—particularly in the *Trinidad Guardian*, the paper Williams accused of concealing his speeches, intimidating potential foreign investors and promoting U.S. and British propaganda.

Only the week before, to Roland's secret delight, Williams had taken the unprecedented step of calling a press conference to show himself cleaning his shoes with the *Guardian*, then publicly burning it.

Since the mysterious events at Teteron Bay when the "revolution" had been averted so peaceably, Roland had no longer trusted Luis or Williams. He seethed that he'd been kept in second place, although the reds *knew* he was recognized by the people, the only one able to rock Williams's government.

Now Roland schemed. As soon as Williams made his retirement announcement he would make his own move.

At 11:00 A.M., Roland received an urgent summons from Luis, rare enough to be obeyed instantly.

Although he raged inside, the meeting with Luis confirmed his belief that Williams really *was* playing a treacherous double game, in reality as much in cahoots with the Communists as he was with the Americans *and* the British, because Luis already *knew* about Williams's wish to retire although Roland hadn't said a word . . . and, worse, he *knew* Roland had nourished, indeed, encouraged Williams's wish.

Luis hissed, "It will be better for everyone but especially for *you* if you put all your energies into changing Dr. Williams's mind. We don't want him to retire, yet! Make him change his mind, or it will the worse for you!"

The announcement was retracted. It hadn't taken much time or effort to convince Williams there was no other man to do the job. Gritting his teeth, Roland entered into what he privately termed "the farce of an election," where at the last minute the proposed union between two groups to form a powerful opposition fell apart, so Williams's PNM ended up with no opposition at all, winning every seat.

Did Jack care?

"Not this year I don't," he told his father cheerfully. "I'm not ready. But I must warn you, Pa, I'm starting to work *now* with a group of young lawyers for the ' seventy-six election—and then, Pa, I'm afraid you must warn your boss to be prepared for defeat."

It had hurt to see Golden Hill again. The beautiful house of Margaret's memory looked so—so unloved, despite all that Obee tried to do. The shine wasn't the shine of the past; the driveway was pockmarked with holes, even the shrubbery had an uncared-for look.

"Mistr'ss Rose, ma'am, sh' say sh' don' wan' spen' nuttin' on de place. It's a pity, miss," Obee had explained dejectedly, sensing Margaret's unspoken shock and sadness.

Rose moved about the house like a ghost, giving Margaret a suffocating hug on her arrival, ignoring her since, talking to herself, stopping every few minutes on the stairway, in the hall, wherever she was to count the money in the purse that was now always with her.

"I'm afraid poor Granny Rose is really failing," Margaret said to Roger as they sat together on the veranda swing facing down the valley.

"Yes," Roger said tight-lipped. "It's a crime that she won't spend a cent on the house, which of course is her right. . . ."

"Can't I, Uncle? Can't I do something about it?"

"If you want to, my child, but perhaps we should wait. Rose hasn't got long for this earth. In another year, maybe less, Golden Hill will be all yours. Then you can decide exactly what you want to do with it."

"I *do* love it here after all," Margaret exclaimed as a hummingbird hovered in the air in front of them. "It's a paradise—at least during the day." She shuddered. "I don't like the nights. They come too fast—and they're too full of ghosts."

The next morning an invitation to a barbecue in Arima came from the Finches. Now that it had arrived, Margaret didn't want to go. "I liked the Tropica lady, Mrs. Finch—she seemed very friendly—but I don't want to be pushed into any . . ."

Margaret paused and Roger supplied the word—"relationship?"

"That's it."

"Why should you be? Don't worry about that. Tommy's at least a year younger than you, I'd say. I'm sure he'd run like a rabbit if he thought his mother was working on establishing any 'relationship' between you." Roger laughed.

"D'you want to go, Uncle Roger?"

Roger frowned. Did he? It probably meant seeing Magdalen Finch, and Paulette had said Theo was there, too. Did he want to accept their hospitality? He decided he did. It was for the best. "I think with the blacks in power, we must all stick together down here. It can't harm us. Let's at least take a look at their place. Perhaps on the way back they'll let you see Orange Grove, where they make all that Tropica perfume stuff I've read so much about."

The difference between the Arima plantation and the way Golden Hill looked now struck both Margaret and Roger forcibly as they drove along the driveway, with neat rows of cultivation on either side—from golden glowing grapefruit and orange groves, to mango trees to cocoa plantings. The beautifully landscaped drive was about two miles long now, as Theo and Magdalen had added piece by piece to the property, once a little oasis buried in a tangled tropical forest, but now stretching all the way to the main road in the northeast.

"It's so beautiful! This is how I remember Golden Hill looking . . . and now it's so shabby. We *must* do something about it. . . ." Margaret sighed.

Roger felt a burning sensation behind his eyes. The darling girl was falling in love with the place after all. Thank God. Golden Hill would be saved!

How he loved her. Today she looked so pretty, with her hair curling around her face, gold like her skin, which she told him with a mischievous look she'd exposed to the sun for the first time. "I was just hungry for it. It felt so good, so warming, but don't worry, I won't sunbathe again in a hurry. It is certainly as deceptive as my mother . . ."—Margaret hesitated for a moment, then went straight on—"as mother always used to warn me it is. Look how quickly I've changed color! I *must* have the right sort of genes!" She laughed again.

Roger still pinched himself at the change in Margaret, the references she made now to Drum and Alicia. There was still a frown, a questioning behind her eyes, but Daniel Siden had been able to bring to the surface the laughing gentle girl inside.

Now they could see the house, with its orderly lawns that were unbelievably green for the tropics. "Watering must go on here around the clock," Roger murmured.

"I feel nervous." Margaret searched for Roger's hand. "It's a bit like coming into enemy territory, isn't it, even though it looks so peaceful, so pastoral. Oh well, into battle we go, Uncle!"

Paulette gave them a wonderfully warm welcome, pressing Margaret to her as if she were a long-lost relation, scooping up the family's new pet, an adorable baby lamb, to put in her arms, before she rushed around introducing them to the other guests from plantations far and near.

Red and blue macaws, guinea parrots, brown-throated parakeets and black and violet creeper birds added their voices to the sound of a soft waterfall somewhere in the distance, while high overhead, looking as if it were flying straight into the surrounding mountains, an Antilles falcon ceremoniously dipped its wings.

"It's like being in heaven," Margaret whispered in an awed voice.

"And you look as if you belong here. . . . Are you an angel?" Margaret blushed as she turned to see the most handsome man she'd ever seen in her life—except, she said to herself, her own beloved father.

Could this be the enemy, the man who as a boy had helped the first Jack Bracken kill her grandfather?

At forty-five, Theo Finch still appeared unaware of his physical presence. He'd inherited all the good things from his parents—from his French father thick brown wavy hair, which he still wore a little longer than most men of his age, extraordinary vivid eyes, as blue as the Caribbean, Margaret thought, and lean, tensile strength showing in his wrists and shoulders. From his mother had come his strong features, which meant Magdalen had always been described more as a "handsome" woman than a "pretty" one.

With his blue shirt open at the neck, dark hair from his chest just showing through, if she'd been told Theo was a film star, Margaret decided, she would have believed it without question. . . .

Theo and Paulette's warm welcome more than made up for Magdalen's stony silence, for during the introductions she wheeled herself onto the veranda, having been told by a servant that Drum Pollard's daughter and half brother were actually on Finch property.

Roger, as courteous as ever, took Margaret over to introduce her to the "matriarch," as he now thought of Magdalen.

Only a fixed, set expression to her jaw gave any sign of the stroke that had come so viciously and unexpectedly the day following Matthew's attack, a stroke Magdalen had fought until now her speech was almost back to normal, although she no longer had enough mobility in her right side to be able to walk.

Excusing herself after a gruff "good afternoon" to both Pollards, she went into her room, her mind in turmoil, having seen Margaret's lovely face. The Pollard girl was not yet a woman, but she was no longer a child. Magdalen prayed with every bit of her being that Tommy wouldn't fall in love with her. "I want Golden Hill for him alone. I want the Pollards out, out, out," she said to a blue violet sky.

Tommy hardly said a word as he sat next to Margaret, stolidly munching down the delicious marinated steak and a salad of avocados, eggplant, Creole yams and spring lettuce. When Theo suggested he show their visitors around the estate he scuffed his feet awkwardly and asked if someone else could do it.

Paulette threw her arms boisterously around her son. "Oh, you're such an old shy boots, Tom Tom. Why don't you go? Can't you see Margaret wants *you* to be the guide?"

Theo groaned inwardly. Just the wrong thing to say to a shy young man, but the words were out and the damage was done as he saw Tommy's face turn the color of their best beets.

To take attention away from his blushing son, Theo picked up his cutlass beside the screen door and said, "All right. I'll do the boasting about this place—although my mother deserves most of the credit. Who wants to come with me?"

Sullenly Tommy tagged onto the end of the group of guests who followed Theo along a narrow wooded path leading to the waterfall and a crystal clear stream, which freshened the air and scent of every flower it touched.

Margaret couldn't remember enjoying herself more, and she joined the others singing "All Things Bright and Beautiful" and "Take Me Home, Country Roads." They must have walked about a mile, exclaiming over the luxuriant vegetation and exotic plants being grown specifically for Tropica, when the guests started to dawdle, idling along more and more slowly, picking flowers and ferns, feeling lazy after the delicious lunch and rum punches. Margaret rushed to keep up with Theo, who never slowed his stride as he made his way through the property as if he were truly the king of the forest.

Suddenly a loathsome smell, which hit with such force she felt sick to her stomach, made Margaret stop to hold on to the slender trunk of a mango tree. "What is it?" she cried.

Theo put up a warning hand telling her to stay where she was, but she crept forward to see what he could see and then froze with fear.

Asleep in a clearing ahead was a boa constrictor at least fifteen feet in length, its middle grotesquely swollen. Moving fast, Theo slashed his cutlass down to slit the snake's belly wide open at its fattest point where, to Margaret's horror, the matted carcass of a wild hog fell out, a hog, Theo told her, the snake had swallowed whole, to digest slowly over the next few weeks.

As Theo kicked the dead snake into the undergrowth, Margaret asked in a frightened little voice, "But what was that ghastly smell? I've never smelled anything like it. I thought I was going to faint."

"One of the most powerful smells in the world," Theo explained.

"The boa constrictor uses it to paralyze its quarry. . . ." He started to say something else, then stopped abruptly.

"What is it? Are you all right?"

"Yes, yes, I was just going to make a silly joke."

"Well, make it then. You see, I'm laughing already. . . ." A flush of color spread across his tanned face.

He was blushing like Tommy. Again she thought how appealing and attractive he was. How could this sensitive man have been her family's enemy?

He placed a hand on her shoulder, saying self-consciously, "I was just going to say we make perfumes for beautiful young ladies—like you—to use to trap *their* quarry, but not to paralyze them."

Margaret was enthralled. "Oh, do tell me more. It sounds fascinating."

He smiled at her enthusiasm. "In the perfume business we try to imitate nature. We're always striving to find natural 'attractants.' They do exist, you know."

They talked all the way back to the house, where Theo needed no persuading to take Margaret over to the Orange Grove plant on her way back to Maracas to show her how many of the tropical oils were extracted.

At the last moment, just as Margaret was about to get into the Tropica station wagon with the logo in large green letters on the side, a servant came to tell Theo his mother urgently needed to speak to him. "I won't be a second," he said, but it was several minutes before he returned, frowning. "My mother isn't feeling too well. If you don't mind, Margaret, let's do it another day—unless, Paulette, you could take Margaret over to the Grove?"

Paulette smiled graciously. "Of course I don't mind, but why doesn't Tommy do his stuff. He's got out of everything today. Come on, old man. Be a good host. . . ."

With poor grace Tommy ambled to his feet and was about to get behind the wheel of the car when Magdalen herself appeared on the veranda, looking agitated and upset.

She beckoned violently to Tommy, who sheepishly went over to hear her whispered message, before she abruptly wheeled herself inside again.

Tommy returned blushing again. "She wants me to say here." Tommy looked at his mother helplessly.

"Oh, well, I've got a better idea. Let's do the same thing we did today at Orange Grove next week." Paulette clapped her hands together like a child. "We'll have more time. None of us will feel so tired and Margaret, you can bring your notebook in case you learn something for your degree. . . ."

"What a wonderful, memorable day, Uncle Roger." Margaret felt sleepy as she curled up in the corner of the car on the way back to Maracas. "I must say I'm glad now we didn't go on to Orange Grove. I *am* tired, but it's funny how old Mrs. Finch suddenly didn't want anyone to leave her. I hope she's all right. . . ."

Roger smiled grimly. "Don't worry about her, pet. She's probably the toughest old bird you could find anywhere. I think she just had a touch of the 'apprehensions.'"

"What does that mean?" Margaret could hardly keep her eyes open. The sun, the food, the rum were all conspiring to send her to sleep.

"Oh, nothing for you to worry about."

"Well, that's good . . . good." She was asleep.

It was the beginning of many visits to Arima and to Tropica's Orange Grove estate when Margaret, knowing the agony of shyness herself, did everything she could to make Tommy feel at ease.

"I think it's all going to work out per-fect-ly," Paulette said to Theo after one of Margaret's visits.

"What is, darling?" Theo replied absent-mindedly. "What's perfect? The new tuberose plantings?"

"No, silly, Margaret and Tommy, of course. Didn't they look sweet together today. Did you see the way she smiled at him?"

"What d'you mean 'Margaret and Tommy'? They're children. What are you plotting, you rascal?"

Paulette smiled broadly. "They're not children, darling. They're grown-up, and don't you agree it would be wonderful if they . . . they fell in love and got married? Then Tommy and she would live at Golden Hill—just think of all that wonderful land for Tropica!" She giggled to make sure he realized that wasn't her main objective.

Theo had to laugh. "You're an amazing Machiavellian lady, Mrs. F. But I can't say I've noticed any 'falling in love' going on. In my opinion they're still children." He shut his eyes. As far as he was concerned it was ridiculous. He was prepared to grant Margaret Pollard was no longer a child, but despite her graceful air and intelligent conversation he sensed she was immature—what was she—twenty or twenty-one years old? She was delicate like a stripling, whereas Tommy was *really* wet behind the ears and would need a lot of shaking up before any woman would put up with him!

But just as Paulette had misinterpreted Margaret's attempt to put Tommy at ease, so had Tommy overreacted—to her smiles and responses.

The next week Tommy asked Paulette to lend him her car to take Margaret to the drive-in movie theater on the road between Orange Grove and Port of Spain. As he expected, his mother was thrilled with the idea. It was almost as if he'd suggested taking Princess Anne or Tricia Nixon! Mothers! What a pain they were.

Margaret hadn't sounded particularly enthusiastic when he'd suggested the movie on the phone, but when he told her Woody Allen's *Bananas* was showing, she'd agreed to go.

Tommy liked drive-ins, usually miles from anywhere, so it wasn't easy for a girl to leave in a huff if she got upset when he tried something. Drive-ins meant opportunities and not many disappointments.

But he was already disappointed when he picked Margaret up and saw she was wearing a straight-laced sheath dress with no sign of any cleavage and no buttons or zippers to open.

At first everything was fine. They held hands. He circled her palm with his finger a few times, which should have told her what was on his mind, and she never once took it away. It was only when he started stroking her knee that she started to move to one side. That was all right, too. He didn't want anything too quickly—but she wasn't cooperating. She kept twitching and moving farther away until she was right up against the door.

There was nothing for it but a major move. He reached over and pulled her roughly to him, keeping one hand on her shoulder while, quick as a flash, he covered her full bosom with the other. Before he knew what was happening she'd slammed her handbag into his face, cutting his eye open.

God, he had blood running down his face! The girl was crazy! She was trying to kill him! He clutched his face, not attempting to stop her as she opened the car door and went running out to the main road.

Zombie, crazy bloody zombie! He was half blinded with blood.

I'll get even with her if it's the last thing I do, he told himself later, as, with dried blood encrusting his eye, he drove back to Orange Grove, waiting until he saw the light go off in his parents' room before creeping into his own room to try to patch himself up.

The next time Paulette suggested inviting Margaret over, he let out such a yelp of protest that she clapped her hands over her ears in mock terror.

"What on earth did she do to you, darling?" Red-faced, Tommy stalked out of the room, slamming the door behind him.

That night she recounted the incident to Theo. "I think they've had a lovers' tiff, but I don't care. I'm going to invite her over again anyway. They'll soon make up."

But Margaret was "otherwise engaged."

"I'd love to see you back in the States sometime," she told Paulette carefully over the phone. "In fact, after I've graduated could I come and talk to you about Tropica? I admire what you've done so much. I'd really appreciate your advice on what I'm going to do."

"Oh, thank you, Margaret!" Paulette cried. "Hold on. I'll let you talk to the business brain, my husband. He'll tell you what to do."

Margaret felt strangely shy, hearing Theo's voice. Again she repeated how much she'd like to learn more about Tropica—that she wasn't sure what she was going to do after college. "I can't help thinking it could be something in the beauty area. I've always loved perfume and . . ."—she laughed self-consciously—"obviously all the kinds of things girls love—creams, lotions, potions. Ever since you told me about the fragrance business, I've been thinking how much I'd love to be involved."

Theo said abruptly, "Would you like an apprenticeship?"

"Really! You mean it?" Her heartbeat quickened. "I can't think of anything more wonderful in the world."

"Get your degree. Then give me a call—probably at the New York office. Miss Shooter's my secretary. Tell her I've told you to call. She'll set up an appointment and we'll work it out. It's not *all* fun and games you know, but . . ."—his voice softened—"it *almost* is for anyone who has a real feel for the business—and I believe *you* may well have a 'nose' for it, too."

Margaret laughed excitedly. "Oh, how wonderful. Thank you so much. I can't wait. You really mean it?"

"I mean it." Theo paused, then said quickly, "You may have a 'nose' for finding just the scent to trap your quarry. . . ."

Nanette
1972

FROM habit Nanette stroked the small stub remaining of the funny chestnut-colored lipstick over her eyelids and cheeks, adding a smidgen to the end of her nose (she'd been taught a darker shade there "shortened" it just the necessary amount), finishing her make-up, as she always did, with a smear of Vaseline petroleum jelly over her lips.

Jack had teased her when he'd seen her sitting at their own dressing table for the first time, just as she was sitting now, naked, making purposeful strokes on her face, sometimes adding a trace of glittering gold powder at night, quickly transforming good looks into extraordinary looks.

"You're certainly not going to be very expensive to keep," he'd said six months ago, kissing her shoulder and grabbing the chestnut-colored lipstick to circle her areolas, leaving her nipples bare because "it's more erotic that way."

She hadn't turned up for what was to have been her first modeling assignment in Port of Spain that morning, and he hadn't kept his appointment with his father either. An appointment, he'd told her more than once, that was important because it involved his cousin Matthew being transferred to an "open" prison for first offenders and those on their way to rehabilitation . . . but apparently it hadn't been so important after all.

Sitting awkwardly, her legs slightly apart and showing her black bush of hair, she'd turned to look at Jack, who'd thrown his hands in the air as if in exasperation—and they'd spent the rest of the day in bed.

Tears of self-pity streaked the cheekbones she'd just contoured so expertly. She didn't bother to pat the streaks away. She didn't know why she'd even bothered to make up at all.

There was only one way for her to be able to steal into the shadows, to merge anonymously with the crowd and disappear without everyone knowing where she'd disappeared to—and that was when she left the funny chestnut color off!

She'd been taught in Paris how to make the most of her face, and that was the trouble—she'd been making up out of habit ever since. Without that one piece of make-up, Nanette considered herself "ordinary" even if nobody else did—and she knew she automatically became what her own brain told her!

Was she really going to run away today? The tears fell faster as she asked herself the question, knowing full well the airline ticket was hidden under the pink sheets in the linen cupboard.

Since Roland, her future father-in-law, the impressive ambassador himself, had told her smilingly he was going to turn their wedding into such a fantastic occasion, inviting guests from far and near and as many dignitaries "as the Country Club can hold, m'dear" she couldn't remember sleeping a wink. And now the wedding day was only weeks away. The truth she'd have to face was coming nearer.

If only she'd told Jack the truth from the beginning, but when was the beginning? She'd never been able to work it out, for it was only in the last month or so that life had stopped being blurred—as the whole of the previous year had been blurred, with only Jack's fierce and unexpected devotion surfacing toward the end like a buoy in a hopelessly foggy sea, a buoy she'd finally turned to cling to, knowing it was her last chance before she sank out of sight.

Nanette went to the window to stare down at the savannah below, as dry as a boneyard. It had been a brilliant green when they'd moved into the apartment in the rainy season, as green and as promising as a badge of fresh courage to look out on every day. It was appropriate that it was so dry, barren and sad looking on the day she'd decided to leave. Jack had told her only the evening before that she had to be prepared for *more* of a public life, not less. At that moment she'd known she would have to use the ticket as soon as possible.

It was a perfect day to run away. Jack was conducting a special symposium at the Council of Legal Education; then he was dashing home to pick her up to attend a reception for Derek Walcott. "The finest poet in the Caribbean," he'd told her, who like Jack had received a fellowship from an American university and also like Jack had been invited to teach in many parts of the world.

Jack had tried to make her interested in Walcott's poetry, just as he'd tried to make her understand so many things she wasn't ready for.

Now she restlessly picked up a copy of "The Train," a poem Jack had expressly asked her to read before meeting Walcott that evening.

> *Where was my randy white grandsire from?*
> *He left here a century ago*
> *to found his "farm,"*
> *and, like a thousand others,*
> *drunkenly seed their archipelago . . .*

She was sure Walcott knew where his white grandsire was from. She knew he had not one, but two white grandfathers, and bright blue eyes shone out from his own black face.

Just like Jack, Walcott's relations were a multicolored lot; perhaps that was why Jack liked him so much.

Nanette shuddered. Color. It had always been the biggest stumbling block of her life. If it hadn't been for her relentless blackness, her mother had told her since she was a little girl, so many things would have been different.

Not that her mother had ever said it accusingly or even unkindly. How could she—although she herself was far lighter skinned—but whichever way she'd chosen to say it—repeatedly—it had rankled, until out of the blue had come the amazing French Prince Charming of a photographer to whisk her away at last from "what might have been" to "what was going to be." As he had described it to both mother and daughter, it was going to be a life of fantastic excitement and luxury in Paris, where her very blackness would, incredibly, be an asset, not a disadvantage.

She'd known from the beginning it wasn't her blackness alone; that it was because her color went with the most "divine *derrière* I 'ave ever seen, *ma petite* . . . and as for those legs! Oh la la!"

Nanette threw on a cotton robe to cover her breasts. She'd never understood what made her body so special. She'd always worried she was too thin, too gawky, too tall. But she'd known how to move—"like a lizard" a beach boy had once described it, and she'd remembered that description, always moving lightning fast, unerringly, with extraordinary slinkiness.

Jack had told her that morning she had to help his mother, Emerald, with the lunch she was giving for ambassadors' wives, and now Nanette went to the cupboard to sort through her clothes, almost as if she were going to attend the lunch.

She was playing a game, she knew, playing for time, saying to herself that if the ruffled suit came back from the cleaners that morning as promised, then perhaps she'd go to the lunch and leave on the plane tomorrow or the day after. But she knew it was just a game.

The next day was not a good day to run away. There was a visiting professor from Harvard whom Jack wanted to charm, and her obligatory appearance as a "top model" to aid one of the prime minister's pet charities. No, tomorrow would not do.

The sight of the rumpled unmade bed, where last night they'd made such beautiful love, started her tears anew, and bleakly she started to pack a few things into the bag she'd brought with her on the flight to a new life the year before.

She had to get out of Jack's life, his brilliant life set on a steady course to success, before her past caught up and obliterated both of them.

She hadn't told Jack about Becky's letter. He'd have been furious to know Becky was writing to her at all, because Jack, she knew, considered Becky a lightweight who had deserted her at her time of need. Perhaps Becky *was* a lightweight, but she usually knew the score. The warning Becky had sent, coupled with her own guilt at not telling Jack the truth, had finally made up Nanette's mind to cut out.

Hadn't she always been told it was better to amputate, to cut off a relationship than let it rot away? She'd had enough experience of rot setting in. As she'd said before to Becky and Jack, she was jinxed. There was something about her that spoiled things.

As quickly as she'd applied the make-up, now she removed it, until her black skin shone with grease, devoid of any color. Now she was "ordinary," easily lost in a crowd, just like any other tall, skinny, black girl. Curiously this was the way Charles had always liked her best—even though it was Charles, the French photographer, who'd taught her in the first place how to use make-up to increase the size of her eyes, make her cheekbones more prominent and her mouth more sensual.

Charles. She'd hardly thought of him in years—the self-styled "professor," who from the moment he'd set eyes on her had set about changing her, insisting she strap her already tiny breasts flat to her body. He "detested women with fat breasts" he said. He'd taken her to Alexandre to have her hair cropped like a boy's, an inch long all over her head. He'd chosen her clothes, made her up and photographed her for *French Vogue, Elle* and *Marie France*. Then, to her bewilderment, just when she'd felt she was at last becoming "chic" and so more appealing to Charles, he'd announced he was sending her to America.

She could still remember the emphatic note in his voice as he'd told her, "I am . . . what is the word . . . 'loaning' you to *mon ami*, an American, a good photographer, not so good as me, but good. He did me a good turn once. Now I am glad to do one for him."

Her tears and pleas to stay had made no difference.

Charles had been adamant and although he'd casually told her he would bring her back "in a month or so" she'd known their relationship was over—that in six short months, although she'd done everything he'd asked her to, he was tired of her.

She'd tried to run away that time too—for such a different reason, but Charles had found out and Charles Marinois was particularly proud of the fact he never let his friends down. He'd promised the black girl to l'Americain, Tony Basser, after Tony had admired her one night in a bistro, and he would deliver the goods or else!

Was it then things had started to become blurred? Nanette had been in a daze, finding herself on an Air France plane bound for Kennedy, Charles having slipped a dose of tranquilizer into her breakfast coffee. He had taken her to the airport where, with the help of an airline stewardess, she'd apparently arrived at the plane in a wheelchair, to be helped aboard suffering from a "severely strained back."

By the time her head cleared, she'd been sitting in a yellow cab with Tony Basser rocking her back and forth like a baby, crooning "Lucy in the Sky with Diamonds" as his hands explored her in the darkness.

Tony Basser had been kinder than Charles, but Nanette had soon found out he was just as kinky in his own way. He'd installed her in his SoHo loft, photographed her day and night for the first few days, then shown her off around town, when just as he'd expected, she was spotted by a Ford talent scout, signed and—whoosh—she was off.

It hadn't occurred to her that this was the way she could become rich and independent. "Tony's looking after all that . . ." she would tell the few model friends who bothered to ask how she was doing. As Tony had instructed, and she had had no reason not to acquiesce, Ford reluctantly sent all her checks to Tony because "He's investing it for me . . ." she'd said, happy at twenty not to have to worry about a confusing subject like money. He'd given her "pocket money" to get her to and from sittings and shows, and, looking back, she remembered she'd been quite happy in a way.

As her services became more in demand, she also remembered how other models had gone out of their way to tell her she was being "used" . . . that "Tony Basser's no good, babe. Please let me introduce you to my accountant . . . to my lawyer. . . ."

But she hadn't wanted to change things. He'd been sweet to her at first, and when he began to change, his "moods"—as she'd called them—had only lasted a few days. Then he'd turned into a master, snarling she was his "goddamn black slave woman," insisting she stay naked around the house, kneeling to him as she served his meals.

Sometimes when he asked friends over for a drink or dinner, she wasn't allowed to put her clothes back on either, but would have to "serve" them the same way—providing Tony gave the orders. If anyone else asked her for anything—even an extra piece of ice for a drink—he or she was out, never to be asked back.

It had taken Nanette a long time to connect Tony's moods to an increasing dependence on drugs, "the habit" that had finally led to the terrible day when once again she'd discovered she was going to be part of a barter deal, a far more deadly one than the "exchange of favors" with Charles Marinois.

This time she was being exchanged for a guaranteed regular supply of top-quality heroin, which at the rate Tony was slipping, wouldn't be required for very long. Everyone in the world of photographers and models talked about her in nervous whispers, about the amazing black model who'd made it to the covers of America's most prestigious magazines, the crazy, sweet but incredibly naive black girl whose career would soon grind to a terrifying halt, unless somebody rescued her from the clutches of Big Man. And somebody had. Jack—Jack Bracken, the boy wonder.

Nanette shook herself mentally. Now she had to do her own "deal"; she had to leave Jack before Big Man sent one of his lackeys to ferret them out and exact his usual form of vengeance—for Becky had written "Big Man's moving up in the world. He's linked up with Joe Gallo, said to be the real boss in town with contacts in his pay all the way to the Caribbean and Caracas. Big Man's vowed to get even with you both. *Please* be careful!"

She was gone. In disbelief, Jack read the short note Nanette had left. It was as if someone had delivered a brutal blow to his stomach. He could feel real pain tearing him apart. He stumbled out to the little terrace of the apartment, staring down at the barren park as Nanette had done hours before.

It was impossible. Why? He rushed to the cupboard to sort through her clothes, her flimsy dresses—pink, green, white, beige. He saw all the clothes he'd bought for her were still there. She hadn't taken one thing he'd bought. He bit his lip in an effort to stop angry sobs from breaking out. That she'd left behind the clothes he'd bought for her increased his pain.

Something had happened to frighten her—but what? Had there been threats she'd never mentioned?

Had she been hiding information from him? Had he missed obvious signals? He felt like a sleepwalker as he emptied the wastepaper basket for clues, finding two other notes she'd written to him, only to tear up, both similar to the one he still held with trembling fingers. "I love you, Jack." The words were a mockery. If she loved him, how could she demolish him like this? ". . . But I'm not good enough for you. It's better I go away before something terrible happens."

He went back out to the terrace to smoke his pipe, trying to think of where she might have gone. He knew she wouldn't risk going back to the States, but she'd been to Venezuela on one modeling job since her arrival. Could she have found someone else in Caracas? Surely not. He remembered last night. He couldn't believe she had anyone else. Their bodies moved in perfect unison, she'd said so herself, although often—too often, he thought now—she'd also said how much she wished their minds could move on the same level too.

Had he frightened her with his talk of intellectuals like Walcott, with lunches for ambassadors' wives, with the correct kind of clothes for the wife-to-be of Mr. Jack Bracken, the up-and-coming young liberal lawyer with such excellent connections?

He was ashamed to let anyone know she'd gone, but he *had* to have help. He'd go out of his mind trying to work out where she might be on his own.

He called the heads of Pan American, Viasa, BWIA. Had Nanette Henry left on any of their flights . . . to Caracas or any other place? In a few hours he had the answers. Nobody of that name had flown out of Trinidad that day. He checked on sailings. Nothing. He called the chief of police.

Finally he decided he had to call on his father. Roland had never seen Jack in such a state. He offered him a glass of brandy but nothing seemed to calm him down. The more he spoke of the girl, the more he seemed to lose control.

It didn't help to talk about "other fish in the sea" or make other trite remarks. It made Roland realize how madly Jack must love the girl, for he'd thought Jack could have any girl he wanted, particularly a gawky one like Nanette. Roland had never been able to understand how she'd made it as a top model, and in America of all places!

After days of nonstop checking, Jack was no further ahead. He'd established that no one called Nanette Henry had booked a passage anywhere out of Trinidad. Could she still be on the island, and if so with whom? Whom had she been particularly friendly with?

No one—and it had bothered him that Nanette was so aloof, so unapproachable. "I'm really shy," she'd told him. She couldn't understand why, with her reputation as a top New York model and her habit of staring into space saying nothing, the local people, her contemporaries, thought she was stuck up, while older people thought she was "weird."

It hadn't bothered her. "I only want you," she would whisper, her touch making him forget everything else. How hollow that phrase rang in his mind as days and then weeks passed without a trace of her. He had made up his mind to return to New York to shadow Big Man once again, when the maid, who only turned up when she felt like it, came in unexpectedly to clean out the cupboard and silently handed him a crumpled up schedule from the interisland airline LIAT that she'd found tucked away between the folds of a pillow case.

Nanette had marked it with three little red checks for different times and days of the week, but the destination was the same. Martinique.

Why Martinique? Now Jack remembered Nanette telling him that was where she'd first been spotted, five years before, by the French photographer, who'd taken her to Paris. Was she hoping to be discovered all over again? What did it all mean?

He kicked himself as he reflected how little he had ever asked her about her early life before Big Man. He'd put his head in the sand, not wanting to learn any more "sick" details. He was also beginning to realize he had taken her far too much for granted, tucking her under his wing safe and sound in Trinidad without thinking of how she might be feeling.

He asked himself now why had she been in Martinique five years before? He vaguely remembered her saying she had been on vacation there with her mother, whom she'd fallen out with and hadn't been in touch with since her arrival in New York. Jack reproached himself bitterly, remembering how easily he'd accepted her firm no when he'd suggested she ought to make up with her mother and invite her to their wedding. He hadn't been interested in her mother. He'd been obsessed with Nanette and no one else.

Now his mind was feverish with questions. Where was the mother from? More important, where was Nanette from originally?

He could suddenly hear his New York friend, Will Tollor, as he'd attempted to sound uninterested while trying to answer his frantic questions that night in the house on Long Island.

"She comes from France. She was Tony Basser's girl—until she became part of a deal he made with Big Man."

France. Suddenly it began to make sense. She must have come from that special part of France several thousand miles away from the Champs Elysées . . . Martinique!

How many opportunities he'd let slip, he told himself, when it would have been so easy to pin her down. He'd liked the fact she was an "orphan by design"—as he'd teased her—pointing out he'd had so much trouble with relations all his life, it was refreshing not to load his life up with any more—refreshing, until she'd disappeared into thin air as completely as smoke from a sugarcane fire.

"If you're determined to go there, at least look up cousin Sam and Gloria, won't you?" his father said reprovingly. Roland was no longer sure he wanted Jack to find Nanette, let alone marry her, a girl who was so unstable, unreliable, who'd already caused premature furrows of worry on his son's face.

Jack frowned at his father's suggestion, but Roland went on. "I feel guilty about them. I was about to invite them to your wedding, because we haven't been in touch for so long. It's terrible how easy it is to lose touch, but then our worlds hardly ever did touch. Jack, they *are* a good pair! I would appreciate it if you'd meet them and give them my best. You've never been in Martinique, have you? Well, then, they may be helpful." Roland put a hand on his son's arm. "You mustn't be disappointed if there's no trace of her. Just because she checked off some flights on an airline schedule, remember there hasn't been anyone of her name on any flight out of this island since you first reported her disappearance."

"It's the only clue I've found," Jack said sharply. "I've got to follow it up. I'll do my best to look up your cousin, Dad, but I can't promise. Don't think I've ever met him and his family, have I? Well, not since I was a kid—and frankly I'm not in the mood for a family reunion."

Jack hadn't been able to eat or sleep properly since Nanette had left. If he'd thought he had his feelings for her under control, her disappearing act had certainly proved how wrong he was. Why, why, *why* had she gone? The same fruitless question tormented him as the small plane hopped, skipped and jumped between the islands, taking all day to cover the few hundred miles separating Trinidad in the south from Martinique to the northeast.

The plane slipped over the hills, as the setting sun turned them a vivid orchid pink. Jack felt tears pricking the back of his eyes. He couldn't believe Nanette would go out of her way to hurt him so deeply. There had to be a sinister reason behind it, and he felt panic rise— sensing Big Man had to be involved.

As a taxi took him to his hotel, he decided he would call on Gloria and Sam Bracken after he'd made all his inquiries. He felt too emotionally worn out to see *anyone*, let alone relations he wouldn't recognize and cared less about, but he'd promised his father, so he had to make some sort of contact.

After he'd checked in, Jack had a quick shower, then called a contact of the Trinidad chief of police to get a list of all the discos and beach bars on the island. He spent until nearly dawn going from one to another, asking if anyone had heard of a young black model called Nanette Henry, showing the pictures he always carried with him, one where she'd been made up for a *Cosmopolitan* sitting, another he'd taken himself when she was sitting on the terrace of their small apartment without a scrap of make-up on. Nobody seemed to have heard of or seen anyone like her, although everyone said something like, "Man, we only wish we had!"

All next day and the next Jack combed the beach bars, the hotels, the duty-free shops, the quayside cafés, where he quickly found more French was spoken than English and sometimes a curious combination of both. He asked questions until he was hoarse and showed the pictures until they were tattered, but he got nowhere.

Dispirited, physically and emotionally worn out, he was lying on his bed when the phone rang about 8:00 A.M. the third day after his arrival.

"Jack?" an unfamiliar female voice asked.

"Yes?" His spirits sank lower as he guessed, correctly, that it had to be Gloria Bracken. Obviously his father hadn't trusted him to get in touch, and his father had probably been right.

Jack tried to be polite for his father's sake, but he was desperate to get out of the invitation he sensed was coming, to pretend he wasn't feeling well but . . . this woman, he thought irritably, is just too damned tenacious. "I have a surprise for you," she said at the end of their conversation. "Someone to cheer you up."

"Who?" He couldn't have cared less about the answer. There was no one Gloria Bracken could provide who would make the slightest difference to his life.

"My daughter," the woman went on. She seemed oblivious to the curt note in his voice. "It's a lucky coincidence you've come, because she knows so few young people of her age. . . ." She rattled on as Jack watched the smoke from his pipe rise to hang over his head in a gloomy cloud.

At noon he stood outside the hotel, a miserable expression on his face, knowing that, however hard he tried, he wasn't going to be able to exert any charm.

A loud horn honking announced Sam's arrival and Jack jumped into a Mini-Moke to discover his father's cousin was a fast and fearless driver. Perhaps foolhardy might be a better description, Jack thought after a few minutes, as the Moke turned round corners on one wheel, screeching as the bends became more and more hairpin.

Gloria was waiting at the door to meet them, looking almost as depressed as Jack felt he must look himself. To his amazement as he went through the motion of kissing her hello, she burst into tears.

"What's wrong? What's happened?" He felt he had to ask the questions, although the woman's tears surely had nothing to do with him. In his anxious state every tear that fell seemed to echo impending doom.

Sam jumped out of the car to rush over to his wife, asking the same questions.

"It's Naomi. . . ." Gloria almost choked. "When I tol' her we had a surprise for her, dat Roland's son Jack was arrivin', sh' . . . just wen' wild, berserk. She wen' runnin' down de mountainside like a crazy person."

"Naomi? You mean your daughter?" Jack looked at the woman, noticing despite her misery that if it weren't for the tears staining her features, Gloria Bracken was a very pretty woman.

He followed her into a well-furnished living room, the sea sparkling far below, a soft wind touching the tops of the tamarind trees on the hillside.

"Naomi. . . ." He repeated the name, as his gaze came to rest on a large photograph on the piano. "Naomi. . . ." There was a rush of blood pounding in his ears; the room was reeling. For the first time in his life Jack understood what it felt like to faint. He fell forward, hitting his forehead on the side of the piano, a spurt of blood shooting up like a fountain. In seconds he had regained consciousness, but blood gushed out of a nasty cut over his temple.

Looking back on his first meeting with Gloria and Sam Bracken, Jack often recounted the sequence of events in a way that had his audience rocking with laughter, but then it hadn't been funny. It hadn't been funny at all.

As he sat in the bathroom and Gloria tried to patch up his wound, he took the tattered pictures of Nanette out of his pocket. Gloria backed away in alarm. "I don' understand? Is dis yo' fiancée, de one yo' father tol' us 'bout who's missin'? But sh' looks lik' . . ."

"But she *is!*" Jack was crying but he didn't care, his tears mixing with the blood that still trickled down his face. "My fiancée Nanette *is* your daughter Naomi. I don't understand it either, but I'm going to find out what it's all about. . . . Which way did she go?"

"I'm here."

She stood in the doorway, disheveled, if possible even thinner than when he'd first set eyes on her that summer evening almost two years before.

No wonder nobody had noticed any "stunning new model" around town, Jack found himself thinking. Nanette—Naomi—whichever name she was using—looked like a waif and a stray. Her hair, always methodically straightened, was looking, well, almost woolly, and with no make-up on she looked no more than twelve—thirteen at the most. She was also wearing what had to be the ugliest, most sloppy-looking pinafore dress Jack had ever seen.

Gloria rushed over to her daughter, trying to clasp her in her arms. "What's all dis 'bout, Naomi? I don' understand."

The girl moved away from her mother, tears pouring down her face, unable to speak, staring at Jack, her eyes wide, frightened, as if she weren't sure it was really the man she'd grown to know and love.

He held the towel soaked in blood to his head, trying to take control of the situation. "Can you leave us, Gloria, for a few minutes? Then you'll have all the explanations in the world."

"Well, young man, don' yo' t'ink we should get yo' t' a hospital first?" Sam had come up behind Naomi and tried to match the note of authority in Jack's voice.

Naomi saw for the first time that Jack was hurt. Her stiffness and tense awkward stance in the doorway disappeared and she rushed over to him. "I didn't know. . . . Oh, my darlin', my darlin', what's happened? What's happened?"

Jack allowed her to lead him to a little outbuilding at the end of the garden where she'd been staying. "Nanette, why?" he asked over and over again.

"Not now. Let me fix you up." She bathed his wound, which at last stopped bleeding, and she wrapped his head with a bandage that made him look so woebegone the tears started all over again. "Oh, Jack, Jack—I've been trying to get over you, to forget you—but—I don't think I'll ever be able to."

"But why should you?" He held her to him, skin and bone, trying to press her body into his flesh, not even aware in his desperation how much he was bruising her. She herself pressed closer, wanting to be one with him, wanting the bruises, the marks of his hands on her skin, knowing the minute she'd seen him she could never be apart from him again. If Big Man found them, they'd at least die in each other's arms. "Oh, Jack. . . ."

They tore at each other's clothes, not caring who might see them through the unscreened entrance. They were two bodies desperate for each other, clinging closer, each movement made out of past torment.

The few minutes Jack had asked for stretched to hours—to twenty-four hours—as again and again they restated their love, their need for each other, and Jack made her realize the agony he'd experienced since her disappearance. Even his anger, when she told him about Becky's letter with the warning about Big Man, quickly evaporated as her hands and mouth begged him to forgive her for her lack of faith in him.

It was only when the sun began to set for the second time since his arrival at the house that Jack realized he was hungry. He was about to chide Nanette—as he still called her—for not suggesting they eat, when in the middle of a sentence he stopped himself. "We have a lot to say to each other. A lot of understanding to do, but tell me, did you also run away because I was always lecturing you on what to eat, to wear, to say, to do? Did it all make you feel you didn't love me after all?"

His earnest expression made Naomi laugh for the first time in weeks. "Oh, darlin', no. I love to learn from you, to do whatever you tell me to do—that's my nature, I can't change. I *wanted* to learn." Her expression darkened. "It wasn't only Big Man's threats that made me feel I had to leave, to protect you. Even *now* you know Gloria's my mother, don't you know who I really am?"

Jack frowned. "I don't understand. I know you're not Sam's daughter. My father told me just before I left that Sam only married your mother a few years back. I don't understand a lot of things—why you changed your name from Naomi to Nanette Henry, or why you never told me your stepfather was a distant relation of mine. But what does that matter?" He nuzzled her cheek. "He's your stepfather—there's no blood relationship, but even if there was, everyone's a little bit related to ev-eryone else in the Caribbean, darling. That's nothing to worry about."

He felt her tense as he spoke, but before he could say more, Gloria's voice came from the doorway, a cool, assured voice, so different from that of the distraught creature who had welcomed him the day before.

"I've bin askin' myself so many questions since yo' arrived, Jack," she said, giving no indication of surprise or embarrassment at the sight of them lying together on the single bed without even a sheet to cover their nakedness.

Jack tried to appear at ease, but he felt distinctly at a disadvantage. "Can't we meet to talk everything out later? Give us a few minutes to get tidied up."

"Jack, I can' let ev'n another minute pass!" Gloria cried passionately. "I wan' yo' t' know what Naomi has obviously *still* not tol' yo' from what I just overheard. Her father, Jack, was my lover when I was very young. He was . . . was . . . Drum Pollard." She went on quickly, as if determined to get the facts out at all costs. "Dat means, of course, dere *is* a blood relationship b'tween yo'. Drum was yo' first cousin, an' Naomi an' yo' are second cousins. . . ." A sympathetic look crossed her face. "I didn' mean t' shock yo', but I t'ink yo' should have known dis at de beginnin'. It'll perhaps make yo' understan' t'ings 'bout Naomi dat she'll nev'r tell yo' herself."

Naomi crouched back against the headboard, defiant, looking as if she were about to contradict her mother, but then thought better of it.

Jack's thoughts were in turmoil. Why had his father never told him? But then why *should* he have told him? His father had no idea that Nanette Henry was, in fact, Naomi Simpson, Gloria's daughter.

After his initial stunned reaction, Jack felt a slow anger build in him. No wonder "Nanette" had always been so nervous, not knowing where she fitted in.

In the minutes after Gloria left them alone, Naomi, still miserable and depressed, whispered to him about the shame she'd always been made to feel about her color. She cried she was sure her mother had never *meant* to hurt her, to make her feel unworthy. But until Gloria married Sam with her constant sighing and expressions of regret over "what might have been"—Naomi pressed her face into Jack's bare shoulder and said, "I was completely demoralized. Isn't that the right word?—until Charles came and took me away. Then when I got to the States, the first thing Ford told me I had to do was change my name! Because there was already a famous black model called Naomi Sims! It would have been a joke to have a Naomi Simpson! Ford chose Nanette and I chose Henry—after Henry Street, where Mother used to work in a beautiful house full of Chinese antiques. You'd have loved it." She looked wistfully at Jack, longing for his approval.

As she spoke of her feelings of inferiority, her unhappiness, her acceptance even of the "slave-girl role," Jack smoldered. He was going to give this beautiful girl her right identity. One day the world would know who she was—who she *really* was.

They washed and dressed and found Gloria busy in the kitchen. She told them she wanted to wait until Sam had gone to work the next morning before they had what she called their "family conference."

She explained, "It's not dat Sam doesn' know now Naomi's Drum's daughter. At first I refused t' tell him, but after Drum's death dere wasn' any reason any more for him not t' know." She gave them a wide, beautiful smile. "We're so happy, Sam an' me, an' he's so good t' me, I didn' want any more secrets between us. All de same, I t'ink Sam might be embarrassed t' hear me speak 'bout Drum wid yo' here, Jack. Even though . . ."—Gloria shot him an arch look—"yo're obviously goin' t' become ev'n more of a member of de family!"

Jack was bursting with questions, but he contained himself, trying to make conversation during what Gloria called their "celebration dinner" of baked crab and a special orange soufflé that she told him proudly she'd learned to prepare at a "real French cookin' school jest opened in Fort de France."

The next morning the three of them settled down on the veranda to talk, Jack so totally recovered from his depression that it was as if the Jack of two days ago had never existed. He asked a barrage of questions, quickly making notes, until Gloria sat back half amused, half alarmed. "What are yo' up t' Jack? I feel as if I'm in a court o' law or somethin'. What 'xactly are yo' gettin at? Drum was very decent t' me. I receive an allowance from some stocks he invested in for me. It isn' worth so much t'day, but nobody can help dat!"

"What was Naomi left in Drum's will?"

Jack's question stunned Gloria for a second. She shook her head slowly. "Why . . . nuttin', but I expect'd nuttin'. Dat was our arrangement. Nobody was ev'r t' know Naomi was his daughter. I gave him my word and 'til his death I kept it. I don' intend t' shout de truth from de rooftops now. Dere's no need."

"Oh, but perhaps there is a need, Gloria. Perhaps there is a very definite need."

Gloria began to feel nervous. What was this strange, indignant young man thinking up? First her daughter had returned out of the blue, saying she was finished with the glossy New York world, that she was sorry for her past behavior, that she'd decided to settle down and spend a couple of years quietly with her mother. There had been no word about a boyfriend, let alone a fiancé bearing the Bracken name!

Gloria had suspected a man had to be behind Naomi's strange reappearance, the sobs she'd heard coming from the garden outbuilding, and the way she'd let her looks slide, not caring what she wore, hardly bothering to comb the hair she'd once been so meticulous about. But Gloria thought her daughter had been thrown over—probably by a white man—as she had been thrown over by Drum. She'd never expected what was really behind everything—and she could still hardly understand how any girl could leave a man who so obviously adored her.

The events of the past week had all been too much and Gloria felt stirrings of fear. It seemed Jack Bracken had something on his mind. Something Gloria knew she wasn't going to approve of at all.

Quickly, to change the subject, Gloria said, "I don' wan' t' talk 'bout it any more. I just want t' say dat Rose—Drum's mother—was always kind t' us. She sent 'long a few checks t' help out—'til Alicia, Drum's wife, found out we'd arranged t' meet 'again for de last time. I often t'ink Rose must have got most of de blame for dat, 'cause I never heard from her 'gain, but I can' help t'inkin' she'll leave somethin' t' Naomi in *her* will. . . ."

"Rubbish!" Jack's incisive tone sliced across her soft, sentimental rumblings like a knife through butter. "Why should a senile old woman remember you, when her supposedly 'brilliant' son did not and had no intention of doing so? It's a disgrace." Jack's tone was bitterly sarcastic, as he jumped up to put an arm protectively around Naomi's thin shoulders. "You've both been treated like outcasts—and Naomi, my darling Naomi, well, she's suffered all these years because of that treatment. Suffered more than you'll ever understand, Gloria," he added pointedly.

Now Gloria jumped up in agitation. "Don' say dat, Jack. You weren' dere. You don' understan' dose years. It's different now. Den color was a mark 'gainst yo'. It would have harmed Drum's career." Tears started to fall down her face again, and it was as if the salt in the tears could break through her soft flesh, aging her instantaneously.

As Gloria spoke, Jack's rage mounted. If Naomi's mother was complacent and indifferent to the cavalier treatment she'd received, well, that was her funeral. As Naomi's fiancé and soon-to-be husband, he would see that his beloved wife, as black and as beautiful as any woman could be, would never, *never* suffer again because of the color of her glorious silky skin.

Now Jack spoke quickly, firmly, stroking first Naomi's arm, her shoulder, then her bosom, his eyes never leaving Gloria's frightened face. "It can be viewed as unconstitutional today for a white legitimate child to inherit all, while a black illegitimate child receives nothing." He boldly covered Naomi's slight bosom, the movement illustrating to Gloria, as it was meant to do, his total mastery over her. He continued evenly, "It's imperative justice is carried out. I intend to see that it is."

Gloria clutched her throat. "What . . . d-d'yo' mean, Jack? What can be . . . done? What d'yo' intend t' . . . t' . . . do?"

He smiled thinly. "It's very simple. My fiancée will have to sue Drum Pollard's estate through the main beneficiary, Margaret Pollard— for her rightful share of *their* father's property."

Naomi and Gloria gasped, both of them particularly affected by the way Jack had stressed the word "their."

Margaret received Naomi Simpson's writ at breakfast one glorious morning at Golden Hill when the vegetation was lush and verdant after recent rain, the air cool and delicious with the scent of frangipani flowers blooming in full glory.

Rose had only just returned to her room, when Obee appeared, his old face a twitching mixture of consternation and respect. "De law'er pusson from dat Mastah Roland Bracken's office, he be here wid an' import'nt message, Mistr'ss Margaret."

"Oh." Margaret was hardly listening, excited that in the next few minutes Theo Finch would be arriving to take her to see the new Tropica property on the coast where research to use plankton and sea algae in cosmetics products was under way for the first time.

Later Margaret would recall that the minutes before Obee's announcement and receiving the writ from the lawyer were, for some reason, among the most special in her life.

Everything was working out so wonderfully. She loved . . . no, she *adored* her job with Tropica. It was hardly a job yet, but Theo had told her she was doing very well in her apprenticeship and had intimated he believed she had a natural gift—rare for a woman—the kind of "nose" that in time with more training would be able to detect one single aroma in a fragrance and label it, analyzing and identifying odors "as different as chocolate is from cheese, and an onion is from an oleander, with a speed no laboratory instrument can yet duplicate!"

Margaret *loved* the way he talked about the business—the way he talked about *anything*, which was the reason, she told herself, she was so looking forward to the day ahead. Even the morning itself seemed especially exquisite.

She'd begun to have breakfast as often as possible with her grandmother, encouraging the old lady to join her on the veranda, where Rose would cry with delight like a little girl as Margaret asked her to help feed the many kinds of birds that swooped and sang and chirped for the small pieces of bread they distributed.

Rose never spoke much, but Margaret knew how much her grandmother enjoyed their breakfasts together and she enjoyed them, too, trying to unlock the deep, dense sadness she sensed in the lined, suffering face, trying to make her grandmother speak about the happy times of the past.

So far she hadn't been successful, but since graduating from college to return to Golden Hill to spend a couple of months at the Tropica essential-oil plant, at least Margaret knew her grandmother now looked forward to getting up in the morning.

So Margaret would remember the precious moments of that day as a slight breeze ruffled the slender immortelle blossoms and a silvery pink haze dipped slowly over the mountains. She shut her eyes, breathing in the sensuousness, savoring the thought of the day ahead, touring the seaweed stations at her boss's side. . . . And then everything changed with the arrival of Obee . . . the beginning of a new nightmare.

The server of the writ was such a fresh-faced, smiling young man, Margaret couldn't believe what she was looking at in her hand.

It was heaven-sent, she told Roger later, that Theo Finch arrived at that moment, his strength bolstering her, for instead of crumbling as she once might have done, she felt a surge of contempt for Jack Bracken and his fiancée, the same contempt, she told herself, that surely her father must have once felt toward Jack's father, Roland.

But Theo *was* there, gripping her arm as for one quick moment she leaned against him, reading and rereading the document the boy had given her, understanding what was written there, yet refusing to accept it could have anything to do with her.

How could it have anything to do with her—or her father?

For two hours while they waited for the call to Roger—that Theo had immediately suggested Margaret put through—she talked while Theo listened and saw for the first time the woman emerging . . . feeling an electricity, unspoken, yet live in the atmosphere like phosphorous, he found himself thinking, that bursts into visibility in the tropical ocean at night.

Margaret felt it, too—but neither acknowledged nor even comprehended what it meant. But from the moment Margaret turned to him in anguish and shock, it was a force—real, there to be reckoned with.

"Can you believe this latest diabolical plot?" As Margaret's anger grew, so did her conviction it was all part of Roland Bracken's nonstop "political machine." "It's almost beyond belief to think human beings can stoop so low." Her mouth tightened. "But nothing is too low for Jack Bracken. This is such an obvious attempt to give credence to Eric Williams's pledges—to his endless diatribe that he's no 'tool of the whites,' that his first thought is for his own people. How dare they! How dare *she!*" Margaret's voice broke for a second, but she went on, her voice rising, "How dare Bracken's loathsome black fiancée . . . link her name with mine! It's incredible."

Theo could hardly believe this fiery spirit was the same gentle Margaret he'd grown to know since she'd joined Tropica three months before. With her eyes blazing with fury as she poured out her scorn, she looked even more beautiful. "Oh, this place is such a paradox! So full of beauty on top, yet so rotten underneath. Yet . . ." Margaret paused and said, blushing, "before you came Theo, I was thinking what a wonderful world I lived in after all, that I'd been so wrong about Golden Hill, that despite the fogginess in my mind, the past was, at last, behind me. I felt so lucky to be here enjoying and loving. . . ."

Again she blushed and Theo felt impelled to go to her to ask gently, "Loving what?"

"My work." She managed to smile. "I was *so* looking forward to being with you today—and now this. . . ." She flung the writ down on the desk, her blush deepening with her anger. The phone rang. At last Roger was on the line from Dallas.

Margaret asked Theo to read the writ to him. It was too painful for her even to say the words "Rightful inheritance—a substantial landholding or equivalent value."

While Theo was speaking Obee came into the room, even more agitated than he had been earlier. He stopped short when he saw Theo on the telephone and was about to back out, but Margaret stopped him. "What is it, Obee? It's all right, you can speak, but speak quietly."

As Obee whispered to her Margaret clutched her throat. "It's the press, reporters! Obee says they're on the main veranda asking for an interview."

Theo quickly thrust the phone into Margaret's hand. "Here, speak to your uncle. He's catching the first plane down. Then go to your room.

I'll deal with the vultures. Stay in your room until I tell you to come out. Don't worry, Margaret. You have nothing to fear."

Twenty-four hours later, as Roger landed in Port of Spain, the headlines were again spelling out the Pollard name in the most eye-catching large print. POLLARD INHERITANCE CHALLENGED, screamed the *Trinidad Guardian*, with a paragraph beneath quoting Margaret ". . . It's a government plot." And Margaret's statement was followed by Jack's viewpoint, word for word, as he'd originally described the situation to his father on his return from Martinique: "It is already being said in top legal circles that it could be viewed as unconstitutional for a white legitimate child to inherit all her father's worldly goods while a black illegitimate child receives nothing. In the *Simpson v. Pollard* case, everything rests on whether Naomi Simpson can prove she is, in fact, the illegitimate daughter of Drum Pollard and Gloria Simpson."

"Can you believe my father could *ever* have had anything to do with a woman like Gloria Simpson, who's hardly better than a prostitute?" Margaret cried to Roger on his arrival. "You remember how we talked on the plane coming down last year? Little did we realize that so long as there's a Bracken left living on this earth he will go on trying to discredit—ruin—the Pollard name. As if arson and death weren't enough. Now Jack and his father are trying to ruin my father's reputation, not to mention steal my land!"

The situation was ugly—and as Roger pointed out to Theo, unfortunately the case had been brought at a time when this kind of litigation would inevitably attract world press attention. But Roger felt great pride in the way Margaret was reacting. He had expected to find her as he'd found her in California—unable to cope, needing to be rushed back to Daniel Siden's clinic—but it wasn't that way at all. Instead, there she was upright, with eyes flashing, defending her father, flaying Jack Bracken and his fiancée with well-chosen words, every day returning to the subject with more anger, more conviction. "Jack Bracken's not only a blackmailer and a terrorist! He's a thief, egging on this . . . this . . . so-called model to steal the Pollard land. Well, it will be over my dead body!"

Margaret had been accurate in her assessment of Williams's reaction to the case. It *was* the kind of publicity that could be put to good advantage, and the prime minister knew it. But she wasn't right about Jack's father's reaction at all. Initially Roland Bracken had been appalled. "You can't mean it," he'd told his son after getting over the first shock of discovering the gawky, overly thin Nanette—Jack's "top model" girlfriend—was none other than the little thumb-sucking girl he'd only clamped eyes on once, years before, Gloria and Drum's daughter Naomi.

Jack had been particularly upset by his father's strenuous objection to the news Naomi intended to sue the Pollard estate for her "rightful inheritance."

"I can't understand your attitude. You of all people," Jack had snapped sarcastically. "Isn't this the kind of 'hard-luck' story that's manna from heaven for Eric Williams? Especially if he gives us his unofficial blessing to proceed, righting the wrongs of the imperial past and all that sort of thing. . . ."

Although Jack didn't receive any encouragement from his father, it didn't stop him from spreading the story among his father's influential friends . . . until word had indeed come that the prime minister could see no reason why Naomi should not use the proper judicial processes to ensure justice was properly carried out.

Why had Roland held back his own support? Because from the beginning he dreaded where it was all going to lead. As he told Jack, he could see the stories that were going to emerge as reporters did their homework—dragging up the facts behind the Mount St. Benedict fire, making it appear as if the Brackens had always carried on a vendetta against the Pollards and always would.

And it was all happening as he'd predicted. It *was* a case made in heaven as far as the press was concerned. Hardly a day passed without a picture of a Pollard and/or a Bracken, past and present, appearing in print. It was all so *unnecessary* and ugly, and, Roland sighed, the devil of it was it could drag on for years and the publicity along with it.

Luis told him to relax, not to worry, that in no way had the case affected the respect he had earned over the years, "working for the Party . . . for the common good." Roland wasn't so sure. He'd been in the doghouse before when he'd least expected it. You could never know with the reds. But he tried to keep cool and quiet, just as one of the key characters in the case, Gloria Simpson Bracken, was doing. She'd steadfastly refused to comment on the situation one way or the other. Without her support Roland couldn't see how Naomi could achieve anything, although he supposed that with modern equipment, blood tests and the like, anything was possible.

As weeks then months passed and the case dragged on, to everyone's relief (particularly Naomi's) Jack decided one weekend they would slip away and get married quietly without any hullabaloo. Becky had written again, this time to report "Big Man 'got his' the day after Crazy Joe

Gallo was gunned down during a birthday party at Umberto's Clam House in Little Italy." Jack decided he could now safely take his newly rounded bride back to New York to show off her extra flesh to all the Beckys and other models who'd given Nanette no chance for a future. "There's no way you can't win this case, pretty one," he told Naomi as he came home unexpectedly one lunchtime, desperate to have sex with her.

As she slipped off her clothes and lay obediently on her stomach, knowing that was how he liked to begin, Jack noticed with satisfaction she was even developing a shapely behind to hold on to.

Even as he started to ram her, heaving her back against him, holding on to her boyish tits, he was brainwashing her for her witness-stand ordeal ahead. "My little mistress of Golden Hill," he panted. "You lovely white man's prize . . . Drum Pollard's little girl, and now mine. I'm your 'Big Man' now . . . oh, oh, oh. . . ."

"I don't want to say it, but the facts don't look too good. Gloria Simpson is going to cooperate with her daughter after all, so we haven't got much chance! I suppose it was too much to expect she'd hold back her support forever, considering who her son-in-law is." Roger looked earnestly across at his New York lawyer, hoping to hear his assessment of the situation was wrong, though his common sense told him there was no way it could be.

He'd brought the best lawyers in on the case from New York, including the celebrated Walter Foy, whose track record was outstanding. They'd huddled for months with some of the best legal brains in the Caribbean, but from the beginning Roger hadn't been optimistic. As delay followed delay, he'd begun to realize that no lawyer, however loaded with degrees and successful cases, could break through the local barriers.

It was how the case was viewed in Trinidad that counted—and viewed by *Trinidad* lawyers, not by hotshots from other places in the Caribbean. It wasn't American land they were talking about or an American inheritance. It was "God's own earth"—at least that was the way most Trinidadian lawyers described it.

As Foy now confirmed to Roger, unless a very large carrot could be produced to make Naomi withdraw the case, it could go on for years, with only the lawyers getting richer. But now, Foy told him grimly, the size of the carrot had to be "extraordinary."

Theo Finch had had the best idea all along, Roger thought grumpily as his chauffeur drove him over to Tropica's office after leaving Foy.

Theo had invited him to lunch in the boardroom, not to talk about the case, he had stressed on the phone, but to answer Roger's recent questions about Margaret's future with his company.

As he went up in the elevator, Roger thought again, that he should have followed Theo Finch's advice in *total*, instead of only half of it, which thank God at least meant he'd moved Margaret out of Trinidad as fast as possible, away from prying eyes and endless attention from the press.

Roger was impressed with the spacious reception room on the thirtieth floor, the good pieces of furniture, even a splendid antique clock ticking away. There was nothing flashy, no sign of "Hollywood" beauty spots and tricks—and the boardroom was even more restrained and elegant, with a spectacular view of Central Park all the way to the George Washington Bridge and the Hudson River. The more he saw of Theo Finch, the more Roger respected him.

Despite Theo's insistence that he didn't want to discuss the case, once he sat down Roger said immediately, "You were right. I was wrong. If only I'd listened to you in the first place. As you once suggested Foy has just recommended we try for a settlement out of court."

Roger could remember how intent, how anxious, Theo had looked as he'd stipulated, "Surely we're all agreed the most important thing is not to involve Margaret in any of the ugly facts. She's been through enough. Wouldn't it be better to settle fast? I bet I'm right that Bracken's determination to continue would weaken if the price is right."

Theo had also believed and said from the beginning that Naomi was *entitled* to receive something substantial from the Pollards. Good God, Roger Pollard is as rich as Croesus, he had told himself then. Surely Roger could afford a fair cash settlement to lay the matter to rest once and for all!

But nothing had happened, and now here was Roger telling him the lawyers were going to do precisely what he'd recommended months ago. It was all too late, of course. The papers had already had a field day.

Theo controlled his anger, reflecting on the harm already inflicted on Margaret. He could only pray it would be a case of "better late than never"—that Roger—and so Margaret—would never have cause to regret their tardiness in coming to what as far as Theo was concerned had always been the only solution.

Over a delicious arugula, basil and endive salad, followed by fresh lemon sole, tiny new potatoes and Chinese peapods, Theo began to tell Roger what a fantastic niece he had. "She's going to be an important perfumer, I'm sure of it." He partly forgave Roger when he saw the look of joy on the man's face.

"Really? That's wonderful news." Roger looked at him with a little-boy smile. "Would you mind explaining what you mean by 'important perfumer'?"

"I'll put it this way. It means having the ability to add one essential oil to perhaps three hundred others in the right order and amount to create a perfume masterpiece, one that's going to sell and sell over the years—a perfume that's instantly recognizable anywhere in the world. That makes what we call a 'nose' as opposed to a good technician and . . ."—Theo held up his finely fluted wine glass to the light before he sipped the delicate wine inside—"your niece is, believe me, a fantastic 'nose.'" They laughed together with the same air of complacency before Theo went on. "Tropica is very lucky to have her, but that doesn't mean one day she won't start her own company. She'll be some competition! But I promise you, Roger, I want her to have everything she wants for herself."

Theo was surprised himself by the depth of emotion in his voice, and Roger looked at him curiously as he attempted to cover it up by adding "Well, she deserves it, don't you think? She's worked like a Trojan."

Over coffee, Roger brought up the case again and by the time he strode out to the elevator to return to his own office on Park Avenue, the arrangement had been made that while Roger worked with the lawyers attempting to negotiate a fair price with Naomi and Jack Bracken, Theo would send Margaret off on her first trip to Grasse, to Roure Bertrand Dupont, one of the most important essential-oil houses in the world. To Roger's relief, Theo said he thought he might even be able to take the time off to go with her.

Rose
1974

THE house seemed very quiet. Rose couldn't understand where everyone was. Since breakfast she'd been looking for Piper and Drum and Rosetta, but they were playing a game with her. Yes, that was it. Piper liked to surprise her and she was sure at that very moment the children were working away somewhere under Piper's supervision; perhaps creating a special table decoration out of the hibiscus—even young Drum was good at that—or painting a painting—that was Rosetta's favorite pastime.

Soon Obee—stupid, fawning Obee—would come to lead her—and she told herself she *must* look as unsuspecting as possible—to the room where, like a grown-up child himself, Piper would be hiding behind the sofa or the curtains to capture the look of pleasure on her face when she saw their children's handiwork.

If only it wasn't so hot. She didn't feel up to acting a role today. Rose looked at the sleeves of her dress with surprise. Why was she wearing such a shabby old dress and one with long sleeves? Had Maize laid it out for her that morning? She couldn't remember. In any case Maize must be crazy when she knew the shipment had come in from Saks with the new lavender silk that Piper was going to love. Lavender was his favorite color—not that the maid would be allowed to know a personal think like that.

Lavender silk by day and black lace at night. She giggled softly—black lace that hardly stayed on her body for more than a few minutes when Piper wasn't preoccupied with business or politics.

She sighed heavily.

She supposed she'd have to go upstairs and change into the lavender silk, but she really didn't feel well. She'd have to talk to Piper about taking her away for the rainy season. She couldn't endure the terrible humidity again this year. She decided she was in need of a change. Perhaps Piper would take her to England where she'd always longed to go.

As she stood at the bottom of the stairs the strangest thing started to happen. The stairs changed into the slopes of Mount El Tucuche.

She didn't know whether she was going to be able to climb them, even though she now knew somewhere at the top of the mountain Piper was watching, waiting for her to climb up to join him.

It was really too bad. Why would he put her through such an ordeal, changing their very own Golden Hill stairs into a steep mountain slope? He knew she wasn't that strong. It was his fault, she thought petulantly. He did nothing to dissuade her from eating her favorite yams which made her fat, and then out of breath when she climbed stairs, let alone slopes!

Now she could see Piper beckoning to her. He couldn't know she had a bad stitch starting in her chest, a stitch that was beginning to numb her legs and her arms. He couldn't know she wasn't going to be able to climb up the Hill again. If he wanted her, why did he make her go to the top of the Hill? Why didn't he meet her halfway? It wasn't fair.

As Rose put her foot on the first step, the stitch in her chest ripped violently across and down her body. "Piper . . ." she whispered. It was the last word she ever spoke.

The morning after Rose's cremation Margaret was up early, walking down the trail leading to the cocoa-sorting sheds where her parents had taken the steps that had changed their lives so completely.

Roger had never seen Margaret look so rosy cheeked as a rain squall sent her rushing back up the east veranda steps. "Where on earth have you been, child? You're wet through. . . ."

"I didn't sleep well last night, Uncle, but I didn't mind. I started thinking . . . I can't explain, but as I lay in the dark I somehow had this new feeling of . . . of . . . responsibility. It was almost as if Grandma Rose was . . . was passing on her love for the house to me, telling me I couldn't leave, that I had to give the house the same care and love Captain Piper and she had once given it when they were young."

Margaret looked anxiously at Roger. "Does that sound silly? I feel so full of . . . feeling . . . of love for Golden Hill this morning. I've never felt this way before. The house is still full of ghosts, and when I'm far away and start to think about the place—and Trinidad—perhaps I'll still think the way I usually think—fearful, apprehensive, full of doubt about that terrible night, still so mixed up in my mind—but maybe not. Now there's something added. A sense of . . . well, I suppose the best word has to be *responsibility*."

Roger hugged her, tears filling his eyes. "I've been longing to hear you say that, Margaret. I've never told you—I haven't thought of it in years, but when I wasn't the old decrepit I am today . . ." He nodded self-consciously as Margaret started to remonstrate. "No, let me go on. I have to tell you. One of the biggest blows of my life was when I learned my father hadn't left Golden Hill to me, but to Rose and . . . to your father—to Drum. I came back to Trinidad after the war determined to challenge the will, to fight for what I considered should have been mine. I was very bitter. I hated Rose. I hated your father, but then, well, something happened to change my mind. I went away if anything more bitter than when I arrived. And then—you know what happened then. My life changed dramatically when oil was discovered on the property my father *had* left me at Cedros." Roger laughed again and with a sarcastic note went on, "If he'd known what he was really leaving me, I doubt I would ever have received it! If early on he'd only carried out a little more prospecting—but it was not to be. All these years I've loved Golden Hill in a way I thought you'd never be able to understand. Now, from what you tell me, you *do* understand. It's wonderful. You don't know how happy it makes me to hear you speak this way—and I suppose you realize this afternoon you'll become Golden Hill's new owner, because obviously Rose *must* have left everything to you. Who else?"

Margaret smiled shyly. "I don't suppose it would be wrong to think that way even before the reading of the will."

"It's as I said yesterday," Roger went on quickly, before Margaret could refuse to listen. "The reading of the will, I'm sure, will solve everything. No mention of Naomi. . . ." Seeing Margaret frown, Roger put up an unusually stern hand. "Margaret, you *must* listen. You must be prepared. Nothing that you'll hear today should make any difference to your feelings for your father. Your memory of him is based on your knowledge of *his* love for you. Whatever happened in his life has nothing to do with that love, nothing can change that."

"Please, Uncle Roger. . . ." Margaret tried to stop him from talking, but Roger was determined to go on.

"Nothing, I repeat, Margaret, nothing can change that. If, as I expect, there's no mention of Naomi in Rose's will, then that's a huge point in your favor and I'm sure we'll reach a settlement this week. It's about time! I know you don't want to consider a settlement out of court—but Theo suggested it over a year ago and he was absolutely right. I could kick myself I didn't listen to him then. We don't want any more newspaper stories. You've got to get on with your career, which Theo predicts is going to be a brilliant one. If you love Golden Hill as much as I'm beginning to think you do, then I'm sure it, too, will have an important place in your plans. Theo mentioned the possibility of your own business one day." Roger looked at her amused. "Golden Hill Cosmetics—how does that sound?"

Margaret kissed him affectionately. "You're right, Uncle Roger, it's a beautiful idea. I can see the new plantings from here to here." She waved her arm expansively from the left to right. "Not so much cocoa but lots and lots of beautiful flowers—for beauty products and perfumes. Well, I'd better go and dry off and decide what I'm going to wear for this depressing visit to the lawyer's office."

"Are you prepared for it?"

Margaret nodded determinedly. "Absolutely. I'm never going to let a Bracken get me down again. I've got new strength."

Edward Gellen, the courtly, elderly gentleman who'd been looking after Pollard business for years, had originally suggested he come up to Golden Hill for the reading of the will, but that idea had been vetoed by Ambassador Bracken. And, as Gellen had explained in embarrassment to Roger, "These days I'm afraid one has to go along with the ambassador's wishes . . . if one wishes to continue one's business."

Margaret hummed cheerfully as Obee drove her and Roger to the lawyer's office in Port of Spain, but like the weather her mood darkened as they drew up outside the three-story building in Aberdeen Street. The rain that had hardly stopped since early morning hadn't freshened the city air. As they stepped across a wide running rivulet in the gutter the atmosphere was stifling.

"Deep breathing?" Roger tried to look confident.

Margaret flashed him a broad smile. "Don't worry, Uncle! I'm all right. I've been practicing deep breathing since yesterday, and it works! I feel much more in control than when we arrived."

Nevertheless, as they went into the welcome cool of the air-conditioned lobby, Margaret clutched Roger's arm to whisper, "D'you think Jack Bracken might dare to turn up here with that . . . that imposter?"

"It's likely!" Roger whispered back, although he wondered why they were whispering. "You must be prepared for anything." However, a few minutes later when Jack sauntered in, a confident, knowing look on his face, Naomi wasn't with him. Perhaps, Roger thought grimly, she herself could no longer face up to the ordeal she'd allowed her husband to perpetrate.

It was so dark in the office that Gellen ordered the lights to be switched on, although it was only three o'clock.

Margaret and Roger had scarcely settled themselves down in an unobtrusive corner before Jack's parents, Ambassador Roland and Emerald Bracken, arrived, followed a few minutes later by James, Carmelita and Frederick Bracken, James's right shirt sleeve pinned back to the elbow, a jarring reminder that his arm had had to be amputated following Matthew's wild swing with the panga, a crime for which he was still in jail.

What a sorry group the Brackens looked, for all Roland's ambassadorial position of authority and dignity. What must he be thinking behind his usual impassive features, his receding hairline making his shiny black face look unnaturally long and sepulchral? As for James, despite his woebegone, dog-in-the-manger attitude, there was still something shifty about the way his eyes darted about.

Why on earth were they all there anyway? Would the youngest Bracken, April, be the next to arrive? Did they really think it was likely Rose had left them a love letter in her will? Or some kind of apologia in the form of money or land? It was insane if they did.

Roger began to look forward to the reading of the will, confident there could be no more shocks in store for his darling niece. It would be interesting to see the reaction of Rose's brothers, sister and nephews when they realized there was no mention of any of them.

He felt Margaret's hand clutch his arm and followed her eyes to the door, where the next arrival stood hovering uneasily, a shy smile around his mouth.

For a moment Roger couldn't make out who he was. Certainly not a Bracken.

He looked at Margaret inquiringly. "Who is it?"

She looked shocked. "Tommy . . . Tommy Finch. I don't understand."

There were two strangers behind him, whom Mr. Gellen quietly introduced as Benton Clark and Thomas Acton, lawyers acting on behalf of the Finch family.

Roger began to feel damp spreading around his collar, uneasy again as he'd felt years before sitting across from Roland Bracken, "eating humble pie," at his father-in-law's request.

What on earth had the Finch family to do with the reading of Rose Pollard's will—and why Tommy Finch? Why not Theo? And why hadn't Theo mentioned at the funeral that Tommy was going to be present? It didn't make any sense.

Roger scrutinized the Brackens as Ed Gellen started to speak. They looked uneasy, too, obviously not expecting young Finch either, particularly turning up with a couple of Finch lawyers.

Although trickles of perspiration were now running down his back despite the air conditioning, as Roger listened to Gellen's flat tones, a new presentiment of something devastating and diabolical about to happen began to give him cold shivers.

"'This is the last will and testament of me, Rose Agatha Pollard of the Independent State of Trinidad and Tobago. I hereby revoke all former wills, codicils and testamentary disposition made by me. I appoint Edward Gellen and Xavier Denotes, both of 16 Aberdeen Street and Benton Clark of 430 Vincent Street in the city of Port of Spain attorneys-at-law in the said Independent Republic of Trinidad and Tobago to be the executors and trustees of this my will. . . .'"

Margaret's hand tightened in his, although what Gellen was continuing to read in a matter-of-fact voice was so far all that Roger expected. "'. . . I give and bequeath to my beloved granddaughter Margaret Alicia Pollard all my real and personal estate wheresoever and whatsoever including my jewelry and all the property over which I shall at my death have any general or special power of appointment or disposition, with the exception of the house known as Golden Hill, in the Valley of Maracas, and one hundred and fifty acres immediately surrounding the house, known as the Picton acres, being the original parcel of land bought by Governor Picton's heir for the establishment of the Golden Hill plantation.'"

Roger heard a man's voice shout out "No!" as the lawyer read on in a low, solemn voice. Had it been Jack's voice? Roland's?

Roger glanced around the room before he turned anguished eyes on the girl he loved so much. She was as still as a statue, eyes glazed, looking straight ahead as if she were seeing an apparition.

There was only one person in the room who looked at ease and that was the boy who usually never looked at ease, Thomas Picton Finch.

He had just heard the words that his grandmother had told him only the night before he *would* hear—that eight years before, following the death of her son, Drum, Rose Pollard had told his grandmother personally she'd made up her mind to "right the great wrong of the past," and would attempt to "mend the breach" by deeding on her death the return of Golden Hill to the Finch family, to Thomas Finch, the youngest descendant of Governor Picton's heir, who had built the property in the first place.

Although he'd been openly skeptical, Tommy had followed Magdalen's instructions dutifully—as he always did. He'd gone to Edward Gellen's office in Port of Spain, where his grandmother had told him Margaret Pollard would be expecting to hear she'd inherited Golden Hill to live there happily ever after, but who instead would learn the Pollards would never again rule from that great roost on the hill, that instead he—as Rose Pollard's carefully chosen heir—was now the recognized, legal owner of the great house and original tract of land.

Tommy was surprised to find he couldn't bring himself to look at Margaret. He'd been looking forward to seeing her crushed demeanor as the incredulous look of defeat spread across her face. But for some reason he hadn't the nerve to look in her direction after all. It was enough, he told himself, that she could see *him* sitting there with a smile that stretched from ear to ear, a smile that said, "Damn you, Margaret Pollard. Now, you walking zombie, we're even!"

It was better he didn't appear to gloat. His grandmother had warned him that even his own father might not necessarily be in favor of the amazing turn of events, that it was essential he act with dignity and decorum. She'd made him promise he wouldn't join in any of the arguments likely to break out in the lawyer's office, and she had taken the precaution of sending her own lawyer along with Benton Clark to make sure he kept his promise. He was to be gracious and simply sign whatever papers Gellen and Clark gave him to sign.

His grandmother had squeezed his hand so tightly, it had momentarily hurt and surprised him that the old lady still had so much strength after all she'd been through. "Remember Margaret Pollard will still own by far the major part of the land up on the Hill." She'd leaned back in her wheelchair watching him closely. "Although you will inherit what should always have been yours—and your father's before you—the original Picton acres and its crowning glory of a house, the house I was born in, Tommy—the house your grandfather was born in. . . ." Magdalen's voice had thickened with emotion and there'd been tears welling up in her eyes, but she'd gone on relentlessly. "The Pollard girl will obviously inherit the rest of the land, just as she inherited the huge parcel from her father, but it's land I'm sure she won't want to keep. Why should she? She has no reason to stay. She'll be shocked, so there's no reason to aggravate her further. It won't take long before she'll want to sell the whole estate and you'll want to buy it." The tears had gone as quickly as they'd come as his grandmother had leaned forward to cackle mischievously, "And if you behave well now, you'll get it at a giveaway price, my boy. You mark my words!"

And he was marking her words, for it was all happening as she'd predicted. There was a sudden hush in the office as Gellen began to read the last paragraph, now in a distinctly unhappy voice. "'As a sign of my beloved granddaughter's approval of my decision to return Golden Hill and the original Picton acres to Picton's descendant, Theo Finch, to hold in trust for his son, Thomas Picton Finch (a decision taken after many months of thought), I am asking her to sign this document as proof she knows and accepts the foregoing provision is in no way a reflection of any lack of love for her, but because of my desire to die knowing I have done everything in my power to "settle old scores" between two fine families.'"

"It's not true! It's not true," Margaret cried out, looking desperately at Edward Gellen as if he could annul the words he'd just spoken.

Roger stood up quickly, pulling her with him. "Not now, Margaret. Say nothing now. Don't worry. This is all absurd. We'll issue a denial through the proper channels."

Margaret wasn't listening. She pulled away to lean over the lawyer's desk, to say in an impassioned voice, "I didn't know what I was signing. I had no knowledge . . . no idea that Grandmother Rose . . ."

Now a babble of voices broke out. Tommy, forgetting his grandmother's urge for caution, vehemently shouted, "Yes, you did know! You told me yourself you were happy your grandmother had made the decision to give Golden Hill back to its true owner. . . ." Both the Finch lawyers told Tommy sharply to be quiet, while Emerald and Carmelita screamed, "It's a bloody disgrace . . . it's disgustin'!" and Jack, his face taut with anger, shouted, "You won't get away with this!"

Margaret hardly knew how she got back to Golden Hill, the house she'd left with such feelings of optimism and love hours before, to return drained, exhausted, waxen as a doll, each limb weighing its true weight, so that she had to be half carried up the veranda steps to her room, where she lay motionless, looking up at the fan whirring lazily above her, a fan that would go on whirring no matter who lay beneath, an uncaring fan, an uncaring house, an uncaring . . . she bit her lip.

She couldn't even let her thoughts go to the deepest hurt of all. To Theo. How *could* he have acted as though he were her real friend, her support, so full of sympathy, never allowing her to fall back into her maudlin, self-pitying moods?

All the time he must have known of Rose's intentions "to right the wrongs of the past. . . ." No wonder he had come to her aid so immediately the morning the writ had arrived from Naomi Simpson. He must have been petrified at losing any of Golden Hill's assests as a result of the lawsuit, assets he'd been waiting for so patiently, knowing as he must have known, the staggering change Rose had made to her will.

Margaret shuddered as she thought of Tommy Finch's profile in the lawyer's office, so arrogant and self-important—and then, when his veneer of calm impartiality had deserted him when she'd challenged the reference to her own signature on her grandmother's last wishes, the vicious lie he'd told: "You told me so yourself—that you were happy your grandmother had made the decision to give Golden Hill back to its rightful owners . . . to right the wrongs of the past!"

How much more did she have to endure before "wrongs were righted"?

What about the "wrongs" done to her? When would she stop being wounded by those she'd grown to trust and love?

She lay listlessly looking up at the fan, whirring away minutes of her life, once more an empty life, wondering what on earth she was going to do with herself now?

"You're a liar. A liar and a thief. What's got into you? I won't have a son of mine lying. . . ." Theo lifted his hand as if to strike him, but Tommy ran out of the room, the sound of his racking sobs making Paulette start to cry as she'd been longing to do since the long confrontation between Tommy and his father had begun.

"Why can't you believe him?" she wailed, crouching back against the sofa like a wounded animal, as the husband she'd thought she knew so thoroughly, in every mood and situation, seemed to grow more hostile and strange before her eyes.

The tension Theo could feel building in his head was unbearable. Misery engulfed him; even his bones ached with the effort of holding back, of not giving in to the mad urge to rush after Tommy and take him by the neck to shake the truth out of him, or to march into his own sick, *evil* mother's room to demand Magdalen tell the lawyers what had really transpired following Drum Pollard's death to precipitate Rose Pollard's astonishing decision.

That *something* had transpired, Theo was certain.

Every word of Rose Pollard's "long thought-out decision" smacked of his mother's influence and intervention, for now, despairing, looking back across the years, Theo was forced to accept that despite the tragic events of the past, including his own imprisonment, his mother's grievance against the Pollards had obviously never waned. And neither had her pursuit of what she perceived to be the Finches' birthright—the ownership of Golden Hill, no matter what the cost to man, woman or child.

Child! He felt a lump in his throat as the thought of Margaret, never far away, hit him anew. He sensed her anguish, her bewilderment, seeing in his mind her great gray eyes misty with tears, remembering the shy way she'd spoken his name, asking him question after question about the business, her enthusiasm and joy at working with him so obvious. Now it was all finished, her trust in him extinguished.

He felt powerless to build it back. He couldn't even influence his son to change the emphatic statement he'd issued through the family lawyer that Margaret Pollard had told him personally what her grandmother intended to do, that he hadn't given it much thought "at the time" because it hadn't "meant much to him," that now he was very "surprised and hurt" Margaret was challenging the bequest on the grounds of her grandmother's senility and her own inability to comprehend what she had then been asked to sign.

Margaret's lawyer had been quick to dismiss the importance of her schoolgirlish signature on the will, releasing her statement: "I was too ill and upset following my parents' deaths to know what I was signing, when my grandmother asked me—as I thought—to witness her signature on a document the day before I left Trinidad to go and live in the United States with my aunt and uncle in August 1966."

Despite begging his mother to tell him the truth, Magdalen had refused to respond, turning her face to the wall like an angry child, until, frustrated and bitter, Theo had slammed out of the room, telling her he would never forgive her and never see her again unless she confessed to what he was sure was an evil, premeditated plot.

Theo had issued his own statement, repudiating the will as the act of a senile woman, refusing to meet with the Finch lawyers to discuss the terms of his trusteeship. Apparently that was no impediment to Tommy's eventually receiving the property if Margaret lost her case.

Worst of all, whatever he said or did, Margaret refused to see or even speak to him, resigning from Tropica the day after the will was read, issuing a statement before she left for the States that any communica-

tion he wished to make should be made through their respective lawyers, that she had no wish to see or speak to any member of the Finch
family again.

Roger had been no help. Despite Theo's protestations, it seemed
Roger also believed that he must have been party all along to the
scheme to regain Golden Hill for Finch generations to come.

Paulette was torn, tortured, on the one hand refusing to believe her
own son could lie about something of such major importance (and, if it
was a lie, to tell it over and over again so publicly), on the other hand
sensing Theo could be right, that it was a carefully contrived plot of her
mother-in-law's, who Paulette had been forced to accept influenced
Tommy much more than either Theo or she ever realized.

This afternoon's long row between father and son was the third—and
something told Paulette it was going to be the last—on the subject. As
Theo stared gloomily out of the large window, Paulette timidly began to
plead as she'd been pleading since the news broke. "Theo, please don't
give up on Tommy. I can't believe our boy's the liar you say he is.
There has to be something in what he says. After all that Margaret
Pollard's been through, perhaps she is a bit unbalanced, just like Rose,
her grandmother."

Theo whirled round furiously. "Shut up!" he cried. "Don't you start
attacking a defenseless girl, who's never said an unkind word or thought
an evil thought in her life."

Paulette flushed deeply, her reddening skin emphasized by her snow-
white hair. "That's not fair. I'm not attacking her. Why should you
stand up for a stranger against your own son—and your mother?"

Theo walked past her, despite her cries. "Don't leave me like this,
Theo. Can't we talk about it?" When the door slammed behind him,
she felt as if he were walking out of her life, as if she'd lost him. He was
a stranger.

"Oh, Theo. . . ." Paulette rushed to follow him. "Please talk to me.
I love you. Don't shut me out."

He turned a tortured face to her. "Don't you know how I hate all
this? It's killing me. I can't believe this nightmare is happening."

He allowed her to lead him to the veranda swing, where they sat in
silence, watching huge butterflies, the brilliant blue morpho, the purple
gold califo, flutter in and out of the flowering hedges. Just as Paulette
felt she couldn't bear the silence a moment longer, Theo covered her
trembling hands with his. "We've got to get away from here—to escape
this sickening heritage. Who cares about the Orange Grove plant? If it
goes up in smoke, I don't care any more. Let's go back to the States and

take Tommy with us. Perhaps once he's there, he'll come to his senses. I tell you, Paulette, this air's poisonous. Just as weeds and flowers here sprout overnight, so do evil thoughts. Let's get back to the real world."

He gestured in the direction of his mother's room. "I gave her the chance to start a new life with us in the States. Instead, somehow she got us to spend more time with her *here*, and look where it's taken us! We never used to have a cross word. To think I was about to knock Tommy's head off a few minutes ago. I've got to get out. This place is killing me—and our family."

But when Paulette told Tommy they were leaving in two day's time, he refused to accompany them. "Why should I?" he snapped petulantly, avoiding his mother's eyes. "Why should I do anything *he* wants me to do? He thinks I'm a liar, a thief. Well, let him think it. I'm going to stay here to prove him wrong."

Despite Paulette's pleas to make it up with his father before their departure, Tommy sulkily refused to go anywhere near him. It didn't make any difference when she tried to explain how Theo felt about the whole matter—whichever way it was finally resolved. "Your father's such an honorable man; he feels there's no way he *or* you should even contemplate accepting such a bequest. Golden Hill was *sold* to the Pollard family by your great-grandfather. It was an honest, straightforward business transaction. . . ."

Tommy stopped Paulette short with the ultimatum, "I'm staying here to look after Granny Mags and *her* interests. She's the only one who's interested in looking after *mine!*"

It was an obvious reference to his father's opposition and Theo didn't make things any easier, refusing to say goodbye either to his mother or Tommy. "I've nothing more to say to either of them," he snapped, leaving Paulette inside the house to say goodbye, while he waited morosely in the car.

As they started down the tree-lined drive, Paulette looked through the car window with tear-filled eyes, wondering if she would ever see Arima again.

She no longer knew what to think or even hope for. If the will was proved, their son would eventually inherit Golden Hill and Theo would never forgive him for it.

If the will was declared void, Tommy would never forgive his father for his lack of support and active part in helping scuttle the inheritance.

Tommy's obdurate attitude had made things intolerable and it hadn't helped, Paulette knew, that Theo had read in the paper that despite the two cases Margaret Pollard was now involved in, she had found the time to "form her own special fragrance company in California, where since her return she has been seen regularly with the distinguished Dr. Daniel Siden."

Paulette could hear herself sighing as the plane carrying them back to New York left behind hazy blue Caribbean skies to plunge into dark storm clouds. To her, the darker the clouds, the more they epitomized everything going on around them.

Theo's inscrutable expression didn't change as the tiring journey went on, until finally Paulette gave up trying to get him to speak, to smile, to show her he still recognized they had a life to live together whatever happened over Golden Hill.

In the year since his sister Rose's death, Roland reflected, nothing had gone right, yet in many ways the cumulative effect had brought him to something approaching peace of mind.

He'd made a fool of himself twice. First he'd listened to Jack when he should have listened to his own inner counsel. He'd gone to Ed Gellen's office because Jack had been so sure Rose would have recognized and named Naomi as her granddaughter in her will, a recognition that would have won the case for them immediately—a case that was *still* dragging on, as Roland had known it would—with now no end in sight, due to the further litigation over Golden Hill between Margaret Pollard and the Finch family.

How could he have expected Rose to do him or any member of his family a single good turn on the happy occasion of her death—when she'd never made an unselfish move in her life?

Roland snorted as he thought back to the undignified scene in Gellen's office, when young Tommy Finch had made monkeys of them all.

As if that hadn't been enough, a month later had come all the trouble with Matthew—again trouble that would never have happened if he hadn't intervened, arranging a transfer for Matthew to the open prison for first offenders because Jack had maintained Matthew had never intended to "hurt a fly," not Magdalen Finch or certainly his own father. "He deserves a chance to be 'rehabilitated,'" Jack had urged, and Roland had believed him.

What a joke! Roland now knew that Matthew Bracken, even if he was his own nephew, was a cold-blooded killer who, since his escape from the open prison after neatly carving up a guard with a kitchen knife, was accurately described on wanted posters throughout the Caribbean and Venezuela: DANGEROUS CRIMINAL. MATTHEW BRACKEN. SIX FOOT

TWO, TWENTY-THREE, CAN PASS FOR WHITE. SUSPECTED OF TER-
RORIST ACTIVITIES . . . MAY BE ARMED.

Roland poured himself an unusually large Scotch and soda, wondering why on earth he was wasting time thinking about Matthew! It wasn't
as if he hadn't anything substantial to worry about!

The realization had only hit him recently that his cat-and-mouse relationship with Luis had given him literally *years* of apprehension, waking up every morning wondering if it might be his last.

Years of training had gone into the apprehensive, even penitent act
he'd put on, when Luis had let it be known he was in disgrace again for
failing to carry out a two-year-old directive—to encourage Eric Williams to put off his official visit to the People's Republic of China, and,
worse, for having the audacity to accompany Williams there. Roland
had received part of the credit in the press for helping establish trade
relations between the two countries, with an agreement to export cocoa,
coffee and asphalt on an experimental basis, as well as expediting the
establishment of a small PRC embassy and nonresident ambassador in
Port of Spain, with a Trinidad mission planned soon in Peking.

Luis switched from a "hot" to "cold" tone of voice, as he'd announced, "Our friends are not pleased that this has taken place. You
will remember in 1965 you helped persuade Prime Minister Williams to
accept an invitation from Moscow to pay a visit to the Soviet Union. It
is now nearly 1975, and that visit has still not taken place. I fear with
the notoriety attached to certain members of your family and your own
failure to act promptly on important matters, despite the time and
money spent on improving your own standing in the community, our
friends' patience is wearing thin."

Luis had then delivered a smile Roland had seen many times over the
years, thin, humorless, parting his lips in such a way his features became almost Oriental. "I don't want to alarm you, my friend, but perhaps you should take stock of your position and reevaluate whether you
have delivered what you *should* have delivered—in view of the many
rewards you have received."

"My friend." Had Luis ever had any friends? If so Roland certainly
wasn't among them. In his own mind Roland believed he had given
more than anyone could be expected to give to the cause. His *own*
position in the community *had* improved a thousandfold, but the leadership that he had been promised year after year was further away than
ever.

When Luis had given him the express command "Make sure Eric

Williams stays . . . encourage him that no one can ever replace him," he had done the job too well.

Now, Roland knew, Eric Williams would never retire; he would die "with his boots on" as the English liked to say. As there weren't that many years between them, that meant *he* could easily die himself with his "second-in-command boots" on!

Already Williams was talking about the 1976 election and what he intended to do in the years that came after. Here was where he revealed his basic lack of understanding of the people. He had been cocooned so well he little realized how out of touch he was, that it wasn't he who was now considered the "real friend of the people." That appellation fell to his sidekick and right-hand man, Roland Bracken!

For the last few months Roland had slowly and carefully (oh, so carefully, even a half step at a time) built even more support for himself, not only among the masses, but from those in positions of power both in and out of government—encouraging in an overt way some of the firebrands who wanted to strike in the oil and sugar industries, funneling money through a number of "laundered" channels to help the "anti-Williams" plans materialize—the bombing of key Texaco officials' homes, the burning of major sugarcane estates.

Williams was threatening another state of emergency, much as he was loath to do so. There was talk of another massive protest march.

The unrest his Communist bosses had once wanted him to instigate, but now strangely wanted him to curb, was going to be much greater this time because it was an unrest that he was creating to produce the needed coup to establish *him* once and for all as the leader.

And Roland knew it *could* happen. The people knew he wasn't a hothead or a frosty intellectual like Williams. He was viewed as an "approachable" man who could get things done for the people, because there were now a number of people out there who could testify as to what he'd already done for them, people who respected him—ironically for the one thing that had always torn at his guts—his patience.

He got up to pour himself more scotch, then decided against it. He had to keep on his toes.

Once the news he'd learned today would have caused him weeks of sleeplessness, as he plotted and planned to avoid falling into the pit he'd have been sure was being dug for him.

Now, through the support system he'd built outside for himself—while appearing to continue to follow Luis's commands—he was cool, calm, assessing what lay behind Williams's casual mention that he

planned to visit Fidel Castro in Cuba in June and would then fly on
directly to Moscow for the official visit he'd been meaning to make for
years. Williams had made it sound as if it was Roland's fault he hadn't
made the visit before, and he'd also made it clear he did not expect
Roland to accompany him, either to Cuba or Russia.

Roland's forehead started to throb. Damn and blast. It was probably
the scotch. He told himself to relax. If he panicked now, he'd be lost.
He had to act like an Oscar winner, in order that Luis should not suspect that from now on he, Roland Bracken, was looking out for his own
interests first and last while at the same time keeping every one of his
senses "on duty" to watch out for danger signals.

Not twenty miles away across the Gulf of Paria in a run-down Venezue-
lan fishing village, Matthew stroked the handle of his brand new gun
with more feeling than he ever lavished on the substantial bodies of the
girls in the leading brothels of Caracas.

He gestured with his head in the direction of Trinidad and the smoky
outline of the mountains of the Northern Range just visible across the
moody stretch of water. "D'yo' t'ink anyone ov'r dere would reco'nize
me, now?"

Luis Delorso smiled his tight-lipped smile. "No, young man, I don't
think so. Shall we say you have 'matured'?"

Matthew liked the Cuban. He always said the right things, brought
him nice presents and so far hadn't asked him to do anything too difficult. He never questioned how Luis had found him and seemed to
know all about him. He was sure it was because of his record, and it was
one he was proud of.

The only thing he regretted was that the panga hadn't sliced off Magdalen Finch's head instead of his father's arm—but in a rum-and-soda
or marijuana haze, even that mistake didn't bother him too much.

"How did you get on with your Uncle Roland over there?"

Matthew looked at Luis stupidly for a moment. Uncle Roland? Williams's cocksucker? Why would Luis be interested in an old fogey like
him?

Matthew snarled, "He be lik' all de rest o' dem. All talk an' no do."
He took a long draw on his marijuana cigarette and started to laugh.
"He don' know de half o' it. He t'inks his son, big Jack's a bloody saint.
He don' know jest what Jack's been up t' dese last years. . . ."

When Luis didn't answer, Matthew twisted restlessly in his chair.
"But I don' know, ev'n Jack, I hear since he's come bac' t' de island an'
got hisself married, an' all, ev'n he's not de same. Mah family . . ."—

he spat on the ground—"dere all de same. I 'pose even me own brud-der, me twin. . . . He's r'form'd dey say, workin' his tail off at de uni-versity an' fer what? So he can be paid tuppence by de whites. Williams ain't done nuttin' fer us an' neither 'as me fancy Uncle Roland. He t'inks he's de big shot wid his guvm'nt limo an' all, suckin' up t' Wil-liams, suckin' up t' de whites. Nuttin's changed. Dere are bloody big holes in de roads, de people's houses get old'r, poor'r an' de whiteys get rich'r an' rich'r. Nuttin' changes. . . ."

Luis put a consoling hand on Matthew's arm. "But we're going to change all that, aren't we, Matthew? We're very pleased with the last hijacking job you did for us. Now we can draw up some long-range plans. How would you feel about—shall we say—getting even with your Uncle Roland one day, the day when you're going to do such a fine job for us in Trinidad?"

Matthew brightened up. "Get ev'n? Yeah. I like de sound o' dat." He fingered the gun suggestively. "He coulda stopp'd me goin' t' jail, de ol' stuck-up bast'rd, but he did nuttin'. When—when? D'yo' mean when de rev'lution comes?"

Luis nodded. "Yes, your Uncle Roland has stood in our way for a long, long time, so *devoted* to the chief minister"—he emphasized the words sarcastically—"encouraging him to bring more and more Amer-ican investment into the island, tying up your natural wealth, giving away so much to those who have so much, while unemployment grows and the people grow poorer. . . ."

Matthew gritted his teeth. "De bast'rd . . . de bast'rd!"

"First we must wait to see how the prime minister reacts to his first trip to the Soviet Union. This is the first important overseas trip he is making without your uncle at his side. It is a good beginning. We will talk again after you return from your next mission for us. You are a wanted man—particularly in Trinidad. We have to move carefully, cleverly. It may be we will take care of your uncle at the same time that we take care of the chief minister. It all depends on whether the chief minister shows he is with us—or against us. . . . But don't worry, Mat-thew—in any case your day of revenge will come . . . sooner than you think."

19

Theo
1977

THE presentiment that something unexpected was going to happen had been with him all morning, so much so that, finding he had an unusual thirty minutes to spare, he'd gone on impulse into St. Patrick's Cathedral, trying to recapture the feeling of peace he'd once always received whenever he'd fallen on his knees and talked to God.

It hadn't happened. He felt hollow, empty. His brain was sharper than ever, but what had happened to his soul?

He'd become too proud, allowing the gulf between him and his only son and aging mother to become so wide, there was no longer even any pain, just numbness whenever he thought about them.

As Theo walked briskly along Fifth Avenue back to his office, he was, as usual, impervious to the glances thrown his way. He looked like "someone," whom passers-by on the most famous street in the Western world noticed and fleetingly wondered who he was, which film or play they might have seen him in, pleased they were in a city where celebrities were part of the everyday crowd.

If anything, the tension in his face most days now had made him more striking. His face was thinner, sharpened with an inner pain that most of the women he met instinctively wanted to soothe. But Theo

Finch had no way of dealing with women who approached him on that basis.

As the secretaries in the Tropica offices said among themselves, "He's too good to be true! Why he isn't a priest beats us! It can't be anything to do with Mrs. Finch, or can it?" He was so fair-minded, so wise and apparently prepared to listen indefinitely to their personal problems. . . . But what about *his* personal problems? Not even the new and glamorous creative director had managed to get close to him in any way. When the female members of the Tropica staff summed up their feelings, most of them felt sorry for Mrs. Finch, although they also wondered why on earth he'd ever married her?

She was obviously older, not that attractive, a nice woman but, not surprisingly, unsure of herself, not good at making decisions. The secretaries knew a groan would go up from their bosses whenever they heard Paulette Finch was going to sit in on an important meeting . . . but that happened less and less these days.

She seemed to tire easily, so that now when Mr. Finch was away, often two weeks out of four, she didn't come to the office for planning sessions as she'd always done once.

Today, Paulette Finch looked more unsure than ever. Something was up but no one would get a peep out of old Shooter, Mr. Finch's secretary. She was as closed-mouthed as he was and not nearly so "fair."

Back to their typewriters and dictaphone machines the girls went, oblivious to the magnificent views from every window of Tropica's thirtieth- and thirty-first-floor offices.

"Mrs. Finch is waiting to see you, Mr. Finch." The note in Marion Shooter's voice told Theo that something serious—and unexpected—*had* happened.

His heartbeat quickened as he opened the door to his inner office to see Paulette standing with bowed shoulders, staring into the distance, where a puff of cloud lit by the sun sat atop the new World Trade Center towers like spun sugar.

"What is it? What's happened?"

She'd been crying again. Theo tried to shrug away the quick irritation he felt, knowing the reason had nothing to do with the reason he often gave her: that she had nothing to cry about; that when she came into the office she should try to pay some attention to the way she looked as the founder and owner of one of the country's most important cosmetics businesses.

He couldn't tell her that above all he was irritated because her sadness provoked his guilt for not loving her the way she deserved to be loved—

something that, however much he tried, he'd found he could do nothing about. Now instead of the broken words he was so used to hearing—adding up to no real reason for tears other than a general dissatisfaction with life, a sense they were drifting apart, a plea for a closeness he had no time to build—Paulette rushed over to put her arms around his neck.

She hadn't been so demonstrative in months.

"Your mother—Tommy—" she choked on the words.

He stiffened. Surely after all this time she wasn't making another useless plea for them to be reconciled? Nothing had changed to make a reconciliation possible. If anything the situation had grown worse as the girl he'd become so fond of, Margaret, had had to endure months of press attention through his own family's machinations, while the tortoise-slow minds in Trinidad debated, agreed, then agreed to disagree, turning the whole case into a monumental farce. At last he'd heard a final decision was now only a week away, but the damage was irreversible, whatever the outcome.

Theo tried to extricate himself but Paulette's arms tightened. "Your mother has had another stroke. Tommy called me this morning. She's asking for . . . for your forgiveness. She's dying."

Theo broke away, a cry escaping from somewhere deep inside him. The pain he'd forgotten broke through the numbness as he thought of the mother who'd always loved him so deeply, lying in Arima in the house deep in the woods, hoping to be forgiven before she died.

"Oh, my God. . . ." Theo covered his face.

Seeing her husband with his defenses down strengthened Paulette's resolve. She had been terrified to tell him the news after months of stifling her deepest needs. Now she cried, "You must go to her. You'll never forgive yourself if you don't."

"Dying?" Theo repeated the word bleakly. Even after her first stroke Theo had never faced the actuality that his firebrand of a mother could die.

Paulette gave Miss Shooter the instructions to get Mr. Finch a seat on the next plane to Port of Spain, telling her to charter a plane if there were no reservations available . . . and to call Tommy to meet his father at Piarco on his arrival.

As they drove to Kennedy, Theo gripped Paulette's hand as he hadn't gripped it in years. She was amazed, no, appalled at her thoughts, which she felt were disloyal . . . that now, Theo would *have* to recognize how hard Tommy had worked during the past year, keeping

Orange Grove working at top capacity, delivering orders on time like a pro, taking all the snags out of the endless government red tape.

Since their return to the States, Theo had adamantly refused to discuss Orange Grove. Paulette knew he saw the figures but that was that! He'd given the Orange Grove/Caribbean business to one of the senior vice-presidents to deal with and had never allowed her to bring up the subject.

As the car approached the terminal, Paulette made him turn his face to hers. "Your mother loves you," she whispered, looking deeply into his eyes. "Everything she ever did was for the family—for you, for Tommy. Don't be hard on her any longer. You'll only be hard on yourself."

Tears glistened in his eyes. He bent to kiss her. "You're right . . . oh, God, I know you're right. If only I'm in time. . . ."

Seated next to a huge black man in tourist class, the journey seemed interminable. He could see for the first time in years the wild, angry face of young Jack Bracken and remembered the terrified young boy he'd been himself, waiting to swing up on the giant branch of the saman tree.

He could see himself looking down from Mount El Tucuche's summit on his release from prison, longing to throw himself into the swelling torrents below, knowing the mother he adored had sold herself to gain his release and was still "selling" flesh to support them.

Even his smooth well-kept hands reminded him of the calluses that had once shocked and depressed her so much.

As the plane dipped down over a violet-colored sea to make the first stop in Antigua, memories still came to torment him as he remembered bouncing along in an old Ford with an excitable tomboy of a girl called Paulette at his side, looking for the cocorico, Tobago's national bird.

How cruel he'd been to her during the past few years. What in God's name had he allowed to happen to himself that he could have shut his eyes to her misery, to a woman who epitomized love in the purest, most giving sense?

His anguish grew as he walked down the plane's steps and inhaled the first intoxicating scents of the tropics. Now, the memories were fresher, more wounding—of a gentle gazelle of a girl who'd followed him through the woods in Arima the day he'd killed the boa constrictor, a girl so hungry for life, for information, so obviously awed he was giving her so much of his time. Margaret.

He had to face the truth. He still missed her; her voice, her gentle touch on his arm. It was useless to dwell on and perhaps it was just as well. She'd made it very clear, more than once, she wanted nothing more to do with him.

Tommy was waiting, his baby face contorted with nervousness among a thick cluster of black faces, and Theo could see the effort his son was making to blink back tears, as he came hesitantly toward him. They fell into each other's arms.

"Oh, Dad. . . ."

"Forgive me, son, forgive me." Theo had never experienced such conflicting emotions, of joy, bitterness, sorrow, even excitement, as the air in Trinidad seemed to emphasize every feeling in his mind and body.

"She's unconscious, Dad. Doc Pellato doubts she'll last through the night." Tommy held on to his father's hand as if he'd never let it go. "She's been so good to me, Dad. She's helped me through these awful months." Tommy started to cry in earnest. "She always did everything for our good, Dad. Please believe me."

"I know . . . I know. . . ." Theo wondered how he could feel so differently all in the space of a few hours. How could he have behaved as he had over what was, after all, just a pile of bricks and mortar? How was it he'd been so unyielding, so lacking in comprehension, insisting Tommy give up Golden Hill, forcing his mother to admit her complicity in Rose's astonishing bequest, without attempting to bring everyone together to talk things over like mature, sensible people? Instead he'd behaved like a dictator, or a self-declared bloody plaster saint, not attempting to see or listen to anyone else's point of view.

He should have flown to California and broken through the security surrounding Margaret, to make her realize how foolishly they were all behaving, that love and friendship were the only things that mattered. He was entirely to blame. No wonder Paulette looked so wan and behaved so nervously. He had a lot to make up for to everyone.

The neat green lawns, the luxuriant, brilliant flowers, even the sight of the yellow birds flying in and out of the breezy veranda, made Theo feel like a new man.

He raced to his mother's bedside, irrationally expecting the force of his feelings to make her well again, longing to pour out, "Mother, I was wrong. Don't talk of forgiveness. I'm the one who should never have let the situation get so out of hand."

The sight of the still figure under the thin sheet shocked the urgency out of him. "Mother, dear Mother," Theo whispered. The tears he'd held back coursed down his face. "I'm here. I won't leave. I love you.

Oh, I love you, Mother. I understand everything. Don't let it be too late for me to tell you. . . ."

Was there a flicker of movement? As he stayed by her bed, he prayed with more fervor than he'd ever prayed, that she would regain consciousness, at least long enough to know he was there, so that he could tell her he understood at long last she'd lived by her own rules to safeguard the future, as she had thought, for him and his son.

As Tommy joined the vigil in the darkened room, to Theo's joy, Magdalen slowly opened her eyes and for one moment appeared to look straight at him, but she gave no sign of recognition before she looked beyond him, over his shoulder, into a distance he couldn't see.

There was a certain irony in the fact that on the day Theo and Tommy met with Thomas Acton to hear Magdalen's last wishes, the Trinidad court at last announced its final decision regarding Rose Pollard's controversial last will.

Thousands of miles away in San Francisco, Margaret was finalizing the acquisition of a new perfumery in a fine location just off Union Square when the phone rang and to her delight Daniel Siden announced he was in town and wanted to see her.

She'd seen him a few times since her return, bringing him up to date on all that had happened over Golden Hill. "You once said I'm a survivor." She'd gone on tremulously when he hadn't answered. "I suppose I must be. I didn't collapse, even when I discovered that . . . that . . . Theo Finch had been using me all along. Golden Hill has never brought me anything but bad luck. I'm fighting the Finches as a matter of principle, but if I lose I'm not even sure I'll be sorry. If I win, I'm almost certainly going to sell the place. Trinidad doesn't mean anything to me."

"Doesn't it?"

She'd known she couldn't brush off any of the doctor's questions. "I . . . don't think so. The strangest thing is, before I received the news about my grandmother's will, I felt such love for the place. I'd been for a walk and came back to tell Uncle Roger how suddenly I realized I loved Golden Hill after all." She'd looked at the doctor shyly. "Uncle Roger even teased me about starting my own cosmetics company—Golden Hill Cosmetics, he called it." Again she'd tried to laugh. "What a joke! Little did we both know what we were going to hear that afternoon—that the Finch family had been plotting for years to get the property back."

At seven o'clock, when the doctor called on the Fairmont Hotel house phone, Margaret told him to come right up.

"Margaret, you look more beautiful every time I see you."

"Doctor Siden, I didn't expect such pretty words from you. . . ."

He took her hand and led her to the easy chairs placed by the picture window with the spectacular view of the bay. In the city sprawling down the hills toward the ocean, the lights were just going on, as the last remaining rays of the sun colored the sky extravagantly with a deep pink gold haze.

"Margaret, I came here to give you some news." Daniel came straight to the point. "In fact, your uncle asked me to come and I wanted to, because I know I can trust you now to accept the news in the way it should be accepted."

Margaret started to get up from the chair, but Daniel lightly touched her shoulder, willing her to remain where she was.

"In a few minutes everything will be behind you—no more lawsuits, no more apprehension, no more waiting for answers." He spoke calmly, evenly, his eyes never leaving Margaret's, hypnotizing her to be calm, to trust him and everything he had to say.

When she started to speak, his eyes told her to remain silent, as they had so many times during her treatment. "In a few minutes you will be able to put all your considerable talent and energy into the future. The past will be over." He saw her hands were trembling and he took them firmly in his. "The news is waiting for you in Los Angeles, but your uncle wanted me to come personally to tell you the Trinidad judiciary announced its ruling this morning that the last will and testament of Rose Pollard was drawn up at a time of uncommon duress, causing temporary insanity." He drew his chair closer to Margaret. "You have won your case. Due to this circumstance, your grandmother's last will has been declared null and void. The Finch family will not inherit any part of Golden Hill"—he allowed a sarcastic note to enter his voice— "despite the fact it was built by their ancestor. As is usual your family lawyer immediately made public the contents of the will your grand- mother made prior to the one just contested."

The intent way the doctor was looking at her meant Margaret still felt uneasy. She had won her case, yet something was not right.

Why had Daniel been sent to deliver what was, after all, good news? Why had her uncle asked him to come, when a simple telephone call announcing the news she'd been waiting for two years would have suf- ficed? She bit her lip. What other shock could possibly lie in store?

She waited, feeling the tension build between them. He continued coolly. "In a valid, recognized will drawn up by your grandmother prior to the 1966 will—I'm told in 1961 . . ."

Margaret interrupted abruptly. "That's the year I . . . Mummy and I left London to go back to Golden Hill to live. Oh, how I hated going back. . . ." She stared out at the darkening sky.

"Yes, I remember you telling me. Do you remember my reminding *you* how totally your feelings had apparently changed two years later? How experience can change everything, turn unhappiness into happiness in the same place with the same people using positive thoughts, not negative ones?"

Margaret blushed. Even to this day, as Daniel Siden well knew, she hadn't been able to talk to him about the night of her parents' deaths. Something still blocked the way, standing between the facts as she'd been told them and the real facts, which in some terrible way she knew involved her.

She tore her mind away. "Go on."

He ignored her building distress as he said dryly, "You are, as you had every right to expect, your grandmother's main beneficiary, inheriting all that was left to you in the 1966 will as well as the Golden Hill mansion and the Picton acreage. There is only one other bequest. From what you have told me and I have learned for myself about your grandmother, it was a surprisingly thoughtful bequest for her to have made."

"Thoughtful?" she repeated slowly. If Daniel had said "thoughtful," then perhaps she really *didn't* have anything to fear.

"Your grandmother left two hundred acres and one hundred thousand dollars to Naomi Simpson to acknowledge her as of her flesh and blood." Daniel went on speaking quietly yet forcefully. "I said 'thoughtful' because it *was* a surprisingly thoughtful act from a woman who wreaked such havoc in other people's lives. The property she left to Naomi is apparently clearly defined—nowhere near Golden Hill or its land. It lies to the west. . . ."

"I don't want to hear. I don't want to hear!" Margaret screamed, white-faced. She rushed to the bathroom to get away from the reasonableness in his voice, the attempt to make her accept once and for all her father's unfaithfulness, a rejection from the grave. Naomi Simpson, her half sister!

Daniel could hear her hysterically crying but he did nothing, knowing it would abate. She would return to him, conciliatory, ashamed for her outburst. He had expected it and so had Roger, which was the reason he'd left an important consultation on receiving Roger's phone call to fly up to San Francisco, to be there because he'd known Margaret would need him.

As he sat looking out at the brightly lit city he thought of the many moods Margaret had presented since they'd first met in 1971, understanding how the convoluted twists and turns in her life had produced pressures so great that in order to maintain her "physical" health, her mental processes had, as he'd explained to her numerous times, been "resting." Now she was well on the way to full recovery.

He thought of Rose Pollard's amazing ability to affect events in death as much as she had affected them during her life. He had concluded that Rose, maddened by her son's decision to bring Alicia back to Golden Hill to usurp her position as mistress of the great house once more, must have made the bequest to Naomi in 1961 as a determined reprisal against both of them. Rose had probably hated her daughter-in-law from the beginning, Alicia's aristocratic background emphasizing the distance between their "stations." He imagined that Rose must have carried that chip with her until the day she died. Then, too, perhaps the bequest to Naomi had really been a subconscious effort to show deep down Rose *had* been aware she was responsible for the tragedies that had marred so many lives.

When Margaret finally emerged, Daniel set about convincing her she had to appreciate in a positive way that her battles were truly behind her. She had won one lawsuit. There was no longer any case to answer on the other. The inheritance demanded by the illegitimate child had been given. Justice had been carried out from the grave.

"Although Margaret Pollard won . . . well, in one way," Tommy said, suddenly shame-faced, "at least Granny Mags never knew we'd lost."

Once Tommy even mentioning "winning or losing" would have infuriated Theo. Now there was a new bond between them, and Theo, looking back on his life, realized how little attention he'd paid to his son. How, he asked himself, could he expect Tommy to act like a man, when he'd never received a man's influence? He'd reneged on his responsibilities as a father, using the telephone as the main form of communication between Tommy and himself, sending presents and postcards from faraway places, using Paulette as the bearer of news, both good and bad.

But something miraculous had come out of the schism between Tommy and himself. Tommy had absorbed a real understanding of the all-important point of difference between their business and other cosmetics houses—the exotic and unusual tropical extracts and oils that made their products unique—and in comprehending and acting on that, Tommy had grown to love Trinidad.

As for Paulette, Theo ruefully reflected, he hadn't spent enough time with her either. It was all going to change.

Tommy and Theo had been astonished to learn the size of the fortune Magdalen had amassed, far larger than had ever seemed possible.

Theo had a lump in his throat as he and Tommy discussed the future, knowing the fervent hopes that had gone into his mother's will. If only he'd reached her bedside in time to tell her how blind he had been, how his stubborn pride had been responsible for so many lost opportunities for a closer, loving relationship between them. He blinked back tears, remembering again the anguish he'd felt as the lawyer had read out the last line of Magdalen's will. "'. . . And Tommy, by your thirtieth birthday, when you will have full use of the inheritance I have left you, I know you will have become the man your father is in thought, word and deed, the most honorable human being I have ever known in this world.'"

He was a sham, but he was glad his mother had never known it. Now he had to redeem himself.

He would have loved to stay with Tommy, but Tommy didn't need him looking over his shoulder. He was more than capable of running Orange Grove. From now on it was going to be a joy—and a privilege—to work with him.

The day of his return to the States, as Theo passed the turn to Maracas Valley on the way to the airport, out of nowhere came an unsettling longing to see Margaret again. Should he fly to California and attempt to see her one more time, trying to prove he had known nothing of Rose's insane attempt to give back the Golden Hill property to his family? Would she listen? And even if she did, where would it all lead?

He tightened his hands on the steering wheel. It was best left as it was. Perhaps time passing would make everything come right and he would no longer feel this strange mixture of emptiness and longing whenever he thought of her . . . and she would relax and no longer think of the Finch family as her enemies.

What he had to do now was pay more attention and give more love to Paulette. As he gave Tommy a bear hug goodbye, he heard himself saying something totally out of character. "I'm going back to give your mother the best time of her life!"

After the night Daniel Siden had broken the news to Margaret about her grandmother's acknowledgment of Naomi (far worse to hear than if she'd lost the case against the Finches), both her uncle and he had tried to make her take an interest in Golden Hill.

When she'd met with her Uncle Roger in New York a month later, he'd made her sit down with an intimidating bunch of accountants and lawyers to impress on her not only her current assets, but the assets she would inherit when he, her beloved uncle, died! As if she could listen to anything as dismal as that!

She'd begged him to take her out of the book-lined room that reeked with the smell of money being made every hour on the hour by, so her uncle kept telling her, the best group of advisers anyone could possibly have!

All right, so she was already rich, but she didn't want to hear about becoming any richer. The important thing was never to be "haunted" by Golden Hill again. She'd fought for it and had regained it. Now she was sure it could only bring her misery, and it really didn't have anything to do with the fact that Jack and Naomi were now living only a few miles from Golden Hill's boundaries.

To Margaret, Trinidad spelled disaster, every beguiling sod of it, impregnated with fertile seeds that blossomed overnight, in the same way that seeds of envy, greed, hate and lust (she would never believe her father could ever have *loved* a woman like Gloria Simpson) sprang up to take hold of people, generation after generation. If she was apt to exaggerate every thought about Trinidad, she didn't care, but she was relieved when Daniel supported her in her decision to get rid of the place.

Uncle Roger had had to accept as final that Golden Hill was to go. He was to sell the house and Picton acres surrounding it, and, if he received a fantastic price for the rest of the agricultural land, that could go too. If not, it could go on accruing profits, and the money could be remitted to the U.S. when the Central Bank gave permission.

There was only one proviso Margaret gave her uncle. If there was any suspicion whatsoever that a Bracken or a Finch wanted to buy Golden Hill, no matter what price was offered, it was to be refused. Other than that, she really didn't care who bought it, and perhaps it was better, she told Roger, if she didn't know.

It had hurt Roger to hear the firmness in Margaret's voice that morning, for he still loved the place, the house where he'd been born. Like a twinge from an old scar, he even felt the sense of loss he'd experienced when he'd learned he'd been passed over by his father for his half brother and stepmother. He couldn't bear the thought of new owners

and he couldn't bear to think of the great old house disintegrating further either—the potholes, already spoiling the sweeping driveway, opening up into great crevasses, golden blossoms from the immortelle trees
falling into the cracks, rotting away to become a breeding ground for
weeds, which would throw out their tentacles until they began to climb
and eat into the coralstone walls.

Roger tossed and turned in bed that night until the obvious solution
came to him. He would buy the property himself, the house and the
Picton acres, and because he was born on the island and was an important shareholder in the now jointly owned oil company, there would be
no impediments to the purchase.

Perhaps it had all been for the best, that just as Texaco had had to
become Textron, so had he been forced to make more and more con-
cessions, until he'd had to shake hands with Roland Bracken and Eric
Williams on the abolishment of United Texas Oil in Trinidad and the
formation in its place of Utotrin.

He would pay the going price for Golden Hill, but nobody, not even
Margaret, would know until his death that he was the owner. He would
never make it public and he would never live there either, but he *would*
restore the house and landscaping to its former prime condition.

It was nearing three in the morning, but Roger felt as refreshed as if
he'd slept soundly all night. He even smiled in the darkness, amazed at
his ability still to be sentimental, knowing to see the Golden Hill deeds
in his name would give him the greatest satisfaction of his life.

If one day Margaret regretted her decision to sell, then it would give
him even more happiness to take her back on a surprise visit to show her
that under his ownership everything had been put back in perfect running order—and that on his death Golden Hill would once again revert
to her ownership. By that time—he smiled to himself in the dark—he
sincerely hoped Margaret would be happily married with children of her
own, who deserved to know about and experience at first hand the background to their strange and complicated heritage.

Paulette hadn't wanted to worry him. She was saying it again, after the
doctor had left them alone for a few minutes, following the devastating
news. Twenty-five, almost twenty-six years of married life, and he'd
allowed them to drift so far apart, Paulette had had to faint away in his
arms before he'd realized she was ill, perhaps very ill.

Cancer. The word hung in the air like deadly gas, snuffing the energy
out of his own legs.

"Perhaps you'd like a second opinion?" the young Afrikaans doctor had asked. "If so, I understand perfectly, but I must insist if you wish to talk to your own doctor in the States, you fly home immediately. You cannot continue on your cruise." '

Theo couldn't get over Paulette's composure. Since his return from Trinidad, determined to put back in their lives all that had been missing for so long, he was the one who'd felt like breaking down, touched by her joy the day he'd told her they were going to celebrate their silver wedding anniversary. He remembered Paulette's screech of excitement as he'd shyly handed her the tickets and the itinerary. "Admittedly a few months late, but then last year there wasn't a world cruise to go on!"

There hadn't been any time for her to feel ill, she'd said defensively weeks later, when, on the high seas, she'd fainted into his arms, as they were about to go to lunch in the Queen's Grill.

The ship's doctor had been alarmed by what he'd found. A lump in her breast, which Paulette had noticed but hadn't paid any attention to. "It doesn't hurt," she'd kept saying during the next few days, the longest days Theo could remember spending, as the great ship slowly sailed down the coast of Africa to its tip.

An ambulance had been waiting at the dockside. "Oh, what a fuss," Paulette had sighed, but Theo had noticed how willingly she'd climbed into the bed in the private ward the *Queen Elizabeth 2* had managed to arrange in Capetown's Groote Schuur Hospital.

She'd kept smiling, trying to cheer *him* up before the result of the biopsy which she'd said she was sure would reveal "absolutely nothing to worry about."

"Speed is of the utmost importance," the Afrikaans doctor had said, not attempting to sugar-coat his words. "It's essential the tumor is removed before metastasis. I would recommend Mrs. Finch be operated on at once."

Theo held Paulette to him, only then realizing she was trembling, that her hands were cold and clammy. Of course she was frightened. Her composure was entirely for his benefit and how grateful he'd been for it, until he'd realized the different fragility about her . . . aware all over again of the lovely stephanotis essence she always wore, one she had long ago decided to keep for herself.

"Oh, Paulette, my darling. . . ."

Her eyes were misty. "Theo, how wonderful to hear you call me darling. Please say it again." Her eyes were luminous with tears as much for his words of love as for what had provoked them.

There was no time to lose. He had to save this wonderful woman, save her from death and protect her with as much love as he could muster for the rest of her days.

When they told the serious young doctor they wouldn't risk wasting even a minute, he smiled for the first time. When Theo left Paulette in the ward an hour later, he learned that following a consultation with another leading cancer specialist, it had been decided to perform a radical mastectomy. It was feared the cancer had already spread to the lymph system.

"What are the chances of recovery? Full recovery?" It was as if someone else was asking the question. Theo was in a daze. He still couldn't believe the terrible knowledge given in the last hour.

Dr. Van Pourren hesitated. "Early diagnosis is the key factor. We're hopeful we are in time." He coughed delicately. "Because of this, Mr. Finch, although this is a terrible shock for you, I am naturally relieved you decided to act at once. It's often difficult to know whether metastasis has occurred or not. Within a month of the tumor appearing for the first time, I'm afraid from our experience, we know it can have already occurred."

Like a sleepwalker he went back to the ship, packed a couple of suitcases, and left the purser to supervise putting the purchases they'd already made in other ports in storage until the ship returned to New York. Sculpture, glass, even packages of things they'd had no interest in but had bought because of a certain lettering on the container or the way a package had been folded.

He hated himself when he remembered how often he'd been bored during the cruise, only really enjoying their forays into the shopping centers of other countries.

Everything Paulette had admired he'd bought for her, but she was so unlike other women, who, at the never-ending cocktail and dinner parties on board, had shown off their finery, the jewelry they'd "found" that day, as if it had all been waiting for them to scoop up in a treasure hunt. The only purchase that Paulette could really call "personal" was a long, bugle-beaded dress. The thought of it now made Theo want to vomit.

It was the most daring dress she'd ever owned, Paulette had exclaimed, even half-heartedly trying to stop him from buying it because it had also been incredibly expensive.

But he'd insisted and she'd flirted with him as they were getting dressed that evening, leaning forward so that her breasts, already tanned golden from sunbathing nude beside their Florida pool, had been totally exposed.

He'd entered into her game of coquetry, pinning her down on the bed, feeling the sharp edges of the beads digging into his bare chest, carefully taking out each breast to suck, long and hard, while she'd moaned beneath him.

When he'd got up to finish dressing, quick as a flash she'd taken the dress off, lying back with her legs open, crying, "Let's forget about dinner. Oh, Theo, take me . . . take me."

He'd started to protest—then, thank God, she would never know it, he'd found himself thinking of Margaret, of all people—and in his guilt he'd plunged into her, the semen pumping out of him before Paulette had had a chance to "drown in love" as she often described her overwhelming need.

And now the bugle-beaded dress hung in the closet, a dress she'd never be able to wear again.

He pressed the bell in the cabin, not realizing that, lost in his thoughts, he kept on pressing. A willowy stewardess knocked on the door. "Is anything wrong, Mr. Finch?"

"Oh, I'm sorry. I didn't realize. . . ." Her sweet face was so full of sympathy he could hardly bear to look at her. "Look, take this dress, will you? I don't want to run the risk of my wife ever seeing it again. I don't want to get back to New York and find it hanging in her closet."

The girl blushed. "Are you sure, sir? Surely there must be . . ."

"Take it," he snarled. "Take it out of my sight."

As the taxi taking him to the Mount Nelson Hotel left the quayside, the ship's siren gave its first alert that it would be leaving in a few hours.

He would never be able to hear a ship's siren again without remembering his feeling of desolation.

"Your wife is making an excellent recovery." By now Theo was used to Van Pourren's nasal vowel sounds and the strange way he clipped off the end of each word.

"When d'you think we'll be able to leave?"

Theo couldn't wait to leave South Africa. The people had been kind, but there was an ominous, heavy feeling in the air, which his logic told him had to be connected to all that had happened to Paulette, but which was also linked in his mind to the reminders everywhere of the apartheid system, "whites only," "blacks only." Thank God, Eric Williams would never set foot there. It could only fuel every antiwhite feeling he'd ever had.

"Early next month . . . without a doubt." The doctor hesitated for a moment. "May I suggest perhaps you take a short vacation together before you return home? I know you're both very successful business people. I'm concerned Mrs. Finch might rush back into her usual hectic schedule without proper rest. You know, there's a certain psychological adjustment to be made."

Theo sighed. The doctor was right. He'd been expecting—and dreading—advice of this kind, but where should they go?

He felt weak at the thought of all the bolstering, loving he would have to deliver on a nonstop basis. He prayed he'd be up to it, that in no way would he ever by accident reveal that if he loved her more now, it was because of his profound pity.

All the joy and happiness that had given Paulette back her confidence, her laughing carefree attitude to life, was no more. Since she'd come round from the anesthesia, she'd been silent, turning her face to the wall, answering him in a tearful voice, only once allowing him to put his arms around her. The doctor told him it was not unusual. "It will take time and a lot of patience, but believe me, this attitude will pass, providing you continue to give your support. There are great strides being made in plastic surgery in this area. It may be your wife will be able to have some breast reconstruction. Talk to her about it. Encourage her, but above all, love her as she is today."

They went to Durban, an overrated spot, Theo thought. They went on sightseeing trips, walked on the long Natal beaches, tried the "best restaurants," shopped until Paulette even found a small shop specializing in bras for mastectomy patients.

She tried to look as if she were enjoying herself, but after three days she broke down. "Let's go home, Theo. I'm homesick. I want to see Tommy. I want to go back to work."

He held her closely in his arms that night, forcing himself to make love to her as she cried piteously there was no way he could want to touch her any more. The imploring note in her voice compelled him to act as a passionate man, but it *was* an act. It had been an act for years, draining him of spirit. She was insatiable, as if she knew he was committed to fulfilling her needs. It was as if she knew she had only to ask and he would obey. He'd finally become the perfect husband.

"Beautiful Botanicals. D'you like it?" Margaret couldn't wait for Daniel Siden's reaction.

He held the streamlined white container up against the light as if he were examining a laboratory specimen. "It looks like opaline, it feels like opaline, it probably *is* precious French opaline, but something tells me at ten dollars a throw, it isn't opaline at all!" He put it down on the desk as Margaret giggled.

"You're right, Dr. S., it isn't. It's the clever invention of Freddy Axelard, my new vice-president of design. He dreamed it up and it was made to his specifications, but . . ."—she impulsively put her hand on his arm—"tell me, I can't wait a minute longer. Do you like the name?"

He moved away, amused at her wide-eyed look of surprise. What a different Margaret Pollard she was these days, growing more and more sure of herself. Had her confidence really grown since the sale of Golden Hill had finally gone through—to an American who'd been born in Trinidad, he vaguely remembered her telling him. It had probably helped, but more important was the growing success of her business. She was branching out, no longer only selling fragrances blended individually for customers, but launching a range of beauty products that, to her excitement, stores across the country were interested in buying.

It was time to answer her question. "I like the name"—the doctor still wanted to tease her—"particularly the BB logo—Brigitte Bardot—a great coincidence. Men will want to buy the products for their women thinking they're going to get a whiff of La Bardot!"

"Oh, you're impossible." Her hand was back on his arm and this time Daniel Siden let it stay there, liking the look of the long pale nails resting against the dark hair on his wrist.

As they walked around her new offices, he silently admired her long legs, her gracefulness, as much as he outwardly praised her for the tasteful decoration and utilization of office space.

"I think you're headed for success, Miss Pollard, and if you need a resident psychiatrist to take care of your employees who are less than dedicated, you know whom to call." He spun her around in a graceful pirouette, allowing her to fall naturally back against him, keeping her there for one brief second before he released her.

"I'll remember your kind offer, dear doctor," she said breathlessly. "After we open for business next week I may give you a call."

As they headed toward the new reception area, the phone started to ring. "That's strange," Margaret said. "I didn't tell anyone we'd be here, and hardly a soul knows we're even hooked up. Hello? Yes?" She frowned. "It's long distance, but it's a very bad line. Hello? Hello? Yes, yes? Oh, my God." She leaned heavily against the desk.

"Yes, yes, yes. Of course I'll leave on the next plane." As she put the phone down Daniel barked out an order. "Deep breathing, please!"

He waited until she'd followed his instructions, inhaling and exhaling before he allowed her to speak. "It's Uncle Roger. He's had a heart attack. Oh, Daniel, I love him so. He's been everything to me. I can't bear it."

"You can bear it. Do you want me to come with you?"

"Yes. No. I don't know."

He glanced at his watch. "You can catch the red-eye with luck." Swiftly he dialed the airline. "One ticket? We'll take it."

He put the receiver down to look at her steadily. "If you need me you have only to say the word, but I know you're going to be all right. Come on, we'll have a quick bite before you catch that inhuman form of transport. By the time you arrive in New York I'll know how serious the situation is and I'll tell you the facts. Where will you stay?"

His fast flow of sentences steadied her and she gave him a rueful smile. "With Aunt Clare, I suppose. That was her secretary, if you can believe it. She couldn't even call me herself, but at least she expects me at the house as soon as I arrive. If I feel as I do now though, I'll go straight to the hospital."

"Of course you must. Your Uncle Roger needs you just as you once needed him."

She did go straight to the hospital from Kennedy, a premonition clutching at her throat that she'd find her uncle dead or dying. "Please God, just this once. Please God, don't let it be true."

She didn't expect her prayers to be answered. Her words weren't meaningless, but she seriously doubted there was a God who wanted to listen to her.

When a nurse directed her to Roger's ward, in the hospital's intensive care unit, to her surprise he was sitting propped up in bed, attached to any number of wires and tubes, but smiling wanly, thanking her with his eyes as well as his lips for coming "all this way to see me."

"I love you, Uncle Roger. You've got to get well for me, d'you hear!"

He closed his eyes wearily. "You're the only reason in this whole world I'd want to get well, believe me. I don't want to leave you alone. I want to see you married, happy, children, before I go. . . ." A tear splashed down on the sheet.

Margaret tried to look as happy as she could. "Oh, Uncle, it's a whole new generation out there. I don't need to be married to be happy. Girls don't need to get married so young any more. They're career-minded. Look, I brought you my first sample. . . ." She opened her tote and brought out the Beautiful Botanicals bottle. "It will make you even more beautiful than you are already."

Roger tried a weak smile. "It's good. Even I can tell that. I like the . . . name. . . ." He leaned back weakly, his breath coming in short spurts. "I'm tired, Margaret, perhaps you can come back later?"

"Of course. . . . I'm going to live in this hospital."

As she got up to go, Roger wheezed suddenly, "One minute, one minute. There's something I must tell you."

She didn't know whether it was her imagination, but he seemed paler, more withered. "Let me get the nurse first, Uncle, please."

"No," Roger gasped, "I'm all right. Just tired, very tired. Listen dear girl, I must tell you something. . . ." The note of urgency in his voice made her sit down again.

"All right, Uncle, don't worry. Whatever you want me to do I'll do." She held his hand lovingly, kissing his wrist.

Roger tried to return her squeeze. "You're a good girl, Margaret. You're the daughter I should have had in more ways than you'll ever know." She looked at him inquiringly, but he went on. "I wasn't going to tell you, but for some reason I didn't expect to get such a good warning that I was going to die. I always thought I'd just drop down— you know—out like a light. It seems it will be just my luck to drag on and on."

"Don't talk of dying. I won't hear of it."

"I'm glad I've got this little bit of time left to tell you. As I've been lying here I realized how unfair I was being, not warning you, letting you in for another shock in a lawyer's office one day. I couldn't do that to you. . . ."

Margaret looked at him so trustingly it twisted his heart. It was a look that said she knew he'd never do anything to harm her, that she knew he'd sooner pull out his life-sustaining plugs there and then than harm one hair on her head.

"I didn't tell you the truth about Golden Hill being sold."

"What d'you mean?" The alarm sounded in her voice as much as she tried to hide it.

"I told you an American had bought the house and the Picton acres, an American born in Trinidad. That was partly true, but it was deliberately misleading. Darling Margaret . . ."

"Yes, Uncle?" She couldn't imagine what he was going to say.

"I bought it."

"You?" She looked at him with amazement. "Why on earth?"

"I couldn't let it go out of the family. I told you when we went back the first time together, that my father had passed me over even though I'd worked so long and so hard for the estate. How hurt I'd been. . . ." His voice was growing weaker and Margaret anxiously looked at the door, willing someone to come in and help him. "When you told me you really meant what you said about selling, I realized I'd never got over the old pain. I had to have the satisfaction—silly I know—of seeing my name on the deeds. Can you understand?"

"Oh, yes, yes, Uncle, but why didn't you say so? I'd have given it to you. It's ridiculous, really. . . ." She found she was crying, touched by her uncle's feelings, knowing she not only understood, but she was actually glad a stranger hadn't bought Golden Hill . . . but she couldn't bring herself to say so.

Roger seemed to summon up strength from somewhere. "There's one more thing you must know. I hope to have many years left—perhaps I haven't after all, but I left the property to you. I know it sounds stupid, but I've always felt you only needed time to understand why Golden Hill had to be yours. Golden Hill Cosmetics. . . ." He tried to smile, but suddenly he collapsed against the pillows, saliva oozing from his mouth.

"Uncle. . . ." Margaret rushed to the door. "Nurse, come quickly."

They assured her he was going to be all right, that her visit had overexerted him, that all he needed was rest, but Margaret felt she couldn't leave the hospital. For an hour she sat in the waiting room, dozing, waking to the realization that Golden Hill was still in her future, if not in her present.

She shivered. It was an omen. She had been happy to know her uncle bought it—but to think she would own it again one day. It was too much responsibility. It frightened her.

The nurse was shaking her shoulder. She'd fallen asleep again. "Really, Miss Pollard, you must get some rest yourself. There's no need for you to stay here. You can go in to say goodbye to your uncle. Then come back again this evening. He tells me you've just arrived from California. You must be exhausted."

Although only an hour had passed, Roger did look better when Margaret tiptoed in. There was more color in his face and his jaw was no longer slack. "Promise me you'll go home and get some rest," he whispered. "Don't let Clare worry you. Your room's all ready. Let everyone fuss over you."

As she left the hospital it was drizzling. She started to walk down Park Avenue looking for a taxi. She felt disoriented, looking at her watch in disbelief. She'd often forgotten to change the time. Twenty to eight,

California time?—that meant it was already twenty to eleven in New York. More than anything she felt she needed a steadying cup of coffee before facing Aunt Clare. She ran to catch a taxi and, recalling a coffee shop near the Pierre Hotel, asked the driver to drop her at Fifth and East Sixty-first Street. The drizzle had turned into a steady downpour when she got out, trying to remember exactly where the coffee shop was.

She was standing under the hotel canopy when she heard her name—a voice—and the tiredness left her as a rush of adrenaline flooded through her veins.

It was Theo, running across the street, shouting her name. He held her at arm's length looking into the face he'd been dreaming of for the past three years, staring, staring into those deep gray eyes.

"Where are you going?" His voice sounded hoarse, rough, even to him. He didn't let her answer but almost pulled her into the Pierre lobby to sit on the stiff upright sofa inside the swing doors. She tried to remain aloof, unfriendly, but the tears that had started at the hospital were pouring down her cheeks.

Words were pouring out as if there had never been any barrier between them. Theo said all the things he'd been wanting to say about a situation he should never have allowed to happen.

Suddenly he didn't need to say any more. Margaret knew he was telling the truth, that her grandmother's will had been as big a shock to him as it had been to her. Quietly, reasonably, he repeated, "How could you think I would ever harm you in any way, little Margaret."

She put her hand over his mouth to stop him from speaking and he hungrily grabbed it to kiss. She asked quickly about Paulette, about Tommy, trying to fill the electrified space between them with conversation.

He waved them away. "They're fine—fine . . ."

She felt dizzy, wanting to lean against him, to feel his cool kiss again.

"Stay with me, have lunch—dinner?"

"I can't. I haven't got time." She told him what had happened to Roger. "I must get to my aunt's house. Then I've got to go back to the hospital."

"Margaret." His eyes seemed to penetrate her innermost thoughts. "We have to meet again. We have three years to make up. Three years of misunderstandings. You know I'm . . . we're . . . I'm so fond of you. Please at least have lunch before you leave me now. . . ."

She started to laugh. "It's only eleven o'clock, Theo. I honestly couldn't eat a thing. I'm so full of—well, emotion. First Uncle Roger, then meeting you." When she broke away she finally promised she would have lunch with him after visiting Roger the next day.

"Come to my suite at the Waldorf Towers for a drink first." He caught her surprised glance. "Yes, Tropica merits a suite there too, now. It's grown even bigger since you left, but I'm sure you know that. Soon you'll be my biggest competitor with—what is it? Beautiful Benefits? No, Beautiful Botanicals," he corrected himself.

"How on earth do you know that?" She felt strangely embarrassed, as if she'd been found using someone else's copyright, but at the same time her anger stirred. "Damn it, I must have spies in the camp already!"

"There will always be spies where there's talent—don't ever forget it—and Margaret Pollard means talent. Remember years ago when I told you that. . . ." She blushed again as he tipped her face up to his. "Those were the days when you were learning to smell the plumbago for me to reproduce in the lab."

He'd planned to catch a plane later that day back to Miami, where Paulette had gone ahead for a long weekend—but when he reached the office he quickly phoned to say he was too overloaded to get away. "I'll try tomorrow, but I can't promise. It may well have to be Friday evening."

"Oh, Theo, I miss you already," she cried. "I didn't sleep last night. I had a funny pain again." She didn't sound too concerned, he decided. Every so often she complained of a pain, "where there isn't anything left to have a pain in." Again the doctors had said it was common. This time, overwrought after seeing Margaret—although he didn't mention it—he spent longer than usual on the phone. "I'll call you tomorrow afternoon, Paulette. By then I'll know for sure what plane I'm catching."

He couldn't sleep that night. He both longed for and dreaded the next day, not knowing what he would do if Margaret failed to turn up, or what would happen if she did.

Margaret found it hard to sleep, too. Once or twice she stretched out her hand in the dark to call Daniel and ask him to come at once, but then she thought better of it. By the time she fell into a deep sleep it was nearly 3:00 A.M. She woke with a start to hear the house phone buzzing. Her aunt's voice, as controlled and as cool as ever said, "It's nearly eleven o'clock, Margaret. I know you told the maid to wake you early, but as you looked dead tired, I felt it would be better for you to sleep on. You'll have plenty of opportunity to visit your uncle later."

Margaret was about to ask her when she was going to the hospital, to make sure her aunt could see her husband in private, when Clare answered the question for her. "I'm glad you're here to take over the hospital visiting chore. I'm going away today to play in a backgammon tournament. I'll be back on Monday." Before Margaret could tell Clare what she thought of her—and this time she felt her anger boiling over, enabling her to do so—her aunt had put the phone down.

Eleven o'clock. Margaret was trembling—with rage at her aunt's insensitivity, with anxiety to get to the hospital and at the thought of seeing Theo again.

What time had he said? He hadn't said. Just "lunch" had been mentioned and a drink beforehand—that could mean anything. Noon? Twelve-thirty? Perhaps it was a godsend that no time had been set. It meant she could relax, she told herself, knowing that to relax was one thing that was certainly out of the question.

She hurriedly bathed, using a new Beautiful Botanicals bath oil with a piquant scent that lingered on the skin for hours. She looked at herself at least a dozen times before she left, regretting she had no "proper clothes" with her, but had just pushed a few things into a tote bag in order to catch the red-eye. Perhaps that meant she wouldn't turn up at the Waldorf Towers after all. She wasn't dressed for it, telling herself as she arrived at the hospital she would stay there all day, then phone Theo to explain why she couldn't meet him.

Fate just isn't on my side, she was telling herself an hour and a half later, when one of the doctors attending her uncle came to see him, and the nurse on duty told her he would prefer that she didn't return until the visiting hour that evening. For the rest of the day it was important her uncle rest quietly.

She stood in the street, trying to hypnotize herself as Daniel had taught her to do in times of stress—but this was a different kind of stress. Despite telling herself fiercely that she wasn't going to the hotel, she was hailing a taxi, telling the driver, "The Waldorf Towers, please. . . ."

It was five to two when she went inside the small thickly carpeted exclusive entrance. Nobody lunches this late. He won't be there. She went past the reception desk as Theo had told her to do. "Go straight up to the thirty-fourth floor. . . ." At two o'clock she arrived outside the suite. She pressed the bell again and again but no one answered.

She felt hysterical, a pent-up longing bursting out of control. She paced up and down the hallway, went down in the elevator and up again. Still no answer. A crushing, destroyed feeling weighed her down as she walked back to the elevator, thinking she'd walk for hours through the city streets, trying to wear the heartache out of her, until she could go back to the hospital to visit her uncle.

The elevator doors opened, and there was Theo, as tense and as strained with anxiety as she. Without words they walked back down the corridor to the suite. Theo threw the newspapers he'd gone down to buy to get away from the endless waiting to the other end of the room. He lifted her up in his arms and carried her into the bedroom.

He was so gentle as he unbuttoned the little buttons at the neck of her dress, carefully lifting it over her head, unfastening her bra to release her beautiful breasts. She felt a wild sense of abandonment, even as she tried to cover them with her hands, as he looked in wonderment at her dark nipples, tracing them with trembling fingers.

She was in ecstasy. She was in another place, in another room, no longer seeing or sensing Theo. She was remembering her father, her wonderful handsome father who had made her delirious with longing when she was thirteen years old, when she hadn't known what great urge of wanting meant.

Who was leading whom? Neither knew. Both were receiving fulfillment for the first time in their lives.

Margaret was smiling up at him, her arms pulling him closer. As Theo slid into her at first slowly, then more and more insistently, aggressively, she wrapped her legs tightly around his back, her whole being wide open for the feeling she'd waited for for so long, expecting, wanting the pain that came as he burst through her physically and mentally.

She was back in her father's dressing room. It was her father who was filling her being as she knew now she'd wanted him to fill her. She saw everything as it had been. Her father backing away from her embrace, her mother's entrance, snatching the gun. Her mother killing her father because of her—because of her rotten craving for sex.

She screamed "Daddy!" as the fevered thoughts came one after the other. She tried to pull away in anguish, but now something else was happening, no longer pain but a mind-bending series of sensations, each one more joyous, more ecstatic than the one before, as Theo, oblivious to her cries, thrust deeper, deeper, deeper. She was coming— the need she had had for years—now she knew what it meant, as orgasm after orgasm thrashed through her body.

She lay on top of him, softly sobbing, whispering about her guilt, explaining what had just happened to her, while Theo painstakingly tried to convince her the guilt was not hers to bear in any way.

The phone rang again and again as the long afternoon went on. They ignored it. They slept locked into each other, awoke to explore each other again, he slowly, methodically licking every part of her, pulling her to him to suck his nipples, his penis.

It was a heaven she couldn't believe existed for other people. It was as if they had invented it for themselves. It was an idyll that surely could never end.

It was daybreak before Theo realized a day and a night had passed. Neither of them had eaten since breakfast the day before and they looked at each other, laughing like children, knowing they were hungry. Theo was calmer now, full of a peace he'd never experienced before. He stopped her from dressing, asking her to stay naked in the rumpled, soiled bed so he could look at her, touch her while he called room service and asked for his messages.

She saw his face change. He moved his hand away from her breast. The idyll was over—but for how long?

"Paulette?" she asked. She felt no guilt. He doesn't love her, I *know* he doesn't love her, she told herself defiantly. It had been a marriage made for the wrong reasons—that much he had told her during the long hours just gone.

He nodded slowly, his striking, sensitive face suddenly haggard, beaten. "She's . . . she's been taken ill. She's been taken to the hospital."

"Is it serious?" She was still flippant, determined not to let anything—or *anyone*—come between the love she now knew they shared.

He crept under the sheets, still warm and wet from their lovemaking. He took her in his arms, stroking the long lovely body, and, as he touched her, he began to tell about Paulette's illness, about the world cruise that had ended so tragically in Cape Town, about the loss of her breast and her long fight with cancer.

She was going to be sick. She ran to the bathroom, trying to cover her own breasts with her hands. How could he have taken . . . given? He banged on the door, insisting she open it or he would break it down.

She couldn't face him. "Go away," she moaned. "Go to Paulette. How could you make love to me knowing . . . knowing. . . ." She started to sob, staring at herself in the mirror, seeing marks of Theo's mouth, hands, on her neck, shoulders, breasts. She felt unclean, full of shame.

And Theo was wrong. She *was* guilty. She was just as responsible for her father's death as her mother had been. Like a curse, she suddenly remembered her uncle's halting words. He had bought Golden Hill and she would one day own it again. She would never be free. The albatross was back and the curse would touch everyone she loved.

Margaret turned on the shower as hot as she could bear it, trying to wash the marks away, to steam out her tumultuous feelings.

When she finally came out of the bathroom, wrapped in a huge bathtowel, Theo was in his robe, apparently calm, reading the *New York Times* at a table set for two. She couldn't believe his look of serenity.

She had to get away. She couldn't face the next telephone message or stand to see him walking out of the door to catch his plane, out of her life once more.

When Theo went to the bathroom, she decided she would make her move. As soon as he closed the door behind him, she threw on her clothes to rush into the first taxi she could find, back to the house, to collect her thoughts, to try to calm down before she returned to the hospital.

What if her uncle . . .? Her hand flew to her throat. Fate couldn't deal her any more blows. He *had* to be the same, if not better. . . . On her arrival, to her intense relief, she found Roger *did* seem better, more alert, eager to talk about the "small deception" as he put it, that he'd practiced over Golden Hill

She could hardly think as she sat at his bedside. Every inch of her body was on fire. While her mind fiercely rejected Theo, her body already ached, longed for him again.

When she left the floor, Theo was waiting in the hospital lobby, taut, tense, afraid she might rush past him without speaking—but too much had happened between them for her to be able to do that.

"Come back to the hotel. Oh, please, darling Margaret." They stood in the street, each one reflecting the other's tension, hurt, anxiety.

"How can you ask me to do that? How can you be so heartless? Why are you still here? You should be . . . at . . . the airport . . . on a plane."

"Margaret, I couldn't leave without seeing you again. The time we've just spent together, doesn't it mean anything to you?"

"What about Paulette?" She cried out the words, her pain making her want to attack, to hurt him as she was hurting.

"I called her. I called the hospital. It's tomorrow. She's to undergo some exploratory surgery. It was all very sudden. She didn't know. I didn't know. Of course I'm going down . . . but I had to see you again first. Oh, Margaret, don't look at me like that. I'm not heartless, but now that I've found you, how can I let you go out of my life?"

They walked aimlessly, not knowing where they were going, or how far they were traveling, like people in love everywhere, oblivious to everyone and everything.

He persuaded her to go into a bar on Central Park South as the rain started again, darkening the already dark, almost empty bar between the lunch and evening rush hour.

"You can't stop wanting me, Margaret. It's real. It's between us. It was there from the beginning, but you were so young. I'm so much older." Theo swallowed hard. "Is that the reason you ran away? I'm too old for you I know, and yet . . ."

"No, no, no. Don't you see, it's Paulette. I could live with myself when I thought you'd never had a real marriage. Everyone divorces these days. I didn't stop to think. I wouldn't *let* myself think, but when you told me about her illness— You could never leave her like that. Neither of us could live with ourselves—with the guilt and the shame. Never!"

Theo stared at the bar ahead. She was right. He could never leave Paulette, but why did he have to *leave* her? Couldn't they still see each other? Other men saw women other than their wives.

He began to speak, then thought better of it as Margaret cried, "I only realized last night—when we made love—the half life I've been leading. I've been an emotional cripple, don't you understand? My feelings for . . . for my father affected my life terribly. I can't share you now with a wife who's already suffered so much, who may be about to suffer more. I *can't* live another life of deception—just when I've discovered what living, feeling, *loving* is really all about. . . ."

Margaret

R OLAND felt a grim satisfaction when Luis told him the assassination date.

August 31, the seventeenth anniversary of Trinidad's political
independence. It would be a day of merrymaking, of bunting
and confetti in the streets, colorful enough to make the people—oh,
how simple they were—forget for one day what a farce it had all been.

Of course, the date had been deliberately chosen, but not because
Luis and those who directed him *cared* about the sad and steady erosion
of all Eric Williams's promises at the time of independence, or because
they *cared* that Williams, who had analyzed the economic roots and
implications of slavery with such brilliance, had so pathetically failed to
ensure a better standard of living for his "unenslaved" people. The
"comrades" didn't care about that, but they *did* care that Williams had
effectively integrated the Trinidad economy into that of the U.S.—despite his well-publicized visit to Moscow and "lip service" to the reds.

As vivid lightning zigzagged across a violet sky and a grumble of
thunder was followed by a discordant and protracted chorus from the
red monkeys high in the hills, Roland picked up his pen to finish his
letter to his son Jack.

It was the one imprudent act he was allowing himself before The
Day. Imprudent, but scarcely reckless—that had never been his style.

If anything, looking back across the years, Roland considered he had always been too cautious, embracing Luis's directives to be "patient" too quickly and too well.

His own rebellion had been short-lived. He had helped build a strong opposition party to Williams's without Williams even knowing it, intending to do the unheard-of, to walk out on Williams and publicly accuse him of letting the people down, intending to take over the reins of the opposition just before the election. But then—to his initial stupefaction—his own boy, Jack, had been elected leader of the opposition not knowing, of course, his father's own "Grand Plan."

It had still seemed the perfect answer, for if and when "Jack's Party" beat the daylights out of Williams, then Roland's secret supporters around the island had promised him they would reveal his true affiliation to Jack and he would at last be able to tell his son about the many covert actions he'd undertaken over the years to topple Williams.

But it hadn't turned out that way. Williams had scored an amazing victory after all, campaigning vigorously against the "bribery and corruption in his own government." Although Roland knew he was considered "beyond distrust" throughout the scourge, he was still amazed, when it was all over, that Williams hadn't happened on his own "double-treble-game."

Eric Gairey had been the turning point.

As Luis told him the coup, in the works for so long, had succeeded in Grenada during "the prime minister Sir Eric Gairey's absence overseas," and the new leader, Maurice Bishop, lost no time establishing diplomatic relations with Cuba. By doing so he made his true allegiance perfectly clear to the world and, Roland believed, in particular to Dr. Williams not so many miles away across the sparkling Caribbean.

But Dr. Williams hadn't seemed to receive the message loud and clear—that Communist influence, now fully at home in Cuba, was now going to spread throughout the tropical isles.

Instead Trinidad's prime minister welcomed with open arms—or so it appeared—the peanut farmer's emissary, Philip Habib, sent by President Carter on a ten-day diplomatic offensive—"aimed at countering Cuban influence in Britain's former colonies" was how the ultraconservative English *Daily Telegraph* described it.

Now Roland wrote quickly to Jack, "Although black progress has surpassed my expectations in many ways, in my heart there remains no safe distance from the wretched past of our ancestors. Racism still blows through the world like an evil wind and we both know Williams achieved a hollow victory in 1962. If I die in my attempt to rid our island of the dreamer who spins dreams but never solutions, I am writing this to say 'never give up, Jack.' I know how tenuous is the black man's grip on a comfortable, dignified way of life and how strangling the grip of the other desperate way of life for a black man can be.

"So long as we are denigrated as a group, not one of us has really made it. With your strength and brilliance, however, you *can* hoist our people up to the heights they deserve. Again, I stress, never give up the fight. Be cautious, but never *patient* with progress.

"If I succeed, you will never read this letter, but you will still learn where my *true* allegiance has always been—to our people, to the end of white domination, U.S. interference, *and* without bending our knees to those in the East."

Roland reread the letter, sealed it and gave it to the only other person he trusted, Emerald, telling her, "I have a special job to do, love. You're not to worry. It involves security and the safeguarding of the prime minister. If anything should go wrong, I want you to give this to Jack with my love."

Her eyes filled with tears, but he couldn't help it. He had to go on. "I'm telling you, old love, nothing *will* go wrong, but, as you know, in war *and* peace there are always risks for those at the top. If anything should go amiss, after our son has read this letter he'll know what to do. Otherwise on September the first you can return this letter to me. All right?" He looked at her levelly, telling her with his clear, steady glance that everything *was* going to be all right, but she *must* follow his instructions, that he was relying on her as he always had.

At last Matthew was going to meet the man he'd heard so much about—"Arc"—who'd been working with the KGB in the Caribbean for three decades. Arc was the man Luis had told him they could no longer trust, who wanted to effect a coup in Trinidad as much as they did—but for the "wrong reasons." Williams was to go and so was Arc, after he'd assisted Matthew in getting through the security surrounding the prime minister.

Matthew whistled twice, paused, then whistled again as he'd been told to do. The "safe house" on the outskirts of San Fernando hadn't been difficult to find, but his feet were killing him. It had been a long trek from the beach where the boat had dropped him. A light went on in an upstairs room, then went out again. It was the signal to say it was safe to enter.

To reassure himself, Matthew stroked the guns in the halter strapped to his body, drew in his breath and put a fixed smile on his face. This was the most important mission of his life. One hundred thousand fat ones awaited him in Caracas if everything went according to plan—and he intended to pocket every one of them.

The Matthew who now carefully approached and entered the two-story house wasn't so different from the wild, unprepared Matthew who'd rushed into Magdalen Finch's Orange Grove house to attack her nine years before. On the surface he showed the results of intensive training, in which he'd literally been knocked into shape in the roughest terrorist school on earth. He looked cool and calm, could move as smoothly as a cat, could hit any target with unerring accuracy, but underneath he was the old, never content Matthew, suffused with a sense of injustice. He was still jealous of his twin brother, who in his eyes had gone over to "whitey's camp," while his "brilliant cousin Jack," although not so flagrantly "pro-Establishment," lived like a white man. Matthew had heard Jack was even building a house "with no expense spared" on land left to his wife by his treacherous "passing for white" aunt.

A match flared in the darkness. He'd made contact. As a cigarette glowed, Matthew put out his hand to shake the mysterious Arc's hand.

Was it a black or a white hand? He couldn't tell.

"Can we put de light on, sir?" He'd been told to be his most respectful.

"Later." The voice was thick, throaty, a disguised voice. "What's your name?"

Matthew jumped. He hadn't expected that question. For a minute he wasn't sure what to say. He decided to use the name on the passport Luis had given him the day before ". . . in case you can't use the escape route arranged by our contact."

"Paul Cullen."

"That's not your name." Again the voice sounded false.

Matthew had had enough. Who did he think he was?

He clicked on his torch and shone it directly at the voice. "Mah God. . . ." He backed away in sudden terror. "Mah God. Yo' . . . yo' . . ."

"Yes, Matthew. I didn't expect you either. Did Luis send you? Are you the man who's going to fire the shot? The man I'm supposed to 'try' to apprehend?"

"Appre-what?" Matthew stuttered, uncongealed fear flooding his body. He didn't know what to say or think.

How could the man he'd heard Luis run down, that crawling, slimy, boot-licking uncle of his, be Arc the KGB plant? How could Roland be the man who once had been so valuable to the Party, but who according to Luis had now grown dangerously "too big for his boots"? Did it mean the "safe house" had been discovered? Had his uncle killed Arc? Was his body lying dead in one of the rooms? Matthew shook as if he had a fever, trying to decide what to do.

Roland went over to the window and looked out carefully. There was no one in sight. He pulled the blinds, the curtains, then switched on the light.

Matthew swiftly pulled out his gun. "Don't t'ink I won' use it. Jest 'cos yo're me relation means nuttin' t'me. . . ."

"I don't think Luis would be very pleased if you wasted time killing me after all our careful preparations." His uncle spoke so softly, Matthew had to concentrate to hear him.

He kept the gun pointed at Roland's head. He wasn't convinced, couldn't accept his uncle was the man who'd supported the reds for so long. "What's your code name?"

Roland smiled at him as if he were his favorite nephew. Matthew felt more frightened than ever.

"Arc," Roland said again very softly, "A-r-c," he spelled out. "D'you trust me now? You see, Matthew, despite all you've heard about me over the years, I was on your side all the time. Your side and Jack's side, because Williams has let our people down."

It was hard to swallow, yet Matthew suddenly believed it. Arc's identity had remained so secret because his Uncle Roland *was* the "last person" anyone would ever suspect. "Yo're de las' pusson I'd 'ave ev'r suspect'd, " he mouthed the words.

Roland was now all business. "We haven't any more time to discuss hows and whys. We have our orders. Where's the ammunition?" Roland looked at his watch and Matthew could see his hand was trembling. It made him believe in Roland more than ever. Grudgingly he even began to respect him.

Roland had been frantically playing for time with every word he'd spoken, every movement he'd made since he first heard Matthew's voice, and to his disbelief seen by the light of his first match his nephew's cunning features.

Why hadn't Luis told him his nephew was the chosen tool of destruction? Was it because even coldblooded Luis hadn't been able to tell him he was going to have to kill his own kin immediately following the assassination? Or had Matthew been chosen because in killing his nephew his story would gain credibility—that he'd "stumbled across" and killed the assassin following the prime minister's murder?

Even as the thoughts came, Roland dismissed them. Luis would have no qualms about killing anyone, and he knew very well how Roland felt about his unstable, dangerous nephew. Matthew's appearance meant something more sinister—yet what?

He looked at his watch again. At least another hour before the dawning of The Day and his breakfast appointment with the prime minister. It was going to be hard to put up with Matthew's company for another sixty minutes, but there was nothing else for it.

They had just finished going over the details when Matthew, his ears trained for the last two years to hear the slightest sound, heard a car door shut.

Roland switched off the light and, kneeling on the floor, shifted aside the blind to peer out.

There was not only one car outside. Two or three were now in the drive, unmarked and without lights.

Was it the police, or Williams's special counterinsurgency unit always on the lookout for guerrillas? Had Matthew been followed or had it been a setup by Luis from the beginning to disgrace and discredit him?

Had Williams suspected him all along and decided in his cool, professorial way that he should hang himself? Roland could feel the noose tightening around his throat.

If he was found inside with Matthew, a wanted criminal, he was doomed. He could hear the accusations—"Harboring a known enemy of the state, traitor to Dr. Williams's government."

He saw one man, two men run stealthily toward the house.

"Out the back door," he hissed to Matthew, who was fingering his trigger nervously. "There's a trapdoor—a tunnel. . . ."

As they stumbled out into the night, a beacon of light transfixed them in its beam for a split second. The second of doom for Roland, as a familiar voice, that of the head of the counterinsurgency unit, shouted, "That's Matthew Bracken all right, and that's his uncle with him, the ambassador. . . ."

Matthew let loose a salvo of shots and Roland heard a sickening scream as he yanked up the trapdoor.

A loudspeaker blared into life. "You are surrounded. Put your hands up. We will count to ten. . . ." They jumped down into the blackness below and heard no more as they raced along a winding subterranean tunnel that stretched for over a mile to a dried-out river bed.

Even as they ran, panting in the foul humid air, Roland couldn't believe all that was happening. He'd been seen. What excuse could he give? His idiot of a nephew had shot and apparently hit someone. He was ruined.

"Wher' we goin'?" Matthew cried hoarsely.

Roland didn't answer, saving his breath until they'd gone about half a mile, when he snapped at Matthew to start shining the torch at the highly arched walls on either side of them. In a few minutes the torch picked out a ladder engrimed with filth and weeds. "After me." Roland climbed to the surface in a dark alley.

"Yo' sur' was ready for anythin'," Matthew gasped.

It was better yet. Not twenty yards away, Roland unlocked a door in a broken-down building and in minutes they were driving in a baker's van toward Bonasse.

As Roland drove, his mind was in turmoil. Williams had been able to counter the "revolution" eight years before by having his Coast Guard's guns ready to fire from the sea on the revolutionaries on the shore road. He must also—somehow—have known about the assassination plot.

Had Luis been playing a double game? He would have to risk that Luis had had nothing to do with it and follow the "abort mission" plan worked out in the event of the assassination attempt's failure.

They had to reach a point on the coast near Bonasse where a Boston whaler was ready for them to join a freighter lying at anchor off Icacos Point, where Trinidad comes close to the Venezuela mainland.

Roland racked his brain one more time to see if there was any way he could explain his presence in the house with Matthew, a known terrorist and killer. The answer had to be no, and, surprised at his own coolness, he accepted that there was nothing else he could do but leave Trinidad. He had money abroad. Later he would make contact with Jack, who would have received his letter by then.

Perhaps he would never see Emerald again. He could bear that, but he couldn't bear the thought of never again seeing Jack.

He fought the emotion tearing through his body. There were others overseas he could work with. The coup still wasn't an impossibility. Eric Gairey had been taken by surprise. So could Williams be—perhaps more easily from without than within.

Roland's confidence started to build as the first red splashes of the sun's fire burned across the sky. "Can you handle the whaler?" he asked Matthew sharply.

"O' course I ca'." They drove the van into a cluster of manzanilla trees and Roland breathed a sigh of relief. On the horizon he could see the squat lines of a freighter, while behind a huge boulder, just as had been arranged, was the whaler.

At first, Roland thought it really *was* going to be plain sailing. Even he could drive the simple little boat if he had to. But as he began to relax, the waters around them changed, one minute calm, the next, swirling, tossing, spinning the boat in a direction away from the freighter.

Neither of them knew that, expendable now, Luis had signed their death warrants in a number of different ways. Both inexperienced sailors, they were going to their deaths as so many across the centuries had done, caught up in the infamous *remous*—the deadly crosscurrents caused by the tide of the Caribbean meeting and clashing with waters from Venezuela's Orinoco River.

As Matthew wrestled violently with the wheel in an attempt to ride the now mountainous waves, the whaler turned on its side, spinning away from him like a child's top.

In vain both he and Roland struggled to reach the boat, their thoughts so different but equally desperate.

I've got t' get t' Caracas t' get dat money, Matthew thought, even as he clawed ineffectually toward the boat, while Roland looked up at the now perfectly blue sky, praying one day his son would succeed where he had so lamentably failed.

> *Here he comes now, here he comes!*
> *Papa! Papa! With his crowd,*
> *the sleek waddling seals of his Cabinet*
> *trundling up to the dais . . .*
> *who will name this silence*
> *respect? Those forced, hoarse hosannas*
> *awe? That tin-ringing tune*
> *from the pumping, circling horns*
> *the New World? Find a name*
> *for the look on the faces*
> *of the electorate. Tell me*
> *how it all happened and why*
> *I said nothing.*

Jack let his tears fall on the poem by his favorite poet, Derek Walcott, and on his father's letter by its side, already crumpled and soiled. He'd read the letter at least a dozen times since his grieving mother had put it into his hands, telling him between her sobs that his father had entrusted it to her care to give to him "in case somethin' happens"!

How he'd longed to cry out the truth at the memorial service, but what good would it have done to let the world know for a few fleeting seconds—before he was probably clapped in jail—that Eric Williams, the scheming, lying bastard, had engineered his father's death?

Even if some believed him, would it help him follow his father's last wishes to go on with the fight . . . as he would go on for the rest of his life? Certainly not: for his father was being treated as a hero.

A plot had been uncovered, the government release stated, "to assassinate our revered leader, Dr. Eric Williams." The details had been sketchy but chilling. A house full of stolen arms, suspected intervention from abroad and . . . who had stumbled into this unknowingly but Ambassador Bracken, who had "given his life so selflessly, in a vain attempt to catch the would-be assassin."

Nobody in the family, not even Jack, ever discovered that Matthew had been the unnamed gunman, that he had drowned as Roland had drowned—for neither body was ever recovered from the shark-infested waters.

"'Aromatherapy—a well-known form of beauty care in Europe and the Orient, where it is literally as old as the hills—is being brought to this country by Beautiful Botanicals, as a natural extension of our work,' says the company's energetic and innovative young president, Margaret Pollard. Aromatherapy is based on the regenerative powers of certain natural oils applied on the nerve centers of the face and body. The object is to stimulate the reproductive action of the skin cells and speed up the renewal process to recapture a 'younger rhythm.' . . ."

Margaret tried to concentrate on the lengthy article, but her eyes were closing. She was so tired. She was always tired these days, and, as both Dan Siden and her Uncle Roger told her regularly, it was no wonder.

She was pushing herself, doing too much, cramming every minute of the working day—which usually stretched long into the night—with one thing after another.

They didn't know the reason, although Dan probably guessed, that she was using hard work as therapy, hard work and a little play—not much play—and it *did* help.

An interviewer had told her the year before that Helena Rubenstein had once said, "Work is the only excitement that lasts." Margaret had laughed politely and made a noncommittal answer, but now she was inclined to agree with the late, great lady of cosmetics, that is, if "excitement" *was* the operative word.

Work, work, work, she had told herself fiercely for days, weeks, months. Don't think about him. Don't even look at the Tropica counter in the stores you visit. Don't risk going near. Send someone else to "look over the competition."

Of course, it was ridiculous. She *had* to get near when Beautiful Botanicals had a chance of moving into a prime location, which inevitably meant counter space near Tropica's square footage, which along with Estée Lauder and Clinique, commanded the best, most visible space in the leading stores.

Not that she wanted BB to grow as big as Tropica.

Then she would remember (oh, how she remembered every word, syllable, forcing herself never to recall his touch) that Theo had once told her that Paulette and he had promised themselves Tropica would never grow "too big," but they hadn't been able to stop its phenomenal growth.

Once upon a time. As she lay her head down on the desk top, half dozing, the phrase rang through her head. Before she fell asleep Margaret promised herself she would stop thinking about "once." She would take Dan's advice and concentrate on living "now" and go with him next week on the sailing trip to Catalina Island.

Dan had known she was a different girl from the one who'd gone racing off to New York on the red-eye.

The day Roger was released from the hospital and she'd convinced herself her uncle was going to be all right, she'd called Dan and asked him to meet her at the airport—for after two painful telephone conversations with Theo she'd been able to convince him she had to get away "to think."

"So much has happened I have to be on my own," she'd cried.

It wasn't true. She didn't want to be on her own. She was frightened she'd give in to her nagging desire to get on a plane to Miami to be with him, to go anywhere with him—to the ends of the earth, to escape from responsibilities, ties, old wounds that wouldn't heal.

But somehow she'd staggered through the first week without him, then the second, and in the middle of the third she'd gone back to Los Angeles.

There were his letters to take with her—such beautiful letters. She'd torn up the first one, then had spent an hour trying to stick it together again, not realizing it was going to be the first of several. But they had all been letters that really said goodbye, and finally he'd written to say she was right. He had been dreadfully wrong.

He loved her, would always love her, but he'd been forced to accept that no love could exist where there was shared guilt.

"Paulette is going to be all right—so the doctors say—but every day is a new day with her dreadful disease. She's going to need all my attention and care. I don't regret our hours together. They were the most beautiful of my entire life. They've given me strength to go on, realizing I've experienced a love as burning as the sun . . . as natural as the flowers growing out of the earth. I hope those hours meant you gained something, too. You're so beautiful, so young, God bless you and the man lucky enough to make you happy."

Work had been the only solution to facing life without him, for Daniel Siden hadn't been able to ease the pain of separation.

Daniel, who knew the old Margaret so well, had sensed immediately that something had happened to her in New York.

"I don't know what you mean." She'd tried to look cool, indifferent. And then to her amazement he'd kissed her—hard, long, probing.

She'd shut her eyes, agonized, trying to pretend it was Theo, but it was impossible. She'd felt nauseated, had gone rigid, until her lack of response had resulted in an embarrassing apology and a coolness in their relationship that hadn't righted itself for months.

"Margaret, you're in love. Tell me about it," he'd demanded more than once, until she'd known she had to get away.

No one was ever going to hear about her meeting with Theo. It was a treasured memory that even she wouldn't be able to enjoy, to savor to the full for years—not until the longing went away.

Like a godsend she'd heard about Roure's first aromatherapy conference in Grasse, and although she'd known it would hurt to return to the city of flowers, where once she'd thought she knew what happiness was all about, she'd fled there to bury herself in the subject, to experience the aromatherapist's art on her own skin.

It *was* soothing and astonishingly relaxing, "inducing not inertia, but a state in which, energy being freed, one's whole concentration can be directed onto a more perceptive plane . . ." one of the practitioners had explained. Miraculously for the first time since her meeting with Theo, Margaret found she could direct all her energies to her business.

She'd stayed in France for three months, learning as much as she could about the use of camomile, mint and lavender oils for sensitive, delicate skin, essence of rose to heal wounds and fade scars, Indian verbena and sandalwood to tighten open pores, geranium oil to stimulate circulation, rosewater for broken capillaries, pulverized tree bark and linseed oil for special problems.

The subject was so engrossing, so fascinating that, when she'd returned to the States, she'd gone to see Uncle Roger and then to her financial advisers to ask their advice about opening an aromatherapy clinic and perhaps eventually several mini-clinics in the specially selected stores already carrying the Beautiful Botanicals line.

Uncle Roger had been encouraging, but she could see he was engrossed in a project of his own. She'd never seen him so excited, although, as usual sensitive to her feelings, at first he'd told her very little—because it involved Golden Hill.

When she'd laughed and said to him, "Let me know the worst! What have you got up your sleeve now?" he'd poured out the details. He was building a frozen-food plant on the northern part of the Picton acres, something he'd wanted to do for forty years, he'd told her, his eyes shining. "Would you like to be a director?" He'd only been half joking.

"Oh, Uncle, you're incorrigible. I know what's going to come next. Golden Hill Frozen Cosmetics!"

"That's not a bad idea. You'd better come in with me early. I can see I'm going to need your input—frozen papaya face packs!"

"You've hit the jackpot. Papaya's a natural enzyme—it's wonderful for the skin. . . " and so they'd gone on, teasing, laughing, without touching on the reality of Golden Hill at all.

That had been fifteen months ago, months of nonstop work for Margaret, traveling back and forth to Europe, finding the right pairs of expensive, trained hands belonging to women who after years of study knew which oils could best help which skins.

At last it was beginning to take shape and her first aromatherapy clinic was about to open in Beverly Hills. The interest from the papers and magazines had been phenomenal, Margaret thought, so much so she had a mountain of clippings to read.

When she woke with a start at midnight to find she was still in the office, her neck and shoulders stiff and cramped from sleeping in such an awkward position, she promised herself again she would definitely accept Dan's invitation to go sailing, and she'd take the clippings with her to read.

Salt was on her tongue, her skin. It felt good. It was, she told herself with a wry smile, a form of aromatherapy—because if the brain was relaying the news the salt felt good, the skin would respond favorably, too.

At anchor in the lee of the land, Margaret idly watched a kingfisher diving from the limb of a tree into the water and back as if it were on a yo-yo string. She was about to bring Dan's attention to the clever bird when a sharp gust of wind caught a bunch of clippings in the basket beside her, scattering them across the deck. She just managed to grab a handful before they went over the side. "Oh, well, there'll be more where they came from."

She settled back so that her face was in the shade, stretching her long legs out into the warmth of the sun. She was so glad she'd come. The thought of being rocked to sleep by the lapping waves was soothing, too, and Dan, since they'd gone through what she called their "difficult" period, was relaxed, easy to be with.

A breeze started to flutter through the clippings again and she brought a bunch of them together between her knees.

As she started to read an interview she'd given to the *Chicago Tribune* some months before, something else on the same page caught her eye. Her heartbeat quickened. Tropica. She'd caught sight of the word "Tropica." What was it?

Margaret put her hand to her mouth. "Oh, no . . . oh, no," she moaned. In a column beside her interview was a tribute to Paulette Cobble Finch, the co-founder of Tropica " . . . whose premature death from cancer last month is a great loss to the beauty industry. Reached at his Miami home, Chairman of the Board Theo Finch said, 'Tropica was entirely my wife's dream. She was its inspiration and true creator. Together with Thomas, our son, we worked to interpret what were always Paulette's original ideas into products for the women of America and today the world. . . .'"

Margaret looked at the date. March 6. Almost six months ago—and he hadn't called her, hadn't written.

Why hadn't Uncle Roger told her? She answered herself. Because she had never told him the war between the Finches and herself was over, ended in twenty-four glorious hours at the Waldorf Towers.

But why hadn't Theo called?

She couldn't stay on the boat. She had to get back to the mainland. She couldn't be tormented for another second with all the questions flooding her mind.

"Dan. . . ." He understood. He knows, she thought, as a fair wind sent the sloop gracefully toward the mainland marina. He's known ever since I came back from New York.

The doctor came to put an arm affectionately around her shoulders. "What are you going to do, Margaret?" When she didn't answer immediately he whispered, "Don't do anything in a hurry. Nothing's going to change. He'll be there. . . ."

If he was going to be there, why hadn't he called her? In the time it took for the yacht to cross the stretch of water back to her waiting car, Margaret realized how illusory her "peace of mind" and "I'll work it out of my system" attitude really was. It was a defense mechanism, that was all, to prevent being hurt or betrayed ever again.

He had been the one to say the final goodbye, not she. If he hadn't written the final letter, would she have been so resolute about staying away, spending her life working, traveling? She knew the answer.

She hardly slept, waiting for six o'clock when on the East Coast the Tropica switchboard would open.

"Tropica. Good morning."

"Mr. Finch, please."

"Mr. Thomas or Mr. Theo Finch?"

"Mr. Theo Finch."

"I'm afraid he isn't in the office today. Would you like to speak to his secrertary?"

"Yes, no, well, yes, please."

"One moment please." The operator came back on the line. "I'm afraid Miss Shooter will not be in this week. One moment please. . . ."

"Yes, can I help you?"

"Can you tell me where I can find Mr. Theo Finch?"

"I'm afraid not. If you would like to leave your name and number I'll certainly see your message reaches him."

Margaret put the phone down, blushing. She couldn't leave her name. She couldn't bear waiting to hear his voice, waiting for the phone to ring—*if* he returned her call.

She had to speak to him, to hear the voice that proved he still cared. Suddenly their love, their secret love, so strong when it was buried within her, was fragile, one-sided.

She dialed the Miami house. There was no answer. She dialed the Miami office. "Is Mr. Theo Finch there?"

"No, I am afraid not. Who's calling?"

"It's a personal friend. I've . . . I've just heard about Mrs. Finch. I've been away. D'you know where I can reach him?" As on previous occasions, Margaret sensed that this operator, like so many outside the main business centers of New York and Los Angeles, was more approachable, less guarded. Perhaps it was also less efficient, but this time she felt a surge of gratitude toward the Florida operator who said quite openly, "Mr. Theo, you said? He's out of the country."

Margaret sighed, the misery in her voice escaping over the wire.

"He's in Trinidad, miss. Perhaps you'd like to try reaching him at Tropica's Orange Grove plant. Would you like the number?"

Relief flooded through her. "No, no, I have it. Thank you very much. D'you . . . know if he'll be there long?"

There was a pause. "Yes, I think he will, miss. Mr. Thomas Finch is here at the moment, and so far I believe there's no date set for Mr. Theo's return."

"Oh, thank you, thank you so much."

Margaret could see herself in the mirror above the phone. She was flushed, glowing with an inner excitement, anticipation, nervousness.

She looked at her watch again. Six-twenty. Nine-twenty in New York—ten-twenty in Arima, where the late-summer rain would be brightening the grass, freshening the flowers. She could smell them already.

Slowly she dialed another number. "Hello? Uncle Roger? I've got wonderful news for you. I'm going back to Golden Hill."